D0752323

"Ron Rosenbaum is among the most thoughtful and insightful interpreters of our fractured fin-de-siècle society. He has a wonderful eye for paradox and always manages to find the significant detail and to suggest the most intriguing conclusion. He pursues the elusive and complicated with great clarity." **—ROBERT STONE**

"I can't tell you the excitement I feel every time I come across a story by Ron Rosenbaum. Not only is he one of the finest investigative reporters of our generation—attacking contemporary Goliaths with a fearless wit and intelligence—but he is a fabulous storyteller. This collection is a treasure." **—TERESA CARPENTER**

"Ron Rosenbaum combines the skills of a terrific investigative reporter and an accomplished literary stylist with an idiosyncratic streak all his own. These pieces take chances, exhibit guts and stake out an edgy territory that will henceforth be known as 'Rosenbaumian.' Grisly, weird, bizarre—I thoroughly enjoyed this book." **—PHILLIP LOPATE**

". . . Rosenbaum is a master of the short form—the 5,000–10,000 word magazine article. They're all as easy to read as spy stories and beautifully written. Rosenbaum's chosen subject is the struggle to find out what really happened—to John F. Kennedy in Dallas, inside James Angleton's CIA, when Adolf Hitler realized he would never know for sure the identity of his grandmother's lover. Other writers drown in such subjects; Rosenbaum turns them into a kind of poetry of doubt." **—THOMAS POWERS**

PENGUIN BOOKS

TRAVELS WITH DR. DEATH

RON ROSENBAUM grew up in Brightwaters, New York; graduated from Yale; got his start writing for Dan Wolf at the *Village Voice* and Harold Hayes at *Esquire*. His first book, *Rebirth of a Salesman: Tales of the Song & Dance Seventies*, collected his chronicles of that confused decade. His portraits of eighties excess for *Manhattan, Inc.* were collected in *Manhattan Passions*, which the *New York Times* called "a sobering perspective on the values of the age." His first novel, a satire of the media world called *Murder at Elaine's*, is being developed into an off-Broadway production by Nora Ephron and Roy Blount Jr. Currently a contributing editor for *Vanity Fair* and a contributor to the *New York Times Magazine* and *Mademoiselle*, he's also at work on a second novel for Viking, set in the anti-Hitler underground of the early thirties. He lives in lower Manhattan near Gem's Spa.

TRAVELS WITH DR. DEATH

And

Other

Unusual

Investigations

RON ROSENBAUM

PENGUIN BOOKS

PENGUIN BOOKS
Published by the Penguin Group
Viking Penguin, a division of Penguin Books USA Inc.,
375 Hudson Street, New York, New York 10014, U.S.A.
Penguin Books Ltd, 27 Wrights Lane, London W8 5TZ, England
Penguin Books Australia Ltd, Ringwood, Victoria, Australia
Penguin Books Canada Ltd, 2801 John Street, Markham, Ontario, Canada L3R 1B4
Penguin Books (N.Z.) Ltd, 182–190 Wairau Road, Auckland 10, New Zealand

Penguin Books Ltd, Registered Offices: Harmondsworth, Middlesex, England

First published in simultaneous hardcover and paperback editions
by Viking Penguin, a division of Penguin Books USA Inc. 1991

1 3 5 7 9 10 8 6 4 2

"Back on the Watergate Case with Inspector RN" first appeared as "Ah Watergate" in *The New Republic*; "The Shadow of the Mole," "The Subterranean World of the Bomb," and "Turn On, Tune In, Drop Dead" in *Harper's Magazine*; "Oswald's Ghost" in *Texas Monthly*; "The General and the Blond Ghost" and "Travels with Dr. Death" in *Vanity Fair*; "The Mysterious Murder of JFK's Mistress"* in *New Times*; "Crack Murder" as "Crack Murder, A Detective Story" in *The New York Times Magazine*; "The Corpse as Big as the Ritz," "Dead Ringers,"† "The Last Secrets of Skull and Bones," and "Secrets of the Little Blue Box" in *Esquire*; "Tales from the Cancer Cure Underground" in *New West*; and "Dream Dancing" as "Richard Hoffman's Unknown Famous People" in *New York*.

* Co-written with Phillip Nobile
† Co-written with Susan Edmiston

LIBRARY OF CONGRESS CATALOGING IN PUBLICATION DATA
Rosenbaum, Ron.
Travels with Dr. Death and other unusual investigatons / Ron
Rosenbaum.
p.   cm.
ISBN 0 14 013845 5
1. Criminal investigation—United States—Case studies.
2. Conspiracies—United States—Case studies.   I. Title.
II. Title: Travels with Doctor Death and other unusual
investigations.
[HV7914.R67   1991b]
363.2′5′0973 — dc20   90–12846

Printed in the United States of America
Set in Granjon
Designed by Michael Ian Kaye

For my father,
Henry Rosenbaum, (1915–1990),
a man who was truly ''born with
the gift of laughter and
the sense that the
world was mad''

ACKNOWLEDGMENTS

Thanks first to my editor at Viking, the peerless Nan Graham, for her belief in this book, and for the intelligence and acuity of her suggestions for improving it. Gillian Silverman and Bob Castillo at Viking also made valuable contributions to the manuscript.

In the course of writing these stories I feel I've benefited from a remarkable array of exceptionally talented magazine editors, including (alphabetically) Martin Arnold, Bob Brown, Tina Brown, Dominique Browning, Jon Carroll, Sharon Delano, Byron Dobell, Lee Eisenberg, Don Erickson, Harold Hayes, Kim Heron, Rick Hertzberg, Michael Kinsley, Lewis Lapham, Jon Larsen, Suzanne O'Malley, Helen Rogan, Duncan Stalker, Bruce Weber, and Meredith White. Thanks again, all of you.

I'm grateful to Susan Edmiston and Phillip Nobile, my coauthors on "Dead Ringers" and "The Mysterious Murder of JFK's Mistress" (respectively), for all the hard work and inspiration they contributed to those stories.

I'd also like to thank the dozens of fact checkers at all these magazines who worked long hours on these stories, confirming facts, correcting errors, and chasing down *tks*.

Particular thanks are due Elise Ackerman, for research and fact checking the Hitler material, and to Waltraud Kolb, for research and German translation work on that story.

My exceptionally able and talented assistant, Katie Karlovitz, has been invaluable in all stages of preparation of this book, and my typist/ word processor, Jay Matlick, has done fast work on short notice with amazing accuracy.

The older I get the more I feel indebted to certain teachers at Yale, particularly Michael O'Loughlin, Henry Schroeder and Josiah Thompson, specialists in the metaphysical poets, Chaucer, and Kierkegaard, respectively, but whose larger gift to me was teaching me how to read.

In addition there are a number of people whose friendship, advice, encouragement, and support in various ways over the years have been particularly valuable. They include Jane Amsterdam, Dick and Robin Bell, Susan Braudy, Betsy Carter, George Dolger, Jan Drews, Mike Drosnin, Lester Faggiani, Ed Fancher, Rebecca Wright Fox, Liz Hecht, Nat Hentoff, Gary Hoenig, Craig Karpel, Caroline Marshall, Stanley Mieses, Kathryn Paulson, Dan Wolf, Ruth Rosenbaum, Evelyn Rosenbaum, Mary Turner, Mayer Vishner, Alan Weitz, Ross Wetzsteon, and Dan Wolf.

Finally, I'm not sure I can thank Kathy Robbins adequately for all the intelligent advice and spiritual uplift I've received from her. My constant regret is that I didn't have the benefit of her guidance much earlier—say about junior-high age; I know my life wouldn't have been as misspent and misguided as it was until she became my agent and advisor. In addition, it's been a pleasure to work with all the others in the Robbins office: Evelyn Rossi, Julia Null, Elizabeth Mackey, and Caroline Gelb.

Contents

Contents

INTRODUCTION: INVESTIGATING THE INVESTIGATIONS

The voice on the tape was pleading for an answer. "You believe this investigation *did* take place? You're the only one in the world who can tell us."

Outside on the grounds of the old FDR mansion up the Hudson at Hyde Park, New York, it was a glorious October day. I was inside, oblivious to it, buried deep in the windowless listening room of the FDR library archives, when I heard that plea. Despite the scratchy static in the earphones of the old reel-to-reel tape recorder, the urgency of the questioner was unmistakable. *You're the only one in the world* who can tell us.

The voice pleading for an answer was that of John Toland, the historian and Hitler biographer. The man he was questioning was Dr. G. M. Gilbert, the American psychologist who'd been detailed by the Allied authorities at Nuremberg to be personal psychological counselor to the imprisoned Nazi war crimes defendants during the trials and executions of 1946. Every night alone with Goering, with Hess, Streicher, Rosenberg, Ribbentrop, and the like, Gilbert would hear the ramblings and ravings, the backbiting, excuses and reminiscences, of the men closest to Hitler—up to the very moment the hangman's noose silenced them.

On the tape Toland was asking Gilbert about something startling one of these "clients" had confided to him shortly before he was taken off to the gallows.

The client was Hans Frank, one-time personal attorney to Adolf Hitler in the years before Hitler came to power; later Frank went on to preside over the slaughter of millions as governor-general of Nazi-occupied Poland.

After being condemned to death at Nuremberg for crimes against humanity, Frank produced, with the encouragement of Gilbert and an American priest, Father Sixtus O'Connor, a thousand-page pencil-written memoir of his life, focusing on his personal experiences with Hitler. Toland had sought out Gilbert to question him about an ex-traordinary story which Frank had recounted in that memoir, a story he'd discussed with Gilbert before his execution.

It was a story about the purported Hitler "family secret." About a "confidential investigation into Hitler's family history" Hans Frank claimed to have initiated in 1930 in his capacity as personal attorney to Hitler in response to a "blackmail" threat to expose the family secret.

In Hans Frank's death-cell memoir, he made the astonishing assertion that his confidential investigation had, in fact, turned up evidence of a potentially embarrassing Hitler family scandal, one that posed a threat to Hitler's political career—indeed, to his whole political persona. Frank claimed he'd found documentary evidence that Hitler's paternal grand-father was not the Aryan peasant laborer Georg Hiedler, as the official biographies maintained, but, instead, that Hitler's grandfather was "a Jew from Graz named Frankenberger."

Needless to say, this bizarre story has proven controversial, but three decades of dispute over it have not fully refuted, nor fully corroborated, its essential elements. The reason for its claim on our attention, of course, is not the relatively trivial genealogical question—who was the paternal grandfather?—but the place the Hans Frank story occupies in a pattern of other incidents, other episodes during Hitler's lifetime, in which questions were raised about his origins, about his "racial purity." And for the role doubts about his own "racial identity" may have played in the origin and pathology, the unique virulence of Hitler's anti-semitism. The Frank story might, if it had veracity, be a clue to the genuinely interesting larger question over which historians and biographers still disagree: When and how did Hitler become an anti-semite? What was there about his anti-semitism that turned it into such a uniquely murderous hatred?

What I've finally come to believe about the Hans Frank story and its significance can be found at length in the concluding essay in this book. Suffice to say here that at one point I was on the phone to John Toland to question his basis for accepting, for the most part, the truth of Frank's story (if not of the "Frankenberger" evidence). Toland suggested I go to Hyde Park and dig up the tape of his interview with Dr. Gilbert in the raw research materials for his Hitler biography, which he'd donated to the FDR archives.

Because, Toland pointed out, while historians and archivists could fight over the text of Frank's memoir for centuries, reading things into words on a page, Dr. Gilbert, Frank's psychologist, had actually questioned him personally on the subject of his "confidential investigation."

And now on the tape I heard Toland pressing Gilbert about the Hans Frank story. Can we believe it? *You're the only one in the world . . .*

There was something arresting about the tone of Toland's voice that struck me then and has stayed with me. Perhaps I'm reading my own pessimism into it, but beneath the urgency for an answer I thought I detected a despair of certainty. A sense that the possibility of really knowing the answer to his question has slipped irretrievably away.

Because, after all, Gilbert is not technically "the only one in the world who can tell us." More precisely, he's the only one still alive who spoke face-to-face with the only man who could *really* "tell us"—Hans Frank, the man who claimed to have conducted that "confidential investigation" and to have spoken face-to-face about its results with Hitler himself.

Gilbert was certainly the last best witness alive who could speak to the question of Hans Frank's veracity and motive in telling his story. Making such judgments was Gilbert's job inside the Nuremberg cells. But still, what Gilbert has to say can't resolve the question with certitude. It's more like a clue than an answer.

The very form of the question—"You believe this investigation *did* take place"—is telling. One more instance of what I've come to think of as the paradigmatic form the search for truth has taken in our time: the investigation of the investigation.

Consider the way the never-ending investigation of the Kennedy assassination for many years took the form of an investigation of the Warren Report. Warren Report dissidents called themselves "critics" and for a long time (until the advent of the Freedom of Information Act unleashed a flood of once-classified material) they tended to attack the text rather than the case beneath the text (they were the first deconstructionists).

The Woodward and Bernstein investigation of Watergate began as a re-investigation of the original U.S. attorney's grand jury investigation—the one that fell for the White House cover-up. Subsequently, the Woodward and Bernstein investigation has itself become the subject of investigation—into the motives of sources like Robert Bennett and Deep Throat for helping uncover the cover-up. Indeed, there are those who've sought to prove that it was Deep Throat, not Dick Nixon, who was the ultimate trickster in the case.

Watergate was the great begetter of investigations of investigations. Out of the material churned up by the congressional Watergate investigations came the "Baker Report" on the role of intelligence agencies in Watergate. Then came the Nedzi House Subcommittee on Intelligence Agencies' re-investigation of the Baker report material. All of which, in the climate of skepticism bred by Watergate and Sy Hersh exposés, generated the momentum for the full-scale Senate Intelligence (Church Committee) investigation of the role of the CIA in assassinations abroad. Which then engendered the Schweiker subcommittee investigation of the role of intelligence agencies in the Kennedy assassination. Which finally produced the critical mass of paranoia-become-reality to bring the whole thing full circle: a full-scale big-budget re-investigation of the Kennedy assassination, which the House of Representatives commissioned in 1977.

An extensive eighteen-month official investigation, the most thorough we're ever likely to get, concluded that JFK *was* "probably assassinated by a conspiracy," a plot probably backed by organized crime, although the committee "was unable to identify the other gunman" it said was firing from the famous grassy knoll opposite Oswald. Unfortunately, it turned out that the proof of the "other gunman," which the committee based on "scientific" acoustical analysis of a static-filled police-radio tape found in an attic, was not persuasive to another group of experts convened by the National Academy of Sciences. They disputed whether the grassy knoll "gunshot" sound isolated from the static by the House committee experts was really a gunshot or just a spike of static within the static.

And so, after all these years, the Warren Report has been thoroughly deconstructed, but no one has been able to reconstruct any definitive alternative to its conclusions. Which should not be cause for smugness on the part of Warren Report loyalists, because even if we believe Oswald did it, we still don't know who Oswald *was*, why he did it, under which of his many guises.

And so investigation begets investigation begets re-investigation, and still the ghost of Oswald lurks in the static with that inscrutable smirk on his face, the specter of uncertainty that seems to mock our best efforts to get to the bottom of things in the world after Dallas. Whose side was Soviet defector Yuri Nosenko really on? How did George Jackson die? Who smuggled him the gun? Who was behind James Earl Ray? Who was Manuchar Ghorbanifar really working for in his Iran-Contra role?

Are we any better off, any closer to the truth, as a result of all our re-investigations? In fact, my nonpessimist side would argue that we have both more truth and more uncertainty. Or to put it another way, more truths, if not the truth.

Take one instance: the fact that we now know, courtesy of the Church committee and others, that the CIA and the Mafia collaborated on assassination plots against Castro. That our government took out a mob hit "contract" on a foreign leader—while JFK was screwing the mistress of mob boss Sam Giancana—may ultimately turn out to have no consequential bearing on the question of who killed JFK (although Lyndon Johnson, for one, thought the Kennedy assassination was the consequence of some kind of backfire from "the damned Murder Incorporated Kennedy was running in the Caribbean"). But if it tells us nothing useful about who killed Kennedy, it certainly tells us a lot of useful things about the true face of power in JFK's America.

A number of the stories herein take the form of investigations of investigations. Very few of them are devoid of supposition, theorizing, speculation. I'll concede there is more uncertainty in these stories than I'd like. I prefer certainty. I prefer questions answered, doubts erased. I grew up reading Hardy Boy Detective Mysteries by the cartonful, longing to leave the uneventful suburb of my childhood, to have adventures and solve mysteries. Which is what I thought a life in journalism would be about.

Instead, while I found myself having more than my fill of adventures, the mysteries I was most attracted to rarely got solved in the old-fashioned sense, in part because the question at issue was often not "Who killed John?" but "Who *was* John?" or "Why did John kill himself?" Or they would be the kind of conceptual mystery that didn't lend itself to simple solutions: the metaphysics of the mole hunt; the theology of nuclear deterrence theory; the process by which the poetics of fraud and faith produces "cancer cures" in the clinics of Tijuana.

I'd find myself entering into clandestine subcultures, immersed in esoteric controversies where the Hardy Boy mysteries were less useful as guidebooks than Pynchon's *Crying of Lot for 49*, Polanski's *Chinatown*.

In fact, you could say the stories in this book represent an education in the varieties of contemporary uncertainty, an education capped by my brief but memorable conversation with James Jesus Angleton, the late legendary CIA counterintelligence chief. A conversation that ended up—or that he skillfully deflected into—a discussion of our mutual fondness for William Empson's classic work on poetic explication, *Seven Types of Ambiguity*.

Empson had made the case that instances of poetic ambiguity were not to be scorned as fuzzy self-contradiction but were, in fact, compressed expressions of the conflicting forces at the heart of a poem. Angleton praised Empson's investigation of the varieties of ambiguity as a model for counterintelligence technique: valuable in decrypting the ambiguous intentionality of double agents and suspect defectors.

Of course, nearly everything Angleton himself said and did was riddled with ambiguities, not the least instance being his mysterious role in leading the search for the personal diary of JFK mistress Mary Pinchot Meyer in the aftermath of her murder.

The officially unsolved murder of JFK's best and brightest paramour is an unusual case in the context of this collection. Because it's one of the rare ones where I believe there is actually less uncertainty than meets the eye. I think I know the solution. Or enough to rule out any conspiracy theories about her death, suspicious as it might seem on the surface.

The facts are that Mary Pinchot Meyer, the talented, lovely, widely admired exwife of CIA luminary Cord Meyer, had an ongoing affair with John F. Kennedy, which began in his second year in the White House. And that in September 1964, nearly a year after JFK's murder, Mary Meyer was also murdered—shot at close range while strolling along the C&O towpath at the foot of Washington D.C.'s Georgetown. In the immediate aftermath of her murder, her close friend James Angleton of the CIA, the wife of Ben Bradlee (later editor of the *Washington Post*), and Cord Meyer converged upon Mary Meyer's painting studio and turned the place upside down in a frantic search for the dead woman's personal diary, which, when found, was removed without knowledge of the authorities, thus ensuring that the secret of her White House affair would not be exposed in the course of the murder investigation.

The police and the prosecution believed a lone gunman was responsible, that the shooting was the byproduct of an attempted rape-robbery, which she resisted. The man arrested and charged with the murder, an unemployed laborer, was indicted, put on trial—and acquitted by a D.C. jury. Which means that the death of Mary Meyer remains officially unsolved.

Does that mean that the real killer of this highly accomplished, highly connected woman is still at large? And that her death had something to do with her secret sexual liaison with the slain president? That it was not the random result of an assault by a lone gunman?

In the years since her liaison with the president became public in 1976, that affair, her death, and the contents of her diary have become the nexus of a web of conspiracy-theory speculation.

One night in the Hollywood Hills, well into the late '80s, a well-known West Coast figure handed me a long missive from a private conspiracy-theory investigator who claimed that the murder of Mary Meyer was the key to just about Everything—all the scandals and tragedies of the post-Dallas world. In essence, it went something like this: Mary Meyer was murdered because of what she knew about the CIA plot to kill JFK; James Angleton seized her diary because it revealed the truth about the assassination; later on, Angleton, as Deep Throat, exposed Watergate to the *Washington Post* to depose Nixon, because Nixon planned to expose the truth about the CIA's role in JFK's death—which was *really* what was erased from the eighteen-minute gap on the Watergate tape. I think I might have left something out—the murder of John Lennon might also figure in—but you get the picture. Mary

Meyer's missing diary, like the eighteen-minute erasure, has become a black hole into which the secret truths of our time have disappeared.

This entire Ultimate Conspiracy Theory fantasy seemed to be founded upon the "fact" that Mary Meyer's murder was "officially unsolved," the only suspect acquitted by a jury. Although according to the L.A. figure who showed me the Letter That Explained It All, there was one further fact that made it look like the cover-up was still going on: the missing transcript.

He'd hired a private eye, my L.A. friend explained. He'd been intrigued enough by the unsolved status of Mary Meyer's death to put a gumshoe on the case. This was more than abstract historical curiosity. He felt he owed it to Mary Meyer. He'd known her briefly—intensely but platonically, he said—and clearly worshiped her. Spoke of her exquisite beauty and intellect, saw her as a clandestine crusader for peace in the hawkish upper echelons of Camelot—on a mission in her White House trysts, to turn JFK's head toward peace.

But the private eye my friend hired hadn't gotten very far before he reached a dead end. The transcript of the murder trial of the man accused of shooting Mary Meyer had disappeared from the D.C. courthouse archives, he said. The obvious conclusion was that it had been removed because it contained a clue to the conspiracy.

Not quite. I'd read the transcript when it was still there in the D.C. court clerk's office—read it with great avidity and attentiveness, read it hoping to find some clue, some evidence of conspiracy, some flaw in the prosecution's lone gunman theory. It certainly would have made a bigger story if there'd been a hole in the case that pointed to a more sinister explanation of the prosecution's theory of a random assault by a stranger.

That night when I told the L.A. guy that I'd actually read what he'd thought of as The Missing Transcript, I had the strange sensation of being addressed, implored in that same tone of urgency John Toland used in pressing Dr. Gilbert: *You're the only one in the world who can tell us.* What did the "missing" transcript reveal? Was there a conspiracy?

What I told him was, in essence: no. That having not only read the transcript but having reinvestigated the whole case, interviewed most of the principals, I'd come to believe in the "lone gunman" theory of this case. That the fatal shot *was* fired in the midst of a random assault by a stranger. That the prosecution may perhaps have indicted the wrong lone gunman on the basis of imperfect eyewitness testimony. But that no evidence was ever adduced that gives the slightest hint there was a conspiracy behind Mary Meyer's murder—or that her death had any relation to her secret liaison with JFK.

Indeed, the only real conspiracy was the one that took shape after her death, the one in which her high-placed friends conspired in a well-meaning attempt to preserve the secrecy of the affair with JFK described in her diary.

What the unsolved murder of Mary Meyer calls for—something I've found essential in a number of these uncertainty-plagued stories—is a quality Keats called Negative Capability. He defined it, in one of his letters, as the capability "of being in uncertainties, mysteries, doubts without irritable reaching after fact or reason" when certitude about neither is attainable. In the Mary Meyer case, the fact that her murder is officially "unsolved" is irritating, yes, but not justification for creating conspiracy theories out of whole cloth.

Nonetheless I've found that state of irritability Keats spoke of can be a powerful investigative tool, or at least a spur to action. A number of the stories herein began with scraps of newsclips, obscure footnotes challenging conventional wisdom, which I'd filed away until finally, often after years of festering in my files, just plain irritated me enough with their unresolvedness into investigating them further.

My year-long journey into the subterranean world of the bomb began with a crumpled four-paragraph *Times* clip I'd saved for several years, a little squib about a Strategic Air Command major fired for raising questions about the theoretical certitude of the fail-safe system for preventing an unauthorized nuclear-missile launch. The attempt to untangle the threads of the Angleton-Philby relationship in the mole story began with a footnote in Thomas Powers's biography of Richard Helms, which referred to a footnote in William Corson's book on the CIA, which offered a startling heretical revision of the "Third Man" story. What finally persuaded me to pursue the Hitler ancestry question was a clipping of a letter in New York's *Jewish Press*, which referred to a letter in Jeddah's *Saudi Gazette*, which presented a poisonously distorted version of the "Jewish ancestry" myth.

In most cases, although I believed I ended up closer to the truth than where I began, I rarely succeeded in eradicating the irritation of incertitude; rather, more frequently I found deeper, more disturbing levels of uncertainty and irritation. And so many of these stories are efforts to map out the boundaries between what can be known and what can't, road maps that take us up to the borders of *terra incognita*, not infallible guides to the entities within it.

Introductions like this tend to go astray when they postulate pervasive unities among disparate stories. Nonetheless, reading these over, it dawned on me that there is a peculiar kind of uncertainty that is common to many if not all of them. An uncertainty produced not by conspiratorial entities but rather, I suppose you could say, by individual entities with multiple identities.

The most egregious, most literal example is in "Dead Ringers," in which the Marcus twins, from birth a kind of multiple entity, led a double life in which they served as each other's secret identity. Double lives and secret identities are second nature in the mirror world of double agents and false defectors in the Angleton-Philby story; playing with identities, aliases, and electronic projections of themselves was the secret vice of the phone freak proto-hackers. Mary Meyer and Deep Throat led secret lives as White House Lover and White House Betrayer, respectively. J. Edgar Hoover was among the first to postulate a "second Oswald," warning in a memo about the possibility of an "Oswald impersonator" using O.'s identity. Indeed, Oswald himself seems to have been, when you add it all up, less a single person than a series of impersonations, harboring second and third Oswalds within him. And Hitler's ravings in *Mein Kampf* against "the Jew within"— how much of his psychotic rage can be attributed to fear of a "Jew within" himself, the need to exorcise the fear of an "alien" entity within his own identity?

In addition, of course, there are a number of stories herein of fantasy identities—the Mechanicals' Play "celebrities" in the Richard H. Roffman story ("Dream Dancing"), the Knights Templar fantasy of the Skull and Bones initiates, the F. Scott Fitzgerald fantasy that star-struck David Whiting thought he was living out in "The Corpse as Big as the Ritz" (with Sara Miles as his Zelda) before he ended up bleeding to death from a star-shaped wound on the back of his head in Gila Bend, Arizona. (I should point out that I don't think Burt Reynolds was the star who struck him; I *believe* Burt's alibi about the Oriental massage.)

It would be tempting to claim that the uncertainty factor generated by multiple identities is the signature of the zeitgeist in these stories, but in fact, I think it's an older, more primal phenomenon. There's a line I came across during a recent unsuccessful effort to make it all the way through Carlyle's *History of the French Revolution*—a line about the prodigies credited to the fictional persona of the king of the Old Regime—the ability, for example, to "appear" in many places at once in his realm.

"For ours is the most fictile world, and man is the most fingent, plastic of creatures," Carlyle says. "Fictile" I took to mean that enduring itch to create fictions about ourselves, and fictional selves. I guess you could say these are factual stories about fictile people.

January 1990

PUBLIC
SCANDALS

•   ▪   •

BACK ON THE WATERGATE CASE WITH INSPECTOR RN

"I am aware," H. R. Haldeman writes, "that there is a cult of people in this country who collect every scrap of information about Watergate because of its many fascinating mysteries." He's more than aware: his memoir, *The Ends of Power*, is a seething nest of almost every conceivable scrap of Watergate conspiracy theory developed to date. The Democratic Trap Theory, the CIA Trap Theory, the Blackmail Demand Theory: you name it, H. R. Bob buys it. Indeed, the former chief of staff is nothing if not a buff himself, and he spices his book with tantalizing buff-to-buff hints for further investigation of the "fascinating mysteries." "I'll only pause to bring out one more fact about the $350,000," he teases, "this one for the Watergate buffs. . . ."

Although such recognition is welcome, the tone of the reference is regrettably uncharitable. By calling serious students of Watergate a "cult" of "buffs," he is, of course, lumping us with the much-abused "assassination buffs" and the aura of bad taste and futility that is associated with their efforts.

But there is a difference between these two domains of buffdom.

Perhaps because—as Nixon partisans like to remind us—"nobody drowned at Watergate," the conjectures and conspiracy theories that have sprung up in its wake lack the taint of ghoulishness that has continued to plague grassy knoll theories, the most recent excrescence of which (David Lifton's *Best Evidence*) insists on conjuring up a grue-some postmortem surgical alteration of the fatal wounds to fit a favored bullet trajectory theory. Although certain Watergate theorists venture equally far into fantasy (I have in my Watergate collection a curious vanity press volume called *The Journal of Judith Beck Stein*, written by a former patient in the Chesnut Lodge sanitarium, which seems to allege that the entire Watergate conspiracy and cover-up was engineered to cheat her out of a legacy and silence her exposure of the banking system), the eyes of Watergate buffs tend to twinkle rather than stare. Ours is a civilized passion.

Who, then, are the Watergate buffs? Not, as you might expect, a coterie of Nixon-haters still savoring each delectable detail of his demise, "wallowing in Watergate," as the ex-President put it. No, many of the most relentless and dedicated Watergate buffs are pro-Nixon revisionists determined to prove that the whole episode was a dirty trick perpetrated upon, rather than by, Richard Nixon. (Reed Irvine's *Accuracy in Media* newsletter has tirelessly pursued the Democratic Trap Theory for seven years now.)

Some of us are reporters who were stationed in Washington for the thrilling Final Days, and have developed a lasting taste for the arcana, however tangential, of the case. I, for example, can claim credit for being the first to uncover both a prophetic mention of Watergate in the Bible and an anticipation of the Plumbers Squad in the historical etymology of the *Oxford English Dictionary*. In the Book of Nehemiah (Ne:8:1) the people of Israel gather after their return from Babylonian exile to hear the prophet Ezra read the law of Moses to them for the first time since they regained their freedom. Where do they gather to hear the Word? At the entrance to Jerusalem known as "the Watergate." And the *O.E.D.* offers an eerie foreshadowing of the substance of the twentieth-century scandal in the eighteenth-century usage of the verb "watergate": *to void urine*. That is, in effect, *to leak*.

Though studies of this sort may seem inadmissibly mystical to some, there are hard-nosed investigators among the buffs as well: former prosecutors, Congressional staffers, politicians—even an ex-President, the greatest buff of them all. All are united by undiminished delight in the "fascinating mysteries" to which H. R. Bob refers. And in fact there *are* genuine gaps in our knowledge that are more extensive than anything any eighteen minutes of tape could supply. There are obvious questions (quick: who ordered the break-in?) and subtle ones (just what was missing from the "Bay of Pigs report" that Richard Helms finally turned over to Richard Nixon, and how did it shape the outcome of the CIA cover story fabricated in the famous "smoking gun" tape?). And there are more esoteric excursions into the ambiguities of the evidence. Did the White House tamper with the birth certificate of the alleged "love child" of George McGovern? Who was private eye Woolsten-Smith's source of information in The November Group? And what was the mysterious "red box" the President keeps harping on in his September 15, 1972, talk with John Dean? ("What is the situation on the little red box?" asks P. "Have they found the box yet?" Could this be a childhood toy—Nixon's Rosebud?) Finally, of course, there are the larger motivational questions: was the downfall of the President pure self-destruction, or was he undermined by subterranean power struggles which have yet to be fully analyzed?

Some buffs will stop at nothing in an effort to find some rational explanation for the actions of Richard Nixon. Consider the heroic efforts of Professor Douglas Muzzio, author of *Watergate Games*, an attempt to translate major Watergate turning points into mathematical game theory decision matrixes. Game theory proves, according to Muzzio, that far from acting as he did "because he was 'mad' or 'needed to fail,' " RN "acted rationally in response to events and actions by other Watergate players." Even if the professor's "payoff matrixes" and "decision trees" fall short of convincing us of that conclusion, he is an extraordinarily well-read buff, and his analysis of the other "Watergate players" is often illuminating. Take, for instance, the game theory rationale he constructs to rehabilitate the much maligned original Watergate prosecutor, Earl Silbert. Muzzio claims that a Silbert prosecutorial "ploy"—tricking Dean into believing Liddy was already talking—was the key to cracking the case. If you find that hard to believe, just study Professor Muzzio's chart.

While such reductionist efforts are good for a chuckle, the idea that all Watergate mysteries were "solved" by the smoking gun is no less laughable. In fact (and this is what raises Watergate cultists from buffdom to scholarship) there is still uncharted territory to be explored. With that in mind, let's take a brisk tenth anniversary wallow in the muddied fields of Watergate theory and survey the state of the art in the kingdoms of conjecture built by the buffs.

●   ■   ●

Foreknowledge Theory, in its many forms, has been a consistent growth area of buffdom over the past ten years—a steady performer compared to, say, Deep Throat Theory, which proceeds by fits and starts of guesswork. Foreknowledge Theory has blossomed into a major revisionist heresy. In its "Democratic Trap" variation, it's become a vehicle for the quest of die-hard Nixon loyalists for historical vindication. Trap Theory traces its origins to seven volumes of executive session testimony taken by Howard Baker's minority staff of the Senate Watergate committee. (The seven volumes, which have come to be known among foreknowledge buffs as "The Seven Volumes," are not to be confused with "The Baker Report," a separate minority staff investigation which, when reinvestigated by the Nedzi Committee of the House, developed into the CIA Foreknowledge Theory.) The Seven Volumes tell a provocative and fairly well-corroborated story of Watergate-eve intrigue among RN's enemies. The story begins with a British-born, New York-based private eye named A. J. Woolsten-Smith, who came to Kennedy Democrat William Haddad in April 1972 with what he said was reliable information that the Republicans had targeted a sophisticated spy operation against the Democratic National Committee. Haddad introduced Woolsten-Smith to Larry O'Brien's DNC deputy and to Jack Anderson. In conversations with them, specific tips about the Watergate target and the Cuban composition of the break-in team were passed along. It also happened that Jack Anderson was an old friend of Frank Sturgis and ran into him at National Airport the night before the break-in, just as Sturgis was arriving from Miami with the Cubans in order to make their second entry into O'Brien's office—the one that would end with their arrest and the beginning of Richard Nixon's fall.

●   ■   ●

At this point, the foreknowledge scenario becomes more speculative. The man who led the cops into Watergate to arrest the burglars, one Officer Shoffler, is said to have signed up for an unusual second eight-hour tour of duty that night. Shoffler turns out to be the closest cop to the Watergate when the guard, Frank Wills, called police headquarters. An acquaintance of Officer Shoffler, one Edmund T. Chung, testifies that in a post-Watergate dinner conversation he got the "impression that Shoffler had advance knowledge of the break-in." According to the Trap Theory, the Democrats learned about the first, May 27, break-in and bugging after it was over and contrived a plan to lure the Committee to Reelect the President (CREEP) team back into Watergate on June 17, at which point they tipped off the cops. How did they lure them back in? With the malfunctioning bug on Larry O'Brien's phone. According to Reed Irvine, that bug "may not have died a natural death." In other words, the Democrats exterminated the bug to lure the CREEP repair team back to be trapped in the act.

Other possible tipsters to Officer Shoffler postulated by other variations of Foreknowledge Theory include Jack Anderson, the CIA, Howard Hughes's p.r. man Robert Bennett, or a double agent on the break-in team itself (usually identified as McCord). If all the people with alleged foreknowledge *had* actually decided to tip off the cops and trap the burglars, you'd think at least one of them would have been able to get through to Officer Shoffler. But Shoffler flatly denies being tipped off, and there is no smoking gun to contradict him. Foreknowledge Theory, in consequence, has bogged down in fanciful embellishments of the supposed Democratic (or CIA or Jack Anderson) conspiracy to trick Dick Nixon. For the most part, foreknowledge has degenerated into inconclusive foreplay.

●   ■   ●

One person who hasn't given up on foreknowledge, however, is Richard Nixon. In *RN: The Memoirs of Richard Nixon*, a volume which is unquestionably the masterwork of Watergate buffery, RN claims that shortly before he resigned he became aware of "new information that the Democrats had prior knowledge and that the Hughes organization might be involved. . . . And there were stories of strange alliances" between his enemies and moles within the White House. It is easy to see the appeal of Foreknowledge Theory for Nixon. It's the embodiment of the darkest Nixonian fantasies: a hideous congeries of his hypocritical enemies use dirty tricks to lure him into essaying a dirty trick himself, then stumble over themselves in the shadows in their haste to call the cops.

In fact, the more you pursue Foreknowledge Theory, the more it begins to seem as if Richard Nixon was the only person in Washington who *didn't* know about the break-in ahead of time. Which brings us to a surprisingly stagnant and neglected subdivision of Foreknowledge Theory, the Richard Nixon Foreknowledge Question: did RN order the break-in or approve it in advance?

Of course, we have RN's word for it that he didn't. Moreover, RN claims that this has been *proved conclusively*. How so? The release of the White House edited transcripts back in 1974, he writes in *RN*, "proved conclusively that I had not known about the break-in in advance." In other words, because RN is not heard *confessing* to ordering the break-in on tape, because he denies it several times (when he knew he was being recorded), it's been proved that he didn't do it. RN frequently shores up this "proof" with copious citations from his "diary entries" immediately after the break-in. Time after time, it seems, he confided to his diary his total bewilderment at the strange and unexpected news that anyone would want to bug the Democratic National Committee.

Most Watergate investigators have been content to let RN by with this Big Surprise version of his reaction, there being no concrete evidence to the contrary. Neither the Ervin Committee, the Impeachment Committee, the Woodstein team, nor the Special Prosecutor's office had evidence or belief enough to conclude that RN knew in advance. The only Watergate observer to take an unequivocal *Guilty! Guilty! Guilty!* stand on Nixonian foreknowledge has been Mary McCarthy. Why so shy, the rest of them? Perhaps they don't want to be perceived as knee-jerk Nixon-haters eager to believe the worst about RN. Perhaps everyone is still waiting for another smoking gun to surface.

Well, another smoking gun *has* surfaced, it just hasn't been obtained yet. I came across a clue to its existence and whereabouts in Haldeman's book. If Haldeman is to be believed, the decisive testimony on the RN Foreknowledge Question may be on tape—but not a White House tape. Haldeman writes that he learned of this potentially explosive tape from

Ken Clawson, the former *Washington Post* reporter who'd become an aide to Chuck Colson and later was promoted by RN to head the White House p.r. operation during the Final Days. According to Haldeman, an anguished, conscience-stricken Clawson came to him in May 1973, shortly after the chief of staff was forced to resign by RN, and told him: "Chuck Colson is blackmailing Nixon. He's got Nixon on the floor. Nixon didn't know that Colson was taping all of his telephone calls with Nixon *before and after* Watergate happened. He's got on tape just what Nixon said all through the whole Watergate mess."

Now, the novelty of this putative evidence is not in the blackmail revelation (everyone in the White House was blackmailing everyone else by that time), nor is it in the fact there are tapes of Colson and RN. It is that, unlike the thousands of pages of White House tapes we already have, RN *did not know his Colson calls were being taped*. He made four calls to Colson from Key Biscayne in the twenty-four hours after he learned about the break-in arrests: nearly two hours of talk with Colson would be on these Colson tapes, but not on the White House tapes. RN tells us that, according to his "diary," Watergate was not discussed in those four calls. He and Colson talked about George Meany. About the polls. About the press. He just can't recall anything about Watergate. "Watergate," RN writes, "was the furthest thing from my mind."

If Colson did make tapes of those calls, and if he didn't destroy them as a relic of his sinful past when he got religion, then it's safe to assume they're stashed in a Colson-controlled safe deposit box somewhere. The contents of that safe deposit box would probably prove in his own words whether RN had that all-important foreknowledge, and how actively and immediately he collaborated in the subsequent cover-up. It would change our entire understanding of the internal dynamics of the collapse of a government.

●   ■   ●

Among the delights of buffdom are the unexpected discoveries one makes about apparently unrelated Watergate mysteries while tracing a single strand of the tangled web. And so it was that, while pursuing the question of Clawson's motives in telling the Colson blackmail story, I came across a surprising Clawson reference in *All the President's Men* which seemed to clinch the case for Clawson as the elusive Deep Throat. To all but the most deeply versed initiates of Deep Throat mysteries, the passage was an innocuous bit of background on Clawson: "Wallace had been shot by Bremer about 4 p.m.," Woodward and Bernstein write. "By 6:30 a *Post* editor had learned the name of the would-be assassin from White House official Ken Clawson."

This sent me searching madly for *Washington Post* (and Woodstein) editor Barry Sussman's book *The Great Cover-up*, where, I recalled, Sussman provides the only intra-*Post* clue to Deep Throat's identity. I found it. It looked like the clincher at last: "On May 15, 1972, hours after George Wallace was shot," Sussman writes, "we at the *Post* had not learned the name of the man who shot the Alabama governor. Woodward mentioned to me that he had 'a friend' who might be able to help. As we began to get into the Watergate scandal, 'my friend' as Woodward called him, came to play a mysterious, a crucial role. Over the months, 'Bob's friend' became more and more important to us and Howard Simons gave him a new name: 'Deep Throat.' "

●　　　　■　　　　●

It looked as though I'd cracked the Throat case: Clawson was the guy who got Bremer's name for a *Post* editor. Woodward's editor says the source from whom Woodward got Bremer's name for the *Post* later became known as Deep Throat. In the movie version of *All the President's Men*, which was made in close consultation with Woodward, Robert Redford appeals to Deep Throat by reminding him, "You helped me out on the Wallace thing."

I was ready to tell the other Deep Throat theorists to close up shop. But I still had just enough doubt—Clawson had a reputation as an unusually rabid Nixon loyalist—that I decided to violate a cardinal rule of buffdom: I made some phone calls. (Buffs, unlike mere reporters, do not make phone calls except to other buffs. They are content with the pleasures of the text, the wealth of resonances already in the literature.)

When I tried to track down Clawson through fellow RN loyalist Victor Lasky (author of *It Didn't Start With Watergate*), I learned that Clawson had fallen ill several years ago and Lasky had lost contact with him. Lasky thought my clue intriguing but had his doubts about Clawson as Throat. "He was one of the last ones to go down in the bunker,"

Lasky told me. "He was defending the Old Man right down to the last minute. It makes no sense to me—*unless he was putting on the act of acts. . . .*" (My emphasis.)

At the *Post*, Barry Sussman confirmed that Woodward had turned to his "friend" for help with the Bremer name, but wouldn't say for sure that "Bob's friend" had actually been the one to *succeed* in getting the Wallace suspect's name—in other words, Deep Friend wasn't necessarily Clawson.

What about the line in the movie: "You helped me with Wallace"? Sussman thought that the director of the movie, Alan J. Pakula, might have gotten that detail from Sussman's own book rather than from Woodward. Or that he might have been wrong about the Bremer source being one and the same as Deep Throat. Sussman didn't like the Clawson theory at all. Of course, Sussman would not *want* it to be true, wouldn't want the clinching clue to have come from a slight detail he inadvertently let slip in his book. He did tell me that the only other person who had ever delved deeply enough to ask him about the relationship between the Bremer passage in his book and the Wallace line in the movie was John Dean. Dean has been a long-time Deep Throat buff, Sussman said, and in fact had called him recently to speculate about a new suspect.

"Oh, I know, Dean's candidate is Dave Gergen," I said smugly, recalling that Dean's ghostwriter, Taylor Branch, had written about Dean's Gergen theory back in November 1976. Not anymore, Sussman told me: Dean has switched suspects, but not directly from Gergen. There was another intermediary suspect before he settled on his brand-new tenth anniversary Throat candidate. (Sussman didn't tell me either one.) I sympathize with Dean. Before I came upon the Clawson clue, I'd been working the Henry Peterson angle, and I'd never *really* given up my lingering Leonard Garment and Seymour Glanzer suspicions. It was comforting to know that Dean too suffered from similar Throat-switching tendencies. It seems that after ten years his wily ex-antagonist is destined to continue to elude definite detection.

●   ■   ●

Some suggest that after ten years the real mystery of Deep Throat is his continued silence. "If he's such a big national hero, why doesn't he step forward and claim all the credit?" Victor Lasky asks. "I'll tell you why," Victor Lasky answers. "Because there is no Deep Throat." One possible explanation for the silence of Throat—and it does lend support to the Henry Petersen theory—is that if Throat were, like Petersen or Glanzer, part of the Justice Department prosecutorial team, the disclosure of his identity might give all the Watergate felons cause to petition for a reversal of the verdicts on the grounds of prosecutorial misconduct. Who knows, they might have to restage all the big Watergate trials. As John Dean said, "What an exciting prospect."

In defense of the non-dottiness of Deep Throat speculation, let me point out that Watergate and its aftermath was a subterranean war of leaks, of attempts by one faction or another to divert press and prosecutorial attention to rival power centers. Several significant civil wars within the White House and within the bureaucracies and agencies acted themselves out in deep background attacks. Deep Throat might have been a conscience-stricken loner seeking absolution in underground garage confessionals. But he also might have been a cynical game-player trying to use the *Washington Post* for some factional gain. Without knowing his identity, our understanding of Watergate history will be incomplete, although I have a feeling we all prefer the continuing mystery to the inevitable disappointments of certainty.

RN certainly does not consider Deep Throat speculation an idle question. He's as big a buff as anyone on the subject. Haldeman gives us fascinating glimpses of RN and his ex-chief of staff batting around Deep Throat theories in buff-to-buff chats. According to Haldeman, RN's personal Deep Throat candidate is Robert Bennett, the Hughes p.r. man who was Howard Hunt's boss in a p.r. firm that also served as a CIA cover. According to Bennett's CIA case officer (cited in the Nedzi Committee hearings), Bennett boasted that he was feeding Bob Woodward information and that Woodward was "suitably grateful," a quote which has become the basis for entire Robert Bennett theories of Watergate, some of them spread by Chuck Colson and all of them misguided.

As a buff, however, I find it troubling to see fellow buff RN mired in the dark ages of Deep Throat speculation. All serious analysts of the question have long since abandoned the Bennett-as-Throat hypothesis. Bennett was a source for Woodward, but a source he acknowledges on the record in *All The President's Men*. In fact, J. Anthony Lukas, who boomed Bennett big in a *New York Times Magazine* article, abandoned him and switched to lukewarm endorsement of Mark Felt (Edward Jay Epstein's candidate), the Deputy FBI director who was feuding with RN's pet, Pat Gray.

Haldeman's own candidate is Fred Fielding, the former John Dean deputy who served President Reagan as White House counsel in charge of ethical questions. There's a wonderful description of ethics counsel Fielding in John Dean's book which depicts the future arbiter of integrity drawing on "rectal gloves" in order not to leave fingerprints on the potentially incriminating contents of Howard Hunt's safe. Fielding, by the way, is one of three key Deep Throat candidates in powerful positions in the Reagan high command. He and the others (communications director Dave Gergen, John Dean's one-time choice, and Alexander Haig, a frequently mentioned contender) will be suitably grateful, I hope, now that my Ken Clawson solution has gotten them off the hook.

●   ■   ●

Of course, no survey of buffdom is complete without an appreciation of the achievements of *RN: The Memoirs of Richard Nixon*. Only fellow buffs can appreciate the indomitable, never-say-die spirit of buffery in this work. If the White House transcripts are the Bible for buffs, *RN* may be considered the Gnostic Gospels, the great heretical reinterpretation of the central sacred texts. One thinks of comparable heroic acts of misinterpretation—William Blake's notion that Milton's Satan is the true hero of *Paradise Lost* comes to mind.

But for the most precise literary antecedent to *RN*, we must consider nothing less than Vladimir Nabokov's *Pale Fire*; for the best parts of *RN*, like Nabokov's novel, take the form of an obsessive, elaborate explication of an established text. In *Pale Fire* we have a mad professor misinterpreting his murdered friend's poem to fashion himself the central character. In *RN* we have a defrocked President doggedly taking on the tape-recorded text of his own words and, with a heroic act of the explicative imagination, transforming guilt-laden utterances into evidences of utter innocence, raising explication to the level of high art.

Consider the balletic leaps of ratiocination he takes with the notorious "I don't give a shit what happens, I want you all to stonewall it, let them plead the Fifth Amendment, cover up or anything else, if it'll save it, save the plan" passage in the tapes. It emerges from the smithy of RN's art as "my oblique way of confronting the need to make a painful shift in our Watergate strategy."

Then there's his marvelous explication of the famous March 21 "cancer on the Presidency" talk with Dean, the one in which he repeatedly insisted he wanted to pay a million-dollar hush-money bribe to keep the cover-up going. This, he explains, was his way of ensuring that the truth would come out "in an orderly and rational way."

But RN is not content with exegetical virtuosity. He has brand new theories to offer buffs. Take his fascinating suggestion about the real culprit in the creation of the eighteen-minute gap. He knows that his explanation of the erasure is a kind of command performance. He knows we're expecting a dazzling effort from him on this one. But he's confident: "I know my treatment of the gap will be looked upon as a touchstone for the candor and credibility of what I write," he begins. It's a breathtaking gesture, almost like Babe Ruth pointing to the stands. He's convinced he can pull it off and make us believe that neither he nor Rose Mary Woods had anything to do with erasing that tape.

What he delivers is less an explication than an epic innuendo implying extended Secret Service conspiracy and treason within the White House:

> I think we all wondered about the various Secret Service agents and technicians who had had free daily access to the tapes, and even about the Secret Service agents who had provided Rose with the new but apparently faulty Uher tape recorder just half an hour before she discovered the gap. We even wondered about Alex Butterfield, who had revealed the existence of the tape system. . . . But it would have taken a very dedicated believer in conspiracies to accept that someone would have purposely erased 18½ minutes of this particular tape in order to embarrass me.

RN is just such a dedicated believer, and the more you study *RN*, the more you realize just how dedicated he is. He suspected Watergate was a set-up from the first. Barely two weeks after the break-in, he was entertaining "the possibility that we were dealing with a double agent who purposely blew the operation."

Indeed, RN is so preoccupied by the idea that he is the *victim* of the break-in and bugging of his opponents that he repeatedly fantasizes that his own party headquarters were bugged. He attributes to Haldeman, in one of his "diary" entries right after the June 17 arrests, the story that "one of Chotiner's operatives had said that a McGovern aide had told him that *they* had our committee rooms bugged." Curiously, he deletes from his diary citation the name of this "Chotiner operative" and that of the McGovern aide who confessed to a Watergate-like crime against RN. RN seems to have an exclusive on this bombshell.

RN's greatest strength as a buff is his generosity as a guide to future 'Gate revelations—the ones destined to keep buffs busy for the next ten years of wallowing. RN's clues to what's in store take the form of elaborate denials of things he hasn't been accused of yet. When one comes across one of these in the text of *RN*, one senses that RN is signaling that there's a truly delicious incriminating morsel on a tape he fears might be released in the foreseeable future.

● ■ ●

One of the best of these coming attractions is the passage in which RN attempts to deny offering clemency to Jeb Stuart Magruder about a year into the cover-up. It's April 1973. RN is in the middle of his famous "personal investigation" of Watergate following Dean's "cancer on the Presidency" talk. Magruder is about to go back before the grand jury he lied to the summer before. If he tells the truth, he can put all the President's men in jail and make a liar out of RN. Assured of clemency, however, he might be willing to risk continued protective perjury. And so, lurking behind RN's unusually detailed account of a chat with Ehrlichman back then, there must be a heretofore unnoted offer of clemency to Magruder; and it's possible to glimpse in the pale fire of his preemptive interpretation the reflected glare of the guilt he's trying to eclipse: "I had been thinking the night before about Magruder's young children," RN tells us, sawing away at the heartstrings, "and about his wife. 'It breaks your heart,' I said. I thought back to Haldeman's comment two weeks before on how pathetic Magruder had been with his plea for clemency. I told Ehrlichman that this was a painful message for me: 'I'd just put that in so that he knows that I have personal affection,' I said. 'That's the way the so-called clemency's got to be handled.' "

The single most tantalizing of these peeks into future revelations, however, is RN's teasing suggestion that he's got a hitherto unknown break-in in store for us, one that he personally ordered, presumably on tape. RN tells us that on Wednesday, June 21, 1972, with the cover-up still in its embryonic stage, he came up with a bold counterattack proposal: "I said that every time the Democrats accused us of bugging we should charge that we were being bugged and maybe even plant a bug and find it ourselves!"

He seems to have been mulling this idea over for ten days when, in a conversation with Colson for which RN feels compelled to offer a preemptive pre-tape-release explanation, he makes it sound as if he gave a definite go-ahead order: "Colson and I talked about the exaggerated publicity that was being given to the break-in. In sheer exasperation I said it would help if someone broke into our headquarters and did a lot of damage—then we could launch a counterattack. Colson agreed. . . ."

●   ■   ●

This sounds like the authentic RN. Two weeks after the Watergate break-in, he's champing at the bit to order a break-in on himself to prove that his break-in on his enemies was retroactively justified by the one he'd blame on them. Of course, no such break-in at RN's campaign headquarters has been reported. But would RN have brought up the subject in his memoirs and tried to excuse it ("in sheer exasperation . . .") in advance if the order did not sound serious on the yet-to-be-released tape?

And it happens that not long after this conversation, a break-in took place at the Long Beach office of RN's former physician, Dr. John Lungren.

According to RN, "No money or drugs were taken but my medical files were removed from a locked closet and left strewn about the floor of the office." Note that RN's medical records were not removed from the office. And if the Lungren break-in team had merely wanted to photograph the records, why leave them so conspicuously scattered around? From the description RN provides, it seems as if the only purpose of the Lungren break-in was to advertise the fact that RN was the target. Such advertising comes in handy to RN. He cites it later as evidence that his enemies used the same tactics against him as he did in having his men break into Daniel Ellsberg's doctor's office. The symmetry is so pleasing to RN that one wonders if he had a share in shaping it. RN seems not at all outraged that damage was done to his doctor's office, only that just one network carried the news of the Lungren break-in while all three made a big deal over a 1973 report of a break-in into JFK's doctor's office during the 1960 campaign (another RN job?).

Yes, while other investigators have retired from the field, RN is still probing these baffling break-ins. Haldeman provides us with a fascinating glimpse of Inspector RN at work on the Ellsberg break-in case. Shortly after the November 1976 election (which would soon put a Democratic Administration in charge of the disputed storehouse of White House tapes), RN summoned Haldeman to San Clemente "to probe my memory," Haldeman says. According to Haldeman, Inspector RN has been toying with the hypothesis that he—RN himself—ordered the break-in: "I was so damn mad at Ellsberg in those days. And Henry was jumping up and down. I've been thinking—and maybe I did order that break-in."

But Inspector RN is not completely satisfied with this deft solution to the Ellsberg case. He'd called in Ellsberg operations chief Egil Krogh, and Krogh told him *he* didn't remember the President ordering him to do it. "Again and again that afternoon Nixon returned to the subject," Haldeman recalls. "Finally he said, 'I'm just going to have to check it out further.' "

Surprisingly, Haldeman has doubts about the good faith of Inspector RN's continuing investigation:

> And then I realized the situation. If Nixon had ordered the
> break-in while in the Oval Office his order was preserved
> on tape. And those tapes might well become public some
> day. Nixon was debating whether to reveal what he had
> really said in that office about the break-in or wait it out.
> It might be years before that particular tape was unearthed.

Now, it seems to me that this is an extremely uncharitable interpretation of Inspector RN's motives. If you recall, RN has told us that as soon as he heard the shocking news of a cover-up in the White House from John Dean back in March 1973, he proceeded to launch his own intensive investigation of the entire affair. So this account of RN probing to see whether anyone remembered *him* ordering the Ellsberg job is just another indication among many that after ten years, RN *is still on the case*. And, at long last, he may be closing in on Mr. Big.

—*THE NEW REPUBLIC*
June 1982

POSTSCRIPT TO "BACK ON THE
WATERGATE CASE WITH INSPECTOR RN"

It's still remarkable to me that the original Watergate burglary remains unsolved. In the seven years since *The New Republic* asked me to do this piece for their Tenth Anniversary Watergate issue, we're no closer to a solution. As the most recent Nixon biography (Stephen Ambrose's 1989 *Nixon: The Rise to Power*) reminds us, "Nobody was ever prosecuted for ordering the Watergate break in, only for participating in it, or conspiring to cover it up."

Ambrose himself is divided on the subject. He's clear that Nixon was frantic to get dirt on Larry O'Brien—and to find out what dirt O'Brien had on him from his Howard Hughes connection. But he believes it was actually John Mitchell, not RN, who gave the order to break into O'Brien's Democratic National Committee office at the Watergate. In other words, he seems to accept RN's repeated denials that he ordered the break-in or knew about it in advance. In his 1985 book *Citizen Hughes*, however, Michael Drosnin quotes a high-level Watergate insider (who sounds like Jeb Magruder to me) to the effect that he was present when Mitchell received a phone call from Nixon, urging the O'Brien office break-in. That's probably the closest we'll ever get to linking RN directly to the command decision, although even that remains an account of a telephone call from a bystander, not a party to it.

In the years since this story appeared, I've come to believe, in effect, that both versions of who ordered the break-in might be technically correct, because it's often forgotten that there were not one but two separate break-ins by the Watergate burglars.

The first, in late May 1972, was successful in the sense that the burglary team went in and out without getting caught. But it was also frustratingly unsuccessful in that the bug they planted on O'Brien's phone malfunctioned, or they planted it on the wrong phone (both versions are told). Still, they did obtain some information, which was stored in the now-purportedly-destroyed "Gemstone" file.

Then in early June 1972 the question arose: Is the Gemstone material promising enough to warrant sending the burglars back in again to fix the O'Brien bug and photograph more documents?

My admittedly conjectural belief now is that Mitchell, under pressure from RN for O'Brien dirt, may have ordered the first break-in himself. But that, before ordering the team to go *back* in, he acquainted RN with the Gemstone material and asked him if he thought it was worth the risk to go in for more. And that RN, tantalized and frustrated by the initial Gemstone product, couldn't resist asking for more and, one way or another, gave the go-ahead. Which accounts for the tortuous dividedness of his pronouncements on his role. He was being truthful in a technical sense when he denied he ordered the break-in. What he actually did, I believe, was *re-order* it.

THE SHADOW
OF THE MOLE

The big mole. The American Philby. Is he still among us, still a trusted figure operating at the highest levels of government, still burrowing ever deeper into our most sensitive secrets, as embittered exiles from our espionage establishment, the losing side in the Great Mole War of the past decade, contend? Is he, even now, sitting in some comfortable Capitol district office and reading these words, chuckling contentedly?

Or did he ever exist at all? Might he be a delusion engendered by the fevered fantasies of the hierophants of counterintelligence theory—a product of paranoid "sick think," as the complacent victors in the Great Mole War, the current chiefs of the espionage establishment, have called it? Worse, might the entire twelve-year-long hunt for the American mole and the civil war within the clandestine world that it created have been a massive deception operation? Might Big Mole merely be a chimera craftily conjured up by the KGB of Kim Philby and Yuri Andropov in order to provoke and profit from the divisiveness and paralysis, the self-destructive finger-pointing futility that followed?

For those of you whose knowledge of mole literature is limited to Le Carré's *Tinker, Tailor, Soldier, Spy*, and who might still assume that somewhere, somehow, some real-life George Smiley has tracked down some real-life Big Mole and mopped up the stain of treachery—well, the real-life case of the Big Mole, the frenzied twelve-year hunt for the American Philby, makes the complications of *Tinker, Tailor* seem like the child's play of the title.

Because we have serious matters to consider here. Deadly serious: charges of treason, unresolved allegations against individuals at the very heart of the heart of the American diplomatic and intelligence establishment, some still in government service. We're talking about careers ruined, about mass resignations of counterintelligence people convinced that the CIA has been irrevocably penetrated by KGB pawns, about men we thought were *our* moles in Moscow arrested and shot, and about schizophrenic distortions of our own perceptions of Soviet policy.

But before we start naming names of Big Mole suspects—and I happen to have a little list—before we plunge into the murky waters of mole literature for some conjectural detective work, let's look at the Big Mole mystery in historical perspective.

●   ■   ●

Since the flight to Moscow in 1951 of British foreign-service moles Guy Burgess and Donald McLean, and the forced retirement of suspected "Third Man" Kim Philby, every other major Western nation has been rocked to its secret core by the discovery that one or more of its highest-ranking clandestine-service chiefs had been a KGB penetration agent. The French had their SAPPHIRE ring; the heads of West German counterintelligence, of Swedish counterintelligence, of Canadian counterintelligence have all been convicted or forced into retirement because of mole allegations. Most recently, in Britain, Sir Roger Hollis, the head of MI5, the British FBI—James Bond's boss, for God's sake—has all but been convicted posthumously of being a mole.

But not us. Not here. Which means one of two things: that we're immune, we can trust each other, the word of a gentleman among the old-school-tie aristocrats who founded our clandestine and diplomatic services has proved its worth against betrayal. Or that we just haven't uncovered our Big Mole yet.

Not that there haven't been suspects. Averell Harriman. Henry Kissinger. Former CIA head William Colby. Former White House speech writer Arthur Schlesinger, Jr. Two former chiefs of the CIA's Soviet Bloc division, three other high-ranking CIA executives. Even the CIA's chief mole-hunter, counterintelligence guru James Angleton himself—all have been named at one time or another as possible KGB penetration agents by CIA colleagues or defectors from the KGB.

None of the allegations against them has been proved. And yet in the absence of a definitive discovery of the Big Mole—or proof that his existence is a sophisticated Soviet disinformation plot—the allegations fester in the files, poisoning the perceptual apparatus of the West, paralyzing—for better or worse—the entire espionage establishment, making it impossible for us to trust what we know about the Soviet Union, or know what we trust.

At the heart of this continuing corrosive confusion, doubt, and ambiguity is the mysterious relationship between British master mole Kim Philby and America's master mole-hunter James Angleton. Although it has been a deadly serious duel that's stretched over three decades, the relationship has come to include elements of an incongruously intimate marriage: not unlike a real-life version of the deadly embrace between Le Carré's Smiley and Karla. But a marriage whose complexities and ambiguities make that one seem like Ozzie and Harriet's by comparison.

On the surface the outcome seems long established. There is Philby, generally acknowledged to be the most successful spy of the century, comfortably established in Moscow, a colonel-general in the KGB, now even more exalted by virtue of his long-time close collaboration with former KGB boss Yuri Andropov. And there is Angleton, the acknowledged genius of counterintelligence—spying out spies—in the West, whose brilliant career bears one ineradicable scar: his failure, by all official accounts, to detect or even suspect Kim Philby's true Soviet loyalties despite years of face-to-face contact with the spy of the century.

Angleton. On the outside now. Fired from the CIA for fingering one too many of his fellow operatives in his search for the American Philby, a crippling obsession his detractors claim was fueled by rage at his failure to discover the perfidy of the original Philby. Angleton, leader of the losing faction in the mole wars, now an embittered exile who occupies his time growing orchids and orchestrating a subterranean information war against the winning side, portraying the powers-that-be at the CIA as doing the bidding of the Big Mole, who is himself doing the bidding of KGB colonel Kim Philby, his triumphant creator.

And yet buried in the literature are provocative hints—sometimes surfacing only in cryptic footnotes—that there is an entirely different way of looking at this picture. Indeed, every element in the Philby-Angleton relationship, every clue to the identity of the Big Mole, is shadowed by an ambiguity that points to certain unsettling and unexpected interpretations.

●   ■   ●

Let's start with a wedding. The year is 1934; we're in Vienna. In the streets outside, Austrian Nazis are gunning down the socialist opposition. Inside, a curious clandestine marriage ceremony is being celebrated. The bride: an Austrian communist named Litzi Friedman, on the run from the fascist police. The groom: a twenty-two-year-old, Cambridge-educated English aristocrat named Kim Philby, the son of famed "Arabist" St. John Philby, a scholar-adventurer who was to the Empty Quarter of Arabia what Lawrence was to Transjordan.

What was Kim Philby doing marrying a member of the communist underground? It was a question that might have troubled his colleagues in MI6, the British secret service, had they known about it when they recruited him a few years later. At that time he had been posing as a sympathizer of the Fascist cause in Spain, and the contradiction might have raised warning flags. Knowledge of a secret marriage to a Stalinist might have caused MI6 to proceed with more caution a decade later, when they promoted Philby to the Soviet desk in counterespionage and put him in charge of telling the Western alliance the secret meaning of Stalin's foreign policy. The implications of the clandestine ceremony might have made the American secret services more wary when Philby arrived in Washington in 1949 and—as chief liaison with the FBI and CIA—was given carte blanche access to every secret our secret services had. It might have helped nail Philby as the mysterious Third Man who tipped off the British Foreign Office spies who fled to Moscow in 1951.

But did that marriage entirely escape the notice of those who might have made use of it? In fact it seems there were at least two who knew.

One was a witness at the wedding. The other was James Angleton, American chief of counterespionage, who learned of it from the witness.

The witness was Teddy Kollek. Now mayor of Jerusalem, then a social democratic activist in Vienna. After the war, Kollek, along with other members of Jewish intelligence, came in contact with Angleton when they were running missions to Palestine from Rome, and Angleton was OSS station chief in the Italian capital.

That liaison became extremely close over the years, an emotional as well as strategic affinity. Later, because the Mossad would not trust anyone in American intelligence other than Angleton, he retained sole command of the Israeli desk in the CIA even when he shifted to being chief of counterintelligence. In 1949, Kollek visited Washington on a "trade mission" for the newly established Jewish state. We know he spent time renewing his close friendship with Angleton. We know that at the same time Angleton was having weekly lunches with the liaison officer for the British Secret Intelligence Service, a man named Kim Philby. Since Angleton was fired from the CIA in 1974, several accounts have surfaced that suggest Angleton was tipped off to the truth about Kim Philby's Soviet mission by Kollek and his colleagues in Israeli intelligence.

The story first appeared in a cryptic footnote. Back in 1977, William Corson, author of a study of the clandestine world called *Armies of Ignorance*, cited an unnamed source in a footnote to the effect that "Israeli intelligence had detected the activities of Burgess, McLean, and Philby and that the CIA and SIS were thus in a position . . . to use them as conduits for false information."

The implications of the footnote were so shocking—requiring a re-writing of the entire postwar history of espionage, and perhaps of diplomacy too—that most experts flatly refused to accept it. In a critical footnote in his biography of CIA chief Richard Helms, writer Thomas Powers suggested the Corson footnote itself must have been "disinformation" planted by Philby's enemies, a black "valentine" sent to Philby by the CIA to arouse distrust of him among his KGB bosses.

But the story would not die. It cropped up again in Andrew Boyle's *The Fourth Man*, a book that attracted the most attention for its public exposure of the Queen's curator, Anthony Blunt, as the "Fourth Man" in the Philby Ring of Five. But the real bombshell in the Boyle book once again involves the purported Israeli intelligence tip-off to Angleton. This time with a potentially more sinister twist to it.

According to Boyle, Kollek (identified only as a London-based Jewish intelligence operative who "still occupies a prominent and respected position in public life") "passed on to Angleton the name of the British nuclear scientist who they had unearthed as an important Soviet agent . . . 'Basil,' the code name of the Fifth Man" of the Philby-McLean-Burgess Ring of Five.

Others have disputed Boyle's candidate for Fifth Man, but the crucial difference between this story and the Corson footnote is that Boyle makes the turning and "playback" of the Ring of Five not a joint CIA and SIS operation but a private Angleton ploy. Angleton ran "the operation out of his hip pocket for at least a couple of years," says Boyle. "Playing a deep game," he kept it from the British entirely, *and* from his fellow Americans. According to Boyle, Allen Dulles himself never learned the "deep game."

●　　■　　●

But just how deep was that game? And why did he keep it to himself? Could it still be going on? The implication of the Corson and Boyle stories is that, contrary to the conventional history, from the late 1940s on, Kim Philby was James Angleton's patsy. And may still be. Angleton did nothing to discourage that impression when I called him to ask for comment. Although he would not confirm or deny it directly, when I asked him if he'd been tipped off about Philby by Israeli intelligence there was a long pause on the line, following which Angleton said, with great deliberation, "My Israeli friends have always been among the most loyal I've had. Perhaps the only ones to remain loyal." He refused to comment further on this or any other substantive intelligence matter, with one cryptic exception.

Deflected from interpretation of intelligence literature, Angleton and I drifted into a discussion of the intelligence of literary interpretation. We expressed our mutual preference for the practitioners of the New Criticism that prevailed at Yale when Angleton was there in the Thirties to the theories of the so-called Yale critics who had come to rule the roost when I arrived there in the Sixties. Angleton boasted to me that he had recruited some of the best minds of the New Critics and poets into the OSS, where their facility at teasing out seven types of ambiguity from a text served them well in the interpretation of the ambiguities of intelligence data. Finally, I returned to the question of Angleton and Philby—just who knew what about whom. Once again he declared he was "unable to comment." Why not confirm or deny the Boyle story, I asked? After all, it was an event that took place thirty years in the past.

"What you have to understand about these matters," Angleton said again, with great deliberation, "is that the past telescopes into the present."

The past telescopes into the present. The implication is that the "deep game" is still going on, that the credibility of disinformation played back through Philby and his Ring of Five, following the Teddy Kollek tip-off, could not be compromised even now by Angleton's taking credit for the success of the ploy.

Needless to say, there will be those among Angleton's many critics who would say that the whole notion of this "deep game" was carefully planted by Angleton and his allies in an attempt to turn his most mortifying failure—the Philby case—into a clandestine success.

But there is an even darker interpretation of the fact that Angleton played this whole game "out of his hip pocket" for so long. Some might be tempted to say Angleton was *protecting* Philby and friends for at least two crucial years between the time his Israeli friends tipped him off and the spring of 1951, when a break in KGB ciphers finally led the British to close in on Philby's cohorts, McLean and Burgess, and to put the Cambridge spy ring out of business. Later, in 1974, when a member of the CIA counterintelligence staff compiled a voluminous compendium of circumstantial evidence suggesting that mole-hunter Angleton was himself the Big Mole, his putative knowledge of that wedding and his hip-pocket treatment of its implications did nothing to diminish the shadows of ambiguity that darkened around him in the final days of the mole wars.

Was Philby running Angleton? Was Angleton running Philby? Does either of them know for sure?

●   ■   ●

Somehow it all comes down to what was really transacted between the two of them during those long lobster lunches at Harvey's restaurant.

Washington, 1949. Harvey's restaurant. J. Edgar Hoover's favorite lunch spot. Philby and Angleton begin meeting there once a week. There is official business to transact. Philby is stationed in Washington as liaison officer for His Majesty's Secret Intelligence Service, Angleton as head of the CIA's Office of Strategic Operations. Their mission: to exchange secrets. Angleton to brief Philby on what the CIA has learned about the Soviets through uniquely American assets, Philby to brief Angleton on what the British have learned from their special resources. All to further the Special Relationship.

But there is more to it than that. There is a special relationship growing between the two men. "Our close association was, I am sure, inspired by genuine friendliness on both sides," Philby writes. "Our discussions ranged over the whole world." Yes. They were teacher and pupil once. Philby had taught Angleton the "double-cross system" in 1943 in London when Angleton was an OSS novice. Now they were equals, two brilliant, highly civilized men who shared a more intimate and knowing view of the hidden reality of world affairs than any other two one could think of, the communion of blood brothers in the most secret of secret societies in the West.

"But," Philby writes, "we both had ulterior motives."

Indeed. In his memoirs, obviously written under the watchful eye of his KGB superiors, Philby assures us *he* knows just what the ulterior ambitions on each side of the lobster-stained tablecloth were.

Philby tells us that he was aware that Angleton was "cultivating me to the full," but he explains Angleton's motive in this as merely a bureaucratic maneuver. British-American intelligence liaison was carried on by bilateral contacts in both Washington and London. Philby tells us that Angleton wanted to give the CIA London station, which Philby says was ten times bigger than the British one, the key responsibility for the two-way flow of secret-sharing between the allies. "By cultivating me to the full" in Washington, Philby writes, Angleton "could better keep me under wraps" and shift the locus of secret-sharing to London, where the CIA would have more leverage.

After giving us this curiously detailed and somehow unconvincing analysis of Angleton's motive, Philby lapses into an uncharacteristic bit of boastfulness, in a memoir otherwise distinguished by a dry and reticent wit when it comes to describing the cleverness of his duplicitous achievements. In a passage that one suspects may have been meant for the eyes of the KGB analysts doing a prepublication check into his manuscript, Philby writes:

> For my part I was more than content to string [*Angleton*] along. The greater the trust between us overtly, the less he would suspect covert action. Who gained most from this complex game I cannot say. But I had one big advantage. I knew what he was doing for CIA, and he knew what I was doing for SIS. But the real nature of my interest was something he did not know.

Or did he? If we accept the implications of the Corson footnote, Angleton was "keeping Philby under wraps" and "cultivating him to the full" for very different reasons. By this analysis, Angleton knew exactly what Philby's "complex game" was about and it was Philby, not Angleton, who was being played for the fool. Angleton was feeding him not real secrets but carefully cooked disinformation along with his crustaceans.

On the other hand, it is not impossible to imagine the two of them together, fellow initiates into the secrets of both sides, playing both sides in the Cold War for fools in a great game of their own devising.

If there is *any* answer to the perplexities presented to an analyst of the Angleton-Philby lunches, I believe it just may have been cryptically encapsulated by Philby in an ostensibly jovial aside on the difference in weight gains the two master spies displayed as a result of their weekly pig-outs.

Angleton, Philby writes, "was one of the thinnest men I have ever met, and one of the biggest eaters. Lucky Jim! After a year of keeping up with Angleton I *took the advice of an elderly lady friend and went on a diet*, dropping from thirteen stone to about eleven in three months." (Italics mine.)

Angleton, in other words, is able to consume and conceal the consequences of consumption—his very metabolism betraying a talent for covertness. Philby, however, finds himself consuming more than is good for him until someone points out that it has disfigured his profile. Is there some self-awareness on Philby's part that Angleton has been feeding him a diet of disinformation—which he only later learns from a mysterious outsider (who was that lady?)—that he must disgorge from his body of knowledge?

Whatever the deeper nature of the game, an observer present at these lunches would have been privileged to witness one of the most extraordinary confrontations—or collaborations—in the history of intelligence. A seven-course feast of seven types of ambiguity.

But of course these were no mere intellectual games being played. Before we get deeper into the ambiguities of the strange marriage between Philby and Angleton, let's look a little more closely at why we should care. Let's look at the absolutely crucial role Kim Philby played in creating the entire perceptual structure of the Cold War from its very inception.

●   ■   ●

In a certain respect, while Le Carré's works have popularized the concept of the mole as the representative of the divided character of the West, the association of Philby with Le Carré's arch-mole, Bill Haydon, in *Tinker, Tailor* has diminished the true significance of Philby's role. In *Tinker, Tailor* Haydon is referred to knowingly as "our latter-day Lawrence of Arabia," an unmistakable reference to Philby, whose father is almost always referred to as "the famed Arabist St. John Philby," and who played a Lawrencian role in the great game of imperial Arabian politics.* There are other touches linking Le Carré's Haydon and Philby—both compulsively seductive, but sexually ambiguous,

---

* Oddly enough, it is none other than the great Lawrence himself who may have given us the missing clue to the origin of Philby's true loyalties. I have come across a piece of evidence I have not seen referred to anywhere else in the literature that sheds intriguing new light on the Philby family's true politics. It's a previously unpublished letter from Lawrence that appears as an offering in the private catalogue of a dealer in rare books and autographs. While the letter, dated 1932, is advertised by the dealer as a missive "linking" Lawrence with "Notorious Communist Spy 'Kim' Philby," this is perhaps an unintentional mistake. The internal dating of the letter (a remark that "Philby took my place at Amman later in 1921"—when Kim Philby was only nine years old) makes it clear that Lawrence is referring to Kim's *father*, the Arabist St. John Philby.

Cambridge-educated aesthetes who became Marxists in the Thirties, men of sensibility who retained the supremely arrogant character and the corrosive self-contempt of the aristocratic ironist.

While this makes for literary interest in Le Carré's recurrent moral debate between sense and sensibility, it reduces our appreciation of the geopolitical significance of Philby's role. Because Kim Philby was nothing less than a visionary, a demonic one, but still perhaps the best-placed and most effective visionary of the postwar world.

Let's recall Philby's precise position in the years 1944–1949. Recruited by the Soviets in 1933, Philby writes in his memoirs: "I was given the assignment to infiltrate counterespionage *however long it took*."

It took him eleven years. By then he had not merely infiltrated counterespionage, he was *running* the entire British counterespionage operation against the Soviets while working for the KGB. What that meant was that during the crucial period when the wartime alliance between the West and the Soviet Union was shifting into the postwar schism, Philby was the one person whose job it was to tell the West about the secret intentions and motivations of the Soviets, and to tell the Soviets about those of the West.

In this absolutely unique, Janus-like role, he was more than any single man able to *create* the reality of each side for the other. How accurate the reciprocal images of East and West he created, how much the character of the postwar world is the result of Philby's double vision, is something only Philby knows. While Philby tells us in his memoirs that he was faithfully serving the Soviet Union's instructions, those memoirs were written and edited in Moscow under the protection and control of the KGB. Which side he was really serving, or whether he was playing a deep game of his own, is something we may never know for sure. But it is useful to recall that his lifelong nickname, "Kim," came from the Rudyard Kipling character—the half-British, half-Indian

---

What is fascinating about the letter for our purposes is Lawrence's characterization of the elder Philby as "rather a 'red'; but decent—very."

Some commentators, including Le Carré himself, have speculated that the younger Philby's Marxist motivations may have had their genesis in a reaction against his father's presumed old-fashioned imperialist "Great Game" politics. Nowhere in the literature is there any suggestion that the elder Philby was "rather a red." Could it be that he too had been playing a great game of concealment, and that Kim was not rebelling against but carrying on a family tradition of grand duplicity?

boy who was initiated into the breathtakingly exhilarating mysteries of "the Great Game" of duplicity, deception, and manipulation as it was played by the British in their vast Asian empire. Those who played it frequently felt less loyalty to their employers of record than to the game itself.

Nor has the possibility that Philby's game was deeper, his vision more personal and individual than ideological, escaped the attention of both sides he was playing with. At crucial stages in his career, even after he was ostensibly exposed in 1951 as the Third Man, doubts have emerged as to the locus of his ultimate loyalty.

●　　■　　●

Take the Otto John case. The year is 1954. Three years after the Third Man case explodes, Burgess and McLean have fled to Moscow, although nobody knows they're there yet. Philby has been repeatedly interrogated as the suspected Third Man who tipped the two of them off, but the best interrogators in the business have not been able to crack his denials. The secret world of the West is divided on the issue of Philby's loyalty. The CIA, the FBI, and MI5 are convinced he's a long-term mole and have forced him into retirement. But Philby's old outfit, MI6, contains a number of old-school-tie partisans of Kim's who believe he's a victim of American McCarthyite paranoia. Although he's been forced into retirement, secret-service contacts have been arranging employment and financing for him.

Meanwhile, on a July night in West Berlin, Dr. Otto John, head of the BND, the West German equivalent of the FBI, goes out for a night of drinking. Sometime during the night he is drugged, kidnaped, and dragged across the border to East Berlin. That's his story. By another version he deliberately defects to the East. For a year nothing is heard of him. Then suddenly he reappears in West Berlin, claiming to have escaped KGB captivity.

To this day no one is sure what the real story is. "Whole careers have been made on the Otto John case," one intelligence-world observer told me, "but still no one can figure the damned thing out."

But of all the ambiguities to be found in analysis of it, none is more fascinating, none more resonant with larger implications than the story John brought back about Kim Philby. According to John, during his marathon interrogation sessions in East Berlin, his KGB inquisitors kept returning to press him on one point in particular: *Who was Kim Philby really working for?*

Now here lies an absolutely delicious feast of interpretive possibilities. Assuming for the moment that Dr. John was telling the truth, were those questions about Kim Philby motivated by genuine doubt, or did the KGB want the West to *think* it had doubts? Did they know at the time of the interrogation that Dr. John would return to the West to tell of it? Did they allow him to escape in order to return to tell of it? If they had doubts, what were they based on?

There is convincing evidence in the literature that back in the Forties the KGB had allowed the atom-bomb spies Klaus Fuchs and the Rosenbergs to be captured, even though Philby knew enough to have warned them, in order to prevent a Philby tip-off from throwing suspicion on Philby himself. Would the Soviets have given up such major assets for the sake of someone whose loyalty they were still uncertain of? Or did they suspect Philby had been "turned" during his 1951 interrogations?

The question of Philby's "turning" or re-turning is a fascinating theme of his mysterious limbo years—the period between his forced retirement in 1951 and his final flight to Moscow in 1963. We know he was employed by one faction of his old colleagues in MI6 as a low-level agent in the Middle East, first based in Cyprus, where there is some evidence he was running agents from the Armenian emigré community out of Cyprus across the Turkish border into Soviet Armenia. Had he been "turned" secretly, and was he being rehabilitated, under the direction of MI6, into major-agent status in order again to entice the attention of the Soviets so that he might infiltrate the KGB apparatus for his British masters?

Bruce Page and his colleagues on the London *Sunday Times* provide perhaps the best summary of the absolutely astonishing murkiness and complexity of Philby's role in those limbo years:

> There could be every reason for putting a man under suspicion of working for the Russians in contact with them. If he *is* the Russians' man they will be unhappy at his demotion from the superb position in Washington and they may feed him some genuine information to help him restore his credit.

If he is *not* their man, they may well think that he is, and act in the exactly same manner, anyway. In fact, in such a situation, the loyalty of the agent is more or less irrelevant to anyone except himself.

Those of you who have been able to follow and appreciate these truly dizzying and delightful ambiguities of the problem of Philby's loyalty in his Mideast limbo are now qualified to appreciate the curious question of our man's final flight from Beirut to Moscow in 1963.

It's there that the ultimate question of his loyalty becomes more than relevant to himself; it becomes crucial to an understanding of the secret history of superpower relations in the past two decades.

The situation is this. It's summer 1962. Kim Philby's living in Beirut, where he's been based for six years, ostensibly operating as a roving Mideast correspondent for the London *Observer* and the *Economist*. And, of course, still in the employ of MI6 *and* in the service of the KGB.

Meanwhile, in Israel in June of that year, an Englishwoman is overheard criticizing Philby's journalism at a cocktail party. She doesn't like his pro-Nasser slant, and she's heard to say that "as usual, Kim is doing what his Russian control tells him. I know that he's always worked for the Russians." Swiftly the woman is returned to England. Interrogated. She admits to having befriended Philby after he returned to England from his Vienna wedding to an underground communist bride. She recalls having asked him why he had suddenly taken on the guise of an anticommunist, pro-Franco sympathizer. His reply, she said, was that he was "doing a very dangerous job for peace, working for the Comintern."

This was enough to make the case against Philby complete. A problem remained: how to get Philby back to England, how to avoid the massive hemorrhage of secrets a public trial would involve. Nicholas Elliot, an old-school-tie colleague in MI6, was dispatched to Beirut to offer Philby complete immunity in return for a complete confession (the same deal that would later be offered to and accepted by Fourth Man Anthony Blunt). Elliot arrived to find Philby expecting him. A tip-off by another, still buried British mole is suspected. But Philby confessed anyway. A limited confession. He asked for more time to decide whether to accept the offer of immunity and return to England to tell all, not just about himself but also about the KGB apparatus that controlled him.

Elliot then flew directly from Beirut to Washington and presented James Angleton, by then CIA chief of counterintelligence, with Philby's typed confession. And then what happened? For ten days, nothing. And on the tenth day Philby disappeared from Beirut. Six months later he reappeared in Moscow, having once again made a laughingstock of the intelligence services of the West.

There has never been a satisfactory explanation of why Kim Philby was permitted to escape. Not a *straightforward* explanation, at least.

One British writer suggests it would have been "out of the question to kidnap him back to England." But even if we accept this kid-gloves approach to a man who betrayed dozens of British agents to their deaths, the notion that the single most effective traitor in British history was given ten days of leisure in which to arrange his escape is difficult to accept.

And where was James Angleton all this time? Think of it: he's wanted to nail Philby since 1951 and at last his archnemesis is at bay in Beirut, apparently ready to begin to talk. A full confession from Philby could well be the greatest intelligence coup of the postwar era. At last—at least—we would begin to know what the Soviets knew about us and when. At last we might learn how deeply penetrated *we* had been and perhaps who the Big Mole, the American Philby, was. And yet with all the resources of the CIA at his disposal for the most important mission of his career, Angleton did not even cover Philby with enough surveillance to prevent his slipping out of the city at his convenience and making his way to the safety and comfort of Moscow.

There are only two possible explanations for this phenomenal circumstance. One is that Philby, particularly Philby with a grant of immunity, would have been too much of an embarrassment had he remained in the West and that the clandestine services of both Britain and the U.S. were happy to see him slip away beyond the reach of the press and publicity. (I have also been told by one mole-watcher that there is some suspicion that the Soviets were so worried about Philby's talking that they removed him from Beirut "at gunpoint.")

The other possible explanation—curiously, one that does not appear anywhere in the literature I've seen—is that sometime in those ten days following his confrontation with Elliot, Philby *was* "turned." Turned and *encouraged* to escape to Moscow—the better to serve those he'd once betrayed. To become *our* mole in the KGB. A more likely version of this variant would be that Philby convinced the endlessly gullible British that he could be turned and thereby earned himself the ability to make a leisurely and unhampered exit from Beirut and laugh over the whole affair with Andropov when he arrived in Moscow. Still, in this regard the dying words of Guy Burgess cannot be ignored. According to Nigel West's history of MI5 (*A Matter of Trust*), Philby's fellow mole and Moscow exile, Burgess, "on his death-bed, had denounced Philby as a British agent." Perhaps this was merely one final example of Burgess's notorious reputation as a prankster. Perhaps Burgess—generally acknowledged to be brilliant and shrewd despite his streak of playful irresponsibility—*knew* something. He died before he could be interrogated further on this question. Only Kim Philby knows the truth.

●　　　　　■　　　　　●

What we do know is that the moment Kim Philby arrived in Moscow marked the beginning of a remarkable change in the personality of the KGB. So striking has been the shift in its operational profile that it is impossible not to see in the complex and sophisticated new character of the mind of the KGB the shaping influence of the mind of Kim Philby.

"Contrary to what was believed in the West, Philby was no retired intelligence agent" when he reached Moscow, writes recent Soviet defector Vladimir Sakharov. "In fact, from the moment he arrived in Moscow, he had become an important member of the KGB's inner circle. . . . In the process, Philby played a vital role in the rise to power of . . . Yuri Andropov. . . . Simply, Andropov used Philby to tell him how the KGB should look and operate, especially in Western Europe and the United States."

And what did Philby tell Andropov? Get a new tailor, for one thing. Away with those "ill-fitting suits" so beloved of spy-fiction portraits of Soviet agents. The new, Philbyan KGB began to attire itself in expensively tailored, stylishly cut Western suits, the better to blend into the sophisticated circles of the Western capitals it was assigned to penetrate.

But the Philby signature can be seen in more than surface sophistication: KGB operations—once mainly distinguished by thuggish tactics of blackmail, bribery, and brute force—developed a level of subtlety and complexity almost baroque, in fact rococo, in the many-layered richness of ambiguity they displayed. Particularly in relation to the American target; particularly in relation to James Angleton.

Sakharov notes Philby's alliance with one Aleksandr Panyushkin, who had served as his control during the crucial years of 1949–1951, when Philby was stationed in Washington, having those long weekly lunches with James Angleton and using their intimacy to steal every secret the U.S. secret services had.

Panyushkin, Sakharov tells us, "eagerly sought Philby's advice on how to deal with Americans." And just how did Philby advise the KGB to attack the American target? It seems clear from the history of the next decade that a conscious decision was made to *target the mind of James Angleton*. The goal: to drive him crazy, destroy his effectiveness as chief guardian of the secrets of the Western world. The method: the double-cross system.

After all, it was Philby who had molded the mind of Angleton when he tutored him in the double-cross system they worked against the Nazis. And it would be Philby, alone among men, who would know exactly how to undo the mind he'd created, using its very double logic to twist his one-time pupil's mind into a pretzel.

Nowhere in the literature of the mole maze has anyone fully credited Philby for the utterly devious brilliance of the web he wove to entangle Angleton. To see it in its proper perspective, we have to look at five schools of counterintelligence theology that have grown up around the Big Mole question. Yes, theology.

"When you get in this deep," one of my intelligence-world sources was saying, "all the real questions become theological."

We had been speaking specifically about the murky nature of the soul of Yuri Nosenko, the maddeningly enigmatic Soviet defector, the locus of whose true loyalty had baffled some of the most brilliant men in American intelligence for a decade. It was a question whose answer might resolve fundamental perplexities of doubt and belief but one that just could not be resolved, it seemed, by means of reason.

Partisans were reduced to a religious faith, skeptics were not so much advancing positions as perpetrating heresies.

And so, as we examine the five schools of thought on the real meaning of the great Mole Hunt, we have to realize that it has become as theological as, say, the sixteenth-century controversies in the Church over transubstantiation versus consubstantiation, the question of the presence of the mole being almost as arcane and inaccessible to mere reason as the question of the nature of the Presence in the Host.

●   ■   ●

Our first school—let's call it the Angletonian orthodoxy—believes in the Real Presence of Big Mole as an article of religious faith, the way the Devil is more real to certain true believers than God. Not only does Big Mole exist, but he is a kind of organizing principle of the perceptual phenomena of this world, running the CIA from deep within the structure of the intelligence apparatus, ensconced as ineluctably as original sin at the center of its soul. The Angletonian orthodoxy has its genesis in what might be called the Gospel according to Golitsyn. Anatoly Golitsyn, the first Big Defector from the KGB. You might call him the John the Baptist of Big Mole theology. Although he defected back in December 1961, he remains "even today, by far the most controversial figure in the world of intelligence," according to Nigel West.

The controversy is not over the number of *genuine* moles Golitsyn exposed. When he defected from his post as a KGB counterintelligence officer in Helsinki, Golitsyn brought with him the names of a number of KGB penetration agents in England, Western Europe, and Scandinavia. And solid clues that helped make the case against others, including Philby. No, the controversy was over *conceptual* moles— supposed deep-penetration agents, particularly in America—for whom Golitsyn had only fragmentary clues and code names.

The mole code-named SASHA, for instance. The SASHA story was the first incarnation of Big Mole, the first shadowy prefigurement that there was a high-level penetration agent in America—inside the CIA headquarters itself. Golitsyn's gospel tale of the Activation of SASHA— which first appeared in Angletonian acolyte Edward Jay Epstein's groundbreaking book, *Legend*—was to become the central credo of the True Angletonian Faith.

Washington, 1957. A top KGB official, Viktor Kovshuk, makes an unexpected flight from Moscow to Washington. He slips into town without surveillance and makes some mysterious rendezvous. Flies back almost immediately.

According to Golitsyn, the sole purpose of this unusual round trip was the "activation" of an extremely high-level mole inside the CIA headquarters. Golitsyn didn't know his real name, he said. Only his code name: SASHA. The search for SASHA began. It is still going on now, at least in the mind of James Angleton.

Belief in the existence of SASHA became in itself a religious test of faith, not only for everyone in the CIA but for every subsequent defector. Those in the CIA who expressed doubts about the existence of SASHA immediately came under suspicion of *being* SASHA. For subsequent KGB defectors, failure to stick to the one true SASHA story became evidence that one was sent to *protect* SASHA.

Such was the fate that befell Yuri Nosenko when he fell into the hands of the orthodox Angletonian inquisition. If you believe the Angletonians and the Angletonian theologians, Nosenko was the single most devious, most fiendishly clever, most successful spy ever encountered by the great spy hunter of the West.

Nosenko was, according to the orthodox Angletonian gospel, the first of the false prophets Golitsyn had foretold would come to throw doubt on him and question the existence of SASHA. And sure enough, not long after Nosenko defected in January 1964, he was telling a story that confused everyone by saying SASHA was actually ANDREY. Nosenko's defection was an offer the CIA couldn't refuse, because Nosenko claimed to be the KGB officer who, in November 1963, was assigned to go through the entire KGB file on one lone American defector, Lee Harvey Oswald. But Nosenko's Oswald story (Nosenko claimed the files showed no direct KGB involvement with the ex-U-2-base radar operator) was merely a red herring, according to the Angletonians. Nosenko's real mission was to shield SASHA, and during his debriefing he casually let slip a revised version of the Kovshuk activation story designed to discredit belief in SASHA's importance.

According to Nosenko, the real purpose of the 1957 Kovshuk trip *was* to activate a penetration, but not that of the exalted and mysterious SASHA. Nosenko claimed never to have heard of SASHA. According to him, Kovshuk had gone to Washington to tend to an agent code-named ANDREY. He gave enough details of ANDREY's identity to lead the FBI to arrest a Sergeant Rhodes, who had once worked in the American embassy motor pool in Moscow. When interrogated, Rhodes admitted meeting with Kovshuk in 1957.

Could this grease monkey be the master mole SASHA of the Golitsyn gospel? Or was Nosenko deliberately trying to protect SASHA by claiming the Kovshuk mole was really this minor-league ANDREY—and that he'd already been caught, and the whole mole hunt could be called off?

It was over this question that the first shots in the decade-long Mole War within the intelligence community were fired. It was over this question that a subterranean civil war would be fought inside the CIA, a war for the secret soul of the West, a war that, according to the Angletonian gospel, the good guys lost.

●   ■   ●

The good guys. Recalling that this is the orthodox Angletonian gospel we are relating here, it's still hard not to remark that the good guys went a little crazy in the final throes of the Big Mole madness. Particularly over Nosenko. Because everything about Nosenko fit perfectly into the prophecies of Golitsyn: the false prophet sent to cast doubt upon Big Mole's existence, the false clues he scattered, the false description of himself, the eagerness of other false defectors to declare all he said was true. Everything fit. Except one thing: even after all his falsities had been thrown in his face, Nosenko would not confess. He still claimed to be a sincere defector. He would not break down and say who sent him and why. He would not reveal what he really knew about the identity of Big Mole.

Enter the bank vault. Perhaps the single most horrifying episode in the entire tortuous Mole War chronicle. Not merely tortuous; it was, in fact, nothing less than torture.

When conventional methods of interrogation failed to get Nosenko to confess his perfidy, the CIA's Soviet Bloc division decided he would have to be convinced of the absolute hopelessness of holding out. And so they put Nosenko in a thick-walled steel cage, with only a single bed and a bare light bulb, nothing to look at, listen to, or react to, no distinction between night and day, no hope of escape except by a confession. They kept him in solitary confinement for two and a half years. There are hints they did more than observe him, interrogate him, and subject him to extreme sensory deprivation. There are hints that they slipped him mind-altering truth-serum drugs. There are hints of harsher, more physical methods brought to bear. And yet, after all that,

Nosenko never cracked. Or at least he never yielded up the "truth" that his inquisitors were certain he was concealing.

Instead, what happened was that when Nosenko wouldn't crack the Angletonians began to crack. The counterintelligence inquisition they were conducting began to get out of hand. They demanded that the entire key Soviet Bloc division of the CIA—the single most important sensory apparatus trained on the Soviet Union—be quarantined from all contact with confidential information, for fear of contamination by the invisible presence of Big Mole somewhere in its midst. In effect, they put the CIA *out of commission* when it came to running operations against its chief target. Then they began to turn on one another. Even Nosenko's chief inquisitors came under suspicion. One of Angleton's deputies made a case against a high-ranking fellow CIA officer who had compiled a report proving the falsity of Nosenko's cover story. In other words, a case was made against him because of his very support of the orthodox Angletonian position. The logic behind this: Nosenko had been sent a false cover story specifically to help promote the career of the man who unmasked its falsity, who would thereby be in an unassailable position to protect the identity of Big Mole.

By August 1966, Nosenko was still in solitary, but the entire anti-Soviet capacity of the CIA was in quarantine, and a subterranean religious schism between the Angletonian believers and the skeptics and agnostics who doubted the existence of Big Mole was tearing the place apart.

At this point the tide began to turn against the Angletonians. At this point, CIA director Richard Helms, seeing his entire agency consuming itself in a cannibalistic civil war, made the classic demand of the organization-minded bureaucrat: resolve the Nosenko case in sixty days *one way or another*.

This was akin to saying prove or disprove the existence of God within sixty days. It didn't happen. A pro-Nosenko faction, based in the CIA's Office of Security, made a case for accepting Nosenko's story at face value. He had, after all, brought over many valuable clues that had led to the exposure of genuine Soviet penetrations all over the world. Would the KGB have sacrificed that many assets just to give credibility to a defector whose mission may merely have been to protect a so far invisible Big Mole?

Absolutely, the Angletonians argued; the value of the agents and assets sacrificed just indicated the value of the Big Secret that Nosenko was sent to shield.

Sixty days passed, and nothing was really resolved. But Nosenko was removed from the bank vault—just as he was about to crack, the inquisitors claimed.

And from that point on the CIA, indeed the entire anti-Soviet intelligence capacity of the United States, shifted, according to the Angletonian gospel, into the hands of the Soviets, under the invisible guidance of Big Mole—whoever Big Mole might be.

●   ■   ●

Now there arose in opposition to Angletonian orthodoxy a Second School of thought, what might be called the "sick-think reformation."

"Sick think." That was the phrase used to characterize the convoluted, contagious logic of suspicion and paranoia that the Angletonians applied in analyzing the accounts of almost all defectors subsequent to the prophet Golitsyn. "Sick think" was the term used in testimony before the House Assassination Committee to characterize the rationale behind the extended isolation and torture of Nosenko.

In the years that followed Nosenko's release from the bank vault, the "sick think" view of the Angletonian gospel became the new official orthodoxy in intelligence circles. Nowhere is the case for sick think made more convincingly than in David Martin's brilliant work of reporting, *Wilderness of Mirrors*, a work that incensed the Angletonians no end, but which—it might be argued—is a compassionate, even respectful view of a powerful mind led astray by its own complexity and sensitivity.

Martin creates a convincing portrait of Angleton as a victim of the mirror-image doubleness of his own counterintelligence logic. The key assumption behind the sick-think theory of Angletonian orthodoxy is that Big Mole probably never existed. That Angleton came to worship its existence as a kind of false idol, a Golden Calf created by Angleton's guru Golitsyn. In fact there is, in the comments Martin elicits from sick-think theorists, a distrust of Golitsyn as a Dostoevskian, Rasputin-like mad monk infecting clear-thinking Americans with dark and murky Slavic speculations; making Americans think like Russians.

Consider, for instance, William Colby's reaction to hearing the Angletonian gospel: "I spent several long sessions doing my best to follow [Angleton's] tortuous conspiracy theories," Colby has written, "about the long arm of the powerful and wily KGB at work, over decades, placing its agents in the heart of Allied and neutral nations and sending its false defectors to influence and undermine American policy. I confess that I couldn't absorb it, possibly because I did not have the requisite grasp of this labyrinthine subject, possibly because Angleton's explanation was impossible to follow, or possibly because the evidence just didn't add up to his conclusions."

After Colby's accession to power in late 1973, Angleton gradually became isolated in an agency that was seeking to purge itself of a murky and tainted past and that saw "sick think" as a symptom, a symbol of those dark ages. But increasing isolation did not deter Angleton from pursuing Big Mole or discovering even Bigger Moles.

Project Dinosaur, first revealed by David Martin, is probably the most shocking example of the extent of the distrust engendered by the Angletonian orthodoxy. Project Dinosaur was the code name for Angleton's attempt to prove that perhaps the single most respected figure in the American diplomatic establishment, Averell Harriman, was in fact a long-term Soviet mole.

Once again, the origin of this suspicion was an apocryphal tale from the Golitsyn gospel. Golitsyn claimed the Soviets had recruited a powerful member of the American establishment as a long-term agent in the Thirties, and on his return to the Soviet Union in the Fifties had commissioned a play dedicated to him. The plot involves the illegitimate son fathered in the Soviet Union in the Thirties by a capitalist prince, who then is reunited with his American father in Soviet solidarity in the Fifties. Now there is some controversy as to the identity of the capitalist. In Martin's *Wilderness of Mirrors* he's clearly identified as Harriman. However, a prominent Angletonian partisan confided to me that *he* thought the play was really about U.S. merchant prince and Soviet friend ———— ————.

In 1974 the end came for Angleton and for the first phase of the mole war. Colby had appointed one of Angleton's Big Mole suspects to be CIA station chief in Paris. The man had been cleared of all suspicion—by all but the diehard Angletonians—but nonetheless Angleton flew to Paris, buttonholed the head of the French counterespionage department, and warned him that the CIA had placed a Soviet mole in his capital city.

When Colby found that out, he fired Angleton. He disguised it by confirming a leak to Seymour Hersh that linked Angleton to an illegal mail-interception program. But the real reason for the firing was his inability to get Angleton off the mad mole hunt.

Soon afterward, Colby's CIA not only rehabilitated Nosenko's reputation and gave him back pay for the time he spent in the bank vault, they even set him up as a paid consultant teaching counterintelligence—Angleton's job—to new recruits.

To the Angletonians, it was a complete coup. A Soviet agent was now shaping CIA counterintelligence operations. There were murmurings from the Angletonians about Colby's own loyalties. There was talk of some kind of liaison Colby had had in Vietnam with a French journalist suspected of being KGB-controlled. Some were quoted as saying that, considering what Colby was doing to the agency, he "might as well be a Soviet Mole." There were scores of resignations and forced retirements from the ranks of the Angletonian loyalists. It was nothing less than a purge. A purge that left the agency in the control of the Big Mole, if you believe the Angletonians. In defeat, they said, the Nosenko case had "turned the CIA inside out."

●   ■   ●

Still, the struggle did not end there for the Angletonians. The struggle is going on now. In the years since his dismissal, Angleton himself has been officially silent, but his acolytes have been generating a steady stream of fiction and nonfiction books that have brought the story of the subterranean civil war to the surface and popularized the Angletonian gospel. First and most importantly there was *Legend*, Edward Jay Epstein's study of the strange career of Lee Harvey Oswald, which was *really* the story of the Nosenko controversy, which was *really* the story of Angleton's search for the Big Mole.

Then there was *Mole*, by William Hood, one of Angleton's deputies in the counterintelligence department. *Mole* is ostensibly the story of the ill-starred career of one of our moles in Moscow in the late 1950s, a Colonel Popov. But the subtext of *Mole* is that all the ambiguities of the case seem to add up to a conclusion that our mole was "blown" by one of *their* moles on our side, and once again we are given the Angletonian gospel about the tragic failure of the bumbling CIA bureaucracy to listen to the warnings of Angleton and his staff about penetrations.

And then there is *Shadrin*, by Henry Hurt, a fascinating account of perhaps the most complex, baroque, almost "overartfully sculpted" (as one CIA officer called it) KGB deception operation. The target of the operation was Nikolai Shadrin, a one-time Soviet destroyer commander who defected to the U.S. in 1959. Six years later, a KGB officer known as "Igor" offered his services as mole to our side. "Igor" told the CIA that if they helped promote his career he'd quickly rise to a top post in Moscow, where he'd funnel a feast of Soviet secrets direct to us. Exactly how should we help him gain this promotion? We should make it seem that he'd recruited Shadrin back to the Soviet side, and have Shadrin (who was then a Defense Intelligence Agency employee) feed him U.S. military information to turn over to the KGB.

According to Henry Hurt, Angleton saw through this immediately as a KGB "provocation," an attempt to seduce or abduct Shadrin back to the U.S.S.R. Angleton encouraged Shadrin to go ahead and meet with Igor, feed him doctored data and disinformation, but warned him never to meet with Igor outside North America. At that point it seemed as if Angleton had turned the devious Shadrin game to our advantage.

But at that point Angleton was fired. The people who believed that Angletonian thinking was "too convoluted" took over the agency, people who began to think that "Igor" was a real find, a high-level KGB agent who might end up working for us in the Kremlin. And so when Igor insisted that Shadrin fly to Vienna to meet with him, objections were raised by holdover Angletonians who feared the worst. But the new regime was so eager to please Igor that they told Shadrin to go ahead. Shadrin left his hotel room in Vienna one night in 1977 for a scheduled rendezvous with Igor. He never returned. The Angletonians are certain he was kidnapped, tortured, and probably executed by the Soviets as an example to those tempted to defect in the future. A victim of those on our side who failed to heed the warnings of the Angletonians.

If at the heart of the sick-think reformation was the belief that Angletonian orthodoxy was too convoluted, the essence of a Third School, a school of which I am, so far as I am aware, the sole proponent, is that *James Angleton's thought was not convoluted enough*. That he was one convolution short of the dazzling complexity of the mind of Kim Philby. That Philby, Angleton's tutor in the double-cross system during the Second World War, simply—or complexly—outsmarted Angleton with a game that might be called the double-double-cross system, a game that depended on the creation of Ghostly Presences that I would choose to call Notional Moles.

●   ■   ●

To explain the notion of notional moles, let me cite two examples from historian John Masterman's study *The Double-Cross System*: PLAN STIFF and PLAN PAPRIKA.

Now the basic method of the double-cross system evolved when the British secret service captured German spies in England during wartime. The spies were quickly "turned," on pain of execution, and forced to send back on their radio transmitters whatever disinformation the British wanted German intelligence to believe. Frequently the German spies, while locked in London prison cells, would be given "notional" adventures to report back to their German superiors. The term notional comes from medieval philosophy, and refers to the class of entities that exist only in the mind.

And so, for instance, Masterman describes the "notional" activities of captured Nazi spy SNOW and his captured spy ring associates SUMMER and BISCUIT. "On 17 September 1940, SNOW dispatched BISCUIT, who met SUMMER. . . . He then *notionally* took SUMMER with him to London. . . . The Germans were told via SNOW's transmitter that SUMMER had fallen ill . . . and was being nursed by BISCUIT. . . ." (My emphasis.) All of these notional adventures are taking place while the actual agents are in jail.

The notional method, Masterman tells us, was also used to create the specter of British moles within German territory. PLAN STIFF, for instance. "This plan was to drop by parachute in Germany a wireless set, instructions and codes, and to persuade the Germans that an agent had been dropped but had abandoned his task. It was hoped that the Germans would have to undertake a search for the missing agent. . . ."

And even more resonant for the American mole-hunt question is PLAN PAPRIKA, which was, according to Masterman, "evolved in order to cause friction among the German hierarchy in Belgium. A long series of wireless messages was constructed containing sufficient indications in code names and the like *to allow the Germans to guess which of these high officials were engaged in a plot* to make contact with certain British persons with a view to peace negotiations." (My emphasis.) In other words, to inspire a Nazi mole hunt.

PLAN PAPRIKA was aimed at creating "notional" traitors, whose conceptual existence would do as much or more harm than real traitors because of the unresolvable suspicion, distrust, and dissension the hunt for the nonexistent notionals would cause among the very real objects of suspicion created thereby.

The advantage of "notional" moles, of course, is that the side employing them doesn't need any real recruits, any long-term cultivation of ideological dissidents, or blackmail to recruit someone within an opponent's intelligence establishment. In fact one is better off *without a real mole*.

Now, imagine you are Kim Philby and you are facing an ultrasuspicious James Angleton across the chessboard in the game of East-West deception. How do you put one over on an opponent who knows you're out to put one over on him?

Assume that your goal has two parts: to neutralize or destroy the effectiveness of counterespionage against your side, and to get inside the secret files of the other side. Now let's make it harder. Let's assume you have no "assets," as they say, on the other side. You have no real mole, no big mole, no little mole already there to help you out. How do you start?

First, let's get into the files. Let's get deep into the most intimate personnel files of the CIA with the psychological profiles of the most secret of secret agents and their case officers, the ones who might be running moles against us. How? Let's send over one of our most brilliant agents, let's call him X. Let's give him the names of some of our genuine moles in other NATO countries. We'll have to make some sacrifices here, blow some people who have been pretty valuable, but look at the prize: the Central Registry of the CIA's Soviet Bloc division. So we'll let X expose some NATO moles and then we'll provide him with a bombshell of a clue. To an American mole. One we know doesn't exist. But they don't. A "notional" mole. We'll have X insist he can't even speak of this clue to anyone but James Angleton and the president of the United States. Everyone else is suspect. And here's what he'll say: "You people have been penetrated. Someone very high up is a KGB agent. My buddies back at Dzerzhinsky Square are so full of themselves over this that they get a little loose in the tongue. I've heard bits and pieces. Some clues. If only I could match them against your files. . . ."

●   ■   ●

At this point you've got Angleton in your hip pocket. You've confirmed all his darkest suspicions about the complete penetration of every other secret service in the West. And now you've got him on the track of the biggest prize of all: the Big Mole within his own organization. You begin to dredge up certain suggestive details from your tour of duty at KGB headquarters, a first initial, a career path, a peculiar operational signature . . .

And then Angleton makes a suggestion. Why don't I let you look through our personnel files, study the details of some of the most important cases, the moles we've run against Moscow? And there you are. All the way in. Certain American CIA execs are horrified at the idea of letting a senior KGB officer—defector or not—get into those files, but that only suggests *they* have something to hide in there. And so in three years you've accomplished all that it took three decades for Kim Philby to achieve: total access to the secret soul of the Western intelligence services.

But that's not enough. Not if you're Kim Philby and your target is James Angleton. Sure, you know his files inside out now, but you want something more: you want to destroy his effectiveness for the future. Forever. You want to paralyze the entire Central Intelligence Agency. So you think back to the first time you met Angleton and the two of you worked together. The double-cross system. You taught it to him. How to make the enemy believe false information is true by putting it in the mouths of false defectors you've turned to work for you. You know Angleton will see right through a *simple* disinformation operation so you've got to give it one further twist.

You've got the mole hunt going, but the question is: how to keep it going? Since there is no big mole, sooner or later one suspect after another will be cleared of false suspicion and questions will be asked about the validity of the original mole-hunt clue.

How to do it? What about making it seem that your notional mole's masters are panicked at the progress of the mole hunt, that they fear Big Mole's exposure, and have mounted a complex diversion operation to protect his notional cover?

Enter the false defectors. A delicate game here. Their falsity has to be exquisitely, carefully calibrated with an eye toward congruence with the rhythms and counterpoints of Angletonian counterintelligence theory.

So you send one false defector after another to approach the CIA. You provide them with some true information and some false, and one common theme: there is no Big Mole, there were a few little moles, but they've already been caught.

You know that with Angleton's double-cross-system mentality he's going to say to himself: if they've sent over a false defector to say there is no big mole, then there must really be a Big Mole they're trying to protect. But if you make it *too* easy to detect the falsity of the defector, if you don't provide him with enough true material to show that you deem the Big Lie about Big Mole important enough to sacrifice some valuable medium-size truths, then Angleton might see through the game, see that at bottom you want him to believe there *is* a Big Mole and therefore the reality might be that there is *not*.

And it is precisely here that Angleton's mind failed to be convoluted enough. He was too obsessed with the certainty that a betrayal had occurred and thus blinded to the possibility that this was *exactly what Philby wanted him to think*. Of course, if Angleton had followed this logic he would have to distrust *any* conclusion he came to as the one Kim Philby wanted him to make. Which would have been the abandonment of reason to an assumption of Philbyan omnipotence. But in fact he ended up abandoning reason anyway—to an irrational faith in the existence of, the omnipotence of, the unseen presence of Big Mole, a presence that could well be just another notional conjuration by the master of double double cross, Kim Philby.

The surprising thing about this is that Angleton himself didn't grasp the possibility that he was the victim of a notional-mole ploy, that his thinking didn't take that one final convolution, particularly when he knew it was Kim Philby he was facing across this conceptual chessboard.

●   ■   ●

The inability to believe that Angleton could have been so thoroughly outsmarted is probably the genesis for the fourth and most shocking and improbable of all the mole-theory heresies: the notion that Angleton himself *is* the Big Mole.

There's a certain insane logic to it if you choose to sit still for it. Angleton's renowned obsession with Big Mole, his finger-pointing at practically everyone else in the agency, can now be seen as the perfect cover for a malevolent mole masquerade of his own. And the effect of the Angleton-inspired mole hunt was easily as destructive of the CIA as any mere information-gathering mole might be.

Angleton a Soviet mole? The possibility is as astonishing and unbelievable as the notion that Philby was a mole before 1951. Or that Philby might be our mole even now.

But it was a man on Angleton's own counterintelligence staff who made the case against Angleton. And not a dreamy novice; no, it was Clare Petty, a case-hardened counterintelligence officer who'd earned a reputation for shrewdness when he was the first to spot the top mole in the West German BND, Heinze Felfe, long before the Germans caught on to him.

What little we know of this bizarre heresy again comes to us from David Martin's *Wilderness of Mirrors*, although the fact of the allegation's existence—if not its credibility—has been confirmed by attacks on Petty from the Angletonian camp, perhaps inspired by information coming from Angleton himself.

In June 1974, according to Martin, Clare Petty delivered to his superior a massive report on Angleton's career. There were boxes of documents and twenty-four hours of tape recordings to support the allegation, but all of the evidence was said to be "circumstantial." And even some of the circumstantial evidence was tenuous at best.

One instance cited, for example, was Angleton's failure to follow up a Soviet defector's allegation that Henry Kissinger was a long-term Soviet mole. The allegation came from a defector named Goleniewski, who had exposed some genuine penetrations in Western Europe but whose credibility had subsequently been damaged by his repeated claim to be true heir to the throne of the Romanov tsars.

The case against Angleton was in a sense a displaced case against his guru Golitsyn, the defector whose mole warning had created the whole mole madness, the KGB agent whom Angleton had allowed to burrow into the most secret and sensitive CIA personnel files, ostensibly in search of mole clues. "How the hell," Martin quotes one CIA division head as saying, "could anyone in his right mind give a KGB officer enough information [from CIA files] to make a valid analysis?" The Great Mole Hunt these two conducted had, one might argue, done more to destroy the effectiveness of the CIA than any ten highly placed moles might have accomplished. But the question remains: if this utterly improbable thesis were true, when might Angleton have been recruited? And why? It is here that we must return to the perplexing question raised by the Corson footnote and the Teddy Kollek tip-off—just what was the "deeper game" Angleton was playing with Philby's Ring of Five? Why was he running it from so deep in his hip pocket? Just what was really being transacted between Angleton and Philby during those two years of long weekly lunches they shared at Harvey's restaurant in Washington, D.C.?

Of course, there is a fifth permutation of these possibilities. Some might call it even more farfetched than the Angleton-as-mole heresy. What if the truth were not that Philby was running Angleton but that Angleton was running Philby? That Philby and even his KGB soul mate Andropov were our men in Moscow?

Wait, you say. How could that be? Angleton has been fired, exiled, and dismissed from intelligence work. Furthermore, Angleton and the Angletonians are constantly proclaiming the defeats that the KGB has inflicted on U.S. intelligence. The Angletonian gospel insists that the brilliance of the KGB and the foolishness of the CIA ruling establishment have created disaster after disaster for our side, that it's practically *run* by the KGB.

But look at it another way. What if Philby was our man in Moscow? Wouldn't we want his KGB associates to think he'd been a brilliant success, that he had even their archnemesis James Angleton on the run, that they'd dealt us grievous defeat after grievous defeat? Wouldn't we want the Soviet presidium to think that Yuri Andropov had been a masterful general in the complex war of moles and disinformation?

Of course, it would require a massive deception operation on our part to create such an impression. Many events—the firing of Angleton, for instance—would have to be staged. The Soviets would have to be convinced that *we* were convinced we'd been utterly defeated in the mole wars. Entire factitious histories would have to be created, which would mean that much of the orthodox Angletonian literature would, wittingly or unwittingly, have to reflect the strategy of the grand deception.

●   ■   ●

Is such a thing possible? I admit I wouldn't have considered it if I hadn't come across two particularly provocative passages in mole-war literature.

The first appears in what seems at first to be an utterly dry and academic analysis of disinformation theory. It's an ostensibly idle flight of speculation in a paper entitled "Incorporating Analysis of Foreign Governments' Deception into the U.S. Analytic System." The paper was delivered to a Washington symposium sponsored by a little-known group called the "Consortium for the Study of Intelligence," and published in an obscure volume called *Intelligence Requirements for the 1980's: Analysis and Estimates*.

The author, however, is not obscure. He's Edward Jay Epstein, perhaps the premier journalist in the mole-war field. As we noted earlier, Epstein's book *Legend* was the first to expose the subterranean civil war within the CIA over Big Mole and to make the Angletonian case that the agency had been subverted and defeated by the intrigue of KGB-sent false defectors.

The paper in question, however, has little of the undercover exposé glamour of *Legend*. It focuses on an abstract and academic analysis of the "bimodal approach" to analysis of deception and disinformation techniques. The paper makes a useful distinction between "Type A Deception," which Epstein defines as "inducing an adversary to miscount or mismeasure an observable set of signals" (the British, for instance, placing dummy aircraft on Scottish runways during World War II in order to scare the Germans into thinking an Allied invasion of Norway instead of Normandy was approaching), and "Type B Deception."

The latter is the most fascinating and complex mode. It aims, says Epstein, at "distorting the *interpretation* or *meaning* of a pattern of data, rather than the observable data itself.

"The main component of Type B deception," Epstein suggests, is generally "disinformation which purports to emanate from the highest levels of decision making: for essentially it must be represented as reflecting the secret strategy and motives of those in command. Such supposedly high-level information must be passed either through a double agent or a compromised channel of communication. . . . The disinformation can be plausibly reinforced by statements to diplomats, *journalists and other quasi-public sources*" (my italics).

While Epstein's paper is purportedly about the importance of acquiring a capacity to analyze and detect the possibility of Type B Deceptions being used on us, his discussions of the requirements for Type B Deception analysis apply also to the capacity for *performing* Type B Deceptions on an enemy. He goes on to propose the creation of a separate Type B Deception team for the purpose, he says, of analysis, but with the obvious capacity for *perpetrating* grand deceptions.

"This unit," Epstein suggests with remarkable confidence, almost as if he were describing something that already existed, "would be capable of generating a wide range of alternative explanations for received information."

While Epstein makes it sound like a mere analytic unit, his suggestions as to the kind of personnel to be employed make it obvious that we are talking about an offensive disinformation capacity: "It might conceivably employ functional paranoids, confidence men, magicians, film scenarists, or whomever else seemed appropriate to simulate whatever deception plots seemed plausible."

Simulate or stimulate deception plots? The importance he attaches to such a unit makes it hard to imagine we don't already have this capacity. And without seeming like a functional paranoid it's possible to imagine it has *already* been used. Perhaps in the service of the grandest, most imaginative highstakes Type B deception ever attempted: the running of Kim Philby and the placement of our mole Yuri Andropov in the ruling seat in the Kremlin.

In other words, it may not be out of the question to speculate that the whole dark Angletonian gospel of defeats—including, wittingly or unwittingly, Epstein's *Legend*—may itself be a "legend," a cover story, a grand Type B deception to preserve the security of an incredible Angletonian victory.

Hard to believe. But to work, such a deception would have to make one think it's impossible to believe. And there is one fascinating further piece of evidence for the fifth or Grand Type B Deception Theory: *The*

Hargrave Deception. A novel by E. Howard Hunt. His most recent one. A fascinating piece of work. In previous novels, Hunt has let drop little tidbits of inside agency gossip. *The Berlin Ending*, for instance, reflected the widespread intelligence-world belief that Willy Brandt was a Soviet-controlled agent.

But *The Hargrave Deception* goes further. It's the whole mole story, the whole Philby-Angleton relationship subtly disguised and with an astonishing twist. The James Angleton figure in the novel is called Peyton James, and he's an angler, a fly-fishing specialist like James Angleton. The Philby type is Roger Hargrave, here an American, but an American educated at Oxford. Without getting into the convolutions of plot, the bottom line is this: the Philby type defects to the Soviet Union for the purpose of infiltrating the KGB. He's our fake defector, our mole in the Kremlin. The problem is that only one man knows the real nature of his mission (everyone else considers him a traitor). The one who knows, Peyton James, eventually betrays his Philbyesque source—which in a sense Angleton may have done through the hints that have appeared in the Corson footnote. The ultimate double, double, double cross.

Of course, you could say this is all a Howard Hunt fantasy.

But so was Watergate.

—*HARPER'S*
October 1983

POSTSCRIPT TO
"THE SHADOW OF THE MOLE"

My "notional mole" theory has received some attention recently as a possible solution to the unending perplexity of the Angleton-Golitsyn mole hunt mess. Robin Winks takes note of it in his excellent recent book on Angleton and other Yale-bred spies, *Cloak and Gown*—although Professor Winks, in trying to explain it, defines the notion of the "notional mole" incorrectly when he refers to Golitsyn as the notional mole.

No: Golitsyn, the KGB defector, in this theory would be the trans-mitter of the notion, the one who plants, either deliberately or inadvertently, the false suspicion that the CIA has been penetrated by a high-level mole working for the KGB. Once he'd convinced counter-intelligence chief Angleton of the truth of this notion, the specter of the notional mole succeeded in paralyzing the CIA with false suspicion of its own personnel, crippling its ability to trust any intelligence about the Soviet Union.

Notional moles, by definition, do not exist; they're specters of un-certainty conjured up by enemy intelligence services to create a climate of distrust in their adversaries.

Looking back on it now, I'm less inclined to believe the notional mole was a deliberate plot hatched by the KGB or Philby, more inclined to believe that it was an ad hoc concoction by Golitsyn to perpetuate his primacy among defectors as top dog mole spotter.

What's changed my opinion on the issue was a conversation on informer psychology I had with the brilliant NYPD homicide detective Al Cachie in the course of reporting the "Crack Murder" investigation (p. 138). Cachie would talk about the difference between the product of the "first squeezing" of an informant and the less trustworthy product of subsequent "further revelations" from the same source. An in-former—whose psychology is similar to that of a defector in his de-pendence for money and survival on his case officer—will inevitably, as time goes on, seek to insure his perpetuation on the payroll, his primacy in favors, by inventing notional crimes and schemes that only he can detect and defeat.

I think that's what happened in the relationship between Angleton and Golitsyn. Here the case officer became the captive of his defector-informer because, however brilliant Angleton was as a theorist, he lacked the psychological savvy a street-smart detective could have applied to Golitsyn's never-ending mole accusations. I think Al Cachie would have seen through Golitsyn's game.

OSWALD'S GHOST

Dealey Plaza. It's a hot morning in August of this year, and motorists whizzing down Elm Street are witnessing a curious, if not sinister, phenomenon. Three people have gathered around a manhole at the foot of the famous grassy knoll. There's an attractive young blond woman, a spry, grizzled older fellow in a Coors cap, and a guy in his thirties with a tape recorder. The older guy is bending down and—demonstrating remarkable vigor—pulling the hundred-pound manhole cover out of its recess in the sidewalk.

Then he stops. Waits for a Dallas Police Department squad car to cruise by and disappear into the darkness of the Triple Underpass. At last he has yanked the massive iron seal clear of the opening that leads down to the storm sewer system honeycombing the underside of Dealey Plaza.

Then he does something really strange. He walks out into the middle of Elm Street traffic, heads uphill between two lanes of oncoming cars, and plants himself in the middle of the road about 25 yards upstream.

"Okay now, Ron. I'm standing right where the president was when he took the head shot. Now I want you to get down in that manhole," he yells at the younger guy, who, not to be coy, is me. "Elaine," he calls out to the woman, "you show him how to position himself."

So here I am, out in the midday sun, lowering myself into this manhole. It's kind of cool down here, though some might call it dank. While it is nice to escape the pounding of the direct sunlight, this is not my idea of summer fun.

But this is no ordinary manhole. This is the historic Dealey Plaza manhole that a certain faction of assassination buffs—led by Penn Jones, Jr., the guy in the middle of Elm Street—believes sheltered a sniper who fired the fatal frontal head shot on November 22, 1963. This manhole is the first stop on a grand tour of Dallas assassination shrines, during which, among other things, Penn has promised to show me the exact locations from which, he says offhandedly, the nine gunmen fired at John F. Kennedy that day. Sort of the Stations of the Cross Fire in conspiracy-theory gospel.

You remember Penn Jones, Jr., don't you? The feisty, combative country editor of the *Midlothian Mirror*. Author of the four-volume (so far) privately printed series called *Forgive My Grief*, the continuing account of his JFK-assassination investigation, which focuses on the deaths and disappearances of the 188 witnesses (so far) who Penn contends knew too much about the assassination conspiracy to be permitted to live.

Well, Penn Jones, Jr., is still on the case. He has retired from his editor's post to a farmhouse in Waxahachie, where he lives with his disciple and research associate, Elaine Kavanaugh, and publishes a monthly assassination newsletter, the *Continuing Inquiry*.

"Elaine," Penn yells out, "get Ron to back up against the wall there. Then he'll know what I mean."

I think Penn has sensed that I have some reservations about his Manhole Sniper theory, and this elaborate positioning is designed to address my doubts. In fact, I am skeptical.

Not the least of my problems with the Manhole Sniper theory is that it requires the putative manhole assassin to have popped up the hundred-pound manhole cover at just the right moment, fired a shot, then plopped it down over his head without any of the surrounding crowd taking notice of his activity. But Penn is determined to set me straight on this misapprehension.

"Okay now, Ron, you've got to move back so's your back is touching the rear of the hole there," Elaine says.

I follow her instructions and find myself completely under the overhang of pavement. In total darkness, except . . . well, damned if there isn't a perfect little rectangle of daylight coming through an opening in the pavement right in front of my eyes, and damned if Penn Jones' face isn't framed right in it.

"That's the storm drain in the curb side you're lookin' out now," says Elaine.

"See what a clear shot he had?" Penn Jones yells out. "Okay, Elaine, now pull that manhole cover back over on top of him. Ron, you'll see that even in the dark you'll be able to feel your way to one of those runoff tunnels he used to squirm his way under the plaza to the getaway."

Elaine begins to lug the heavy seal over the hole. Over me.

"Well, actually, Elaine, I don't think that'll be necessary. I get the picture," I say, hastily scrambling out, visions of the glowing eyes of sewer rats sending shivers through me.

Penn Jones hustles over, dodging traffic, and drags the cover back into place. He gives me a look that says, "Uh huh—another one not prepared to follow the trail all the way," and then he sets off on a trot up the grassy knoll to what he says is the next point of fire.

But before we follow Penn Jones up the grassy knoll, before we get any deeper into the labyrinthine state of the art of JFK-assassination theory, let's linger a moment on the manhole demo, because we've got a metaphor here for my own stance in relation to the whole web of conspiracy theory that the assassination buffs have spun out over the past twenty years. Because I'm going to be your guide in this excursion, and I want you to trust my judgment and powers of discrimination, I want you to know my attitude toward these people, which can be summed up by saying that I'll go down into the manhole with them but I won't pull the cover over my head.

You need a connoisseur when you're dealing with the tangled thicket of theory and conjecture that has overgrown the few established facts in the years since the events of that November 22. You need someone who can distinguish between the real investigators still in the field and the poets, like Penn Jones, whose luxuriant and flourishing imaginations have produced a dark, phantasmagoric body of work that bears more resemblance to a Latin American novel (Penn is the Gabriel García Márquez of Dealey Plaza, if you will) than to the prosaic police-reporter mentality I prefer in these matters.

You need someone with something akin to what Keats called negative capability—the ability to abide uncertainties, mysteries, and doubts without succumbing to the temptation of premature certainty. You need someone like me. I rather fancy myself El Exigente of conspiracy-theory culture, like the "Demanding One" in the TV coffee commercial. I've covered the buff beat since the early seventies—you might call me a buff buff—since the time, before Watergate, when everybody laughed at the idea of conspiracies.

So with El Exigente here as your guide, let's look at who's still on the case after twenty years and whether they have anything worth saying. What are the real mysteries left, and is there any hope we'll ever solve them?

●   ■   ●

Remember the way the residents of the little coffee-growing village in the Savarin commercial gather, buzzing nervously around the town square, awaiting the arrival of El Exigente, the white-suited coffee taster whose judgment on their beans will determine the success or failure of their entire harvest?

Well, the buff grapevine had been buzzing furiously for days before my departure for Dallas. Cross-country calls speculating about the nature of my mission. My past writings on the subject extricated from files, summoned up on computer screens, and scrutinized suspiciously. Indeed, angrily in some cases, as I learned the morning of my departure, when I received an irate call from newly ascendant buff David Lifton, author of the most successful of the recent buff books, *Best Evidence*. He accused me of plotting to trash his cherished trajectory-reversal theory.

As I set out for Dallas on the eve of the twentieth anniversary of the Dealey Plaza shooting, I was aware that I was heading into a buzz saw of buff factionalism. Long-festering rivalries and doctrinal disputes were dividing the Dallas-area buffs after years of beleaguered unity. Some of the bitterness can be attributed to the aftermath of the British invasion of Dallas-area buff turf in the past decade. First there was British writer

Michael Eddowes with his KGB-impostor theory: the Oswald who returned from the Soviet Union in 1962 wasn't the same Lee Harvey Oswald who defected to the USSR in 1959 but instead was a clever KGB impostor who used the name "Alek Hidell" (one of Oswald's aliases in Dallas and New Orleans). A few years later British writer Anthony Summers came to Dallas to research his theory that Oswald was not a Russian but an American intelligence operative. Both writers swept through town, wined and dined the local buffs, wrung them dry of their files and facts, and departed to publish completely contradictory conspiracy theories.

Eddowes' book, *The Oswald File*, left the most lasting legacy of divisiveness; it launched the epic embarrassment of the Oswald exhumation controversy. Eddowes maintained that his KGB-impostor theory could be proved by examining the body buried in Fort Worth's Rose Hill Cemetery under Oswald's name. Dental and medical evidence would show that the body belonged to an impostor, he said.

A number of Dallas buffs invested a lot of credibility in the exhumation crusade. Mary Ferrell, for instance. The great archivist. For years she had labored diligently to collect and index everything ever written about the assassination, every document, every clipping, every scrap of potential evidence. Her husband built a room in their back yard to hold the ever-expanding files. They bought two German shepherds to protect their stock. And for all those years, unlike the publicity-happy buffs who used her work, she had never sought to publish a theory of her own, had never abandoned her archivist's neutrality, had just gone on compiling her ultra-authoritative, supercomplete name index to the JFK assassination. Sample entries from the name index indicate its comprehensiveness:

> Boyer, Al—Hairstylist. He accompanied Josephine Ann Bunce, Jayme Bartlett and Bonnie Cavin to Dallas from Kansas City, Missouri. Warren Commission, vol. 22, p. 903.
>
> Boykin, Earl L. Wife, Ruby O. 1300 Keats Drive. Mechanic at Earl Hayes Chevrolet. Probably the same as Earl Boykin, who gave his address as 1300 Kouts at the Sports Drome Rifle Range one of the days Oswald was allegedly there. *Texas Attorney General's Report*.

But then this dashing Englishman swept into town and away went her meticulous scholarly neutrality. "This Eddowes was some character," one rival buff remarked. "He had his own Rolls-Royce flown over from England. He'd chauffeur Mary around. Then she'd fly over to England, and he'd drive her around London in Rolls-Royces."

It was the old story. Mary Ferrell ended up enlisting in the exhumation cause, drawing a flotilla of Dallas buffs behind her. They were all convinced that the authorities would never let the body be exhumed because of the terrible dual-identity secret it would reveal.

Then in 1981 Oswald's wife, Marina, was somehow enticed into the exhumation battle, and it was Marina's lawsuit that finally opened the tomb. And so out they went to Rose Hill Cemetery with cape and shovel to see just who was buried there.

The body they dug up seemed to have Oswald's teeth—the American Marine Oswald's teeth—down to the tiniest detail. The medical examiner said that the Oswald buried in Oswald's grave was the same Oswald who had been in the Marines before he defected to Russia. The second-body buffs weren't satisfied, of course (they're still demanding a ruling), but the credibility of the whole Dallas buff community went right down the tubes.

●　　　■　　　●

Arrive in Dallas with a suitcase full of current buff literature, most of it newsletters. I've got the *Grassy Knoll Gazette*, put out by Robert Cutler. I've got Penn Jones' *Continuing Inquiry*. I've got Paul Hoch's *Echoes of Conspiracy*. And I've got *Coverups!* from Gary Mack of Fort Worth.

The last is new to me. But buried in a buff gossip column, there's a tip-off that it too is a product of Dallas-buff fratricide: "Gary Mack and Jack White were dismissed by Penn Jones as consultants to *The Continuing Inquiry*. No explanation was given."

I've heard a lot about Gary Mack. He is the industrious young turk of the new generation of high-tech audiovisual-aids buffs who have supplanted the old-style document-indexing types. Over the years, they've blown up, enhanced, and assiduously analyzed every square millimeter of film and tape taken that day, and they've discerned lurking in the grainy shadows shapes and forms they say are gunmen. Leafing through Mack's newsletters, I come upon a fascinating photomontage of Grassy Knoll Gunmen on the front page of *Coverups!* There is Black Dog Man—I've seen him before—and a new one to me: Badge Man. I am familiar with various suspicious characters of their genre, such as the Babushka Lady and the Umbrella Man, to whom the photographic buffs have attributed various mysterious roles. I decide to call Gary Mack and check these guys out.

Black Dog Man. At first he was a furry shadow on top of the concrete wall behind the grassy knoll. Certain audiovisual-aids types saw in blowups of that furry shadow a manlike shape. In some blowups, they said, they could see a man firing a gun. Skeptical photo analysts on the staff of the House Select Committee on Assassinations thought that the furry shadow looked more canine than conspiratorial and dubbed the dark apparition Black Dog Man.

And there he is on the front page of the October issue of Gary Mack's newsletter. Next to Black Dog Man is Badge Man; an extreme blowup of a tiny square of what seems to be a tree shadow is accompanied by a visual aid, "a sketch of what he might look like if this photo is computer-enhanced." And suddenly—in the sketch at least—Badge Man leaps out of the shadows and takes explicit human form. He's a man in the uniform of a Dallas police officer, complete with badge and shoulder patch. He appears to be firing a rifle concealed by what looks like a flare from a muzzle blast. In the foreground of the Polaroid from which this blowup was made, the Kennedy limousine is passing the grassy knoll and the president is beginning to collapse. It is less than a second after the fatal head shot. Am I watching Badge Man fire it? The House Select Committee photo panel reported, "Although it is extremely unlikely that further enhancement of any kind would be successful, this particular photo should be re-examined in light of the findings of the acoustics analysis," which placed a gunman behind the grassy knoll.

What does your guide, El Exigente, make of Black Dog Man and Badge Man? Much as I would like to have an enhanced portrait of the assassin at the moment he fired the fatal shot, I'm afraid my instinct is that these photos must be classified as an artifact of the Beatles-in-the-trees variety. Recall that when Bob Dylan's *John Wesley Harding* album came out—the first one after Dylan's near-fatal motorcycle accident—there were stories of cryptic messages embedded in the album-cover

photograph? There was supposed to be a group shot of the Beatles—
their four heads anyway—hidden in the shadows of the trees. I saw
the Beatles in the trees once they were pointed out to me. But I don't
think they were there, if you know what I mean. The same can be said
for the thereness of Black Dog Man.

When I reach Gary Mack, he says he has something exciting to show
me if I visit his Fort Worth home and investigatory headquarters: a
beautiful blown-up enhancement of the Bronson film.

The Bronson film. The last, best hope that we'll get a motion picture
of the "other assassins." Sort of the Shroud of Turin of the buff faith.
Dallas onlooker Charles Bronson was taking home movies in Dealey
Plaza that day. He caught the assassination in color. Showed it to the
FBI. Nothing of interest, they said. Fifteen years later an assassination
researcher named Robert Ranftel came across an FBI report, buried in
100,000 pages of declassified documents, about this film. Dogged Dallas
assassination reporter Earl Golz tracked down Bronson—now in Ada,
Oklahoma—checked out the film, and discovered something no one
noticed before. Up there in the left-hand corner of the frame, the
Bronson camera had caught the sixth-floor windows of the Texas School
Book Depository. Not just the sniper's-nest window on the corner where
Oswald was said to be perched but also the two adjacent windows. It's
those two windows that Gary Mack wants me to see.

He also fills me in on his continuing struggle to rescue the Dallas
police tape from being reconsigned to the dustbin of history. Gary thinks
he can save it. I'm not so sure. For a glorious period of about three
years, the Dallas police tape represented a triumphant official vindication
of everything—well, almost everything—assassination buffs had been
saying since 1964. The tape (actually a Dictabelt made of transmissions
from a motorcycle cop's open mike to police headquarters on November
22) was excavated from a box in a retired police intelligence officer's
closet in 1978, after Mary Ferrell reminded the House Select Committee
of its possible existence and probative value.

Acoustical analysis of the sound patterns submerged in the static on
the police tape led the House Select Committee to the spectacular conclusion that "scientific acoustical evidence establishes a high probability
that two gunmen fired at President Kennedy" and that the assassination
was "probably a result of a conspiracy."

Not only that. The highly respected acoustics scientists who analyzed the tape concluded from their reconstruction of echo patterns and test firings in Dealey Plaza that the second gunman was actually on the grassy knoll. Yes, the much ridiculed assassination-buff obsession, the grassy knoll. The longest, most thorough official government investigation of the JFK assassination concluded that the buffs were right all along.

The vindication was short-lived, though. In 1982 a new panel of acoustics experts, this one convened at the request of the Justice Department by the National Academy of Sciences and known as the Ramsey Panel, blasted the police-tape findings out of the water. Its determination was that the so-called shots heard on the Dictabelt, including the grassy-knoll shot, took place a full minute after the shootings in Dealey Plaza that day and thus couldn't be shots at all.

And so we're back to square one. The acoustical evidence doesn't rule out a grassy-knoll gunman or a conspiracy or even the nine gunmen Penn Jones posits. But the mantle of scientific proof the buffs had downed now seems to be in shreds.

Not so, says Gary Mack. "Are you familiar with automatic gain control, Ron?" he asks me, and he launches into a highly complex, technical critique of the Ramsey Panel critique of the House Select Committee acoustics report. The Ramsey Panel misinterpreted automatic gain control in their retiming thesis, he says. They neglected to analyze the sixty-cycle power hum to see if the Dictabelt in question had been rerecorded. They neglected certain anomalies of the Dictabelt that could be cleared up by further analysis of echo-pattern matching and corroborated by a more precise jiggle analysis of another gruesome home movie, the one taken by Dallas dressmaker Abraham Zapruder.

Gary sounds like he knows what he's talking about, and perhaps he can make his case. But listening to his technobuff talk, I get a distinct sinking feeling that the Dallas police tape—like almost every other piece of "definitive" evidence in the case—is now forever lost in that limbo of ambiguity, that endless swamp of dispute that swallows up any certainty in the Kennedy case.

This morass of technobuff ambiguity leaves me utterly exhausted and depressed, but Gary Mack shifts the conversation to a missing-witness story. It isn't the greatest missing-witness story I've heard. Nothing like the classic Earlene-Roberts-rooming-house story. Nothing like the second-Oswald-car-salesman story. But it has enough of that *misterioso* provocativeness to give me a little thrill of that old-time buff fever and remind me why the whole hopeless confusing case has continued to fascinate me for two decades.

This particular missing-witness story concerns Oswald's whereabouts at the time of the shooting. No witness has ever placed him on the sixth floor any later than 11:55 a.m., 35 minutes before the gunfire. Oswald maintained that he was on the first floor throughout the shooting. And one witness, Bonnie Ray Williams, who was eating fried chicken on the sixth floor, stated that as late as 12:20 p.m. he was alone up there, that there was no Oswald on the sixth floor. Where was Oswald? The Warren Commission implied that he must have been hiding on the sixth floor in his sniper's nest from 11:55 on, while the Fried Chicken Man was chomping away.

But Gary Mack tells me about a witness, never questioned by the Warren Commission, who contradicts that hypothesis. She is Carolyn Arnold, now a resident of Stephenville. Back in 1963 she was executive secretary to the vice president of the Book Depository. She knew Oswald well by sight. She says that she came upon Oswald sitting alone, eating a sandwich in the employees' second-floor lunchroom at 12:15, just ten minutes before the motorcade was scheduled to pass the building. Her timing of this sighting has been corroborated convincingly by other employees, who noticed when she left her office to go to the lunchroom.

If Oswald was planning to assassinate the president from the sixth floor, what was he doing calmly eating lunch four floors below, right before the president was supposed to come into view? Could he have been that hungry, that calm? And if that was Oswald in the lunchroom, who were the figures spotted moving around on the sixth floor by witnesses across the street from the building at just about that time?

Whatever the significance of the Carolyn Arnold story—and perhaps it can be explained by eyewitness error—just listening to Gary Mack tell it brings me back to that peculiar sense of dislocation that attracted me to the JFK case in the first place. That frisson of strangeness.

●   ■   ●

Bring up the *Twilight Zone* theme. It's summer 1964. I'm seventeen, and I'm in a small crowded theater in New York's Gramercy Park section. A fierce man strides across the stage with a pointer, gesturing contemptuously at a huge blown-up slide projection of Lee Harvey Oswald. It's the famous *Life* magazine cover photo, the one with Oswald posing in his back yard with a rifle in one hand, a copy of the Socialist Workers Party paper, the *Militant*, in the other, and a pistol on his hip. He's got that weird, glazed, grim-faced grin.

But there's something else going on in this picture, the man with the pointer is saying. Something going on with the shadows. Look at the direction of the shadow of the gun, he commands us. Now look at the direction of the shadow cast by Oswald's nose. Different angle. Something's wrong. This picture has been faked. It's part of the frame-up. That's Lee Harvey Oswald's head but someone else's body. The man with the pointer is, of course, Mark Lane. He has just come from Washington, where he has been representing Oswald's side of the story before the Warren Commission at the request of Oswald's mother, Marguerite. And investigating the case himself. Already he has turned up some stories the authorities don't want us to hear, he says. Stories that suggest deep currents of complicity between the Dallas police and the conspiracy to frame Oswald.

The Earlene Roberts story, for instance. Roberts was the landlady of Oswald's shabby Oak Cliff rooming house. She recounted an incident that occurred a half hour after the shooting. Oswald had returned home and disappeared into his bedroom, and she was sitting in her parlor watching coverage of the assassination on TV when a Dallas police squad car pulled up in front of her place. The car paused, then honked its horn twice and left. Shortly thereafter, Oswald emerged and headed off in haste, only to be intercepted—accidentally, according to the Warren Commission—by Officer J. D. Tippit, who was shot dead while attempting to apprehend him.

The police department denied that any of its vehicles passed or stopped at Oswald's address. The only car in the vicinity at the time, they said, was driven by none other than Officer Tippit. Just what was going on between Oswald and Tippit?

Whoa. *Twilight Zone* again. Most Americans remember exactly where they were and what they felt when they first heard that John Kennedy had been shot. I'm no different; I do, too. But I have to confess that I remember even more vividly where I was and what I felt when I first heard the Earlene Roberts story. I remember feeling a chill, feeling goose bumps crawling up from between my shoulder blades. There was a kind of thrill too, the thrill of being let in on some secret reality. Shadowy connections, suggestions of an evil still at large that ordinary people were not prepared to deal with. Dangerous knowledge.

That Earlene Roberts story certainly struck a nerve. And not just with me. Brian De Palma's second film, *Greetings*, while ostensibly about the draft, featured a character obsessed by Kennedy's assassination and by the Earlene Roberts story in particular. This guy was convinced, as is Penn Jones, that Earlene Roberts' death, before she was able to give testimony to the Warren Commission, was the work of the People Behind It All.

Dangerous knowledge. It's the recurrent theme in almost all the assassination-conspiracy films that followed De Palma's first. In Alan Pakula's *The Parallax View*, in William Richert's *Winter Kills*, in Michelangelo Antonioni's *Blow-Up*, in De Palma's later *Blow Out*, the hero begins by investigating the death of a Witness Who Knows Too Much, and soon he becomes a Witness Who Knows Too Much himself. His attainment of a darker, more truthful vision of the way things really are makes him a target for assassination. A way, perhaps, for us to approach the horror of being assassinated, the unassimilable horror of what JFK experienced at Dealey Plaza.

Let me return to 1964, because in the fall of that year, just two months after hearing the Earlene Roberts story, I was fortunate enough to get to know the assassination researcher whose methods and judgment I still respect above all others in the field. His name is Josiah Thompson, and he was my freshman philosophy instructor at Yale. At the time I knew him, he was becoming increasingly preoccupied with two mysteries: the often misinterpreted nature of the mind of the gloomy Danish antirationalist philosopher Sören Kierkegaard and the numinous hints of an alternate interpretation of the truth lurking in the shadows of the Warren Commission's 26 volumes.

His investigation of Kierkegaard resulted eventually in a highly acclaimed biography and a study of Kierkegaard's pseudonymous writings called *The Lonely Labyrinth*. His investigation of the teeming labyrinth of the Kennedy case took him into the *Warren Report*, then out into the world and down to Dallas, where he reinterviewed the witnesses, reexamined the evidence, and found new witnesses and new evidence. He produced what many regard as the most scrupulously researched and carefully thought-out critique of the official conclusions, a book called *Six Seconds in Dallas: A Micro-Study of the Kennedy Assassination*.

And so with Thompson as my model, I came to think of critics of the *Warren Report*—the best of them, anyway—as intellectual heroes, defying conventional wisdom and complacency to pursue the truth. I had lost track of Thompson during the past ten years, and I was having trouble tracking him down to see what he thought of the JFK case after twenty years. It wasn't until I got to Dallas that I heard a strange story about him from one of the West Coast buffs who had found me in my hotel room through the buff grapevine. He'd heard that Thompson had abandoned his tenured professorship of philosophy and chucked his whole academic career to become a private eye somewhere on the West Coast. What the hell could that mean? Had he become a casualty of dangerous knowledge? Or had he fallen in love with it?

●   ■   ●

Next morning. Rendezvous with Penn and Elaine at the Book Depository for the grand gunmen tour. The Texas Historical Commission plaque at the base of the building still astonishes with its frank rejection of Warren Commission certainty. This is the building from which "Lee Harvey Oswald allegedly shot and killed" JFK.

"You ever been in the military, Ron?" Penn Jones is asking me. We've moved to the top of the grassy knoll, and Penn is pointing out snipers' nests in the buildings surrounding the killing ground down below.

There was hardly a building or tree that hadn't bristled with guns that day, according to Penn's vision of things. There were gunmen on top of the Dal-Tex Building, gunmen in the Records Building, even gunmen up in the skies.

"Look over there," Penn says, pointing toward the top of the Post Office Annex. "That was an observation post. They had a man there overlooking things so he could assess the damage done" by the first nine gunmen in Dealey Plaza. If they failed, Penn says, he could alert the multiple teams of backup gunmen farther along the parade route. Or if necessary call in the airborne team.

"They," for Penn, is the military. He believes that the military killed Kennedy. Not the Mafia, not the CIA, not Cuban exiles, not some of the fusions of all three currently fashionable among buff theorists.

"Why the military?" I ask Penn. "Because they thought he'd withdraw from Viet Nam? Or—"

"Shit, no. So they could take *over*," he says.

Penn was in the military, a World War II transport officer in the North African campaigns. In some ways Penn is still in the military. Only, he's a general now. A master strategist. As he surveys the landscape of Dealey Plaza, pointing out the teams of gunmen, as we retrace the motorcade route through the streets of Dallas, examining the locations of backup gunmen teams, Penn is like a general reviewing his troops, a battlefield strategist pointing out the logic of his deployments.

Of course, Penn's army of gunmen doesn't spring entirely from his overactive imagination. We're standing on the railroad tracks now, the ones that cross over the Triple Underpass. Penn points out the famous railroad signal-tower perch of the late Lee Bowers. Up there on November 22, 1963, Lee Bowers had a clear view of the area behind the stockade fence that crests the grassy knoll. Right about here, where Penn, Elaine, and I are standing, police officer Joe Smith stopped a man who was exiting the scene with suspect haste, as Smith testified before the Warren Commission. The man showed Secret Service credentials to Smith. The Secret Service says that none of its agents could have been there at that time.

As for the late Lee Bowers, it was his "mysterious death," shortly after his Warren Commission testimony, that set Penn off on his twenty-year chronicling of deaths and disappearances of witnesses with dangerous knowledge.

"Lee Bowers was killed in a *one-car accident* in my hometown of Midlothian, Texas," Penn tells me, his drawl just crawling with embittered sarcasm. "The doctor in Midlothian who examined him told me that when he admitted him, Bowers was in some sort of strange shock."

And we cruise by the site of the old Highlander Hotel in Highland Park. Now replaced by some big new condo tower: "The paymaster stayed here," Penn tells me. "It's also where the gunmen stayed the night before. They tore it down completely. I think it's significant that all these buildings were torn down."

Penn is fascinated by the first-class treatment the gunmen got before the day of the shooting.

"They treat the gunmen real well, *before*," he tells me. "They're mighty important. Every wish of theirs must be complied with."

Almost wistfully he describes the wish-fulfilled life of the gunmen in the secret, safe houses he says they occupied the nights before the Night Before.

"There was one up in Lake Lugert, Oklahoma," he says. "That was some damn place. They had anything they wanted. Gambling, women. Lobsters flown in *daily. Shee*it."

Of course, Penn says, things changed for the gunmen the Day After.

"They loaded them in the two getaway planes and then just blew up the planes—one of 'em over the Gulf of Mexico, the other one down there in Sonora Province, old Mexico."

Not every shrine has been torn down. Some have been quietly disintegrating. The Oak Cliff sites. The Earlene Roberts rooming house to which O. returned shortly after the shooting. The house, where he and Marina had lived as their marriage disintegrated that year. Jack Ruby's raunchy apartment and motel pads. The Texas Theater, where O. was finally cornered.

"They just let this area decay," Penn says—as if even the inexorable organic breakdown of wood fiber is due to a conscious decision *they* made.

I'll never forget pulling into the driveway of this Oswald-and-Marina abode. It isn't so much the shock of discovering around back the hauntingly familiar outside staircase that served as a background for the controversial O.-with-rifle-and-nose-shadow pix.

No, it is the expression on the face of the ancient Mexican man who apparently lives in the decaying shrine now. Evidently Penn is a regular, fairly well tolerated visitor here; when we arrive, the man—who is sitting on the sagging, splintered front porch with a child who appears to be his grandson—waves familiarly at Penn. But as we pass, I notice a deeply puzzled expression come over his face. Why do these crazy Anglos keep cruising my driveway? What kind of satisfaction is it they're after, that they never get?

But the thing I'll remember most about our tour this day is not the haunted landmarks or the ghostly gunmen they conceal. The thing I'll never forget, for its intensity and authenticity—an intensity that explains the shadowy world they've created—is the grief of Penn and Elaine.

Actually, it's Elaine's grief. I already know about Penn Jones' grief. It is all there in *Forgive My Grief*, his saga of murdered witnesses to the truth. The title is from Tennyson, by the way, from a passage of *In Memoriam* addressed to God, who took away the poet's closest friend:

> Forgive my grief for one removed,
> Thy creature, whom I found so fair.
> I trust he lives in thee, and there
> I find him worthier to be loved.

Elaine's involvement in this whole thing is hard to figure out, though. Why would a bright, young, attractive woman—young enough to have hardly known who JFK was when he was shot—why would she immerse herself in the buff biz after two decades, when it doesn't look like the case is on the verge of being cracked and all Penn offers is the despair and futility of mourning one lost witness after another?

I begin to get a clue to what might be motivating Elaine during the course of the tour, on our way back from the Oswald-and-Marina house, when Elaine spots a fat woman on the street.

"That looks like my stepmother," she says. "God she was unfair to me. Every time I see a fat woman, I think of her and how unfair she was."

"Look at that concrete bridge abutment up ahead," Penn is saying. "That's where William Whaley [the taxi driver who took Oswald from downtown to Oak Cliff] died in a crash just after he tried to testify about Ruby and Tippit."

"My mother died when she was twenty-five," Elaine says. "Most of the rest of my close relatives are dead now. All I have left is my grandmother."

And so it continues as the tour winds down, a counterpoint of Penn's public grief and Elaine's personal grief.

Later, after the tour is over and we are cooling off with some beers, Elaine tries to explain why she has made Penn's project her life's work.

"From the moment I met Penn, I knew that's what I was gonna do—work on the case with him," she tells me. "And when I started, I was so excited."

"What happened?" I ask.

"Then I met all these people, and I saw there was no hope."

"Which people?"

"The other people on the case." She reels off a list of prominent buffs.

"What's wrong with them?" I ask.

"They none of them really *loved* John Kennedy. I remember meeting David Lifton and asking him point-blank, 'Did you love John Kennedy?' And he wouldn't give me a direct answer. And that's the real question: did you love the man? If you didn't love him, why work on the case? Then it's just a hobby or some kind of excitement.

"We're down to two hundred subscribers now," she says. "And most of them are old. Pretty soon they'll die, and in a few years we'll be down to fifty. And that's what we have to look forward to. In two more years it'll be all over. It's pretty sad."

But Elaine isn't going to give up.

"You get used to people laughing at you. You get used to the scorn and the ridicule. You put up with it because if you really believe in something, you don't stop, no matter what. It's like a religion."

She and Penn drift into a talk about religion, specifically about Thomas Merton, the Trappist monk and philosopher, Penn's idol.

"When Penn's gone, I'm gonna become a hermit like Merton," Elaine says. "Why should I bother with people anymore? I've lost everyone I loved except my grandmother and Penn. When they're gone, there won't be anyone.

"But I guess you've got to keep up the fight," she says, rather unconvincingly. "Still it's pretty sad. It's heartbreaking, depressing. There are days when Penn and I both weep over it. We both grieve over it."

"Over it?" I ask. "You mean—"

"It's sad for the state of the country. But really it's more sad for John Kennedy. That's what we can't get over."

It is then that I realize that these people are not buffs. They are mourners. Their investigation of the assassination is their way of mourning, a continuation of his last rites that they can't abandon. Unlike the rest of us, they haven't stopped grieving.

●   ■   ●

While the poets peopled the world of that November 22 with a grief-generated galaxy of hostile ghosts, the official investigators narrowed their focus to one man. Somehow lost in the controversy over the acoustical evidence is that the House Select Committee actually came up with a prime suspect. A candidate for the Man Behind It All. And testimony to back that up. It all comes down to what you think of the tail-and-the-dog story.

The tail-and-the-dog story is at the heart of the hottest area of assassination theory still thriving after all these years: mob-hit theory. In the past few years, mob-hit theory has succeeded in shouldering aside such other rival contenders as CIA-anti-Castro-hit theory, pro-Castro-hit theory, and KGB-complicity theory and in pushing itself to the forefront of consideration.

The rush to the mob-hit judgment began in 1979 with the publication of the final report of the House Select Committee. Written by organized-crime expert and chief counsel Robert Blakey, the committee report comes within a whisker of calling the events of November 22, 1963, a gangland slaying and within a whisker of a whisker of pinning the contract on New Orleans mob boss Carlos Marcello.

"The committee found that Marcello had motive, means, and opportunity to have President John F. Kennedy assassinated, though it was unable to establish direct evidence of Marcello's complicity," the report states. "The committee identified the presence of one critical evidentiary element that was lacking with other organized crime figures examined by the committee: credible associations relating both Lee Harvey Oswald and Jack Ruby to figures having a relationship, albeit tenuous, with Marcello's crime family."

The key here is Oswald's uncle Dutz. Ruby's organized-crime ties—to teamster thugs connected with Jimmy Hoffa, to Sam Giancana and guys like John Roselli who were in on the CIA-mob plots to assassinate Fidel Castro—had long been known. What the House Select Committee established was an Oswald organized-crime connection: his uncle Charles "Dutz" Murret, of New Orleans, whom the committee described as both "a surrogate father of sorts throughout much of Oswald's life in New Orleans" and "an associate of significant organized crime figures affiliated with the Marcello organization."

The abstract connections are all there. We know that Marcello hated the Kennedy brothers with a deep bitterness that grew out of much more than fear of the threat that Bobby Kennedy's organized-crime prosecutions posed to his billion-dollar racketeering empire. Marcello had experienced the kind of physical humiliation at the hands of Kennedy justice that can brew a passion for revenge surpassing mere calculation of profit and loss.

Just two months after John Kennedy's inauguration, Marcello was virtually kidnaped in New Orleans by immigration officers acting at the direction of Bobby Kennedy's Justice Department. Arrested, handcuffed, he was dragged without a hearing to a Border Patrol plane and, according to Robert Blakey, "flown 1200 miles to Guatemala City and dumped there, without luggage." When his presence became known to the authorities in Guatemala, he was expelled and "unceremoniously flown to an out-of-the-way village in the jungle of El Salvador, where [he and his lawyer] were left stranded. Salvadorian soldiers jailed and interrogated the two men for five days, then put them on a bus and took them twenty miles into the mountains. . . . They were hardly prepared for the mountain hike, as they were dressed in silk shantung suits and alligator shoes. . . . Marcello fainted three times. . . . During a downhill scramble, Marcello fell and broke two ribs" before reaching an airstrip and managing to reenter the U.S. illegally.

Indubitably, in all this unaccustomed humiliation at the hands of the Kennedys, the motive is there.

But where is the direct connection? That's where the tail-and-the-dog story comes in. The teller of the tale is Ed Becker, whom Blakey describes as "a former Las Vegas promoter who had lived on the fringe of the underworld."

The scene is Churchill Farms, Marcello's plantation outside New Orleans. It is September 1962. Becker is there to discuss a business proposition, but the talk turns to the Kennedy campaign against organized crime. The mention of Bobby Kennedy's name drives Marcello into a rage. "Don't worry about that little Bobby son of a bitch," he shouts, according to Becker. "He's going to be taken care of."

How? Becker testified before the House Select Committee that the plan was to "take care of" Bobby by "taking care of" his brother and that Marcello "clearly stated that he was going to arrange to have President Kennedy murdered in some way." Becker said that Marcello compared Bobby to the tail and his brother Jack to the whole dog, citing a proverb: If you cut off the tail, the dog will keep biting; but if you chop off the head, the dog will die, tail and all.

The committee took a lot of time painstakingly and convincingly corroborating the circumstantial details of the story. Then they called Marcello in to testify about it. He denied it. But he also testified before the committee in executive session that he made his living as a tomato salesman, testimony that his recent Brilab conviction calls into question.

The tail-and-the-dog story may not be enough evidence to indict or convict, although I have been told that the committee staff forwarded its Marcello material to the Justice Department in order to encourage it to do just that. But Becker's story takes mob-hit theory a step beyond motive, means, and opportunity in the abstract.

●   ■   ●

That night. Back in my hotel room after Penn Jones' tour, recovering from the plunge into undiluted grief. I continue calling my buff contacts across the country. A long midnight talk with Bay Area buff Robert Ranftel is the most provocative.

Ranftel is a codiscoverer of a fascinating new piece of information about the case. The Gillin story. The Psychedelic Oswald theory.

Don't laugh. It's based on careful research, and it addresses perhaps the most enduring and perplexing mystery remaining in the case: the mind of Lee Harvey Oswald.

Because, after all these years the question for most researchers is no longer whether Oswald was involved but who he was. Was he KGB or CIA? Was he a pro-Castro partisan infiltrating anti-Castro groups, or was he an anti-Castro activist setting up false pro-Castro fronts? Was he informing for the FBI or being informed on? Did he support JFK or hate him? There is convincing evidence on both sides of each of these questions. How could one man have created so much ambiguity about his true identity in so short a time? And why? Was he just confused? Or was he out to confuse?

Ranftel unearthed a clue to this dilemma, an episode that took place during Oswald's mysterious sojourn in New Orleans the summer before the assassination. The Gillin story first surfaced in a document that wasn't declassified until 1977, an FBI memo about an interview with a New Orleans assistant district attorney named Edward Gillin. On the day Oswald was killed, Gillin phoned the FBI to report a strange encounter he had had in the summer of 1963 with a man calling himself Lee Oswald. How this skinny guy named Oswald had come into his office and started talking about a book he'd read by Aldous Huxley. A book about psychedelic drugs. "He was looking for a drug that would open his vision, you know, mind expansion," Gillin recalled. He had come to the assistant DA, Oswald said, because he wanted to know if such drugs were legal. And how to get them.

Oswald and Aldous Huxley. What a bizarre meeting of minds. Oswald and psychedelic drugs. What a combination of ingredients. And yet Ranftel and his collaborators, Martin Lee and Jeff Cohen of the Assassination Information Bureau, came up with several other periods in Oswald's career during which the psychedelic connection might have been made.

The U-2 base in Atsugi, Japan, for instance. Where Oswald served as a Marine Corps radar operator before he defected to the Soviets. Ranftel and company discovered that during the time Oswald was stationed there, Atsugi base was a storage and testing facility for the drugs used in the CIA's Operation Artichoke. Artichoke was the forerunner of Operation MK-ULTRA, the CIA's search for a foolproof truth serum—at first called the Twilight Zone drug—which led to the testing of LSD, often on unsuspecting military personnel. Ranftel and his colleagues located a Marine who was stationed at Atsugi at the same time as Oswald and says that he himself was given LSD and other psychedelics.

And then there was Oswald's curious bad-trip episode at Atsugi. Ranftel, Cohen, and Lee described it last March in their *Rolling Stone* article, "Did Oswald Drop Acid?": "While Oswald was on guard duty, gunfire was heard. He was found sitting on the ground, more than a little dazed, babbling about seeing things in the bushes . . . what in the Sixties would become known as a bad trip."

Ranftel and company point to the widespread suspicion that Oswald's defection to the Soviet Union may have been staged with the connivance and encouragement of the CIA or military intelligence, both of which were at the time repeatedly trying to plant "defector" operatives inside the USSR. They cite CIA sources revealing that agents dispatched into situations with the potential for hostile interrogation—including the use of psychedelic interrogation aids—were often exposed to such drugs before setting out on those missions, so they would be able to recognize and cope with the effects of the drugs. People so exposed were known in the intelligence world as enlightened operatives.

Oswald an enlightened operative? Oswald a Huxleyan psychedelic mystic?

For one thing, as Ranftel remarks tonight, "it might explain that strange, quizzical smile you see on the guy's face in so many of his pictures."

What was going on behind that smile? The Psychedelic Oswald hypothesis offers an explanation, a way of reconciling some of the intractable contradictions he left behind. CIA or KGB? Pro-Castro or anti-Castro? Perhaps the answer is neither and both. Perhaps the answer is that he enjoyed the game of posing as both, of playing at infiltrating one side on behalf of the other, of playing both sides against the other, the pleasures of the enlightened operative. We know that as a boy Oswald's favorite TV show was *I Led Three Lives*. Had drugs given a psychedelic twist to the solemnity of that classic of role playing?

The Psychedelic Oswald hypothesis might go a long way toward explaining some of the mysteries of Oswald's strange summer in New Orleans—those months before the assassination when he began playing the dangerous game of pro- and anti-Castro politics and which climaxed with his mysterious pre-assassination trip to Mexico City.

●   ■   ●

New Orleans. The French Quarter's decaying fringe. 544 Camp Street, to be specific. The most intriguing address in the whole JFK case. Only it's not here anymore. I came all the way to this steamy, sweaty late August swamp of a city to enter the building at 544 Camp Street because some buff or other told me it was still here. Because, of all the shrines in the story of O., this one might hold the clue to what was going on in his mind in the summer of 1963, when he fled Dallas, arrived here, and began to act weird.

One thing almost all conspiracy theorists, even Warren Commission defenders, agree on is that though the assassination was an act executed in Dallas, it was conceived in the contagion of intrigue that infected the mind of Oswald that August in New Orleans.

The mind of Oswald. I'm beginning to feel some inkling of the turmoil therein as I stand before the curious sculpture that has replaced the now-demolished building at 544 Camp Street.

I fled Dallas yesterday, sick of brain and body. A bad case of food poisoning got to my body. So bad that for a while I thought I'd end up as number 189 in Penn Jones' list of suspicious casualties of the case. (Of course, how could they know I would stuff myself with barbecue in that particular place on Mockingbird Lane?)

It was Gary Mack's assassination film festival that got to my brain. Drove me out of town. Not the goat's-head hypothesis, not the eyestrain from the Bronson-film blowups. No, it was the Oswald craniotomy controversy that took me out of the merely maddening world of *Blow-Up* right into *Texas Chainsaw Massacre* horror.

Should I tell you about this experience, or will you think it too ghoulish, too gruesome?

Notes on the assassination film festival. Arrived Gary Mack's lovely suburban Fort Worth tract home. Eager to see the Bronson film, but first there was Gary's critique of the goat's-head hypothesis.

The goat's-head hypothesis is the official explanation of the most horrible moment in that horror-filled home movie known as the Zapruder film. The moment when the fatal head shot appeared to slam the president back into the seat of his car as though it had been a frontal hit.

Gary ran and reran that moment for me on his home projector and screen set.

Not that I objected. After all, it could be argued that if you haven't seen the Zapruder film, you haven't actually experienced the assassination. You know a president was shot, an office vacated, but you haven't seen the man's head brutally blown apart, you haven't seen John Kennedy die, and so perhaps you haven't had a chance to confront the loss.

It was the sudden appearance in the seventies of bootleg copies of the Zapruder film and the showing of high-quality copies to congressmen that did more than anything to get the Senate and the House to launch their own investigations of the shooting.

Because, watching that shot knock Kennedy backward, all the senses cry out that it came from the front. But Oswald, we know, was behind. Which would mean a second gunman and therefore a conspiracy.

And yet from a restudy of the autopsy evidence the House Select Committee concluded—just as the Warren Commission had—that the head shot was fired from behind.

"How could that be?" I asked Gary Mack.

"Well, they cited the films of the goat's-head tests," Gary said. "Back in 1948 the Army did filmed studies of the impact of bullets on goats' heads that demonstrated what they called a neuromuscular reaction, which in certain circumstances will cause a backward motion even with a shot from behind."

"And do you accept that?" I asked.

"Well, the thing they fail to take note of," he told me, "is that in the neuromuscular reaction, the extremities are supposed to go rigid. Now if you look closely at the president at the moment he's hit—here, I'll slow it down so you can see that doesn't happen to Kennedy; he's all loose and wobbly."

Next, the Bronson film. Real *Blow-Up* stuff. There was the limo turning the corner onto Elm Street right below the Book Depository, beginning to head downhill toward the Triple Underpass and the spot a hundred yards farther down Elm, where the shots would hit. The real mystery of that particular moment, a mystery that becomes apparent once you've walked the motorcade's route in Dealey Plaza, past the Book Depository and down toward the fatal spot, a mystery neither the official inquiries nor the amateur critics have satisfactorily explained or even addressed, is this: why didn't Oswald, or whoever was up in the Book Depository, shoot the president when he was coming right toward the sniper's-nest window, when he was heading down Houston Street straight into his gunsight, a mere thirty yards away? Why did the assassin wait until the president's car turned the corner onto Elm Street and began pulling away? Was there an inner struggle, some crisis of conscience going on in the assassin's mind? Did he almost decide to let his target slip away unharmed?

The Bronson-film blowup that Gary Mack showed me that afternoon did not address that question. The Bronson film was really a kind of ghost story. Because in the early footage, six minutes before the limo reached the fatal turn onto Elm Street, there, up in the corner of the frame, in the windows six floors above the street, pale, ghostly, eva-nescent shapes flickered.

Gary had blowups of the crucial frames. They showed dim gleams of shadowy shapes in the corner sniper's-nest window. And pale, ghostly presences moving, blotches and blurs, in the two windows next to that. Windows that should have been empty at the time of the shooting, according to the lone-assassin theory.

Assassins? Or artifacts in the photo-sensitive emulsion?

Gary Mack thinks they're men wearing pale green and magenta shirts. They could be. They could be John, Paul, George, and Ringo, for all I can tell. As a matter of fact, does anyone know exactly where the Fab Four were that day? If we go by the cui bono, or who-benefits, theory of the assassination, the finger of guilt could well swing toward the lovable Liverpudlian lads, since it's always been my belief that the Beatlemania that swept America just eight weeks after the assassination was really a hysterical transference of repressed JFK-assassination shock and grief. The link being the hair—both John Kennedy and John Lennon being loved for the look of their locks.

I refrained from exploring this theory with Gary, but he had convincing technical answers to my other objections. He was certain that he had prima facie evidence of conspiracy right there on his screen, the kind of evidence no goat's-head shoots can refute, and that costly computer enhancement, which he can't afford, might even show us human features as well as the shirts of the assassins.

But scientific evidence alone is not enough here. This case requires what Kierkegaard called a leap of faith. The existence of God, K. argued, can never be proved by constructing a scaffolding of rational argument. Faith can only come through a leap from that scaffolding into the realm of what he called the absurd. And El Exigente here is not ready to make that leap. He is troubled also by the question of what happened to the green and magenta men and, if they were up there shooting, what happened to their rifles and bullets?

No leap of faith required in the craniotomy controversy, though. No, this one requires a leap back into the grave. Oswald's grave. Or, as Gary prefers, the grave of Oswald's impostor. Because Gary had new evidence that very well might be enough to cause people to open up Oswald's grave *again*. That's right. Just two years after the notorious Eddowes-Marina exhumation seemed to establish that Oswald was the guy buried in Oswald's grave, Gary came upon a key discrepancy in the exhumation evidence.

He began to explain the thing to me in great and gruesome detail, a tale that might be called the Clue of the Assassin's Skull.

To understand the importance of his new discovery, Gary said, you have to know what they did to Oswald's skull during his first autopsy back in 1963.

"It's part of the record they did a craniotomy on him, back then,"

Gary told me. "They sawed off the top of his skull with a power saw. They reached underneath the brain, cut it off, and lifted it out, and they noted in the official record that a craniotomy had been done.

"Now, when they did the exhumation this time, no mention was made of a craniotomy. And then Paul Groody, the mortician, said it had suddenly struck him after they had reburied the corpse that he hadn't noticed that a craniotomy had been done on the skull of whoever it was buried in Oswald's grave. The skin had rotted away, leaving a naked skull. But with a craniotomy, the top of the skull should have fallen off. It didn't. In fact, there are videotapes of the exhumation showing them handling the skull, even holding it upside down, and nothing falls off. And at one point they severed the head and placed it on a metal stand. Somebody bumped it and it rolled onto the table, but the top still didn't fall off. Which proves that it can't be Oswald's skull down there, that it must be an impostor. Wouldn't you like to see that tape, Ron?"

At that point I made an excuse and fled town.

●   ■   ●

And so I am here at 544 Camp Street. Trying to forget about Oswald's skull. Trying to get inside his head. Let me explain why this particular address is so important.

Shortly after Oswald arrived in New Orleans in April 1963, he embarked on a mystifying campaign of dangerous and duplicitous political intrigue whose motive is still obscure. One of his first acts was to contact the national headquarters of the pro-Castro Fair Play for Cuba Committee (FPCC) to get a charter to set up a New Orleans chapter. He gave the name "A. J. Hidell," one of his false identities, as president and only member of the chapter.

At the same time, he was approaching anti-Castro Cuban-exile groups, declaring that he shared their feelings, boasting of his marksmanship and his Marine training in guerrilla warfare, and telling them that he wanted to be sent on a paramilitary mission to Cuba.

Then, in August 1963, one of the anti-Castro activists he had been soliciting came upon Oswald distributing pro-Castro pamphlets in his role as one-man Fair Play for Cuba Committee. A fight ensued. Oswald was arrested and jailed. Demanded to see an FBI agent. Told the bureau he was willing to inform on the pro-Castro movement.

Just what was he up to? And on behalf of whom? That's where that address 544 Camp Street becomes so interesting. It's at the heart of the paradox of O.'s simultaneous pro-Castro and anti-Castro activity. The address first surfaced in the case when it was found rubber-stamped on one of the pro-Castro tracts Oswald was handing out. It identified 544 Camp Street as the headquarters of the Fair Play for Cuba Committee. And yet not only did the building at that address never house the FPCC but it also swarmed with right-wing anti-Castro groups and was the headquarters of a right-wing ex-FBI agent named Guy Banister, who was that very summer recruiting people to infiltrate pro-Castro movements.

What was Oswald up to? As far back as 1964, Warren Commission staffers were scratching their heads over that and writing memos to each other about the possibility that Oswald's paper FPCC group was a front set up to infiltrate the pro-Castro movement on behalf of the anti-Castro group based in 544 Camp Street.

They never were able to resolve it. When the staffers presented their memo on Oswald in New Orleans to the harried chief counsel of the Warren Commission, it came back with these words scrawled on it: "At this stage we are supposed to be closing doors, not opening them."

Subsequent Senate and House assassination investigations tried to reopen the doors to 544 Camp Street but found only doors within doors.

"We have evidence," then-Senator Richard Schweiker declared, "which places at 544 Camp Street intelligence agents, Lee Oswald, the mob, and anti-Castro Cuban exiles."

Yes, behind those doors Oswald had gotten himself entangled in some of the darker strands in the fabric of American life. And yet what does it all prove? Perhaps there is a clue behind another set of doors— *The Doors of Perception*.

Consider this passage from Huxley's classic account of the psychedelic experience, based on his mescaline trips:

> The schizophrenic is like a man permanently under the influence of mescaline . . . which, because it never permits him to look at the world with merely human eyes, scares

him into interpreting its unremitting strangeness, its burning intensity of significance, as the manifestations of human or even cosmic malevolence, calling for the most desperate countermeasures, *from murderous violence at one end of the scale* [italics mine] to catatonia, or psychological suicide, at the other end. And once embarked upon the downward, the infernal road, one would never be able to stop. . . .

"If you started the wrong way," I said in answer to the investigator's questions, "everything that happened would be a proof of the conspiracy against you. It would be self-validating. You couldn't draw a breath without knowing it was part of the plot."

This last paragraph strikes me as a good description of the mind of the assassination buff as well as of the assassin.

Up until now there have been three theories relating to Oswald's strange immersion in the subcurrents swirling around 544 Camp Street: (1) he was a pro-Castro activist infiltrating anti-Castro movements on behalf of Cuban agents, (2) he was an agent of anti-Castro forces using a pro-Castro front to infiltrate Cuba, perhaps to kill Castro, and (3) he was a pro-Castro activist being cultivated and set up as a patsy by sinister anti-Castro-mob-intelligence-world operatives.

These contradictory theories have one thing in common. They all make Oswald a pawn in someone else's game.

If, however, we go through the doors of perception and look at New Orleans through the eyes of an "enlightened" O., another way of thinking about the ambiguities suggests itself.

Look at New Orleans through the eyes of an O. whose favorite TV program as a child was *I Led Three Lives*. Who may have absorbed the dark conspiracy-obsessed consciousness of that Huxley passage. Someone who has been a U.S. Marine, then a Soviet citizen, then a U.S. citizen again. Someone for whom change of identity has become second nature, someone who has seen the world from both sides and been disillusioned by both. Someone who—with his doors of perception opened—thinks he sees through it all. Someone for whom the only pleasure now is in the posing, the plotting, and the counterplotting. Look at O. as a pre-assassination assassination buff. Not a lone nut but a lone mastermind, deploying identities the way Penn Jones deploys gunmen. What a paradise New Orleans would have seemed that steamy summer to someone like that, with its murky web of plot and counter-plot.

How convenient 544 Camp Street would have been. So many strands of intrigue so close at hand, so many strings so easy to pull.

How inconvenient for my purposes that 544 Camp Street has dis-appeared from the face of the earth. How I wanted to walk its halls and get a feel for its atmosphere. But the building was torn down some years ago to make way for a new federal court building. The old building's exact location at the corner of Lafayette Street is now a concrete plaza empty except for a large, abstract, federally subsidized sculpture.

And yet that sculpture . . .

The best way to describe the sculpture would be to call it a sixteen-foot twisted helix of black painted steel. Military-industrial-complex-size *damaged chromosomes*. Its title: *Out of There*. Hard to believe its creator did not know the significance of the place in which his work was installed. A better monument to the tortuous doubling and redou-bling of the mind of Lee Harvey Oswald could not be imagined.

I wander south on Camp Street, passing comatose derelicts, disin-tegrating warehouse buildings, and dingy rooming houses. Come upon the Crescent Street Garage, where O. used to drop in and read gun magazines in the office. Next to the Reily Coffee Company, where he was employed, greasing coffee-grinding machines. The garage was also, according to the testimony of a mechanic, a depot for unmarked FBI and Secret Service cars. The mechanic said that he saw envelopes pass between agents in unmarked cars and Oswald.

Back up the street, past *Out of There*, to the all-night drugstore on the corner of Canal. Another O. hangout that summer. Horrible glaring fluorescents that must have been around since that summer, truly a depressing place, the nature of whose clientele can be surmised from a scrawled sign over the prescriptions counter: "Due to Uncertainties All Drug Sales Are Final."

Due to uncertainties. I push through the sweaty atmosphere back toward my hotel, mired in the maze of uncertainties surrounding O.'s Camp Street summer. His sojourn there suggests everything, proves nothing. Provides support for almost every conspiracy theory; proves none.

●   ■   ●

And so there it is. After all these years. Theories, uncertainties, possible connections, suspicious coincidences. Yes, the Warren Commission investigation was inept and incomplete, relied on information supplied by agencies with a stake in covering up their role. And yet, twenty years later, several minor and one major congressional inquiry down the line, there is only more uncertainty.

I speak to Robert Ranftel again. This time about the dismaying question of whether it is time to call it quits, admit defeat, and give up the whole intractable case. Perhaps even concede that—in the absence of any proven alternative—Oswald may have acted alone; the Warren Commission, for all its bungling, might have gotten it right after all.

"What about the mob-hit theory," I ask Ranftel. "Isn't there any hope for that? I mean the House Committee pretty much endorsed it?"

"Well, mob-hit theory is where the action is now," Ranftel says. "Everybody's writing their mob-hit book. Did you see the latest—*Contract on America* [by David Scheim, subtitled *The Mafia Murders of John and Robert Kennedy*]?"

"Do you think mob-hit theory is just another buff trend?"

"I think the organized-crime theory is sort of a halfway house out of the Kennedy case for a lot of buffs," he says.

"A halfway house?"

"Well, it solves a lot of problems. You look at the typical mob hit. It's a murder that goes unsolved. And the people who did it typically never talk. So you can almost use the fact that the JFK case remains unsolved as evidence it was a mob hit. It allows a lot of people to walk away from the case and say we've brought it as far as it can go. You see a lot of assassination buffs now turning into organized-crime buffs."

A halfway house out of the case. Ranftel's phrase suddenly clarifies for me a persistent subtext I thought I'd been picking up in my conversations with some of the best of the buffs. Take Paul Hoch, for instance. Almost universally regarded as one of the most careful and meticulous researchers in the game. A computer programmer by profession, he specialized in looking into an area of ambiguity and searching the thousands of cubic feet of declassified documents in the archives until he found the single document that clarified the point in question.

He was still working on the case—publishing his *Echoes of Conspiracy* newsletter—but his work now was filled with echoes of echoes. Reports of reports. Clippings. There seemed to be no edge, no direction, no sense that any of this was leading to anything.

"I get the impression that you're shifting from being an assassination investigator to something more like a commentator," I told Hoch.

"I think that's true. A historian might be more accurate. I try to keep the record straight."

"But what about solving the case?" I asked.

"I just don't know," he said. "I just don't know if it's too late now."

●   ■   ●

Too late? Would it matter if it weren't? Maybe that's the real question. Maybe, after all, there's no big secret, no clandestine conspiracy there to uncover. Immersed once again in the frustrations of the case, the frequent foolishness and apparent futility of the buff biz, I find myself almost longing to succumb to the simplicity and conventional comfort of lone-assassin certainty. To be able to stuff all the seething ambiguities, strange coincidences, provocative hints, all the suggestions, implications, curious connections, and mysterious sightings that the critics have turned up, just stuff them all in a drawer and say, "Case closed."

Before I do that, though, there is one man I want to track down and talk to. A private eye. My onetime philosophy prof turned buff turned shamus: Josiah Thompson. What will the author of *The Lonely Labyrinth* have to say about the JFK case now, after twenty years, when it has grown more labyrinthine—and lonelier.

I have some misgivings about calling him. Afraid, I guess, that he has become another casualty of the case. Picturing him in some seedy Sam Spade-like office, embittered and cynical over his failure to crack the JFK case, trudging through the fog, doing divorce work or something similarly dispiriting. But after the first five minutes on the phone with him I know that Thompson is just the person I am looking for. He has emerged from the maze with his lively intelligence, judicious wit, and wry humor intact. And his private-eye work has given him new insights into the problems of the Kennedy case.

He begins by explaining why he chose to make the switch from professor to private eye. After the publication of *Six Seconds in Dallas*, after serving as a consultant on the evidence for *Life* magazine's JFK reinvestigation in 1966 and 1967, he returned to a prof job at Haverford College, disillusioned by the fiasco of the Garrison investigation.

"Garrison just blew the critics out of the water," Thompson tells me. "So I sort of gave up for a while in the late sixties."

After completing his Kierkegaard biography in 1973, he turned his attentions to the complexities of that other twisted and tormented late-nineteenth-century thinker, Friedrich Nietzsche.

While he was on leave out in San Francisco writing a biography of Nietzsche, he had dinner with famed private investigator Hal Lipset. At the time, Lipset was being considered as a possible chief investigator for the newly formed House Select Committee on Assassinations. But Thompson found himself enthralled by Lipset's discussion of his own cases.

"Just on a lark I hit him for a job," Thompson tells me. "And he gave me one. Before I knew it, I was working for five dollars an hour doing surveillance in Oakland."

He was good enough that when Lipset's partner David Fechheimer formed his own firm, he asked Thompson to come to work for him and gave him a murder case for his first assignment.

"I started working on a really great case," he tells me. "And I couldn't give that up. It was too much fun."

In a short time, it seems, he turned into an absolute ace of a private eye.

There's one case in particular that pleases him. A Korean-born prisoner. Jailed for five years on a murder rap. Thompson reinvestigated the original case. Got it overturned. Got his man out of jail.

"He didn't do it," Thompson tells me. "I know who did it."

Interesting: he got an innocent man off, and he knows the identity of the real killer, who is presumably still walking around.

Dangerous knowledge. It is gratifying to find that Thompson hasn't fled from the frustrations of the seemingly insoluble but has instead embraced them. I envy him; I am tempted to hit him up for a private-eye job myself. But first I want to get his private eye-philosopher's assessment of the state of the art of the JFK case.

A few years ago it looked as if Thompson might get credit for cracking that one too. When the House Select Committee came out with its report on the acoustical analysis of the Dallas police tape, it placed a gunman behind the stockade fence on the grassy knoll, exactly the spot Thompson pointed to in his book.

But, refreshingly, he's willing to concede that the acoustical evidence that once promised such certainty now looks muddied.

"Uncertainty has replaced clarity," he says wistfully. "We're back in the swamp. Back in the morass again."

"The lonely labyrinth?" I ask.

He just laughs.

And refreshingly, considering that he was one of the original *Warren Report* critics, he is prepared to concede that in crucial aspects of the case, further investigation has proved him wrong and the commission right.

The much-ridiculed single-bullet theory, for instance. The whole lone-assassin theory depends in complex but definite ways on the Warren Commission's belief that one bullet went through JFK's body, smashed through John Connally's fifth rib and wrist, and emerged unscratched. I have actually handled that so-called pristine bullet myself in the National Archives, felt how smooth and unmarked its surface is, and scoffed at the idea that it could have emerged so utterly unscathed.

But, as Thompson points out, recent neutron activation analysis of the bullet and the tiny fragments left in Connally's wrist make it almost a scientific certainty that they came from the same bullet.

"That's very powerful evidence that the single-bullet theory is correct," he says. "It absolutely astonishes me, but you gotta look at what the evidence is. One thing I've learned from these years of being a private investigator is that I no longer place much faith in most eye-witness testimony to prove anything. If you're gonna rely on anything, it's the physical evidence and photographs. Another thing I've learned is that it's a waste of time to try to prove anything with government documents, the endless nit-picking that was done by the critics in the JFK case comparing discrepancies in what a witness said to the police or the FBI in a deposition and what they testified to later. You learn that the police get it wrong all the time and that nit-picking doesn't get you closer to the truth."

The truth. What *does* Thompson think is the truth in the JFK case? Is he actually leaning toward accepting the Warren Commission verdict that Oswald acted alone?

No, Thompson says. In fact, he still doesn't think the evidence adds up to Oswald's firing *any* shots that day.

"I think it's maybe sixty-forty that he didn't," Thompson tells me. "Although I can see reasonable men taking the other position."

"What, then, do you think Oswald's role was that day?" I ask him.

"I've stayed away from analyzing," he tells me. "What you have when you look into him is puzzle boxes within Chinese puzzle boxes. In the logic of intelligence circles, anything can mean anything. I think he was scheming in ways I don't understand, and finally, when the president was shot, the curtain opened and he recognized a lot more was going on than he knew."

And who does he think O. was scheming with? Thompson leans toward the mob-hit school of thought because of the new evidence developed by the House Select Committee about Ruby's connections and movements. "If Ruby was given access to the jail, if Ruby was *stalking* Oswald, as it seems they've demonstrated, one has to ask the question, why? And you have to look at the statistics on organized-crime prosecutions and how they dropped off after the assassination. One thing you can say about the assassination is that it's been enormously *effective*. It worked. They blew his head off, and they got away with it."

They?

"Why has nobody broken? And what group can enforce that kind of discipline? Nobody's turned. Of course, maybe there's nobody to turn."

Is there anything his private-eye's instinct tells him about the case that might solve it or explain why it's unsolved?

"That goddam bullet," he says, "that bullet just doesn't fit. You have to consider the possibility that evidence was tampered with. I know when I was working on the *Life* project they left me alone with that bullet for fifteen minutes. I could have done anything with it. But once you raise that possibility—that some pieces of the puzzle have their edges shaved off or pieces never in the puzzle have been brought in— you're never gonna put that puzzle together. In my heart of hearts, that's what I believe happened. And since we no longer have objective criteria of physical evidence, we're left with an epistemological conundrum."

An epistemological conundrum. Yes, that's what it has always seemed like to El Exigente. Somehow the JFK case is a lesson in the limits of reason, in the impossibility of ever knowing anything with absolute certainty. Gödel's Proof and Heisenberg's Uncertainty Principle all wrapped into one. That's why El Exigente has always stayed above the battle, observing the foibles of the buffs from a position of amused detachment, resisting the impulse to become obsessed with knowledge maddeningly dangerous for its unknowability. I've seen too many brilliant people—some of them my friends—self-destruct in the attempt. I've always been too cautious to risk becoming a passionate casualty of the case.

But now Thompson, El Exigente's mentor, turns the tables on the Demanding One. In his modest but insistent Socratic way, he demands to know what I think.

I tell him I've gone into this most recent journey through the state of the art with the vague feeling that the mob-hit theorists probably have come closest to the truth of the case, but I've come out of it feeling that they have failed to nail it down. That the tail-and-the-dog story is as close as they'll ever come but it falls short of being proof, and that the rest is all the usual suggestive connections of the sort that can support any number of unproven theories.

And, I tell Thompson, I find myself longing—because of the advent of the two-decade anniversary—to come to some conclusion instead of suspending judgment on the crime of the century forever. And that although I am resisting it, to my dismay I find myself tempted after all these years to give in and embrace the *Warren Report* conclusions.

"You're right to say the conspiracy explanations are unsatisfying," he replies. "And you're right to recognize the urge to push it all into one pattern or the other for the satisfaction of having a conclusion. But," he adds, "you're also right to resist that temptation."

And so—for another ten years at least—I will. As far as I'm concerned, the case is still not closed.

—*TEXAS MONTHLY*
November 1983

POSTSCRIPT TO "OSWALD'S GHOST"

"Mysteries that Matter" was the title of the lead editorial in the Sunday *New York Times* for January 7, 1990. Among the six "intriguing questions" still "awaiting answers" was "*Who was Lee Harvey Oswald?*" (Among the others were "Was there a Fifth Man?" and "Was Otto John kidnaped?"—both discussed in "The Shadow of the Mole.")

The thrust of the *Times* editorial was that the newly liberated Eastern European governments should open up their espionage archives, which might "finally resolve conflicting stories from various Soviet defectors about Oswald's links or lack of them with Soviet intelligence."

I too remain convinced that "Who was Oswald?" *is* a mystery that matters, although I'm not confident that the solution is to be found in the archives of Eastern Europe. In the seven years since I undertook this twentieth-anniversary survey of the state-of-the-art of Oswald studies for *Texas Monthly*, the real growth area has continued to be mob-hit, rather than KGB-link theory. The most persuasive, most responsibly researched recent version of the mob-hit hypothesis can be found in John Davis's *Mafia Kingfish: Carlos Marcello and the Assassination of John F. Kennedy*.

Give Davis credit: he's done more than merely re-investigate, more than collate Kennedy-hating quotes from recently declassified FBI wire-taps of mobsters. He's also done some original reporting; he's worked on the case beneath the text. The connections he's established between Oswald, Ruby, David Ferrie (O.'s bizarre, sometime Svengali), and Marcello are legion, going beyond even the House Select Committee's investigation, which singled out Marcello for suspicion (because of his outspoken reaction to harassment by Kennedy's Justice Department). Yet they remain connections, skeletal links, conjectural lines of command, not a fleshed-out assassination plot. And Davis falls victim to the disease of assassination researchers: he tries unconvincingly to use connections, links, to associate Marcello with the assassination of Martin Luther King and of Bobby Kennedy, even with Watergate too. The One Big Plot syndrome. (Marcello, who denied any link to any assassination plot before the House Select Committee, remains in federal prison serving out his labor-racketeering sentence in the BRILAB corruption case. Reportedly suffering from Alzheimer's, he may no longer know who he is, according to Davis, much less answer further questions about what he did or didn't do.)

Despite the absence of a smoking gun, Davis's may be the best conspiracy scenario we'll get. Still I'm somewhat suspicious of conspiracy theories that make Oswald a pawn in somebody else's game. From the time I spent in Dallas and New Orleans following in O's footsteps, trying to keep track of his shifting guises, aliases, cover stories, I still feel he was more of a manipulator—if only of his own impersonations—than a pawn. (And I think the voice we hear in Don DeLillo's *Libra* is probably the best Oswald impersonation of them all.)

THE GENERAL AND
THE BLOND GHOST

The General is still at war. Despite his recent plea-bargain truce with the Iran-contra special prosecutor, General Richard Secord still has scores to settle, blasts he wants to level.

Blasts at the special prosecutor for what the General calls "asinine" misstatements in the explanation filed with his guilty plea (to one count of making false statements to congressional investigators). And blasts at the press for "false" reports that he "pleaded guilty to lying to Congress."

"It was a *false statement*," he insists angrily to me. "Not 'lying to Congress.' And also it was *not* to Congress."

"It was to what, a congressional investigator?"

"Yeah, in a deposition. Not a hearing, not testimony before Congress."

The General is ready to go to war over these distinctions; he's planning a press conference to launch a counterattack. But in the meantime he has lots of other targets he's happy to blast away at. There's super-heavy lawyer Arthur Liman ("a sleaze"), Ronald Reagan ("chicken" for not pardoning Ollie North), the C.I.A. ("shoe clerks" who "lied" about their knowledge of the General's arms-dealing "Enterprise"), and a certain prominent senator ("Check out the circumstances of his divorce—any of your colleagues in the press will tell you about his proclivities") to name a few. The General hits high and low.

He's at war to defend his honor and his conduct not just during Iran-contra but during his entire career; he's launching lawsuits, attacks, and counterattacks against the barrages of what he calls slander, fabrication, and lies perpetuated by malicious rivals and "dishonest" reporters. Particularly against the "slander" he hates more than any other. The one he hates so bitterly a deep brick-red glow of rage spreads across his countenance whenever he speaks of it. The one he hates more than anything he's been accused of in Iran-contra. The one that links him to the reviled arch-renegade C.I.A. agent Ed Wilson.

Indeed, the General wants so desperately to demolish that "fabrication" that he does a remarkable thing. He persuades "the Blond Ghost"—legendary C.I.A. clandestine-side operator Ted Shackley, the spectral godfather of the C.I.A.'s secret warriors—to materialize for me in the flesh to help the General exorcise the Ed Wilson allegation.

A fascinating pair, Secord and Shackley. Not, perhaps, the conspiratorial "Secret Team" they have been described as by some, but an extraordinary couple of covert operators. Talking to them in succession, listening to their accounts of three decades of secret wars and clandestine missions, was like having a door open on a hidden chapter in contemporary history, an unexpected glimpse into the murky culture of clandestinity that grew out of the dark side of J.F.K.'s Camelot.

●   ■   ●

The two years since the spotlight was on Secord at the height of 1987's Iran-contra frenzy have not been kind to him. Most people recall the General as the defiant, combative leadoff witness with the almost weirdly ramrod-stiff demeanor who fought committee attorney Arthur Liman in a brutal cross-examination battle over whether the General was a profiteer or a patriot in running the Enterprise for Oliver North.

Two years later he's still battling, but he's taken some losses, not least among them the kind of enterprise he's now able to run. At the time the Iran-contra operation was exposed, the General was running a globe-spanning arms network that reached from Teheran to Tegucigalpa with tens of millions of dollars in revenues flowing through Swiss bank accounts. Before that, when he'd been a deputy assistant secretary of defense in the Pentagon, he'd presided over billions of dollars of U.S.-government arms transfers on three continents.

When I first met the General this fall, shortly before his plea-bargain deal, in his Tysons Corner, Virginia, office, the dramatic reduction in his worldly circumstances was immediately apparent.

The General operates out of a bare, windowless eight-by-ten-foot cell of an office attached to a nearly empty office suite. There is no sign on the door, no official title for this enterprise. "We just call it 'Mr. Secord's office,' " his receptionist says. No associates are evident. He's just moved into Tysons Corner, the General says, but he looks as if he's been driven here, cornered in Tysons Corner by his troubles. He's still got the ramrod-stiff posture, the bantam-rooster combativeness, but the nonstop combat has taken a toll on his temperament, never particularly sunny to begin with. The Washington press has reported two drunk-driving arrests in the past twelve months (which he's appealing).

One of the first things I ask the General to do is clarify what kind of business he is actually in.

Before Iran-contra, he says, "I specialized in ballistically hardened airfield shelters," selling mainly to Arab-world clients, many of whom he got to know when he served as the Pentagon's point man for the Reagan administration's bid to sell AWACS planes to the Saudis.

" 'Ballistically hardened' means . . . ?"

"Shelters you put over airplanes and airport facilities that can withstand direct hits from certain missiles and free-fall bombs. We were working on contracts to sell to the Emirates. Then we lost it to a European consortium" about the time Oliver North enlisted him in the Iran-contra operation.

These days things seem slow at Mr. Secord's office. There doesn't seem to be anything actually in the pipeline, although the General says he's once again "very close" to an attractive opportunity.

"I'm very close to closing a deal to broker imports of Chilean fruit," he tells me, "mainly stone fruit—you know, peaches and plums." The General strikes me as the kind of guy who will always be "very close" to a deal; he lacks the smooth-tongued con-man glibness of an Ollie North. The General's too prickly, too *martial*, to be a good hustler.

Aside from the impending stone-fruit deal, Secord depicts himself as debt-ridden, hundreds of thousands in the hole from lawyers' costs. (In addition to fighting the special prosecutor, he's "vigorously" pursuing a libel suit against Atlantic Monthly Press and writer Leslie Cockburn over her book, *Out of Control*; he's beaten the Christic Institute lawsuit that named him and Blond Ghost Ted Shackley, among others, as leaders of a Secret Team that used assassination and drug money to mastermind evils from the Kennedy assassination to Iran-contra. While the Christic suit was thrown out of court last fall, Secord has got his lawyers pursuing the Christics to make them cough up his legal fees.)

The Iran-contra special prosecutor claims that $1.5 million in profits from the Secord-run enterprise went to Secord personally, but Secord calls that "a fantasy, it was all frozen, I never got that money." Says he's broke now.

The General has tried some fund-raising efforts on his own, but— let's face it—he's not the charismatic charmer and top-dollar fund-raising phenom Ollie North is. He didn't emerge from Iran-contra the Jimmy Stewart national hero. North did. The General was a much more ambiguous figure. People are still divided over whether to think of him as profiteer or patriot; celebs and politicians never rallied to him the way they did to North. Ironically, one of the only "names" who did rally to Secord's support is the liberal pacifist folk-singer Buffy Sainte-Marie, author of the anti-war anthem "Universal Soldier." She watched the General's frontal-assault testimony before the Iran-contra committee (he'd marched in unarmed, without the cloak of immunity Ollie North wrapped himself in) and came to believe that here was a basically truthful soldier who was getting a raw deal from the committee because they were afraid to go after Ronald Reagan.

Indeed, the question of the president's role in Iran-contra still lacks a satisfactory answer, as the *New York Times* recently noted in its account of the Secord guilty plea. The General's plea "is peripheral to the central issue in the affair," the *Times* pointed out, "and seems to underscore how *the Iran-contra prosecution has failed to produce an authoritative explanation of who in the administration of Ronald Reagan was responsible for authorizing the arms scheme* [italics mine]."

This is no mystery to the General. He's certain he knows the answer to that. "Everything I did was authorized by the president," he tells me. That's *why* he did it. A pip-squeak colonel like Oliver North could not order the General around if the General didn't believe, *know*, the orders were coming from his commander in chief.

He has no doubt about it. He was on a mission for the president, on behalf of his country's national security. He'd been called upon to undertake extraordinary missions before. In fact, he told me about a couple of them at least as extraordinary in their own ways as Iran-contra. I'm thinking in particular of his mission during the Cuban missile crisis and his top-secret "Santa Claus" plan for a commando invasion of Iran. It was in the course of listening to Secord talk about these unpublicized past missions that I began to get a better sense of who he was. And why he didn't understand what happened to him when his final mission crashed and burned.

●   ■   ●

In all the hours I spoke to him, the General told only one joke. Actually, technically, he told me *about* the joke. It's not that he's a humorless guy; he's capable of an extremely dry—to the point of bitterness—deadpan sarcasm. But he never struck me as, you know, a man *given to jest*. What stayed with me about this particular joke was the way it defined the gulf between the General's world and mine.

The joke came up in the context of the General's unusual mission in the Cuban missile crisis. Which was to fly the first wave of the planned U.S. air strike on the Soviet missiles in Cuba. The mission that Kennedy, Khrushchev—and a couple of billion other souls—feared would touch off World War III.

It was October 1962. War was just a shot away. Captain Richard Secord was stationed a Hurlburt Field, Florida, as part of an air-commando squadron four hundred miles from Cuba. As Kennedy demanded that Khrushchev remove the missiles, the Pentagon prepared the famous "surgical strike" plan: an airborne attack to blast them out if the Soviet leader refused to remove them voluntarily.

Down at Hurlburt Field, Secord and nine other pilots were put on round-the-clock standby alert. Their AT-28 "Jungle Jim" prop fighters were armed with napalm rockets. Ready to take off and head for Cuba, the tip of the scalpel of the surgical strike. If global nuclear war were to start then and there—as many thought it might—Dick Secord was prepared to fire the first shots.

He was thirty then, seven years out of West Point and already one of the most experienced combat pilots in the air force, having flown 285 combat missions in Vietnam in the opening phase of the plunge into the quagmire there. In all I'd read about the Cuban missile crisis, the watershed event of the nuclear age, I'd never read a detailed description of what the surgical-strike plan actually involved. According to Secord it was a two-stage plan. His wing of ten solo-piloted AT-28s would go in low and hit the missiles first.

"We were going to mark them," he says, for a follow-on strike by jet fighter-bombers.

"Mark them? What does that mean, mark them?" I ask Secord.

"Lay down napalm and fire rockets into the missile sites," he says. "Then the heavy fighters would come in and knock them out. They wanted us to go in first because they wanted people with combat experience. Only we had it. The jets didn't have any experience. I thought it was a real sensible plan," he adds.

"And then after you napalmed the missiles they would come in and take out whatever was left?"

"Right. We used to joke—you can imagine what we'd joke about . . ." He shifts into clipped cockpit-radio tones, imitating what they'd joked about: how after they'd napalmed the Soviet missiles they'd radio back to the combat-virgin jet pilots, "*You may bomb my smoke now, fearless leader.*"

Well, sure, top-gun, right-stuff fly-boys never miss an opportunity to rib one another, and the prospect of post-surgical-strike "bomb my smoke" gloating over the combat-virgin jet pilots must have been appealing as hell. But was that the General's *only* reaction to the nature of his mission?

"Didn't you talk about your mission being the beginning of the Big One, World War III?"

"Talked of little else," he says laconically.

"What was it like? Weird? Strange?"

"Well, it was, but we were doing a job, we were concentrating entirely on that. We were confident of our ability. This was 1962 and we had overwhelming power. The Soviet Union couldn't stand up to our power at that time."

"But missiles could have flown. Bombs would have—"

"Yeah, but they would have been *ours*. I mean, they would have fired back, perhaps, but Khrushchev didn't have a chance and he knew it."

"Wouldn't Khrushchev have moved on West Berlin?"

"At his great risk," the General declares. "At his great peril. We had the power to utterly destroy all the Soviets and they knew it. Knew it better than we knew it."

It finally began to dawn on me that part of the General—at least the pure military strategist within him—apparently *regrets* that he didn't get to complete his mission, even if it did start World War III. Because he has *no doubt* we could have won a smashing victory and saved ourselves a lot of trouble.

The General downplays his role in the Cuban missile crisis.

"I was only a gnat," he says.

"But the forward gnat," I say. The forward gnat of the apocalypse.

●   ■   ●

The General was no longer a gnat in April 1980 when the Desert One Iranian-hostage rescue mission crashed and burned on the Iranian steppes. He was a major general then, when he became acting commander of the planned *second* hostage-rescue strike, in the aftermath of the Desert One failure. The General was chosen because he had the airborne-special-ops logistic experience required, and because he knew the turf and the enemy. He'd flown missions with the Shah's air force in the war against the rebellious Kurds. In the late seventies he'd headed the Military Assistance Advisory Group in Teheran that was funneling billions of dollars in weapons and advanced technology into the buildup of the Shah's army (all of which promptly ended up in the ayatollah's hands). In effect, he'd have to be running the new hostage-rescue mission, the Secord Plan, against an enemy he'd trained and armed himself.

The Pentagon gave him carte blanche to draw on all the resources of the U.S. short of nuclear weapons. By August 1980, the General told me, he'd put together a sledgehammer force that was on standby alert to blast its way into Iran and take the fifty-two hostages out.

How was he going to do it? His plan, the Secord Plan, or, as I've come to think of it, the Santa Claus Plan (for reasons that will become evident), is probably the best indication of the General's signature style as a military planner. No surgical strike, this: the General's preferred instrument was not a scalpel but a meat-ax.

Here's how the General describes the difference between the failed Jimmy Carter rescue plan and his:

"In Desert One they had eight helicopters. I had ninety-five in the force I assembled. I had something on the order of between four to five thousand men in my immediate force. I had fighter cap over their airfields—with my gunships, if they started to taxi any fighters, we'd destroy them on the ground. I had airborne tankers, AWACS, the entire first wing of the special-ops command under my command. I had it *all*. At that time there were two battalions of rangers in the entire U.S. Army. I had both battalions *in addition* to all of those other things. As far as I know, they are the only troops in the world trained for night airfield assaults. That was the battalion that took Grenada, those were my men. My preference was for direct assault. Nothing fancy."

"Just go in there?"

"Just like Santa Claus," he says.

"Just like Santa Claus in his sleigh?" I say, not quite seeing the analogy between Jolly Saint Nick and the Secord Sledgehammer over Teheran.

Upon reflection, though, the analogy becomes crystal-clear. Santa, after all, *does* make use of a nocturnal airborne delivery system, and indeed Secord's plan called for his sledgehammer commando force to drop right down the ayatollah's chimney and come out blasting. Secord is so breezily sure of the Santa Claus Plan—I can hear him briefing the president confidently and persuasively—that I almost don't ask the obvious question, but after a pause I do.

"And once you're in there, how do you know they're not just going to kill all the hostages as soon as they hear you coming?"

"It's unlikely," he says. "These are pretty cowardly people. If they killed them [the hostages] they were going to go V.F.R. direct to see Allah."

"V.F.R. direct? What does that mean?"

"It's a fighter-pilot term. It means no instrument flight, nothing. Just going straight to Allah."

He says his mission wasn't going to go forward until they knew the hostages were in three or fewer locations. There had been a moment— the "Eureka Briefing"—when they thought they'd gotten such intelli-

gence, but it turned out to be false. But given good intelligence, the
General had no doubts he could have pulled it off.

Still, his feeling that the hostage keepers wouldn't kill the hostages
for *fear* of "going straight to Allah" seems to ignore the fact that, for
religious extremists, going straight to Allah might be regarded as a
blessing and *incentive* to kill the hostages, if they felt it served the
ayatollah's will.

"It's a judgment call," Secord concedes. "It's arguable. You always
recognize the distinct possibility that the people you're trying to rescue
might get killed and hurt. I think the people who have been held for
so long in Lebanon, for instance, would certainly welcome a rescue
attempt. I mean, I think I would, rather than the living death of it."

●   ■   ●

Iran-contra has been a kind of living death for the General. He's
been hostage to the crisis for five years now, two when it was secret
and three after it broke. But despite the ordeal he still has no doubts
about his conduct. Not only that the whole thing was "authorized by
the president," but that it was not a crackbrained illicit scheme but a
Good Plan, another "sensible plan." A plan that would have worked.
That's working even now, the General believes. He contends that the
much-scoffed-at "Iranian moderates" *did* exist. Believes in the arms-
shipment "opening" to Iran. Believes history has already *vindicated* him
in the recent triumph of the Rafsanjani "moderate" faction against the
"hard-liners" in Teheran.

Yes, he tells me, the whole thing "might still have worked"—he
might have been able to pull it off, get the hostages in Lebanon back—
"even after it became public." In fact, the General thinks the whole
tragic farce all came down to one heartbreaking moment when—if he'd
only been able to grab the phone away from Ollie North in time and
get on the line with Ronald Reagan—the whole thing could have been
turned around.

The pivotal moment came on November 25, 1986, when Reagan's
attorney general, Ed Meese, had just gone on television to declare he'd
discovered the Iran-contra "diversion" and the entire administration
from the president on down was shocked—*shocked!*—by it all. A few
hours later, the General was in a hotel room with Oliver North; North

was on the phone with the president, and the General was signaling frantically to put him on the line. If only he could talk to the president, the General thought, he might save the mission from self-destructing. But in fact by the time North put the phone in his hand, the line had gone dead. Ronald Reagan had rung off, and thereafter his aides erected a wall around him to prevent the General from getting through.

"What would you have said if you had gotten the president on the line in time?" I ask the General over lunch one afternoon at a place called Twenty-One Federal in downtown D.C.

"I would have said, 'Mr. President, this is Dick Secord—you know, General Secord. One of the principals in this controversy. This is *insane*. I demand to see you immediately.' "

"And what if he said, 'Come right over'?"

"I would have been there in twenty minutes. I would have said, 'You're badly advised and a lot of people are going to be hurt.' That's what I would have said. What they did was take a covert operation and turn it into a scandal."

He would have had the president tough it out, keep the now overt covert operation going. "It still could have worked," we could have had the hostages home, the General maintains. "Instead, what they did by appointing the Tower Commission was like calling in artillery fire on your own position after the enemy has left."

The General says they turned a covert operation into a scandal, but in fact covert operations have a habit of turning into scandals all by themselves. Conversely, people who get caught in scandals have a habit of claiming they were actually involved in a "fully authorized covert operation" to cover their tracks. The famous "smoking gun" statement in the Watergate case was Richard Nixon's self-taped admission that he ordered the F.B.I. to cut short its investigation of the break-in at Democratic Party headquarters because it might expose a sensitive "C.I.A. covert operation"—when it actually threatened to expose *him*.

But the covert-operation cover story cuts both ways: it's a double-edged sword and the General himself has been wounded by it in the Ed Wilson affair, a wound that seems to cut deeper than any other.

Ed Wilson was an ace secret operative, "a hero," the General says, of the clandestine world, for the supersecret operations he conducted throughout the world.

Then something happened. He turned. He became a renegade. Not a K.G.B. mole but a demented capitalist. He resigned from the C.I.A. and began merchandising his Agency connection shamelessly to get lucrative arms-shipping contracts. The whole thing blew up in 1980 when Wilson's multimillion-dollar dealings with Muammar Qaddafi were exposed. He'd provided the Libyan dictator and bankroller of terrorists with tons of deadly C-4 terror explosives and other deadly matériel. All along Wilson claimed that his dealings with Qaddafi were authorized and monitored by the C.I.A. After his conviction (and a fifty-two-year jail sentence) Wilson expanded his claims: he said that then deputy assistant secretary of defense Dick Secord was a "silent partner" in one of his multimillion-dollar arms-dealing enterprises.

Secord's skyrocketing career was grounded by the investigation that followed. He was suspended from the Pentagon by Caspar Weinberger, then reinstated by Frank Carlucci. He's never been charged with anything on the basis of the Wilson allegations, but he's been tarred by them. In fact, the Wilson taint was the source of his trouble in the Iran-contra affair. Early on, while the resupply effort was still secret, rival contra operative Felix Rodriguez denounced Secord to George Bush aide Donald Gregg as part of the old Ed Wilson crowd. The suspicion of venality from an Ed Wilson link is probably what prejudiced the Iran-contra committee against Secord's claim of pure patriotic motives and led to Arthur Liman's hammer-and-tongs attack on the General on national TV.

The General can barely contain his rage when the subject of the Renegade is raised. I ask him about the Rodriguez claim that he was part of the old Ed Wilson crowd.

"Well, that's a laugh," he says, mirthlessly. "I'm glad you brought that up. You know, I *didn't* work for Ed Wilson. You know, I was *exonerated*."

The General is bitter about the Wilson slur. He's successfully sued a Wilson associate for slander for going on *60 Minutes* and claiming that the General was one of Wilson's "silent partners." (The million-dollar slander judgment was awarded to the General by default because the Wilson associate, now in the Federal Witness Protection program, refused to drop his protective identity to show up in court.)

But a deeper reason for his outrage about the Wilson link, I believe, is that Wilson the Renegade with his Qaddafi connection is almost a demonic parody of—or parallel to—the General's Iran-contra role. Wilson sold explosives to Qaddafi; Secord sold rockets to Khomeini. Wilson says *his* was an authorized covert operation; Secord says *his* was the real authorized covert operation.

Which is perhaps why he sent me to see the Blond Ghost. There's no better expert witness in the world on covert operations, authorized or unauthorized, than Ted Shackley. And Ted Shackley too has been unjustly tarred for his association with Ed Wilson, the General says. The Blond Ghost might have been chief spook, head of the C.I.A., right now if it hadn't been for whispers about him and the Renegade.

"Go see Ted Shackley," the General said that afternoon at Twenty-One Federal. "He'll set you straight. You know, the Christic suit singled him out as one of the arch-criminals of all time, an evil genius. But he's a nice man. Call him up. Tell him I sent you. He'll talk to you."

I had my doubts about that. The Evil Genius/Nice Man—revered as a god by some, reviled as a Kurtzian *Heart of Darkness* figure by others—is one of the single most fascinating behind-the-scenes figures in the secret history of our times. But as far as I knew, the man known as the Blond Ghost, the godfather of secret warriors, confided in reporters less often than John Gotti.

In the course of his rise to number-two man in the C.I.A.'s clandestine "dirty tricks" division, Shackley had run not just covert operations but whole secret wars for the C.I.A. from the early years of the Kennedy administration. As torch-bearer of the Kennedy brothers' passionate romance with counterinsurgency, covert action, "special operations," the Ghost's presence had been felt with deadly force in Cuba, Laos, Saigon, and Chile, to name a few places.

Indeed, you could look upon him, like the General, as one of the last surviving knights of J.F.K.'s Camelot. And not just rusting in his armor, according to some. His legend as a clandestine operator was so potent that in 1987, nearly a decade after he'd left the C.I.A., he was said by some to be the ghostly "father" of the Iran-contra covert operation.

The next morning I tried the number the General had given me for Shackley. It turned out to be the office of his international risk-assessment consulting firm, Research Associates International.

"Dick Secord says I should go see the evil genius face-to-face," I told Shackley. "I'm trying to separate the fact from the fiction about you two."

He laughed, a high-pitched laugh, a bit short of—but not far from—maniacal. It seemed to be provoked, at least ostensibly, by my line about separating fact from fiction.

He told me he'd get back to me. First he wanted to do some checking on me. He didn't say that, but he admitted it later. He admitted a number of surprising things later.

Shackley called me back at my Washington hotel on Friday the thirteenth, the day of the 190-point market plunge. He'd be willing to see me the following morning. He'd be working in his office all day Saturday dealing with his overseas clients "in the oil-producing countries," as he put it. They would all be demanding to know whether to pull their funds out of the U.S. Whether the market would crater Monday morning. The Evil Genius/Nice Man gave me an address in a high rise across the Potomac in Rosslyn, Virginia. There would be one restriction on the interview, he said. It would be on-the-record, I could take notes, but there could be no tape-recording.

He had to take precautions, Shackley explained later. There had been dirty tricks played on him in the aftermath of his being named a defendant in the now dismissed Secret Team lawsuit. There had been break-in attempts at his office; there had been impostures, people posing as reporters for antagonistic ends. There could be no tape-recording because he didn't want to risk the tape's "ending up in some Christic video"—referring to the various Secret Team videos which Christic crusader Danny Sheehan has used to whip up a fund-raising frenzy among the Hollywood left.

●   ■   ●

Rosslyn, Virginia, is a spooky place on a Saturday morning. A thick cluster of supercontempo high rises perched like birds of prey within reach of the Capitol and the Pentagon. It's virtually deserted today: all the beltway bandits, procurement-consortium consultants are drinking Bloodies at brunches in the Virginia horse country.

Security is tight in a low-key way at Shackley's high rise—despite, or because of, its apparent vacancy. A separate, privately keyed elevator takes me from the twelfth floor to the penthouse office suite of Research Associates International, where a security camera focuses discreetly on me before the door is opened by Ted Shackley himself.

No longer blond, the Ghost is graying these days; but he's still pale, spectral. Not the shocking pallor of legend. The Blond Ghost nickname, the mystique of the dead-white pallor seem to date back to Saigon, when Shackley was chief of the massive C.I.A. battle station there, from 1969 until 1972, and was said to roar around the streets of the city with a phalanx of motorcycle escorts looking "like a proconsul," making the Empire's presence felt. "More power than a god" is how an awed Felix Rodriguez described Shackley in Vietnam.

Another C.I.A. operative who knew Shackley in Saigon once described his ghostly appearance: "Tall, thin, real white skin, real white. . . . He never went out in the sun, man. He never went out in the sun."

These days Shackley looks less, well, mythic. These days he presents the dyspeptic mien of a harried academic on a New England campus in his loosely hanging tweed sport coat, high-water pants, and the open-collar shirt of weekend Wasp informality. Less like Mr. Kurtz than a bilious Cheever melancholic. There is an air of being besieged about him, yes. Perhaps it's the pressure to come up with the right call on the market for his foreign-capital clients before Monday morning.

But there's another sense in which he seems besieged. Not so much by the dirty tricks that followed in the wake of the Christic suit, but by what must have seemed to him a profoundly dirty trick played on him by history. On him and his fellow enlistees in the Camelot crusade. It had started with a kind of idealism. The use of counterinsurgency, clandestine wars, covert operations—"the Third Option" between overt war and diplomatic inaction, as Shackley called it in his book of that title—was going to be the lean, mean, pragmatic action arm of liberal democracies. The way to fight Communist insurrections in the Third World was by winning the hearts and minds of the peasants. In most cases what it came down to was counting their bodies. And now with the idealism gone, the hopes dashed, Kennedy dead, Shackley is called upon once again to defend Camelot's twisted legacy.

He ushers me into his command post, a spacious corner office featuring beveled-glass structural walls and a dramatic view of the District spread below us.

"My clients are mainly from the twenty-two oil-producing countries," Shackley begins by explaining. "But the focus of Research Associates International has shifted recently," he says, "as the global petroleum market has shifted from wet barrels to paper barrels."

"Wet barrels to paper barrels?"

"The oil market is no longer primarily driven by real-world market conditions of supply and demand—wet barrels—which calls for political and economic intelligence. Instead it's increasingly driven by futures-index trading—paper barrels—of what we call 'the Wall Street refiners' like Salomon Brothers."

So Research Associates has shifted more to executive security, he says. Protection. If you're a brokerage exec going to meet an Arab oil client in a Pacific Rim venue, for instance, Research Associates will check out the likelihood of the Arab's being a terrorist target, make an assessment of local security, and tailor a security-system package to the intelligence as well as provide the personnel, i.e., bodyguards.

Shackley's telling me this from behind the vast desk that appears to be part of a suite of newly minted Pacific Rim Consultant Victorian furniture. (It feels as if we could be in Singapore or Abu Dhabi, which I think is the point.)

The setting conjured up for me *Out on the Rim* or one of those other Ross Thomas novels about dicey doings in the international-consulting game among ex-generals, ex-intelligence guys, arms dealers, and off-shore bankers. And there was something about Shackley in this setting, with the talk of wet and paper barrels, a whiff of my favorite Ross Thomas character, "Otherguy Overby." Otherguy got his nickname from the way, whenever some international house-of-cards deal collapsed, he'd always be the one to say it was "the other guy" who ran away with the Swiss-account numbers—when he wasn't being somebody else's other guy.

Not that there's anything bogus about Shackley's risk-assessment business. (Indeed, he surprised me that Saturday by telling me he was advising his foreign clients to keep their money in the market, which I thought at the time was a foolish, certainly risky call for a risk-assessment consultant, but which turned out to look remarkably prescient, a tribute to his intelligence, of one sort or another.)

But it's the Otherguy ambiguities of international-consultant culture that are at the heart of Shackley's explanation of why—even though others might have linked him to renegade terror-bomb supplier Ed Wilson—in fact there was no such link.

"Wilson was a great salesman, a great name-dropper," Shackley tells me. "You know the type, always leaving the impression he was your best friend. We know he was saying this kind of stuff, that he was a big buddy of Ted Shackley."

So some people might have gotten the wrong idea. It's true, he says, he used to visit Wilson's grand estate in the Virginia horse country; their wives were social friends. And it's true that while Shackley was still in the C.I.A. he'd allow Wilson to chat him up about the international arms trade, because one of the Agency's big concerns in the late seventies was locating the vast store of arms the U.S. left behind in Vietnam after the fall of Saigon. Shackley thought Wilson might know where these missing arms might turn up. But otherwise they had no official relationship, he insists, and after he left the C.I.A. and Wilson got in bed with Qaddafi, he had no knowledge of the terror-explosives trade and no business relationship with the Renegade, nor did Secord. And, Shackley insists, he was never a consultant to the Secord-run Iran-contra Enterprise.

●   ■   ●

Since we are on the subject of Iran-contra I ask Shackley about the allegation that he was the real "father" of the whole Iran-contra affair. (I thought I would take the opportunity to get the Ghost on record on as many of the allegations swirling around his name as I could.) There's a bit of Otherguy in his response to the secret-father allegation. According to Shackley, the whole mistaken notion about him arose because "as part of my business I monitor developments in the oil-producing countries and I had a dialogue going" with a certain Iranian General Hashemi, former head of the Shah's secret police, a man said to have excellent contacts within Iran. In November 1984, General Hashemi persuaded Shackley to meet him in Hamburg, where Hashemi introduced him to the now notorious con man/fixer Ghorbanifar. Who, Shackley says, happened to make "a flip comment" about the Lebanese hostage situation, a flip comment that made reference to the tractors-for-prisoners exchange deal the U.S. had made with Castro for the return of the Bay of Pigs prisoners. Since one of the Lebanese hostages of the pro-Iranian Hezbollah was a high-ranking C.I.A. agent named William Buckley, who once worked for him, Shackley sent a memo of the Ghorbanifar conversation and the "flip comment" about a deal to the State Department when he got back from Hamburg.

"They told me, 'We're not gonna do anything about it.' That was in December '84." Six months later at lunch with National Security Council consultant Michael Ledeen, Shackley says, he mentioned the Ghorbanifar "flip comment" and—at Ledeen's urging—gave Ledeen an update on Ghorbanifar's view that a deal might be done.

But, Shackley insists, it was the other guy—Ledeen, not he—who pushed the idea on the National Security Council. It was Ledeen's memo, not his, that got the deal under way, got the Israelis and North into it. He seems to think this clearly establishes that he wasn't the father of Iran-contra.

"Imagine my surprise," he tells me, when a reporter called him after Iran-contra broke and asked him if his memo to the State Department was the origin of it all.

" '*Oh my gosh!*' " he says he exclaimed to the reporter. "I hadn't put the two together." He claims he's suffered "a nightmare of grief and aggravation from this apocryphal" father-of-Iran-contra charge, which he feels he's conclusively refuted.

Strangely, though, the Iran-contra committee's final report makes what Shackley calls a "flip comment" sound much more explicit: "At one meeting on November 20 Ghorbanifar told Shackley that for a price he could arrange for the release of the U.S. hostages in Lebanon through his Iranian contacts." Strange, because in a footnote the committee identifies the source of *this* version as "Shackley interview 2/27/87." Indeed, even Shackley's version to me makes it sound as if he might have planted both the idea of a trade and the name of the Iranian "first channel" in Ledeen's mind. Perhaps he didn't actually father Iran-contra; maybe he just stepfathered—or godfathered?—it.

There's also a bit of Otherguy in Shackley's response when I ask him about the C.I.A.-Mafia assassination plots against Fidel Castro that the Church committee exposed in the 1976 Senate hearings. Shackley had been chief of the C.I.A.'s Miami station in 1962, running the no-holds-barred C.I.A. secret war against Castro, the "Kennedy Vendetta" that followed the Kennedy humiliation of the Bay of Pigs.

"The C.I.A.-Mafia plots," I put it to Shackley directly, "myth or reality?"

"There was a dialogue, yes," he says carefully. "But I was not a dialogue partner."

Not a dialogue partner? "Were you aware it was going on?"

"No."

"Was it authorized?"

"The guy who was dealing with it was my superior. It was not in my purview."

"Who was the superior, the dialogue partner?"

"William King Harvey. He was the one who would have had approval for it. He was in direct contact."

A remarkably candid admission of intelligence failure here, it seems. The Ghost is saying that as C.I.A. chief of station in Miami he was utterly unaware higher-ups in the Agency were coming down to meet with Mob guys in the Fontainebleau Hotel to plan the assassination of Fidel Castro and to pass them poison pills to do it. (The Church committee found that there was more than just a "dialogue" with the Mafia and that in addition there was a series of non-Mafia C.I.A. assassination schemes.)

But, as he says, he was busy. Busy running a secret war which, if anything, managed to consolidate the Castro regime and which, according to Taylor Branch and George Crile in their study of Shackley's war, "may have persuaded Castro to welcome Russian nuclear weapons in Cuba as a means of guaranteeing his own survival."

●   ■   ●

On to Laos. Here it's not precisely the other guy, it's the *other warlord*, who's to blame in the Shackley version. In Laos the long-standing charge has been that the C.I.A., at the very least, countenanced opium growing and smuggling by Laotian warlords who were its tribal allies against the Communists.

The Ghost really galvanizes himself into action when I ask him about the opium charges. First he calls out to his wife in the outer office. A sturdy, dignified woman with a steely-gray bun appears, and Shackley asks her to bring me a copy of the Senate-committee report that he claims "cleared" the C.I.A. of the opium charges. Then he leaps up from behind his desk and begins searching the office for a proper map of Indochina. Finds one, and brings it over to the couch where I'm seated, spreads it out.

To understand why the opium charge was false, he says, he first has to explain to me the disposition of forces in the two-front secret war he was running as C.I.A. chief of station in Laos. Once again I feel I'm being briefed by a master. At last we come to Vang Pao, the Laotian warlord who was closely allied to and supported by Shackley's C.I.A. battle station in Laos, and who has been the target of opium-trade accusations. "Vang Pao," says Shackley, "was actually commander of Military Region 2 here in northern Laos, the Plaine des Jarres area in the center. Over *here* in the West is where you see the Golden Triangle opium-growing area. Which was a different military region under an *entirely* different commander. Vang Pao was *not* in charge in the Golden Triangle area." It was the *other* warlord who was in the poppy business.

Shackley's wife returns.

She seems embittered by her husband's having to defend himself all the time. "This is the 50-millionth copy I've made of this," she says as she slaps the Xeroxed pages of testimony onto his desk and exits.

Shackley shows me the committee testimony that "cleared" the C.I.A. I didn't have a chance to read it then. When I did look at it more closely later, it was not as conclusive an exoneration as the Ghost seems to think it is. The committee report quotes the C.I.A.'s own inspector general as having asked C.I.A. personnel who were stationed in Laos whether they knowingly abetted opium smuggling. They denied it, and the inspector general accepted their denials. But the committee investigation does seem to suggest that controls over their allies weren't airtight.

●   ■   ●

When we come at last to Vietnam and the notorious Phoenix program, Shackley doesn't deny he was involved. He defends the Phoenix program. But he does insist that once again this is a case where not he, but another guy, is the real "father" of the program. The other guy being, in this case, the man they call "the Blowtorch."

Phoenix remains one of the most controversial and hotly disputed episodes in the whole tragedy of America in Vietnam. It's been attacked as a massive "assassination program" that claimed 20,000 to 40,000 Vietnamese victims. It's been defended as the single greatest success of the American "pacification" program in Vietnam, the program that would have won the war if only we had cut off the Ho Chi Minh Trail in Laos.

Shackley is not ashamed of it at all, he says, but once again there is the question of paternity. He does seem rather insistent that I get straight that he didn't father it.

"I want to put that to sleep once and for all," he says. "I was *not* the father of Phoenix. The Christics have long claimed I'm the father. I'm not."

"Who is the father?" I ask.

"Ambassador Komer. Bob Komer. You can go ask him, he'll tell you."

Ambassador Bob "the Blowtorch" Komer, as Henry Cabot Lodge dubbed him, was L.B.J.'s special deputy to Vietnam, charged with getting the liberals' dream of a hearts-and-minds pacification program off the ground. (It's often forgotten how many of these dark episodes were dreamed up by liberal "best and brightest" types.)

Phoenix was about pacification, not assassination, Shackley insists. About intelligence evaluation and assessment. To explain the difference between an evaluation program and an assassination program he uses the example of the killing of a hypothetical Vietcong cadre he calls "Ron Rosenbaum."

"Phoenix was targeted against the Vietcong political-military infrastructure in South Vietnamese villages. The first task was to identify the members of the infrastructure. You know, they were great ones for using aliases—for instance, you, Ron Rosenbaum, might be a member of the VC," he says somewhat pointedly. "But you might go by the alias Tom Smith, and have four other names, and we want to know whether there were one or five of you. Then we'd locate where you are, which village, which house, and have the South Vietnamese police go out. And if they found good old Ron, they'd arrest him, detain and incarcerate him for questioning. Now, if good old Ron grabbed his trusty AK-47 when they came for him, they were authorized to return fire. As a result people got killed—on all sides."

Former C.I.A. chief and onetime Phoenix administrator William Colby has testified that about 20,000 alleged VC cadres died as a result of these deadly visits to their villages.

But were they all the Enemy? One charge against Phoenix is that the South Vietnamese authorities—in order to meet the quotas the Americans set for Phoenix—would fill jails (the notorious "tiger cages") and graves with personal enemies, innocents who failed to pay bribes to the list-makers, non-VC dissidents.

But the C.I.A. was not responsible for these deadly mistakes, Shackley says, because it just collated the lists. "We did not have operational control over Phoenix," he says. It was the other guys, "the South Vietnamese military and police, that did the shooting. We did collecting, collation, we were the evaluation mechanism," he says. "Assassination was not part of our charter."

The essence of the Ghost's style in Vietnam was numbers, lists, and quotas. Felix Rodriguez recalls that about Shackley in Saigon: "He had a reputation as a tough guy, very results-oriented, very rigid and ruthless in an intellectual way. He also had a reputation for levying requirements on subordinates that could be measured or quantified. For example, X number of intelligence reports about X number of penetrations, with X number captured and X number killed, was how he liked to see things submitted. The figures made it easier for him to deal with the bureaucrats back at Langley."

And how does a results-oriented guy judge the results of his career as a whole, of the two decades since the Bay of Pigs, during which he was running secret wars and covert actions for the Agency?

Like the General, the Ghost is a man of few, if any, doubts. He sees the record of his Third Option methods as one roaring success after another.

In his book, summing up what he's learned, he tells us flatly that "our experience over nearly two decades in such diverse areas as Cuba, the Dominican Republic, Vietnam, Laos, Cambodia, the Philippines, Zaire, and Angola proved that we understood how to combat 'wars of national liberation' " with the Third Option methods he recommends.

Cuba, Cambodia, Laos, Vietnam—successes?

There's a black wall in Washington, D.C., with 60,000 names on it, the names of military men who died vainly trying to make up for the failure of Third Option tactics in Vietnam, Laos, and Cambodia.

A more skeptical view of the results of the results-oriented Ghost's career can be found in former *Wall Street Journal* reporter Jonathan Kwitny's book *The Crimes of Patriots*, in which he observes that, "looking at the list of disasters Shackley has presided over during his career, one might even conclude . . . a Soviet mole probably could not have done as much damage to the national security of the United States with all his wile as Shackley did with the most patriotic of intentions."

Toward the close of our nearly two-hour-long conversation (I would have gone on, but he cut it short before I could get to Chile, Australia, and the rest), I try to get the Ghost to step back a bit and put Third Option operations from Cuba to Iran-contra in historical perspective. See if he'll talk about the origin of the counterinsurgency gospel in J.F.K.'s Camelot. Because it's my view that the real Otherguy, the ultimate historical Otherguy, in all those operations is John F. Kennedy with his deadly obsession with covert operations. (I suspect J.F.K. liked them because they were as sexy and dangerous and secret and illicit as his own covert liaisons with gangster chicks like Judith Exner.)

"Doesn't it all go back to J.F.K.?" I ask Shackley.

Shackley quibbles a bit about J.F.K. as the *intellectual* author of Third Option theory. He traces it to a series of theoretical "articles in classified journals in the late fifties" that argued for an American response to Third World insurrections modeled on the successful British counterinsurgency program in Malaysia.

But he concedes that J.F.K. was the *effective* godfather of the Third Option.

"It took on a greater sense of urgency when Kennedy came to power. J.F.K. reached out and embraced the Special Forces and the like." Secord too says his career was shaped by J.F.K.'s embrace. "It was the strategy of the time, and I was the right age," he tells me.

●   ■   ●

"Embrace" has just the right connotation of the erotic ardor which, by all accounts, the Kennedy brothers brought to Third Option solutions. Some might call that embrace a fatal attraction, considering the body count from the Bay of Pigs to Iran-contra and the results thereof. Maybe America will never be really good at performing dirty tricks on foreigners, and maybe it's to our credit that we're bad at it.

Ever since my encounters with the General and the Ghost, I've been looking for a way to put extraordinary figures like Secord and Shackley in perspective. (To me the things they admit are far more astonishing than any Secret Team conspiratorial fabric woven about them.) Finally I found myself rereading Graham Greene's 1955 Vietnam novel, *The Quiet American*, and discovering in Greene's gung ho idealist American, Pyle, an eerily prescient resemblance to the Ghost.

Pyle's the American agent who gets a fanatical glean in his eye at "the magic sound of figures: Fifth Column, Third Force. . . ." Pyle falls in love with a Vietnamese girl named Phuong, which is Vietnamese for Phoenix, the all-seeing bird. His love for her brings destruction, of course, like the American "love" for Vietnam would. Greene's epitaph for the Quiet American could be the epitaph for the General, the Blond Ghost, and all the rusting knights of Camelot:

"I never knew a man who had better motives for all the trouble he caused."

—VANITY FAIR
January 1990

PRIVATE
INVESTIGATIONS

• ▪ •

THE MYSTERIOUS MURDER OF JFK'S MISTRESS

The paint was still damp on Mary Meyer's final canvas when she left her studio for a walk. It was a circular canvas. In her recent work she had been exploring the effects of swaying velvety semicircles of color across unprimed circles of canvas.

She pointed an electric fan at the undried painting. It was a chilly fall day; she put on gloves, pulled on a sweater and a sweatshirt over her blouse and covered those three layers with a heavy blue cable-knit angora, complete with hood.

From the outside, the studio looked like the garage it had once been. It was one among a row of garages along an alleyway behind the backs of two rows of brick townhouses fronting on N and O streets in George-town. Since her divorce, she had spent three or four days a week working in her studio, a few steps away from some of her closest friends, whose homes abutted that alley. Her sister, Tony, and Tony's husband, Ben Bradlee, lived on one end; Mr. and Mrs. John Kennedy lived on the other end until they moved to the White House. Occasionally, Mary

Meyer would take walks with Jackie along the towpath paralleling the old Chesapeake and Ohio barge canal.

That was where she was heading now, in fact: out the alley, left on 34th Street, down to the foot bridge that leads across the canal and onto the towpath between the canal and the wooded embankment that descends to the Potomac.

She reached the towpath about noon that day, Monday, October 12, 1964. John F. Kennedy had been dead almost a year. It was two days away from Mary Meyer's 44th birthday.

●   ■   ●

Air Force Lieutenant William Mitchell left the Pentagon Athletic Center on the Virginia side of the Potomac about noon, crossed over the Key Bridge, exited down the steps to the towpath and began his regular run 2 miles west to a fishing spot on the river called Fletcher's Landing and back again. He passed three people on his way west—a middle-aged couple and a young white man in Bermuda shorts.

He passed two more people on his way back east to Key Bridge. First there was the woman in a blue hooded sweater. He met her just as she was crossing the wooden footbridge a mile from Key Bridge. He came to a full stop in front of the bridge and allowed her to cross it alone to avoid jostling her in mid-passage. Picking up speed again, 200 yards farther east, the lieutenant came upon a black man walking in the same direction as the woman. The man seemed to the lieutenant to be about his size, wearing a light-colored windbreaker, dark slacks and a peaked golf hat. The man's face didn't leave much of an impression on the lieutenant.

●   ■   ●

Henry Wiggins had just raised the hood of the gray Rambler when he heard the screams. Wiggins had been pumping gas at the M Street Esso station when he got a call to take his truck over to Canal Road, where a Rambler with a dead battery was stalled on a shoulder across from the canal.

The screams were coming from the vicinity of the canal. It was a woman. "Someone help me, someone help me," she cried. Then there was a gunshot. Wiggins ran across the road to the stone wall above the canal. A second gunshot. When he looked over the wall, Wiggins saw a black man in a light jacket, dark slacks, and a dark cap standing over the body of a white woman in a blue sweater. Wiggins saw the man place a dark object in the pocket of his windbreaker, then watched him disappear down the far side of the towpath into the wooded incline dropping down to the edge of the Potomac.

●   ■   ●

James Angleton was angry at his wife, Cicely. Here he was in the middle of a big conference at CIA headquarters—Angleton was then chief of counterintelligence for the CIA—and his wife was interrupting the meeting with a silly fantasy. According to a radio bulletin, an unidentified woman had been slain on the towpath that afternoon, and Cicely was sure the victim was their old friend Mary Meyer. She had often warned Mary not to go there alone.

Angleton dismissed his wife's anxiety. That evening they had planned to drive Mary Meyer to a poetry reading and he saw no reason to change anything.

When they arrived at Mary's home that night, her car was in the driveway, yet the lights were out inside. A sign hanging on her door said "Free Kittens—Ring Bell or Call." No one answered the bell. At his wife's insistence, Angleton checked Mary's answering service. They told him Mary had been murdered. The Angletons hurried to the Bradlees' home, where they helped make funeral arrangements. Later that night, Angleton returned and rescued three kittens from the empty house.

Soon the CIA chief would learn he had a mission of great delicacy to perform. An intimate of Mary Meyer's had charged him with recovering and disposing of her secret diary, a diary that contained references to a very special affair.

●   ■   ●

The manhunt began less than five minutes after the murder. When Henry Wiggins phoned the D.C. police from the nearby Esso station, the dispatcher sent squad cars full of men from all over the precinct racing to seal off the five well-marked exits from the towpath across the canal to the streets of Georgetown. With the exits sealed off soon enough, police figured they'd trapped the murderer on the hilly wooded strip of bank between the canal and the river (which was chilly and too wide at that point to afford an escape).

Officer Warner was heading east through the underbrush along the roadbed of the old C & O tracks. He emerged from a detour into a shadowy spillway to find standing, in the middle of the tracks, a short wiry black man, dripping wet and covered with grass and twigs. Water ran out of the wallet the man offered as identification. He said his name was Raymond Crump Jr. He had been fishing around the bend, he told the officer, had fallen asleep on the riverbank and woke up only when he found himself sliding down the bank into the water.

Officer Warner asked Raymond Crump Jr. to show him exactly where "around the bend" he had been fishing. Raymond Crump started to lead him west along the shore. They didn't get far.

● ▪ ●

When he arrived at the body with the medical examiner and eyewitness Wiggins in tow, Detective Bernard Crooke was struck immediately by how beautiful the murdered woman was. "I've seen a lot of dead women," Detective Crooke says, "but none who looked beautiful when dead. She even looked beautiful with a bullet in her head."

Crooke didn't have much time to reflect upon this. A few minutes after he arrived, as he was still trying and failing to find some identification on the body, a cry went up from Henry Wiggins, who was peering down the bank that descended from the towpath to the C & O roadbed and then down to the river. Wiggins was pointing at two figures on the roadbed below. One was Officer Warner; the other was Raymond Crump Jr. "That's him," shouted Wiggins, pointing at Crump.

Five minutes later, a handcuffed Crump was brought before Crooke. "Why is your fly open?" Crooke asked Crump.

"You did it," Crump said. Crooke didn't like that. He didn't like the fishing alibi Crump told him, but Crump stuck to his story. As he was led past Mary Meyer's body toward a squad car to be booked, Crump looked down at the blue-angora-clad body.

"You think I did that?" he asked.

Crooke thought he did it. Then came what was for Crooke the clincher. He was interrogating Crump back at the stationhouse when one of the men who had been searching the shoreline for the still missing murder weapon brought back to Crooke something he had found in the Potomac—a light-colored windbreaker jacket with a half empty pack of Pall Malls in one of the pockets. Crooke told Crump to try it on. According to Crooke, it fit Crump perfectly.

"It looks like you got a stacked deck," Crooke recalls Crump telling him. Then Crump began to cry. Crooke says he patted him on the back, but the sobs only increased.

●   ■   ●

Ms. Dovey Roundtree is a black woman, an ordained minister of the African Methodist Episcopal Church and one of the best homicide lawyers in Washington. She claims an acquittal rate of 80 percent for clients accused of murder. In addition to a steel-trap legal intellect and an aggressive courtroom style, she brings to the task of winning over a jury some of the righteous fervor and persuasive eloquence of the pulpit.

One day in December 1964 a black woman, a church-going A.M.E. Christian, came to Ms. Roundtree's law offices and asked for her help. Her son, Raymond Crump Jr., stood accused of first-degree murder and couldn't make bail. Her son was innocent, the mother told Ms. Roundtree. She knew in her heart he was a meek, gentle boy. He had had some hard times—a bad accident a year ago, troubles with his wife, some problems with drinking and work—but he was not a murderer. Roundtree took the case. She started her own private investigation: she was determined to find out who this woman Mary Meyer was, and who her friends were.

●   ■   ●

It was a wedding of special grace and promise. When Mary Eno Pinchot and Cord Meyer Jr. married in the bride's Park Avenue home in the spring of 1945, life seemed rather splendid. They were both monied, talented and justly full of expectation. She was the most beautiful girl in Vassar's class of '42. He graduated Yale Phi Beta Kappa, summa cum laude, and won the Alpheus Henry Snow Award as "the senior adjudged by the faculty to have done the most for Yale by inspiring his classmates."

Mary came from one of America's prominent political families—the Pinchots of Pennsylvania. Her uncle Gifford Pinchot, a two-term governor of his home state in the twenties and thirties as well as a noted forester, was often mentioned as a dark horse for the Republican presidential nomination. Her father, Amos Pinchot, a radical lawyer, helped organize the breakaway Bull Moose Party for Teddy Roosevelt in 1912. He later became a pacifist and an American First critic of FDR's internationalism. Our declaration of war against the Axis drove him to attempt suicide. The Pinchot fortune, based on the lucrative dry goods business of Mary's paternal grandfather, James, and augmented by the large inheritance of his wife, Mary Eno, reached into the millions.

Cord's blood lines were less illustrious but similarly marked by wealth and politics. His great grandfather grew rich in sugar and his grandfather, a state chairman of the New York Democratic Party, in Long Island real estate. Cord Meyer Sr. served as a diplomat in Cuba, Italy and Sweden before retiring from government service when he fathered a second set of twin sons in the twenties.

At the time of the marriage, Cord was serving as a military aide to Commander Harold E. Stassen, then a U.S. delegate at the drafting of the United Nation's Charter in San Francisco. He had lost an eye to a Japanese grenade on Guam and published "Waves of Darkness," a moving, often anthologized short story of the disillusions of war, in the December 1945 *Atlantic*. In 1947 the Junior Chamber of Commerce named him one of the ten outstanding young men in the United States. As spokesman for the liberal United World Federalists, he crusaded across the country for the idea of world government. After listening to one of Cord's speeches, Merle Miller noted in his journal: "If Cord goes into politics he'll probably not only be President of the United States; he may be the first president of the parliament of man. And if he does become a writer, he's sure to win the Nobel Prize."

Cord did not fulfill Miller's prophecy. At the urging of Allen Dulles, he joined the Central Intelligence Agency in 1951 and developed into a determined anti-Communist operative, eventually rising to the post of assistant deputy director of plans, better known as the dirty tricks department.

By 1956, after 11 years of marriage, Mary, then 36, could no longer tolerate living with Cord and the CIA, a business she hated. She divorced him and moved across the Potomac from McLean, Virginia, where RFK was her next-door neighbor and friend, to a Georgetown townhouse around the corner from her sister, Mrs. Benjamin Bradlee, and their mutual good friend Senator John Kennedy.

It was Mary, not Cord, who eventually attained the White House. The grace and promise of their wedding was twisted in unforeseen fashion. While he sulked in the CIA, even briefing JFK on occasion, she became the secret Lady Ottoline of Camelot.

Jack and Mary first met at Vassar. Kennedy (Harvard '40) dated several members of Mary's class, including her chum Dorothy Burns. "Everybody knew everybody then," says Scottie Fitzgerald Smith, F. Scott Fitzgerald's daughter and Mary's classmate. The women closest to Mary on campus refused to reminisce about her. But interviews with acquaintances indicate that she did not particularly distinguish herself at Vassar. Selection for the daisy chain, a wreath of daisies borne at graduation by the comeliest and most personable sophomores, seems her only honor. "Mary wasn't very gregarious," Scottie Smith remarks. "She didn't mingle about. She was an independent soul. I always thought of her as a fawn running through the forest."

A short story entitled "Futility" in the April 1941 *Vassar Review and Little Magazine*, the single extant sample of her campus writing, suggests a free and wildly imaginative spirit. A young lady, bored with the "chicly cadaverous" women who are "being too killing about Noel Coward's love life" at a Park Avenue cocktail party, runs off to a hospital for a strange operation. She wants to have the ends of her optical nerves attached to the hearing part of the brain and the auditory ends to the seeing part so that everything she sees she hears and vice versa. The surgery was a success. The young lady returned to the apartment now empty of partygoers and lay down on the hostess' sofa. Mary concluded the fantasy: "The lighted aquarium, like a window to a green outdoors, shone above the mantle in the dark room. The copper fish undulated aimlessly among the other weeds, and as she watched them, she heard the far off buzz of men's and women's voices chattering in the room, the sound of glass clinking against ice, Beatrice's voice rising and falling. The low murmur hummed on and on, and Ruth fell asleep. And because her eyes were closed, she heard nothing to disturb her, and slept forever on the chartreuse couch."

After Vassar, Mary went to work for the United Press in New York City, and there fell in love with Bob Schwartz, a home-front staffer for the GI newspaper *Yank*. For the sake of Mary's mother, they maintained separate quarters, but their intense three-year involvement was public knowledge. The Pinchots accepted the relationship. The couple traveled together and passed many weekends at the several-thousand-acre Pinchot estate in the Poconos. Now an entrepreneur in Tarrytown, New York, Schwartz would say only that he was Mary's first love and that he had ended it in 1944, before Cord returned from the Pacific. "Mary was unbelievable to behold," Schwartz avowed. "She was uncompromising about her view of the world and had great strength about it."

Although Mary considered medical school, she took her $30-a-week feature writing job at U.P. seriously. In 1944 she free-lanced three well-turned pieces on "meteorbiology," venereal disease and college sex courses for *Mademoiselle*. Criticizing squeamish public attitudes toward the wartime epidemic of syphilis and gonorrhea, she wrote, "Though the spirochete is better barred from the body, there's no reason to ban awareness of it from the mind." In "Credits for Love," she endorsed sex education "as a means to a happier and less hazardous private life."

Scottie Fitzgerald Smith was at *Time* during this same period and saw a lot of Mary. They lunched and partied together. Scottie recalls that Mary enjoyed skinny-dipping *ensemble* in the bubbling "champagne pond" under the idyllic waterfall on the Pocono property. "She was unconventional and broke the rules of our generation. But her unconventionality was quiet and disciplined. She was never a showoff." Asked to describe Mary's appeal to men, her old friend remarked, "Mary had perfectly lovely skin and coloring. She always looked like she had just taken a bath. A man once told me that she reminded him of a cat walking on a roof in the moonlight. She had such tremendous poise. Whether she was merely shy or just controlled, I don't know. She was very cool physically and psychologically, a liberated woman long before it was fashionable."

Mary's first son, named Quentin after Cord's twin who had died on Okinawa, was born in 1946. She thereupon combined motherhood and manuscript-reading at *Atlantic Monthly* while Cord studied at Harvard. Soon she retired from her literary career to assist her husband's world government efforts and bear two more sons, Michael and Mark. After the divorce was all but decided in 1956, Michael was killed by a car in McLean. This tragedy affected both parents deeply, but it did not bring them back together; it could not salvage the marriage. "She respected Cord but wanted to make it on her own as a painter," explains a Washington intimate. "Why should she have to go to dinners with the director of the CIA when she'd rather be in her studio?"

After the separation, Mary fell under the influence of Kenneth Noland, a painter who was one of the founders of what became known as the "Washington Color School." Inspired by Helen Frankenthaler's revolt against the "too painterly" qualities of Abstract Expressionism, Noland and the late Morris Louis, both residents of Washington in the fifties, began experimenting with new techniques of applying paint to canvas. They made color, rather than structure or subject, their primary concern. They and their disciples tended to concentrate on a single format. Louis worked with the bleeding edge, Noland on targets and Gene Davis in stripes. This small community significantly affected the history of American art and made some of its members famous and wealthy.

Mary chose to paint in *tondo*; that is, on rounded canvasses. Like her lover Noland, four years her junior, she focused on swaths of circular color. Her painting *Blue Sky* hangs in the Manhattan apartment of poet Barbara Higgins, a friend from the early sixties. *Blue Sky*, a very early work, is a 6′ by 5′6″ rectangle, but large semicircular bands of green, blue and orange color resting above and below two hard-edged horizontal lines show evidence of her later direction. "When Mary started painting large pictures, she began freeing herself," Mrs. Higgins says. "She felt she was making a breakthrough and was happier than I'd ever seen her."

●   ■   ●

Mary's long friendship with John F. Kennedy continued throughout their respective marriages. She regularly attended Kennedy White House soirees in the company of her sister, Tony, and Ben Bradlee. We now know, originally through the *National Enquirer*, that a sexual relationship began in January 1962. In September 1963, Mary and Tony Bradlee flew with JFK in the presidential helicopter to the Pinchot estate in Milford, Pennsylvania, where JFK officially accepted on behalf of the government the donation of a mansion and some land.

"That in itself was probably not enough to command the President's presence," writes Ben Bradlee in *Conversations with Kennedy*, "but a chance to see where his friends the Pinchot girls had grown up, and especially a chance to see their mother, was apparently irresistible. . . ."

A few weeks later, in the awful month of November 1963, Mary Meyer's first show opened at Washington's Jefferson Place Gallery. The reviews were quite good, recalls Nesta Dorrance, then director of the now-defunct gallery. She feels it was too soon for Mary's potential as an artist to be judged.

The friends of Mary Meyer choose words like "warmth . . . vibrance . . . loyalty . . . mystery and strength" to describe her.

"Mary had a half-sister, Rosamond, a Broadway actress who committed suicide in 1938," one friend remarked. "Rosamond used to go down to the Pinchot stables at midnight, saddle a horse and gallop at full speed across the estate. Mary was awed by her, she thought it was poetic. That was the feeling we all had for Mary."

●   ■   ●

On the Saturday following Mary Meyer's murder, five people gathered at her Georgetown home and tore it apart searching for the secret diary. Sometime before she died, Mary had entrusted to her friends James and Ann Truitt the fact of her affair with JFK and the existence of a diary recounting some of her evenings with the President. Truitt was then a vice-president of the *Washington Post*; his wife, Ann, was a sculptor and confidante of Mary. Before they departed for Tokyo in 1963, where Truitt was to become *Newsweek* bureau chief, Mary discussed the disposition of her diary in the event of her death. She asked them to preserve it, and to show it to her son Quentin when he reached the age of 21.

The Truitts were still in Tokyo when they received word of the towpath murder, and the responsibility for the diary was communicated to their mutual friend James Angleton, through still uncertain channels. Mary Meyer was accustomed to leaving her diary in the bookcase in her bedroom where, incidentally, she kept clippings of the JFK assassination. The diary was not there after her death.

Angleton therefore brought some of the specialized tools of his black-bag trade—white gloves, drills, etc.—to the task of combing the house. Also there to aid in the search were other members of Mary Meyer's circle: Tony Bradlee; Cord Meyer; a former college roommate, Ann Chamberlain; and Angleton's wife, Cicely.

They tapped walls, looked in the fireplace and turned over bricks in the garden, finding nothing and exhausting themselves in the process. Cord lit a smoky fire, Angleton pitched in washing dishes and the whiskey flowed. One frustrated seeker went out into the garden and yelled up to the sky, "Mary, where's your damned diary?"

It wasn't in the house at all. Tony located it in Mary's studio later, along with the canvasses she was readying for what would have been her second gallery show. The diary was in a locked steel box filled with hundreds of letters.

●   ■   ●

Neither the police nor the prosecutor was aware of the existence of a diary when Raymond Crump went on trial for the murder of Mary Meyer on July 19, 1965.

"This is a classic textbook case of circumstantial evidence," Prosecutor Albert Hantman told the jury.

Prosecutor Albert Hantman was missing certain direct links in what seemed on the surface an airtight case. He didn't have the murder weapon. He'd had the riverbank searched, he'd had scuba divers rake through the muck at the bottom of the Potomac. No gun. And his eyewitness, Henry Wiggins, would only testify to a "glance" at the man he saw standing over Mary Meyer's body. Hantman's case had many strengths despite this. Crump's fishing alibi sounded implausible in many ways. He claimed he'd lost his fishing pole and "chicken hair" bait in his fall into the Potomac. But a nosy neighbor had observed him leaving home that morning carrying no fishing tackle at all and wearing a dark plaid cap and a light colored windbreaker which matched those worn by the assailant.

Hantman decided the only way to prove that Mary Meyer's murderer and Raymond Crump were one and the same man was to reconstruct in detail the movements of each before, during and after the murder, and to prove that no one but Raymond Crump was present on or about the towpath when Mary Meyer died.

Hantman even went so far as to try to introduce a large tree branch into court as evidence. Hantman justified this unusual request by claiming that the position of the bloodstains on the tree—and he waved about in open court a vial of Mary Meyer's blood scraped from the tree—would support his reconstruction of Mary Meyer's death struggle.

The murderer first tried to drag Mary Meyer down into the bushes on the bank behind the towpath, the prosecutor told the jury, hinting strongly at a sexual motive for the initial assault. Then, Hartman said, "she grabbed the tree . . . holding on for her life. She didn't want to lose sight of the people; and he was attempting to pull her down behind the canal. She struggled and fought. His jacket was torn. Her slacks were torn. His finger was cut. She had abrasions and contusions on various parts of her body. He shot her once and she resisted. She broke away from him. She ran across the towpath. She fell. She was alive and he had to shoot her again so she couldn't identify him."

By trying to prove everything so precisely from circumstantial evidence, Hantman left Roundtree several opportunities to challenge successfully any absolute interpretation of such elements as the bloodstains and hair fiber analysis. She forced a National Park Service mapmaker to concede that there were other possible exits from the riverbank area that had not been sealed off by the police. In the end she rested her case without calling a single witness. Instead, she presented a powerful final summation that came down hard on Air Force Lieutenant Mitchell's description of the man following Mary Meyer on the towpath as "about my size." William Mitchell's size was 5′8″, 145 pounds. Roundtree told the jury: "Look at this little man, Ray Crump. He is your Exhibit A." Crump, she said, was only 5′3″. She reminded the jury that "only the official exits had been sealed" and raised the specter of "a phantom" killer who escaped the manhunt by way of an unmarked exit.

Dramatic as Roundtree's summation was, Prosecutor Hantman pushed the pitch of the drama almost over the edge into farce in his rebuttal argument. He decided to take on directly Roundtree's Exhibit A—Ray Crump's short stature as compared to the 5′8″ height of the man William Mitchell had observed following Mary Meyer. Hantman played his trump: the elevator shoe demonstration. "The defendant," Hantman said, "was 5′ 5½″ when he was taken to identification."

Then Hantman dramatically placed government Exhibit 17 on the lectern in full view of the jury. Government Exhibit 17 was a pair of Ray Crump's shoes—the pair he was wearing when he was arrested.

"Look at the heels of these shoes," Hantman cried. "They are practically Adler-heel shoes. There are at least . . . two inches of heel on that pair of shoes. . . . This is what gave Lt. Mitchell the appearance that this defendant was his size."

The case went to the jury on July 29, 1965. After five hours of deliberation the jury foreman sent to the judge for answers to the following questions: "Was Ray Crump right-handed or left-handed? Did the police ever permit Crump to show them where he claimed to be fishing and from where he fell?"

The judge told the jury they would have to depend upon their own recollection for the answers to those questions. The jury deliberated for a few more hours, then sent a second note to the judge informing him they were deadlocked eight to four. They did not say which way. The judge instructed them they were not "hopelessly" deadlocked and ordered them to return to their deliberations. At 11:35 a.m. on July 30, after a total of 11 hours, they sent word they had finally reached a verdict. They found Raymond Crump not guilty.

●   ■   ●

The acquittal left the murder of Mary Meyer officially unsolved. But Washington police never reopened the investigation. They closed the towpath murder file after the trial. "Without a full confession and witnessing it myself," remarks Inspector Bernard Crooke, "there's no question in my mind that Ray Crump shot Mary Meyer." Like the detective in the film *Laura*, Crooke became somewhat captivated by the victim. He leafed through several old homicide notebooks stored in his current office at Third District Headquarters on V Street to refresh his recollection of the case. Homicide detectives interviewed at least 100 friends of Mary Meyer. Apparently, nothing untoward turned up; any prior association with Crump was ruled out after a check of her personal belongings. Crooke recalls going through her deep, narrow townhouse and being amused by the contrast of the exquisite antique furnishings and the starkly functional bathroom with a sunken tub. Crooke was also struck by the formal written invitation to a simple date with a gentleman that he found on her desk. "We learned that she was seeing several men," he says, "and when you look 25 and you're free . . . She would have quickened the pulse of many men."

Crooke discovered a diary-type calendar in Mary Meyer's home, but not any larger diary. "I'd have been very upset at the time if I knew the deceased's diary had been destroyed."

Dovey Roundtree believes Mary Meyer's murderer is still at large, although she has no particular person in mind. In her pretrial investigation, Roundtree pursued the ghost of Mary Meyer in the hope of locating another suspect or a suggestion of one. If her client was innocent, as she truly believed, then somebody else, perhaps a boyfriend, committed the act. Although she despised making sexual innuendos about dead women in court, she was prepared to raise the matter. "She had a lot of different men," Ms. Roundtree comments in her law office at Roundtree, Knox, Hunter and Pendarvis. "Some were younger. For a woman her age, you'd think she'd just have one person. I thought it was unusual even though she was an artist. I was looking for motivation. I narrowed it down to people who knew her and her habits, who may have argued with her and had a confrontation. I thought we were getting close to something sexual or some other reason which I didn't understand myself. But after the prosecution introduced a mountain of evidence, I decided to keep my case as simple as possible. Hantman was a most frustrated man. He wanted Ray Crump on the witness stand and would have destroyed him. Ray had goofed off from work and took a six-pack of beer fishing to get away from his bitchin' wife. They wanted to massacre and burn this boy. If I failed, he would die."

Ms. Roundtree recalls a number of anonymous phone calls in the course of the case, directing her to secret meetings. Wary of a trap, she stayed away.

The trial proceedings seemed rushed to her. She learned that Mary Meyer had a high White House clearance and that her diary was burned before the trial. "I thought the government had something to do with the whole case," she says. Her client, Ray Crump, left Washington after the trial. He thinks he was framed the first time, she says, and lives in fear that someone will come after him again.

●   ■   ●

Fourteen years after the murder, the *National Enquirer* disinterred the untold story of Mary Meyer in its issue dated March 2, 1976. The bold front-page headline read "JFK 2 YEAR WHITE HOUSE ROMANCE . . . Socialite Then Murdered and Diary Burned by CIA." The tabloid's eager source was James Truitt. According to Truitt, whose quotes comprised almost the entire text, JFK first asked her to go to bed with him in the White House in December 1961. A current involvement with an artist caused her to reject his proposal. But beginning in January she kept regular sexual rendezvous with the president until his assassination. "She said she had to tell someone what was happening," Truitt informed the *Enquirer*. "So she confided in me and my former wife, Ann."

If Truitt's revelations are to be believed, Mary loved JFK but realized their liaison would be limited to brief encounters even though, as she told Truitt, he felt "no affection of a lasting kind" for his wife. Their arrangement apparently had its comic moments. Truitt's notes record an episode in July of 1962 during which Mary turned on JFK with two joints of marijuana. He laughed as he mentioned an imminent White House conference on narcotics. "This isn't like cocaine," he reputedly said. "I'll get you some of that."

Furthermore, the *Enquirer* disclosed that Mary's personal diary, containing references to JFK and several love letters from him, was discovered by her sister, Tony Bradlee, in her garage studio and surrendered to James Angleton of the CIA, who had aided in the search.

The *Enquirer* account raised the question of an official CIA connection to the death. The tabloid called the murder "unsolved" and suggestively characterized the official view of the case as "a lone gunman" theory. Immediately after the acquittal of Ray Crump there was talk in Georgetown circles of the possibility of conspiracy in Mary Meyer's death— one person close to the case heard speculation about "KGB sacrificial murders." And Patrick Anderson's recent novel, *The President's Mistress*, postulates a Georgetown paramour of a Kennedyesque president murdered by an overzealous aide in a struggle over a memoir of the White House affair. But no evidence to support such talk has ever been uncovered, and no one has ever pointed to a better suspect than Ray

Crump. Even if someone other than Ray Crump did kill Mary Meyer—another black man in a light windbreaker, dark slacks and golf cap—in the absence of evidence to the contrary from any source, the violence done to her on the towpath that day is more likely to have been random rather than conspiratorial. None of the many friends of Mary Meyer we spoke to has suggested any other motive.

The real questions left unanswered in the wake of the *Enquirer* revelation circle around Mary Meyer's diary: What was in it, who read it, what became of it, what if anything did it reveal about the nature of her relationship with JFK and why did the people involved in the search for the diary behave so strangely when its existence became public after 14 years of silence?

The close circle of friends that linked Mary Meyer and JFK had gathered at her home in the wake of her murder to search for the diary in order to fulfill one of her final requests. Some of them had even, several years later, attended a seance in Upper Marlboro, Maryland, at which some attempt was made to establish "contact" with her departed spirit. And for 14 years all of them had kept the story not only out of the public press but for the most part out of the mainstream of subterranean Washington gossip. For years before Judith Exner or any of the women with whom JFK consorted became household words in the mass media, the names of many of them were quite familiar to the Georgetown Camelot set.

But the Mary Meyer revelation shocked even some veteran observers of that scene. "It was a bombshell," said one, "not because it *happened* but because nobody I know ever heard a whisper."

After the secret legacy shared by that circle of friends became tabloid headlines in 1976, all the resentments, hatreds, bitterness and infighting that had been building among the members of the circle since the deaths of the secret lovers suddenly broke out into the open. Without that shared secret they appeared to have nothing to unite them. James Truitt betrayed his confidence to get Ben Bradlee, Bradlee's newspaper questioned Truitt's mental health, Bradlee accused Angleton of a lock-pick "break-in" at Mary Meyer's studio, Angleton called Bradlee a liar, Tony Bradlee, now divorced from Ben, contradicted her husband's version of some of the key events.

The aftermath is a tale of disappointed expectations, revenge and disloyalty, as sad and pathetic in its way as the death of Mary Meyer and the destruction of other illusions of Camelot.

James Truitt strongly resents Ben Bradlee. The fact that he would trample the memory of his beloved friend Mary to embarrass Bradlee is one measure of his animus. In happier days, Truitt held a position of some importance at the *Washington Post*. He was the right-hand man of its publisher, Philip Graham. After Graham shot himself in the summer of 1963, Truitt wound up in the Tokyo bureau of *Newsweek*, another *Post* company. Bradlee, transferred to the *Post* from *Newsweek*'s Washington bureau in 1965, brought Truitt back to Washington, where he worked on the paper's new "Style" section. Unfortunately, he did not perform especially well and had a nervous breakdown in 1969. Truitt believes that Bradlee conspired to have him fired and that the *Post* did not keep certain promises to him after Graham's suicide. Truitt told *Enquirer* researcher Bernie Ward that he exposed the Mary Meyer affair with JFK in order to show up Bradlee. "Here is this great crusading Watergate editor who claimed to tell everything in his Kennedy book," Ward quotes Truitt as saying, "but really told nothing."

If the executive editor of the *Post* covered up for JFK, his paper did not extend the same courtesy to Truitt. The *Post* gave front-page attention to Truitt's crack-up in its February 23 story on the Mary Meyer revelations.

After reporting the *Enquirer*'s assertions in detail, including confirmation of the upcoming narcotics conference that JFK supposedly referred to while stoned in the White House, *Post* staffer Don Oberdorfer cited a doctor's certification contained in court records that Truitt had suffered from a mental illness "such as to impair his judgment and cause him to be irresponsible." An anonymous Washington attorney added that Truitt had threatened Bradlee and others in recent years with exposure of the "alleged scandals." Thus the *Post*, while giving admirable play to an extremely touchy subject, created the hard impression that Truitt was an unreliable source—even though Bradlee knew that Truitt was essentially truthful about Mary Meyer and JFK.

The motives behind the Bradlee-Angleton clash are less clear. They also had been friends. But as far back as 1965 Bradlee seems to have hurt Angleton in the *Post*. According to one source, in 1968 Bradlee took the initiative to write an unsigned *Post* story on a book by Kim

Philby (Britain's counter-intelligence chief in the pay of the KGB), a story that purposely ignored all favorable references to Angleton while quoting the unfavorable mentions. When Angleton asked him why he treated a friend like that, Bradlee denied authorship.

Their feud burst forth again over the matter of Mary Meyer. A *Post* reporter close to Bradlee recalls that Bradlee informed him long ago that he, Bradlee, had caught Angleton breaking into Mary's studio in quest of the hot document. "Ben was surprised to see him there with his lock pick," he says. *Post* columnist Nicholas Von Hoffman cited the same hearsay in *The New York Review of Books* (June 10, 1976), where he observed that the residence of a presidential paramour "was broken into by a CIA agent and her diary burned." During Seymour Hersh's attempt to pin down his CIA domestic surveillance scoop, a man from the *Times* called Angleton and accused him of the studio break-in.

Ben Bradlee, who seems to have been telling the Angleton lock-pick tale around town for some time, stood by its accuracy. "Angleton was trying to get in," he affirmed in a phone interview, "but ultimately he was invited in." But Bradlee, while he could not account for Angleton's lock-picking zeal, quickly disavows any CIA angle. "If there was anything there," Bradlee said regarding the agency's shadow over the case, "I would have done it [written the story] myself."

Angleton angrily denies the break-in charge. "It is a total lie," Angleton told us. "I was never at the studio."

One source, who tends to take Angleton's side in the Angleton-Bradlee dispute, also accuses Bradlee of disloyalty to Mary Meyer. According to the source, Bradlee considered exposing her affair with JFK himself in *Conversations with Kennedy*, until others pressured him against it.

In fact, Bradlee did allude to JFK's fascination with Mary Meyer in the following passage:

> The conversation ended, as those conversations often ended, with his views on some of the women present—the overall appeal of the daughter of Prince Paul of Yugoslavia and Mary Meyer. "Mary would be rough to live with," Kennedy noted, not for the first time. And I agreed, not for the first time.

What did JFK mean? "I don't know," Bradlee told us. What sort of woman was Mary? "She was marvelous," he said. (The Bradlee-Kennedy exchange on Mary Meyer took place in February of 1962—just a month after the affair was inaugurated in Truitt's chronology.)

Also, according to the same source allied to Angleton, Mary Meyer herself was not on speaking terms with Bradlee for the last six months of her life because she felt he had given away a confidence of hers in *Newsweek*. Bradlee continues to deny that he was aware of the JFK-Mary Meyer affair before the *Enquirer* story—even though, as he admitted to us, he read through the diary in 1964.

"Were you surprised to learn of the liaison?" we asked Bradlee.

"Of course I was surprised," he said. "I was amazed."

●   ■   ●

The whole story of the life, death and resurrection of Mary Meyer is immensely complex and is not complete here. Many friends and relatives understandably drew back from the public controversy. Many refused all comment, others misled and misspoke. However, from unpublished materials and interviews with intimate sources, we have found certain things that can be said about the contents of the diary and the letters and the nature of the affair itself.

James Angleton read those letters. He also read the diary. He catalogued the letters. He took notes on some of them. He offered certain people the opportunity to repossess letters they had written to Mary Meyer.

In a letter Angleton wrote to Truitt after the diary search, he said two other persons whom Angleton identified only as "M" and "F" had read the diary. "M" and "F" told Angleton they wanted to preserve certain edited parts.

One other person was permitted to see the diary: Mary Meyer's older son, Quentin, then 18, read deeply in the private papers and subsequently wrote his brother, Mark, about the contents.

In an unpublished draft of the *Enquirer* story, Mary's sister, Tony, reveals far more about Mary, JFK and the diary. (Publicly, Tony denies corroborating the *Enquirer* story.)

"Mary and JFK did have a close relationship. You obviously know that much and that's true," she told the *Enquirer*, according to this draft. She continues:

> I didn't know anything at all about it at the time. What I understand of it afterwards, it was a fling, another of Jack's flings. If Mary had any relationship of the kind she went into it with her eyes open.
>
>   We did find it [the diary] in the studio. I don't remember where. It may have been in a filing cabinet. I was the one who found it. We were going through her belongings and there it was. Yes, it's true we were looking for it. None of us read it. We were all honor bound not to. [Here Truitt wrote "no" in the margin.] The diary was a slim volume. All I remember is that it was like a sketchbook with a nice paisley-colored cover on it. It was kind of a loose leaf book, nothing like Ben's book he was taking things down in, just a woman's notes about what she had been doing. I swear I don't remember what was in it, I went through it so quickly. And I remember there were some JFK's in it. There were some references to him. It was a dreadful time but as I remember it had pencil marks. It was very cryptic and difficult to understand. Not much there but some reference to JFK. I felt it was something we shouldn't look at. There were some references to him. But the diary was destroyed. I'll tell you that much is true.

When James Angleton read the diary, he thought that although Mary Meyer's prose was informal, the implications in the entries were transparent. Angleton decided that in the wrong hands the diary might be troublesome to the children and others. (Angleton had a fatherly relationship to Mary Meyer's sons, and later, when Cord Meyer left for London to assume his present post as CIA station chief, Angleton became trustee for the children.)

"I burned them," Angleton later wrote Truitt. Yet Angleton also wrote Truitt that he had informed certain members of Mary Meyer's family that the papers still reposed somewhere at the Pinchot estate in Milford.

Does the diary still exist? Unless it shows up again somehow, only those familiar with its contents can help us form a judgment about the real nature of the 20-month relationship between Mary Meyer and John F. Kennedy.

One person who is in a unique position to comment authoritatively on that relationship, and who has never before spoken to the press about it, agreed to entertain a limited number of questions about the affair:

"How could a woman so admired for her integrity as Mary Meyer traduce her friendship with Jackie Kennedy?"

"They weren't friends," he said curtly.

"Did JFK actually *love* Mary Meyer?"

"I think so."

"Then why would he carry on an affair simultaneously with Judy Exner?"

"My friend, there's a difference between sex and love."

"But why Mary Meyer over all other women?"

"He was an unusual man. He wanted the best."

—*NEW TIMES*
October 1976

CRACK MURDER

The anonymous call came into the 71st Precinct shortly after 9 one evening last November. It was a male voice, and the message was simple: there's a dead body in a black Mercedes parked on Rutland Road near Wingate High School.*

The precinct patrol-car team dispatched to the site found an adult black male in a leather jacket and jeans slumped forward in the front passenger seat of the Mercedes. Blood from bullet wounds in his head, neck and chest had spilled out onto the front seat, soaking into the soft leather and drenching the double stack of tape cassettes next to the body. When Detective Albert E. Cachie of the Brooklyn South Homicide Squad arrived on the scene shortly thereafter, he found the body in the car shrouded in a sweet-smelling cloud of strawberry scent. One

* The events described here are true, the people are real. However, the names of witnesses and suspects had been changed at the request of the New York City Police Department.

of those powerful little "fragrance trees" dangling from the dashboard mirror was still pumping away for dear life.

In fact, a few days later, when Al Cachie opened the door of the Mercedes (it was now parked in the basement garage of the 71st Precinct house) to show me the location of the bullet marks within, the stale odor of industrial strength strawberries still pervaded the interior. The stacks of tapes were still there, too, glued together now by the dried blood into a single mass. The titles on top: "Love Songs by the Commodores" and "Rap Attack."

In the last few days, more has been learned about the now-deceased owner of the Mercedes than his taste in sound and scent.

He was known by the street name Halfback, and he was said to be a rising star in central Brooklyn crack-dealing circles. He'd moved rapidly to the top ranks of one of the most powerful and well-established crack combines, the Eddie Holmes crew. Halfback's ascent from street dealer to what might be called the marketing-executive level in the corporate hierarchy of the crew had been abetted by a certain mystique.

For one thing, the word on the street was that Halfback never used drugs himself, certainly not crack, the highly addictive cocaine derivative, nor anything else. He didn't drink, didn't gamble, didn't chase women, although he was not exactly a monk in this respect: he would, it is said, allow *them* to come to him, and Detective Cachie had already interviewed two frightened women, each of whom thought she'd been his current girlfriend.

Halfback's refusal to use the substance he sold allowed him to hold on to his profits. And there was something else about him that set him apart from the average crack entrepreneur. Detective Donald Gregori, the precinct detective Cachie was working with on the case, noticed it: up on the wall in the apartment of one of Halfback's girlfriends were two academic-looking certificates with his name on them.

One was for completion of a course in Gestalt psychology, the other for success in a course in transactional analysis. It's true that Halfback had earned these certificates in prison while he was doing time on auto theft charges. But there is reason to suspect that he had applied the psychological sophistication he acquired in these seminars to the transactional Gestalt of the crack-dealing world. If so, it seemed to have served him well. The word was that Halfback had become so successful that he had recently decided to break away from the institutional constraints of the Holmes organization and go out on his own—become an independent crack tycoon. This career move, Cachie suspects, may have proven fatal to him.

It's taken Detectives Cachie and Gregori four days of patiently interviewing witnesses just to piece together an outline of the complicated sequence of events of that night. "The body is found in the car on Rutland Road," Cachie tells me. "You can see these bullet marks on the inside of the door frame here on the passenger side," he says, pointing out pockmarks in the metal. "And the M.E."—medical examiner— "tells us he was shot four times on the left side of the face and neck from close range, so it's pretty clear he was shot while in the car. But he wasn't shot *first* in the car.

"You see, we've got witnesses on Saratoga Avenue, a couple of miles away, who say Halfback is standing on the sidewalk outside this hangout which is a known crack-dealing location, and someone with a silver revolver comes up to him and starts firing five or six shots. At least one hits him, because he's seen bleeding and staggering over to the Mercedes, and he's heard saying something like 'I'm not gonna make it.' Then a friend or associate, a guy whose street name is TNT, helps him into the Mercedes and drives off, telling people he's gonna take Halfback to the hospital. There are also reports of another car, a blue Olds 98 also belonging to Halfback, following the Mercedes and being driven by one or two other friends or associates, including a fellow named Ricky. About half an hour later, TNT appears back at the scene of the original shooting and tells people Halfback died before he got to the hospital."

Cachie slams the door of the Mercedes.

"Now the question we're left with is: who was the first shooter, the guy with the silver revolver? People are kicking out TNT's name, people are mentioning Ricky, but none of the witnesses say they recognized the first shooter. Then the question is, these friends or associates who drove off with Halfback—were they really planning to take him to the hospital, or were they finishing him off, and if they put the four bullets into him, were they in on it from the beginning? There are a lot of questions on this one," he says, as we head upstairs to meet Detective Gregori. "This is turning out to be an interesting mystery. A good murder."

When Detective Cachie characterizes this as a "good murder," when, a bit later, Detective Gregori refers to it as "one of the better homicides," these phrases do not constitute praise for the deed. A good murder is, rather, one that brings out the best in them, one that challenges their skills as detectives, unlike cut and dried homicides that are referred to dismissively by detectives as "grounders" or "ground balls"— easy outs.

But a truly good murder offers more than mere complexity. The better homicides also offer the potential for larger significance. The killing of Halfback, for instance, might lead to the conviction of a major crack crew leader and the possibility of penetrating the crack-dealing underground that has become a kind of breeding ground for homicides in the city.

Last year, the citywide murder rate made a sudden leap upward— about 20 percent over 1985. Most of the detectives I talked to believe this jump can be attributed mainly to crack-related killings. Crack-world homicides present a special set of difficulties to detectives. They find themselves confronted with a secretive criminal underground that is heavily armed and trigger-happy. They find that witnesses knowledgeable about a crack crime frequently have something to hide themselves, and even those who don't are fearful of the consequences of talking to detectives.

●   ■   ●

Detective Al Cachie brings certain special assets to a case like this. For one thing, this is his turf. He grew up in central Brooklyn, in Bedford-Stuyvesant, a short drive from the scene of Halfback's shooting. As he moved up in the department—through the plainclothes and narcotics squads to the rank of detective—he was detailed to Brooklyn precincts. He knows the streets, knows the people. He can listen to street talk and judge the credibility of a speaker from the nuance of his inflection, distinguish jive talk from truth in a way few outsiders to these neighborhoods can. Because he can talk their language, people are more willing to talk to him, to confide in him.

Cachie brings something else to the Halfback case: an analytic ability that grows out of 10 years' experience investigating major homicides. While Brooklyn homicides don't get the publicity high-profile Manhattan murders do, Al Cachie has become a legend among those who know his work.

One afternoon, in the 77th Precinct station house, as Cachie was taking me up to the detective unit to show me the case files on a cop killing he'd solved, a lieutenant by the name of Duffy stopped him to see what he was up to. Cachie is something special, Duffy tells me.

"This guy," says Duffy, indicating Cachie with his thumb, "you're with the greatest—no, one-half the greatest team of homicide investigators around here."

The team Duffy refers to consisted of Cachie and another Brooklyn-born detective, Paul Weidenbaum. In the 10 years they worked together, the two of them handled dozens of major homicides. Among precinct commanders, they became known as the team to ask for when the department was faced with a particularly difficult murder. Among cops in the field, they became known as the "I Spy" team, after the black-white secret-agent team played by Bill Cosby and Robert Culp on television.

But the Cachie-Weidenbaum partnership no longer exists. It was a casualty of the introduction in Brooklyn last year of a new system for structuring the investigation of homicides. The police department seems chronically unable to make up its mind about how best to organize murder investigations, and the new one is the third system in the last 15 years.

Under the previous systems, the basic unit for investigating a homicide was a two-man team composed of experienced detectives who generally worked together on case after case. Under the new system, which, so far, has been introduced in the Manhattan North and Brooklyn South jurisdictions, a new kind of ad hoc two-man team is formed for each new homicide. These teams are composed of a detective from the precinct in which the corpse is found, and a homicide specialist from the boroughwide homicide command.

In effect, the previous systems promoted long-term "marriages" between detectives of similar temperament, while the new system sets up a series of "blind dates" between the experienced homicide man and the relatively inexperienced precinct detective, partnerships in which the chemistry is not always predictable.

What's lost in this ad hoc arrangement, according to several homicide detectives I talked to, is the rapport, the coordination of tactics, that years of working as a team can develop between veteran detectives.

Still, in the Halfback case, the blind date between Cachie and Gregori seemed to have some advantages. Gregori was familiar with the cast of characters in Halfback's life. He'd become a precinct detective after serving on the aggressive "buy-and-bust" narcotics squad. So he knew the way crack crews operated. And he'd worked on a case involving Halfback before. There had been a kidnapping in October: the 6-year-old child of Eddie Holmes, the head of the major crack crew in the area, had been snatched from his school, and anonymous calls had demanded $50,000 to spare his life. The child had been returned unharmed, but in the investigation afterward Gregori had come across the name Halfback and the names of several of his associates. Nothing had been proven, but Gregori suspects a connection between the child's kidnapping and Halfback's murder.

The two detectives' different temperaments seem to complement each other. Gregori is short, wired-up with a needling sense of humor and still some of the attack-dog impulsiveness he put to use on the buy-and-bust squad. Cachie, on the other hand, is tall, judicious and analytical. He's also older than Gregori (48 to 39) and has almost twice as much time (22 years to 13) on the force. While Gregori tends to make dramatic statements ("I'd love to nail Eddie Holmes if he's behind this"), Cachie tends to reserve judgment and approach the tactical considerations in the case—whom to talk to first, whom to bring in for questioning—with the disposition of a chess player trying to think many moves ahead.

●   ■   ●

Tonight, five days after the murder, the two detectives are planning to drive over to the funeral home to check out the crowd at the viewing of Halfback's body. When we meet Gregori at the 71st Precinct station house, he's eager to report a promising development. He's gotten a call from Halfback's main girlfriend (the one with the Gestalt certificate on her wall). She's been planning to make an appearance at the funeral home tonight. But she's gotten word that threats have been made to disrupt the ritual.

"She says people in the family have been getting calls warning them to stay away, the funeral place is gonna get shot up," says Gregori. "She wants to go, she wants to take her children but she's scared, so she asked if we'll stop by to escort her."

Both detectives are pleased that she's turned to them. They're both convinced she knows a lot more about the circumstances of Halfback's life, and his death, than she's been willing to tell them so far. The fact that she's turned to them for help means that their efforts in building a relationship with her have not been in vain. Building relationships is the key tactic in cases like this, which are seldom solved through the unveiling of some Agatha Christie-like clue or the exercise of Sherlockian deduction. If they're solved at all, they're most often solved when the perpetrator—or someone else who knows the truth—is somehow persuaded to "give it up."

"I'm always surprised," a veteran police sergeant told me, "at how often these guys talk the perps into giving it up. You take a guy like Al, you take any one of your better homicide cops, put 'em in sales they could be makin' millions on the outside."

The skills of the clever salesman, of the street preacher, indeed of the transactional/Gestalt therapist—the ability to be both confidant and confidence man—are what the homicide cop needs in a case like this.

A homicide, Cachie told me, creates, in the immediate aftermath of the death, a sudden community of highly charged but dangerous knowledge. People who have it, have that knowledge, feel a pressure to discharge it, to share it, to talk about it. Friends of the victim, friends of the perpetrator, witnesses and friends of witnesses, in a case like this they all feel the external pressure to be silent, but they also feel an internal pressure to say something to somebody.

Homicide detectives want to be that somebody. To become so, they must insinuate themselves into the social circuitry by establishing bonds of trust.

As they set out tonight in Cachie's unmarked Buick to pick up Halfback's girlfriend and escort her to the funeral home, the detectives feel they've begun to get somewhere with this case. The viewing of the body of the deceased is frequently a ritual that brings together into a kind of critical mass all those people who feel the pressure to talk. In their role of escorts, the detectives won't be outsiders at this ritual, they'll be part of it.

●   ■   ●

That urge, that pressure to talk—when Cachie and his former partner Paul Weidenbaum get together to discuss past cases, they talk about the urge as if it were some kind of palpable biophysical reality.

One evening over dinner in the back room of an Italian place in Greenpoint, the two former partners were recalling for me some of the more bizarre and extreme effects of that force.

"Did you tell him about the sleeping bit, Al?" Weidenbaum asks.

"The sleeping bit," says Cachie, "you mean. . . ."

"When the perps go to sleep on us."

It's a corollary effect of the internal urge to talk, Weidenbaum explains. Guilty suspects, even if they repress the urge to "give it up," nonetheless exhibit surprising behavior as soon as detectives let them know *they* know the facts.

Time after time, Weidenbaum says, "When we put him in a cell and lock the door and tell him 'you're in for murder,' within a half-hour or so they're fast asleep."

"They go to sleep?"

"They go to sleep on us. And the only thing I can feel about this to explain it is that if the person *wasn't* guilty, they'd be so excited, so nervous—how can they go to sleep? But in this situation they've got it off their chests, they just lay down and go to sleep."

"It happened with that fellow in the Palm Sunday massacre, Christopher Thomas," Cachie says.

The Palm Sunday massacre was the 1984 slaughter of 10 women and children in a house on Liberty Avenue by a coke-crazed killer named Christopher Thomas. Cachie and Weidenbaum worked on that one together for two months as part of a task force.

"As soon as we locked him up, he just lay down and went to sleep," Cachie says. "I remember his sister came to see him, and she kept saying, 'How can he sleep? How can he sleep?' "

Powerful as the internal pressure is, the Miranda rule and other constraints on questioning suspects have placed some limits on a detective's ability to exploit it. Nonetheless, there's one ancient technique that still has a place in the modern detective's repertory: trickery.

"We can still deceive them," Weidenbaum tells me. "We can use trickery as long as it doesn't violate their rights."

He then proceeds to give me a classic instance of what he called permissible deception in a case he and Cachie worked on, a case they call "The African Queen."

"She cut her husband's head off," Weidenbaum begins. "What happened was, this man was, well . . ."

"Retarded," says Cachie.

"He was a veteran from World War II with 100 percent disability. She was an immigrant from . . ."

"The Cameroons," supplies Cachie.

"In any case, she met him and decided she's going to get his Government insurance. And one day she calls the police and says, 'Look what happened to my husband.' And the police come there, and there he is, a bloody mess on the floor, the only thing holding his head onto the body is maybe a little piece of skin. If you lift him, the head's going to roll right off. And so how do we investigate this? We start talking with her, and she thinks she's smart enough to fool everybody. Every day she comes to the precinct to talk to us."

The more she talked to them, the more suspicious they became. The blackberry brandy story was the last straw for the two detectives.

She had set the table in the apartment as if to show there were four people up there drinking the night of the murder, a night she claimed she was "away." She had put out an empty bottle of blackberry brandy and four glasses.

The problem was, the glasses in which the four people were supposed to have downed the bottle of blackberry brandy "were sparkling clean," says Weidenbaum. "She hadn't thought through her deception very thoroughly."

Convinced now that she'd murdered her husband, but handicapped by the lack of any witnesses or conclusive physical evidence, the detectives decided to use some deception of their own.

"I explain to her that when a person is murdered the last thing a person sees is the person who killed them. And this image remains on the lens of their eyes after they die, and with all this modern technology that we have, at the time of the autopsy we have the eyes removed and they are sent to a special lab, and in this lab they develop them like you would develop film, and we get a picture back of the murderer."

"That isn't true, is it?" I say, almost gulled by his deceptively sincere recitation.

"No, this is what I'm telling her," Weidenbaum clarifies for my benefit. "And she's sitting there listening to the story, and then she says to me, 'I guess you're going to find my picture.' The next day she goes back to the morgue and asks somebody at the morgue, 'Can you do this with the eyes?' And they thought she was crazy. She insisted on having the body immediately cremated with the eyes in it."

Her guilty reaction to the detectives' ruse helped convince a grand jury to indict the woman, Weidenbaum says. She subsequently plead guilty.

●   ■   ●

The night of the wake: We're on the third-floor landing of a once-elegant apartment building, the one where Halfback's main girlfriend lives. Detective Gregori is standing with his gun drawn and his back pressed against the wall of the landing to remain out of firing range from within.

There has been, at least, some misunderstanding here. There is some concern that something worse has happened.

The concern has been aroused by the threats the girlfriend has been hearing. Not just the threats to shoot up the wake. The death of Half-back has left her in a precarious and unprotected position. Word has gotten around that Halfback kept a safe in her apartment in which he stashed his crack-dealing profits. Already there has been an attempt to break into her apartment. Then there have been visits by "friends" of Halfback. One left with several thousand dollars in cash, supposedly to deliver to Halfback's mother. The girlfriend is worried about the safety of her two children (not Halfback's); she's afraid to leave the apartment, afraid to stay.

And so when Cachie and Gregori knocked on her door and were told by an unfriendly male voice inside, "Donna's not here," when repeated demands of "Open up, police!" were met with silence from within, concern rose to alarm.

Gregori now reaches down and slips underneath the door the modern detective's most effective weapon: his business card.

In this respect, too, detectives are like salesmen. After every interview with witnesses or suspects, Cachie makes it a point to give them his card, asking them to call if they hear something new or have something more to say. People who don't want to be seen talking to a detective will often call the number on the card to arrange a rendezvous away from the neighborhood or to give anonymous tips.

The misunderstanding at Donna's door has finally been cleared up by the card. The door slowly opens and someone who identifies himself as a cousin of Donna lets us in. Gregori, however, doesn't return his gun to his holster until he has made a quick check of all the rooms. The cousin explains that Donna has been playing it safe, staying in another apartment in the building; he and Cachie go off to get her while we wait in the living room.

This is unlike any of the previous apartments we've visited on this case. Most of them have been more or less brave struggles to maintain some semblance of civility against the seemingly inexorable deterioration that afflicts these poverty and crack-stricken neighborhoods. But this one is different, this is the *luxe* life that crack-dealing profits can buy, for a brief time at least. The floors are carpeted wall to wall in rich chocolate brown. There's an expensive stack-type tape deck and sound system and a fairly plush set of matching sofa and chairs. Still displayed on the wall are the deceased's psychology certificates.

In the living room, as Donna gets her kids groomed and dressed up for the wake, the detectives are skillfully orchestrating a low-key but purposeful exchange of rumor, gossip and hearsay with Donna, a female relative and the cousin. They're just as curious about what the cops have heard as the cops are about what they've heard. But, as it turns out, most of what everyone has heard seems to be secondhand. One name keeps emerging in the discussion as a source of all the hearsay. "Roy's been saying that," "I heard that from Roy." "That's what I hear he told Roy." This Roy, an associate of Halfback, seems to have been everywhere, conducting a kind of personal investigation of the death of his friend, talking to everyone except the detectives. They have a description of him, they've been looking for him, but so far he's eluded them.

Donna's two children are dressed now in what look to be expensive little matching outfits. She helps them into their well-cut matching overcoats. It's possible to see the trade-off she's made in life from the way she pampers her kids with fine clothes and constant attentiveness.

Before she met Halfback, as an unwed mother of two on public assistance, she could see the grim future her kids faced every day on the streets around her. Her liaison with a powerful crack tycoon was a way of providing them with a comfortable home, good clothes, insulation from the abyss outside. But it was a precarious kind of protection, founded on the profits of a trade that was digging the abyss even deeper. It's left her exposed to a dangerous situation, her security and prosperity disintegrating rapidly, her kids exposed, not only to poverty, but to danger from her deceased boyfriend's enemies. And "friends."

In dealing with the detectives it's clear she's still holding something back. She is still divided between her allegiance to the code of silence that rules the world of her deceased boyfriend, and her desire to find some new source of protection for herself and her children. The detectives play upon this. Before we set out for the wake, each of them takes her aside for a serious, one-on-one talk about her future, her plans—talks designed to build the trust that will be a bridge from Halfback's world to theirs.

●　■　●

At the wake: The funeral home people have done a superb job of reconstructing Halfback's face. They've situated the coffin on a raised platform at one end of the viewing room and laid out the body in such a way that the left side of his head, the side that took the bullets, is not visible.

Seeing him like that, with the damage concealed, his powerfully built body attired in a lustrous blue suit, an expression of great seriousness of purpose on his face, it's possible to understand the charisma he was said to have projected when he was alive. At a low rail in front of the coffin, three teen-age girls are holding on to each other, intermittently breaking into collective fits of sobbing. Other mourners stand and gaze respectfully at the dead crack tycoon.

In the reception hall outside the viewing room, a larger crowd mills about, chattering nervously, gazing curiously at the two detectives who are escorting Donna and her children into the viewing room. Leaving them there to make their peace with the body, Cachie and Gregori circulate through the crowd, speaking casually with those they recognize from previous interviews.

Cachie points out a couple of teen-age boys mingling with the crowd who are conspicuous because they're wearing prominently displayed beepers on their belts.

"Crack runners," he says, "All the big operations use those beepers." It's not clear, he says, whether these runners are still functioning remnants of Halfback's crew or observers from rival operations. The mood in the reception room is tense. Although the promised violence has not materialized, many people are aware of the threats; they're reluctant to talk.

But later, after we drop Donna off and head over to the crack location, Gregori reveals that she *has* "given up" something that night, at the wake: Halfback's gun. It had been hidden in the apartment, she'd told him. After the shooting she'd given it to a friend for safekeeping. She promised tonight she'll try to get it back and give it to the detectives. This is a breakthrough, because, not only is it possible the gun will tie Halfback to other unsolved shootings, but also, by giving up the gun to them, Donna has given them a symbolic token that their patient courtship of her has begun to bear fruit.

●   ■   ●

Later that night at the crack location: We park across the street from the place where Halfback was shot. His blood still stains the sidewalk, although the heavy rain tonight is likely to wash away the last traces. It's a neighborhood of rubble-filled lots surrounded by torn and twisted chain-link fences; we're parked next to one such lot. Across the street from us is a block full of crumbling walk-up apartment buildings with ground-floor storefronts. The storefront opposite us, the one with the boarded-up windows, announces by means of a crude handpainted sign that it is a "Game Room."

Inside the game room we find a front room occupied by several teenagers (a couple wearing beepers) shooting pool on a battered table to the accompaniment of the boops and beeps of video games installed in the dim corners. The back room is occupied by two very unfriendly, very uncomfortable looking dudes who make it clear they neither saw nor heard anything about the shooting; they were "away" at the time, they say.

Farther down the block there's a convenience store the detectives refer to as "Eddie Holmes's store." It's like just about every convenience store in central Brooklyn in that it has a bright red and yellow crenelated tin awning with little painted light bulbs outlining its edges. But it's unlike most convenience stores in that its shelves are mainly empty and its entire inventory consists of a few dusty cans. Nonetheless, through the sheets of rain that are now sweeping down the street it's possible to see the shadowy outlines of at least two figures lounging inside the store.

Rain has diminished the level of activity on the block tonight, but some will not be deterred from their appointed rounds. An anomalous couple emerge from a weedy gap in the chain-link fence fronting the rubbishy lot next to us. The two are anomalous because they're white and because they have no umbrella, no hats; so intent are they on their errand they just trudge forward as if they don't notice the streams of water pouring down their faces.

The detectives decide it's time they paid a visit to Eddie Holmes's store. But before they even reach the other side of the street, they get a lucky break. There's a teen-ager loitering under the tin awning of the store. As the detectives approach, this teen-ager spots another teen-ager he knows coming toward him on the opposite side of the street. Maybe he just wants to say hello, maybe he wants to warn his buddy about the presence of the cops, but, whatever the reason, he calls out "Yo! Ricky!"

Cachie and Gregori stare at the fellow being hailed as Ricky, then look back at each other. A rapid exchange follows:

"Ricky? That's *Larry*."

"Larry *is* Ricky."

"That little bastard."

"Hey! You get over here," Cachie yells to the Ricky-Larry kid.

Instead, Ricky-Larry turns on his heels and breaks into a run in the opposite direction. Both Cachie and Gregori set off after him.

To understand the genesis of this incident, to understand how irritated the detectives are to discover "Larry is Ricky"—and why they care—you have to understand an encounter that took place in a central Brooklyn apartment two nights ago.

It's the apartment of a very frightened young woman who was said to be one of Halfback's other girlfriends. As the detectives were standing in her kitchen talking to her, she stood, practically frozen, staring at the floor in front of her refrigerator, responding, if at all, in an inaudible murmur. In the next room of the cramped apartment, a youth she identified as her brother Larry was sitting on a couch looking pensive and distracted. After the unhelpful talk with the terrified girlfriend, the detectives spent some time chatting up Larry. They ask him about his job, and he says he's working as an apprentice to a carpenter. They're pleased they've come upon at least one kid in the course of the investigation who's learning a legal trade. They talk to him about school; he responds with sincerity about finishing up high school. They encourage him, and as they leave, you can tell they're pleased he seems to have responded.

And now suddenly, here he is at the crack location. They realize his street name is Ricky, and that, in all likelihood, he's the same Ricky their informants have been saying followed Halfback to his death in the blue Olds. And when they see him turn and run in a guilty panic— it all makes them furious. Suddenly *they've* been the object of a deception; their earnest attempts to be "Larry's" confidants have allowed them to be taken in by the confidence man who's "Ricky."

In addition to being quick-witted, Ricky-Larry is fleet of foot, and it doesn't take the detectives long to realize they don't have a chance of catching him. They head back, feeling foolish and annoyed, sweaty and rain-soaked, and they proceed to make that visit to Eddie Holmes's store.

The two characters hanging out in the store are not pleased to see the detectives enter the premises. They are not eager to talk to them. They object strenuously to being separated for these proposed chats. Cachie has taken one by the elbow and is guiding him out of the store so they can talk outside under the awning, leaving Gregori to confer alone with the other fellow inside.

Outside, under the dripping awning, Cachie's guy proves no more willing to engage in a dialogue about the case; he's sullen and monosyllabic. He barely even looks at Cachie. In fact, it turns out he's looking over Cachie's shoulder at a third fellow who has appeared out of nowhere and is now loitering behind Cachie's back. Cachie whirls around and starts pointing at the loiterer, yelling to him to get lost, but the fellow refuses to retreat.

Cachie doesn't like this a bit. He strides over to this third individual, stands toe to toe with him and begins to make his point in more explicit terms.

It's not clear to me, since it happened so fast, who raised whose hands first or if hands were raised. But in the blink of an eye the loiterer was reeling backward as if he'd been given a powerful shove. He staggered backward, regained his balance but did not abandon his position completely. He yelled something at Cachie, and this time Cachie practically leaped forward at him; this time the loiterer had the practical wisdom to turn and run.

Back in the car afterward, Cachie is a bit abashed at losing his temper in this fashion. It is rare for him, a reserved phlegmatic type, to show his emotions that way. He tries to explain it to me and to himself.

"I was telling him I wanted to speak to his friend in private and he refused, and something he said just got me mad."

"What was it?" I ask.

"He just came back at me saying, 'I don't have to leave, this place is 'legal.' This place is legal—can you beat that? *That place!* There was just something about the way he said it that set me off. I don't know why, but it did."

It's possible to speculate, from what we know about Cachie's background, why he blew up over that exchange.

Cachie lives out in Suffolk County now, but when he drives through his old central Brooklyn neighborhood, and others like it, he can't help feeling pain and frustration over the way his hometown turf has been torn and ravaged by poverty, drugs and guns. It's not merely the physical deterioration, but the loss of the web of community there once was and the effect it's had on the generations of kids being destroyed by it all.

There's a conservative side to him that puts the blame for the situation on the failure of families to raise their kids right. But there's another side of him that sees the ravaged families, the whole ravaged community, as victims of malign neglect by a society that no longer feels the need to care very much about the destruction of generations of black children.

Things were bad enough before crack, now they look close to hopeless in many of these neighborhoods. Crack may be a symptom of a deeper disease, but it's no minor inflammation to the homicide cops who deal with its consequences. They all say there are more guns out on the streets—not cheap Saturday night specials, but the heavy 9 millimeter weapons favored by crack and coke dealers. One day in the Brooklyn morgue, Cachie picked up a bullet recently removed from a corpse whose case he was working on. The bullet casing looked shiny and undamaged.

"Teflon," he said.

"A Teflon bullet?"

"No, Teflon-coated. They're designed to go right through bulletproof vests. We're finding a lot of these lately."

The crack epidemic is something cops take personally. Not only has it made their caseload more dangerous, it's also damaged their reputation. The indictment last year of a dozen officers and former officers from Brooklyn's 77th Precinct on crack and corruption charges has made all cops touchy about crack cases.

And so, when the defiant loiterer at the crack location told Cachie, "This place is legal"—a phrase that carries a smirking insinuation that there's been a payoff to the law—it's not surprising it touched a raw nerve in the detective. It's almost as if that one remark triggered all the anger and frustration he's been feeling, not just over this case, but about what has happened to what was once his hometown.

Of course this case itself embodies a kind of touchy contradiction for Cachie. Because, after all, here he is, out in the streets of crack territory getting drenched in the rain, barging in on armed trigger-happy coke heads—for what? To bring the killers of a crack dealer to justice, to solve a murder which—although he personally does not use the phrase—fits into the category cynical detectives call "a community service homicide," the killing of someone who's been poisoning a community and making a cold-blooded profit on the destruction of a lot of lives.

So what's Cachie's motivation? It's the job he's paid to do, yes, it's a "good homicide," but there's something more than an intellectual challenge that keeps him going up dark staircases with gun at the ready looking for potential leads as he and Gregori do for two more hours tonight despite the downpour.

He's evidently given some thought to the question of his own motivation in a case like this. On the way back to his headquarters that night, after we drop Gregori off at the 71st Precinct, he tries to explain his thinking to me.

"Do you remember that fellow, Mr. Marshall, the gentleman on the ground floor with the broken lock?" Cachie asks me.

It was a scene that was hard to forget: the ground-floor apartment in a building overlooking the street where Halfback was first shot. Mr. Marshall was a tall dignified gentleman in his late 50s who made his living "in construction." He was still strong but it looked like a life of manual labor had begun to take its toll on him. So had the deterioration of the neighborhood. There was no lock on his apartment door. It had been broken off so many times by intruders that he could no longer afford to keep replacing it. Besides, he figured it was by now common knowledge there was nothing left in the apartment worth taking. In fact, the only appliance in his kitchen was a battered hotplate; the only furniture a peeling wooden table. He had a lot of sorrows, this man, but he bore them with dignity, and Cachie made a point of staying, listening and sympathizing—the guy seemed grateful for the company.

"Now there's a guy," Cachie is telling me, "who's worked all his life, paid his taxes, lived an honest life and what does he get for it? He gets a neighborhood where he can't keep a lock on the door and he can't afford to leave. So you ask me where's the motivation in a case like this where the deceased is a crack dealer? What it's really about is that gentleman there in that apartment. What's he got back? What's he got back? But at least if he sees, here I am, the representative of the law, I'm going around, I'm talking to people, I'm working on this case, it's not as if it's completely gotten to the point where people are shooting each other in the streets and nobody cares, nobody even notices."

"So you're saying that by being a presence, by showing him some element of the system is working, it's a signal to him that the situation here hasn't been completely abandoned?"

"That something is still functioning, yes."

"So, in a way, *he's* the victim you're working for?"

"That's one way of looking at it, yes."

●　　　■　　　●

Two days later in the squad room of the 71st Precinct: Cachie and Gregori are discussing the motive for Halfback's killing. The two detectives appear to be leaning in different directions on that question.

Gregori points to talk they've picked up that there was a contract out on Halfback's life—that his split with Eddie Holmes and his link to the kidnapping of Holmes's child "has got to be the factor."

Cachie now tends to believe that robbery was the motive. Halfback was known to have carried money and drugs in the Mercedes and, he believes, someone killed him for that. Cachie's established—by interviewing Halfback's girlfriends and determining what items of jewelry he habitually wore—that two rings and a neck chain were most likely ripped off his bleeding body in the car.

They're hoping to get some answers today as they head out, once again, to the crack location. After several hours of fruitless attempts to locate elusive figures in the case, they're parked opposite the game room trying to figure out their next move, when they spy someone drifting down the middle of the street toward them. They have a hunch they know who it might be.

"Well, will you look at that," says Gregori.

"Looks like he's been smokin' his brains," says Cachie.

Indeed, the person they're referring to does seem to be drifting rather than walking down the middle of the street, with a faraway crack-brained look in his eyes. He doesn't notice the detectives' car until he's right alongside. Cachie leaps out and takes him by the elbow.

In a few seconds they have him sitting in the front seat of their car. By this time he's snapped out of the crack cloud he's been in, and he's not happy about his situation. He's got his head in his hands, and he's staring down at the floor of the car.

This unhappy individual turns out to be Roy, the Halfback associate they've been trying to locate for a week now, the one who figured as a source of much of the rumor and gossip about the case, the one who seems to have been conducting his own personal investigation of his buddy's death.

"How'd you know I'd be here?" Roy demands sullenly, apparently under the impression they'd been lying in wait for him.

In fact, finding Roy was a lucky break, the sort that often occurs after detectives spend days pursuing fruitless leads. But the two men do not disabuse Roy of the notion of their omniscience. "We know *everything* about you, Roy," says Gregori.

Now they begin the process of trying to win Roy over. They suspect he may have the inside story of the case if they can get him to give it up.

Cachie puts the car in gear and heads off to the station house. It's going to be a delicate task getting Roy to give it up. What they've got going for them is Roy's predisposition to want to make trouble for the people who murdered his pal. Working against them is Roy's distrust of the police and the legal process. The decisive factor may well be that urge—the urge Roy feels to talk, to show off to the professional investigators just how much he, an amateur, has learned from *his* investigation.

On the drive over to the precinct house, the detectives make no mention of the case or the purpose of their drive. Instead, they try to engage Roy on a personal basis, and by the time they get to the precinct house, there's a kind of grudging rapport among them all. But it's still not easy getting him to give up what he knows.

There is, for instance, a moment, shortly after they've installed themselves and Roy behind the closed door of the windowless interrogation room at the back of the 71st Precinct detective unit, when they ask Roy who was driving the Mercedes that carried the wounded Halfback away.

"I didn't see," Roy says.

The detectives look at each other and frown at Roy.

"Remember what I told you about honesty," Cachie says sternly. "Now we know who's driving the Mercedes. I know it. The whole world knows it. In fact, I'm going to write it down on this piece of paper. Now you tell me who it is, and I'll show you what I've written, and I bet it's the same name."

"TNT," Roy mutters.

Cachie shows him the slip of paper on which he's written "TNT."

"See what I mean, I knew that, I know a lot more than you think. We've been talkin' to everybody on this case, we've got most of the pieces of the puzzle already, we just want your version."

Then Roy proceeds to tell them something they don't know, something that could be the key to the case. The way Roy tells it, it all began when a crack supplier by the name of Little Wayne "beat Halfback" for a couple of hundred dollars—shorted him on a dope delivery. Halfback then decided to teach Little Wayne a lesson; to beat him in return, but for $7,000. What Halfback did, Roy says, was make a newspaper-wrapped package just like the one he ordinarily made up to wrap his regular $7,000 payment to Little Wayne. Only this package contained no cash, just more newspapers. It was this ploy, says Roy, which led to the shooting.

It was not Little Wayne, however, who did the shooting. The guy with the silver revolver went by the street name of Surf, says Roy.

"Yes, we heard that," says Cachie, his face expressionless. In fact, this is the first time anyone they've talked to has given a name of any kind to the first shooter. But Cachie has told me that an important tactic detectives use when receiving a new piece of information is always to pretend they already know it. This serves two purposes. It reassures the person who tells them that he isn't out there alone as the only supplier of potentially dangerous information. And it encourages him to come up with something more, something to add to what is already "known."

What about the aftermath of the shooting on the street? Cachie asks Roy. What about the role of the "friends" of Halfback, the ones who were ostensibly taking him to the hospital?

Roy wasn't a witness to the final moments inside the Mercedes, wasn't a witness to the moment in which the final four bullets were fired into Halfback, but from all his sources, from the people who've talked to people who know, there's no doubt in his mind that it was the "friends" who did it. In fact, he says, he's even seen one of them wearing one of Halfback's rings. Another one, he says, showed up later wearing Half-back's beeper, a device Roy recognized by a telltale-dent in one corner. He also says there was money in the Mercedes that night belonging to Halfback, and he's sure it wound up in the same hands.

Once they've taken Roy through his story, Cachie and Gregori confer outside the interrogation room.

"We've got to get this guy down to the D.A. to give a sworn statement," Cachie says.

They realize this is not necessarily going to be an easy task: Roy is still suspicious of the legal process. They've established a conversational rapport, but will he back off when they take him down to the district attorney's office and ask him to give the kind of sworn testimony that carries more evidentiary weight than a precinct room rap?

Cachie walks back into the room and says to Roy, "Hey, you're gonna buy me lunch now, right?"

Roy grins. He likes Cachie, but he's smart enough to sense that something else is up.

"Don't have no money for lunch," he says warily.

"Don't hand me any bull," says Cachie, "you're the businessman. Come on, let's go, we're gonna get some lunch . . ."

Something happens on the way to "lunch" that may well be the decisive factor in getting Roy's cooperation. We are back in the detectives' car heading for "lunch," although Cachie means to make lunch downtown next to the D.A.'s office a preliminary to the taking of a statement. It seems to me that this might be a hasty move, that Roy is too jumpy and suspicious to go along with this.

But then Roy sees the Mercedes. We have taken a route through the precinct parking lot that leads right toward the black Mercedes sedan that had been Halfback's prized possession—and his death-bed.

Roy, who's sitting in the back seat, sits up and leans forward when he sees it.

"Half's Benz," he says softly, almost reverently. "Can I look?" he asks the detectives.

"What's there to see?" Cachie asks him.

"I just wanta look, man, let me out."

Cachie stops the car. Roy throws open the door and runs out. Both detectives stiffen a bit as they wonder whether he's just conned them into an opening to run away.

But, in fact, he runs directly to the door of "Half's Benz," opens it and gazes in.

It's not clear what's going through his mind as he stares at the bloodstains on the leather seat and the blood congealed on the cassettes. But it appears to have had some effect on him. He walks back to the detectives' car slowly, looking pensive.

Seeing the bloodstains that are the only visible traces of his crack-dealer hero's gaudy dream may have been a turning point in Roy's relationship to the cops. He sits in silence the rest of the way downtown and doesn't raise any objection when he learns the true nature of his final destination.

—*THE NEW YORK TIMES MAGAZINE*
February 1987

POSTSCRIPT TO "CRACK MURDER"

It was nearly a year after the breakthrough that concludes this story that indictments were filed and arrests made in the Halfback murder case. By then a special task force of Brooklyn detectives had been established, and the investigation was widened to include a series of related murders committed by one of the boldest and most sophisticated crack operations in Brooklyn, "The Wild Bunch," the Drexel Burnham of the new crack-dealing corporations in the borough. Shortly thereafter, Detective Al Cachie received a long-overdue promotion to Detective First Class.

THE CORPSE AS BIG AS THE RITZ

SARAH MILES, BURT REYNOLDS, AND THAT DIRTY LITTLE DEATH IN THE DESERT

Sergeant Forrest Hinderliter of the Gila Bend (Arizona) Police had been up since two in the morning with a dead body and a shaky story. He'd found the body—a black man with a bullet hole in his back—lying on the floor in Apartment 44 of the North Euclid Avenue project at the western edge of town. He'd also found a woman there, and this was her story:

She woke up after midnight to find a man on top of her, making love to her. She'd never seen the man before. She told him to get off and get out; she warned him she was expecting another man. A car pulled up outside and flashed its lights. A minute later the other man came through the door. Explanations were inadequate. In the scuffle a gun was drawn, a .38 revolver. A shot went off, the first visitor died.

An accident, the woman told Sergeant Hinderliter, the gun had gone off by accident. An accident, the other man, the one who owned the .38, told the sergeant.

Sergeant Hinderliter had the body tagged and carted off to Phoenix for an autopsy. He took statements until six thirty in the morning, then returned to the station house to check in for his regular Sunday tour of duty.

He was drinking black coffee at Birchfields's Café at six minutes past noon when the phone rang. It was Mrs. Steel, the station-house dispatcher, on the line. She had just taken a call from a man at the Travelodge Motel. There was a dead body in room 127, it was reported, an overdose of something.

●   ■   ●

Up until 1965 Gila Bend showed up frequently in National Weather Summaries as having registered the highest daily temperature in America. One hundred twenty in the shade was not unusual. Occasionally Gila Bend was referred to as the hottest place in America.

It was hot in Gila Bend, but not that hot, the Mayor of Gila Bend confided to me one evening at the Elks Club bar. Someone in Gila Bend had been doing some fooling around with the thermometer readings to make Gila Bend look a few degrees hotter than it was. In 1965, the Weather Bureau did some checking and put a stop to the matter. Since then Gila Bend has been just another hot place.

There's an old narrow-gauge railroad that runs south from the town to the open-pit copper mines near the Mexican border. The Phelps Dodge Corporation uses the railroad to run copper anodes from their foundries up to the Southern Pacific freight siding at Gila Bend. Hollywood Westerns occasionally use the railroad's ancient steam locomotive and the cactus wastes surrounding the tracks for "location" work.

On January 28, 1973, an MGM production company shooting *The Man Who Loved Cat Dancing*, a high-budget, middlebrow Western starring Sarah Miles, Burt Reynolds, and Lee J. Cobb, arrived at Gila Bend. Forty members of the cast and crew checked into the Travelodge Motel on the eastern edge of town.

●   ■   ●

There was no pulse. The skin had cooled. Pale blotches on the hands, the neck, and the forehead suggested to Sergeant Hinderliter that death had come to the body several hours before he had. Rigor mortis, in its early stages, had stiffened the arms which were wrapped around an empty polyethylene wastebasket. It was twelve thirty P.M.

The young man lay curled up on his left side on the floor of the partitioned-off "dressing-room" area of Travelodge room 127. His nose touched the metal strip which divided the carpeted dressing-room floor from the tiled floor of the bathroom. His feet stuck out beyond the end of the partition.

The capsules were big and red. There were about a dozen, and most of them lay in two groups on the floor. Burt Reynolds would later testify he saw pills lying on top of the dead man's arm.

The sergeant wondered why the man on the floor had decided to collapse and die in what was clearly a woman's bedroom: the vanity counter above the body teemed with vials of cosmetics, a woman's wardrobe packed the hangers, a long brown hairpiece streamed across a nearby suitcase. As he stepped out to his squad car Sergeant Hinderliter felt a hand on his arm. The hand belonged to an MGM official.

"He'd been drinking," the MGM man told the sergeant in a confidential tone. "He'd been drinking, he swallowed a lot of pills, he took a bunch of pills and he was dead. He took an overdose," the man said.

The sergeant asked the MGM person for the dead man's name and position.

The name was David Whiting, he told the sergeant. "He was Miss Miles's business manager. You see, that was Miss Miles's room he was in. It was Miss Miles who found him, but . . ."

"Where is Miss Miles?" the sergeant asked.

"She's over there in 123, Mr. Poll's room, now, but she's much too upset to talk. She's had a terrible experience, you can understand, and . . ."

"Yes, he was my business manager," the sergeant recalls Miss Miles telling him a few minutes later. "He was my business manager, but all he wanted to do was f—— me all the time and I wasn't going to be f——ed by him."

Sergeant Hinderliter is a mild-mannered and mild-spoken cop. He has a round open face, a blond crew cut, and a soft Arizona drawl. His dream at one point in his life was to earn a mortician's license and open a funeral home in Gila Bend, but after four years' study he dropped out of morticians' school to become a cop because he missed dealing with warm bodies. In his off-duty hours Sergeant Hinderliter is a scoutmaster for Troop Number 204. He recalls being somewhat surprised at Miss Miles's language. "Now I've heard that kind of talk sitting around with some guys," he told me. "But I never heard a lady use those words." (Later, as we shall see, Miss Miles denied she had used those words.)

Miss Miles was stretched out on one of the twin beds in room 123, her head propped up by pillows. Her face was flushed, her eyes streaked and wet. She was upset, she told the sergeant, but she was willing to talk.

I might as well tell you the whole story, she said.

The sergeant took notes, and this is the whole story she told that afternoon, as he remembers it:

It all started at the Pink Palomino café. There were a dozen of them there, movie people; they had driven thirty-six miles to the Palomino for a kind of pre-birthday party for Burt Reynolds who was to turn thirty-eight the next day, Sunday, February 11.

She had driven to the Pink Palomino with Burt Reynolds, but she left early and drove back to Gila Bend with Lee J. Cobb. She had wanted a ride in Cobb's impressive new car—a Citroën on the outside, a powerful Maserati racing engine within. Back at the Travelodge she proceeded to the cocktail lounge. She had one drink. She danced.

It was close to midnight when she started back to her own room. Halfway there she decided to stop by and apologize to Burt for failing to return to Gila Bend with him.

When she entered room 135, Reynolds's room, she found a Japanese masseuse there too. Sarah asked permission to remain during the massage. The Japanese woman rubbed, Sarah talked. Around three A.M. she left and walked around the rear of the building to her own room. As soon as she stepped into the room, she told the sergeant, David Whiting jumped out of the dressing room and grabbed her.

Whiting demanded to know where she'd been and whom she'd been with. She told him it was none of his business. He slapped her. She screamed. From the next room, the nanny Sarah had hired to look after her five-year-old son rushed into Sarah's room through a connecting door.

Sarah told the nanny to call Burt. David Whiting released Sarah and ran outside. Burt Reynolds arrived shortly thereafter and took Sarah back to his room where she spent the remainder of the morning.

Sometime later that Sunday morning, it may have been eight o'clock, it may have been ten, Sarah left Reynolds's room and returned to the nanny's room, number 126. She spoke briefly with the nanny, reentered her own room to use the bathroom, and found David Whiting's body on the floor. She gasped, ran back to the nanny's room, and told her to call Burt.

●   ■   ●

Gila Bend Coroner Mulford T. "Sonny" Winsor IV was still in bed Sunday afternoon when the dispatcher called him with news of the Travelodge death. He too had been up all night with the shooting death in the Euclid Street project. He had some questions. Had the dead black man, in fact, been a total stranger to the woman and the man with the .38, or had there been a more complicated relationship?

Coroner Winsor—he is also Justice of the Peace, Town Magistrate, Registrar of Vital Statistics, and a plumbing contractor on the side— wasted no time with the second body, the one he found at the Travelodge. There was nothing in room 127 to suggest anything but suicide. He rounded up a coroner's jury, including three Gila Bend citizens he found eating in the Travelodge Coffee Shop, and took them into room 127 to view the body for the record.

Next Coroner Winsor looked for some piece of identification for the death certificate, some proof that the dead man was in fact David Whiting. He bent over the body on the floor and reached into the pockets of the dark trousers. Nothing. Nothing in the right front pocket. He rolled the body gently over to look in the left front. There—no ID, but a key—a Travelodge key to room 127, Sarah's room, the room in which the young man died.

Coroner Winsor decided to check the young man's own room for identification. He ran back through the rain to the motel office, learned that David Whiting was registered to room 119, and ran back with a key.

He saw bloodstains as soon as he crossed the threshold of 119. There was blood on the pillow at the head of one of the twin beds. There was blood on the bath towel at the foot of the bed. There was blood, he soon discovered, clotted upon wads of toilet tissue in the bathroom. There was blood, he discovered later, on a Travelodge key on the other bed. It was a key for room 126, the nanny's room.

The death of David Whiting suddenly became a more complex affair. Had he been beaten before he died? The coroner called the chief of police over to room 119. The chief of police took one look and decided to call in the professionals from the Arizona State Police. There was the possibility of assault, even murder, to consider now.

●   ■   ●

Sarah Miles had a boil. The year was 1970 and Sarah Miles had come to Hollywood to do publicity for *Ryan's Daughter*. She had two appointments that afternoon: the first at noon with the show-business correspondent of *Time*, the next at three o'clock with a *Vogue* photographer. It was the *Vogue* appointment which worried her: *Vogue* wanted to feature her as one of the three most beautiful women in the world, and there, on her cheek, was a stubborn boil.

So she was not in an especially good mood as she sat in her bungalow at the Beverly Hills Hotel, waiting for the man from *Time* to arrive. Nor had her mood improved thirty minutes later when he finally showed up.

He wore a dark, three-piece English-cut suit, a luxuriously proper Turnbull and Asser shirt. He flashed a burnished-gold Dunhill lighter and a burnished-bronze hothouse tan. He removed a bottle from his suit coat, announced that it contained his personal Bloody Mary mix, and began the interview by discoursing at length upon the inadequacies of all other Bloody Marys. His name was David Whiting. He was twenty-four years old.

The subject of Sarah's boil came up. David Whiting confessed that he too had, on occasion, trouble with his skin. However, he told Sarah, he knew the *very best dermatologist in Hollywood*, and knew of an extraordinary pill for boils. Take one and ten minutes later, he promised Sarah, her boil would vanish.

He disappeared for ten minutes and returned with a bottle of the magic boil pills. She took one. The boil lasted much longer than ten minutes. The interview did not. As she went off to be the most beautiful woman in the world for *Vogue*, she assumed she had seen the last of David Whiting.

The next evening they met again. He requested the meeting, but despite his strange performance the first time, she didn't turn him down. She was amused by his pomposity, intrigued by his intelligence. She began calling him "Whiz Kid."

A few days later she was sitting in the V.I.P. lounge of the L.A. airport awaiting a flight to New York when David Whiting showed up and announced that he was taking the same flight. He secured the seat next to her. The next morning in New York he showed up in her suite at the Sherry Netherland. He took a room on the same floor. She never encouraged him, she says, but neither did she tell him to get lost.

Maybe it was the Vuitton luggage.

"He always had to have the best," she remembers. "All his doctors were the best doctors, his dentist was the very best dentist, Henry Poole was the very best tailor in London, everything with David had to be the best. If your agent wasn't the very best agent, then you had to change; if your doctor wasn't right, change, and he couldn't understand me because nothing I had was the best. . . . He'd spend hours at a restaurant choosing the best wines. . . . Suddenly he'd say to me, 'Do you have Vuitton luggage?' and I honestly had never heard of it. I said what was that word, and he said, '*Vuitton!* Come on! Don't pretend with me.'"

She wasn't pretending, she said. "It was funny. He was a *joke* in that he made people laugh. He was the sort of person you could send up . . . But David was the first person who awakened me to what was the best and what wasn't the best."

Then came the Working Permit Crisis. There was panic in the Sherry Netherland suite. For ten days Sarah had been unable to appear on American television because her working permit had not come through. A small army of MGM PR people scurried in and out of her suite reporting new delays and new failures, receiving scornful tongue lashings from Sarah.

"I began to get quite angry. I remember calling Jim Aubrey, the head of MGM you know, and telling him this is ridiculous, I've been here ten days, and this is ridiculous, all the money that's being wasted through these silly, interminable delays. And David Whiting was in the room with all these others and he started going, 'What's the matter? What happened? What happened? Working permit? Good God!' And he went straight to the phone and rang up a number and in half an hour my working permit arrived. . . . Literally in one telephone call I had a working permit which these other people hadn't been able to get for ten days. And I sort of thought, hmmmm, that's not bad. . . ."

Then there was the eye infection. "I came up with an eye infection and couldn't go on the Frost show . . . and he said, 'Oh, don't worry, I'll see to that,' and he took me across New York to an eye specialist, who gave me special stuff that cleared up my eyes. He was terribly efficient in certain areas, really terrifically efficient. Then he'd go over the top. Whenever he'd done something good, he'd get euphoric, and he'd suddenly go higher and higher and higher until he suddenly thought he was some sort of Sam Spiegel-cum-President-of-America and he'd go berserk in thinking he was terrific."

He followed her everywhere in New York. He was going to get *Time* to do a cover story on her. He arranged a lunch with Henry Grunwald, editor of *Time*, for her. Things didn't go smoothly. "You f——ed the whole thing up. You f——ed the whole thing," David screamed at her when she reported back to him. He continued to follow her.

A few days later he waved good-bye to her at Kennedy Airport as she took off for England, her country home, her husband, and her child. The next morning he knocked at the front door of her country home in Surrey. He was stopping by on his way to a skiing holiday, he told her. He stayed for a year.

● ■ ●

Sergeant Hinderliter didn't see the "star-shaped wound," as it came to be called, the first time he looked at David Whiting's body. Nor had he seen blood. But when he returned to room 127, Sarah's room, he was startled to see a pool of blood seeping out onto the tiles of the bathroom floor. The body seemed to be bleeding from the head.

Sergeant Hinderliter found the "star-shaped wound" at the back of the head, to the right of the occipital point. The wound had apparently stopped bleeding sometime after death, and resumed when the coroner rolled the body over to search for identification.

This "stellate or star-shaped contused laceration one inch in diameter . . . is the kind of injury we frequently see in people who fall on the back of the head," the autopsy doctor would testify at the coroner's inquest.

"This, of course, does not preclude," he added, "the possibility of the decedent having been pushed. . . ."

There were other marks on the body. Two "superficial contused scratches" on the middle of the abdomen. One "superficial contused abrasion" on the lower abdomen. Several scratches on the hands. There were "multiple hemorrhages"—bruises—on the chest and the left shoulder.

"Would those be consistent with someone having been in a scuffle or a fight?" the autopsy doctor was asked at the inquest.

"Yes," said the autopsy doctor.

But despite the suggestive marks on the outside of David Whiting's body, the cause of death, the autopsy doctor concluded, was to be found within.

A CATALOG OF THE VARIOUS DRUGS IN SARAH MILES'S BEDROOM
AS COMPILED BY DETECTIVE BARNEY HAYES AND CHEMIST JACK
STRONG OF THE ARIZONA STATE POLICE

ITEM ONE: some pills, multivitamin preparation

ITEM TWO: capsules, antibiotic drug

ITEM THREE: capsules, Serax Oxazepan, for treatment of anxiety and depression

ITEM FOUR: A—capsules of Dalmane which is a hypnotic and
B—some capsules which were not identified

ITEM FIVE: tablets, Methaqualone, which is a hypnotic antihistamine combination

ITEM SIX: some capsules, Ampicillin Trihydrate, which is an antibiotic

ITEM SEVEN: some further capsules which were not identified

ITEM EIGHT: some pills, Compazine, a tranquilizer

ITEM NINE: A—yellow tablets, Paredrine, which is a hypotensive and
B—some gray pills, Temaril, an antipruritic and antihistaminic

ITEM TEN: tablets of Donnatal which is antispasmodic and sedative

ITEM ELEVEN: white tablets, a yeast
ITEM TWELVE: a liquid, an anticough mixture

One item was missing from the scene. Burt Reynolds told Sergeant Hinderliter that when he had been summoned by Sarah to look at the body, he had noticed a pill bottle clenched in one of David Whiting's fists. He had pried it loose, Reynolds said, and rushed in to Sarah who was, by then, in room 123. He had shown her the bottle and asked her, "Do you know what these are?" She was too upset to reply, he said.

The pill bottle disappeared. Burt Reynolds doesn't remember what he did with it. He might have thrown it away in room 123, he said. He might have had it in his hand when he returned to 127, the room with the body in it. He remembers seeing a prescription-type label of some sort on it, but he doesn't remember what the label said. The pill bottle was never found.

And the pills on the arm: nobody seems to have explained the pills on the arm. David Whiting may have knocked some pills on the floor, but there would be no easy way for him to knock pills down onto his own arm while lying curled up on the floor. No one else in the case has admitted knocking them down onto his arm, or dropping them there.

●   ■   ●

There are other unanswered questions about the pills David took on his last night. Item Five on the list of Sarah's drugs is a pill called Mandrax. Mandrax is the English trade name for the formulation of two drugs. One—the main ingredient—is Methaqualone, which is described in medical literature as a "hypnotic," and as such occupies the drowsy middle ground between the barbiturates and the tranquilizers. The second ingredient in Mandrax tablets is a small amount of diphenhydramine which, under the more familiar trade name Benadryl, is marketed as an antihistamine and mild depressant.

American drug companies sell pure Methaqualone—without the Benadryl—under several trade names, including the one which had become a household word by the time David Whiting died: Quaalude.

The autopsy doctor found Methaqualone in David Whiting's body.

(There were 410 milligrams in his stomach, 7.4 mg. in his liver and .88 mg. per hundred milliliters—about 45 mg. altogether—in his bloodstream.) The doctor also found some Benadryl in his blood, along with half a drink's worth of alcohol and "unquantitated levels" of a Valium-type tranquilizer.

Where did that Methaqualone come from? Because of the presence of the Benadryl, it is possible to surmise that the pills David Whiting swallowed were Mandrax, rather than an American version of Methaqualone. Sarah Miles would later testify at the coroner's inquest that she "believed" she found "a few"—she was not sure how many—pills from Item Five, her Mandrax supply, missing after David Whiting's death. Sarah would also testify that she believed David Whiting no longer had a Mandrax prescription of his own because, she says, David's London doctor had taken David off the drug. But if David Whiting did take Mandrax that night it still cannot be said with absolute certainty that the tablets he swallowed did come from Sarah Miles's "Item Five."

Nor is there any certainty about the number of tablets David Whiting swallowed that night. Adding up the quantities of Methaqualone found in his stomach, blood, and liver, one finds a total of less than 500 milligrams. Since each Mandrax tablet contains only 250 milligrams of Methaqualone, it would seem that the residue of perhaps two, and no more than three, tablets was present in David Whiting's system at the time of his death. But there is no data available on how long he had been taking Methaqualone before that evening, nor whether he had developed a tolerance or sensitivity to the drug.

Was there enough Methaqualone in David Whiting's body to kill him? The autopsy doctor, you will recall, found less than one milligram per hundred milliliters in his blood. According to one traditional authority—*The Legal Medicine Annual* of 1970—it takes three times that amount, three milligrams per hundred milliliters, to kill an average man. However, about the time David Whiting died, the literature on Methaqualone had entered a state of crisis. The Great American Quaalude Craze of 1972 had produced a number of overdose deaths, and, consequently, a number of new studies of the kill-levels of the drug. The results of one of those studies—summarized in an article in a publication called *Clinical Chemistry*—was making the rounds of the autopsy world at the time of David Whiting's death. The *Clinical*

Chemistry article challenged the traditional 3-milligram kill-level, and suggested that less Methaqualone than previously suspected could cause death.

The Maricopa County autopsy doctor who first examined David Whiting cited these new, lower figures, plus the combined depressant effect of Benadryl, alcohol, and the "unquantitated levels" of another tranquilizer to explain why two or three tablets' worth of Methaqualone could have killed David Whiting. He called the old figures "insufficient and antiquated evidence."

But affidavits from a leading pharmacologist and a leading forensic pathologist introduced at the inquest by David Whiting's mother challenged the certainty of the original autopsy doctor's conclusion, especially his willingness to abandon the traditional authorities. "These reports have not been established in the literature," one of the affidavits said.

So great is the conflict between the new and old figures that a certain small dose cited in the new study as a poisonous "minimum toxic level" qualifies as a "therapeutic dose" under the old system.

These uncertainties placed David Whiting's final Mandrax dose in a disputed netherland between therapy and poison, leaving unanswered the questions of whether he took the tablets to calm down or to kill himself, or whether he killed himself trying to calm down.

SOME ITEMS FOUND IN DAVID WHITING'S TRAVELODGE ROOM (NUMBER 119):

—fifty-nine photographs of Sarah Miles
—a large leather camera bag stamped with a LIFE decal, four expensive Nikons inside
—a six-month-old *Playboy* magazine, found lying on the bottom sheet of the unmade, bloodstained bed, as if he had been reading it while he waited for the bleeding to stop
—a piece of luggage—a medium-sized suitcase—lying open but neatly packed on the other bed, as if in preparation for a morning departure and a two-day trip
—two bottles of Teacher's Scotch, one nearly empty, on the night table between the beds. Also a can of Sprite

—an Olivetti portable typewriter with the ribbon and spools ripped out and lying tangled next to it

—a book called *The Mistress*, a novel, the film rights to which David Whiting had purchased on behalf of Sarah Miles. He wanted her to play the title role.

—a copy of a screenplay called *The Capri Numbers*, a romantic thriller David Whiting had been working on with an English actor. Sarah Miles was to play the part of Jocylin. In the screenplay's preliminary description of Jocylin we learn that "this story will teach her the meaning of 'there's a vulgarity in possession: it makes for a sense of mortality.' "

—a Gideon Bible. The Bible is not mentioned in police reports, but when I stayed in David Whiting's motel room a month after his death, I looked through the Bible and found three widely separated pages conspicuously marked, and one three-page section torn out.

The upper-right-hand corner of page 23 has been dog-eared. On page 23 (Genesis: 24–25) we read of, among other things, the death and burial of Sarah.

The lower-left-hand corner of page 532 has been dog-eared. It contains Psalms 27 and 28—each of which is headed, in the Gideon edition, "A Psalm of David." In these two psalms, David pleads with God not to abandon him. ("Hide not thy face far from me; put not thy servant away in anger . . . leave me not, neither forsake me.") David declares he wants to remain "in the land of the living" but warns that "if thou be silent to me I become like them that go down into the pit."

The upper-left-hand corner of page 936 has been dog-eared. The Last Supper is over. Christ, alone on the Mount of Olives, contemplating his imminent crucifixion, asks God, "If thou be willing, remove this cup from me." He prays feverishly ("his sweat was as it were great drops of blood"), then descends to his disciples, whereupon Judas betrays him with a kiss.

Torn out of the Gideon Bible in David Whiting's motel room are pages 724 to 730. Consulting an intact Gideon

Bible, I discovered that those pages record the climactic vision of the destruction of Babylon from the final chapters of the Book of Jeremiah, and the despairing description of the destruction of Jerusalem from the beginning of Lamentations.

"I shall make drunk her princes and her wise men," says the Lord in regard to his plans for the rulers of Babylon, ". . . and they shall sleep a perpetual sleep and not wake." "I called for my lovers but they deceived me . . . my sighs are many and my heart is faint," says the weeper in the torn-out pages of Lamentations.

—Police found no suicide note.

Four months after he moved into Mill House, her country home in Surrey, David Whiting threatened to kill himself, Sarah Miles told me. The threat was powerful enough, she says, to prevent her and her husband from daring to ask him to leave for six more months.

Just what was David Whiting doing, living in the household of Mr. and Mrs. Robert Bolt, Mill House, Surrey, anyway?

At first he was just stopping off on his way to a European ski resort. Then he was staying awhile to gather more material for his *Time* story. His "angle" on this story, he told them, was going to be "the last happy marriage" or something like that. He did not believe in happy marriages, didn't believe they could exist anymore, yet here Sarah and Robert Bolt had what appeared to be a happy marriage and he wanted to find out just what it was they had.

Then David thrust himself into the *Lady Caroline Lamb* project, a kind of family enterprise for Robert Bolt and Sarah. When David arrived in the summer of 1971, *Lamb* was only a screenplay. Robert Bolt—the forty-nine-year-old playwright who wrote *A Man for All Seasons* and several David Lean screenplays—had written it, he wanted Sarah to star in it, he wanted to direct it himself. He was having trouble getting the money for it.

As soon as David arrived he jumped in, started calling producers, money people, studios, agents. He whisked Sarah off to Cannes, rented a villa there for the film festival the better to make "contacts." He went to work on her finances, clearing up a "huge overdraft" in Sarah's account. He talked her into getting new lawyers, new accountants, new agents. He flattered Robert Bolt about his writing, Sarah about her acting. He quite his job at *Time* to devote himself to helping them make *Lamb*, he told them. He persuaded Sarah to make him her business manager, which meant he got ten percent of whatever she got. He persuaded Robert and Sarah to give him a salaried job in their family film company—Pulsar Productions Ltd. On the Pulsar stationery he became "David Whiting, Director of Publicity and Exploitation."

Lamb is a triangle. A year after he moved in with Robert Bolt and Sarah, David Whiting produced a publicity book about the film. This is how he describes that triangle:

There is Lady Caroline, to be played by Sarah Miles: "On fire for the dramatic, the picturesque . . . a creature of impulse, intense sensibility and bewitching unexpectedness," David wrote. "On those for whom it worked she cast a spell which could not be resisted. . . . Such a character was bound finally to make a bad wife." She ends up dying "for love." "And so at the end of her short life, she achieved the ultimate gesture which all her life she has been seeking."

Then there is her husband William Lamb, ultimately to become Lord Melbourne, the Whig Prime Minister: "A Gentleman, self-controlled and decent," David wrote. "A capacity for compromising agreeably with circumstance . . . When Caroline threw herself into her notorious affair with Lord Byron, William refused to take it seriously. . . . He detected in Byron all that was specious in the poet's romantic posturing . . . he was not jealous but his spirit was wounded."

And finally there was Byron: "He was a raw nerve-ridden boy of genius," David wrote, "a kind of embodied fantasy . . . emerged from obscurity . . . born to nobility and relative poverty. With his pale face, extreme good looks and pouting expression . . . the public was entranced with the personality of its twenty-four-year-old author. Nevertheless," twenty-four-year-old David Whiting added, his "divine fire gleamed fitfully forth through a turmoil of suspicion and awkwardness. His sophistication was a mask for shyness. . . . At the most elementary level he was a poseur."

Halfway into an interview with Sarah Miles I read her that passage about Byron from David's book about *Lamb*, and asked her if that was, perhaps, David Whiting writing about himself.

"I think he got that from Lord David Cecil, actually," she said. "Most of it you'll find is from other books, I'm afraid."

I tried again: "What I mean is, did he see the family he moved into at Surrey as a kind of reflection of the Lamb triangle?"

"The Lamb triangle? I see what you mean. It hadn't crossed my mind until you said it. Maybe you're right. I hadn't thought of it like that at all."

At this point I felt compelled to ask directly, and yet if possible with some delicacy, the question that had been on my mind.

"It seems, uh, a probably fortuitous coincidence that this *Lamb* thing was going on at the same time David was, uh, well, what *was* your, what was his relationship, was he sexually possessive or . . .?"

"Nope," Sarah interrupted briskly. "Not a bit. You see, this is the area which is weird. He never made a pass at me, he never spoke of me sexually, it was just a sort of"—pause—"I don't quite know how to put it—it seems so self-*brag*ging, you know, to say the things he said—I can't really, because I don't really—I think he, he wanted to put me up *there*, because it would sort of excuse himself from any sort of reality. I think if he had really made an ordinary mundane *pass* and been rejected, it would have ruined this other image that he had. You know what I mean, I mean if at one time we really *had* had an affair, it would have probably been the best thing for David. I mean he probably would have realized that I was just an ordinary girl like the rest of them."

At this point I thought of what Sergeant Hinderliter had told me Sarah had told *him* on the afternoon of the death, about David Whiting "always wanting to f—— me all the time. . . ."

Now that statement did not imply that Sarah Miles had, in fact, slept with David Whiting. It did however raise the question in my mind about whether David Whiting had or had not ever made "a mundane pass" at Sarah, and I felt I had to ask her about it.

"Sarah, uh, I feel I have to ask you this, it's, uh, a difficult question," I faltered, toward the close of the interview. "But, uh, this sergeant in Gila Bend told me that you told him that all David Whiting wanted to do . . ." I repeated what the sergeant had quoted her as saying.

She skipped, at most, one third of a breath.

"There have been some *extraordinary* reports from those policemen, I mean there really have." She gave a small sigh. "I mean I don't understand what this is *about*. Well I went back into the room, well, there's a whole area in there the police were . . . *very odd indeed*, and I don't *understand*, I mean that quote. . . . What time? When?"

I told her when the sergeant said he heard it.

"I mean, can you imagine, can you imagine me saying this to a policeman, that anyone in their right mind could say that. . . ."

"I can imagine you being upset and—"

"But to say *that!* I'm terribly sorry but I'm not the liar in this case."

●   ■   ●

It was not sex David Whiting wanted so desperately, Sarah told me, it was family. He'd never had a real family before, he'd told the Bolts. His parents divorced when he was a child, he'd hardly seen his father, who, he said, was some sort of director of Pan Am, a position which gave David the right to fly the world for next to nothing. He'd been a child prodigy, he told them, and his mother had sent him off to one boarding school after another. He'd had some unpleasant years in boarding schools. He was too smart for any of them, but they'd treated him badly. Once he said he had been forced to submit to a spinal injection to cure a "learning deficiency" because he'd been stubbornly pretending he didn't know how to read. So painful was this spinal injection that he'd immediately picked up a volume of Shakespeare and started to perform from it just to forestall repetition of that pain. He'd gone to the finest prep school in Washington, D.C., with the sons of the famous and powerful. He'd become an extraordinary ladies' man among the debutante daughters of the famous and the powerful, he told them. He dropped names of his conquests.

His pre-school classmates thought he would become President, he told the Bolts. But what he wanted to be, he told them, was the greatest producer there ever was. At an early age he had taken off from school to make movies in the Libyan desert and the hot spots of Europe. He had been the youngest man ever appointed full-fledged *Time* correspondent, but he had given all that up for Sarah and Robert and for what they could become under his management. He wanted to make Sarah the greatest star there ever was. For all that, he told them, but also for their home, and for the feeling of being part of a family at last.

But after three months things started to go wrong in this family.

David became dissatisfied with mere "publicity-and-exploitation" duties. He wanted to do more. Nobody understood how good he was, nobody gave him a chance to show how much he could do. He decided to show them. Without the consent of the producer of *Lamb* he arranged a deal to produce a movie of his own—a documentary about the making of *Lamb*. This didn't go over well with the real producer. He made enemies. He started staying up in his room for days at a time, according to Sarah, worrying about his skin problem, his weight problem, his falling-hair problem, claiming all the while that he was working on scripts and deals, but failing to do his publicity work on time. Finally, according to Sarah, he was fired from his publicity job. She was the only one to take his side, she says. She kept him on as business manager, but both she and Robert suggested to David that he might be happier and get more work done if he moved out of their country home into Sarah's London town house.

It was at this point, September, 1971, according to Sarah, that David told them that if they ever forced him to leave their family he'd kill himself.

She found it hard to take this threat lightly, Sarah says. Twice before she'd been threatened that way, and twice before she'd ended up with a dead body on her hands. Sarah tells the story of the first two suicides.

First there was Thelma. Thelma had gone through Roeder, the exclusive Swiss finishing school, with Sarah. Since then Thelma had gone through hard times and electroshock treatment. She'd read a newspaper report that Sarah had taken a town house at 18 Hasker Street, Chelsea; she showed up there one day and asked to move in for a while.

Thelma stayed three years. She moved her young son in with her. Sarah gave her a "job" to earn her stay—walking Sarah's Pyrenean mountain dog—but Thelma forgot about it half the time. At night, according to Sarah, "she turned the place into a brothel," admitting a stream of men into her basement quarters. Finally, after Thelma had taken two messy overdoses, Robert Bolt came into Sarah's life and told her she had to get rid of Thelma.

"I told Robert if I chucked her out she'd kill herself," Sarah recalls. "And Robert said, 'Christ, Sarah, grow up. They all say that but not all of them do it.' Robert got to arguing with Thelma one day and said,

'Look, for Christ sake Thelma, can't you see what you're doing to Sarah? If you really mean business you'll jump.' "

Sarah asked Thelma to leave. Thelma jumped.

Then there was Johnny. Sarah had been kicked out of her Chelsea town house because of the obtrusive behavior of her Pyrenean mountain dog. Sarah and Robert had married and were moving to a country home in Surrey. Johnny came along. He was a landscape gardener and owner of three Pyrenean mountain dogs. "I decided to sublease the Chelsea house to him. I thought it would be a very funny joke, having been kicked out for one, to move in somebody with *three* Pyrenean mountain dogs. That tickled me. I liked that," Sarah says.

Johnny was very well dressed, and told the Bolts he was very well off. "But I let him have it for almost nothing, he was a friend, we'd have him up for weekends, he was a very charming fellow, he was a queer but a very nice man—boy."

After nine months Johnny hadn't paid a cent of rent.

"Robert told me, 'Sarah, you're crazy to let this go on. . . . Go up there and get the money.' So on a Friday I went up. The house looked lovely . . . he had a fantastic deep freeze, fantastic food, new carpets—he lived very high."

She asked him for the money. He said of course he'd give it to her—the very next day.

The next morning, back at her country home, she received a telephone call from a policeman. "He asked me if I were Sarah Miles, and did I own 18 Hasker Street, and I said yes, and he said Mr. Johnny W—— has put his head in the oven, he's gassed himself to death. . . ."

In mid-February of 1972, David Whiting moved into 18 Hasker Street.

On the second day of March, 1972, David Whiting was rushed to St. George's Hospital, London, unconscious, dressed only in his underwear, suffering from an overdose of drugs. After his release, Sarah and Robert took him back again.

One evening later that year David Whiting was drinking in London with a woman writer who was preparing a story about Sarah Miles. He began confiding in her about his dream. Robert Bolt was nearing fifty, he observed, while he, David Whiting, was only half that age. He could wait, he told her, wait for Robert Bolt to die, and then he knew

Sarah would be his at last. The woman writer seemed to think David Whiting was being deadly serious.

●   ■   ●

Not enough people die in Gila Bend to support a funeral home. So when the autopsy doctor in Phoenix completed his work on David Whiting, he sewed the body back up and shipped it to Ganley's funeral establishment in Buckeye—thirty miles north of Gila Bend—to await claiming by next of kin.

There was some question about next of kin. David Whiting had filled in the next-of-kin blank on his passport with the name "Sarah Miles." No other next of kin had stepped forward. For three days no one seemed to know if David Whiting's parents were dead or alive. Finally on Wednesday the Gila Bend chief of police received a call from a woman on the East Coast who said she had once been engaged to David Whiting. Among other things she told the chief the name of a person on the West Coast who might know how to reach the mother. After several further phone calls, the chief finally learned of a certain Mrs. Campbell of Berkeley, California.

On Thursday, February 15, a small gray-haired woman stepped off the Greyhound bus in Buckeye, Arizona. She proceeded to Mr. Ganley's establishment on Broadway and introduced herself to Mr. Ganley as Mrs. Louise Campbell, the mother of David Whiting. She persuaded Mr. Ganley to drive her into Gila Bend to see the chief of police.

There was trouble in the chief's office that day. As soon as she walked in Mrs. Campbell demanded to know how the chief had located her. No one was supposed to know where she was. She demanded to be told who had tipped him off. The chief asked her about David Whiting's father. She told him they had been divorced long ago. She told him that three weeks before David's death the father had suffered a near-fatal heart attack and was not to be contacted under any circumstances. Her present husband, David's stepfather, was spending the winter in Hawaii for his poor health and she didn't want him contacted either. She said she wanted David Whiting's personal property. The chief told her he couldn't release it to her until after the completion of the inquest, scheduled for February 27. He agreed to allow her to select a suit for David to be buried in.

"The chief opened up the suitcase and she grabbed everything she could and ran outside to the car with it, clutching it in her arms," Mr. Ganley recalls with some bemusement. . . . "Oh, she went running from one room to the other in the police station and finally the chief said, 'Get her the hell out of here, will you?' She grabbed everything she could get before they could stop her. I was picking out certain belongings in which to bury him. She just grabbed them. . . ."

Ten days later, Mrs. Campbell reappeared at Mr. Ganley's funeral home. It was nine o'clock at night. She was accompanied by an unidentified man.

She asked Mr. Ganley to take the body out of the refrigerator. She wanted to examine it, she said.

Mr. Ganley protested, "I said, 'Well, lady, why don't you take him into the County Mortuary . . . we don't like to show a body like this, he isn't clothed, he's covered with, uh . . . he's been in the refrigerator.' She said, 'Well, that's all right.'"

Mr. Ganley took the body out of the refrigerator and wheeled it out for Mrs. Campbell's inspection.

"She wanted to know if all his organs were there," Mr. Ganley recalled. "She said, 'Could you open him up?' I said no, we won't do that. Well, she wanted to know if the organs were there and I said well I presume they are."

A few days later Mrs. Campbell showed up at Ganley's funeral home again, this time with a different man, whom she introduced as a pathologist from a neighboring county. Again she demanded that the body be brought out of the refrigerator for inspection. Again, with reluctance, Mr. Ganley wheeled it out.

Mr. Ganley asked this pathologist if he had any documentary proof that Mrs. Campbell was, in fact, the boy's mother.

"He told me that he just assumed that she was. So I said well, okay, go ahead. So he opened him up and checked the organs, to see if they had all been returned after the first autopsy."

It was during this session, Mr. Ganley recalled, that Mrs. Campbell did some checking of her own. She examined the star-shaped wound on the back of the head and found it sewn up. She complained to Mr. Ganley about that.

"She asked me why we did that, and I said, well, to keep it from leaking all over the table. And she said, 'Don't do anything else to it.' And then she'd probe up in there with her finger."

"She actually put her finger in it?"

"Oh yeah . . . She never expressed one bit of grief except when I first saw her and she sobbed . . . well, one night she kissed him and said poor David or something."

●   ■   ●

How badly had David Whiting beaten Sarah Miles? You will recall that Sergeant Hinderliter remembers Sarah telling him on the afternoon of the death that David Whiting had "slapped" her. It was the sergeant's impression that Sarah meant she had been slapped just once. He had asked her where Whiting had slapped her. She had pointed to the left side of her head. The sergeant does not recall seeing any marks, or any bruises, or any blood. Eleven days later Sarah told the police and the press that David Whiting had given her "the nastiest beating of my life."

This is how she described it:

"He started to throw me around the room like they do in B movies. . . . This was the most violent ever in my life. I was very frightened because all the time I was saying, 'Hold your face, Sarah, because you won't be able to shoot next day' . . . he was beating me on the back of my head . . . there were sharp corners in the room and he kept throwing me against them . . . I was just being bashed about . . . he was pounding my head against everything he could . . . it was the nastiest beating I've ever had in my life. It was even nastier because it was my friend you see."

A lot had happened between the Sunday afternoon of February 11 when Sarah told Sergeant Hinderliter about being slapped and the evening of February 22 when she told the Arizona State Police about the "nastiest beating."

On Monday morning, February 12, an MGM lawyer named Alvin Cassidy took an early plane from L.A. to Phoenix, drove out to Gila Bend, and advised members of the cast and crew of *The Man Who Loved Cat Dancing* that it would not be wise to talk to detectives from the State Police without the advice of counsel. MGM people stopped talking.

On Monday afternoon the cast and crew of *Cat Dancing* began checking out of the Travelodge and heading for a new location two hundred miles southeast in the town of Nogales on the Mexican border.

On Monday evening Rona Barrett broke the story on her nationally syndicated Hollywood gossip show.

Rona had sensed something funny going on the night before when she attended the Directors' Guild premiere of *Lady Caroline Lamb*. Someone had given Rona a tip that Robert Bolt, who was attending the premiere of his film, had received a "very upsetting phone call."

Monday morning Rona began talking to her sources in Gila Bend. By Monday evening she was able to tell her national audience of a report that Sarah Miles had been beaten up in her motel room by her business manager, a former *Time* correspondent. Rona called it "the alleged beating"—alleged because, according to Rona's sources on location, Sarah Miles was "on the set the next day showing no signs of having been attacked."

On Wednesday of that first week, MGM hired two of the best criminal lawyers in Arizona—John Flynn of Phoenix and Benjamin Lazarow of Tucson—to represent Sarah, Burt, and the nanny.

The MGM legal armada at first succeeded in working out a deal with the detectives. Sarah, Burt, and a few others would tape-record informal, unsworn statements about the night of the death, and answer, with the help of their attorneys, questions put to them by detectives. The detectives and the County Prosecutor made no pledge, but MGM hoped, through this taping device, to avoid having Sarah and Burt and the rest of the cast subpoenaed to testify publicly at the forthcoming coroner's inquest.

These recorded interviews with the detectives, which have come to be known as the "Rio Rico tapes," took place on Thursday, February 22, at the Rio Rico Inn of Nogales, Arizona, where the MGM people were quartered. Sarah's description of the violent, nasty beating, quoted above, comes from one of these tapes.

The deal fell through. Gila Bend Justice of the Peace Mulford Winsor, who was to preside at the inquest, was not satisfied with this absentee-testimony arrangement. He issued subpoenas for Sarah, Burt, Lee J. Cobb, the nanny, and the two other MGM people, commanding them to appear in person in Gila Bend on February 27 to take the stand and testify.

MGM's legal forces promptly went to court. They asked that the subpoenas be quashed on the ground that appearances at the inquest would subject the six people to "adverse publicity and public display."

On February 27, just a few minutes before the inquest was about to open in Gila Bend, Justice of the Peace Winsor was served with a temporary restraining order barring him from calling Sarah or Burt to testify. Justice Windsor decided to proceed with the inquest without them, and called Sergeant Hinderliter to the stand as the first witness.

But the movie company had not counted on the determination of tiny, gray-haired Mrs. Campbell, who turned out to be a shrewd operator despite her fragile, grief-stricken appearance.

Early that morning in Phoenix Mrs. Campbell had hired her own lawyer, presented him with a thousand-dollar retainer, and told him to contest the MGM injunction. Then she caught the first bus out to Gila Bend. On the bus she sat next to a reporter for the London *Sun* who was on his way out to cover the inquest. She introduced herself to the English reporter as a correspondent for a Washington, D.C., magazine and asked him for the details of the case. She wanted to know whether it were possible to libel a dead man.

When she arrived at the courthouse, a one-story concrete all-purpose administrative building, Mrs. Campbell began passing out to the press Xeroxed copies of a document which she said was David Whiting's last letter to her, a document which proved, she said, that David Whiting was neither unhappy nor suicidal. (While this "last letter" certainly did not give any hint of suicidal feelings, neither did it give a sense of much intimacy between mother and son. David Whiting began the letter by announcing that he was sending back his mother's Christmas present to him, and went on to request that she send instead six pairs of boxer shorts. "I find the English variety abominably badly cut," he wrote. "Plaids, stripes, and other bright colors would be appreciated, and I suggest you unwrap them, launder them once, and airmail them to me in a package marked 'personal belongings.'"

Next Mrs. Campbell approached Justice Winsor and asked him to delay the start of the inquest until her lawyer, who she said was on his way, could be present to represent her. She didn't give up when he refused and opened the inquest. She continued to interrupt the proceedings in her quavering voice with pleas for a recess to await the appearance of her lawyer. At one point Justice Winsor threatened to have her removed.

It came down to a matter of minutes. By midafternoon the two men from the County Attorney's office conducting the inquest had called their last witness, and the Justice of the Peace was about to gavel the inquest to a close and send the coroner's jury out to decide the cause of David Whiting's death. At the last minute, however, the judge received a phone call from the presiding Justice of the Superior Court in Phoenix. Mrs. Campbell had secured an order preventing the coroner's jury from beginning its deliberations until a full hearing could be held on the question of whether Sarah, Burt, and the nanny should be forced to appear in person to testify. Justice Winsor recessed the inquest, and Mrs. Campbell walked out with her first victory. She'd only just begun. On March 7, after a full hearing, the court ruled in her favor and ordered Sarah, Burt, and the nanny to appear at the inquest. Finally, on March 14, the three of them returned to Gila Bend and took the stand, with Mrs. Campbell seated in the front row of the courtroom taking notes.

There were strange stories circulating about Mrs. Campbell. There was a rumor that she might not be the boy's mother at all. Other than the "last letter," she hadn't shown any identification to Mr. Ganley. The copy of the last letter she was handing around showed no signature. Mrs. Campbell said she herself had written the word "David" at the bottom of the copy. She had left the original with the signature at home, she said. "Naturally I treasure it . . . that's why I didn't bring it."

Mrs. Campbell refused to give me her home address or phone number. She insisted on keeping secret the whereabouts of both David Whiting's real father and his stepfather, her present husband. She implied that anyone attempting to contact the real father, who was recovering from a recent heart attack, might cause his death: she was protecting him from the news, she said.

She described herself as a free-lance science writer, as a former writer for *Architectural Forum*, as a member of the faculty of the University of California at Berkeley, and as retired. She insisted at first that her married name was spelled without a "p" in the middle. Then suddenly she began insisting that it was spelled with a "p."

She described herself frequently as "a woman without means," and a "woman living on a fixed income," but she hired four of the top lawyers in the State of Arizona to work on the case. She claimed to have flown to England with her aging mother to visit David a few months before he died.

"My only interest in this whole affair is to protect the name of my son," she maintained. "He was not a suicidal type, he was not the type to beat up women."

She was curiously silent about certain areas and curiously ill-informed about others. There was his marriage, for instance. Mrs. Campbell led me to believe that I was the first person to tell her that her son had been married. This revelation took place in the Space Age Lodge, a motel next to the Gila Bend Courthouse building, a motel distinguished by the great number of "life-sized" Alien Beings crawling over its roofs and walls. The second session of the inquest—the one at which Sarah and Burt had finally testified—had just come to an end and Mrs. Campbell was seated at a table in the Space Age Restaurant handing out copies of various affidavits to reporters and occasionally responding to questions.

"Mrs. Campbell, has David's ex-wife been in touch with you?" I asked.

"His what?" she demanded sharply.

"His ex-wife, the one who—"

"David was never married," she said firmly.

"What about the London *Express* story which said he was married to a Pan Am stewardess, and that he used her Pan Am discount card to fly back and forth to England?"

"What wife? What are you talking about? Where did you read that? I never heard of any marriage."

(It is possible that she may have been feigning surprise here, although to what purpose is not clear. The mother of the girl he married told me she herself was certain her daughter never married David Whiting. Nevertheless there *is* a marriage certificate on file with the Registrar of Vital Statistics, Cook County, Illinois, which records the marriage of David Andrew Whiting to Miss Nancy Cockerill on January 29, 1970. Apparently there was a divorce also, because the wife is now remarried and living in Germany.)

Later that same day I had a long talk with Mrs. Campbell in the coffee shop of the Travelodge Motel, where she was staying during the inquest.

He was born in New York City on either August 25 or 26, she told me. "I'm not sure which is the right one, but I remember we always used to celebrate it on the wrong day." She leaps quickly to prep school. "He did so well at St. Albans that he was admitted to Georgetown University on a special program after his junior year and . . ."

When I asked her where David lived, and where he went to school before prep school, she cut off my question. "I don't see what that has to do with anything. I prefer not to tell you." She proceeded to attempt to convince me to drop my story on David Whiting and instead write an "exposé" of one of the Arizona lawyers hired by MGM, and "how these attorneys use their power and influence in this state." She would give me inside information, she said.

"It was always expected that David would go to Harvard," she began again when I declined to drop the story and returned to the subject of David Whiting. "For a boy of David's ability it was perfectly obvious he was headed for Harvard."

He didn't make it. Something about too many debutante parties, and not quite terrific grades in his special year at Georgetown. David Whiting went to tiny Haverford College instead. He majored in English there and wrote an honors thesis "on F. Scott Fitzgerald or Hamlet, I can't remember," Mrs. Campbell told me.

"There was a line from *The Great Gatsby* I do remember," she told me. "That was David's favorite book, and it's a line I think applies to what I saw here today. It was about the kind of people who always have others around to clean up the mess they leave."

I later checked the Scribner edition of *The Great Gatsby*: "They were careless people, Tom and Daisy—they smashed up things and creatures and then retreated back into their money or their vast carelessness, or whatever it was that kept them together, and let other people clean up the mess they had made."

●   ■   ●

A Fitzgerald Story of Sorts:
She met him at Mrs. Shippens' Dancing Class. Her name was Eleanor,

and she was a granddaughter of F. Scott Fitzgerald and Zelda. He was—well, she never knew who he was, in the sense of family, but it was assumed that the dancing students at Mrs. Shippens' were from the finest families of Washington, Virginia, and Eastern Shore society. He certainly acted the part. His name was David Whiting.

When the male pupils at Mrs. Shippens' reached a certain age, they were placed on Miss Hetzel's list. Miss Hetzel's list was a register of eligible males worthy of being called upon to serve as escorts and dancing partners at the finest debuts and cotillions.

Eleanor met him again at a Hunt Cup weekend. She found him sometimes witty, sometimes amusingly pretentious in his efforts to be worldly. In November, 1963, she wrote him inviting him to be her escort at a holiday dance at Mrs. Shippens'. She still has his letter of reply, because of a curious device he employed in it.

Centered perfectly between the lines of his letter to her were the unmistakable impressions of what seemed to be a letter to another girl. This ghostly letter in-between-the-lines was filled with tales of nights of drinking and lovemaking in expensive hotel suites with a girl named "Gloria." Eleanor is certain there was no Gloria, that the whole thing was an elaborate fake designed to impress her, if not with its truth, at least with its cleverness.

"He was always worrying about the way he looked—we'd be dancing or something and he'd always be checking with me how he looked, or giving me these, you know, aristocratic tips about how *I* looked, or *we* looked."

And how did he look?

"Well, he was very fat at first, I think."

"Fat?"

"Oh, quite tremendous. I mean pretty heavy. He'd make jokes about himself. But then all that changed. He spent a summer in North Africa and Libya with a movie production company. He came back from that summer looking much more thin and intense," she remembers. "He came back and all he was talking about was taking over that movie company, and oh, he had great dreams. I remember taking a walk with him—we were at some party and we were both nervous, and we took a walk through this garden and he just went on and on, just—it was the first time I'd seen him thin and he was talking about how he was gonna take over that movie company, and how great he'd been and how he was going to be a producer. . . . He'd always talked about movies, he could name every movie and every movie star that was in them—I mean, some people do that but he was *good*, he knew them *all*."

She drifted away from him—"He was never my boyfriend or anything," she says pointedly—and didn't hear from him for almost two years when one day she got a phone call in her dorm at Sarah Lawrence.

It was David Whiting, then a student at Haverford. "Well, I hadn't seen him and I didn't know where he was at school, and he said, 'Will you come and see me, I'm at Princeton.' So I took the bus down. I got there I guess about nine in the morning, and called him up and he said could I come over to the room—I didn't know it wasn't his room—so I walked in and he just poured this tall glass of straight gin and no ice and said, 'Will you have some?' And I said, 'No, I don't really think I'm in the mood, I was sort of wondering what we're gonna do today,' and he said, 'Well, I think we'll stay in the room until tonight when we'll go over to some clubs.' I could sort of see the day's program unfolding. . . ."

For the next two hours he tried to convince her to sleep with him. "It could be really boring the way he talked about himself so much and how his ego would be damaged if I didn't sleep with him. I remember it was this scene of me sitting up, you know, every once in a while, and we'd talk and we'd stretch out and I'd say, 'Well, I'm going,' and he'd *throw* me down. And he finally got in a real bad mood, and I went."

"Did he ever admit to you that he was just posing as a Princeton student?"

"Oh yes, at the end I think he did."

"Did he think he could get away with it?"

"Well, I guess if we'd never left the room he could have."

SOME LAST EFFECTS OF DAVID WHITING: AN INVENTORY OF ITEMS LEFT BEHIND FROM HIS EIGHTEEN-MONTH CAREER AS HOLLY-WOOD CORRESPONDENT FOR *Time*.

—One 275-watt Westinghouse sunlamp. Left in a file cabinet in his old office in the *Time* suite on Roxbury Drive in Beverly Hills, across from the "House of Pies." "He used to come in after midnight and sit for hours with the sunlamp on—I don't know if he was working or what," the *Time* switchboard operator recalls. Once he didn't turn it off. "I came in in the morning one day and I smelled smoke, and I checked in David's office, and it was his sunlamp. He'd left sometime early in the morning, and he'd just put it in his drawer without turning it off. It was smoldering in there, he might have set the place on fire."

—One pocket memo book with the notation "Cannes No. 6" scrawled in Magic Marker on the front cover. From the same file cabinet. Not long after he had been transferred to the Hollywood job, David Whiting took off for Cannes to "cover" the film festival. A Paris correspondent for *Time* had been under the impression *he* had been assigned to cover it. There was some dispute. The Paris man filed the story. David Whiting took many notes. Interviews with producers, directors, starlets. Memos to himself. A sample memo to himself from "Cannes No. 6":

> General Memo:
> –morn. look good
> –pics
> –people

—One magazine story, written under an interesting pseudonym, for *Cosmopolitan*. The pseudonym is "Anthony Blaine," a synthesis of Amory Blaine and Anthony Patch, the heroes, respectively, of Fitzgerald's first two novels, *This Side of Paradise* and *The Beautiful and Damned*. The *Cosmopolitan* story by "Anthony Blaine" is about Candice Bergen. He met her in Cannes in 1970. He fibbed about his age to her, he played the worldly bon vivant for her, he followed her to Spain where she was making a movie, he continued to see her back in Beverly Hills. He was possessed with her, he told friends. He was just a good friend to her, she told me.

—One box kite, still in the possession of Paula Prentiss. David Whiting was doing a story for *Time* about Paula and her husband, Dick Benjamin. The angle was going to be the idea of a happy marriage, he told them. He visited them a second time in their apartment in New York, and "there was a big change from the first time we met him, I could tell something was wrong," Paula recalls, "that he needed something from us. He wouldn't come out and say it, but we could tell, he'd sit and drink martinis and pop pills all the time. But we did have some good moments with him. I remember he brought us a box kite and he took us out on the beach and showed us how to fly it." (The story about Dick and Paula never appeared in *Time*. It did show up in the November, 1971, issue of *Cosmopolitan*, this time under David Whiting's real name. *Cosmopolitan* also published a David Whiting story about Sarah Miles, the one he had been "research-ing" when he began following Sarah around for *Time*. The story, published in December, 1971, is titled *Sarah Miles: The Maiden Man-Eater* and the subtitle reads: "She uses words that would make a construction worker blush, but from her they sound refined.")

—One list of all the girls David Whiting had ever kissed. "I walked into his office one day and he had his big debutante album out—it had all his invitations and dance programs, and dashing photos of David and the debs," a woman who writes for *Time* recalls. "And he was work-ing on a list he told me was a list of all the girls he'd ever kissed—just kissed, that was enough—and he was going to add it to the album I think."

—One Bekins Warehouse storage number, the index to the artifacts David Whiting left behind when he left for En-gland. Included are some of his many Savile Row suits he decided not to bring back to London with him. "Let me tell you about his suits," the friend who has custody of the Bekins number told me. "He used to fly to Lon-don—on his wife's Pan Am card, of course—fly there on a Thursday to have a fitting done. He'd come back Monday, then fly back again the next weekend for the final fitting and bring back the suit."

—One copy of *The Crack-Up* by F. Scott Fitzgerald, a battered, underlined paperback bequeathed to a woman he knew. Two passages have been cut out with a razor blade. One of the underlined passages: "I didn't have the two top things: great animal magnetism or money. I had the second things, though: good looks and intelligence. So I always got the top girl."

A passage cut out with a razor blade: the fourth verse from a poem called "The Thousand-and-First Ship," a Fitzgerald attempt at a modern version of Keats's "La Belle Dame Sans Merci": "There'd be an orchestra/ Bingo! Bango!/ Playing for us/ To dance the tango,/ And people would clap/ As we arose,/ At her sweet face/ And my new clothes."

They checked into the Gila Bend Travelodge on Monday, January 29. At first David Whiting took the room adjoining Sarah's. Hers was number 127, his 126; an inner door connected the two. He didn't last there very long. Rooms 126 and 127 are in the section of the motel most remote from traffic. They could be reached only by walking back from the highway, past the Travelodge bar, past the length of the larger two-story rooming unit, all the way to the rear of the parking lot and around the back of a smaller, single-story row of Travelodge cubicles. The bedroom windows of numbers 126 and 127 face nothing; they look north upon miles and miles of cactus and mesquite waste. Closer at hand to numbers 126 and 127 is the Travelodge garbage shed.

On Friday, February 2, four days after David and Sarah checked into these adjoining rooms, David was forced to move. Sarah's five-year-old son Thomas and the nanny hired to care for him were arriving from England that evening. So, on Friday afternoon, nine days before his death, David Whiting moved out of number 126 and into number 119, a room across the parking lot in the two-story motel building.

He seems to have chosen this place of exile with some care. The view, for instance, had two peculiar advantages. For one, the line of sight for someone looking straight out the bedroom window of number

119 runs straight across a short span of parking lot and then directly along the walkway in front of the row of rooms he left behind, right past the doors to numbers 126 and 127. No one entering or leaving Sarah's room could escape the notice of an observer looking out the window of number 119.

The other, more subtle advantage to this observation post had to do with the placement of a staircase. A broad openwork staircase of wood planks and iron bars descends from the second floor of motel rooms above number 119 and touches ground on the sidewalk in front of the room, forming a slanting screen in front of the bedroom window. Outsiders in the Travelodge parking lot can't see through the confusing lattice of horizontal steps, diagonal banisters, and vertical railing supports to the bedroom window of 119 behind it. But someone peeking out from *within* the bedroom window of 119, from behind this sheltering screen, can see quite well, although at first it is something like looking out from within a confusingly barred cage.

Sarah says she never knew where David had moved. She'd never bothered to find out, having no occasion to visit him.

But she knew he was watching her. Keeping track of her movements. She'd return from a day on the set and as soon as she walked into her room, the phone would ring and he'd want to know what she'd be doing that night, and with whom.

He had been acting extraordinarily possessive from the moment they arrived at Gila Bend. She hadn't been prepared for anything quite like it. Before they'd left England he'd seemed in better shape than he'd been in a long time. He'd been working on a screenplay, he'd been going out with women, he'd been less obsessed with managing her personal life.

"But as soon as we touched down in America he was back to square one," she says. "He was the old David again."

Sarah speculates it might have something to do with the way she worked. "When I'm on a picture I'm—see, he had known me as a girl who lived in the country, who loved horses, and who lived a quiet life," Sarah told the inquest. "When I get on a film I like to get to know everybody. The wranglers—I never met wranglers before. Christ, they're marvelous people, you know. I mean I want to spend all my time with cowboys."

So Sarah went out at night. Going out in Gila Bend didn't mean going far. It meant eating at Mrs. Wright's Colonial Dining Room, next door to the Travelodge, then walking back across the parking lot to the Travelodge Cocktail Lounge for drinking and dancing to a country-and-western jukebox. For Sarah—according to Gila Bend locals who hung around with the cast and crew—going out meant dancing a lot, flirting, tossing off four-letter words in a merry way. (A *Women's Wear* profile of Sarah, published a week before David Whiting's death, features a picture of Sarah perched in a sex-kittenish pose on one of the black Naugahyde banquettes in the Travelodge Cocktail Lounge. *The Lady with the Truckdriver's Mouth* is the title of the story.)

Meanwhile David Whiting stayed in. At first she'd invite him to come to the bar with her, Sarah says, but he'd refuse and stay in his room and watch for her return. He kept to himself, remote from everyone but Sarah, and Sarah began keeping her distance from him. Waitresses at the Travelodge Coffee Shop recall David Whiting coming in alone night after night, sitting at the counter, and ordering, night after night, a shrimp cocktail and a club sandwich.

During the day he'd haunt the shooting set in the desert, a dark and formal figure amidst the real and costumed cowboys and the casual MGM production officials. He'd have one of his Nikons with him, and he'd hover around Sarah clicking off stills. Or he'd have some papers he wanted her to look at, other papers he'd want her to sign. He began getting on the nerves of the MGM people. There are reports he'd been getting on Sarah's nerves.

The first big fight broke out in room 127 on the evening of Tuesday, February 6. The nanny was in the middle of it. Janie Evans is her name, she is twenty-three years old, dark haired, dark eyed, and rather sexy. She had been hired for this Gila Bend trip one week before Sarah and David left England. Sarah had hired her on the recommendation of David Whiting, and there is good reason to believe that David Whiting and the soon-to-be nanny had been seeing each other before the hiring.

In any case David and the nanny had mutual friends in London, and one of them was a woman named Tessa Bradford, and it was a curious story about David and this Tessa Bradford that led to the Tuesday-night fight.

The nanny had been talking to Sarah about David. That winter in London, the nanny told Sarah, David had developed an obsession for Tessa Bradford. He had haunted her house, followed her car, called her at all hours, rented a Mercedes limousine to take her to the theater. After all this Tessa Bradford had dropped him, the nanny told Sarah. She had thought David was crazed.

That Tuesday night in room 127 Sarah asked David about the story. He became enraged, rushed into room 126, dragged the nanny back to Sarah's room demanding that she "tell the truth."

"Why didn't you tell the truth? Why did you say it was a Mercedes when it was only a mini cab? Why did you say I kept phoning her, I only phoned her five times," Janie Evans recalls him yelling.

Then he turned on Sarah. He grabbed her. "He had her—his hand on her neck like this," the nanny testified at the inquest, "wallowing her head backward and forward, and I shouted at him and Sarah pushed at him, and he went through the door and she threw a vase right after him . . . it didn't hit him, it smashed on the concrete outside."

"He got upset that I didn't get upset about him seeing another woman," Sarah explains. "But I couldn't take his private life seriously."

Other things started going wrong for David Whiting. On Wednesday, February 7, the producer of *Cat Dancing*, Martin Poll, approached David on the set. As usual David had been recording Sarah's performance with his Nikon. Poll hinted strongly that David's presence was not entirely welcome.

"He wasn't in anyone's way," Poll told me, "but for myself I like to have a very private set and it was a closed set from the beginning of the picture, and it was distracting to have photographs taken all the time."

"Did you ask him to stay off then, or what was the actual conversation?" I asked Poll.

"I am really not interested in sitting on the griddle," was all Poll answered.

On Thursday, February 8, Sarah saw David Whiting for the next to last time.

"He came into my room that evening and his face was ashen and white, and more sallow than I've ever seen it. And he put the script on the bed and he said, 'I've just read it and it's no good at all. I can't write anything.' "

After that, nobody remembers seeing David Whiting outside his motel room.

On Friday morning David Whiting called the motel manager to

complain about the reception on his TV. He was getting sound but no picture, he said. But when the motel manager came to the door of number 119 to see about getting David his picture back, he found the DO NOT DISTURB card hanging from the doorknob. He kept checking, the manager recalls, but the DO NOT DISTURB sign never came down.

There are indications that David Whiting was trying to get out of Gila Bend. Thursday night he placed a call to a woman in Washington, D.C. He talked to her for eighty-four minutes. They had been engaged once. He had continued to confide in her after he left her behind for Hollywood. That night he told her that "the particular situation there in Gila Bend was over for him," she recalls. He didn't sound overjoyed about things, but neither did he sound suicidal, she says. He did say he wanted to see her and talk to her "about this situation in Gila Bend and about him and me." He talked about flying to Washington to see her.

Two nights later, Saturday night, about an hour before midnight David Whiting received a call from a friend in Beverly Hills. The friend wanted to know if David was going to attend the Directors' Guild premiere of *Lamb* Sunday evening. "No," David told the friend, "Sarah and I think it will be a bummer."

Nevertheless, David told his friend, he was thinking of leaving Gila Bend for Hollywood sometime in the middle of the next week.

David's voice sounded slurred that night, the friend recalls.

"It sounds like you're into a couple of reds," he told David.

"No," David replied. "Mandrax."

●　　　■　　　●

Burt Reynolds wanted a massage. It was close to midnight when he returned from the Pink Palomino, picked up his phone, and asked the desk to ring the room of the Japanese masseuse.

Reynolds was staying in room 135. It was in the same single-story block of cubicles as Sarah's room. The two rooms were no more than six or eight yards apart, almost back to back, in fact. However, as close as they were physically, it was still necessary to go all the way around the building to get from one to the other, and going around the building meant passing directly in front of David Whiting's screened-in bedroom window.

The Japanese masseuse was staying in room 131. Her name was Letsgo (an Americanization of her Japanese first name, Retsuko) Roberts, and she had been summoned to the Travelodge on Friday afternoon to tend to Sarah, who had suffered a bruising fall from a horse. Letsgo and Sarah got along so well that she was plucked from her regular tour of duty at a place called The International Health Spa in Stockdale, Arizona, and installed in a room at the Travelodge.

About midnight on Saturday Letsgo received a phone call from Burt.

He asked her to come over to room 135 and work on him. When Letsgo walked into Burt's room she found Sarah there, she told me. She had the feeling the two of them had been drinking.

"They were kind of—kind of, you know, not drunk—but kind of happy, you know, after drink," Letsgo recalls.

Burt, attired in a white terry-cloth dressing gown, proceeded to lie on the bed, and Letsgo proceeded to give him a two-hour massage.

Meanwhile Sarah chatted with Burt. She apologized for leaving the party early with Lee J. Cobb. She told him about an old boyfriend of hers. He told her about an old girl friend of his. Sarah turned on the TV, watched a British film; she ate an apple and banana; she lay down next to Burt on the double bed and dozed off, according to Letsgo.

About two A.M. the masseuse offered to walk Sarah back to her room, but Burt told her he'd see that Sarah got back safely. The masseuse left.

An hour and fifteen minutes later Burt walked Sarah around the back of the building to her room.

Back in his own room, Burt had hardly slipped off his clothes and slipped into bed when the phone rang. It was the nanny. She was saying something about Sarah being beaten up, something about David Whiting. He heard a scream over the phone, Burt told Sergeant Hinderliter the following afternoon. He heard no scream over the phone, Burt testified at the inquest four weeks later.

Scream or no scream, Burt put his clothes back on and headed around the building to Sarah's room. It was at this moment that the paths of Burt Reynolds and David Whiting may have crossed. David's violent encounter with Sarah had just come to an end. He ran out of her room just about the time the nanny called Burt for help. If David Whiting was proceeding to his own room while Burt was on his way to Sarah's,

David and Burt might have met in the parking lot at the northwest corner of the building.

When Burt first told the story of the events of that night to Sergeant Hinderliter, he did not mention encountering David Whiting or anyone else on his way to Sarah's room.

Ten days later in the "Rio Rico tapes" and then again on the witness stand at the inquest—much to the surprise of Sergeant Hinderliter—Burt testified that he did see "someone" as he was heading around that corner.

"It was to my left as I came around. . . . I saw someone going in the door, and the door slammed very hard behind him. . . . At the time I didn't know whose room it was, nor could I identify him since I'm not very good at identifying backs, but it looked like a man, and the door slammed behind him. Later I found out, the next day, that that was David Whiting's room."

And then, a few minutes later, leading the wounded Sarah back to his own room, something caught Burt's eye. "As I rounded the corner to go to my room I saw the drapes open and close," in the window of the same room whose door had slammed behind a man a few minutes ago. There was no light on in the room behind the drapes, he told the inquest, a detail which makes his observation of the moving drapes all the more acute, since the window of that room is well-screened from view by a staircase.

At this point, Sarah testified at the inquest, Burt told her, "If I was not as mature as I am now, I would lay him out."

The following afternoon, after the body of David Whiting had been discovered, the masseuse heard this story from Sarah. Sarah and Burt were back in Burt's room. "Mr. Reynolds wanted to go down and fight him, Mr. Whiting, but Sarah, she stopped him. . . ." the masseuse told me. "She told Mr. Reynolds it would cause more trouble."

Sarah testified that shortly after she arrived at Burt's room she became worried about the well-being of the man who had beaten her. She told Burt she wanted to call up David Whiting "to see if he was all right." It was not physical injury she was concerned about, it was injury to David's *feelings*, she says. "Because whenever he has hit me he has always been so ashamed afterward, so remorseful. . . ."

But Sarah did not make the call. Burt advised her to "deal with

everything in the morning," and she went to sleep. Had she in fact
made that call she might have saved his life.

●   ■   ●

Not much is known of the movements of David Whiting that night.
Sarah did give David a call early in the evening to inform him that
Burt had invited her to attend the birthday celebration at the Pink
Palomino in Ajo. Sarah says she invited David to come along and that
David refused. He was in his room at eleven P.M. calling Hollywood.
It is reasonable to speculate that he stayed up waiting, as usual, for
Sarah's return. He may have spent these hours peering out from behind
his sheltered observation post. In the absence of anyone crossing his line
of sight, the picture outside his bedroom window consisted of the empty
walkway past Sarah's room and a blank brick wall, the narrow end of
the one-story unit containing Sarah's room.

At night the management of the Gila Bend Travelodge switches on
an intense blue spotlight implanted among the dwarf yucca palms which
line that blank stucco wall. The blue spot illuminates the sharp green
spears of the yucca palms and casts confusingly colored shadows of their
fanlike arrays upon the wall, an effect apparently intended to create an
air of tropical mystery in the Travelodge parking lot.

If David Whiting had been watching at just the right moment, he
might have seen Sarah cross the parking lot from the Travelodge Cocktail Lounge and head toward Burt Reynolds's room.

Three things are known for sure. Sometime before three thirty A.M.
David Whiting entered Sarah Miles's bedroom. Sometime after she
encountered him there, he returned to his own room, where he left
bloodstains. And sometime before noon the next day, he returned to
Sarah's room and died.

He had a key to Sarah's room. "I kept on saying, 'David, are you
taking my keys, because they're not here anymore,'" Sarah told the
inquest. "And he said, 'I don't need to take keys. You know me, I can
pick a lock.' He was very proud of the fact that he could pick locks."
Nevertheless a key to Sarah's room, number 127, was the only item
found on him after his death.

The only witness to the goings-on in room 127 was the nanny, Janie

Evans. "I think you'll find that the nanny is the key to this whole thing," Sarah's lawyer in the case, Benjamin Lazarow of Tucson, Arizona, told me, as he slipped a tape cassette—one of the "Rio Rico tapes"—into his Sony. "You listen to this cassette with the nanny on it. Listen to how scratchy and worn out it sounds. You know why? It's because the detectives kept playing it over and over again. They were *very* interested in the nanny's story."

The first thing she saw in room 127 that night, says the nanny, on the tape, was Sarah lying on the floor with David Whiting on top of her bashing her head on the floor. "That'll teach you!" David was yelling at Sarah, the nanny says. (Ten days before the "Rio Rico tapes," on the afternoon following the death, the nanny had told Sergeant Hinderliter that Whiting had slapped Sarah, but that she didn't know if she had actually seen it or not.)

The nanny ran over and tried to pull Whiting off Sarah, she said. She failed, and finally, responding to Sarah's plea, picked up the phone and called Burt.

When Burt arrived, the nanny returned to her bed in room 126. Twenty minutes later she was dozing off when she heard noises in Sarah's room. It sounded like someone opening and closing a drawer in there, she says. She called out, "Sarah?" but no one answered. This led her to assume that David Whiting had returned. "I was scared. I mean he had been violent. I didn't want to see him so I didn't say anything more."

She went back to sleep, she says.

After he finished playing the "Rio Rico tapes," Attorney Lazarow took out a tape he made on his own of an interview with the nanny. At the end of the interview, Lazarow suddenly asked her a peculiar question:

"Did you hit David Whiting over the head with anything?"

She did not, she replied. I wondered what had prompted Lazarow to ask the question in the first place.

"Oh, I don't know," Lazarow said. "Maybe I was just trying to shake her, see if there was something she was leaving out of her story. We were trying to figure out how he might have gotten that star-shaped wound, and we figured maybe it happened when the nanny was trying to pull Whiting off Sarah during the fight, but both she and Sarah said no."

•   ▪   •

The star-shaped wound on the back of David Whiting's head has yet to be explained away.

An MGM lawyer attempted to explain it away by suggesting that in a fit of rage David Whiting simply smashed the back of his head against a wall. Others suggest that David Whiting was, literally, star struck that night, and that Burt Reynolds was the star. Reynolds has a reputation in Hollywood for an explosive temper and an itch to fight. Before the death, he regaled Gila Bend locals with tales of past punch-outs, adding that he had decided to leave that part of his life behind now that he had become a big star. A woman who knew Reynolds intimately for years told me that he used to blame it on his spleen. His spleen had been removed after a high-school football injury, and ever since then he'd been unable to control his violent temper because, he said, the spleen had something to do with controlling the rush of adrenaline. All of which helps explain why Reynolds became such an obvious target for suspicion; none of it is evidence.

Spleen or no spleen, if Reynolds *had* lost control of his temper and given Whiting a beating, it seems likely that the body would show more evidence of violence than it did.

According to Dr. Robert Wright, who performed autopsy number two on the body of David Whiting, the most violent interpretation that can be made from a reading of the marks left upon the body is this: someone grasped Whiting firmly by the shoulders, shook him, and either shoved him back against a wall causing him to hit his head, or threw him down causing him to strike his head on the ground.

State Police crime-lab people found no evidence on either the walls or the bathroom floors of rooms 119, 126, and 127 to suggest that a bloody bashing had taken place in any of those rooms. (The bedroom floors are carpeted.)

The parking lot outside is covered with asphalt. If it happened, it could have happened out there in the parking lot. But a hard rain swept through Gila Bend in the early morning hours of that Sunday. Any bloodstains that might have been left upon the parking-lot asphalt would have been washed away. The mystery of where and how, and by whose hands, if any, David Whiting received his star-shaped wound remains unsolved.

Does it matter? Dr. Wright thinks it matters. Dr. Wright is a forensic pathologist for the Coroner's Office of the City and County of San Francisco, and a professor of forensic pathology at the University of California Medical Center. He was called upon by Mrs. Campbell, David's mother, to perform an autopsy after she had the body shipped out of Arizona and installed in the refrigerator of a funeral home in Berkeley, just one day before the third and final session of the inquest.

"The force of the impact to the head," Dr. Wright declared in his autopsy summary, "could well have caused a temporary loss of consciousness (a brain concussion), and may have caused him to behave in a stuporous fashion, and to be unmindful of his subsequent acts."

He could have been knocked silly, in other words, and in that state of silliness taken two or three too many pills, killing himself unintentionally. It was a borderline overdose. David Whiting might have been unaware he was crossing the border.

Dr. Wright's conclusion must, of course, be weighed against the milder conclusion of the original autopsy doctor who had not been selected by the boy's mother. But his report does give some substance to something the mother said to me in the coffee shop of the Travelodge.

"The horrible part is, severe-intoxication doses of this drug can produce deep coma. And the horrible thing is if these people thought he was dead—the pulse would have been faint—they could have been drunk or high, suppose they didn't know how to take a pulse—they could have sat around for hours, while his life ebbs away."

The nanny woke up at seven thirty in the morning, she said. She was very cold. She walked through the connecting door into Sarah's room and found the outside door wide open to the chill morning air. She shut the outside door and headed back for the inner door into her own room.

The nanny said she never saw a body in the course of this little expedition. When Sergeant Hinderliter came upon the body about twelve thirty he found the legs from the knees down sticking out beyond the end of the dressing-room partition. Walking back from closing the outside door that morning, the nanny was walking straight toward the end of the dressing-room partition and, presumably, straight toward the protruding legs of David Whiting. There was light: the lights were still on in the room from the night before. But she was drowsy, the nanny said, and she saw no body.

This means one of three things:

The body was not there.

The body was there and the nanny did not, in fact, see it.

The body was there, dead or alive, the nanny saw it and went back to sleep without reporting it. Or else she reported it to someone, and that someone waited four hours before reporting it to the police.

Which leads to another unresolved question: how long before she reported it did Sarah find the body?

"At one time she told me she went back to her room at eight o'clock in the morning," Sergeant Hinderliter told me, recalling his interview with Sarah the day of the death. "And the next time she turned around and said it was ten o'clock. I didn't question her on the time at that time because she was upset, and because at the time of my interview I was just working on a possible drug overdose."

Eleven days later, in the "Rio Rico tapes," and then again at the inquest, Sarah said it was around eleven fifteen when she returned to her room and found the body.

●   ■   ●

Sarah was on the witness stand. The Deputy County Attorney had just led her gently through her account of the death, eliding over any discussion of her stay with Burt Reynolds.

Now came the moment many of those following the case closely had been waiting for. The Deputy County Attorney seemed to be approaching, gently of course, the subject of Sarah's Sunday-afternoon statement to Sergeant Hinderliter. People wanted to know, for instance, whether Sarah had been slapped or beaten.

"Now, do you remember talking to the policeman that came the next morning?" the Deputy County Attorney asked her, meaning Sergeant Hinderliter, and afternoon, not morning.

"Well, I was terribly shook up the next morning. Do you mean the policeman?"

Yes, said the Deputy County Attorney, he meant the policeman.

"By the time I saw the policeman I had heard that Mr. Whiting was dead," Sarah replied. "This was when I was in a bad way."

"Do you recall that conversation with the officer at all?" the Deputy County Attorney asked.

"No. I just told him what had happened."

"But you remember what you told him at this time?" the Deputy County Attorney persisted.

At precisely this point Sarah burst into tears.

"The truth," she sobbed urgently. "The same as I'm giving you now, I think."

The courtroom was silent. At his desk, the Deputy County Attorney looked down at his hands as if in remorse for having trespassed the bounds of decency with his ferocious questioning. From his bench, the Justice of the Peace leaned over toward Sarah and patted her hand comfortingly. When Sarah had wiped the tears from her eyes, the Deputy County Attorney started an entirely new line of questioning and did not venture near the subject again.

There was one final moment of high melodrama at the inquest. The questioning was over, and Sarah, face flushed and stained with tears, asked to make two final statements. First, she declared, she had never resisted testifying before the inquest. "I was bulldozed by my husband, producers, Burt Reynolds, MGM," she said. "I wanted to go as soon as I could . . . and I was not allowed to do this and for this I feel a grudge."

And second, she said, there was the matter of David Whiting's body, still languishing at that time in Mr. Ganley's refrigerator wrapped up in a sheet. (As of this writing, about three months after his death, the body is still languishing unburied in the refrigerator of the Bayview mortuary in Berkeley, "awaiting further tests" and further word from Mrs. Campbell, who hasn't been heard from in some time, an employee of the mortuary told me.)

"I hear from my attorney," Sarah told the Gila Bend courtroom, "that somebody doesn't want to bury this boy and that the state is going to bury him."

Sarah rose up in the witness stand, eyes wet. "*Well, I would like to bury him!*" she cried. With that, she rushed from the courtroom.

Sarah Miles never contacted him, Mr. Ganley told me. "No sir. I've never heard from Miles or anyone of that type. In fact," said Mr. Ganley, "they weren't even interested in David Whiting after his death."

I asked him what he meant by that, and he told me this story.

It was the afternoon of the death. Mr. Ganley was in room 127 with the body of David Whiting, helping the investigators prepare it for shipment to the County Morgue in Phoenix for an autopsy.

"Miss Miles was in the room next door, and she sent word over she wanted to come in and get a dress because they were having a party up at the bar and she wanted to get up there. And the investigators wouldn't let her have the dress. They told her when they were through with the room she could get anything she wanted out of it."

"But that was what she wanted—a party dress?"

"Yeah, she wanted to go to the Elks Club, they were having a barbecue for Reynolds's birthday," Mr. Ganley said.

Meanwhile, Burt Reynolds was in his room talking with a couple of his friends, trying to decide whether to go to that Elks Club party or not. The party was for him, of course, and he would disappoint a lot of the Gila Bend people if he didn't show up. But then, there had been that unfortunate death, and that made it hard for him to feel like celebrating.

Finally, according to one of the people in the room with Burt, the decision came down to this. "Burt said something like if it had been an accident, that was one thing, then it was tragic, you know, and it was no time to party. But if it was suicide, if this guy was so worthless he didn't have the guts to face life, then why spoil the party?"

Burt went to the party.

—*ESQUIRE*
August 1973

TRAVELS
WITH
DR. DEATH

Three lives hang in the balance this morning as Dr. James Grigson pulls up in a gleaming white Cadillac, ready to make his rounds. The tall Texan with one hand on the wheel and one hand on his flamboyant golden cigarette holder, the legendary forensic psychiatrist known as "Dr. Death," is about to head out for the West Texas prairie to do some testifying. Indeed, for the Doctor—the traveling expert witness for hire, the courtroom terror of death-penalty foes—this is going to be the most extraordinarily concentrated stretch of testifying he's ever done. Three death-penalty trials in three Texas towns in two days.

If things go according to plan, if jurors follow his advice and vote for death—as they usually do when the Doctor takes the stand and, in effect, prescribes it—three convicted murderers will be sent to death row to face the Big Needle, execution by lethal injection.

In fact, if the Doctor can adhere to his demanding schedule of appearances, he'll succeed in doing something even he has never done before: dispatch two lives in a single day.

Dr. Grigson's lopsided record over the past twenty years favors his chances: going into these three trials he has testified against 124 murderers, and acting on his advice, juries have sentenced 115 of them to death. He is the death penalty's cutting edge in Texas, its circuit rider. Opponents call him "the hanging shrink." But even he has never done so many so fast.

This morning in Dallas, the Doctor swings open the door of the Sedan de Ville to admit me into the chocolate leather interior. We're off to Love Field, where we'll catch a flight to Lubbock, four hundred miles west. He's agreed to allow me to accompany him on these hectic, history-making rounds, to observe him game-planning his testimony with prosecutors, plotting against defense witnesses. And blasting defense attorneys out of the water: the Doctor has a reputation as a lethal weapon on the witness stand in Texas, which has sent more defendants to death row than any other state. Indeed, one defense attorney calls him "a killing machine."

Grigson, a perpetually grinning, relentlessly gregarious type, gives me a vigorous handshake and puts the Caddy into gear. We begin a journey that will take us deep into the heart of Texas, deep into the minds of three murderers, and deeper into that poorly charted borderline realm between evil and madness that is the Doctor's special turf. Because, despite his controversial methods (the American Psychiatric Association has denounced his practice of telling juries he can "guarantee" that a defendant "will kill again"), despite his embarrassing setback in the Randall Dale Adams *Thin Blue Line* case (the Doctor, who had predicted Adams would "kill again," *still* believes the now absolved defendant is guilty and "will kill again"), it cannot be denied that the Doctor has looked longer and deeper into the minds and hearts of more murderers (1,400 so far) than just about anyone else. One may disagree with where he draws the boundary lines between evil and madness, criminality and sickness. But one can't deny he knows the territory.

●　　　■　　　●

On the evening of March 17, 1989, a twenty-one-year-old white kid named Aaron Lee Fuller was drinking beer over at a girlfriend's apartment in Lamesa, Texas, when he had an idea. Which was that the easiest way to make quick money was to roll old ladies. Some of Aaron Lee Fuller's previous ideas, about how to commit burglaries, for instance, had not turned out well, and he'd ended up spending a couple of stretches in the state pen in Huntsville. This was his worst idea of all.

Before long Aaron Lee Fuller found himself at Loretta Stephens's house, staring through her screen door at the sixty-eight-year-old widow, who was sound asleep on a recliner in her living room. Word on the street had it that Loretta Stephens kept large amounts of cash at home. Fuller used a house key to rip a hole in the screen door and let himself in. Tiptoed past the sleeping figure, proceeded to her bedroom, where, sure enough, he found more than $500 in small bills stuffed into various envelopes.

When he emerged with the money, Loretta Stephens was still sound asleep. All Fuller had to do was make a quick exit and he'd be home free with the cash. The perfect petty crime.

But he didn't make that quick easy exit. Something drew him to the sleeping woman on the recliner. According to a videotaped confession he later made, he stopped in front of her. Stood over her. Stared at her for a full ten minutes. And then began smashing her face in with his fists, shattering her jaw, causing massive hemorrhages and multiple blunt-force traumas to the brain.

He went into the bathroom, washed the blood spatters off his face, and returned to Loretta Stephens's side. Noticed her stirring, still breathing through her broken face. Which caused him to go back to the bedroom, get a pillow, and use it to smother the remaining life out of her.

She was dead, but he wasn't through with her. According to his original confession, he proceeded to sexually assault her dead body.

When he took the stand at his trial, Fuller retracted parts of his confession. Claimed that although he punched Loretta Stephens's face it was not he, but a friend who'd accompanied him, who smothered her to death. And that it was this friend who'd committed the sexual assault.

The jury didn't believe him and convicted him of committing the murder himself. But what may have sealed Aaron Lee Fuller's fate— what made him a prime candidate for the Doctor's death-penalty diagnosis of "future dangerousness"—was Fuller's behavior immediately following the crime. Because it is the Doctor's belief that the special sub-species of murderers who are likely to kill again (unless the state kills them first) betray their "severe sociopath" nature by their emotional reaction—or lack of it—in the aftermath of the killing.

To severe sociopaths, "killing someone is less emotional than eating a plate of scrambled eggs," the Doctor maintains. To them "it's not much different from having a meal at a good restaurant. If you like it, you'll come back again."

What Aaron Lee Fuller did in the immediate aftermath of Loretta Stephens's murder was, essentially, *party hearty*. With the body tied up in a bundle in the back of her car, he and a friend tore off for the bright lights of Lubbock to spend the woman's cash.

They drove to a convenience store, flirted with the cashier, flashed her the roll of bills, and headed off for Lubbock. Almost as an after-thought they dumped the body in a patch of tall weeds by the roadside. When they got to Lubbock they bought a keg, checked into a motel called the Koko Inn. There, Aaron Lee Fuller commenced the last best party of his life.

It took a jury in the tiny West Texas county-seat town of Lamesa (pronounced La-meese-ah) all of twenty-seven minutes to convict Aaron Lee Fuller of "capital murder"—a murder done in the course of com-mitting another felony—the most severe degree of the crime, the one that carries only two possible sentences in Texas: life imprisonment or death.

But the real trial only began with the guilty verdict. On Thursday, February 1, 1990, the Lamesa jury reconvened to begin hearing argu-ments on the question of whether to put Aaron Lee Fuller to death. U.S. Supreme Court decisions and death-penalty law in Texas require this separate "penalty phase" trial for all candidates for capital punish-ment. A pure trial on the life-or-death issue.

The thrust of Supreme Court death-penalty decisions since the Court reformed capital punishment in 1976 has been to permit the state to kill, but to revise the process that selects who is sentenced to die and who isn't. Make it less a single, emotional pull-the-switch decision; make it more the end product of a multistage decision-making process that emphasizes "informed selectivity" and supposedly ensures that the ultimate sanction is not applied arbitrarily or capriciously, but is reserved for the worst, most dangerous killers, the ones who "deserve" to die by some well-defined criteria of just deserts.

How do you decide who really deserves to die? In Texas, a jury never actually votes life or death up or down. Instead, it is called upon to decide three questions about the murder and the murderer, three "Special Issues."

The jurors must agree unanimously, first, that the murderer "deliberately" sought the death of his victim; second, that there is "a probability that the defendant would commit criminal acts of violence" in the future, acts which would "constitute a continuing threat to society"; and, third, that there was no reasonable "provocation" for the defendant's murderous conduct.

In practice, it's Special Issue No. 2—the question of future dangerousness—that has become the battleground on which the life-or-death struggle of Texas death-penalty trials is fought.

What makes Special Issue No. 2 so thorny and contentious—what makes Dr. Grigson's testimony so controversial within the psychiatric profession and among death-penalty foes—is that it asks jurors to make a life-or-death decision based on a prediction of the future. It allows the jurors to punish the defendant with the extra, ultimate sanction of death, not only for the crime he's been convicted of but for crimes he *might* commit later. (It's a novel but not unique requirement. Two other states of the thirty-six that have a death penalty require a finding of future dangerousness.) In doing so, Special Issue No. 2 asks a lot more of jurors than merely looking into a criminal's record. It asks them to look into his soul—indeed, into the evolution of his soul in the future, into the life he *might* get to live, if they don't give him death.

This is where the Doctor comes in. He'll take the stand, listen to a recitation of facts about the killing and the killer, and then—usually without examining the defendant, without ever setting eyes on him until the day of the trial—tell the jury that, *as a matter of medical science*, he can assure them the defendant will pose a continuing danger to society as defined by Special Issue No. 2. That's all it takes.

But the Doctor's impact on a jury is more profound than the mere content of what he says. A death-penalty decision is far more emotionally unsettling to jurors than a mere guilt-or-innocence vote. It's a grave and even terrifying decision to make, in which the desire to exact collective vengeance upon a killer may conflict with the reluctance to pull the trigger personally—which, in effect, death-penalty jurors must do for us all. What makes the Doctor so effective—both prosecution and defense lawyers will tell you this—is his bedside manner with the jury. His kindly, gregarious, country-doctor manner, his reassuring, beautifully modulated East Texas drawl, help jurors get over the hump, and do the deed.

Says one bitter defense lawyer, "He's kind of like a Marcus Welby who tells you it's O.K. to kill."

And as a bonus for the prosecutors who hire him, the Doctor also does his lethal best to destroy defense attorneys and defense witnesses who challenge him.

Which is why, as soon as Lamesa County prosecutor Ricky Smith got a trial date for Aaron Lee Fuller, he put in a call to the Doctor. He knew a conviction would be easy. But death-penalty deliberations can be trickier, even in the conservative West Texas countryside in which Lamesa is situated. There is always a danger of a holdout juror. And the Doctor has a way with holdouts.

On our flight from Dallas to Lubbock, the Doctor tells me about how, in a recent trial, he worked on one stubborn holdout who, he was convinced, had her mind set against voting for death.

"I was watching her and I could tell she didn't believe what the first [prosecution] psychiatrist told her, and she wasn't gonna believe what I'd say. She just had her legs crossed, wasn't gonna hear what we had to say. So we took a coffee break after the first psychiatrist, and I told the prosecutor, 'You got trouble. You got one woman who's gonna hang up this jury, because she's not buying it.'"

The prosecutor then dug up some biographical information on the reluctant woman from the jury questionnaire.

"We discovered she had a fourteen-year-old daughter. And I got back on the stand and had the prosecutor ask me [about the defendant], 'Is this the kind of man that would rape and kill fourteen-year-old girls?' And we went into that. And she uncrossed her legs." The jury voted unanimously for death.

The Doctor repeatedly contends under oath that he testifies neither *for* nor *against* the prosecution or defense, that he testifies only as to what his scientific objectivity tells him. (Indeed, the Doctor points out, he's diagnosed future dangerousness in only 60 percent of the potential death-penalty defendants he's examined. Many other defendants owe their lives to him because the Doctor was willing to predict they wouldn't be dangerous.) Nonetheless, what makes him popular with prosecutors is that he will go the extra mile; he will go for the jugular to score points to win. He's so popular, in fact, that as his plane touches down in Lubbock he's the subject of a tug-of-war between two prosecutors: Ricky Smith in Lamesa, seventy miles south of Lubbock, wants him on the stand to testify against Aaron Lee Fuller tomorrow, Wednesday. But prosecutor Travis Ware in Lubbock wants him to take the stand in *his* death-penalty trial on Wednesday, too.

Travis Ware has tried a half-dozen death-penalty cases—four of them with the Doctor—and never lost one.

"Defense lawyers *fear* Dr. Grigson," Travis Ware explained to me. "They fear his effect on juries. He knows more about the criminal mind than anyone else in America, and he can put it in layman's terms. His demeanor, his sincerity, his charisma is absolutely uncontrollable by the defense. It drives them crazy."

Indeed, the Doctor's scheduled testimony drives them so crazy that during this particular week in February it has created a remarkable, unprecedented phenomenon on the West Texas prairie. Total shrink gridlock! Defense teams in both Lubbock and Lamesa are flying psychiatrists, psychologists, sociologists, and penologists in from all over America to do battle with the Doctor. They're shuttling back and forth between Lubbock and Lamesa, causing scheduling nightmares.

Finally, after two days of shuffling and shuttling and reshuffling, the order of battle has sorted itself out: the Doctor will take the stand in Lamesa first, in the Aaron Lee Fuller trial. Which means leaving Lubbock before dawn Friday morning, driving the seventy miles to Lamesa, facing Aaron Lee Fuller for the first time and pronouncing on his life, then racing back to Lubbock to take the stand and pronounce on the life of defendant Adolfo Hernandez in the afternoon. It will be the Doctor's first-ever double-header. And if all goes well we'll be back in Dallas Monday morning in time for the Doctor to take the stand in a *third* murder trial—which will make it three in two working days.

●   ■   ●

Dawn on the road from Lubbock to Lamesa. The sunrises are spectacular on this part of the West Texas prairie, spanning a horizon line virtually unobstructed by tree, barn, or settlement. One lonely sign advertises one lonely tourist attraction on this stretch of road, the Dan Blocker Memorial. The sign is in the shape of the big hat Hoss wore on *Bonanza*. The chief treasure of the museum in the Big Guy's tiny hometown of O'Donnell is a pair of size 44 trousers Hoss wore at age eleven.

It was about the time we passed the Dan Blocker Memorial sign that the Doctor made his Rock of Ages revelation. He was talking about growing up in the thirties in Texarkana, five hundred miles away in East Texas.

"The Grigsons had the Rock of Ages franchise," he said, "for the four-state area, of Arkansas—"

"Rock of Ages is what?" I asked, not comprehending at first.

"It's a particular—Rock of Ages is a trademark or name of a thicker type of marble. During the Depression and after, you would only bury your loved ones under Rock of Ages marble."

The amazing fact slowly began to dawn on me: Dr. Death's family was in the tombstone business. You could say that the Doctor is still traveling in the family business. Not Death's traveling salesman exactly, but surely his jurisprudential franchisee.

Indeed, there's a bit of the old-fashioned Willy Lomanesque commercial traveler you can't help but notice in the Doctor. None of the downbeat, defeated Loman stuff, but the salesman's relentlessly cheerful glad-handing style. Nothing phony about it—it appears to be his natural temperament, the nonstop pepster with a cheery word for strangers in elevators and airports. Once, at a happy hour in a motel courtyard in Lubbock, the Doctor made all the hardened investigators and prosecutorial personnel at his table stand up and clap for the "Feelings"-type cocktail pianist.

Because, the Doctor confided to me later in a Lubbock steak house, his whole philosophy of life is to "try every day to make at least one person's life a little better, a little brighter."

To that end, with the aim of spreading good-natured laughter, the Doctor's the kind of guy who loves to goose conversations with women in a mildly salacious way, almost invariably introducing me to women prosecutors by saying, "Ron's down here to do an exposé on *your* sex life." And then there's his lambada thing. In the past couple of days of waiting around in courthouses, bars, and steak houses, the Doctor would ceaselessly seek to promote spicy small talk with courthouse women about the leg and thigh positions of the lambada.

But the Doctor's corn-pone Dale Carnegie sweetness and light can be extremely deceptive, as I would discover later that morning in La-mesa. Beneath the good-ol'-boy guise there's a steel-trap mind. The Doctor may be an East Texas country boy on the surface, but he's a country boy like L.B.J. was a country boy. A country boy with a killer instinct.

It's an instinct he began to develop in his youth when he and his brother would come home from work and lock themselves into epic fratricidal chess matches, hour after hour, night after night. The Doctor's brother went on to become a professional pool shark and gambler. And while the Doctor chose a more conventional career path, graduating from Southwestern Medical School in Dallas and doing a psychiatric residency at Parkland Hospital, his restless competitive nature, the pool shark in *him*, was not satisfied by the passive, couch-centered life of a private practitioner of psychoanalytically based psychiatry. He sought out something that satisfied his appetite for competition. He found it in forensic psychiatry, in the high-intensity combat of criminal-trial testimony and cross-examination. He found it in the duel of wits with dangerous criminals. He began to specialize in examining killers.

At first they were mainly competency exams—judging whether a killer was sane enough to stand trial or not. And at first, he says, he got fooled a lot.

"At first I got the shit conned out of me. In medical school I was as liberal as any psychiatrist you'll ever meet. You know, most psychiatrists will say if you commit a crime there's something *wrong* with you." But after thousands of hours in jail cells with killers, he came to believe that most of them were not suffering from mental diseases or disorders. "They were just mean. I often think there ought to be a diagnosis, you know: *'mean son of a bitch.'* "

He became less easily conned, fell less often for tears of remorse or faked madness, he says.

"These days when they'll have tears falling down from their eyes, I've learned to give this response: *'You can knock that shit off, you're not fooling me a bit.'* And you can't believe—tears will dry up just like that."

As for fakers of insanity, well, to illustrate just how hard it is to get him to believe somebody's really crazy these days, the Doctor tells me what is clearly one of his favorite stories, the one about the fellow in jail who sliced off his penis and one testicle.

"Judge called me up and he said, 'Jim boy, have we got a crazy one.' And I go examine him, and even one of the jailers there said, 'Boy, Dr. Grigson, that guy is crazy.' Anyway, I went back and examined him. And I didn't think he was crazy. I called the judge up and said, 'Judge, he's faking [insanity].' And the judge said, 'Jim, *nobody's faking who cuts their dick off!*' And I said, 'Judge, I promise you he's faking.' And they insisted on having a competency hearing. And I got up and told the jury, which was made up of six men and six women, that he cut off his penis and one testicle and that he was faking. They looked at me like 'Man, you know, not only is *he* crazy, but you're crazy, too.' "
But then the Doctor explained to the jury what he'd gotten the prisoner to confide to him in his exam. "I explained to them that every time he had been caught—and he'd been in the pen four or five times—each time he'd cut his wrist, cut his finger, cut his throat. This time he was up for a habitual [a life sentence for repeated felonies] and he said, 'I knew I had to cut something serious!' He said, 'God Almighty! Damn! I wished I hadn't done it.' Well, the jury just laughed and they voted with me and found he was faking."

The Doctor thinks this is an extremely funny story. In any case, it certainly illustrates the extreme lengths to which he takes the notion of personal moral responsibility for conduct, his reluctance to ever excuse or forgive criminal conduct on the ground of mental debility.

"You take the guy that screwed all those dead bodies [a reference to one of several necrophiliac serial killers he's dealt with]. Ask a hundred, a thousand, people on the street, 'Is this guy sick?' They'll say, 'Shit, yes. He is crazy. No question about it. Anybody that does this *is sick.*'

"But we cannot have that concept in law. And as for forgiving, you can say society's at fault, you can say education is at fault—we project the blame, rationalize the behavior. You can ask, How do you *understand* a person committing this kind of act? You can say, If you can *understand*, you can forgive what happened. But I don't forgive."

"You don't—"

"I don't forgive."

●   ■   ●

Lamesa is an old-fashioned Texas town out of *The Last Picture Show.* It even features one of those classics from the James Dean/Buddy Holly era, a Sonic drive-in, the kind with loudspeakers that look like parking meters for you to call in your orders to the carhops. Our directions were to take a left at the Sonic and look for D.A. Ricky Smith's blue pickup in front of his office on a side street.

When we arrived for the Doctor's pre-trial conference with Smith, the D.A. had a word of warning for the Doctor: the hotshot defense attorney brought in from Lubbock, Floyd Holder, "has done his home-work on you. He's read all the propaganda, probably gonna bring up that Dr. Death stuff."

The courtroom was packed. The jury was seated. The defendant looked shockingly young. Cleaned up and clean-cut for his trial, Aaron Lee Fuller looked less like a killer facing death than one of the Brady Bunch facing after-school detention.

Photos taken at the time of his arrest show Aaron Lee Fuller with a greaser pompadour—the Texas version of the white-trash low-life look he affected back then. Today, seated straight up, hands folded formally and politely in front of him at the defense table, Aaron Lee Fuller was wearing a crew cut and a crew-neck sweater, and looking more like an all-American college sophomore than a granny-murdering necrophiliac.

The image, of course, was more than a fashion statement. It was Aaron Lee Fuller's plea, his last resort, a petition to the jury for his life. One that said he'd done bad, he'd gone wrong, but he wasn't beyond hope of redemption. If he could clean up his image, at least there was a chance he could cleanse his soul.

It was an appeal on an emotional, not legal, level, but death-penalty decisions, despite all the multistage decision-making processes, are made on an emotional as well as legal level. And so the Doctor was there to combat that image, to help the jury get past it, beneath it, to see Aaron Lee Fuller the way he did: as the moral and medical equivalent of a rabid dog who must be destroyed.

What troubles his critics in the psychiatric profession most is that the Doctor would take the stand today and make his diagnosis of future dangerousness with complete certainty, yet without ever having ex-amined Aaron Lee Fuller. Indeed, without even seeing him—barely thinking about him before taking the stand. In fact, in the two days I spent with him waiting around to testify, the Doctor spent more time talking about the lambada than he did about Aaron Lee Fuller.

In the first half of his career as a forensic-psychiatrist expert witness, in the sixties and seventies, the Doctor almost always would examine the murderers he'd testify against. Frequently when they were first brought in, he'd be called upon by a court to give them a competency exam—to see if they were rational enough to stand trial. Then, fairly often, prosecutors would call him to take the stand at the death-penalty trial of the same defendant, and the Doctor would use information and insights he had obtained in the pre-trial competency exam against the defendant in the death-penalty phase.

The Supreme Court rejected that practice in 1981 in *Estelle* v. *Smith* (and dozens of death sentences obtained on the basis of the Doctor's testimony were subsequently invalidated as a result) because, the Court said, it violated the defendant's Miranda rights against self-incrimination.

After that the Doctor continued to testify in murder trials, but rarely performed any personal examinations. What replaced it was a curious, carefully choreographed ritual built around him, something known as the Hypothetical. The purpose of the Hypothetical is to allow the Doctor to diagnose the defendant without having seen him or heard the details of his crime until the very moment of Judgment.

The Hypothetical in the Aaron Lee Fuller case was a single question that took no less than *forty minutes* to ask. A vast Moby Dick of a question that swallowed up all the ugly details of Aaron Lee Fuller's crime, everything bad he'd done before in his life, all the bad things he'd been overheard saying to others in jail *after*, and then regurgitated them, laid them before the Doctor for his inspection, and finally asked him—*if*—*if* he, as a scientist, came across such a sorry human specimen, would this sorry specimen present a continuing danger to society?

And so the epic Hypothetical began. *Assume, Doctor*, the D.A. began, that in the early hours of March 18, 1989, Aaron Lee Fuller ripped open Loretta Stephens's screen door, and *assume, Doctor*, that he proceeded to steal her money, and *assume, Doctor*, that he beat her, smothered her, sexually assaulted her dead body—all of these "assumptions" repeated for the jury in clinical detail and all of them reflecting the prosecution's version of events—and *assume, Doctor*, that he dumped the body and partied all night long at the Koko Inn, and *assume, Doctor*, that his prior criminal record consists of such and such crimes and arrests, and *assume, Doctor*, that he told so-and-so he wasn't sorry about killing Loretta Stephens, "that he felt he'd done her a favor," and *assume, Doctor*, that he bragged about his plans to go after other victims . . .

The forty-minute question was coming to a close now. The Doctor leaned forward in the witness stand, smiling equably. *Assuming* all that, Doctor, do you have an opinion about such an—

Objection!

A booming voice from the defense table interrupted the impending climax of the ritual. Floyd Holder, the big, burly, white-bearded defense attorney from Texas Tech law school in Lubbock, rose to speak.

"Your Honor, I would like to take the witness on voir dire [preliminary examination]."

The judge granted the request. And suddenly big Floyd Holder launched a furious attack on the Doctor.

"Doctor," he boomed out, "I understand that it is your opinion that the board of trustees of the American Psychiatric Association are a bunch of liberals who think queers are normal."

Whew. Everyone in the jammed courtroom sucked in a little air as it became clear that a real courtroom mano a mano had begun.

The Doctor demurred mildly to the liberal/queers charge, but before he could finish, Holder demanded, "The board of trustees of the American Psychiatric Association has reprimanded you for your expression of an opinion as to predictions of future dangerousness, have they not?"

Seemingly unperturbed, the Doctor replied, "They sent me a letter saying that this will serve as a reprimand."

"And the American Psychiatric Association has labeled your predictions as *quackery*, haven't they?"

"No, sir, they have not," the Doctor said, still smiling. A majority of the profession is "in agreement with me, that you have to predict dangerousness every day" in commitment proceedings and the like.

"And isn't it true that the A.P.A. filed an amicus brief in which they labeled your opinions as quackery?"

"The Supreme Court disagreed with them," said the Doctor, "and thought that my testimony was appropriate."

"I would object, Your Honor, to any testimony, as not being recognized within the field in which he practices."

"I will overrule the objection," said the judge. And at last prosecutor Smith was able to ask an answer to the killer question.

"Doctor, based upon that hypothetical, those facts that I explained to you, do you have an opinion within reasonable medical probability as to whether the defendant, Aaron Lee Fuller, will commit criminal acts of violence that will constitute a continuing threat to society?"

"Yes, sir, I most certainly do have an opinion with regard to that."

"What is your opinion, please, sir?"

"That absolutely there is no question, no doubt whatsoever, that the individual you described, that has been involved in repeated escalating behavior of violence, will commit acts of violence in the future, and represents a very serious threat to any society which he finds himself in."

"Do you mean that he will be a threat in any society, even the prison society?"

"Absolutely, yes, sir. He will do the same thing there that he will do outside."

And that was it. All the "medical," "scientific" testimony the jury needed—in any case all they'd *get*—to justify a judgment that Aaron Lee Fuller was too dangerous to live, beyond hope of redemption, and ought to be put to death.

But Floyd Holder wasn't quite finished with his assault on the Doctor. He still had cross-examination. He still had one more shot at saving Aaron Lee Fuller's life.

Do you recall the Randall Dale Adams case? Holder began.

The Doctor nodded warily and said, "I recall it well, yes, sir."

Are you as sure about this defendant as you were when you declared Randall Dale Adams was guilty and would kill again? Holder asked.

Again the courtroom tensed up. Even out in the prairie the papers had reported on the Adams case. How Adams, an accused cop killer, was sentenced to death with the help of the Doctor's testimony; how New York filmmaker Errol Morris came down to Dallas (originally to do a film about the Doctor) and began digging into the Adams case, eventually getting Adams's chief accuser—on death row for another murder—to claim that he, not Adams, had fired the fatal bullet at the cop. How this, and holes in purported eyewitness testimony uncovered in *The Thin Blue Line*, resulted in Adams's conviction being thrown out and Adams being freed last year after twelve years in prison.

Looking totally unperturbed, the Doctor said dramatically, "Those people that were involved in the case know that he is guilty. I examined

Mr. Adams . . . there is no question in my mind as well as [the mind of] the jury who convicted him that he is guilty."

And did you say of Randall Dale Adams that he will continue his previous behavior? Holder asked.

"I most certainly said that," the Doctor said defiantly. "And he will."

(Later, he told me that, despite everything, he *still* has no doubt about it: the new confession by Adams's accuser was a sham, a lie by a death-row inmate with nothing to lose who "wanted to jack the system around." And then the following week, in the Dallas trial, the Doctor went even further: he testified not only that he believed Randall Dale Adams did the killing, but that he was certain Adams "will kill again.")

For a brief moment there in Lamesa, it looked as if Floyd Holder might have some momentum going in his assault on the Doctor. But then Holder made a fatal mistake. He fell into the Doctor's death trap, one of the patented devastating counterpunches that have earned the Doctor a reputation as a killing machine on cross-examination. Many lawyers told me the best thing to do is not to cross the Doctor at *all*, to minimize the damage he can do.

The Doctor had told me of the particular relish he has for doing damage on cross-examination. "I always hold something back for cross," he said one evening in Lubbock.

But Holder had done a lot of homework he didn't want to go to waste. He began as he had with the Adams question, a bit smugly. "In the case of *Rodriguez* v. *Texas*, 1978, [did you say of Rodriguez,] 'No matter where he is he will kill again'? . . . Do you remember that?"

Now, this might have been a good question because it was clear the Doctor couldn't recall who the hell Rodriguez was. But the Doctor— a poker player as well as a chess player—shrewdly calculated that Holder didn't know the details either. And so he felt free to spring a trap of his own.

The Doctor replied as if searching his memory and then coming upon a grim recollection. "Is Rodriguez the one that killed four women and raped thirty-eight?"

Of course, he had no idea what Rodriguez had done. But what the jury heard was: killed four, raped thirty-eight. In the silence that followed it became embarrassingly clear that Floyd Holder had no idea whether the Rodriguez he was citing had killed one or a hundred.

Holder tried to conceal how taken aback he was, but he didn't conceal it well. He looked down and shuffled some papers. He said something huffy about "I have no idea" who Rodriguez is, as if that wasn't the point.

But the point had been made, indelibly. And it wasn't his point. The point the jury got was that the Doctor was trying to protect society, protect *them*, from multiple rapist-murderers, and that Holder hadn't troubled to find out how many women Rodriguez had raped and murdered (five of the twelve jurors were women). He was only interested in some kind of legal loophole that let a monster like that loose on the streets again.

It was all over then. Holder had lost not only the moment but his composure, and he never did get it back. He continued briefly; he even brought up the nickname "Dr. Death." ("The jury may not appreciate how famous you are, sir. . . . They call you Dr. Death, don't they?") But he never recovered from the deadly land mine the Doctor had detonated under his feet with his Rodriguez reply.

A day later the Lamesa jury took two hours to agree unanimously on a death sentence for twenty-one-year-old Aaron Lee Fuller.

One down, two to go.

●   ■   ●

Flocks of sandhill cranes roost on the flanks of the empty highway leading back from Lamesa to Lubbock. The fragile endangered birds apparently like the arid isolation of the bare prairie flats as a winter resting ground before their journey north. Midway on his hasty journey between death-penalty trials the Doctor is pumped up by his victory in Lamesa, primed for fresh battle this afternoon in Lubbock.

"By God, if it isn't war," he tells me, "I don't know what war is!"

If it's war, why is he fighting it? He says that he's "taken a lot of shit over this Dr. Death crap," and that if he had it to do over again he might have stuck to uncontested competency hearings. But the Doctor doesn't see himself fighting just to put an end to the life of the defendant. He sees himself fighting to save the lives of potential future victims, the ones the defendant will kill—even inside the pen—if he's not put to death.

To illustrate, he tells me the story of the Zimmermann study and the tree-branch rapist—probably his most heartfelt statement about why he becomes a death-penalty partisan in the courtroom.

Back when his practice of predicting future dangerousness in death-penalty trials first became controversial, the Doctor says, "a Dallas judge named Zimmermann decided to see how I'd done in my record of predictions in *his* courtroom. So they went back and looked at the people I'd examined in court. And there were only two people I said would kill again: Terry Turner and Jesse Eugene Woods. Because it's *rare* for me to say someone will kill again. Most murderers aren't going to—a majority of them will never kill again. Spouse-passion-type killing, you know, after going through all that they'd do almost anything in the world to avoid trouble. Passion killers often make model prisoners. That's one of the things that's misleading. Most murderers on the whole make model prisoners. But that's not true of these sociopaths."

Like, for instance, Terry Turner and Jesse Eugene Woods.

"Terry Turner was a little sociopath—he was, oh, nineteen, twenty years old and a forty-five-year-old woman took him in. She felt sorry for him. Gave him a place to stay, got him a little job. He raped and killed her. They didn't find him guilty of capital murder—something got screwed up, I can't remember. Anyway, Terry got out of the pen in three years. *On the way home* from the pen he raped a woman. Within thirty days he'd taken a fourteen-year-old girl, raped and killed her. And took a tree branch and shoved it all the way up in her vagina.

"Then there was the other one, Jesse Eugene Woods. I'm trying to think what Jesse did the first time. I believe he killed somebody in a fight. [Actually, the charge was aggravated assault and sexual assault, not murder.] Anyway, I examined Jesse and I said, 'I guarantee this guy is going to kill again.' Anyway, Woods got out and beat, I think it was, an old woman to death. And after Judge Zimmermann looked at those cases he said, 'Well, I can testify that Dr. Grigson has been 100 percent accurate in this court.' "

The Doctor does not offer the two-case Zimmermann story as serious statistical vindication. What he's saying is that he's got to be aggressive, persuasive, he's got to *sell* his testimony to juries, so they won't let people like Terry Turner and Jesse Eugene Woods loose to kill again. That's why, he says, he feels compelled to go the extra mile. Not just to testify, but to win—in order to protect potential victims from horrific fates like that suffered by the fourteen-year-old girl.

The problems the psychiatric profession has with the Doctor concern not so much his motives as his claims to be testifying *as a scientist*. In a blistering attack on the Doctor's testimonial practice in its 1983 brief to the Supreme Court in *Barefoot* v. *Estelle*, the American Psychiatric Association, the governing body of the profession, flatly states:

> Psychiatrists should not be permitted to offer a prediction concerning the long-term future dangerousness of a defendant in a capital case, at least . . . where the psychiatrist purports to testify *as a medical expert* possessing predictive expertise. . . . The large body of research in this area indicates that, even under the best of conditions, *psychiatric predictions of long-term future dangerousness are wrong in at least two out of every three cases.* The forecast of future violent conduct . . . is, at bottom, a lay determination . . . made on the basis of essentially actuarial data to which *psychiatrists* qua *psychiatrists can bring no special interpretive skills.* . . . The use of psychiatric testimony on this issue causes serious prejudice to the defendant. By dressing up the actuarial data with an "expert" opinion the psychiatrist's testimony is likely to receive undue weight. . . . [It] provides a false aura of certainty . . . impermissibly distorts the fact-finding process in capital cases. [My italics.]

Equally objectionable, the A.P.A. brief charges, is the Doctor's practice of diagnosing a defendant as a severe sociopath on the basis of a prosecutor's hypothetical question, without examining him—and then telling the jury that the sociopath "diagnosis" is scientific basis for guaranteeing future dangerousness.

"Such a diagnosis simply cannot be made on the basis of a hypothetical question. . . . The psychiatrist cannot exclude alternative diagnoses [such as] illnesses that plainly do not indicate a general propensity to commit criminal acts.

"These deficiencies," the A.P.A. told the Supreme Court, "strip the psychiatric testimony of all value in the present context."

In a six–three decision in that case the Supreme Court majority held that—even granting the truth of the A.P.A.'s objections—the Doctor's testimony should not be barred as constitutionally impermissible because the adversary process of the trial would permit other psychiatrists to challenge his conclusions in court, allowing the jurors as fact finders to decide the merits.

But Justice Harry Blackmun, ordinarily a middle-of-the-roader in death-penalty cases, wrote a furious dissent declaring, "In capital cases the specious testimony of a psychiatrist, colored, in the eyes of an impressionable jury, by the inevitable untouchability of a medical specialist's words, *equates with death itself*." (My italics.)

The Doctor disagrees. The Doctor believes the A.P.A. condemnation is based not on science but on the emotional animus of liberal psychiatrists against the death penalty—and against *him* for being the death penalty's cutting edge in Texas.

The Doctor says he's better qualified than any American Psychiatric Association committee to pronounce upon the science involved because of his unmatchable data base—the examinations he's done of 12,000 criminals, 1,400 murderers, 391 capital-murder defendants.

The Doctor has a hyperbolic counter-argument for those who criticize future-dangerousness predictions: "It's ridiculous to say you can't predict future dangerousness. After Hitler killed the first Jew, would you say he was dangerous? After the second? After a million? How many do you need to know for sure?"

True enough, perhaps, but what if instead of Hitler we look at twenty-one-year-old Aaron Lee Fuller. Is he incorrigibly evil? His defense attorney introduced evidence that Fuller had been physically abused as a child. Is he beyond rehabilitation? Should a jury be told there's a "medical certainty" he's too dangerous to live?

Curiously enough, considering the Doctor's Hitler analogy, the next defendant, the one the Doctor is racing back to Lubbock to pronounce upon this afternoon, is sometimes called "Adolf." The defendant usually refers to himself as *Adolfo* Hernandez, but on his rap sheet, his list of a.k.a.'s included "aka *Adolf* Hernandez." And Lubbock prosecutor Travis Ware invariably refers to him as Adolf Hernandez.

Adolfo Hernandez was a thirty-eight-year-old ex-con with a long history of glue sniffing and house burglaries when he committed his first murder—beating an elderly woman to death with a baseball bat, a big, heavyweight Louisville Slugger type. Just so the jury wouldn't forget, throughout the Lubbock trial, or at least during the death-penalty portion of it I saw, D.A. Travis Ware stalked around the courtroom questioning witnesses with the menacing bloodstained Louisville Slugger resting on his shoulder.

Lubbock's a big town compared with Lamesa; it's the jewel of the West Texas prairie, with major cotton and cattle money, home to the Texas Tech Red Raiders. The Lubbock trial featured a larger-scale cast of characters. There was D.A. Travis Ware—a Texas boy who was educated in England and returned home to become a hard-line law-and-order prosecutor. He drives around with a machine gun in his sports coupe, and has never lost a death-penalty trial.

When we arrived back at the Lubbock courthouse around noon on the day of the Doctor's doubleheader lambada of death, Travis Ware was stalking the courtroom with the Louisville Slugger murder bat over his shoulder, beating up on one of several defense experts who had been flown in to beat up on the Doctor before he even took the stand. The courtroom seemed filled with shrinks taking notes, with lawyers who had upcoming death-penalty cases scoping out strategies against the Doctor. And indeed they'd thrown everything in the book at him this time—psychologists, sociologists, penologists.

This time, Brian Murray, an aggressive young lawyer on the Hernandez defense team, led the direct assault against the Doctor. He began confidently by asking the Doctor about the accuracy of future-dangerousness predictions. He began confidently because he was building on two days of testimony by defense experts who had recited studies all saying you couldn't do it—you couldn't scientifically, medically, accurately predict the dangerousness of any given killer.

"Did you follow up on [your predictions]," Murray asked the Doctor, "to see whether your analysis was correct?"

The Doctor smiled almost beatifically at the question as it came floating up to the plate, stepped into it, smashed it out of the park.

"The only study I know," the Doctor said mildly, "was done by Judge James Zimmermann in Dallas, who conducted a study of all those [times] where I'd predicted a person would kill again in his court. And

I had only predicted two of them. And both of them did again." He didn't go into the tree branch. He didn't need to. It would have been overkill.

What he said, in the mildest of tones, was: "Both of them *unfortunately* had been released from the pen after committing murder. And both of them within a very short period of time committed murder again."

He might as well have given Adolfo Hernandez a lethal injection right then and there. He was throwing the bodies left for dead by Turner and Woods in the jury's lap and telling each juror: Twice before I told juries these men would kill, and both times those juries ignored me and both times innocent people were murdered because *those* juries didn't listen to me. If you let Adolfo Hernandez live and if—*when*— he kills again, don't say I didn't warn you.

In the mildest, friendliest, courtliest, country-doctor, Marcus Welby way he was telling them: *The blood will be on your hands.*

Once again the poor defense attorney who'd stepped into this trap found himself demoralized, disoriented, the wind knocked out of him, stumbling through the remainder of his examination of the Doctor. Stumbling eventually into a final, extra-cruel trap the Doctor sprang on him at the end.

Defender Murray was asking the Doctor about the absence of any neurological or mental-test evidence on the defendant.

Isn't it true, he asked the Doctor, that in the absence of any neurological studies you can't rule out that organic brain damage or retardation might be at the bottom of Adolfo Hernandez's problem, not your diagnosis of sociopathy?

"An attorney representing a client in a capital-murder case *not knowing* a possibility that would be a defense?" the Doctor replied. "That would be absurd."

Bad enough. But the doomed defense attorney wouldn't withdraw from this disaster area fast enough.

"The question was, what if that [testing for retardation, etc.] was not done? Would that affect the result?"

"Are we talking about a mentally retarded *attorney*?" the Doctor asked.

The whole courtroom rocked with laughter. Attorney Murray was left standing there glaring, humiliated, paralyzed.

The Doctor smiled benignly. Murray sat down, defeated. A day later the jury voted unanimously for death. It took them two hours.

Two down, one to go.

●   ■   ●

By the time we got back to Dallas for the final trial of the Doctor's triple-header I'd begun to believe that he was invulnerable, unstoppable on the stand. That the death-penalty process in Texas was fatally skewed whenever the Doctor took the stand to testify—his skills as a witness unbalanced the scales of justice.

The problem is, the Supreme Court decision in *Barefoot* v. *Estelle* (which permitted the Doctor's hypothetical future-dangerousness testimony) envisioned a vigorous adversarial process in which defense psychiatrists and lawyers could present their case to the jury, dispute, refute his "science." In reality, the Doctor's charisma and deadliness as a witness just overwhelm the process and create an intrinsic unfairness.

But finally, in Dallas, I saw the Doctor take a hit. Not a fatal one, but one that threw him off his stride. Even left him speechless on the stand for a moment—something nobody's ever seen before. For that one moment the Doctor's mask of utter confidence and geniality, of Marcus Welby-like disinterested benevolence, slipped.

It happened in the death-penalty trial of Gayland Bradford, a twenty-one-year-old black man accused of murdering a twenty-nine-year-old security guard in a Dallas grocery store.

There was little doubt about the nature of Gayland Bradford's deed. It's all there in the sickly-gray cinema verité of the security-camera videotape they played at his trial.

The tape was particularly devastating because in its opening moments it captured something about the security-guard victim's life as well as his death. It showed him, moments before he was blown away, horsing around with the cashiers, doing a bit of an Oliver Hardy imitation, arms akimbo, saying, with mock outrage, "*I hate this tie.*"

Enter Gayland Bradford. A black-clad figure cuts purposefully through the gray static of the videotape, swiftly reaches the security guard. Sticks a gun into his spine and, before he knows what's happened, blows a hole in him.

There's a sickening POP on the sound track.

The guard sprawls backward beneath a checkout counter, bleeding but alive. "O.K., O.K., *O.K.!*" he pleads, holding up his hand, as if to fend off the gun Gayland Bradford is pointing at him. "*O.K.!*" he says one last time.

It's not O.K. with Gayland Bradford. He pumps three more shots into the guy, quieting him forever.

An open-and-shut case. To nobody's surprise, the jury took twenty minutes to bring in a guilty verdict.

But the death-penalty phase of the trial brought two surprises. First, the Doctor would get to do something he rarely does these days. He'd get to go in and examine the murderer before testifying against him. (The judge had granted a prosecution motion that would have barred defense shrinks from introducing mitigating evidence from their exams unless the prosecution shrink—the Doctor—got to examine Bradford, too.)

That was the first surprise. The other surprise in this case was the Doctor's attitude toward Gayland Bradford. It seemed to me from the moment he showed up at the trial and got a look at Bradford that the Doctor brought more than his usual competitive zeal to this case—he brought something extra, an almost personal animus, to the crusade to get Gayland Bradford executed.

I'm not sure why. Perhaps in part because we were back in Dallas, the Doctor's home turf, but also a place where widespread publicity about his role in the Randall Dale Adams case had revived the Dr. Death image, challenged his reputation for invincibility and certitude. Perhaps also because he would be facing a particularly wily and experienced opponent on the defense team—Paul Brauchle—who'd tangled with the Doctor before and knew his tricks.

Or maybe it was just cultural, maybe it *did* all come down to Gayland Bradford's lightning-bolt haircut, which, as we shall see, was certainly the flash point at the climax of the trial.

Whatever the source, I first noticed the Doctor's extra-aggressiveness in this case on the Monday afternoon following the big Friday doubleheader. He was sitting in court furiously scrawling notes about the defense psychiatrist's testimony, urgently passing the notes up to Dallas D.A. Dan Hagood to use in his cross-examination of the defense shrink. It was as if the Doctor wanted not merely to refute the defense psychiatrist's testimony, he wanted to destroy him.

And, oddly enough, for different reasons I was feeling outraged about the defense psychiatrist, whose ineffectual performance on the stand typified what seemed to me the bankruptcy of conventional psychiatry in dealing with the life-or-death urgency of death-penalty trials.

Because this case had a real, arguable psychiatric issue. Unlike the Aaron Lee Fuller case, unlike the Adolfo Hernandez case, in which there was very little the defense could find to mitigate the horror and cold-bloodedness of the killings (Fuller was very young, Hernandez was very drunk—that was the best they could do), here there was a quantifiable mitigating issue: the possibility that Gayland Bradford was retarded. The defense psychologist who examined him had tested Bradford at an I.Q. of 75, borderline retarded; the Texas penitentiary had tested him at 68.

Retardation does not excuse a killer from responsibility or punishment. But a recent, very important Supreme Court decision in a Texas death-penalty case—the *Penry* decision—held that a death-penalty jury must be asked to consider evidence of diminished capacity such as retardation in deciding whether a killer deserves the maximum sanction of death.

But a number, 75 or 68, wasn't enough. The Supreme Court decision did not hold that some arbitrary number disqualified a killer from capital punishment, merely that it could be *used* in the advocacy process of the death-penalty trial to argue for his life.

What Gayland Bradford needed was a powerful advocate to make the case that his lack of mental capacity diminished the degree of cold-blooded deliberation he brought to his crime.

What he got instead was a shrinking violet of an academic psychiatrist who clung to jargon-encrusted textbook clichés, who cowered behind his pose as an objective scientist and refused to *contend* for the life at stake, the way the Doctor contended for Gayland Bradford's death.

When this defense shrink came under furious attack on cross-examination by D.A. Hagood, he acted petulant, insulted, and irritated that a scientist of his stature and dignity should have to defend himself in the sweaty arena of the courtroom.

Even the defense team was dismayed by its witness's performance.

"This fucker is so stupid," Paul Brauchle confided to me after the slaughter was over, "that he doesn't even *know* how stupid he really is."

I asked the Doctor what he might have said if he'd been hired to testify in Gayland Bradford's defense. And he said, in effect, that he could probably have saved Gayland Bradford's life.

How?

"What you do," he said offhandedly, "is tell the jury, 'Look, it's an awful crime, a tragedy, but this is a scared retarded kid.' Sure the prosecution objects to your injecting this, but you've reached out and planted something the jury can hold on to, not all that bullshit about the *Diagnostic Manual*."

Of course. Suddenly it seemed obvious. But in none of the three death-penalty trials I'd observed had any of the supposedly liberal psychiatrists had the will or the skill to reach out to the jury's heart the way the Doctor does. I began to think the only way a death-penalty trial in which he testifies can be fair is if the Doctor is forced to make the case for *both* sides.

That was not the case in the Gayland Bradford trial. After demonstrating how he might have saved Bradford's life, the Doctor proceeded, over the next forty-eight hours, to throw himself with redoubled vigor into the effort to ensure his death.

To this end he focused his sights on the unusual one-on-one, head-to-head "examination" of Gayland Bradford the court's ruling had mandated.

Before the exam, he had two objectives. First, he wanted to refute the notion that Bradford was retarded. He didn't buy the 75 I.Q. figure.

"That's bullshit," he told me. "I know it's higher than that."

"Based on what?" I asked him.

"Based on what I've heard," he said vaguely.

He didn't disclose the other objective to me right away, but it became the main objective of his exam. He wanted to pin *another murder* on Gayland Bradford. He wanted to prove he'd killed more than once before—all the more reason to guarantee he'd kill again.

He's played investigative shrink before with great success, he told me. A number of times he has examined killers arrested for the first time for murder and—acting on a hunch, on experience, on his data base—he's not only tumbled to the fact these people have killed before, he's gotten them to confess it. He can smell a repeat killer when he sees one, he says. He thought he saw one in Gayland Bradford.

And so it came to pass that at 4:35 P.M. on February 7, 1990, the Doctor was ushered into a conference room in the Dallas County jail. He introduced himself to Gayland Bradford, who was advised of his Fifth Amendment rights against self-incrimination. The Doctor gave Gayland Bradford cigarettes; he gave him coffee; he gave him a ninety-minute "psychiatric examination" that was less like a medical procedure than a third degree in a precinct detective tank.

●　　　■　　　●

"He's killed before. I know it."
Those were the Doctor's first words when he and his wife joined me for a previously scheduled dinner—right after leaving Gayland Bradford in jail.

And as soon as we sat down to dinner at the Mansion on Turtle Creek, the posh Dallas nouvelle-southwestern-cuisine mecca, the Doctor, flushed with victory, spilled out the extraordinary story of his invasive investigative probe into Gayland Bradford's psyche.

It certainly was a curious dinner: the Doctor, ordering celebratory martini after martini (I counted four); the Doctor and his (third) wife, Vicki, describing their courtship on a Singles Bon Appetit cruise to Jamaica; the Doctor picking apart Gayland Bradford's psyche the way he picked apart the limbs of his honey-roasted quail.

Vicki's an attractive blonde pipeline-company executive, seventeen years younger than the fifty-six-year-old Doctor. She says he won her heart on the cruise when he tried to fix a kite-flying contest on her behalf. The Doctor, it seems, had bought hundreds of dollars' worth of kites to give away to the poor Jamaican children; he organized kite-flying contests for the gourmet singles; and—this was the thing that sealed her love—he even contrived to surreptitiously tie *an extra role of twine* to her kite string, to ensure hers would fly the highest and win the contest. She loved that gallant, competitive instinct about him. Still, they have some conflict because the Doctor seems to be a bit set in his ways about investments. Vicki, who's done quite well for herself, wants the two of them to buy a house together. The Doctor's also done well. He makes more than $200,000 a year from his private practice and his expert-witness fees ($150 an hour). Nonetheless, he wants to keep his capital in some investments he's made in gold. Neither seems willing to back down, and despite mutual declarations of love, they're considering splitting up over the house-buying issue.

●   ■   ●

I'd never seen the Doctor so animated, so thrilled with the chase, the hunt, as he was that night in his dramatic fresh-from-the-jail account of going head-to-head with Gayland Bradford.

He came on strong, he said. Forgetting about the conventional psychiatric procedure, which usually begins with a history and leads up to the crime, the Doctor early on got Gayland Bradford to take him through the murder step-by-step.

It was so fresh in his mind—and he still had his notes with him—that the Doctor recounted whole chunks of dialogue verbatim.

"Gayland goes through the whole killing bit," the Doctor began. "How the guard's saying 'O.K., O.K.,' and he's shooting him a few more times. At this point I say, 'Gayland, where did you get the gun?'

" 'Well, I had it.'

" 'How long have you had it?'

" 'Well, I don't know.'

"Finally I say, 'What did you *do* with your gun?'

" 'Well, I ditched it.'

" 'Well, *why?* Why did you do that? You didn't ditch the security guard's gun?'

" 'I wanted to get rid of it.'

" 'Look, something doesn't make sense here. You've made your confession, but you didn't tell them where the gun is. How come?'

" 'I just wanted *me* to know.'

"You hear that?" the Doctor asked us. "He says, 'I just wanted *me* to know.' It had already dawned on me that *he's killed somebody else* with it. Ballistics would show that. So because he doesn't want to be connected with the other killings, he won't say where the gun is. I don't say that to him. My mind's turning like mad. I said, 'Gayland, how come you won't tell them where the gun is? It doesn't make any sense. *Why, Gayland? Why?*'

"Of course, I'm giving him cigarettes and coffee and we almost smoked the defense psychiatrist [there observing] out of the room.

"And by the way," the Doctor added, "this kid's not retarded. This kid's vocabulary—I told him, 'I've heard doctors say that you have a 75 I.Q., that you are mentally retarded, but I want you to know whoever made that stupid statement is 100 percent wrong.' This with the defense psychiatrist who made the statement sitting right there," the Doctor chortled.

But the Doctor hadn't finished with the missing-gun question, and things soon built to an angry climax.

"I kept going, 'Why, Gayland? Why won't you tell me where the gun is?' Well, after the fourth or fifth time he said the reason he wouldn't say where the gun was is 'I don't know what the man who sold it to me might have done with it.'

"And of course I've got my wheels working, and I said, 'What do you mean, what he might have done with it?'

" 'Well, he might have killed somebody with it.' I said, 'Oh, now I understand. You were afraid that if they found the gun, and it had killed somebody else, they might put that killing on *you?*'

"He said, 'Yeah.' I said, 'Hey, that makes sense.' Turned to him and said, '*Gayland, this isn't the first time you ever killed anybody!*'

" 'What do you mean, man?'

" 'Gayland, this isn't your first one.'

"I tried another avenue. Started taking him through his past criminal record. Then asked him, 'When was the first time you broke the law and didn't get arrested? Didn't get caught?' He looked at me like 'You son of a bitch.' Said, 'I quit.' "

And that was it. "Well, he did say one more thing. As we were walking out, I kind of joked, I said to him, 'Hey, man, I know more about you than your own mother.' He said, 'Bullshit.' I said, 'I guarantee you I know you a whole lot *better* than your mother, because I know what you've done.' And as I was leaving he pointed his finger at me and said, 'You're slick.' "

"You're slick?"

"Yeah, it was 'Hey, man, you're slick.' It's the sociopath's compliment. It's the recognition of the sociopath for somebody who appreciates what he really is."

He's slick, the Doctor, yes. But almost too slick in this case. Because as it turned out, the Doctor's trial appearance the next morning in the

Gayland Bradford case was not the expected triumph he'd been brimming over with the night before.

Something happened that next morning on the stand. The Doctor made a serious misstep, went a little too far in his avidity to nail Gayland Bradford.

What happened could perhaps be attributed to the four martinis over dinner the night before. The Doctor did look a little pale and irritable as he took the stand. It was that irritability, I believe, that caused him to stumble.

Not at first, not during direct testimony. There it was possible to detect an edge, but it came across as aggressiveness. Indeed, he was more aggressive than I'd seen him before. Not only did he predict future dangerousness, not only did he attempt to demolish the "I.Q. 75" defense, not only did he inject his uncorroborated suspicion that Gayland Bradford had killed more than once before, he also told the jury, "Gayland Bradford is one of the most dangerous killers I've *ever* examined or come in contact with."

With all that, the Doctor didn't need the haircut remark. But he just couldn't help himself.

Paul Brauchle has a deceptively easygoing manner. Slight, extremely soft-spoken, with a puckish sense of humor, he's cordial to the Doctor, but he has some very strong feelings about the Doctor's practice.

"If you ask me, *he's* the sociopath," Brauchle told me in a courthouse-corridor conversation. "He's the one who, despite reprimands, goes around making pronouncements which have been condemned by his profession. He's the one who does it over and over again with no remorse," Brauchle added. "Just like a sociopath."

Brauchle told me he's learned to be wary of the Doctor on cross, so I wasn't expecting great things; I was surprised when he took the Doctor's haircut comment and blasted it out of the park.

Now, earlier, while discussing the defendant with me, the Doctor had remarked a couple of times upon Gayland Bradford's haircut. It was something of an advanced fashion statement, Gayland Bradford's look. Unlike, say, Aaron Lee Fuller, who tried to craft a whole new, penitent image out of his crew cut, Gayland Bradford was *not* making a fashion statement calculated to ingratiate himself with the all-white jury deciding his fate.

It was a carefully sculpted flattop with shaved sides, common enough in urban areas everywhere by now. But with an added, less common touch: into each stubbly, shaved side of his head Gayland Bradford had had inscribed the unmistakable outline of a lightning bolt.

Despite the fact that his life was hanging by a thread, that thread consisting of the jury's judgment of whether he might be dangerous in the future, Gayland Bradford had chosen a fashion statement that—whatever its private meaning to him—seemed to announce to the jury, "*I am one dangerous dude.*"

It was, however, certainly something the jury was already aware of. The Doctor didn't need to point it out to them.

Still, the Doctor couldn't resist taking a shot at it. It happened in the middle of cross-examination. Brauchle was questioning him about whether he'd prejudged the Gayland Bradford case, before he had walked in to examine him.

Perhaps the Doctor knew he was on thin ice on this subject and saw the haircut wisecrack as an escape.

In any case, when Brauchle asked him if he'd formed any *other* opinions about Gayland Bradford before he examined him, the Doctor said, trying for a laugh:

"Well, I thought that was the weirdest haircut I'd ever seen."

There was a bit of nervous laughter in the courtroom which stopped dead when Paul Brauchle shot back:

"*Pretty good reason to kill him, right?*"

Then there was silence. It was one of those courtroom moments of truth that cut to the heart of the matter.

The Doctor himself was speechless for a moment.

Then lamely, plaintively he volunteered:

"Well, I'd never *seen* a haircut like that."

At this point the judge, mercifully, decreed a recess.

But for one revealing moment the Doctor's mask had slipped. The image of geniality and nonpartisanship he was so good at projecting to juries was betrayed by what seemed to be hostility. Not just to a haircut, but to Gayland Bradford himself. Not merely to Bradford's crime, but to what he saw as Bradford's cultural *alienness*. It seemed to call into question the Doctor's ability to get inside Gayland Bradford's head if he couldn't get past his haircut.

Pretty good reason to kill him, right?

Nonetheless, if it bothered the jury, it didn't bother them for too long. The moment of exposure passed rapidly. The Doctor looked shaken during the lunch recess; he knew he'd been roughed up by Brauchle, told me he knew he had to suppress his emotions, cool himself out. When he returned to the stand, he'd adopted a totally Gandhian tactic: softspoken, barely audible one-word answers to Brauchle's sallies. No combativeness, total agreeableness. Brauchle gave up and the cross ended with a whimper, not a bang.

As it turned out, this jury did take longer than the Lubbock and Lamesa juries to make up its mind. Not two hours as in Lamesa and Lubbock, but six hours. Still, when they came back they'd followed the Doctor's orders. They'd voted yes unanimously on the Special Issues.

Gayland Bradford was sent down to death row in Huntsville to join Aaron Lee Fuller, Adolfo Hernandez, and 322 other condemned murderers waiting out the appeals of their appointments with the Big Needle. In the fifteen years since the Supreme Court gave the go-ahead for the resumption of capital punishment, Texas has executed 33 of its death-row population. In the past, it's generally taken six and a half years before a death-row inmate gets strapped onto a gurney and hooked up to the lethal intravenous infusion.

But there are signs that the pace may quicken for Fuller, Hernandez, and Bradford. Two March 1990 Supreme Court decisions may cut years off the average length of time spent before execution by cutting off secondary avenues of appeal previously available in the form of habeas corpus hearings. In a recent Texas gubernatorial-primary campaign, two Democratic candidates tried to outbrag each other in promising how many they'd execute how fast. And it's not just in Texas—heart of the "death belt," as foes call the five southern states with the largest death-row population—that the rate of executions may be about to make a quantum leap. This month, California has scheduled its first execution in a quarter-century and will begin the inexorable process of bringing its huge backlog of 273 death-row inmates to the gas chamber.

For those who believe the death penalty is a deterrent to murder and who favor more death sentences executed more quickly, the Doctor is something of a hero of productivity. Almost like an Old West marshal riding into town to swiftly string up evildoers. To those who oppose the death penalty, he's the embodiment of all that's arbitrary and capricious about how we select who gets killed.

But few would disagree with Gayland Bradford's awed assessment of the Doctor: He's *slick*.

Or Justice Blackmun's: He *equates with death itself*.

—*VANITY FAIR*
May 1990

DEAD RINGERS

A BIZARRE CASE OF THE DEATH OF TWINS

It was the striped shorts that caused the mix-up at the morgue. When the cops and the maintenance man broke into apartment 10H, slogged their way through the debris covering the living-room floor and found the bodies in the bedroom, they found themselves with an identity problem as well. The maintenance man was certain the bodies in question were gynecologist Cyril Marcus—the tenant of 10H—and his twin brother, gynecologist Stewart Marcus, but he wasn't certain which body belonged to which twin.

Visibility was not favorable to making any kind of identification. The warm moist July air that rushed into the apartment with the cops hit the bone-dry chill within, precipitating a mist which rolled across the living-room floor into the bedroom, picking up fumes from rotting chicken salad sandwiches and human excrement on the way, fogging up the death scene with its sickly vapors.

Not the sort of atmosphere to encourage leisurely speculation about the identity of twins, not that they looked at all identical in death. One twin lay facedown across the head of one of the twin beds, the other faceup on the floor at the foot of the other twin bed. The face of the face-up twin retained the frozen clarity of recent death. The other twin had no face. Dead longer, his features had been blotted out by decomposition. The face-up twin on the floor wore nothing but a pair of long black socks bunched down around his ankles and a flimsy shroud of paper toweling he had apparently pulled across his body in the moments before death. The face-down twin had only a black sock dangling from his left foot and a pair of blue striped shorts on his body.

The maintenance man thought those striped shorts might be a clue; he thought he had seen them once before. Some time ago he had been doing some minor repair work in this apartment and he recalled Dr. Cyril Marcus walking around in shorts much like the ones on the body facedown on the bed.

That's what he told the cops, and that's what the cops told the man from the morgue wagon who arrived later to bundle up the bodies and take them away for autopsy. The man from the morgue wagon wrote CYRIL MARCUS on the red ID tags he attached to the toe and wrist of the twin on the bed and STEWART MARCUS to the tags he put on the other.

It was the other way round. Stewart had either been wearing his brother Cyril's striped shorts when he died or a similarly striped pair of his own. In any case, when the two bodies were finally wheeled into the basement receiving room of the morgue, the clerk there assigned the body tagged CYRIL to body locker #109 and the one tagged STEWART to locker #33.

That night at the morgue when the ex-wife of Cyril Marcus could not identify the faceless body from locker #109—the one tagged CYRIL— the medical examiners suspected a mix-up. They summoned a forensic odontologist, a specialist in making identifications from dental charts, to examine X rays of the twins' teeth. When he finally declared that CYRIL was Stewart and STEWART was Cyril, someone went back and corrected the body-locker registration cards, switching the numbers rather than the names. The body-locker entries on the registration cards now looked like this:

STEWART MARCUS	CYRIL MARCUS
Locker #109	Locker #33

By this time it was too late. The story had hit the papers on Thursday, July 17. The *Daily News* gave it the full front-page-headline treatment reserved for spectacular deaths in luxury buildings: FIND TWIN DOCS DEAD IN POSH PAD. The *Times*, more reticent at first, subsequently moved the twins story up to the front page when the issue of the regulatory practices of the medical profession grew out of the deaths. Most of the original stories had one thing in common: dependent as the reporters were on police and morgue sources, they had Cyril on the bed in shorts and Stewart on the floor in socks. Even a *New York Post* follow-up story four months after the deaths—purporting to set the record straight on the original mix-up—managed to get the right twin on the floor and the right one on the bed but had the order in which they died reversed. Feature pieces that followed up the front pages tended to treat the twins as if they were as interchangeable as their body-locker numbers. One writer seemed to get so carried away with the concept of fused twin identities that she fused the twin *beds* into one. Her description of the death scene featured instead "a big double bed."

In the waning weeks of that summer, it seemed that every citizen of New York City who had ever been to a gynecologist, every person who had ever known a twin or twins, and many who had done neither, had a theory or two about the Marcus twins and how they died.

●   ■   ●

They called themselves infertility specialists, but in the eyes of many of their grateful patients they were nothing less than fertility gods. The God of Genesis, one recalls, was a busy gynecologist and fertility specialist. The wives of Abraham, of Isaac, and of Jacob all suffered from barrenness until God intervened and caused them to conceive. Bringing fertility out of barrenness is, in fact, a distinguishing metaphor of the Old Testament: the fertility of the promised land is only for those who obey the commandments delivered in the barren desert. In almost all cultures, anyone who has the touch, the divine inspiration, or whatever it takes to induce conception, is regarded as a holy man. The Marcus brothers were secularized heirs of this tradition, using a whole repertoire of medical techniques—hormones, surgery, fertility drugs—to accomplish the magic that shamans had performed in the past.

"They were like gods," said one woman who had gone to several gynecologists and spent years of hopelessness before treatment by the Marcus brothers helped her conceive and give birth to her first child. "They were miracle workers," said another woman. "It was like magic," said a third.

Women from all over the East made pilgrimages to the Marcuses' office and to the Gynecological Infertility Clinic they presided over at New York Hospital. Women who had been to gynecologist after gynecologist, taken test after test, drug after drug and had yet to conceive. Women who were approaching or passing forty and desperately wanted a child before it was too late. Women who were able to conceive, but who had suffered miscarriage after miscarriage, hoping to deliver just one healthy child. "A lot of the women in that office were last-chance Charlies," said one patient, who eventually gave birth to two healthy children under the supervision of the Marcus brothers.

There are, in fact, hundreds of healthy children all over the country who wouldn't exist today had it not been for the Marcus brothers—children named Stewart and Cyril, even Marc, by grateful parents. Some women are so grateful they speak as if, in some ghostly way, the twins had actually fathered their children. "I had my first baby by Cyril," they'll say, or, "Stewart finally got me pregnant. He did everything but plant the seed."

●   ■   ●

The homicide cops ruled out murder almost immediately. The door to the death-scene apartment was double-locked from the inside, which meant either that one of the dead twins within murdered the other and took his own life, or—more likely, since there were no signs of violence on either body—both took their own lives in one way or another.

At first the way seemed obvious. The man from the morgue found a number of yellow Nembutal (a common barbiturate sleeping pill) capsules scattered on the floor around the body. The homicide cops found a number of empty vials labeled Demerol throughout the sea of rubbish elsewhere in the apartment. The maintenance man discovered dozens more empty Nembutal bottles in a kitchen cabinet.

Then an odd development. The toxicologist in the medical examiner's office reported that *no* Demerol and *no* barbiturates had been found in either body. The findings seemed to rule out suicide by any well-known drug.

"I don't mind telling you we have a major medical mystery on our hands," said acting Chief Medical Examiner Dominick DiMaio. "We've exhausted all the regular possibilities and now we're going for rare things—exotic is the word, I guess."

One week later, when all tests for exotic killer drugs turned out negative, too, the medical examiner's office proposed an exotic theory instead: the twins didn't die from drugs, they died from lack of drugs; they were both chronic barbiturate addicts who died from the convulsions and seizures accompanying "acute pentobarbital withdrawal." This explanation didn't satisfy many people. It assumed the twins went into simultaneous comas from heavy barbiturate *use*; stayed in the comas long enough to metabolize all the barbiturates in their systems; emerged from the comas to go immediately into seizures so simultaneous and incapacitating that neither could make use of the anti-convulsants also found at the death scene. It also assumed neither twin could call for help or help the other. The theory apparently didn't even satisfy the medical examiner himself. He quietly sent Marcus-twin tissue samples out to another lab for further analysis.

Meanwhile, an even more exotic possibility—the bleeding hemorrhoid theory—came from an unlikely source: Dr. Hugh Luckey, the president of New York Hospital-Cornell Medical Center, where the two doctors had practiced for fourteen years. Dr. Luckey and his hospital—one of the oldest (1771) and most highly respected in the country—were under considerable pressure at the time. Questions had been raised by the Marcus brothers' bizarre death about New York Hospital's practices to protect patients. A *New York Times* story strongly suggested that the twins had been drug abusers for years and cited a report that one of them—apparently under the influence—had staggered into a hospital operating room and ripped an anesthetic mask off a patient's face. (The hospital denied it ever happened.) A *Times* editorial attacked the hospital for "stonewalling" inquiries about the Marcuses' role at the hospital; a Queens congressman called the Marcus affair "a medical Watergate" and called for a cutoff of federal funds to the hospital until all questions were answered.

So it is understandable that Dr. Luckey and hospital officials might want to cast doubt on barbiturate-related theories of the twin doctors' deaths.

"Just because there were barbiturate bottles doesn't mean they died of barbiturate withdrawal," Dr. Luckey said. "I will tell you something: any smart physician could dispose of himself by a mechanism which could never be discovered by anyone, including his insurance companies. . . . No relationship to the Marcus brothers, I have no evidence, but I know the way I'd do it if I were going to."

How would Dr. Luckey do it?

"By injecting something in places where you'd never find it [the injection mark]. Like in a hemorrhoid. A hemorrhoid bleeds you know. . . ."

Dr. Luckey and fellow hospital executives seemed to relish the mystery surrounding the Marcus brothers' decline and death. Toward the close of a lengthy interview during which Dr. Luckey claimed he had not the slightest clue to the mysterious malady that destroyed the twins' brilliant careers, Dr. Luckey and hospital administrator Dr. Mel Platt engaged in a curious dialogue, apparently to discourage further inquiry, reproduced here, verbatim:

> PLATT: If I could figure it out I'd write the greatest novel of all times, because this is an enigma that's going to be with us for a long time.
> LUCKEY: And I'd buy the movie rights. You're damn right. I can tell you this: you're not gonna find out.
> PLATT: You're not gonna find out.
> LUCKEY: You're not gonna find out.
> PLATT: I wish I could find out.
> LUCKEY: That's the honest-to-God truth. You're not gonna find out.

The homicide cops found something out. They were able to piece together the bare outline of the sequence of the deaths, enough to uncover the most perplexing question of all. The smell of a decomposing body, a smell the maintenance man swore he could not mistake after combat service in World War II, was detectable as early as Monday, July 14. Yet on Tuesday, July 15, two separate doormen saw a man they identified as Cyril Marcus stagger out of the apartment building, disappear and return, weaving and stumbling, to another entrance, where a relief doorman accompanied him up the elevator to the tenth floor. He declined any assistance entering the apartment and shortly thereafter told his answering service he wanted no further calls.

What was Cyril doing when Stewart died? Why did he stay with the body at first, then leave it? But most of all, *why did he go back?*

Dr. Alan Guttmacher might be able to suggest an answer to that last question—if he were alive. Twenty years ago, Guttmacher, himself a twin, an expert on twins, and a gynecologist, too, intervened forcefully in the lives of the Marcus twins: he succeeded in splitting them apart for the first and last times of their lives.

Dr. Guttmacher had strong views about twins. He called them monsters. That's the quasi-medical term—descended from an eighteenth-century midwife's manual—for twins who are physically conjoined at birth, a phenomenon we now call Siamese twins.

"All separate identical twins may be regarded as monsters who have successfully escaped the various stages of monstrosity," Dr. Guttmacher wrote. Monsters lucky enough to escape physical conjoinment must constantly be on guard against slipping back into some sort of monsterhood through *psychic* conjoinment. Because of the constant peril of mutually confused identities, Guttmacher comes close to calling physically conjoined monsters *healthier* than most ordinary identical twins. "No Siamese twins have ever been known to succumb to dementia," he points out. "Nor have any sought to end the lives they are doomed to live together."

●   ■   ●

They were born on June 2, 1930 (yes, Gemini), Stewart leading the way, Cyril following two minutes behind, a pattern of dominance that continued into their childhood and adolescence—Stewart the natural leader, outgoing, effervescent; Cyril more withdrawn and quiet, unlike his brother a left-hander, but otherwise apparently content to serve as his brother's right-hand man.

When the two of them ran for class office at Bayonne, New Jersey, high school, it was Stewart who ran for president, Cyril for treasurer. (Both lost.) Both were selected for the National Honor Society, but it was Stewart who won the B'nai B'rith essay contest. Both were considered extremely bright, but it was Stewart who became valedictorian, Cyril who settled for salutatorian. Both got the usual laudatory yearbook captions, but it was Stewart who was described as the twin "bound to win." Both went to the senior prom, but it was Stewart and his date, not Cyril and his, who got their pictures published in the school paper.

They shared the same group of bright, highly competitive friends, but went everywhere together. Although a story about them in the Bayonne High School paper notes that "they wouldn't be seen in each other's clothes," they both wore the same *kind* of clothes and, in fact, seem to have developed a practice of wearing matching outfits of different shades—Stewart light, Cyril dark.

"The Marcus brothers look shrewd in their corduroy jackets, Stewart in tan and Cyril in dark brown," said a report on high-school fashions in the school paper. In many of their yearbook photos Stewart wears a light double-breasted suit, Cyril a dark one. And in a group picture of six sets of twins accompanying a school-paper story entitled DOUBLE TROUBLE AT BAYONNE HIGH, Stewart wears white, Cyril black.

In this double-trouble story there's a provocative statement about the Marcuses' childhood: "If one of them got into mischief both were spanked by their mother to be sure that the right one was punished."

This is exactly the sort of thing that Guttmacher had in mind when he wrote that identical twins reared together can't develop the sense of "my." Making each suffer for the acts of the other makes the difficulties twins have developing separate identities even more severe. One psychoanalytic theorist holds that "the confusion this creates may make them feel that nothing is personal and unique about them . . . misunderstood, lonely, angry . . . there is only one person for whom they are unique: that is their own twin."

Eight years after high school, the Marcus twins were confronted by Dr. Guttmacher. Stewart and Cyril were both first-year residents at New York's Mt. Sinai Hospital, where Dr. Guttmacher was chairman of the gynecology department. Their careers since high school, Guttmacher could see from their résumés, were nearly identical. Same college (Syracuse). Same fraternity. Same academic honors. Same medical school (also Syracuse). Shared the same cadaver in first-year anatomy class. Same medical honoraries. Same internship program at Mt. Sinai. Same residency program in gynecology at Mt. Sinai. Twenty-six years together, and they were expecting to spend at least three more years together at Sinai.

To Guttmacher, steeped in twins research, it must have looked as if Stewart and Cyril were heedless of how they were imperiling the psychic separation that distinguished them from—Guttmacher's word—monsters. Already the all-too-easy insularity and self-sufficiency of their twinship seemed to be causing them difficulties getting along with outsiders. "They were arrogant, resentful of criticism, disobedient of orders . . . there were tremendous conflicts with the other residents," recalls Dr. Joseph Rovinsky, former chief resident in gynecology at Sinai.

Dr. Guttmacher decided to try to sever the psychic monster conjoinment he saw crippling their individual development. He declared that he would prevent them from continuing their residencies together at Sinai or anywhere else. "He absolutely refused to recommend them to the same hospital. He absolutely insisted that they apply to separate programs," Rovinsky recalls. Not only that, he arranged it so that there would be a whole continent separating them: Stewart was exiled to a program at Stanford's University Hospital, while Cyril was transferred to New York's Joint Diseases Hospital.

The traumatic three-thousand-mile separation seems to have lasted but a year. Stewart's superior at Stanford, Dr. Charles McLennan, is certain Stewart left Stanford to continue his residency somewhere else, "in some sort of orthopedic hospital," he thinks. Oddly, Stewart's curriculum vitae omits any mention of where he spent this missing year. Could it be that—as in classic tales of star-crossed lovers—he slipped away from Stanford and made his way back to Cyril's side at the orthopedically oriented Joint Diseases Hospital?

The year after that found Stewart back at Stanford again. Could Dr. Guttmacher have discovered a reunion at Joint Diseases and ordered Stewart back to Stanford? No one has been able to say what Stewart was doing that missing year; and Dr. Guttmacher died one year before the Marcus twins.

Whatever the case, the second separation proved to be the longest time they would ever be apart. Cyril, it appears, reacted more strongly to being alone. After two years away from Stewart he got married. After a third year he fathered a child and accepted a position at New York Hospital. But by the end of that third year Cyril had arranged it so that he and Stewart would be back together again: he had found a sympathetic patron in the head of the department of obstetrics and gynecology at New York Hospital, someone who had none of Dr. Guttmacher's reservations about twin togetherness and who agreed to bring Stewart back to Cyril's side again.

This reunion signaled the beginning of another kind of marriage for the twins. They seem to have consented to wed their individual career ambitions into a single two-headed unit. As in most career-oriented marriages, one partner ended up making the sacrifices and doing the day-to-day drudgery to permit the other to work for the greater glory of them both. In this one, Stewart did the glamorous laboratory research, getting foundation grants, delivering papers at academic medical conferences all over the world, while Cyril stayed "home" and did most of the messy clinical housework, doggedly building up a big income-earning private practice for both of them.

"In order for Stewart to conduct his laboratory work, Cyril did more than his share in the office; he sacrificed some of his own ambitions to work in the lab," recalls Dr. Fritz Fuchs, who became chairman of the department of obstetrics and gynecology at New York Hospital in 1965.

Despite the unfair division of labor—particularly the obstetric labor that had to be attended to at all hours of the night—the twins' career marriage was a fertile one at first. Cyril's clinical experience stimulated Stewart's research and Stewart's research gave birth to new ideas for treatment of infertility in the private practice Cyril presided over.

They delivered a number of scientific papers under both their names. They conceived and edited a large collection of contemporary research in their field that was published in 1967 as *Advances in Obstetrics and Gynecology*, a book that gave them a national reputation as scholars and practitioners. New York Hospital put them in charge of its infertility clinic.

Meanwhile, their private practice began attracting well-born and well-known women, the wives of celebrities. The twins delighted in the limousines that would pull up to their office; they liked to let certain patients know that they could discriminate between the styles of Mainbocher and Norell. They didn't like to let certain people know they grew up in Bayonne; Stewart told one they were from Short Hills. In one sense they were doted upon as a doubly interesting version of a peculiarly New York institution—the fashionable Park Avenue gynecologist. In a more special sense, through their infertility work, they were becoming objects of awe, even worship, of patients who benefited from their green thumb for babies. If they recalled Dr. Guttmacher's warnings about the consequences of failure of twins to separate, it would only have been to laugh at how wrong he was.

●   ■   ●

Sometime after 1967, signs of strain began to show up in both Cyril's marriages. That year Stewart accepted an offer of a full-time associate professorship at New York Hospital-Cornell Medical Center. Cyril was not given one. Accepting the offer meant that Stewart had to give up private practice outside the hospital. It was an important step toward his ultimate goal of becoming department chairman at a teaching hospital. But when he accepted, the entire weight of the private practice suddenly fell upon Cyril. It came at a bad time. Cyril's wife had just given birth to her second child, but Cyril now had even less time for his family. He had to abandon entirely his own limited research efforts, work more hours than ever at the painstaking infertility work at his office and lose more sleep than ever from the emergency obstetric calls at night. According to one nurse who worked for him back then, he began taking amphetamines.

Stewart, on the other hand, was enjoying more freedom than ever. He never married. He told people who asked he never would and wasn't "missing anything" by not having a wife and children as did his twin. He no longer had to spend time with the anxious, despairing, barren women Cyril had to face. He continued to travel to gynecological conferences all over the world, while Cyril's wife complained that Cyril couldn't get time off from his practice to take her anywhere. And, according to friends, she found Cyril too much of a perfectionist (not so surprising a flaw to turn up in one who had spent his entire life up until his marriage in the shadow of a brother-partner who was always a shade more perfect than he).

In late 1969, Cyril's wife asked for a divorce. People who knew him described Cyril as shattered, painfully depressed. In April, 1970, he moved out of their East End Avenue home and into apartment 10H at 1163 York Avenue, alone for the first time since Dr. Guttmacher separated him from Stewart. He got himself a dog for a companion, hoping that the presence of the pet would encourage his children to visit him more often. But neighbors in the building complained about the dog's barking and forced Cyril to get rid of it. Lacking close friends, he took to confessing his unhappiness to puzzled patients in his private practice, occasionally calling them at home late at night from places like Danny's Hide-A-Way and P.J. Clarke's to ramble on about such obsessions as French restaurants and Catherine Deneuve. He started taking sedatives.

Then one morning, in the summer of 1972, Stewart got a phone call from a man who identified himself as Bill Terrell, the handyman at Cyril's apartment complex.

"I think we have a problem here," Terrell said. "I'm pretty sure your brother's in trouble; I'm inclined to think he's unconscious."

" 'Just a minute,' " Terrell recalls Stewart replying. Terrell heard the sound of the phone receiver on Stewart's end being set down. He waited a moment. He waited a minute and a half.

"Then I said, 'Hey, Doctor, you know I'm talking to you.' Then he said, 'You're right,' and I said, 'I'm right about what?' And he said, 'You're right something's wrong.' "

It took Terrell a while, he recalls, to break through the strange passivity that settled over Stewart and to convince him to hurry over to Cyril's building. When they broke through the door, they found Cyril fully dressed, motionless on the floor of the foyer of apartment 10H, looking as if he had lost consciousness while crawling toward the house phone in the hall.

"He's dead," said Stewart, without approaching the body.

"I got down close to him," Terrell recalls, "and I said, 'He's not dead, but he's just about gone.' "

"Give him mouth-to-mouth resuscitation," Stewart said.

"I said, 'You're the doctor, you do it,' " Terrell recalls. "He was kind of dumbfounded. Still standing there."

Fortunately, at this point, according to Terrell, some other doctors in the building arrived and gave Cyril mouth-to-mouth resuscitation. "I'm positive it wasn't the brother who did it," Terrell says.

It didn't appear to be a suicide attempt. Cyril was fully dressed and apparently ready to leave the apartment when he collapsed, and he seemed to be trying to call for help when he lost consciousness.

What happened to Cyril? Hospital treatment records remain confidential. However there are two phone calls that suggest an answer. An anonymous call came to the medical examiner's office not long after the Marcus brothers' death hit the papers last July. The caller suggested that the medical examiner look into the possibility that Cyril suffered a stroke back in 1972 and was hospitalized in a coma. The anonymous caller's information seemed to fit in with the substance of a revealing telephone conversation Stewart had with a friend, just one day after Cyril's mysterious collapse.

It was nip and tuck with Cyril's life, Stewart told the friend. He was not sure exactly what happened, Stewart said, but he was terribly concerned about brain damage Cyril might have suffered from cerebral anoxia—lack of oxygen for brain cells—while he was unconscious.

The friend, who also knew Cyril, couldn't be sure himself whether Stewart's brain-damage fears were justified. After the collapse, the friend said, "Cyril was functioning, but as time went on, in other matters, in the course of a telephone conversation, he'd repeat himself. Something had happened to alter his functioning in some way. It was just not the same old Cyril."

The friend is convinced that Cyril's collapse, Stewart's fear of brain damage to his brother and the crippling conjoinment that grew out of the aftermath led inevitably to their mutual decline.

"It was all down down down after that. . . . The more Cyril deteriorated, the more Stewart involved himself in trying to bail him out and maintain a good front. Maybe Stewart was hoping that by not letting down the front, things would work out. He would always reassure me, Cyril's fine, he's fine. Maybe it was wishful thinking, like trying to save a drowning man who pulls his rescuer down with him."

Physically, they drew closer in the months that followed Cyril's collapse. Stewart quit a recently assumed post as chief of obstetrics and gynecology at Nassau County Medical Center and moved back into New York City fulltime to an apartment just three blocks away from Cyril's. Stewart had taken the Nassau County post with the expectation that with it would come the chance to head the ob-gyn department at an important new teaching hospital being built at Stony Brook, Long Island. When that promise was not fulfilled, he quit to return to commit himself to preserving Cyril. The last separation was over.

In the fall of 1972, they signed on as surgeons in a big abortion clinic. The shift from the promotion of conception to abortion may have had something to do with money. Abortions are quick and simple to perform, and for the amount of time they take, the fees are very high. An infertility case can take many months of painstaking tests, office visits, exploratory procedures, and often complex and delicate operations. Cyril had alimony to worry about. Stewart had Cyril to worry about. But the shift from top-rank infertility research to hack abortion work must have been devastating to Stewart's self-esteem. In November, 1972, Stewart's altered behavior so antagonized his publisher that the proposed second volume of the brothers' book had to be canceled. He alienated the top-name contributors to the volume by failing to return their manuscripts. His research career began to disintegrate.

Why did he do it? Why did Stewart allow his career to slide down the drain to prop up Cyril? Is it possible he blamed himself for the anoxia he thought Cyril might have suffered? Brain-cell death is a question of seconds, and Stewart had hesitated twice while his brother lay unconscious—once on the phone and once in front of Cyril's body when he refused to give his brother the resuscitation needed to save his life. Could Stewart also have blamed himself for the sacrifices his twin had made for his research career, sacrifices that may have contributed to the break-up of Cyril's marriage, and could Stewart have decided on some level to sacrifice that career in return?

Or was it no sacrifice at all? Some theories of twinship say that behind the apparent closeness of twins is "an intense rivalry situation . . . hostile death wishes which in turn demand repression that again brings the twins together." Such a theory suggests the possibility that Stewart hesitated that morning because, at some level, he wanted Cyril to die.

The pressures of the aftermath of Cyril's collapse began to affect their private practice. Patients began to report instances of bizarre, even terrifying, behavior. There were the mutual impersonations for instance. One twin would leave his patient in the middle of an examination and the other would return to the stirrups to complete the job. Once Stewart confided to a patient whom he had failed to fool with a Cyril impersonation that the two of them had played the impersonation game with fourteen patients so far that day and that they'd been able to fool nine of them. "Our mother has trouble telling us apart," he said.

There are indications that after Cyril's collapse, Stewart began impersonating his brother in earnest. Some patients recall leaving messages for Cyril and getting a return call from someone who may have been

Stewart. Then another call from the real Cyril, who seemed unaware of his brother's impersonation.

And one patient reported that she called Cyril for advice and heard him reply to her questions in a slurred halting voice, frequently pausing to wait for answers from a voice in the background. She was certain it was Stewart telling Cyril what to say.

Then there were the temper tantrums, occasionally violent. One patient, who had been hospitalized toward the end of her ninth month of pregnancy, recalls complaining to Cyril that her intravenous needle gave her pain. "He picked up that bottle of intravenous fluid and he slammed it down on the tray." When another patient disobeyed Cyril's orders and got out of bed, subsequently suffering a miscarriage, he berated her almost vengefully. In fact, patients began to characterize the twins' behavior in terms reminiscent of the God of the Old Testament: they were wrathful, they flew into rages when their medical commandments were violated or even questioned, they were jealous ("Thou shalt have no gynecologists before us," was one commandment), they demanded unquestioning faith and obedience.

As their office became less crowded they began to spend more of their idle time engaged in long rambling discourses with certain patients. Cyril startled one with a detailed story about a woman he claimed to have treated for certain aftereffects of intercourse with a large dog.

Even with all this odd behavior, it was a seemingly innocuous insurance-form phobia that did more than anything to hasten the twins' downfall. The Marcuses had a powerful aversion to filling out insurance forms for their patients and would go to bizarre lengths to avoid doing so.

As far back as 1965, one patient reported, she had had to go through months and months of calling, pleading, and personal visits to get them to sign one simple form. Over the years the twins seemed to have developed an elaborate hierarchy of defenses against signing forms they did not want to sign. They'd refuse to respond to phone requests. They'd refuse to receive requests sent by registered mail; they'd tell patients who came to the office to get their forms signed that they'd already sent them out by mail; when the forms never arrived by mail they'd claim the post office lost them; or their mailbox must have caught fire. When the tormented women turned the problem over to their husbands, the twins would make them jump through the same hoops all over again.

Toward the end, they began with increasing frequency to make use of an even more ingenious scheme to avoid forms: they refused to send bills. In many cases they seemed to prefer forgoing a fee to filling out the forms that went with it. This was no real advantage to the patients: many were billed by the hospital as well, and insurance companies required the doctors to bill them or fill out forms before reimbursement was issued.

It was an ingenious device, this no-bill method of avoiding forms, and they might have gotten away with it had it not been for Mrs. Evelyn Chait, a housewife in New Jersey and an early victim of the form phobia. Starting in 1971, she waged a four-year campaign to get her forms filled out. She wrote letter after letter, suffered through excuse after excuse, sent her husband on countless missions. She took her case to outside agencies, amassing a foot-high file of correspondence on the Byzantine twists and dodges Cyril employed to avoid her forms. She stalked him through one ineffectual bureaucracy after another. At last, late in 1974, she found an agency that was willing to take some action. The New York State Department of Professional Conduct assigned an investigator of medical scandals to the case. He set in motion a process that would result in a formal presentation of charges against Cyril and Stewart Marcus by a panel of doctors.

●   ■   ●

Sometime in April, 1974, Cyril Marcus took a headlong fall. He would take a number of falls in the year to come—the autopsy doctors found a number of old abrasions on his knees characteristic, they said, of chronic alcohol or drug users. This fall was the most unfortunate. It came outside an operating room in New York Hospital where he was scheduled to perform an operation. He staggered and collapsed in a way that suggested he was under the influence of drugs.

They wheeled Cyril, sweating and pale, to the emergency room, where a staff doctor treated him and hospitalized him. An agitated Stewart appeared on the scene. Dr. Fuchs, who was present, asked Cyril to take a medical leave of absence and suggested that it would be a good idea if Stewart, too, took a vacation since he was so concerned about his brother and looked tired himself.

The following August, when the twins were permitted to return to the hospital, they had the feeling people were watching them and talking about them. They were right. Hospital administrator Luckey had ordered the twins placed under "extremely close one-to-one surveillance" every moment they were near a patient. "We have great agents in this hospital," Dr. Luckey would later boast. "This place would make the C.I.A. green with envy. Everything gets back to us."

The twins began to withdraw from this scrutiny, admitting only eighteen patients in the eleven months between their return in August and their death in July. They retreated to the relative privacy of their private practice. There, things began to grow stranger by the month. The nurse who began working there toward the end of 1974 found it hard to believe some of the things that were happening in that office.

In the spring of 1975, the nurse confided to a patient what it had been like. When they first came back from their leave of absence, she said, the twins had "tried to straighten up and get better, but it didn't last long." They were taking amphetamines in the office, she said; they would become irrationally angry and blow up at some patients. Their form-filling-out phobia continued. The twins asked her to fend off frustrated form-seekers for them, creating one situation so explosive she began to fear for her life: an enraged husband who had been fighting his way for months through evasions and postponements seeking to get his wife's records transferred to another doctor finally burst into Cyril Marcus's inner office. In the argument that ensued, someone drew a gun.

Then there was the spontaneous-abortion incident. Late that spring, one of Cyril's patients checked herself into New York Hospital in the midst of a spontaneous abortion. The woman and her husband (a doctor) raised questions about whether Cyril's failure to follow through on certain progesterone tests had been a factor in the miscarriage. When Cyril arrived at the hospital, according to the nurse's story, the patient "was lying there bleeding, and Cyril came in—he was really out of it—and he looked at her and said, 'Do you want to go home now?' She obviously needed some attention, and what happened was a couple of the doctors sent him away and took over and took care of her."

The nurse said that things had been getting worse that spring; the practice was deteriorating, the office rent in arrears, the air-conditioner unrepaired. The twins frequently called, telling her in slurred voices that they would be unable to come in for the day's appointments. Cyril in particular, she said, had been losing weight and acting more and more strangely. The nurse was convinced that everyone at the hospital was talking about the twins and their odd behavior—that, in fact, the constant gossip about them was one factor contributing to their drug-taking—but that no one at the hospital would do anything about the situation in their private practice. The nurse said she had been to see Chairman Fuchs twice about the situation, that she told him she wanted to leave but that Fuchs had said, "Why don't you stay with them so you can at least help out the patients."

Meanwhile, the investigator for the state's Department of Professional Conduct was beginning to close in on the twins. Pursuing the complaints of Mrs. Chait, the investigator found himself getting the same runaround the patients and their husbands were complaining of. The twins wouldn't come to the phone when they *were* in, twice when they finally came to the phone they hung up on him. Finally the investigator threatened to slap Cyril with a subpoena if he failed to make an appearance to explain himself. On the appointed day in October, 1974, someone who identified himself as Cyril Marcus showed up in the investigator's office.

"He was very cordial, he was very polite, and he was obviously not Cyril," the investigator recalled. "Cyril was a damaged individual, and in tight situations Stewart took over from Cyril," a colleague explained.

By June, the investigator had eleven more unresolved allegations against the twins; this time he hit them both with subpoenas for appearances on the same day. Neither showed up. Belatedly the twins called and asked for an adjournment. Then another. On June 27, 1975, the director of the agency authorized presentation of charges against them to a special panel of five doctors. The panel voted unanimously to charge the twins with "unprofessional conduct" and ordered them to appear for a trial.

By this time Stewart must have known that the secrets of Cyril's behavior were slipping out. In June he received a disturbing call from Dr. Roger Steinhardt, chairman of the New York County Medical Society Board of Censors. The board, too, had been investigating increasing complaints about the twins' failure to fill out forms and had finally produced—after the usual months of postponements—an appearance at the board's office by one of the twins, who identified himself as Cyril. "All of us sensed something strange . . . awry" about the appearance of this twin, Steinhardt recalls. They found him "affable and easygoing," which does not sound like the emaciated and sickly Cyril. Acting on an informal basis, after getting a hint of Cyril's condition since his 1972 collapse, Dr. Steinhardt called Stewart and asked him if his twin was ill or emotionally disturbed or if perhaps he had suffered a "cerebral accident." Stewart denied everything, but Steinhardt's tactfully phrased inquiry must have tipped Stewart off that his front for Cyril was crumbling. (Nor was Steinhardt completely satisfied with Stewart's denial: he contacted the twins' department chairman at New York Hospital and set up an appointment to discuss the situation. But Dr. Steinhardt's secretary got his calendar confused; Steinhardt failed to show up for the meeting, and before it could be rescheduled the twins were dead.)

The twins didn't know about the panel's investigation of them, they didn't know about the planned Steinhardt-Fuchs rendezvous, but in late May, 1975, department head Fuchs ordered them to appear at the hospital and told them something even more devastating.

"I called them into my office," Fuchs recalls, "and said, 'Look, there is someone on the hospital staff who thinks that you might have a drug problem.' I asked them if there were anything I could do to help them get treatment and offered to let them take a medical leave of absence."

The twins denied the drug allegation, but Fuchs's offer of a leave was more like an ultimatum. He gave them three choices: they could accept a medical leave for treatment; they could voluntarily resign; or they could do nothing and Fuchs would be forced to recommend to the hospital's medical board that they be dropped.

The twins protested that Fuchs had given them unacceptable choices—they'd lose their livelihood if they had to take a medical leave, they'd lose their livelihood if they had to resign their hospital privileges, and they'd lose their reputation either way because leaving would confirm everyone's worst suspicions about them. Unmoved, Fuchs gave them two weeks to decide.

In the difficult days that followed the ultimatum they began to withdraw even further from their practice, sometimes failing to show up at all. One of the last patients to see one of the twins in their office describes a sad and revealing encounter with Cyril. It happened sometime close to their forty-fifth birthday, June 2, 1975. She found herself alone in the office with Cyril. "There was no one else there in the two hours I spent with him. It was a little peculiar," she recalls. "He looked thinner and he looked sick, I would say, physically, and he seemed lonely. He was very upset about Ozzie Nelson's death."

The woman asked Cyril what troubled him so much about Ozzie's death. "Well," Cyril said, "it's just a shame. The good, like Ozzie Nelson, die and then people like Nixon and Mayor Beame are still around."

Cyril then shifted this cheerful conversation from Ozzie (could he perhaps have been thinking about where Ozzie's death left Harriet, the other half of that inseparable couple?) to twins, cancer and death.

"He got into this cancer business," the woman recalls, "and he said, 'Do you know who dies of the same thing?' and I said, 'What?' and he said, 'Twins.' He said identical twins often come down with the same thing, cancer or whatever, and die together or close. Identical twins, or even twins, are very joined emotionally and whatever, and he said, 'Of course my brother and I are not identical.'" Nor were Ozzie and Harriet.*

●   ■   ●

Stewart Marcus had a cancer theory. It didn't involve twins, but it did involve paired organs. Back in 1960, when Stewart was a promising young research gynecologist, he researched and wrote—with the aid of Cyril—a paper on the gynecological implications of "the theory of multicentric origin" of cancers. The paper warned gynecologists to be alert to the fact that when any one organ develops a carcinoma, its

---

* Almost everyone who knew the twins assumed they were identicals, and until the Ozzie Nelson conversation there is only one indication on record to suggest otherwise. Thirty years earlier the "double trouble" story in their highschool paper described the Marcus brothers as "fraternal twins who happen to look very much alike." The possibility must be allowed that the Marcuses were fraternal twins who relished being mistaken for identicals, perhaps even *posed* as identicals because of the special awe identicals evoke. Certainly by the time they reached Dr. Guttmacher their lives had been lived as identicals, and by the time of Ozzie Nelson's death, they may have wondered whether it was too late to escape the common fate so often suffered by identicals.

paired organ—or any other organ composed of tissue "with the same embryological origin"—is likely to have a latent precancerous fertility and may suddenly give birth to a similar malignancy.

The story of the final siege is Stewart's story.

June 12 was the day the twins were supposed to reply to Dr. Fuchs's ultimatum. Fuchs heard nothing from them all day. Finally he called them, reached Stewart and asked if they had decided to take a leave, resign, or allow themselves to be dropped from the hospital staff. Stewart told Fuchs they still hadn't been able to make up their minds, asked for more time, and promised to call Fuchs with the decision on June 16. He didn't. Fuchs called him again, and again Stewart told him the twins hadn't been able to make up their minds. "Well now it is out of my hands," Fuchs told him and proceeded to write the hospital medical board recommending against rehiring the twins.

Still Stewart could have saved himself. Fuchs's recommendation was not final and both twins were entitled to contest it before the medical board. Stewart might have won. "If they had fought it, we might have had a tough time making it stand, especially on Stewart," one member of the medical board conceded. "Hell, Stewart hadn't done much more than miss some clinic appointments."

●   ■   ●

Sergeant Breen of the Fourth Homicide Squad paid a visit to Stewart's Sixty-fifth Street apartment after taking an inventory of the death-scene mess at Cyril's place. According to Sergeant Breen, the scene at Stewart's place was "a repeat" of the one at Cyril's: the same pills, the same piles of newspapers and unopened mail, the same half-eaten food scattered about. According to the doorman in his building, in the past year Stewart had had no visitors to his apartment other than his brother Cyril, and for a full year Stewart had forbidden anyone from the building to enter his apartment at any time. In addition, the doorman said that for about a month before Stewart's death he hadn't seen him at all.

What all this suggests is that in their last year the prophecy of Stewart's cancer paper and of Cyril's Ozzie Nelson story was coming true: the emotional malignancy that had seized upon Cyril some time ago had begun to take possession of what remained of Stewart's private life. For a year he saw no one but a sick mirror image of himself. Until that last month the twins had, at least, locked up their paired afflictions in separate secret compartments. But Stewart's decision not to fight for his job, to make Cyril's losses his losses, made any further separation superfluous, and in mid-June Stewart moved out of his apartment and into a final folie à deux at Cyril's place.

The piles of papers began to accumulate as far back as April: found beneath Cyril's dead body was a full-page ad from an April 7 issue of The *Times*, appealing for aid for Saigon war orphans. Appointments had been neglected for long before that. Taped on Cyril's bathroom mirror were an "Important Notice" from the I.R.S. dated November, 1973, and a reminder about an appointment with a neurologist who had been dead since the fall of 1974.

But even amid the final chaos they created, there were clues that in the last month the twins made pathetic efforts to maintain a life outside the double-locked doors of apartment 10H. It was possible to glimpse amongst the debris the implements of cleanliness and grooming that had always produced the "immaculate" and "meticulous" impression the Marcus brothers invariably made on others. Even at the very end when everyone noticed Cyril losing weight and Stewart growing pale, their suits were freshly creased and their faces closely shaved.

At the time of their death, the bathtub and bathroom sink in 10H were encrusted with spilled instant-coffee powder, but resting on top of these stains was a spray can of Right Guard deodorant, a can of shaving cream, a squeeze bottle of Q.T. quick-tanning lotion, razors, even nail clippers. These all suggest a continuing effort up until the end to save face—the Q.T., in fact, may have been used to cover the pallor that had begun to attract attention to their faces.

Even the state of dress—or undress—in which the dead twins were found may reflect the undying efforts of one segment of their psyches to preserve some last bit of fastidiousness in the face of the filth about to engulf them. The relative nakedness in which the twins were found has inspired some prurient speculation about their activities together, but there's a less lurid explanation for it: the only way to keep clothes clean from contamination and presentable for wearing outside that apartment would be to avoid wearing them at all inside. And wearing over-the-calf socks can be seen as a last-ditch survival of that part of their psyches that would not allow itself to be tainted by stepping in the debris tolerated by whatever disorder possessed the rest of their personalities.

They may have made one last effort to clean themselves up in a more fundamental way. Among the barbiturates on the floor, police also found an emptied prescription bottle of Dilantin, an anti-convulsant drug sometimes used to treat the seizures characteristic of narcotic withdrawal. It's possible that Stewart tried to get Cyril to kick the barbiturate habit with the help of Dilantin or that they were both preparing one last attempt to salvage their medical careers—Cyril called at least one colleague that summer to ask about the possibility of a job in another city. If there was an attempt, it failed: dates on prescription bottles indicate that they went back to buying barbiturates not long after they brought the Dilantin home.

On July 10, 1975, the New York Hospital medical board met to consider the cases of Cyril and Stewart Marcus. Neither twin appeared to defend himself. The decision of the board to drop them from the staff became final. Considering the pending state agency indictment, for all practical purposes they were through as doctors. The twins had finally been driven, by circumstances of their own creation, back into the kind of isolation and conjoinment they had not shared since childhood, indeed since the womb.

The remnants of their last days together suggest that in some respects the twins lived out a kind of nightmarish children's party. There were dozens of bottles of sweet soda pop all over the place—wild cherry, strawberry, vanilla cream, Rooti root beer, Coca-Cola. There were cookies, cakes, and ice cream, too. And they never had to clean up.

As he had with their delivery into the world, Stewart led the way in delivering them out of it. Sometime between July 10 and July 14, he took an overdose of barbiturates and died. That's the final official theory of the medical examiner about Stewart's death. (Samples of Stewart's tissue sent to an outside toxicologist revealed that the original toxicological report had been in error.) The official report does not say whether it was an accidental overdose or a deliberate suicide. It just states "Circumstances Undisclosed."

Clues at the death scene point a different way. Found on the floor beneath the sock dangling from Stewart's left foot was a metal box with the words WILLS/INSURANCE on it. The presence of the opened box suggests there may have been a realistic discussion of the consequences of accidental and intentional death for heirs and beneficiaries. Stewart died without a will and his possessions reverted to his parents, but Cyril seems to have made provision for his two daughters. Circumstances suggest a complex, harrowing chronology. It goes like this: on July 10, the twins pass up their last chance to save their hospital careers and decide to take a final leave of absence together. They take large doses of Nembutal together and go into a barbiturate coma. Stewart dies. Cyril doesn't. Perhaps because of a higher tolerance, his dose is not fatal and he awakens hours, even days, later to find himself alone with the dead body of his brother.

Since the story of these twins is more a love story than a comedy of errors, one thinks of the desolation of Juliet when she wakes from her drugged sleep in the crypt of the Capulets. She finds her lover dead of an overdose and herself alone in a "nest of death, contagion and unnatural sleep."

On Tuesday, July 14, Cyril lurches one last time out of the twins' final nesting place. He stumbles as he is about to cross the threshold to the outside world. The doorman who offers to assist Cyril thinks he "looks like death." Out on the sidewalk Cyril looks at life without Stewart. The first thing he will have to do, he knows, is explain things. It's not hard to explain why he returned so soon to that crypt in 10H. Only in those two minutes he languished in the womb after his brother's departure could Cyril have been more alone.

He double-locked the door behind him. He pushed an armchair up against it as a further barricade. He took off the clothes he had worn for his last venture outside. He may well have clothed Stewart's body in a pair of his own striped shorts. He put a sheet of paper in his typewriter and typed his ex-wife's address on it. He left the rest blank.

The only thing we know for sure about the way Cyril died is that he didn't take the easy way out. He didn't take pills. He may well have paced the apartment keeping watch over his brother's body. For the first time in his life, he was truly his older brother's keeper.

How he finally died is still a mystery: the medical examiner has no positive proof, he offers only "diagnosis by exclusion": circumstantial evidence that indicates Cyril was a barbiturate addict, there were no barbiturates—even after three series of tests and retests—found in Cyril's body, therefore Cyril must have died from barbiturate withdrawal.

But the medical examiners concede that Cyril's body showed no signs of the bruises, mouth and tongue bites or brain hemorrhages that characterize the fatal convulsions of narcotic withdrawal. One source in the medical examiner's office suggests that inanition—exhaustion from lack of nourishment—and a failure of the will to live may have contributed. And the literature of twins is filled with cases in which one member of a pair of identical or conjoined twins sickens and dies and the other, though perfectly healthy, slips into death for no good reason but reunion.

Dr. Guttmacher, the twin who first tried to separate the Marcuses, describes the touching death of Barnum's original Siamese twins, Chang and Eng: When Eng was awakened and told that Chang had died, Eng sighed and said in a resigned fashion, "Then I am going also." And he did, although there was nothing physically wrong with him.

But perhaps the best clue from literature could be found right in the middle of the littered living-room floor of the death scene. Facedown on top of a pile of papers was a paperback novel by Iris Murdoch, opened as if someone were holding the place. It was the only novel visible in the apartment, in fact it was the only book removed from the shelves, which mainly contained scientific literature. The Marcus twins were not known among their colleagues as big novel readers, and the prose of Iris Murdoch does not seem like their cup of tea in any case. It is reasonable to assume that whichever twin was reading that particular book in the last days of his life had chosen it for some good reason.

It's a novel about two brothers, one of them part of a heterosexual couple, one of them part of a homosexual couple. The other central figure is a malignant scientist who makes a bet that he can separate both pairs. He succeeds and fails. The heterosexual couple splits and the heterosexual brother kills himself. The homosexual couple survives. Looking at the story of the Marcus brothers in its kindest light, as the story of twins for whom separation was always a fate worse than death, the title of that novel might serve as an epitaph. It was *A Fairly Honorable Defeat*.

—*ESQUIRE*
March 1976

POSTSCRIPT TO "DEAD RINGERS"

In the years since "Dead Ringers" was published, two other controversial episodes have focused attention on the adequacy of the supervision of medical personnel at New York Hospital where the Marcus twins practiced. There was the question of who was—or wasn't—attending to Andy Warhol in his last hours there. And the controversy over who or what was responsible for the sudden death of Libby Zion, journalist Sidney Zion's daughter, after an emergency admission there.

As for the question of how and why the Marcus twins chose to embrace death together, I still believe the most telling clue is the presence of that peculiarly relevant Iris Murdoch novel atop the garbage midden they made their final resting place. Nonetheless the question of the nature of the love between them in this incredibly sad love story is one that will always be shadowed by uncertainty.

Which hasn't prevented a number of fictionalizers from offering their versions of it. I think it might be worthwhile, since we're dealing with questions of confused identity, to distinguish between "Dead Ringers" the magazine story, and *Dead Ringers*, the David Cronenberg film of 1988. Cronenberg's film was ostensibly based on a novelization of the Marcus twins case called *Twins*—and was itself originally called *Twins*. But shortly before its release, Universal Pictures approached Cronenberg's production company and informed them that Universal was soon to release a big-budget comedy-buddy movie also called *Twins*, starring Schwarzenegger and DeVito. Two nonidentical movies called *Twins* would be too confusing, so they reached an agreement. Cronenberg's production company abandoned their *Twins* title. And simply lifted "Dead Ringers" from the magazine story to take its place.

Oh well—standard operating procedure in Hollywood. But what's more disturbing about Cronenberg's *Dead Ringers* is the way it cheapens the Marcus twins' story. Cronenberg turned the two of them into a cartoonish Jekyll-Hyde pairing (gimmicked up by having Jeremy Irons play both parts) and invented a clichéd love triangle, with a sexy actress as the source of the trouble between the twins. The real love story, the one not captured in the film, was the one *between* the two of them.

CLANDESTINE SUBCULTURES

. ∎ .

THE SUBTERRANEAN WORLD OF THE BOMB

Did anyone ever tell you about the last letter of Our Lady of Fatima? It's more than a dozen years since the night it was revealed to me, but I remember the circumstances exactly. I was in an all-night place called the Peter Pan Diner with a high school buddy of mine. It was 1964, I was 17, and we had been arguing for hours, as we often would, about such matters as the nature of Time before the creation of the universe and the mystery of the afterlife, when this guy hit me with the Fatima prophecy. He said he'd heard it from some seminarians who said they'd heard it from people in the church hierarchy, who said it was a hush-hush matter of intense concern to the Vatican, and to His Holiness himself.

Back in 1913, the story goes, a holy apparition appeared to three Portuguese children near the shrine to the Virgin at Fatima. The heavenly messenger handed the kids three sealed letters for transmittal to the Pope. Eyes only.

The first letter—marked for immediate unsealing—astonished Pope Pius X with a graphic description of a horrifying world war, this just months before the guns of August opened fire. The second letter, said to be marked "Do not open for twenty-five years," shocked Pius XI in 1938 with its vision of an even more terrible tragedy about to engulf civilization.

And then just last year—and here my friend's voice dropped, presumably to avoid frightening the people drinking coffee at the next table—just last year, he said, that wonderful man, the late Pope John, unsealed the third and last letter.

The last letter. The chill I felt creeping over me could not be ascribed to the Peter Pan Diner's creaky air conditioner.

"What was in it?" I asked.

"Nobody knows," my friend said.

"What do you mean nobody knows? They knew about the other ones."

"Yes," said my friend. "But this one is different. They say that when the Holy Father opened it and read what was inside he fainted on the spot. And that he never recovered. And that Pope Paul ordered the letter to be resealed and never opened again. Want to know why? Because the letter tells the exact date of when a total nuclear war that will destroy the entire human race will break out and the pope can't let it out because of the mass suicides and immorality if people were to learn exactly when they were going to die."

●   ■   ●

On January 13, 1975, the *New York Times* published a brief dispatch headed AIR FORCE PANEL RECOMMENDS DISCHARGE OF MAJOR WHO CHALLENGED "FAILSAFE" SYSTEM.

"What Major Hering has done," according to the lawyer for the ICBM launch officer, "is to ask what safeguards are in existence at the highest level of government to protect against an unlawful launch order . . . what checks and balances there are to assure that a launch order could not be affected by the President gone berserk or by some foreign penetration of the command system."

The major was not a hysterical peacenik. A combat veteran of Vietnam, he insisted he would have no moral scruples about killing 10 million or so people with his fleet of missiles. He just wanted to make sure that when he got the launch order it wasn't coming from an impostor or a madman.

Sorry, major, the Air Force replied, a missile crewman like you at the bottom of the chain of command has no "need to know" the answer to that question. In fact, you have no business asking it. When the *Times* story appeared, the Air Force already was on its way to hustling the major into suspension and early retirement.

Interesting, I thought to myself back in '75 as I tore out the story. But so many years after *Dr. Strangelove* and *Failsafe*, how was it possible that this question did not have a satisfying, reassuring answer, even if the Air Force did not want to disclose it to this troublesome major? And so I filed the clipping away in the semi-oblivion of my "possible stories" file.

Two years later I was prowling the corridors of the Pentagon with that now-tattered clipping and a need to know. I was trying to find someone who could give me a satisfactory, reassuring answer to Major Hering's question. I wasn't getting any answers. What I was getting, I realized, right there in the Pentagon, was an onset of Armageddon fever unlike any since that night in the Peter Pan Diner when I heard about the Fatima prophecy.

I think it had something to do with seeing the man with the black briefcase face to face. It happened in a parking lot in Deerfield Beach, Florida, in January, 1976. I was traveling with and reporting on President Ford's Presidential primary campaign. The man with the black briefcase was traveling with President Ford, ready in case the President had to interrupt his Florida primary campaign to wage a nuclear war.

You know about the black briefcase, don't you? Inside are the Emergency War Order (EWO) authentification codes, which are changed frequently and are supposed to ensure that only the President, their possessor, can authorize a thermonuclear missile or bomber launch. When then-President Richard Nixon boasted to a group of congressmen shortly after the Saturday night massacre that "I could go into the next room, make a telephone call, and in twenty-five minutes seventy million people will be dead," he left out one detail: he would have to take the black briefcase into the room with him.

That day in Deerfield Beach, Commander in Chief Ford was making his way through throngs of suntanned senior citizens and pale Secret

Servicemen out onto a fishing pier to pose with a prize marlin. Passing up a glimpse of the big fish, I was ambling back across a parking lot toward the press bus when suddenly I came upon the man with the black briefcase.

Somehow he seemed to have become separated from the Presidential party in the procession toward the pier, and now he stood fully and formally uniformed in the midst of baggy Bermuda shorts and tropical shirts. Peering about, looking for his lost Commander in Chief, the nuclear-briefcase man looked cut off, detached, uncertain how to respond. And in a different sense so was I. I felt a peculiar sense of dislocation staring at that briefcase. (In case you're interested it's a very slim and elegant one: supple black pebble-grained leather with a flap of soft leather fastened by four silver snaps.)

If you wanted to get technical you could say that if the word of a surprise attack on the way reached the President while he was posing with the prize fish, the fact that the man with the black briefcase was here with me and not out on the pier might delay our potential for nuclear retaliation by several, perhaps crucial, seconds. On the other hand some half-a-billion citizens on the other side of the world might enjoy two or three more breaths before their lives were snuffed out by missiles sent by the black-briefcase code. Silly to make these calculations, but what is the proper response to the intimate presence of a key element of the doomsday trigger system? Scream bloody murder? Or should one take, as I did at the time, a detached, esthetic approach to the tableau—relish the piquant frisson of irony at that artifact of instant apocalyptic death standing like a scarecrow amidst the sun-ripening age of the retirees?

Last year when I came upon the Major Hering clipping and read it again, that unsettling vision of the man with the black briefcase came to mind. And my response was different. This time *I* felt possessed by a "need to know," a compulsion that eventually led to a 4,000-mile tour of the nuclear trigger system, a pilgrimage that led me down into the Underground Command Post of the Strategic Air Command, up into B-52 bomb bays, down into missile silos, and deep into the heart of the hollowed-out mountain that houses our missile-attack warning screens.

My first stop was Washington, D.C., where, in the course of doing some preliminary research, I came upon a very unsettling document that has kept me up for many nights since. Entitled "First Use of Nuclear

Weapons: Preserving Responsible Command and Control," it is the transcript of a little-noticed set of congressional hearings held in March, 1976. The transcripts represent a concerted effort by the International Security subcommittee of the House Committee on International Affairs to get the answers to Major Hering's question (indeed, it seems the Hering controversy in part provoked the hearings) and to questions about the curious behavior of then-Defense Secretary James Schlesinger in the last days of the Nixon Presidency.

As the impeachment process wore on and reports circulated about the President's potentially unstable temperament at the time, Schlesinger took an extraordinary action: he sent out orders to the various communications centers in the nuclear chain of command to report back to him, Schlesinger, any "unusual" orders from the President. The implication was that Schlesinger wanted to know about and, perhaps, veto, a potentially deranged Nixon whim to nuke Vladivostok or the House Judiciary Committee.

The brief flare-up over the Schlesinger order illuminated little more than the extent of consensus ignorance on just how we actually will do it when we do it. Like the facts of life to a bemused child, the facts of nuclear death, before it comes, are more like vague notions than actual clinical details.

We know there is no button wired into the Great Seal in the Oval Office. But that one phone call, the one that kills the seventy million— just where does it go? Who answers? Will the people who answer be loyal to the President or to the Secretary of Defense if the President's mental condition is suspect? If the Secretary of Defense could veto a launch by a mad President, could a Secretary of Defense *initiate* a launch if he felt the President was playing Hamlet and was mad *not* to launch?

The Command and Control hearings document reprints in its appendix a disturbing analysis of these questions by a professor of government at Cornell named Quester. Among other observations, Professor Quester suggests that it is the very precautions taken to thwart a madman general like *Strangelove's* Jack D. Ripper that have left us at the mercy of a madman President. Making sure that no one *below* the President can launch a nuclear war means giving to the President alone more unchecked power to do it himself on a whim and a single phone call. But the more power placed in the President's hands alone, the more vulnerable the entire U.S. nuclear arsenal is to being disarmed .

by simply knocking off the President. There must be some provision for a retaliatory threat to be credible in the event a "suitcase bomb," for instance, results in the death of the President, Vice-President, and most of the Cabinet, and no one can remember whether it's the Secretary of Agriculture or Commerce who is constitutionally mandated to decide whether we bomb Russia or China or both.

If such contingency plans—for physical rather than constitutional launch orders—exist, as Quester believes, then in effect we are almost back where we started. Because "Plan R," the linchpin of General Jack D. Ripper's surprise nuke attack plan in *Strangelove*, was just that sort of contingency plan—devised to ensure that our bombers would attack their targets even if the U.S. command authority were vaporized in a surprise attack.

Professor Quester's analysis opens up a dismaying number of disturbing paradoxes in "Command and Control" theory as well as practice. More disturbing than any one of these questions is the fact that these problems haven't been solved to everyone's satisfaction by this time. I felt a sinking feeling reading Quester and the other documentary analyses attached to the hearings: O God, did I really have to worry about this? Weren't people scared enough that it had been taken care of completely by now?

I went through the hearing testimony without much consolation. Some admirals and generals complained to the subcommittee that the new failsafe systems were too stringent—that, in fact, they were worried that they might not be able to launch their nukes when the time came because of all the red tape the bureaucrats had put between them and their missiles. But when the committee tried to get the answers to questions such as those raised by Quester about the actual control of nuclear weapons at the top of the chain of command and the mechanics of the transfer of constitutional succession, they were told either that such information was classified and they had no "need to know," or that "no one was sure" what would obtain.

So I took my underlined and annotated copy of the Command and Control hearings transcript over to the Pentagon. Most questions were referred to the Strategic Air Command headquarters in Omaha, Nebraska, and that's when SAC gave me the big invitation.

Would I like, the SAC people asked, to visit the Underground Command Post buried beneath the Nebraska prairie? Would I like a tour through a Looking Glass Plane—one of the curiously named "airborne command posts" that would take over the launching of missiles if the SAC Underground Command Post suffered a direct 5-megaton hit? Would I like to go to a missile base in North Dakota and descend into an operational launch capsule and crawl into a B-52 bomb bay? Would I like to enter the hollowed-out mountain in Colorado that housed the headquarters of the North American Air Defense Command, the supersensitive safety-catch on the nuclear trigger?

THERMONUCLEAR PORN REVISITED

The nearest motel to the SAC Command Post is a Ramada Inn in a place called Bellevue, Nebraska. I stayed up late the night before my descent into the underground war room rereading *Failsafe*, spellbound once again by the scenes in the war room—half the book takes place there—the very underground war room to which I was to descend the next morning. Rereading *Failsafe* was one of the final assignments in the task of preparation I'd given myself in the month between my visit to the Pentagon and my actual departure for triggerworld. The overall task had been to recapitulate the ontogeny of the thermonuclear fever I suffered as an adolescent by rereading, in the order I'd originally devoured them, all the classics of a genre I've come to call thermonuclear pornography. Back when I was a kid I'd read it all.

I'd started with the soft-core stuff: the tear-jerking, postattack tristesse of the slowly expiring Australian survivors in *On the Beach*, spiced as it was with a memorable seduction ploy in which a doom-maddened woman goes so far as to unfasten her bikini top on a first date, a hint of the unleashed inhibitions the end of the world could engender. This only aroused my appetite for the more explicit stuff: such nuclear fore-play novels as *Red Alert* and *Failsafe* with their mounting urgencies as the stiffening finger on the atomic button brought the trembling world to the brink of "going all the way," to use a metaphor from another adolescent preoccupation whose urgencies may indeed have fueled this one. To a bored and repressed high school student, nuclear war novels were not about skin-searing blast-burns but were dramas of inhibition and release. In that sense the foreplay genre was somehow unsatisfying, ending, as most of them did, with some chastening and guilty retreats and vows of eternal nuclear chastity forevermore. Fruitlessly, I scoured the subgenres of post-World War III science fiction (mutants stalk humans in the rubble; wise aliens sift through ruins for clues to the extinction of life on Planet III) for at least a retrospective fantasy of what the actual outbreak of Armageddon would be like, but all they delivered were teasing references of the sort Woody Allen parodied in *Sleeper* ("We believe that the individual responsible for touching off the thermonuclear catastrophe was a man named Albert Shanker but . . .").

It was not until I began reading the truly hard-core stuff—the strategists—that I found some measure of voyeuristic satisfaction. Reading Herman Kahn's *On Escalation* was like coming upon an illustrated marriage manual after trying to figure out sex from Doris Day movies. I followed the exquisitely fine gradations on the forty-four-step escalation ladder erected by Herman Kahn, with its provocatively titled rungs like No. 4, "Hardening of Position"; No. 11, "Super Ready Status"; No. 37, "Provocative Counter Measures"; all the way up to the ultimate and total release of No. 44, "Spasm War."

That night in Bellevue I felt a renewed rush of that thermonuclear prurience when I reread the first big war-room scene in *Failsafe*.

Do you remember the war-room scenes in *Failsafe*? Do you remember *Failsafe*? That was the trembling-on-the-brink novel that wasn't funny like *Strangelove*. Or witty. But powerful. In *Failsafe*, a condenser burnout in a war-room machine fails to send a "recall message" to a nuclear-armed B-52 as it approaches its "failsafe point," and the bomber heads toward target Moscow as men in the White House and the SAC war room try to defuse the fateful, final explosion.*

Back to the war-room scenes in *Failsafe*. Here's something you might *not* remember about those scenes, something I recalled only on rereading the novel. When the big crisis occurs, the war room is sealed off and

* *Failsafe* and *Dr. Strangelove* are based on mistaken premises, as Sidney Hook pointed out in his contemporaneous polemic *The Failsafe Fallacy*. The Air Force never had a policy of ordering planes to strike their targets unless recalled at a certain point. Bombers would fly to designated points outside Soviet airspace during alerts, but the policy, now known as "positive control" rather than the tainted "failsafe," required that a bomber turn around and head back unless it received a direct voice-communication order to strike. A mechanical failure might cause a plane to turn back by mistake but not to head for Moscow. Unfortunately Hook falls victim to a fallacy of his own in *The Failsafe Fallacy*,

two civilian visitors touring the place, just as I will be, are trapped inside as the greatest drama in history unfolds before them.

Before falling asleep that night in my Ramada Inn room, I must admit I entertained myself with some old-fashioned nuke-porn fantasies. After all the SALT talks had broken down, détente was crumbling into recriminations about human rights. Jimmy Carter was flying around in his nuclear emergency command plane and running nuclear-alert escape drills at the White House. Did he know something we didn't? Alarmist articles with ominous titles such as "Why the Soviet Union Thinks It Can Fight and Win a Nuclear War" were appearing in sober journals. A Soviet surprise attack could happen at any time, warned Professor Richard Pipes in *Commentary*. What if it were to happen tomorrow? I fantasized. What if, as in *Failsafe*, I was to find myself trapped on the Command Balcony when the real thing began and the footprints of incoming missiles began stalking across the big war-room screens?

●   ■   ●

What an exciting prospect—that memorable phrase of John Dean's on the White House tapes leaped to mind. I wouldn't mind it one bit; I realized that in some small way I might be hoping for it. That I could entertain such shameful speculation indicates not only that nuclear annihilation appeals to infantile fantasies of grandiosity but also that it is almost impossible to take the idea of nuclear annihilation to heart, so that it can be felt the way other deaths are feared and felt. What sane human could be excited at the prospect of his friends and loved ones dying on the morrow? Yet there is something in the totality of the way we think of nuclear death that not only insulates but appeals. I think it has to do with some early extreme ways of phrasing and thinking about it.

---

assuming that by discrediting a key assumption in a speculative novel he has somehow discredited the notion that we have *any* reason to fear a nuclear war caused by mechanical failure. In fact, warnings of possible surprise attacks have been triggered on NORAD radar screens by flights of Canada geese and the reflection of the moon under peculiar atmospheric conditions. Under certain contemplated alert postures—the hair-trigger, or launch-on-warning, stance, for instance—such mechanical errors could be enough to launch our entire arsenal mistakenly.

When early strategists began to talk about the totality of nuclear war, they used phrases like "the death of consciousness" on the planet. Kissinger used the only slightly more modest phrase "an end to history." Without consciousness not only is there no history, there is no sorrow, no pain, no remorse. No one is missing or missed. There is nothing to feel bad about because nothing exists to feel. A death so total becomes almost communal. The holocaust of the European Jews left behind millions to feel horror, bitterness, and loss. When people began applying the word "holocaust" to nuclear war they meant a holocaust with no survivors, or one in which, to use the well-known phrase, "the survivors would envy the dead." Even now when a much-disputed scientific report argues the probability for long-term post-holocaust survival, at least in the southern hemisphere, one does not, if one is an American, think of surviving a total nuclear war. One thinks of dying in a flash before there's time to feel the pain. Could that be the attraction, if that word may be used, of nuclear war? Is there some Keatsian element "half in love with easeful death" in our fantasies of the end?

Back in 1957 Norman Mailer wrote in *The White Negro* that the absoluteness of the idea of nuclear annihilation will liberate the psychopath within us, and indeed, Charles Manson wrote of the welcome cleansing prospect of atomic war. In a curiously similar passage in a letter home from Korea, David (alleged "Son of Sam") Berkowitz wrote of his desire for release from atomic fear.

Such theories perhaps account for the perverse fantasy "attractions" of Armageddon, but how to account for the desensitization to the reality? As the demons of nuke-porn fantasies gathered about me in my Bellevue room that night I began to wonder if the very structure of the nuke-porn genre I'd been rereading that had been so stimulating in my adolescence—that thrilling sense of the imminence of release it created—might contribute to the problem of response I felt as an adult. The cumulative effect of pornography, particularly on a virginal sensibility, is to arouse expectations of intensity that reality sometimes fails to deliver. Back in junior high and high school saturation with nuke porn led me to a preoccupation with the dates and deadlines, with that familiar adolescent question, "When will it finally happen?"

Of course there was always an erotic component to the original thermonuclear fever. According to one study of the premillennial fevers that have swept religious communities (from the early Christians, who castrated themselves to avoid the heightened temptation to sin in the little time remaining before the Second Coming, to the wave of ark-building that swept the Rhine when a noted sixteenth-century astrologer predicted a Second Flood), in almost every instance the terror at the prospect of the end of the world was mingled with "fierce joy, sexual orgies, and a kind of strange receptivity."

Back in October, 1962, when it seemed at last it *would* happen, it was with thrilled anticipation and fevered fantasies that my (male) high school cronies and I regarded the Soviet ships approaching the imaginary line in the Atlantic Ocean, breach of which could shortly trigger all-out war. The chief fantasy engendered in the giddiness of the lunchrooms and locker rooms was this: As soon as the Absolute Final Warning came over the P.A. we'd steal a car and approach one of the girls at the other lunch table with the following proposition: The bombs are gonna fall in twenty-four hours. You don't want to die a virgin, do you?

But the October crisis passed and we were all still virgins. There still remained homework to do before graduation. The famous *Bulletin of the Atomic Scientists* doomsday clock has hovered close to the witching hour for three decades and we still haven't heard the chimes of midnight. The Fatima prophecy still had power to chill me when I heard it in 1964—after all, hadn't C.P. Snow declared in 1960 that nuclear war was a "mathematical certainty" by the end of the decade? But by 1970, when the C.P. Snow deadline passed, I'd forgotten there was something special to celebrate.

It's not that these people were false prophets—indeed, at worst they may have been merely premature, at best they may have issued self-*un*fulfilling prophecies; by arousing enough concern they helped prevent or postpone that which they predicted. But whatever processes of internalizing, eroticizing, or numbing were responsible, there is no question that the Seventies have been a decade almost totally de-sensitized to the continued imminence of doom that caused hysteria fifteen years ago.

       ●   ■   ●

What happened to the superheated apocalyptic fever that pervaded the national consciousness from the mid-Fifties to the early Sixties?

The bombs are still there, and the Threat, but when was the last time you had an opinion on the morality of massive retaliation? Can you even recall having an opinion on the gun-in-the-fallout-shelter question? Ban-the-bomb marches? The better-Red-than-Dead debate? Does anyone live his life as if the End were really twenty-five minutes away? Why did we say Good-bye to All That? Or did we?

In his study of Sabbatai Sevi, the fabulous false messiah of seventeenth-century Palestine, scholar Gershom Scholem distinguishes between two strains of eschatological (end of the world) sensibilities: the apocalyptic and the mystical. In the apocalyptic mode, the various revelations of cataclysmic messianic advents, and, to shift to a Christian example, the visions of the titanic last battle at Armageddon (an actual place in the Holy Land, by the way), are taken to represent actual physical upheavals, literal military battles that will be waged on the surface of the earth. In the mystical mode, on the other hand, these climactic wars between the forces of God and His Adversary, and similar upheavals described in sacred books, are said to be waged *internally*—within the mystical body (*corpus mysteriosum*) of the believer—for possession, not of the world, but of the soul.

After reading the literature of nuclear annihilation it seems clear to me that what happened in the mid-Sixties was an internalization of the apocalyptic fevers and their transformation into mystical symptoms.

When the test-ban treaty drove the visible mushroom clouds underground in 1963, it was not long before there sprang up among post-Hiroshima progeny the impulse to ingest magic mushrooms and their psychedelic cognates. The experience of "blowing the mind" from within was an eroticized replication of the no-longer-visible explosion. The once-feared death of consciousness on earth threatened by nuclear annihilation was replaced by the desire for the annihilation of the ego. It's possible that the concept of "bad vibes" can be seen as a cognate of invisible radiation. A generation that grew up with the fear of the ineradicable contamination of its mother's milk by fallout has developed a mystical obsession with the purity of all it ingests, and it can be argued that Jack D. Ripper, the nuke-mad commander in *Strangelove* obsessed with the purity of his "precious bodily fluids," is the spiritual godfather of the health-food movement. The guru who offers a short circuit to "the clear light" is particularly seductive to a generation that expected to be shortcircuited to heaven by the "light brighter than a thousand suns."

That short-circuiting of time had long-term characterological effects that are only now being revealed: a belief that one would never live to be a grown-up discouraged any patience for the acceptance of the need to grow up. Indeed, like Peter Pan (not the diner), the bomb allowed the transformation of the present into a never-never land in which no gratification need be postponed and one could celebrate here what Tom Wolfe aptly called the "happiness explosion" instead of the unhappy one we once feared.

In a similar way the antiwar movement, which grew in part out of the ban-the-bomb fervor, found part of itself seduced into a mystical fascination with making bombs. One of the women survivors of the Weather Underground townhouse-bomb-factory explosion wrote a poem called "How It Feels to Be Inside an Explosion"—perhaps the ultimate internalization.

The persistence of the explosive word "blow" in the slang of the late Sixties and early Seventies may in itself be a residue of the internalization of the apocalyptic. Why else do we describe ourselves as feeling blown away, and getting blown over, blown out, getting the mind blown, getting blown (sexually). And is it an accident that the moving epitaph Ken Kesey spoke for the climactic failure of his attempt at a mystical group-mind fusion that failed to transcend fission was, as Tom Wolfe records it, "We blew it."

There is an undeniable but puzzling erotic element in the mystical symptomology. As I was trying to explain my theory of nuclear pornography to a onetime SDS activist, now a feminist, she did a double take and said that the transformation I was talking about paralleled an explanation she had been developing for the persistence of rape motifs in the sexual fantasies of purportedly liberated women. Rape, she said, in the imagination of many women is an analogue of the unthinkable in nuclear terms, a traumatic, disarming surprise attack that leaves the consciousness devastated. Since there is no certain defense, and constant fear of psychic annihilation is impossible to live with, a transformation occurs in which the constantly terrifying specter of the external rapist is internalized and transformed into an erotic actor in sexual fantasies.

Tomorrow morning at last I would be able to stop fantasizing about the nuclear trigger. I was going to put my finger on it.

ALONE WITH THE SANEST MEN IN AMERICA

They call it the "Command Balcony" of the war room, and it was to be, after two preparatory briefings, my first vision of triggerland. The Command Balcony—I loved the lofty theatricality of the name— was where the President's phone call would be answered when he decided the time had come to unleash the missiles.

Uneasy is the descent into the war room. One is led down steel corridors where hard-nosed security-detachment men wearing blue berets and conspicuously displayed pearl-handled pistols guard the blast-proof doors which are marked NO LONE ZONE. The doors, my guide reassures me, are also gas-and radiation-proof and able to withstand a direct hit with a five-megaton warhead. This is not totally reassuring. In order to take my mission to the command post with proper seriousness, I had absorbed a full-scale "Briefing on Soviet Strategic Capabilities," which emphasized the growing threat from larger Soviet missiles able to deliver a "throwweight" up to twenty megatons with increasing accuracy. But no matter. Provisions have been made against the sudden vaporization of these underground premises. The instant the circuits begin to melt, all command-post functions will instantly revert to "The Looking Glass Plane." This curious code name is given to the "airborne command post," one of a rotating fleet of planes that have been circling the Midwest since February 1961 ready to take over the running of the war from above the blasts.

At first I thought the code name "Looking Glass" must refer to the postattack function—reflecting messages back and forth to surviving authorities at various points on the ground, or perhaps to the mirror-bright aluminum bottom half of the plane designed to deflect the glare of the nuclear blasts from the battle below. I couldn't believe the Air Force would deliberately advert to that dark Carrollian fantasy of hallucinatory chess. But when I asked my guide, an Air Force major, about the origin of "Looking Glass" he told me, "Sir, I can't say for sure but I assume they had that Lewis Carroll book in mind." Later that day I would be taken through an actual Looking Glass Plane on standby for an eight-hour shift aloft, but that morning when I went through the blast-proof doors and out onto the Command Balcony, then I was truly through the looking glass—although, as I would soon find out, not the side I thought.

The Command Balcony is a glassed-in mezzanine of the small two-story theater that is the war room of the Strategic Air Command. In the orchestra pit below, the "battle staff" works away at computer terminals and radar displays complete with all the glowing dials of dimly lit, melodramatic movies. Looming over all, of course, is the fourth wall of the theater—the "big board." Its six two-story-high panels dominate the view from the Command Balcony. Above the open panel closest to me the alert-status indicator reads 1 on a scale of 5. During the October War of 1973 it read 3. A whirling red light flashed above the big board and a message flashed on ordering the battle staff to cease all unnecessary tasks and stand by for orders.

This morning as I walked in the big board was blanked out. For security purposes, I was told. It was not until some moments later that I was to look up and see that fateful sign on the big board. First I wanted to sit in the command swivel chair. There it was ahead of me, a big black swivel chair in the central well of the Command Balcony. The chair is reserved, in time of nuclear war, for the commander in chief of the Strategic Air Command, or CINCSAC as he's known on the Command Balcony. It's from this chair that CINCSAC will gaze at the big board and make his moves in the decisive first minutes of nuclear war. On a panel in front of the CINCSAC swivel chair are the red phone and the gold phone. The President and the Joint Chiefs call in the orders on the gold phone. CINCSAC executes them on the red phone.

"The President can make you a General," observed onetime CINC-SAC General Curtis Lemay, who sat in this chair for many years, "but only communications can make you a commander."

I seated myself in the swivel chair. I picked up the gold phone. I picked up the red phone. The battle staff was humming away beneath me. And for a moment, sitting there in the CINCSAC swivel chair, indulging myself in the seductive grandiosity of this position in the last synapse between command and execution of that awesome final order, for a moment I felt like a commander.

I also felt like a child, let loose with the war toy I'd always wanted.

And I also felt like a potential war criminal. Will some tribunal in the rubble see this article and condemn me posthumously for failing to rip both gold and red phones out of their sockets?

But suddenly, when I looked up from my command-chair reverie to the big board, I felt foolish. A three-line message had flashed onto the big board. Could this be It? Not quite. When I read it I cringed. All my fantasies fled in embarrassment. This is what the message said:

> WELCOME MR. RON ROSENBAUM
> FROM HARPER [SIC] MAGAZINE
> TO COMMAND BALCONY SAC HEADQUARTERS

Then an Air Force photographer stepped forward to take my picture in the command chair as a memento, and then a whole dog-and-pony show of a briefing began, featuring a call on the red phone from the Looking Glass Plane airborne with a preprogrammed "Greetings from the captain and crew to Mr. Rosenbaum, distinguished visitor to SAC's command post."

I could go on. It was in many ways a fascinating briefing but from the moment I saw that first WELCOME sign on the big board I had the sinking feeling they had turned this place, this focal point of nuke-porn fantasies, into a tourist trap. It might as well have been Disneyworld or some bankrupt and bogus "astronaut-land" in some bypassed south Florida subdivision for all the magic that remained. Suddenly all that had seemed forbidden, awesome about the stage upon which civilization's final drama may be played appeared like cheap stage tricks. Even the dimmed lights, "the pools of darkness" that in *Failsafe* "gave the sense of immensity of almost limitless reach," were dimmed only for the duration of my stay on the Command Balcony. They were dimmed to make a slide show, complete with flashlight pointer, more visible as it was projected on the screen. I felt cheated, teased with the illusion of command, then brought down to earth feeling like a cranky, disappointed tourist. A thermonuclear crisis would just not seem at home here on the Command Balcony any more than on a high school auditorium stage.

And that perhaps was the point. The Strategic Air Command is proud of its command-and-control system, does not think of it as an exotic, thrilling Strangelovian mechanism. It's *just* a mechanism, a sophisticated one, but a neutral mechanism they administer, certainly not an evil one—it hasn't done any evil, it hasn't really done anything except be there so long it's become routine.

●　■　●

That moment on the Command Balcony, I later realized, was the point at which I passed through to the other side, a Looking Glass of sorts. I was the one who had been living in a fever of Carrollian nightmares. The world I'd stepped into was relentlessly sane, its people very well adjusted. The paradoxical metaphysic of deterrence theory had become part of their ground of being. No one gave it a second thought, seldom a first. They spent little time in reflection of any kind, much less a Looking Glass sensibility. They were not there to shoot missiles and kill people. They were there *to act as if they would* shoot missiles and kill people because by so doing they'd never have to actually do it. They were content that their role was ceaselessly to rehearse, never perform that one final act.

They could have fooled me. I was fascinated by the aplomb of the missile crewmen I met. These are the guys who will actually pull the trigger for us. Of course they don't pull a trigger, they twist a key. Each two-man crew of "launch control officers" must twist their respective keys simultaneously to generate a "launch vote" from their capsule, and the two-man "launch vote" of another capsule is required before the four twisted keys can together send from ten to fifty Minutemen with MIRVed warheads irrevocably on their way to their targets.

These men will not be voting alone of course. When we pay our income taxes we are casting our absentee ballot in favor of a launch vote, and, should the time ever come, in favor of the mass murder of tens of millions of innocents. Morally, metaphorically, our finger is on the trigger too. But theirs are on it physically day in and day out for years.

I tried to get them to talk about it. Up at Minot AFB the Fifty-fifth Missile Wing helicoptered me out to an operational Minuteman-missile launch capsule nestled in the midst of vast fields of winter wheat. Fifty feet below the topsoil in the capsule I tried to edge into larger subjects— does it make a difference being able to know your target?—but there seemed to be nervousness on both sides, perhaps because of the presence of a senior officer and a tape recorder. Fortunately at the last minute

I was able to arrange, as the final unofficial stop in my tour of the nuclear fortifications, a different kind of meeting with missile crewmen.

Let me tell you about that last stop. Because it was there that I finally got the feel of those brass launch keys—I actually got to twist them and get the feel of launching a nuke—and it was there that I first discussed such issues as nuclear surrender and the Judo—yes, Judo—Christian ethic, and it was there that I first learned the secret of the spoon and the string.

I can't tell you exactly where it was—I agreed to keep the name of the base and the names of the missile men I spoke to out of the story. But I can tell you it was a Minuteman base and the men I spoke to were all launch-control officers. And these are no ordinary missile crewmen. Even among the highly skilled Minutemen men these are the crème de la crème I'm visiting with this Saturday morning. These six guys in their blue Air Force fatigues and brightly colored ascots are a special crack crew of missile men culled from capsules all over the base into a kind of all-star team. This morning they are practicing in a launch-capsule "problem simulator" for the upcoming "Olympic Arena" missile-crew competition out at Vandenberg AFB, where they will represent the honor of their base in a kind of World Series of missile-base teams.

You see, the Air Force goes to some length to imbue the men in its missile squadrons with a military esprit—a task rendered difficult by the sedentary and clerical nature of military-capsule duty. Missile men never need learn to fly a plane and most don't. The romantic flyboy spirit is something of a handicap for men condemned to spend twenty-four hours in a twenty-by-nine-by-ten-foot capsule. There's no need to develop that special brand of nerve and confidence Tom Wolfe, in his study of astronauts, called "the right stuff." The right stuff for a missile crewman is a disposition far more phlegmatic and stolid. So the typical missile crewman of the sample I met was often a pudgy bespectacled graduate of a Southern technical school with a low-key, good-ol'-boy sense of humor, who volunteered for missile duty because the Air Force would pay for the accounting degree he could earn in his spare time in the launch capsule. The Air Force is still run by flyboys who tend to treat the missile crewmen as junior partners. Still the Air Force tries to incorporate the missile men into its traditional gung-ho spirit. It gives them all dashing ascots to wear, as if they were units of some Australian Ranger battalion trained to kill men with their bare hands, when all they actually are expected to do with their bare hands is twist a key. (One almost suspects some deadpan tongue-in-cheek flyboy parody in the ascot touch.) And there are all sorts of patches and merit badges for the annual "Olympic Arena" competition, which is strenuously promoted and prepped for all year round.

This morning these missile men have been practicing for "Olympic Arena" in a special glass-walled launch-control capsule "simulator" that replicates the conditions of the big missile Olympic games. These are not as dramatic as they might sound—no jousting between Titans and Minutemen, no target shooting, no actual launchings at all, in fact. Instead the competition consists of "problems" computer-fed into the capsule simulators, and the crews go through the checklists in their capsule operations manuals to solve the problems. Problems thrown at them can be anything from retargeting half their missiles from Leningrad to Moscow to putting out a fire in the capsule trash bin. For every possible problem it seems there is a checklist to follow, and the activity I watch in the capsule consists mainly of finding the right checklist in the right briefing book and following the instructions. Victory goes to those who follow their checklists most attentively. More like a CPA competition than an Arthurian tournament.

During a break in the problem-solving I am invited into the capsule simulator to look around. It is exactly like the working missile capsule I had been permitted access to a few days ago in every respect but one. The keys. In the working missile capsule the keys are locked securely in a fire-engine-red box that is to be opened only in time of high-level nuclear alert. But as soon as I walked into the simulator that morning I caught sight of the now-familiar bright red box with its little red door wide open. And then I saw the keys. They gleamed brassily, each of them inserted into their slots in the two launch consoles, just as they will be in the last seconds before launch. Apparently the keys had been left there from a launch-procedure problem. I looked at the key closest to me. It had a round brass head, and looked like an old fashioned apartment key. It was stuck into a slot with these positions marked upon it: SET on top, and LAUNCH to the right. This particular key was turned to OFF.

I asked one of the crewmen if I could get a feel of what it would be like to turn the key.

"Sure," he said. "Only that one there, the deputy commander's, the spring-lock mechanism is a little worn out. Come over here and try the commander's key." First I tried the deputy's key all the way to the right from OFF to LAUNCH. Almost no resistance whatsoever. Very little tension.

"Come over and try the other one," one of the crewmen suggested. "That'll give you the real feel of a launch."

To launch a missile, both launch-control officers in the capsule must twist their respective keys to the right within two seconds of each other and hold them there for a full two seconds. The key slots are separated by twelve feet so no one man can either reach over or run over from one key to another and singlehandedly send in a "launch vote." Even if this were to happen, a two-key-twist, two-man "launch vote" from a second capsule in the squadron is still required to send any one missile off.

I sat down in the commander's chair—it's not unlike an economy-class airline seat, complete with seat belt. I turned the key to LAUNCH. This time it took some healthy thumb pressure to make the twist, and some forearm muscular tension to hold it in LAUNCH. Not a teeth-clenching muscular contraction—the closest thing I can compare it to is the feeling you get from twisting the key in one of the twenty-five-cent lockers at Grand Central Station. Nothing special, but the spring-lock resistance to the launch twist is enough to require a sustained effort of will from the person doing the twisting. For two seconds that person and at least three other people must consciously believe they are doing the right thing killing that many millions of people. Two seconds is perhaps time for reflection, even doubt.

Later, outside the simulator, I asked the missile crewmen if they'd ever imagined themselves having a doubt about their grip on the keys when the time came for that final twist of the wrist. What made them so sure they'd actually be able to do it, or did they just not think of the consequences?

"No," one of the crewmen said. "During training out at Vandenberg they'd show the whole class films of the effects of nuclear blasts, Hiroshima and all that, just so we wouldn't have any mistake as to what we're getting into. It's true that they ask you if you will carry out a properly authenticated launch order, and they check your psychological reaction, and the checking doesn't stop there. We're constantly required to check each other for some signs of unusual behavior. But you have to understand that when the launch order comes it won't come as a sudden new trauma. We get practice alerts and retargeting procedures all the time, and the launch will just be a few more items on a procedural checklist we've gone through thousands of times."

By this time we'd adjourned to a small, concrete-floored room containing vending machines for Coke and candy and a few scratched metal folding chairs. Being in a room with the sanest men in America can be disconcerting. And these men were—officially—extremely sane. That constant psychological checking of each other they spoke about is part of the Air Force's Human Reliability Program, which is supposed to be a kind of mental early-warning system to catch people with access to nuclear warheads who are going insane, before their madness turns violent or, worse, cunning.

Of course the Air Force definition of sanity might seem a bit narrow to some, involving as it does the willingness to take direct part in the killing of, say, 10 million people by twisting a key when the proper order is given, while insanity means trying to kill them without proper orders or refusing to kill them despite orders. Nonetheless it is fascinating to read through Air Force Regulation 35-99, Chapter 7, "Psychiatric Considerations of Human Reliability," which is the missile-base commander's guide to early detection of "Concealed Mental Disorders." Regulation 35-99 divides these hidden threats into four categories: "The Suspicious," "The Impulsive," "The Depressed," and "Those with Disturbances of Consciousness." Regulation 35-99 then details "the early signs in observable behavior that strongly suggest the possibility of present or emerging mental disorder" in each category.

Now the trickiest category, according to Regulation 35-99, is "The Suspicious" (don't ask me what school of psychopathology this taxonomy comes from), which enumerates thirteen "clues to paranoid traits." Tricky, because as the Air Force points out "the following clues are sometimes seen in normal everyday behavior." Indeed, it is difficult to read the description of the thirteen clues without thinking of the "normal everyday behavior" of nuclear powers.

There is, for instance: "a. Arrogance—wherein the individual assumes or presumes the possession of superior, unique, or bizarre abilities, ideas, or theories."

Now, one would think that a man able to participate in the launch of up to thirty separate nuclear warheads and help extinguish human civilization with a twist of his key would be a bull goose loony not to "presume the possession of superior, unique, or bizarre abilities." The implication here is that sanity in a launch means *not* thinking about this reality, sanity means the kind of studied insanity or fugue state that ignores one's true relation to the world. Then there is: "b. Lack of humor—especially the inability to laugh at oneself, one's mistakes or weaknesses." Now that is pretty funny. When you think about all the occasions for merriment there must be down there at the controls of an ICBM launch capsule, it's hard to believe anyone would be crazy enough not to see the humor in it all. It's good to know that Regulation 35-99 will keep an eye out to yank the occasional gloomy gus right out of there, so we can be assured that when we go we'll die laughing.

Now clue "l."—"legal or quasilegal controversy about pay, time, accidents, unsatisfactory purchases, or matter of authority"—is an interesting one for a couple of reasons. This "paranoid trait," according to the regulation, "is often seen in conjunction with 'letters to the editor,' 'to the president of the company,' or 'to senior commanders.' " One can immediately see the appeal of this definition to the senior commanders who administer the regulation. But it raises interesting questions. One does not want the launch capsules filled with teeth-gnashing irritable cranks, yet the presumption of irrationality that attaches to any question about "matters of authority" assumes that all authority is rational, an assumption that was implicitly challenged by Secretary of Defense Schlesinger when he tried to ensure that if President Nixon went batty and decided to launch a few nukes during the impeachment crisis, someone would question his authority.

But for the moment let us leave Regulation 35-99 behind with a parting glance at the Air Force's official characterization of the Mad Bomber. He comes under subsection 7-14, which cites "Some Specific Cases of the Paranoid Schizophrenic" for the missile-base commander to have in mind when he's checking out his men. The only other "specific case" mentioned in this subsection is an unnamed "would-be assassin of President Roosevelt [who] came to Washington to shoot the President and thus to draw public attention to the buzzing sensation in his head."

"To the Mad Bomber of New York," according to the regulation, "the need for revenge seemed paramount, dating back to an ancient grudge against a public utility company."

And yet isn't our nuclear retaliatory policy based on our belief in revenge—that any strike against us must be avenged with nuclear warheads even if it means destroying the rest of human society? Just as planting bombs in public places did not restore the Mad Bomber his pension rights (apparently the source of his grudge against Con Ed), neither would a retaliatory nuclear strike restore the lives or freedom lost from the strike we suffered first. Could this analysis of the Mad Bomber have been a sly comment on the sanity of the nuclear balance of terror slipped into the Air Force insanity definitions by some military shrink with a sense of irony?

In any case let us return to that vending-machine room off the launch-capsule simulator, where indeed a discussion ensues with the sanest men in America, which gets into the basic question of revenge by way of Las Vegas and leads us to the secret of the spoon and string.

I don't want you to get the wrong idea about these missile crewmen. I soon discovered that the Human Reliability Program in practice does not necessarily eliminate all but docile automatons. The missile men have lively responsive intelligences and very upbeat personalities. And despite their devotion to pure professionalism, even they are not entirely unconscious of the ironies of their particular profession. They, too, occasionally get that sense of dislocation at the awesomeness of their position and the ordinariness of their life. I got that sense from listening to one of the crewmen tell me a story about a curiously dislocating encounter he had in a Las Vegas hotel.

He'd accumulated some leave time from the long hours of vigils he had spent down in his launch-control capsule, and he'd decided to spend it in the gambling palaces of Vegas.

"I went alone and one night I wanted to get into one of the big floor shows they have," he told me. "Well, when I asked for a ringside table they told me that as I was by myself, would I mind sharing with another couple. I say okay and these two people introduce themselves. The guy says they're from North Carolina where he's a dentist. Then he asks me what I do."

Introductions can sometimes be awkward for a Minuteman launch-control officer. A stranger will casually ask him his line of work and if he just comes out and says "I'm a Minuteman-missile launch-control officer," well, it's not as if everyone will stare into his eyes for signs of incipient missile-shooting madness, but there is, sometimes, a feeling of wary scrutiny. People don't know exactly how to respond to the un-prepossessing presence of a man who is the most powerful and deadly warrior in human history.

"But not this dentist." He displayed none of the usual fears about Strangeloves in disguise, no suppressed whiff of awe at the personified presence of the end of the world.

"Hell no," the missile crewman was telling me. "The only thing this guy was worrying about was whether the thing would actually take off when it came time for wartime launch. He kept saying, 'I just want that bird to fly when the time comes.' He kept saying, 'I want that bird to fly.'"

The crewman shook his head. "It was funny because when the bird flies that means he and his family are probably vaporized. I couldn't figure it. It used to be people you'd run into would worry we'd go off half-cocked and start a war. Now this guy was all excited like he couldn't wait to see it."

"Fact is," said another missile crewman, "most of us have never even launched even a test down at the Vandenberg range. And nothing's ever been test-launched from an operational silo. Once they had a program that was going to let us launch from one of our silos. No warhead of course. From here into the Pacific. But some Indian tribe objected to missiles flying over their sacred burial ground or something and they canceled it. I can maybe see what that dentist was getting at. You sit down there and you know you've got launch capability and you know when you and your buddy turn the keys she'll fly all right but you sure would feel more comfortable if you had it happen once. I tell you I've spent a year and a half underground and I'm halfway to my M.S., but for all those hours down there, when I get out I sure would like to be able to say 'I launched a missile.'"

Again I asked these sanest of all men how they could be sure they'd be able to launch when they knew it was for real.

"One thing you have to remember," one of the crewmen told me, "is that when I get an authenticated launch order I have to figure my wife and kids'd be dead already up above. The base is ground zero.

Why shouldn't I launch? The only thing I'd have to look forward to if I ever got up to the surface would be romping around with huge mutant bunny rabbits." We all laughed. It seemed funny at the time.

"Okay, then, put it this way," I said. "If you assume that when you get the launch order everyone on our side has been devastated by a Soviet first strike, is there any purpose served by destroying what's left of humanity by retaliating purely for revenge?"

"What it all comes down to," said one of the older crewmen, "is the Judo-Christian ethic."

"You mean Judeo-Christian," one of the others murmured.

"Right, like I said, the *Judo*-Christian ethic teaches that you never strike first but if someone hits you, you can strike back."

"Wait a minute," I said. "Isn't it Christian to forgive, turn the other cheek, rather than seek revenge? Say you're Jimmy Carter, a serious Christian, and you're President when the whole deterrence thing fails and for some reason the Soviets are tempted to strike or preempt our strike. You see those missiles coming in on the radar screen and know mass murder is about to happen to your people and nothing you can do will stop it. Is there any point in committing another act of mass murder?"

"You think he should surrender?" one of the crewmen asked me.

"I don't know," I said, taken aback by the abruptness of his question.

"That's the thing, you know," another crewman said. "Once you start thinking about all that your head starts going in circles. You got to change the subject. There's a point where you gotta stop asking questions and go to work. You've just got to have faith that you're doing the right thing. It all comes down to professionalism. We know our presence here helps deter war and . . ."

"Course we thought about the problem if we get a launch order if one of us in a capsule crew suddenly turns peacenik at the last minute," one of the crewmen interrupted to say. "And we came up with a solution. We figured out that the whole two-key thing is really bullshit when you get down to it because we figured out how to get a launch with just one man and a spoon and a string."

"Spoon and a string?"

"Well," the crewman continued, "what you do is rig up a thing where you tie a string to one end of a spoon and tie the other end to the guy's key. Then you can sit in your chair and twist your key with one hand while you yank on the spoon with the other hand to twist the other key over." Now this guy was talking about using some old-fashioned ingenuity to carry out an authorized "execution order." It could of course be used in the service of an unauthorized launch conspiracy. Since launching an ICBM still requires a launch vote from two separate launch-control capsules, it would require two men in cahoots with two spoons and two strings—and probably two pistols—to carry out such an unlikely caper; however, since the two-key system is at the heart of the credibility of the entire command-and-control system, someone in the Air Force just might want to get out a spoon and string, go down into a capsule, and see whether someone might have overlooked a little safeguard.

Nevertheless, I actually found myself more reassured by the missile crewmen's willingness to tell me about the spoon-and-string trick than I was frightened by its possible application. The kind of person who'd cheerfully volunteer the spoon-and-string story is not the kind of person who'd be likely to conspire to use it to try to provoke World War III.

In fact I was quite impressed with the robust psychological health of the missile crewmen. If they didn't engage in rigorous analysis of the moral consequences of their triggerman role, none of them seemed at all the type to want to conspire to start a nuclear war. They put in a lot of idle hours down in the capsule studying for accounting and law degrees, and a nuclear war would seriously disrupt their professional prospects when they got out. Meeting the missile men was the most reassuring part of my trip.

●   ■   ●

Major Hering, you'll recall, was likewise not the least concerned with the mental health of his fellow crewmen. He was worried about the upper links in the chain of command. And unhappily, as one studies those upper reaches more closely, the chain of command seems less like a chain than a concatenation of spoons and strings.

How will Vice-President Mondale, off in Hawaii when a suitcase bomb blows up the White House, wage nuclear war from Waikiki with no black-briefcase man at his side? And don't think President Carter, notified of what looks on the radar screens like a surprise attack, will be able to dip into Russian literature to help him decide whether to retaliate against Moscow and Leningrad, or Leningrad and Kiev. If, in fact, the Joint Chiefs do decide to consult the Constitutional Commander in Chief on the nature of a retaliatory response (faced with a "use it or lose it" situation military commanders tend to shoot first and consult the Supreme Court later; the Joint Chiefs have no need of the President to launch the missiles physically if they feel he's wavering when the time has come to strike back), the consultation will consist of presenting the Commander in Chief with comprehensive preprogrammed attack options generated by our chief nuclear war-gaming computer, the SIOP machine.

SIOP, I should explain, stands for "Single Integrated Operating Plan." It is *the* basic nuclear war plan for all U.S. forces and details exactly which missiles and which bombers will blow up which targets in case of nuclear attack. The SIOP machine is a vast computer complex in a subbasement of the Underground Command Post that generates the Emergency War Orders for transmittal to each element of the SIOP attack. In addition, the SIOP machine is constantly war-gaming its own war plan against its own estimate of the Russian war plan, which SIOP calls RISOP, and updating itself after it counts the computerized death score.

What this means in practice is that the key decisions about how we will respond *in every conceivable nuclear crisis* have already been made by the SIOP machine. Most of us may not think of nuclear war at all these days. The SIOP machine thinks about nuclear war for us twenty-four hours a day. The SIOP will run our nuclear war for us.

In fact, the only moment in my entire sentimental journey I felt genuinely "in touch" with nuclear war was the time I felt the SIOP machine. I don't think it's on the regular tourist trail in triggerworld but I made a special request to see the SIOP machine after reading so much about its awesome capabilities. Even in sophisticated strategic literature the SIOP is spoken of with reverential, almost Delphic, awe, and its pronouncements are surrounded with Delphic mystery. No one even knows how many targets are on the SIOP hit list. One scholarly study of recent nuclear targeting strategy devoted a long footnote to examining whether a fragmentary declassified report which declared that there were 25,000 targets in the SIOP really might have been a misprint, perhaps deliberate, for 2,500 targets.

The secrets inside the SIOP machine, our actual war plans, are perhaps the most secret secrets in America. According to a two-part report by Seymour Hersh in the *New York Times* (December, 1973), a story whose implications were lost in the Watergate deluge, the Nixon Administration's hysterical and ultimately self-destructive reaction to the Ellsberg affair may have been triggered not by his release of the Pentagon Papers but by the possibility—explored secretly in the highest councils of the Nixon White House—that Ellsberg might also release some of the sacred SIOP secrets. In 1961, in the days when he was an eager young Rand Corporation analyst, a fledgling Strangelove who had already made a highly respected debut with a pamphlet on the "Art of Nuclear Blackmail," Ellsberg had been summoned by the Pentagon to review the existing system for the command and control of the nuclear trigger weapons. As part of that work Ellsberg was permitted to review the SIOP and the Joint Strategic Target List. In a recent talk on "the nature of modern evil" at the *Catholic Worker*, Ellsberg, now repentant, described his first look at the primitive SIOP. It shocked him, he said, to learn we had only one nuclear war targeting plan: hit 400 targets in Russia and China. Estimated casualties 325 million. Whether Ellsberg went on to help redesign the SIOP he would not say, and whether he had any significant knowledge of the SIOP secrets as it evolved into a sophisticated computerized targeting system Ellsberg would not say. But according to Hersh's unnamed source (who sounds like Ehrlichman), the very possibility that Ellsberg would reveal sacred SIOP secrets the way he revealed the Pentagon Papers—the possibility that he would thereby show the Russians our hand in the bluffing game that is deterrence strategy—was enough to drive Nixon and Kissinger up the wall. According to this theory all the seamy things done to Ellsberg and the Watergate cover-up that was necessary to cover *them* up can be traced to fear for the sanctity of the SIOP.

Well, you might say, doesn't everyone know what we'll do when attacked? What difference does it make which missiles go where when they all go boom and make everyone dead? It makes a difference to the strategists. For them the game of deterrence, the delicate balance of terror, is not a stalemate but an ongoing poker game in which the dynamics of bluff, ambiguity, and esoteric as opposed to declaratory policies are constantly shifting. As Bernard Brodie, the elegant grand master of civilian nuclear strategists, notes, "Good military planning should distinguish between what the President says he'll do and what he's likely to do." Kissinger, an unreconstructed Machiavellian among strategists, called the latter—our real plans as opposed to what we say we'll do—the esoteric strategy.

Inside the SIOP machine are not only the secret war plans of our esoteric strategy but, in addition, a wide array of targeting options based on computerized war-gaming of possible Soviet responses to our responses to their responses. One missile crewman I spoke to, overwhelmed by the majesty and complexity of the SIOP, burst into a veritable ode to its chivalric, jousting-like possibilities. "Just think," he said, "we're engaged in a test of wills with the Soviets somewhere and they push us too hard and push comes to shove, we don't have to choose between incinerating the planet and giving up. With the new SIOP options we can pinpoint a shot across the Kamchatka Peninsula and if they don't start listening to reason just walk those Nudets [Air Force word for nuclear detonation] across Siberia till they start to feel the heat in Moscow. Course they'll probably start on the Gulf of Mexico with theirs, walk 'em across to Houston, and start to head north, but we'll have our response to that all programmed in the SIOP. You know something else? I understand that before Carter took office he was given a detailed SIOP briefing and the guy was so shaken by it, that's why he suddenly comes out and says we got to abolish all nuclear weapons. The SIOP was too much for him. He just couldn't handle it."

So what actually goes on within the SIOP machine? Many nuclear wars: "practice" wars between SIOP and RISOP. After each battle a computer program counts the dead, estimates the damages, and looks for a way to improve the score in our favor in the next nuclear war. The predictive value of the nuclear wars waged within the SIOP machine is handicapped since it has to match itself against its own estimate of RISOP, which, like SIOP, consists of preplanned reactions that can be changed or rejected by national leaders in the heat of crisis. So the wars within SIOP can become a tenuous solipsistic affair, like a computer playing chess with itself. Still it is awesome being in a room in which the world has ended so many possible ways, perhaps even the precise way it will.

Toward the end of my tour of the SIOP machine I asked the colonel guiding me through the warrens of computers in the SIOP subbasement if I could touch the machine. He looked at the captain accompanying me and shrugged. Not far from me was a first-generation computer element of the SIOP machine. On top of its stacked magnetic tapes was a red "Top Secret" sign, but there was nothing secret for me to see. Only to feel. So I put my hand on its gray alloyed surface and felt in my palm the residual hum and tremor of the thousands of nuclear wars waged by SIOP and RISOP, those ceaselessly clashing computer programs, locked like Gog and Magog in endless Armaggedons within its ghostly circuitry.

●   ■   ●

That was the closest I came to the answers. The answers to Major Hering's question. To my questions about the nitty-gritty details of our actual as opposed to our declared or bluffed targeting strategy. All the answers but one. What happens if we lose?

It was at the very end of my tour of the SIOP machine that I happened to ask an innocuous question that led me down the road into the swamp of "surrender studies."

"In all these wars between SIOP and RISOP," I asked the colonel in charge of the SIOP room, "do we always win?"

The colonel seemed taken aback. He said something about "programming optimum outcomes" or something like that.

"Well, does SIOP ever admit defeat to RISOP or surrender to it?"

"I should hope not," he said.

I had heard whispers about forbidden "surrender studies" when I was down in Washington, whispers about people who have been hounded out of government for daring to suggest that, despite our endless contingency planning and war-gaming, we wouldn't know how to surrender if forced to because we're not permitted to consider the possibility of a loss. It sounded silly, and until that brief exchange in the SIOP room I'd assumed—as I had when I first read of Major Hering's question—that someone somewhere had the answers. But now I was told that even the SIOP machine was not programmed to consider surrender. And so when I returned from my pilgrimage I decide to track down these "surrender studies" I'd heard about.

What I discovered was that in the entire exotic garden of nuclear-war-fighting strategy theory, surrender is the one forbidden fruit. A subject more unthinkable than The Unthinkable itself. In fact, thinking about it has actually been declared illegal in some cases.

Indeed, the short, sad history of surrender studies in the nuclear age reveals that the few intrepid theoreticians who have ventured into that *terra incognita* have come back scarred by the charge that just talking about it can cause it. Back in 1958 a Rand Corporation analyst by the name of Paul Kecskemeti published a modest scholarly monograph entitled *Strategic Surrender*. Beginning with the premise that surrender, like war, is an extension of politics by other means, Kecskemeti explored the various strategies of twentieth-century surrenders—what each party to a surrender was able to win and lose (yes, a loser can "win" a surrender by getting more concessions than his actual strength should command). High marks go to the Vichy French and Germans for their eminently professional disposition of the surrender of France in 1940; a pathetic failing grade to the Americans and Italians who botched the surrender of Italy in 1943. Though his is largely a historical study Kecskemeti did append to the work a section on "Surrender in Future Strategy," with a subsection on "Surrender in Nuclear War"—the latter slightly more than one page long. That was enough. When his book appeared, the great post-Sputnik, Red-or-Dead debate still raged across the land and Kecskemeti had been gracious enough in his preface to acknowledge that "this study was prepared as part of the research program under-taken for the United States Air Force by the Rand Corporation." Swift and massive retaliation fell upon the book. You could call it overkill. There were outcries from the warlords of Congress that taxpayer money was being used to pave the way for capitulation to the Soviets. President Eisenhower was described as upset and horrified as he demanded an immediate explanation from the Pentagon. "I've never seen Ike more mad," said one aide. Everything at the Pentagon stopped for two hours while they tried to get to the bottom of the surrender-study flap. The *New York Times* reported a "tumultuous session" of Congress, and "the most heated debate of the year" brought forth near unanimous passage of one of the strangest resolutions ever to issue from that body. This one, attached as a rider to an appropriations bill and passed in August, 1958, specifically forbade the use of any federal funds to finance the study of surrender.

On the inside cover of the library-battered copy of *Strategic Surrender* I have in my hands, some outraged reader has scrawled: "Americans would rather die on their feet than live on their knees." It's an attitude that has made even the boldest nuclear strategists a bit gun-shy about discussing surrender. In what seems like a characteristically black-humored recognition of the delicacy of using the forbidden word, the index to the second edition of Henry Kissinger's early study of *Nuclear Weapons and Foreign Policy* contains the following laconic citation: "Unconditional Surrender. See Victory, Total."

Even the fearless Herman Kahn, forever urging us to call a spade a spade and a grave a grave in matters of nuclear war, prefers to discuss "responses to postattack blackmail" rather than "surrender negotiations." In his treatise *On Thermonuclear War*, Kahn grumbles that "the investigation of the feasibility of various [postattack] blackmail tactics is not only a difficult technical question, but seems contrary to public policy as set forth in recent legislation forbidding use of federal funds for the study of 'surrender.' " But the master strategist is something less than his usual crusading self when he quits the subject with the terse comment that "such research is important." When he publishes research on surrender problems, Kahn talks of "conflict termination." He talks of "crisis resolution," and, most ingenuous of all, "de-escalation." None, not even he, dares call it surrender.

Officially anyway. Inconclusive inquiries to the Defense Department failed to turn up any indication that the surrender-study ban had ever been repealed, although no one there seemed to know of its existence or was prepared to believe its existence, even after I read them several front-page *New York Times* stories on the controversy.

Kecskemeti remembers. I spoke to him last summer, almost two decades after the big fuss, and it sounded to me as if in his scholarly way he was still steamed up about what happened to his book. He blamed it on "a stupid article in the *St. Louis Post*," leaked, he said, by Missouri Senator Symington, the former Secretary of the Air Force, who was preparing to run for President on a Strengthen-America's-Defenses platform.

Kecskemeti described the Senate debate on surrender. "Sensational, demagogic—and silly," he says. "My book was totally misunderstood. The question is whether great powers are able to end a war short of total annihilation. If this is to be done it must be thought about ahead of time."

THE SEDUCTIONS OF STRATEGY

My pursuit of what might seem like the arcana of surrender studies led me next to a question, another one of those Carrollian rabbit holes in the landscape of nuclear strategy, that is even more fundamental and immediate: Will we respond to a Soviet nuclear attack at all? Is it possible in some circumstances, despite our declarations, that we just won't retaliate?

I first came upon this notion in an elegant analysis of "War Termination" by Fred Ikle, the hawkish former head of the Arms Control and Disarmament Agency. (Ikle took over after the doves there were purged in exchange for Henry Jackson's support of the original SALT agreement.) In the conclusion of his analysis Ikle argues that deterrence—the threat of nuclear retaliation if we are attacked—commits us to a morally abhorrent, genocidal, retaliatory vengeance if the threat fails and we *are* attacked. The logical implication is that in the aftermath of a Soviet surprise attack, we might surrender without firing a shot.

Turn the other cheek and give in.

No less a person than Richard Nixon acknowledged the possible wisdom of such a course of action. Consider the situation I'd be in, Nixon said, "if the Soviet Union, in a surprise attack, were able to destroy all of America's fixed land-based missile force and would confront the U.S. with a choice of doing nothing or launching air- and sea-based nuclear forces only to see the U.S.S.R. inflict even more damage upon us in return." The implication is that Nixon would have surrendered in such circumstances.

I used to have long arguments on this point back in high school. What good would pure vengeance do you if you're dead, I'd ask. Ridiculous, my friends would say: if they knew someone like you was running things and bluffing they'd be more likely to attack. So don't tell them, I'd say, make them think we will strike back but if it does happen, don't. What is to be gained by killing off the rest of the human race?

I had long dismissed this as a naive adolescent hobbyhorse of mine until I tried the question out on the missile crewmen that morning and found it provoked an interesting discussion about the Judeo-Christian ethic. I was even more surprised to find, when I plunged back into the literature of nuclear strategy upon return from my tour, that "Deterrence as a Great Big Bluff" is discussed by some of the most sophisticated nuclear strategists as a very real possibility.

The most rational deterrence policy, writes Bernard Brodie, perhaps the most authoritative and rational of the first generation of strategists, involves convincing an enemy that we are utterly inflexible, vindictive, and even irrationally committed to retaliation against a potential attack, no matter what.

But, argues Brodie, that most rational deterrence policy "involves commitment to a strategy of response which, if we ever had to execute it, might then look foolish." In other words, a rational person may decide it's foolish to retaliate. "It remains questionable," Fred Ikle tells us, "whether the execution of a retaliatory strike can serve the national interests once it has failed as a threat." And there it is again, in the most graphic terms possible, in, of all places, *Strategic Review*, one of the most militantly—albeit scholarly—hawkish nuclear-strategy journals. In the February 1976 issue of *Strategic Review* military strategy writer R. J. Rummel asks, "If deterrence fails would a President push the button? Of course not."

What does this mean? Is Jimmy Carter, who pledged never to lie to the American people, bluffing us along with the Russians? Is that part of the esoteric strategy? Has he secretly decided he won't push the button in that situation? Do the Joint Chiefs know? Would they let him get away with it? Do we want him to tell us, and thus the Russians, making an attack at least marginally more likely?

As you can see, once you get into the Looking Glass world of esoteric strategy, answers become elusive as the questions develop elaborate mirror images: What do we think they think we think they think about what we plan to do? Nuclear war is waged these days not with missiles but with conceptions of missile strategies, with manipulations of perceptions and metaphysical flanking maneuvers. Mental nuclear war (after Blake's Milton: "I shall not cease from mental fight . . .") goes on all the time, often in obscure and veiled forms.

Consider the esoteric implications behind the appearance and disappearance of a single footnote from the prepared text of a speech Henry Kissinger delivered to the Commonwealth Club of San Francisco on February 3, 1976. Appended to his otherwise unremarkable address on "The Permanent Challenge of Peace: U.S. Policy Toward the Soviet

Union" was an eight-line footnote—appended, that is, to some printed versions of the speech and not to others. The official version delivered to the Soviet embassy by the State Department did have the footnote, and there was a message for the Soviets in that footnote, a veiled threat of great consequence between these lines:

> To be sure, there exist scenarios in planning papers which seek to demonstrate how one side could use its strategic forces and how in some presumed circumstance it would prevail. But these confuse what a technician can calculate with what a responsible statesman can decide. They are invariably based on assumptions such as that one side would permit its missile silos to be destroyed without launching its missiles before they are actually hit—on which no aggressor could rely where forces such as those possessed by either the U.S. or the U.S.S.R. now and in the years ahead are involved.

Now the real subject of this footnote is a declared U.S. nuclear strategy known as the "ride out" doctrine. Under it, we have committed ourselves not to respond immediately to a Soviet missile attack we see developing on our radar screens. Instead, incredible as it may sound at first, we are pledged to just sit back and track the incoming missiles, presumably aimed at our missile silos, watch as they blast holes in the Great Plains, ride out the attack, count up the number of missiles we still have left in working order, and *then*, and only then, strike back.

There are several strategic considerations behind what sounds like very odd behavior. First, we have confidence that our silos, for now at least, are sufficiently "hardened" so that the Soviets could not confidently expect to knock enough of them out to cripple our ability to retaliate. Second, confidence in our ability to ride out an initial attack allows us the luxury of not having to fire off our missiles merely on the basis of a radar warning that our silos are under attack; which means that we are less likely to be put in the "use it or lose it" dilemma, as the strategists call it, and precipitously launch our missile force on the basis of perhaps mistaken warnings or small accidental or unintended Soviet launches. Finally, declaring that we'll keep our missiles in their silos during a first strike against us almost compels the Soviets to target on them rather than on our large cities. They are bait of a sort.

Between the lines of that footnote there was an explicit message for Soviet nuclear strategists: a warning to them that if they attempted to develop a silo-busting missile capability—warheads accurate and powerful enough to destroy our Minutemen *inside* their hardened silos—they'd be making a big mistake and wasting billions of dollars. Because if they did develop that capacity we could simply renounce our "ride out" policy and shift to a "launch on warning" stance. This would make them look silly because under that posture, at the first sign of attack our missiles would let fly and the billions of dollars the Soviets had spent on a silo-busting capacity would be wasted busting empty silos.

Of course there are grave dangers to a launch-on-warning policy. Critics call it a "hair trigger" posture. And indeed if the Soviets thought we had shifted to it, they would, in the event of an accidental launch on their part, feel compelled to launch the rest of their arsenal because they'd know our hair trigger would be sending ours their way before we'd have time to verify whether it was an accident.

When the footnote set off a controversy over a possible U.S. "hair trigger" stance, and the footnote was dropped and then restored again, the State Department blandly denied there had been any change in U.S. policy. And officially there had not been. But Kissinger was playing what his former aide, Morton Halperin, calls the game of "the clever briefer." The footnote was designed to frustrate the ambitions of a hypothetical wily Kremlin advocate making a brief for a silo-busting capacity. "You want us to spend billions for this," a Soviet leader would reply to "the clever briefer." "But Kissinger has declared they will go to launch-on-warning if we do it and we will have gained nothing for our billions. What do you say to that?"

There is no good answer. Even though the footnote was deleted and the veiled warning shrouded in ambiguity, raising the possibility should be enough to defeat the arguments of "the clever briefer." That doesn't mean that the feint worked, that we won the War of Kissinger's Footnote. Indeed some military critics argue that Kissinger's subtle Machiavellianism was no match for the Soviets' mushrooming megatonnage. But that, in any event, gives you an idea how the game is played.

●   ■   ●

By this time, several months after my return from the nuclear shrines, several months of immersion in the literature of nuclear strategy, pursuing the paradoxes of esoteric and declaratory strategy ostensibly to write about the state of the art, I realized something was happening to me. I was becoming obsessed by the art, hooked again as I was as an adolescent by the piquant intellectual seductiveness of nuclear strategy. Finally, last August, I felt compelled to make a second pilgrimage. I was looking for some way to escape from the accumulation of nuclear esoterica I had submerged myself in and all of which seemed to be insulating me further from rather than bringing me more "in touch" with nuclear war, whatever that meant—I was sure I would know it if I felt it.

So I flew up to Boston on Hiroshima Day. A small item in Boston's *Real Paper* had attracted my attention: someone was actually going to hold an old-fashioned ban-the-bomb-type demonstration up there to commemorate the Hiroshima and Nagasaki bombings. I'm not talking about one of those anti-nuclear-power demonstrations. These have become very fashionable of late after the organizational success of the Clamshell Alliance's mass civil disobedience on the site of the proposed Seabrook nuclear reactor. There's no shortage of anti-nuclear-power demonstrations.

But a demonstration against nuclear weapons. How odd. As a sometime chronicler of the antiwar demonstrations of the late '60s and early '70s I knew that the only people who still did that were the small and aging band of the pacifist faithful, the War Resisters League, and other, smaller, old-fashioned peace groups; and I couldn't recall the last time I'd heard of them doing anything. This demonstration, part of a series of Hiroshima Day actions, seemed to have been engendered by many of the old peace-movement people hoping to rebuild the kind of mass movement that had disappeared after the test-ban treaty was approved. Apparently this was causing some ruffled feathers among the anti-nuclear-power partisans. According to a friend of mine in Boston, the Clamshell Alliance had refused to give its support to the Hiroshima Day demonstration because "some of them think it's just these old peace-movement people trying to take advantage of the energy the Clamshell people have established. The Clamshell people believe it's important to organize a base in the community rather than just to demonstrate." This snooty attitude confirmed a theory I'd had that the anti-nuclear-power movement was a way for activists to sublimate their feelings of impotence in the face of the massive nuclear-weapons establishment. You can prevent a reactor from being built, you can even shut it down if it's unsafe, but the nuclear warheads are already there, they are extremely unsafe, but no one believes they'll ever go away.

I remember how far gone into the swamp of strategic thinking I was by the time I arrived at Faneuil Hall for the opening speeches of the Hiroshima-Nagasaki ban-the-bomb demo-commemoration. I can remember because my first few pages of notes on that event are devoted to a four-line joke I found written on a wall of the men's room at Faneuil Hall and an analysis of the way that particular joke illuminated the dilemma of just-war theologians who employ the principle of "double effect" (developed in the thirteenth century to justify the use of the catapult as a siege weapon) to justify the "unintentional" slaughter of innocents contemplated by certain nuclear retaliatory strategies.

The joke on the men's-room wall was unusual only in that it was not really dirty, just mildly "sick."

"How did you get that flat tire?" it began.

"I ran over a milk bottle."

"Didn't you see it?"

"No, the damn kid was carrying it under his coat."

Get it? Now let me explain what this has to do with nuclear war. The late '50s and early '60s were full of heady debate for theologians with almost everyone wrestling with the problem of whether conduct of thermonuclear war could, or should, be guided by the same moral principles that were used to define a "just war" or whether thermonuclear war must be considered beyond the bounds of anything justifiable under any circumstances. Even thornier was the question of whether possession of nuclear weapons for deterrent purposes without use, but with the threat of potential use, could be moral if use was immoral. And were some kinds of use, some kinds of threatened use, better than other kinds of threats? No one wrestled more heroically with these problems than Protestant theologian Paul Ramsey. No one tried more strenuously to demonstrate that the application of complex Judeo-Christian moral principles to the most esoteric elements of nuclear strategy was a possible, indeed important, enterprise. Differing with Christian pacifists and "international realists," both of which schools insisted that no moral distinctions could apply to such an essentially immoral or amoral (respectively) enterprise, Ramsey plunged into the thicket of targeting strategy. For my money his finest or most ridiculous hour is his attempt to synthesize an acceptably Christian deterrent posture: he calls for a declared policy of massive countercity retaliation that will really be a bluff.

Here the milk-bottle joke is instructive. According to Ramsey's just-war reasoning (and assuming the milk bottle is some deadly weapon), it is okay to run over the boy as long as you *intend* to run over only the milk bottle. Or to apply it now to nuclear targeting, it is okay to respond to a nuclear strike by hitting an enemy's military targets (counterforce targeting) and killing tens of millions of people who happen to live within radiation range—it is okay so long as you *intend* to knock out only the military installations and the killing of innocent civilians is "unintentional" collateral damage resulting from the "double effect" of an ICBM on both combatant and noncombatant elements of the population.

This rationalization was developed to justify the use of the catapult as a siege weapon since it was impossible to see over the besieged walls to make sure the catapulted projectile hit only the combatants within a city. Ramsey also endorses a modified "bluff of deterrence" position: he believes that an *efficacious* deterrent threat requires that we declare we will wreak retaliation on cities, but that when the moment for retaliation comes we should adhere to counterforce military targeting or none at all.

Ramsey's efforts are a heroic act of rational apologetics, but one can't help but wonder if they don't serve to legitimize all forms of nuclear response since only a few scholastic quibbles seem to separate the sanctified from the unsanctified bomb blast.

I have been staring at blast wounds and radiation burns on and off for two days. The organizers of the three-day demonstration had assembled every major Hiroshima documentary film and they were running them over and over in various church basements around Boston.

In addition, there was a round-the-clock three-day vigil in memory of the victims of Hiroshima and Nagasaki. At first, rather than standing in public I preferred to sit in anonymity and watch the wound films. I felt that after all the intellectualizing over the metaphysics of deterrence theory I might have lost a sense of compassion and that a good dose of Hiroshima horrors might bring me back to my humanity.

I was wrong. Too many pictures of wounds end up blurring the distinctions between the agony left behind by *any* war and the potential for utter annihilation to be feared from the next one. After all, the missile crewmen told me they had been shown graphic films of Hiroshima before being asked if they'd be willing to twist those keys. And still they'd said yes.

At last, driven by shame, perhaps at my lack of response to the wound watch, I headed for the plaza outside Faneuil Hall, where I resolved to spend the hours until dawn standing silently in the memorial vigil for victims of Hiroshima and Nagasaki. The vigil—a semicircle of people standing still around a mushroom-shaped memorial—had been going on round the clock since the anniversary hour of the Hiroshima bombing, and would continue until eleven the next morning, the time the bomb hit Nagasaki. I had actually resolved to stay up all night in the vigil on each of the previous two nights, but it was raining one night and there were some friends to see the second night and I never quite made it out onto the plaza. But this time I was determined to make it nonstop through to the dawn, hoping to do some quiet thinking about the whole matter. Instead of running around looking for another esoteric document, another trigger icon to touch, another fantasy to explore, I needed to stand still and think for a while.

The sociable sounds of a late-night singles-bar complex and the aromas of an all-night flower market wafted over to that part of the plaza where memories of mass death were being memorialized in defiance of the summer merriment. The semicircle around the mushroom-cloud memorial was manned mainly by members of the old peace-movement crowd sprinkled with some young Boston Brahmin pacifist types. On a nearby bench, apparently keeping an intermittent vigil on the vigil, were two shopping-bag ladies. They spent most of their time endeavoring to fix the mechanism of a rusty, skeletal umbrella someone must have discarded many rains ago. There was a rambling discussion in some obscure mode of communication in which I could make out references to cancer of the thyroid, which one or both of them thought she was getting. About 2 or 3 A.M., a wino tried to challenge the silent vigilants to argument on nuclear strategy but he tired of the lack of response. The singles bar closed up and until dawn there was little but silence to disturb the thinking I wanted to do.

For the first three hours I tried my best to think about the victims of Hiroshima and Nagasaki, but I was thinking mainly about my feet. Should I shift my weight from the right to the left and back again, or divide it between the soles of both. Which strategy was more likely to get me through the morning with the least discomfort? (Ever since high school days working in a supermarket job I've had trouble standing up for prolonged periods. I have high arches, you see, and . . .)

God, how inhumane, you must be thinking to yourself. This guy is at a memorial for 180,000 people blasted and burned and he's talking about his high arches. In my defense I would say I was aware of the absurdity of it—the emblematic absurdity at least. By spending an inordinate amount of time thinking about my physical stance I was avoiding what I felt was my duty in this story, in life, to find a comfortable stance, *the* correct strategic stance, or at least a moral position, on the subtleties and the stark crudities of nuclear war.

As I shifted about for a stance I recalled my final phone conversation with Major Hering. It had taken me some time to track him down. He's an ex-major now and he and his family have had to shift location more than once as he looks for the right position, readjusts to the civilian job market. In the meantime he'd been doing some long-haul trucking in order to make ends meet.

At first the Air Force had tried to disqualify him for missile-crewman service under the provisions of the human-reliability regulation: because he wanted to be reassured a launch he executed was constitutional, he was, they tried to say, unreliable. When that failed the Air Force removed him from missile-crewman service and tried to transfer him to other duties. The major appealed that decision all the way up to the Secretary of the Air Force, lost, and then took an early retirement. He really had *wanted* to be a missile crewman and he fought his appeal fiercely with copious research into command-and-control problems to support his thesis. He told me he had a number of filing cabinets filled with documents that supported his position and revealed new unanswered questions, and he felt I should read through the files and the transcript of his hearings and appeals before I spoke to him. "It'll take you about a week or more of reading," the ex-major told me. I'd have to wait until after his next truck run, and after his new job was resolved. Then he'd be prepared to get back into it with me. "This whole thing has taken a lot out of me, as you can imagine, so I'd want to know you're serious before getting back into it all again," he said. The next time I called his number he'd moved to another city and I decided to pass up the filing cabinets.

I had a feeling that Major Hering's question had cost him a lot, cost him a comfortable couple of years down in the cozy launch-control capsules, years in which as it turned out he never would have had to face the constitutional command question his stringent conscience compelled him to ask. Cost him a promising military career and a couple of years of his life trying to extract from fragmentary unclassified sources what were the contingency plans for constitutional succession problems at the top of the chain of command and control. Finding himself alone among all missile crewmen in thinking independently on such questions must have been a burden.

SHOULD WE CALL OUR OWN BLUFF?

Kecskemeti, Ramsey, all those who try to think about nuclear war as more than the three-dimensional chess of the strategists suffer for their efforts.

There are two kinds of "unthinkables" in the thinking on this subject. There is the fashionable "unthinkable" of Kahn and company (how many million casualties are "acceptable" in a nuclear war: twenty? forty?), which in fact was never unthinkable at all to the Defense Department and defense contractors who funded this self-proclaimed daring intellectual adventure. And then there are unfashionable unthinkable questions. Major Hering's question. Unilateral disarmament. Remember that? While Herman Kahn's unthinkables have bankrolled him into a comfortable existence giving posh seminars on the shape of centuries to come, a man like David McReynolds, the War Resisters League organizer who helped lead the big ban-the-bomb demonstrations in the Sixties, sits in a drafty old room near the Bowery and speaks to an audience of five. He's raising again the question of unilateral disarmament at an anarchist-sponsored "Freespace University." In addition to the moderator and me, there are two men off the Bowery with shopping bags who seem mainly interested in getting out of the rain. There's an unreconstructed Stalinist who keeps changing the subject to a long-winded defense of the legitimacy of Soviet intervention in Czechoslovakia (counterrevolutionary provocation, he says) and an ex-Marine who begins all his questions with long quotations from Marcus Aurelius.

Despite it all, McReynolds delivers a brilliant polemical analysis of deterrence theory, in which he argues that unilateral disarmament is the only moral alternative to the mass murder for vengeance our declared retaliating policy calls for. Despite Air Force Regulation 35-99, McReynolds may be the sanest man in America on this subject, yet he has me and a Marcus Aurelius freak to listen to him, if you don't count the shopping-bag men.

Speaking of shopping-bag people, it's getting close to dawn now at this vigil we've drifted away from. I've drifted into a trance after settling into a more or less comfortable stance, but the shopping-bag women bring me out of it with a vociferous discussion of the skeletal umbrella and more talk of thyroid cancer. I recall a groggy illumination at this point: here, before me, was a perfect emblem of what I'd been trying to think about—how the shopping-bag ladies were not unlike sophisticated nuclear strategists, arguing in their peculiar language over the operation of that rickety contraption of an umbrella which, like the contrivance of deterrence theory, provides only symbolic protection for the two powers who seek shelter beneath its empty framework. Suddenly, I realized that the fact that these women had been talking about cancer of the thyroid as they watched the vigil was no accident. An increased incidence of thyroid cancer was a much-feared consequence of strontium 90 in the fallout-scare days of the late '50s and early '60s. They were *thinking* about it. Maybe, unlike the rest of us, they never stopped thinking about it. Maybe that's what drove them to the streets and shopping bags. Maybe they were among the unfortunate few who have not been afflicted by that mass repression we've used to submerge nuclear arousal in our consciousness.

Who else do you know who talks about it?

Well I figured it all out after dawn. My stance.

The illumination I finally received that morning came in the notion of a simple modest proposal. Open up the SIOP. The most frustrating barrier to intelligent thinking about the strategic and moral consequences of our nuclear policy is our continued preoccupation with esoteric strategy—with bluff, ambiguity, and mirror-image metaphysics.

Every targeting strategy, every targeting option the SIOP machine presents to the National Command Authority, represents a profound moral choice. An eye for an eye. Or two eyes. Two cities or one. Total vindictive retribution. Symbolic response or none at all. It's impossible to calculate the moral consequences we as individuals bear for such choices made in our name if the actual content of the choice is hidden behind the sleight of hand of esoteric strategy.

Should we resign ourselves and allow the SIOP machine and its think-tank tenders to make perhaps the most important decisions ever made, to churn out "optimum outcomes" according to definitions of "optimum" values that remain hermetically sealed in its program? We have no way to engage the machine or those who program it in debate over those values or the options they generate. If we were to move toward a democratically determined SIOP, we would have to reveal our bluffs, lay our cards on the table. Games of bluff are inevitably incompatible with democratic decision-making since an electorate can't vote to bluff by policy without, of course, betraying any possible success to an adversary.

Well, let them know. Let us know. Let us no longer be insulated from the master target list, from the master targeting strategy, from the moral options. We are all missile crewmen—all of us who pay taxes pay for the twin brass keys, even if we won't twist them ourselves when the time comes. But in one way or another we all have our finger on the trigger, and it's about time we knew where we're aiming, who's really giving the orders to fire, and whether we ought to obey.

—*HARPER'S*
March 1978

POSTSCRIPT TO "THE SUBTERRANEAN WORLD OF THE BOMB"

It would be comforting to think that concern about the nuclear command-and-control issue has been obviated by the ostensible end of Cold War tensions and the liberation of Eastern Europe. Regrettably, that does not seem to be the case.

Indeed, by coincidence, on the very same day—December 6, 1989—which saw the Czech communist party leadership give up power with the blessing of Moscow—both the *New York Times*'s William Safire in his column and ABC's Ted Koppel on prime-time TV presented doomsday nuclear scenarios founded upon continuing command-and-control uncertainties.

Safire noted the apparent absence from Gorbachev's side at the Malta summit of the customary minion bearing the Soviet version of the "nuclear football" briefcase with the missile launch control codes. (His alarm recalled my own when I saw President Ford separated from the black briefcase man in Florida.) From this pregnant absence Safire conjured up a nuclear war nightmare about Soviet nuclear command-and-control disintegrating in the midst of civil strife or a hardline coup attempt. And the reciprocal nightmare that this situation would present to our own command-and-control system—not knowing whether an incoming missile or bomber flight path signaled an authorized attack or the unauthorized act of a lone madman commander. How absolute is Gorbachev's control over launch orders? Can our decisions whether to retaliate be rational if their command-and-control is not? Safire was not reassuring.

That evening Koppell presented a dramatization of another similarly disturbing scenario, "The Blue X Conspiracy." Two groups of real U.S. and U.S.S.R. decision makers in Washington and Moscow were shown wrestling with a command-and-control crisis scenario involving a terrorist attack that incapacitates the president and vice-president and presents the remaining command structure with the problem of how to respond to what seems to be Soviet sponsorship of the attack. It's clear, as things escalate, that uncertainties built into command-and-control logic generate the dangerous crisis instability.

All of which further convinces me that ex-launch officer Hering was a hero of the nuclear age for sacrificing his career to warn of the disturbing *lacunae* in command-and-control logic. As for the absurd but scary "spoon and string" flaw in the failsafe launch control system that the missile men in Montana disclosed to me, I hope the Pentagon has taken care of that. I'm sure they have, aren't you?

TURN ON,
TUNE IN,
DROP DEAD

The curious tale of the Queen of Death and the lustful "entities" of Escondido is one of those little disturbances of man you may have missed if you haven't been tuned in to developments in the fast-growing "death awareness" movement. The scandal that developed over the erotic escapades of the "entities" represented a serious image crisis for the movement. Defenders of death awareness feel that the incident is merely an aberration being used unfairly by the medical establishment and its pawns in the press—servile minions of the "cure-oriented," "interventionist," "high-technology life-prolonging" old regime—to discredit the work of the dedicated devotees of death and dying. But a case can be made that intercourse with entities—okay, let's call it sex with the dead—is not an aberration but a summation, a consummation, of the whole misbegotten love affair with death that the movement has been promoting.

The Queen of Death, of course, is Dr. Elisabeth Kübler-Ross, who reigns over a mountaintop "Death-and-Dying Center" in Escondido, California, whose work single-handedly created the death-and-dying movement, and who, until now, endowed it with respectability.

Author of *On Death and Dying, Living With Death and Dying, Questions and Answers on Death and Dying*, and *Death: The Final Stage of Growth*, recipient of twenty honorary degrees, Kübler-Ross is now taught, in her estimation, in 125,000 death-and-dying courses in colleges, seminaries, medical schools, hospitals, and social-work institutions. She has come to be regarded as the last word on death. Not only do "death professionals"—hospital and hospice workers, clergymen, and psychiatrists—get their basic training from Kübler-Ross in order to counsel the dying, but her books are so widespread that most people who *die* these days are familiar with her "five stages of dying."

Kübler-Ross's thought has given birth to whole new academic industries—"thanatology" and "dolorology"—helped create the hospice movement, "Conscious Dying Centers," and, more recently, an increasingly cultlike exaltation, sentimentalization, and even worship of death.

In the past, like most sensible people, I've been content to leave strenuous thinking about death in the capable hands of others. Somehow I assumed from all the acclaim from varied quarters that Kübler-Ross couldn't be *too* foolish, assumed that she embodied the typical post-Enlightenment secular consensus on the subject: awareness of death giving an urgency and intensity to life, etc. Probably sensible, caring, and boring. But I have a feeling that the rest of you must have been averting your eyes from what Kübler-Ross was saying all this time, and that we're beginning to see the consequences. Because something's gone awry with the death-and-dying movement Kübler-Ross helped create. Things have gotten out of hand: Kübler-Ross herself has become the guru to a nationwide network of death 'n' dying centers called "Shanti Nilaya"; the "Conscious Dying movement" urges us to devote our life to death awareness and also opens up a "Dying Center"; a video artist kills herself on public television and calls it "artistic suicide"; the EXIT society publishes a handy, do-it-yourself Home Suicide guide that can take its place next to other recent Home Dying and Home Burial Guides; a pop science cult emerges around the "near death experience," which makes dying sound like a lovely acid trip (turn on, tune in, drop dead); attempts at two-way traffic with the afterlife abound, including a courier service to the dead using dying patients and even phone calls *from* the dead; belief in reincarnation resurfaces as "past lives therapy."

Is this multifaceted flirtation with death and suicide—you could call it the Pro-Death movement—some self-regulating, population-control mechanism surfacing as the baby-boom generation gets older, the better to thin its ranks before its numbers begin to strain nursing-home and terminal-ward facilities? And how did Kübler-Ross—saintly, respected, a *Ladies' Home Journal* "Woman of the Decade" for the 1970s—end up running a dating service for the dead in Escondido? Part of the problem may be heroin. Not Kübler-Ross's problem, but the problem in the very origins of her American death-and-dying movement. You see, Kübler-Ross and the American death-and-dying movement took their inspiration from the British "hospice" idea but neglected to import one crucial ingredient that made it work.

The hospice movement in Britain was a practical, no-nonsense alternative to the increasingly complex, painful, and isolating process of death in modern hospitals, where, in the hectic process of prolonging life with tubes and machines, patients aren't able to enjoy peace and quiet and the company of friends and relatives as they die. The British movement offered instead cozy, small "guest houses" for the terminally ill, with a sympathetic staff and medical treatment designed to ensure comfort, dignity, and alertness rather than an artificially prolonged life.

But your basic British hospice was able to offer its dying "guests" one thing American hospices could not, one thing that made these hospices more than merely pleasant places in which to expire without the aid of "high-technology life-prolonging intervention." The attraction of British hospices, the *sacrament*, in fact, that made them so popular, was the special painkilling mixture they dispensed, a potion described by some as the most powerful euphoriant experience available to the human senses: the "Brompton's Cocktail."

A combination of equal parts of pure heroin and pure cocaine, with a dash of chloroform in an alcohol-and-cherry-syrup base, Brompton's Cocktail became legendary for its ability to bliss out patients suffering from pain so intractable that no amount of mere morphine was able to subdue it.

Not surprisingly, dying hospice patients who were fortunate enough to receive the soothing sacrament were known to make all sorts of warm and endearing remarks when in its embrace; words of wisdom and spirituality and love that hospice professionals tended to attribute to the "caring and sharing" environment of their cozy death hotels, and to the visionary insights unique to the dying process, but which probably owed more to the elation and euphoria of the heroin-cocaine combo.

The problem was that while the "caring and sharing" ideas of the British movement could be imported, the drug laws in this country made it impossible to prescribe heroin for even the most terrorizing bone pain. In addition, the use of cocaine as a euphoriant is discouraged. So as a substitute for the real Brompton's Cocktail, American hospice doctors have concocted a bizarre and stunted version of that sacrament: a combination known as "Hospice Mix," which substitutes morphine for more potent heroin, and frequently uses thorazine—liquid lobotomy, as it's sometimes called by mental-health professionals—instead of cocaine.

For all their ostensible reverence for the wisdom of the dying and the integrity of the dying process, American hospices that use thorazine in their "mix" are treating dying patients as if they were psychotics. Unable to offer their dying clients the kind of truly effective and humane pain relief available to the British, American death professionals seem to have overcompensated for this failure by subjecting their dying clients—and afflicting us all—with massive injections of sentimentality, a syrupy overdose of sanctimony about the "beauty" of the dying process, about "learning from pain," to use some typical clichés, and about the wonderful wisdom that makes dying the "final stage of growth."

In doing so, the death-and-dying people have elevated the terminally ill into a new sort of oppressed class—oppressed by "inhuman, cure-oriented" doctors who don't recognize that dying is something to be *celebrated* for its intrinsic worth rather than feared and fought. Death professionals have begun attributing to the dying all the qualities of instinctual wisdom, primitive visionary insight, spontaneous vitality, and organic closeness to the ground of being with which oppressed classes are condescendingly endowed by their more privileged supporters.

"Many Native Americans died with great clarity," declares the co-director of a group called the "Dying Project," a statement that embodies perfectly the identification of the dying with a persecuted minority and, in its lofty condescension, is not far removed in spirit from "The only good Indian is a dead Indian."

●   ■   ●

While this billing and cooing about death did not originate with Kübler-Ross—the cult of "the Beautiful Death" is a recurrent one in stagnant societies—she did come up with one concept that single-handedly revolutionized and *restructured* the worship of death in America and gave it an up-to-date "scientific" foundation: the five stages of dying.

Dividing dying into stages was a stroke of genius. Kübler-Ross brought forth her five stages at just about the time when people were dividing life into "passages," stages, predictable crises. Getting dying properly staged would bring every last second of existence under the reign of reason. As every student of elementary thanatology soon learns, the famous five stages of dying are: denial, anger, bargaining, depression, acceptance.

What's been lost in the general approbation of Kübler-Ross's five stages is the way her ordering of those stages implicitly serves a *behavior control* function for the busy American death professional. The movement from denial and anger to depression and acceptance is seen as a kind of spiritual *progress*, as if quiet acceptance is the most mature, the highest stage to strive for.

What Kübler-Ross calls bargaining, others might call a genuine search for reasons to live, to fight for life. But she has no patience with dilly-dallying by the dying. She disparages "bargaining" that goes on too long, describes patients who don't resign themselves to death after they've gotten the extra time they bargained for as "children" who don't "keep their promises" to die.

Yet by "acceptance," Kübler-Ross means the infantilization of the dying: "It is perhaps best compared with what Bettelheim describes about early infancy," she says. "A time of passivity, an age of primary narcissism in which . . . we are going back to the stage we started out with and the circle of life is closed."

Certainly this passivity makes for a quieter, more manageable hospice. Crotchety hospice guests who quixotically refuse to accept, who persist in anger or hope, will be looked on as recalcitrant, treated as retarded in their dying process, stuck in an "immature" early stage, and made to feel that it's high time they moved on to the less troublesome stages of depression and acceptance.

Now let's look at the practical effect of this premium on passivity on an actual encounter between a dying person and a "death professional." Let's look at a little hand-printed pamphlet entitled *It's Been a Delightful Dance*: the story of Ellen Clark as told in a sermon by Dr. Richard Turner.

This is an account of the therapeutic relationship between Turner and Clark, who was dying of cancer when she approached the Cancer Project of "Life Force," Turner's therapy organization, for counseling.

The California-based Life Force was one of several holistically oriented therapy groups that specialize in what has come to be called "cancering." Turner charged forty-five dollars an hour for such counseling.

I came across Turner and his group in 1980, in the Grand Ballroom of the Ambassador Hotel in Los Angeles, at a convention of the Cancer Control Society, a national organization that supports scores of "unorthodox" and forbidden cancer "cures"—everything from apricot kernels and coffee enemas to secret-formula serums and salves. I was somewhat puzzled to find someone like Turner speaking here, since the acceptance-oriented death-and-dying rhetoric in his speech contrasted with the feverish never-say-die, last-minute, miracle-seeking emphasis of the unorthodox-cancer-cure movement. "With certain patients I've counseled it becomes clear that at some level they are ready to die," Turner told me, when I questioned him after his talk. "They've made their choice, they feel they've lived their life. There was one patient of mine who'd done the holistic cures. But as I counseled her on her dying experience, it was as if this was what she wanted, it was as if she was releasing all her barriers and becoming fully human for the first time. She turned into a living, beautiful person so that by the time she died she'd done all her life's work in her last few weeks. Her name was Ellen Clark. In fact I wrote up my experience with her in a sermon I delivered. It's in our literature."

Reading Turner's description of the progress of his therapy with the late Ellen Clark, it's impossible not to notice the influence of Kübler-Ross in the way he idealizes the progressive infantilization of the dying.

The big breakthrough that Ellen Clark achieves as she's wasting away with cancer is, according to Turner's sermon, that she "develops a childlike transparency." How does Turner deal with this in his counseling session? He's eager to encourage it, eager to "reinforce those feelings that we were like children in kindergarten." His technique for reinforcing this? He responds completely only to Ellen's "childlike," "magical" looks; even when she's trying to tell him something in adult sentences he makes sure that "only part of my attention went back to what she was saying. . . . The result was that heavy subject matter such as life and death and problem-solving progressively lost its dominance and an air of lightness pervaded our meetings."

No wonder. Dealing with an adult who's been turned into a happily compliant dying child is much more fun for friends and family than facing the complexities presented by a stubborn adult who's frantically fighting to live.

As in other tales in the contemporary Beautiful Death literature, an element of parasitism seems to creep into the stories told by the selfless survivors. Turner tells us that after Ellen became the "transparent child," *he* really started getting off on the sessions. He reports feeling "light and alive" after each session. "I was gaining as much from our meetings as her." (Maybe he should have been paying *her* $45 an hour for the privilege.) Ellen's friends also "reported quite consistently being touched and healed in her presence." Touched and healed: the magical powers of the dying are frequent causes for amazement in the literature.

By turning herself into an agreeable, transparent, loving child with Turner's encouragement, by refusing crankily to seek out some new cure or make a desperate gamble for her life, Ellen made it easy for people to be around her and feel loving. The message for dying patients in that sermon is, to revise Dylan Thomas, "*Do* go gentle into that good night."

And then the climax of the *Delightful Dance* sermon: "The morning after I heard about Ellen's death I went out for my daily jog," Turner tells us. "A beautiful orange butterfly landed in front of my foot. I immediately felt *as if I knew this butterfly*, and apparently it had this same connection with me. . . . The butterfly and I were doing a get-acquainted dance. . . . I felt I was doing a get-acquainted dance with the butterfly within me. I feel I am ready to let go of being the caterpillar. . . . I am more ready to dance with my life. . . ."

And so, according to Turner, Ellen's pretty little death turned out to be a plus for everyone: Ellen got to be a butterfly and he got to dance during his daily jog. The whole thing sounded like a dance of death to me.

•   ■   •

   This is only the beginning, this reverence for the life-giving holiness of the compliantly childlike death object. It's a long way from there to going to bed with the dead, but the route is direct, and after reading the recent profusion of death-and-dying literature, I've divided it—in homage to Kübler-Ross—into five stages:

> Stage 1: worship of the dying;
> Stage 2: longing to *be* dying;
> Stage 3: playing dead;
> Stage 4: playing *with* the dead;
> Stage 5: going to bed with the dead.

   We've already seen Stage 1, with its reverence for the wisdom of the terminally ill. In Stage 2, death 'n' dying is seen to be an attractive option for healthy people. Why let the dying get all the benefits of facing death? To maximize the high of the dying experience when it comes, healthy people are urged by Stage 2 literature to devote their life to preparing for a beautiful death. Stage 2 advocates range from the Conscious Dying movement and its subsidiaries, the Dying Project and the Dying Center in New Mexico, to the "rational suicide" advocates. The London-based EXIT group is only one of several that put out practical do-it-yourself guides to painless suicide; other books tell you how to arrange the particulars of your death or burial at home. The late Jo Roman, evangelist of "creative suicide," went one step further—she did it on TV.
   Stage 2 advocates tend to be the nags of the death-and-dying movement. Since we are not fortunate enough to be terminally ill, they tell us, we must make strenuous efforts to overcome our handicap by concentrating our lives on death and suicide.
   It is never too early to start. "Should schoolchildren be asked to write essays on 'How I Would Feel if I Had to Die at Midnight' or compositions envisaging why and in what circumstances they propose to end their lives?" asks Mary Rose Barrington, past chairman of EXIT.

"The answer may well be that they should," says Mary Rose, who, oddly enough, is also "Honorary Secretary of the Animal Rights Group." (Do they favor the right to suicide for parakeets?)

Missing out on early-childhood death education is no excuse to avoid the subject now. And that means today. Tomorrow may be too late if you believe the nagging of Steven Levine, director of the Dying Project. "Tomorrow," he points out, "could be the first day of thirty years of quadriplegia. What preparations have you made to open to an inner life so full that whatever happens can be used as a means of enriching your focus?" The first day of thirty years of quadriplegia. It's a particularly ironic formulation of the challenge because Levine and the Dying Project, and the Dying Center (where people check in to check out) are spiritual descendants of ex-Harvard professor and psychedelic pioneer Richard Alpert (now Ram Dass), and thus of a brand of spiritualism that expressed its incurable optimism with the slogan "Today is the first day of the rest of your life." Sure, but tomorrow the wheelchair and the catheter. Such a shift says something about this branch of the Pro-Death movement—either they've run out of good acid and have been dipping into the melancholy Hospice Mix, or, as they grow older, they're suddenly scared of death and afraid to admit it.

If you read Levine's testament, *Who Dies*, a bible for the Conscious Dying movement, you begin to suspect he's trying to smother his fear of death in protestations of his devotion to it. He's constantly hectoring the reader for having failed to do his death homework: "If you should die in extreme pain how will you have prepared to keep your mind soft and open?" he scolds. "What have you done to keep your mind present, so that you don't block precious opportunity with a concept, with some idea of what's happening, open to experience the suchness, the living truth, of the next unknown moment?"

You could dismiss this scolding as mere schoolteacherish sanctimony, or life-insurance-salesman scare tactics (buy my theory of dying now or you'll be condemned to die inauthentically), but there's something more frightened and frightening in this prose. I think it comes out in the Dying Project co-director's description of the ideal Conscious Dying movement-approved death:

> I've been with people as they approached their death and
> seen how much clarity and openheartedness it takes to stay

soft with the distraction in the mind and body, to stay with the fear that arises uninvited, to keep so open that when fear comes up they can say, 'Yes, that's fear all right.' But the spaciousness from which they say it is not frightened. Because the separate 'I' is not the predominant experience, there's little for that fear to stick to. Clearly a useful practice would be to cultivate an openness to what is unpleasant, to acknowledge resistance and fear, to soften and open around it, to let it float free, to let it go. If you wrote down a list of your resistances and holdings, it would nearly be a sketch of your personality. If you identify with that personality as you are, you amplify the fear of death; the imagined loss of imagined individuality.

This is metaphysical heroin, a Brompton's Cocktail of the mind, the same basic anodyne for the tears of things that all Eastern cults offer: if you detach yourself and experience all passion at one numb remove, in the context of the infinitude of being, nothing hurts as much. If you go the whole route and cease being a person—that "imagined individual" Levine disparages—then you won't even die because there won't be a you to die. You'll never be a person afraid of death because you won't be a person. You'll be, instead, "the spaciousness" that is not frightened. Nonbeings can't cease being. If you make life as spacious and empty as death, you won't notice any transition between living and dying; you might as well be dead.

Which is exactly what the "creative suicide" people say. Or they might call it "CREATING ON MY OWN TERMS THE FINAL STROKE OF MY LIFE'S CANVAS," as video death artist Jo Roman wrote in her last letter to friends. ("By the time you read these lines I WILL HAVE GENTLY ENDED MY LIFE on the date of this letter's postmark," she announces with typical gentleness.)

Roman's trend-setting originality, of course, was not in her committing the act or justifying it on artistic grounds. It was in doing it so publicly. Suicide-proud self-murderers have in the past been content to have their feverish last thoughts and justifications publicized. But Jo Roman insisted on making a federal case of the act itself and the whole tearful "dying process," summoning friends and forcing them to grovel at the altar of her honesty while the videotape cameras rolled. She made the additional breakthrough of claiming for suicides the status of an oppressed *lifestyle* group in need of televised validation: "I want to share it with others in order to raise consciousness. Also, and importantly, because I am averse to demeaning myself by closeting an act which I believe deserves respect."

Of course, creative suicide is not the exclusive province of sick and exhibitionistic video artists. There were the healthy young teenagers in Seattle, a boy and a girl, who, inspired by the transcendent optimism about the indestructibility of the soul in *Jonathan Livingston Seagull*, proceeded to get into a Pontiac and drive it at eighty miles per hour flat out into a stone wall, in order to ensure they spent eternity together.

●   ■   ●

Suicide and suicide pacts are a predictable enough consequence of the death 'n' dying movement. By romanticizing dying, by making death more "authentic" than life, suicide is made to seem an attractive, artistic, even heroic choice.

Another way of promoting the attractiveness and allure of death is through the creation of an inviting, reassuring, sugarcoated vision of the afterlife. Which brings us to Stage 3 in the development of contemporary death worship: the romance of the Near Death Experience (NDE), or playing dead.

At first the NDE seemed to be a freak, based on a few isolated reports. People who had been pronounced "clinically dead," people who "died" on the operating table, in the ambulance, or the intensive care ward, whose heart and vital functions ceased for ten, twenty minutes, would sometimes, after miraculous "resurrections," tell tales of leaving the body and traveling through a remarkable, otherworldly realm.

Aside from the *National Enquirer* ('DEAD MAN' SPEAKS!), no one paid much attention to these isolated reports until a philosophy professor named Raymond Moody compiled 150 of them into a book called *Life After Life*, which was published in 1975 with an endorsement by none other than Elisabeth Kübler-Ross, who claimed that she had been doing exactly the same kind of research and that Moody's findings duplicated hers.

The "NDE" became the semi-official afterlife vision for the death-and-dying religion. It was appealing because it made death seem like something to look forward to. The "undiscovered country from whose bourn no traveller returns," whose mysteries had long terrified the human imagination, now seemed, from the reports of Raymond Moody's travelers, to be about as frightening as a day trip to the Jersey shore.

Let's look at Moody's "theoretically complete model" of the life-after-life experience, which I have here divided into seven easy-to-follow steps.

1. *A streetcar named death*: Our traveler hears himself pronounced dead. Next he hears "a loud ringing or buzzing and at the same time feels himself moving very rapidly through a long dark tunnel."

2. *The fly on the wall*: "He suddenly finds himself outside of his own physical body. . . . He watches the resuscitation attempt from this unusual vantage point . . . in a state of emotional upheaval."

3. *Family reunion*: "He glimpses the spirits of relatives and friends who have already died."

4. *The heavenly customs inspector*: He meets "a loving warm spirit of a kind he has never encountered before—a being of light. . . . This being asks him a question, nonverbally, to make him evaluate his life. . . ."

5. *The highlights film*: The "being of light" helps him along by "showing him a panoramic instantaneous playback of the major events of his life."

6. *Heaven can wait*: "He finds himself approaching some sort of barrier or border apparently representing the limit between earthly life and the next life. Yet, he finds that he must go back to the earth, that the time for his death has not yet come."

7. *Deportation*: "He is taken up with his experiences in the afterlife and does not want to return. He is overwhelmed by intense feelings of joy, love, and peace. Despite his attitude," though, he's forced to rejoin the unpleasant world of the living.

Of course, it's possible that this pallid panorama of sweetness and light may actually *be* the afterlife and the ultimate riddle of existence has been solved. There are certainly millions of people who would like to believe its reassuring, nondenominational, downy-soft delights: Moody's book and his sequel *Reflections on Life After Life*, and its paperback rackmates *Life Before* and *Reliving Past Lives*, have all become big dime-store and drugstore best sellers, creating a popular NDE-based cult.

The only stumbling block that prevents the NDE from becoming the center of a new popular religion for the living has been that the actual ecstatic death trip experience seemed to be restricted to those privileged few whose heart, breathing, and vital functions had ceased for a certain period, or who were fortunate enough to be survivors of a plane crash, car wreck, or other near death trauma.

Enter the ever helpful Elisabeth Kübler-Ross, who not only endorsed Moody's NDE but took the NDE cult a crucial step further by staking out that bright landscape and its loving beings of light for routine visits by the living—those among the living who learned the correct way of *playing dead*.

She discovered this pastime from her own travels in that realm of bright beings, she says. Her first "out-of-body experience" came at a time when she was, if not near death, at least by her account, dead tired from several years of exhausting nonstop travel, lectures, seminars, and workshops promoting death 'n' dying awareness. Drifting off into a trancelike sleep, she says, "I saw myself lifted out of my physical body. . . . it was as if a whole lot of loving beings were taking all the tired parts out of me, similar to car mechanics in a car repair shop. . . . I experienced a great sense of peace and serenity, a feeling of literally being taken care of, of having no worry in the world. I had also an incredible sense that once all the parts were replaced I would be as young and fresh and energetic as I had been prior to this rather exhausting, draining workshop. . . . Naturally I associated this immediately with the stories of dying patients who shared with me their near death experiences. . . . Little did we know then that that was the beginning of an enormous amount of new research, which ultimately led to the understanding of death and life after death."

While this first experience was involuntary, she discovered, after hooking up with some out-of-body occultists in Virginia, that she could learn to repeat it at will. She could play dead. Whenever her bodily vehicle needed a tune-up, whenever she wanted to set back the old odometer, rejuvenate the spark plugs, she could take a revitalizing dip into death, that refreshing fountain of youth.

●   ■   ●

But Kübler-Ross did not stop there. She sailed right on into Stage 4: playing with the dead.

Remember that benevolent "being of light" who greets you when you alight from the streetcar named death? Well, he has friends up there. Plenty of them. Spirit guides. Guardian angels. The enlightened "afterlife entities."

The way Kübler-Ross describes it now, all the while she was garnering her honorary degrees, her acclaim from clergy, shrinks, and academics for working with the dying, she was spending an ever increasing amount of her time playing with the dead. She made her own decisions only in consultation with her guardian angels and spirit guides. She counseled the living to make their decisions based on the guidance of entities from the Other Side.

In Stage 4, the implications of the previous stages become explicit: *death is much more wonderful than life*, the dead are much wiser, and, since two-way communication with the Other Side is now possible, it's better to consult with them about the tiresome business of getting through life. By Stage 4, the dead are not really "dead" at all. They're more alive than we, the living, can hope to be. They're not even called "dead" anymore. For Stage 4 death worshipers they are "afterlife entities"; by the time we reach Stage 4 there is no such thing as death.

This was another Kübler-Ross discovery, I learned from her "media person" in Escondido. "Elisabeth doesn't like the term 'near death experience,' " he explained to me, "because she doesn't believe that death exists."

Doesn't believe in death?

"No such thing," he said. "She believes there are just . . . transitions. So it's not a near death experience because it's available to normal living people every day if they tune in to it."

Turn on, tune in, drop dead.

Playing with the dead has become a rapidly expanding national pastime. Spirit guides and guardian angels are becoming for many adults the comforting imaginary playmates they had to abandon as children, the perfect loving parents they never had. This two-way traffic takes some curious forms. According to a *Washington Post* story (apparently not a hoax), a California company has hired a number of terminally ill patients who will, for a fee, act as couriers, memorizing messages to be delivered to the dead as soon as they arrive on the Other Side. A whole new category of spiritualist phenomena is chronicled in the book *Phone Calls from the Dead*, which cites reports that phones all over America are practically ringing off the hook as chatterbox "entities" from the Other Side pester their friends and relatives among the living. (These days they're probably jamming the switchboards to find out if they can get a date for the next Kübler-Ross "workshop.")

We're also witnessing a revival of the old-fashioned table-rapping spiritualist epidemic that swept America in the mid-nineteenth century. The modern version, which dispenses, for the most part, with tables and props, is known—appropriately enough for the TV age—as "channeling," and this narrowcasting from the Other Side is growing as fast as cable TV. And, like cable, it's a franchising operation. I discovered this when a woman announced to me on the phone that she'd "finally gotten her channel." It seems that she'd been a paid student of a medium who was a "channel" to an afterlife entity somehow related to "Seth," the extremely popular, extremely long-winded afterlife entity whose empty maunderings somehow mesmerize middle-class airheads with pronouncements such as: "For in the miraculous spontaneity of the sun there is discipline that utterly escapes you."

After paying the Seth-related medium for months of trance training, this woman had finally been granted an authorized, franchised "afterlife entity" of her own, which would speak through her when she went into a trance and which would allow *her* to charge others for the privilege of getting its utterances on their problems.

I witnessed one such channeling session in a SoHo loft, and a sad spectacle it was. The woman seemed to have been granted a channel with very poor reception, or else there was an exceptionally thick-headed entity in the control room on the Other Side. After ten minutes of "going into trance," complete with head rollings, eye rollings, and all the most clichéd eyelid-batting expressions of the stage spiritualist, the woman finally snapped to and began speaking in the voice of her "channel" (a voice barely distinguishable from her own). But the hapless entity couldn't answer a single question she posed. I'd never seen an entity hem and haw so haltingly and ignorantly. Apparently, the slick and accomplished spiritualist franchiser who sold this gullible woman her channel hadn't even bothered to polish the entity's act enough to make it a good investment for the franchisee. It's probably a common spiritualist scam, taking advantage of such blind devotion to the wisdom of the dead to dump defective entities on the market the way swindlers sold underwater swampland lots in the Florida land boom.

●   ■   ●

Considering this feverish eagerness to be in touch with entities one way or another, it's not surprising that some death 'n' dying cultists have carried worship of the dead to Stage 5: going to bed with the dead.

It seems as if there has always been a subtext of eroticism in the growth of the death 'n' dying movement. Take the story behind Kübler-Ross's first big break into the national awareness.

"She was doing her seminars with dying patients virtually unnoticed in Chicago," her media person told me over the phone. "But then *Life* magazine heard about her and was going to send someone to see if there was a story in her work. There was this elderly man dying who was going to be the subject of the seminar when *Life* was there, but the old man died the night before."

There followed a hasty search for an understudy dying patient, and what happened next was in the best Broadway tradition: "They found a beautiful young girl to replace the old man." She was twenty-four or twenty-six, the media person told me. "And then *Life* knew they had a story. A real heartthrobber." It was this dying-heartthrob story in *Life*, he said, that made Kübler-Ross a sudden national sensation and enshrined her as Queen of Death.

If the dying can be heartthrobs, if the afterlife entities can be warm and loving and intimate with the living, why would anyone hesitate to go to bed with the dead?

By the time the sexual scandal broke in 1980, Kübler-Ross seems to have been bewitched into buying every last spiritualist trick in the book. She had no less than four personal entities—she called them "Mario," "Anka," "Salem," and "Willie"—attending her. She now believed in reincarnation and claimed to have memories of being alive in the time of Jesus. Where once her seminars had helped the dying, their friends, and their relatives live with despair, she now offered them a grab bag of Big Rock Candy Mountain fantasies of "life after life" to escape from life. And, finally, she'd allied her personal organization with a local sect that called itself the Church of the Facet of Divinity, hailing its minister, faith healer, and medium Jay Barham as "the greatest healer in the world."

Although accounts differ as to who actually did what to whom, allegations of seductions by entities did not arise until the merger with Barham's church. According to one report "Barham regularly conducted seances in which he acted as a medium to communicate with what he called 'afterlife entities.' At many of these sessions, the former female members of the group asserted, they were instructed to enter a side room where they were joined a few minutes later in the dark by an unclothed man who talked convincingly of being an 'afterlife entity' [who] . . . then proceeded to convince the women that they should engage in sex with him. . . ."

According to another report, the seductive entity mispronounced certain words in a manner remarkably similar to that of Barham. Some of the women began to suspect that the aroused afterlife entity had earthbound limitations when five of them came down with the same vaginal infection after being closeted with him. And then there was the woman who actually turned on the light in the entity-visiting chamber and claimed to see Barham, naked except for a turban.

Barham had a wonderful explanation for his resemblance to the turbaned apparition. He denied engaging in sexual activities with any of the women but said that in order to materialize, certain entities might have *cloned themselves* from Barham's cells, which would explain how they might resemble him in materialized form.

Believe it or not, Kübler-Ross seems to have bought that too. For a year after the affair of the erotic entities, she defended Barham and continued to work with him, franchising death, dying, and entity-encounter sessions throughout the country. She now insists, however, that she was no fool, that nobody had pulled the wool over her eyes, that unbeknownst to everyone "I have been conducting my own first-person investigation of . . . Barham." This investigation, which she must have pursued with all the stealth of Richard Nixon's personal "investigation" of the Watergate cover-up, finally uncovered unspecified conduct by Barham that "did not meet the standards . . . of Shanti Nilaya."

None of this substandard behavior, she insisted, took place on her premises or involved her workshops. The clincher in her investigation, Kübler-Ross told a writer, was her decision to have a doctor "measure" Barham's faith-healing power. This test, whose exact nature she did not disclose, revealed to her that his healing skills had declined measurably and that the decline was proof of his misuse of his powers.

"There are those who might say this has damaged my credibility," she conceded. "But it's not important whether people believe what I say. . . . I'm a doctor and a scientist, who simply reports what she sees, hears, and experiences."

Although Kübler-Ross has consistently stonewalled all inquiries about her reported presence at the scene of the assignations with the aroused afterlife entities, there is every indication that her disillusion with Barham has not diminished her swooning worship of death.

In a copyrighted interview with sympathetic questioner Joan Saunders Wixen, Kübler-Ross brushes off the Barham activities and instead boasts of some new benefits troubled people can look forward to as soon as they die. Death is a cure-all, the ultimate panacea: "People after death become complete again. The blind can see, the deaf can hear, cripples are no longer crippled after all their vital signs have ceased to exist."

If this encouragement to euthanasia as a quick solution to all physical imperfections were not so stupid and dangerous, it would be an occasion for regret: death has claimed another victim, the mind of Kübler-Ross. Another sad but predictable triumph of death over reason, another case of an interesting mind committing suicide. It begins to seem that thinking about death is, like heroin, not something human beings are capable of doing in small doses and then going about the business of life. It tends to take over all thought, and for death 'n' dying junkies, the line between a maintenance dose and an O.D. becomes increasingly fine. When Kübler-Ross finally makes her "transition," I'm certain all her nagging physical ailments will clear up, just as she says, but they'll have to mark her mind D.O.A.

—*HARPER'S*
October 1982

TALES FROM THE CANCER CURE UNDERGROUND

IN WHICH WE ENCOUNTER MODERN-DAY ALCHEMISTS, PROPHETS, HEALERS, HERBALISTS, BIOMYSTICS, DOCTORS OF METAPHYSICS AND DOCTORS OF MEDICINE IN OUR QUEST FOR THE ULTIMATE CURE

> *. . . terrible apprehensions were among the people.*
> —DANIEL DEFOE,
> *A Journal of the Plague Year*

The captain rapped on the door of my hotel room promptly at 6 A.M. He was eager to get this expedition under way. He had a decision to make, and his time was running out.

First of all, just 30 hours remained on his VA hospital pass. If he didn't make it back in time, they might find out about this peculiar below-the-border mission. Worse, they might search his room and confiscate whatever magic potion he managed to bring back.

And the time was fast approaching when they were scheduled to do that CAT-scan on the Captain's liver, get a picture, give a local habitation and a name to that vexing shadow on his last X ray. They had already cut a malignancy out of his intestines—this shadow could be the dread metastasis.

"No use pretending you're brave or whistling past the graveyard," the Captain told me as we headed south on 405. "I know I've got it again."

But this time the Captain was going to be ready with a plan of his own. That's why he'd asked to hitch a ride with me on my exploratory trip to the cancer clinics of Tijuana. There were at least a half dozen establishments down there offering every kind of exotic therapy and esoteric substance driven below the border by U.S. authorities—everything from the mysterious decades old Hoxsey elixir to coffee enema cures, fetal sheep cell injections and three varieties of metabolic enzyme treatments. The Captain wanted to scout them all so he'd have his escape route ready when the CAT-scan delivered its diagnosis.

"I know surgery is not the answer," the Captain declared. "I can say that from experience. I took chemotherapy and it was rough. I couldn't take it anymore, and from experience, from the statistics, I know it doesn't work. So they told me, 'Why don't you try immunotherapy?' That was equally rough. They inject dead cells in an alcohol base into your back. I still have the scars. Devilish rough. You can see it in the doctors' eyes—they know they're up against something they can't beat."

The Captain does not say the word "rough" from the perspective of a man who's lived a life of ease. Not counting his wartime Marine Corps service, he's spent most of his 60 years working as a mining geologist in one rough place or another, prospecting for platinum in the Bering Strait, seeking rare earths and precious metals in the feverish interiors of Central America. The Captain never minded the physical privations of the prospector's life, he told me—it was malignant fate that had treated him roughly.

"Had a reef of platinum off the Aleutians," he sighed. "Would have made my fortune. I was back in the States getting ready to sell shares of it when a goddamn earthquake wiped it out."

The same thing happened down in Yucatán, the Captain said. Titanium this time, a sizzling vein of it. Another earthquake and it was gone.

These reverses left the Captain—who has no fortune or family to fall back on—at the mercy of the VA when the malignancy first showed up. He complains bitterly of the degrading, no privacy, prisonlike confinement at the hospital, but he has nowhere else to go.

Still, circumstances have not deprived the Captain of his drive, his prospector's instinct, and this time he is on the trail of something more valuable than any of the precious metals he sought in the past. This time the Captain is prospecting for a cancer cure.

●   ■   ●

So are we all, of course. Who hasn't felt the crablike pincers of cancer panic? In Defoe's time those who spotted the first deadly tokens of the plague on themselves ran madly through the streets shrieking their despair. In our time cancer patients commit suicide on public TV.

While cancer itself is not contagious, the fear is. Defoe's plague year narrator reports that the weekly bills of mortality often featured two or three unfortunates whose cause of death was inscribed: "*frighted*, that is, frighted to death. But besides those who were so frighted as to die upon the spot, there were great numbers frighted to other extremes, some frighted out of their senses . . . and some out of their understanding."

While only one in four of us will get cancer, who among the other three is not "frighted"? Who, today, does not suffer from some degree of cancerphobia—a disease that does not cause death but does exact subtle ravages upon life.

Yes, cancer is just another disease, as Susan Sontag strenuously reminds us in *Illness as Metaphor*. We shouldn't attach any special mystery or dread to it. But we do. And until our medicine men can come up with the magic bullet to kill it, we can't help thinking about it as something more than a disease—some dark curse in the chromosomes, perhaps the symptoms of original sin let loose at the cellular level, a clue to the bittersweet mystery of life.

There would be less temptation to indulge in such speculation if medical science were offering us evidence of inexorable progress toward a cure, or at least an explanation. But no . . .

In the temples of orthodox medicine even the high priests are acting confused and uncertain these days. Public bickering broke out this year between the American Cancer Society and gynecological specialists over such elemental matters as how frequently women should have Pap smears, whether mammographies do more harm than good, even over the once sacred ritual of the annual checkup—leaving laymen confused over how often they should see a doctor or whether it makes a difference if they do.

At a synod this fall commemorating the tenth anniversary of the launching of the great war against cancer (remember when Nixon predicted victory by the end of the seventies?), Dr. Vincent DeVita Jr., the director of the National Cancer Institute, conceded that despite a decade of heavily funded holy war, the overall incidence of cancer appears to be creeping relentlessly upward at the rate of nearly 1 percent per year, while the cure rate has risen little more than 2 percent in 25 years. And the nature of the enemy still remains shrouded in mystery. "We still don't know whether it's something that goes wrong with a single switch within a cell or whether it's many different switches for different cells," Dr. DeVita said. "We don't know what the heck it is" that causes the continued rise in cancer rates, Dr. Frank Rauscher, the research director of the American Cancer Society, added.

While cure rates (actually five-year survival rates) have risen for certain types of cancers—some childhood leukemias and certain localized tumors—two out of three stricken with cancer still die of the disease when treated with what the American Cancer Society calls "proven methods" (surgery, radiation, chemotherapy). And many people suffer more from the side effects of these proven methods of treatment than from the disease. Even the American Cancer Society concedes that "standard management . . . unfortunately may be so fearsome in itself that many people are strongly tempted to seek unproven methods of treatment."

Unproven methods: Defoe's narrator reports that in those plague years, when people despaired of their physicians, they turned to "charms, philtres, exorcisms, amulets and I know not what preparations . . . as if the plague was not the hand of God but a kind of a possession of an evil spirit."

Today, again, the fear of evil spirits—those insidious, invisible carcinogens that possess our precious body fluids—is upon the land. The faith of the people in the cathedrals of orthodox cancer cures is falling away, and thousands are turning for exorcism to the heresies, the sects, the cults, the curious theories of unorthodox cancer cures.

We're not just talking about laetrile here, we're talking about a whole subculture that has existed in this country for at least the century and a half since "Doctor William A. Rockefeller, the Celebrated Cancer Specialist" set himself up for business in the 1840s and sold some black viscous gunk that he claimed would result in "all cases of cancer cured unless too far gone, and they can be greatly benefited." (Doc Rockefeller never made his fortune from his cancer cure; it was only when his son John D. Rockefeller found other uses for the black gunk that petroleum made a little money for the family.)

Still, the popular impression about the unorthodox cancer cure world is that it is composed mainly of cash hungry charlatans and snake oil salesmen eager to make an easy killing off the sufferings and hopes of cancer victims.

In fact, among the healers, the prophets and the alchemists, you find less greed than evangelical fervor—the rapturous conviction of religious visionaries. Each healer has his own biomystical theology, a eucharist that may be apricot kernels or sheep cells, his own vision of the nature of the beast, of the evil spirits that possess the flesh and ravage the body with tumors. Each cancer cure prophet suffers the sublime torment of having absolute knowledge of the secrets of life and, yet, being disbelieved. Let me cite, for instance, the agony of the author of *The Grape Cure*. This book, still sold in health food stores, was first published in the twenties by a South African immigrant named Johanna Brandt. Unable to convince stiff-necked doctors that a diet of grapes and water would cure cancer she cries out: "To hold the key to the solution of most of the problems of life and to have it rejected untried as worthless, that is to pass through the dark night of the soul. . . . To offer the gift of deliverance from pain . . . and to see it spurned—that is crucifixion—Calvary."

But wait. There's one kicker to this, to gazing condescendingly at the cancer cure subculture as a case study in the anthropology of religion: One of them might be right. What if one of the alchemists or biomystics in this murky nether world may have somehow stumbled on to something that has eluded the one-track minds of orthodox cobalt and cyclotron technology? We all know the French Academy laughed at Pasteur and his ridiculous "invisible organism" theory of disease.

Even the American Cancer Society concedes that there is something going on with "unproven methods" of cancer management: "A common pattern is that of the proponent who has tried a remedy in several people with what seems to be good results." The American Cancer Society disparages such good results as "often based entirely on the subjective response of the patient, which may result from the false hope instilled in him."

Whatever the explanation, false hope cures seem to spring up and sweep the nation like religious revivals, a new one at least every decade. In the twenties it was Coley's toxins and Koch's glyoxylide injections; in the thirties it was the Coffey Humber extract and Hoxsey's herbs; in the forties, the Gerson coffee enema and liver extract regimen; in the fifties orgone energy and Krebiozen. The sixties saw the birth of the laetrile cure, the seventies, the Wobe-Mugos and other metabolic enzyme cures, and the eighties seem to be headed for a revival of mind cures—some synthesis of self-hypnotic visualization and psychic self-healing techniques—but who knows what's next.

The natural history of these cancer cure cults is, curiously, not unlike the natural history of the tumors they attack. First they swell rapidly with the revivalitic fervor of the faithful and the testimonials of the cured, then they undergo fierce attacks from orthodox medicine. But at a certain point—just as a malignant growth succeeds only in destroying itself when it kills its host—these cults either collapse of their own pathology or go into remission, shrinking and retreating to below-the-border clinics, surviving or providing in their demise a fertile subculture of unorthodox adherents ready to nourish the next eruption.

Although relations between rival healers within the subculture are frequently characterized by fierce infighting and subtle character assassination, they tend to suspend their intrigues once or twice a year and assemble for mass ecumenical rallies of the unorthodox believers, gatherings that are part therapy theory tournaments, part Renaissance Faire and part revival crusades for the cancerphobic faithful.

And so it came to pass that on the Fourth of July of this plague year, I joined more than a thousand pain-filled pilgrims, healers, herbalists, alchemists, doctors of medicine and doctors of metaphysics converging on the Ambassador Hotel in Los Angeles for the eighth annual convention of the Cancer Control Society, one of the leading unorthodox alliances. It was there that I met the Captain and we made our plans for a caravan to the clinics below the border.

THE LOS ANGELES CONVENTION:
STRANGE ALLIANCES AND PALACE COUPS

Breakfast with Peter Chowka in the basement coffeehouse of the Ambassador: I'd known Chowka off and on in the seventies as an antiwar activist and journalist. Since we'd last seen each other on George McGovern's press plane he had become a leading figure in a new kind of antiwar movement—the growing protest against the medical establishment's war against cancer. Chowka thinks that the new movement will become in the eighties what the antiwar and no nuke movements were in the sixties and seventies, that the medical establishment is the last bulwark of authority to have escaped the exposures and upheavals that have shaken almost every other establishment in American society, and that now its number is up.

The alliances in this new movement are far more complex and peculiar than those in the antiwar movement. Here you have laetrile lovers of the John Birch persuasion lined up with postsixties holistic health food fanatics to defend freedom of choice and the purity of their precious body fluids. You've got laetrile smugglers and marijuana smugglers (for chemotherapy patients) and little old ladies in Adidas on the same side of an extraordinarily emotional issue.

Stiil, Chowka tells me, the similarities to the struggle over Vietnam are striking. The generals in the medical establishment's war against cancer are, he argues, using the same doomed, destructive strategies against an enemy they just can't figure out, much less defeat. The cancer patient undergoes, he says, "a Vietnamization of the body." He's hit with surgical strikes, burned, poisoned with toxic chemicals, while in most cases the elusive enemy melts away and soon surfaces in more deadly forms elsewhere. The generals destroy the body in order to save it and accompany the process with ceaseless proclamations of the nearness of victory, the need for more funds and hardware.

The new critique of orthodox cancer cures is based not on religious allegiance to some single alternative cure, Chowka tells me, but on the work of the growing number of dissident scientists, disillusioned doctors and Ellsberg-like dissenters from the pentagons of medical orthodoxy (doctors Dean Burke, formerly of the National Cancer Institute, and Ralph Moss, formerly of Sloan-Kettering, for instance). The new critics are less likely to claim that they have the one true cure than to attack conflicts of interest built into the economic structure of orthodox institutions. For instance, one of the financial supporters of the now revered Memorial Sloan-Kettering Cancer Center made his fortune as head of Phelps Dodge mining company and invested heavily in the future profitability of radium mining. Orthodox medicine's subsequent enthusiasm for such radium-based cancer treatments as radium implants in the ovaries, the new critics believe, is subject to suspicion—and surpassed in its destructiveness by few of the outright fraudulent practices of unorthodoxy.

Unfortunately, Chowka tells me, some sectors of the new opposition movement are plagued by financial conflicts of interest of their own, and the movement is as schism ridden, sectarian and all around factious as the antiwar movement was in the sixties. "Wait till you get upstairs; you'll see," Chowka warns.

It doesn't take long. I pass the registration desk of the Ambassador lobby, and before I can advance very far toward the entrance to the ballroom someone thrusts into my hands a copy of a paper called *Public Scrutiny*. A banner headline assaults me: PALACE COUP FAILS AT NATIONAL HEALTH FEDERATION.

I make my way toward the ballroom and come upon a woman wearing something I'd never seen before. . . .

An Ultrasuede sandwich board, that's the best way to describe it. Kind of a two-sided suede apron on which large white messages have been printed in big block letters. The front side reads: WHY WAS IDA HONOROF'S NAME REMOVED FROM THE PROGRAM? And on the back: BETTY LEE STRIKES AGAIN.

It is quickly evident that the suede lady is one of the participants on the losing side of the palace coup, and *her* newsletter consists of vitriolic attacks on the people in the palace: "The deposed executive director, who like a vampire continues to suck every drop of blood that is left! . . . entrenched on their own gravy train . . . snake oil exhibits . . . in no way related to health. . . ."

Bad Thoughts and Cosmic Kicks

Inside the ballroom at last. It's hard to forget the look of the place from all those clips of Bobby Kennedy at the podium delivering what were to be his last words. But I'm early, and the action isn't around the podium. The action is around the vast gold-draped periphery of the near empty ballroom, where exhibitors are rushing to unpack the wares they'll display for the next three days of the show.

At the back of the ballroom, in a prime position for crowd flow, I spy a big banner pinned to the wall proclaiming the availability of Betty Lee Morales "Signature Brand" Supplements. And there, below the banner, I spot Betty Lee herself, a large, jolly but formidable woman, president of the Cancer Control Society, our hostess for this convocation and the object of the suede lady's sandwich board attack.

Betty Lee is busy helping her husband unpack the Signature Brand samples he will be taking orders for during the convention. Betty Lee has put her personal signature on her spouse as well as her vitamins— both she and her husband are wearing identical bright-blue Polynesian-style shirts. Betty Lee designed these matching husband and wife outfits, a different one for each day of the convention.

Of course, Betty Lee and her husband are not the only entrepreneurs busily setting up wares to display for the health seekers now streaming into the ballroom for the opening session. Along the three sides of the ballroom and spilling over to two adjoining indoor and one outdoor room you can find tables and booths offering the following goods and services, to name a few: Lone Star Cancer Only Life Insurance Policies, Cancer Book House, air ionizers, water distillers, Vit-Ra-Tox Seven-Day Cleansing Program, Gerovital (GH3) rejuvenation tours, Novafon Ultrasound vibrators, DMSO, Hydrazine Sulfate, three kinds of laetrile, Vita Florum healing water, Britannica 3, Polarity Therapy, Computer Nutritional Analysis from Donsbach University, Wheat Grass Therapy at the Hippocrates Health Institute, Biomagnetic Therapy in Puerto Rico, two clinics from Tijuana, trampolines (rebound physiology energizers), slanted posture beds, Selenium, Iridology, Holistic survival food, Moksha Prem (massage and polarity specialist), Dr. Cayenne (laxative specialist), Silica B-15, Bee Propolis, Gerson Therapy, and Life-Force.

This Bartholomew Fair atmosphere is a little confusing to the new-comer. Betty Lee's remarks from the podium this morning concede that the unorthodox forces don't present the seeker with any single answer. "You'll hear contradictory advice in the next few days," she tells the thousand or so people gathered for the opening. "You'll hear some people say low protein is the only way, others will say it has to be high protein, same with vegetarian and nonvegetarian." But Betty Lee, whose Signature Brand happens to include animal gland extracts, has a peppery piece of advice of puritanical veggies who speak of the sacredness of animal souls. "I'd advise you to read *The Secret Life of Plants*," she says. After reading about the terror and anguish plants feel at being plucked, you'll never again blame yourself for taking the life of an animal, she tells us.

●   ■   ●

Terror and toxicity, anguish and blame are the recurrent themes of the morning's program, which concentrates on the prevention of cancer rather than the cure. Betty Lee strikes the keynote of blame when she says, "Our hearts go out to those who have already produced cancer in their bodies." If you've got it, it's your fault—you produced it.

Some even go so far as to say you're practically seducing an otherwise innocent carcinogen into performing an unnatural act within your flesh. Thelma Arthur, a little gray-haired M.D. who's spent 40 years advo-cating mass screening of the population with her controversial Arthur Metabolic Immuno-Differential, describes the seduction this way: "A wandering little carcinogen happened by your system. He wasn't strong, but you were weak. He looked around for some real estate. Found a place to build a cocoon." He's just a cuddly little creature until he's turned into an insatiable beast by your own sinful toxicity.

Whence comes this shameful toxicity? For years the constipated colon has reigned supreme in the realm of the unorthodox as chief seat of the carcinogenic enemy within, and colon-cleansing advocates are out in strength at this year's convention.

"You don't read much in the newspapers about bowel movements," Dr. Harold Manner, keynote speaker at the CCS banquet, tells us in the middle of our meal. "But it's not really true that you are what you eat. You are what you digest, assimilate and properly eliminate."

While the late cancer cure theorist Wilhelm Reich had been ridiculed for his assertion that regular orgasmic spasms of sufficient potency are essential to preventing cancer, are the connection to the healing rhythm energy of creation, the current cancerphobic fanatics seem to have regressed in asserting that intestinal peristalsis is the central rhythm of life and the key to curing cancer. I think my appreciation of one of the world's great paintings has been forever besmirched by the colon-connected comment Count Anton Schenk makes at this convention. The count specializes in fetal lamb cell cancer cures. Nevertheless, he feels compelled to go into a panegyric on the central importance of colon cleansing to human happiness, concluding, "When I see the famous picture of the Mona Lisa . . . the reason she seems to smile so, I think I have found it. She must have received a successful enema."

But there are signs of a shift lately, signs that the new locus of terror will not be the bowels but the brain, the new focus of cure will not be the cleansing of the colon but of the cortex—brainwashing, some might say. There's a terrifying new enemy in the unorthodox cancer world— *bad thoughts*. Our own thought processes may be as deadly as processed foods. Guilt, repression, anxiety not only make you a drag at parties, but these negative emotions also add up to a vaguely defined "carcinogenic personality." To be healthy one must think healthy thoughts all the time or face dire physiological consequences. This analysis has opened the way for all sorts of new age shrinks, encounter-group therapists, meditation, visualization and hypnosuggestive healers to enter the cancer cure field. One of the most sophisticated syntheses of all these approaches is represented at the convention by a group called Life-Force, whose cancer project offers psychotherapeutic counseling to cancer patients.

One of the leaders of Life-Force, a charismatic minister and psycho-therapist named Dr. Richard Turner, goes so far as to tell the cancer conventioneers that even when one does contract cancer, one should not allow oneself bad thoughts about the diagnosis. One should, instead, welcome it, embrace the malignant growth as an opportunity for personal growth. Dr. Turner cites one client who came to him for counseling after a cancer diagnosis and "realized it gave her a cosmic kick!" Another Life-Force cofounder explains, "When you have cancer you can do anything you want!"

OF FATHERS AND SONS AND APRICOT KERNELS

During the intermission following the first block of speakers, thousands of conventioneers and scores of cancer cure subculture celebrities mingle amidst the exhibits and swirl through the corridors with the noise of ionizers, massagers, juicers and food millers buzzing away in the background.

It's late morning, and in the midst of the corridor swirl I am privileged to witness the grand entrance of Ernst T. Krebs Jr. Krebs bears himself with the immense dignity of a hereditary prince in exile come to survey the squabbling disarray of his émigré rabble. He glows with a grandiose serenity that is, in part, a hereditary legacy. Krebs and his father, E. T. Krebs Sr., were the first to apply an apricot kernel extract called amygdalin to the cure of cancer. Krebs's father's father was a German *apotheker*, and both son and grandson inherited the magisterial dignity, the imperious certitude of that elite class of chemists.

Now, at last, 35 years after father and son collaborated on the discovery that led to laetrile, several states, including California, have legalized the apricot kernel compound, and four of the nation's top cancer centers—Mayo Clinic, Sloan-Kettering, UCLA and University of Arizona—are, under the auspices of the National Cancer Institute, administering it to human cancer patients in controlled clinical trials. The patients are mostly terminal cases on whom orthodox therapies have failed. If there are any positive results, Krebs may well be elevated to the instant sainthood status of great healers like Jonas Salk. The man who cures cancer will stalk the earth like a colossus, and strong men will weep to see him as he passes by.

If the tests go badly Krebs will be condemned to spend the rest of his life at conventions like this, a pretender to the throne recognized only by terminal true believers.

Krebs radiates total confidence of vindication. A large man with luminous straw-colored hair, pale jowly flesh encased in a luminous blue suit, he exudes a combination of W. J. Bryan's passion (thou shalt not crucify mankind on a cross of carcinogens) and W. C. Fields's imperious grandiosity. Buoyed by the prospect of imminent transfiguration Krebs's voice swells as he describes his father's and his discovery of B-17 as "a Copernican revolution" in the biological sciences. "Laetrile offers hope for not just cancer but for the entire range of degenerative diseases that affect mankind." The discoveries of the Krebs family will return human health to what Krebs claims was once, long ago, an Edenic state.

There is a whole theology of a Fall implicit in Krebsian biology. Once, Krebs tells the throng around him in the corridor of the Ambassador Hotel, once, long ago, "the flesh of all the fruits we know today contained sufficient quantities of B-17" to prevent the development of the diseases that plague us today. But civilization and hybridization tainted these trees of life and the fruits thereof, driving the redeeming biochemical essence deep within the kernel, inaccessible to the bite. The final fall came with the Romans, says Krebs. "When they grafted the sweet almond shoot onto the bitter almond root, the last dietary source of laetrile was lost because the bitter but not the sweet almond kernel contained B-17." The fall of Rome followed soon thereafter.

Not until 1,500 years later did Krebs's father rediscover that which had been lost, and he died without seeing his healing vision fulfilled. The son has dedicated his life to liberating the promise of redemption encapsulated in the kernels and to restoring to mankind this enzymatic eucharist that has the power to transubstantiate tumors and make possible the remission of civilization's carcinogenic original sin.

If you think I am exaggerating the religious dimension of the laetrilists' cause, that's obviously because you haven't read a book called *Thank God I Have Cancer!* It is the work of the Reverend Clifford Oden of Garland, Texas, who says he cured his colon cancer with laetrile but whose more important contribution is to make explicit the religious righteousness of the theory of laetrile cytochemistry.

The Reverend Oden argues that since God created all flesh, benign and malignant, cancer cannot be bad. God made cancer. It must have a meaning, a purpose. A malignancy is, in fact, a message from God embedded in the flesh.

●   ■   ●

In the midst of Krebs's triumphant laetrile litany, a short, intense, dark-eyed figure persists in interrupting him with a passionate and unorthodox dissent from Krebs's own unorthodoxy. He says that the laetrile of the father hath not the magic of the laetrile of the son, that the son has betrayed his father's legacy.

The dark-eyed dissenter is a naturopath from Pasadena named Richard Barmakian, and his story of a lost laetrile formula clearly disturbs Krebs's serenity. Barmakian describes a quest he went on when "a dear friend of mine was dying of cancer." It took him down below the border to Tecate, Mexico, to see a man he regarded as a kind of wizard of unorthodoxy. Tracking the wizard to his Tecate lair, 34 miles east of Tijuana, Barmakian begged him to reveal "anything he knew about curing cancer that I didn't because I just wasn't going to let my friend die. I was determined to save her.

"He was very hesitant to come out with this information. It took him over an hour before he finally opened up and began to explain certain things to me. He told me how when he had lung cancer he had gone to see Krebs Sr., who gave him some little tiny capsules. In very short order his lung cancer disappeared. This was the original effective product with all the enzymes in it. Finally he opened up and told me the story of the real product versus the so-called laetrile of today." Unfortunately Barmakian left Tecate empty-handed; the wizard had none of the real stuff left.

As soon as he got back Barmakian "called a source I knew in Krebs's lab. The source was reluctant to talk, and when he finally realized I knew what I was talking about he yelled, 'How did you hear about this?'

"After much persuasion he sent me two vials, one of which I sent to my friend airmail special delivery. In three months time—she'd already been taking laetrile, the present kind, for her adenocarcinoma without results—she recovered."

In the corridor I ask Krebs whether his product differs somehow from his father's potion. "No," Krebs the younger thunders. "No. I have never deviated one micrometer from the original formula my father and I perfected."

Still, Krebs acknowledges the confusions about real laetrile and false laetrile. I ask Krebs as he makes his way, throng in tow, into the ballroom, which of the laetrile brands is the best. He frowns. "The question is which is the worst."

DR. SIERRA'S MAGNETIC MYSTERY TOUR

The final hours of the first day's program offer a special sort of strangeness: Dr. Ralph Sierra's magnetic mystery tour de force.

He's a spry little guy, Dr. Sierra. He operates a biomagnetic research clinic in Puerto Rico, where, he claims, he cures cancer by the application of north magnetic force and the ingestion of north magnetically charged water.

The belief in the healing power of magnetism goes back to the rogue aristocrat Austrian doctor Franz Anton Mesmer, who used iron magnets over the bodies of afflicted patients—including many susceptible women in Marie Antoinette's court circle. Before long Mesmer decided it wasn't the magnets but his own "animal magnetism" that induced the convulsive healing crisis his patients went through.

Dr. Sierra has put the magnetism back in mesmerism, and, indeed, contemporary biology is hot on his heels in returning to serious investigation of the somatic effects of magnetic fields on living organisms. But Dr. Sierra's prescriptions seem, shall we say, almost too simplistic to be true. "Take a glass of magnetized water two or three times a day . . . because when that water becomes part of your body it's charged with energy and will keep you well," he tells the audience in his evening lecture. "We cure cancer, we cure heart diseases, all the degenerative diseases with the magnetism."

I might have been able to take the magnetic practitioner more seriously if it weren't for his weird demonstration. But here is Dr. Sierra bustling around the stage of the ballroom setting up something that looks ominously like an electric chair with a gleaming copper disk for a backrest, and there is a woman volunteer seating herself in the chair, and now Dr. Sierra is hooking up some wires and electrodes to some kind of generator. He then places goggles—big, weird, space welder goggles—over her eyes and calls for the houselights to be dimmed.

Suddenly the place is dark and there is a strange, loud buzzing sound. Sparks begin to explode from the goggles, and it looks like sparkler sticks are burning inside each goggle eye. I don't think the volunteer is prepared for this.

"Don't worry," Dr. Sierra reassures her, "Every cell in your body is being revitalized by the magnetic polarity we are inducing." The next thing we know he brandishes a yardlong fluorescent bulb and asks the sparkler-goggled lady to put it in her mouth.

She does. Apparently the revitalized magnetic potential in her body is supposed to light up the bulb.

More sparks. More buzzing. Not a flicker from the tube. Anxious, apologetic reactions from Dr. Sierra. He scurries about, frantically making adjustments in the buzzing spark generators. Still nothing.

The audience becomes restive. Some are visibly nervous about the fate of the volunteer in the electric chair. Finally, Betty Lee steps forward to try to rescue the situation. She takes the microphone from the frantic Dr. Sierra. She takes the sparkler goggles off the woman's head and the fluorescent tube from her mouth.

"Do you feel any differently yet?" she asks the electric chair volunteer. "Of course, it's very quick, but I'm sure people would like to know if you feel different."

There is an inaudible response from the woman in the chair.

"You feel more relaxed?" Betty Lee interprets. Cheers from the audience. Who wouldn't feel more relaxed with several major electrical appliances removed from her body orifices?

MISSING PERSONS AT THE FEAST

There is a ghost hovering over the great Cancer Control Society banquet, haunting Dr. Ernesto Contreras even as the smiling Tijuana clinician steps forward to accept his Humanitarian of the Year award at the climax of the ceremonies in the Ambassador's Coconut Grove.

No one at the banquet has the bad taste to touch on the troubling presence of the phantom at the head table. But the death of little Chad Green—whose parents resisted court-ordered conventional chemotherapy and who fled with him to Dr. Contreras's clinic in Tijuana—the conflicting stories surrounding the child's final days, have cast shadows on the humanitarian reputation of the man who's been called the godfather of laetrile.

Every effort had been made to spare Dr. Contreras the indignity of having to confront questions about Chad's death. During last year's convention Chad's name was on everyone's lips, and everyone loved and blessed the little bambino in his brave struggle. This year Chad's inconvenient death makes his name something of an embarrassment. He's no longer a live martyr, no longer a dead person. He's become a virtual nonperson.

Nor have Chad's parents, Jerry and Diana Green, been made to feel particularly welcome anymore. While the convention program had promised their appearance, they turned out to be no-shows—and under puzzling circumstances at that. Jerry and Diana Green had been scheduled to speak just prior to Contreras's presentation. It turned out that the young couple could not afford travel expenses to the convention, and the CCS declined to help, forcing them to cancel.

Peter Chowka, who was with the Green family shortly before Chad's death, is not surprised at this development. Bitter acrimony, angry charges and countercharges broke out between Contreras and the Greens when Chad died. Even the actual cause of the child's death is still, Chowka says, a subject of dispute between the doctor and the parents.

Contreras sheds no new light on this mystery during his appearance at the convention. He never once mentions Chad's name. But three days later, below the border at Contreras's clinic, we would confront the godfather of laetrile with the ghost of Chad.

THE MEXICAN CONNECTION:
GOAT GLANDS AND HORSE-SORE SALVES

It was on the final afternoon of the convention that the Captain and I made our connection with the woman who would guide us on our below-the-border odyssey. Her name is Marilyn Merrill, and our first stop the next morning was her home in Laguna Hills, where we were scheduled to rendezvous with the other pilgrims and curiosity seekers who would make up our border-crossing caravan.

As we took a Laguna Hills exit off 405, the Captain was in the middle of telling me a surprising story about the premedical uses to which the legendary Ernst T. Krebs the elder had applied apricot kernels. It seems that back in the twenties, before Repeal, the Captain's father was running a small distillery and sought out Krebs in San Francisco.

"That's when I first met Krebs," the Captain explained. "He was supplying apricot kernel extract, essentially amygdalin, to bootleggers."

"Why would bootleggers want laetrile?" I asked.

"This was before it was laetrile," the Captain said, before it became a cancer cure. "Back then it was just an apricot pit extract they used to improve the taste of bootleg liquor. Took the edge off."

Although fashions in prohibition have changed—with liquor now legal and laetrile bootlegged—a Prohibition atmosphere still prevails in the cancer cure world with the prohibited elixir the object of smuggling, adulteration and intrigue. In its *Unproven Methods* pamphlet, the American Cancer Society warns darkly against "the 'underground railroad' whereby cancer patients from all over the United States are directed to Mexico . . . for treatment with worthless or unproven methods." Reading that, I had visions of frightened cancer patients crouching in dank basements, moving only at night, the FDA hot on their heels.

But there were no dank basements in Laguna Hills, a prosperous Orange County suburb. In fact, the gathering of patients and guide at this "underground railroad" way station looked more like an angry suburban kaffeeklatsch.

They were angry because we were late. When the Captain and I pulled into the driveway we found that our fellow pilgrims—two women cancer patients, the husband of one of them and Peter Chowka—had been pacing around for an hour, impatient to get our Tijuana safari under way. Our schedule called for us to see no less than five clinics in a single day and, considering the difficulty of finding one's way below the border and the urgency that the possibility of redemption on the journey promised, they were in no mood to waste any more time.

Indeed, there was some grumbling as efforts to consolidate cars into a more compact caravan caused confusion. All this and an unexpected seat switch caused one of the eager pilgrims, a pleasant middle-age woman we'll call Renee, to burst into tears.

None of this seemed to faze our jolly guide, Marilyn, who finally got us straightened out and under way. How did Marilyn get into her strange business of being travel agent for the underground railroad?

It began with the phone calls. A few years ago, when she became head of the Orange County chapter of the International Association of Cancer Victims and Friends, she began to get calls from time zones all over the world, sometimes in the middle of the night. They were pleas from cancer patients eager for something to hope for below the border, fearful of the unknown, asking her, "What's it really like *down there* on the other side?" not just "Will this save me, or my mother?" but "Is it safe? Is it clean? Is it for real?"

She began ferrying friends across the border to see for themselves. When some local clubwomen asked her to take the whole club, Marilyn rented a bus. It became a regular practice, then a kind of business: bus-along tours to the Tijuana cancer clinics with Marilyn acting as tour guide, speakers from the cancer cure subculture, lunch at the Gerson clinic, chats with patients and doctors.

For all her boundless cheerfulness, Marilyn's work is not a light-hearted lark. Many of the bus-along people are cancer patients. She's come to recognize certain characteristics of the cure seekers who come to her.

"Take that woman Renee," Marilyn said to me, "the one who burst into tears because there was some confusion about car assignments." I had been assigned the front seat of Marilyn's car, which was the lead car of our three-car caravan. The backseat was piled high with sandwich-stuffed coolers, Thermoses full of hot coffee and cold juices, plastic bags dewy with well-scrubbed fruit—enough, more than enough it seemed, to take Cortés to the Seven Cities of Gold, just enough for a Jewish mother guiding her brood to Tijuana.

"Now, I like Renee," Marilyn went on, "but that's behavior you see a lot from some of these cancer patients.

"One of the things you discover when you read about the personality studies they've done with cancer patients is this sense of confusion and uncertainty. And you can imagine what it's like for them when they're trying to choose from all the alternative therapies. Now, she's typical. When she arrived she had to take off her blouse, show me all her scars, tell me about her operations in detail, and it turns out she's been on several different therapies and hasn't stayed with any one. I run into this type all the time. It's as if they're reluctant to give up their disease. I call them 'shoppers.' They shop around, they do a little of one, a little of another, just enough to stay alive, not to ever really get well. They don't want to, they don't have the will to go through the incredible discipline some of the alternative therapies require. I mean, Charlotte Gerson's coffee enemas are not easy. But the ones who really want to live, they'll stick with a decision."

That's Marilyn's theory about the cures people report from unorthodox treatments. She thinks that those who go below the border with the will to fight will come back up with a greater chance to live regardless of which therapy they choose: It's the border-crossing process itself that is decisive—the decision to go beyond the bounds of the death-sentence certainties of orthodox medicine.

Still, Marilyn is, in effect, a connoisseur of cancer clinics, and I was eager to find out from her which one she'd choose if she faced a personal emergency. While she wouldn't commit herself unequivocally, she did confide that when her mother was diagnosed with skin cancer Marilyn wasted no time in dragging her down to the Hoxsey clinic in Tijuana where, Marilyn said, the Hoxsey tonic cured her. She'd go there herself, Marilyn said, if she had a similar malignancy.

I was somewhat taken aback: the Hoxsey cure is—especially when considered in light of all the sophisticated, holistic, enzymatic, crypto-scientific cures and prevention regimens mushrooming in the alternative cancer cure world—the oldest and purest throwback to the age of magical elixirs, secret potions, snake oil peddlers with cancer salves. I wasn't even aware a Hoxsey clinic existed anymore, although I had read something of its colorful, controversial history.

The legend of the Hoxsey elixir takes us back to the 1840s, when "celebrated cancer specialist" Rockefeller was still selling his cancer salves at medicine shows. The Hoxsey cure had an even humbler origin: as a horse-sore salve.

Great Grampa Hoxsey had this prize stallion, you see, who developed a big cancerous growth on his hoof. He put him out to pasture to die. Well, suddenly, the story goes, the old stallion started to get better. The tumor shrunk, and Grampa Hoxsey decided it was because of something the horse had been eating out there in the far pasture. He watched what herbs he went for, compounded them into a salve and started to treat other farm animals with it.

The formula stayed in the family as a horse cure until Harry's father began to try it out on human cancers with amazing results. When the father died the story takes a kind of biblical turn. Seventeen-year-old Harry was the youngest of twelve children, and because he was his father's eager assistant in the cancer salve business, it was to him that the dying old man passed the birthright for the secret formula. He made him memorize it. Later the other brothers and sisters greedily tried to wrest the rights to the formula from Harry, but it existed only in his head—and he kept it there.

Harry Hoxsey built his birthright into a headline-making healing empire. His clinics swelled with devotees claiming cures every place he set up shop, but Hoxsey never bothered to get an M.D. degree and ended up in fractious litigation with the AMA wherever he went, eventually making his last stand in Dallas. Hoxsey won most of his legal battles—including a sensational slander suit against AMA spokesman Morris Fishbein—but eventually the fierce struggles took their toll, and after two heart attacks he moved his clinic below the border in the early sixties and put it in the care of his longtime chief nurse, Mildred Nelson. Now on a hilltop in Tijuana, she presides over a little adobe house that is the shrunken remnant of the once vast Hoxsey empire. It was to be, Marilyn told me, our first stop.

Marilyn is worried about Nurse Mildred's situation, she told me. She's worried about the whole future, in fact, of what remains of the Hoxsey enterprise. Unlike Harry Hoxsey, Nurse Mildred isn't evangelical. She's content to cure whoever happens to come to her. She doesn't have promotional booths at the cancer cure conventions the way the other unorthodox healers do. The only pamphlet she's printed up is primitive compared with those of other clinics.

There are some clinics inside and outside the United States that peddle what they purport to be Hoxsey elixir, but according to Marilyn only Mildred has possession of the original formula. Marilyn fears for the preservation of the true Hoxsey formula in Mildred's fragile exile outpost.

●   ■   ●

Just before we reached the border our cancer cure caravan stopped to regroup in the parking lot near Motel 8 in San Isidro. This particular Motel 8 has become a popular way station and outpatient residence for cancer victims. They go for below-the-border treatments during the day and return for a good old-fashioned cheapo American motel at night. Motel 8 offers shuttle-bus service to most of the clinics, some of them driven by the Jehovah's Witnesses, who for religious reasons prefer the unorthodox treatments.

In the parking lot Marilyn opened up the back of her car and offered sandwiches, coffee and snacks from the massive supply she'd packed. The Captain emerged from the black Cadillac he'd switched to and offered a selection of the plastic, foil-sealed, watery fruit juices he brought from his VA hospital stash. Across the parking lot, across a mile or so of scrub, the hills of Tijuana rose in a jumble ahead of us, a maze of crooked streets and alleys covering their contours.

For years Tijuana and other Mexican border towns have been a refuge for an extraordinary array of health dissidents and quacks whose prescriptions and procedures had gotten them in trouble with U.S. authorities. First and still perhaps the strangest of the border town healers is the notorious Dr. Brinkley who pioneered the goat gland operation and built up a huge medicopopulist following in the Midwest and South during the thirties, twice coming within a few votes of getting elected governor of Kansas.

Dr. Brinkley's goat gland operation—he actually transplanted the testicles of goats into the scrota of men for what he claimed were curative and rejuvenative effects—never really went over big with established U.S. medical men. So he was forced to pioneer some of the border town clinical protocols that cancer cure dissidents would later emulate, using one of the ultrapowerful clear channel X stations based below the border to evangelize half the nation with his messianic medical messages, thus attracting attention to the clinic in a way FCC and FDA authorities couldn't control.

Forbidden cures, like forbidden thrills, have become an enduring part of the lore and the lure of border towns in the popular imagination. Since things have loosened up above the border these days, there aren't too many fantasies or forbidden visions—give or take a donkey or two—you need to go to Tijuana to fulfill, and cancer cure cults are the last refuge of the strange and forbidden exoticism that once seduced people below the border.

IN WHICH WE GET TO TASTE THE TONIC

We got lost for about five minutes after we crossed the border. The route to the Hoxsey clinic goes through a part of town that has no street signs, and none of the passersby we asked knew the way to General

Ferreira street. Marilyn usually has a hired Mexican driver for her bus-alongs who knows the way. "I'm facing backward giving the lectures, so I never know the route except from the back," she said, explaining her difficulty. But she's a remarkably calm pathfinder, and, suddenly, as we struggled up a crooked road whose potholes seemed to have been the work of land mine blasts, we crested a hill, and she shouted, "There it is."

There it was, indeed. Not an impressive edifice from the outside, certainly not when compared with the huge Hoxsey clinic in Dallas. Marilyn recalled that when she first took her mother to the modest adobe and stucco building with the chipped and peeling exterior, the poor woman burst into tears and sobbed, "Why have you brought me *here?*" She changed her tune, said Marilyn, as soon as she met Nurse Mildred.

Inside, three or four patients sat in the rather dilapidated waiting room, which is graced only by a small black and white portrait of the late Harry Hoxsey, the vigorous hatchet-faced healer in his prime. Nurse Mildred was in the middle of a diagnostic conference with the Mexican doctors when we arrived.

While we waited for her I spoke with one patient in the waiting room. His name is Mr. Thomasina, he said in the accent of his native Greece. He lives with his wife in Canoga Park, California. His case history in brief: a diagnosis of prostate cancer with pelvic bone metastasis. "They wanted to operate," Mr. Thomasina said, "but they didn't give me much hope. I knew somebody who'd been cured by Hoxsey back in the fifties. So I came down here instead. That was last spring. I'm in good shape again. Take the tonic four times a day, come back every six months for a checkup."

It wasn't merely the apparent medical miracle of Mr. Thomasina's recovery that struck me—orthodox scientists routinely dismiss this as mere anecdotal evidence. No, it was the similarity in his diagnosis to that of another stranger I had met in a hospital room in my hometown 3,500 miles away—and the difference in outcome.

I had been visiting my father, who was in a Long Island hospital for minor surgery. The guy in the bed next to him had the same diagnosis as Mr. Thomasina—prostate cancer with suspected pelvic bone metastasis. But this guy, Johnny, was following his doctors' orders and, as he cheerfully put it, was "gonna let them carve me up." He made much of the fact that his surgeon had a reputation for bluntness, for slapping his patients with downer diagnoses without any kid gloves.

"Yeah," Johnny told us while I was visiting, "he just came out and said they were gonna carve me up, take out the testicles, see what they could carve out of the bones but that I shouldn't expect much if the bones were involved. And I shouldn't get too hopeful.

"I've been lucky with my health all my life," Johnny went on. "I can't really complain about this." Somehow he seemed to take consolation in the fact that his cancer would balance out his previously good karma, and he seemed almost satisfied with the justice of it all.

I don't know what was more astonishing—that kind of resignation or the kind of daring it took for Mr. Thomasina to defy convention, the advice of doctors and family, and come to this desolate hilltop in Tijuana for his cure.

I was talking to another patient who'd come all the way from Canada to get a lump in her breast treated when Marilyn appeared in the waiting room and told us that Nurse Mildred Nelson would see us now.

She was not what I'd expected. By this time I thought I'd run into just about every variety of cancer cure person you could imagine—the pseudoscholarly didact, the charismatic mystic, the martyred medico. I thought I'd heard every possible sophisticated, holistic, anticancer, megavitamin, nutritional supplement rap going.

Yet here on a hilltop in Tijuana was an old-fashioned nurse with an old-fashioned tonic—a tall, angular Texas woman who said she'd cured 80 percent of her cancer patients. She projected no charismatic healer vibes, she didn't even feel it necessary to attack the claims of rival cures ("They may be doing good for people for all I know"). She just sat next to her battered metal file cabinets ignoring the paint peeling from the ceiling, the ringing phones and the chatter of the Mexican doctors scurrying back and forth, and told us how back in the year 1946 she'd left her quiet life as a practical nurse in the tiny west Texas prairie town of Jacksboro and gone to work for the notorious Harry Hoxsey.

Her mother had cancer, and her father devised a plan that he wanted to hide from his practical nurse daughter. "My dad was haulin' heavy machinery into Dallas a lot so I didn't think too much of it when he asked me to bring mom in on one of the trips," Mildred recalled. "Then he tells me about this new doctor we're goin' to see, and we'd already been to every doctor far as San Antone, but when he starts describing this Harry Hoxsey, I said, 'You're going to a quack.'" She spit out the word "quack" with severe west Texas contempt.

She had no hesitation telling the great Hoxsey himself "You're a quack" when he handed her mother his bottle of tonic. She was stunned when Hoxsey responded amiably by offering her a job in his clinic. "He said, 'If I cure your mother's cancer, will you come work for me?'" He did. She did.

At first, Mildred said, she couldn't believe some of the results she was seeing. "Harry was quite the talker, you know, and he'd tell me one after another, each bigger than the next, and I wouldn't believe it. Took me a year working there to get my feet on the floor, see the improvement month by month in the people coming in before I'd begin to believe it."

The memory of the late irrepressible founder brought some warmth to her eyes, and the severe chief-nurse frown softened. But then I asked what seemed to be *the* wrong question around the place, and she snapped at me like I was some fool patient who couldn't keep his mouth shut on the fever thermometer. "Isn't one of the criticisms of the Hoxsey therapy that the formula's a secret?" I asked. "What happens if, uh, you should pass away without—I mean, might it end up being lost to the world?"

"That's not true," she snapped at me. "For the longest time we've printed the ingredients right on the bottle. And that has been published a number of times."

So would it be possible for someone to formulate it on their own?

"No, I have to put it together in a particular way," she said.

"Well, what will happen if—"

"I'll have someone right here who will do it. That's in the works right now. When Harry died five years ago I wasn't responsible for it, but at his death I became responsible for it."

"Why has it been the feeling that the process should be kept a secret?" Peter Chowka asked.

"He wanted them to recognize it, and then he would turn it all loose."

"So, you feel that because it hasn't been subjected to a fair test, there's no reason to let anyone know how it's prepared?" Chowka asked.

"Right. Not only that, there are a number of them today who will tell you, 'We're using the Hoxsey medicine,' and they know nothing about it. There are herb places that tell you they have the Hoxsey formula, but it isn't the Hoxsey formula."

Mildred's assurances about the preservation of the genuine formula left me feeling uneasy. Was it in a safe deposit box somewhere or still in her head while the transition was "in the works"? So powerful is the aura of integrity of this woman, yet so strange and fragile the circumstances in which she works, that I found myself terribly worried that this elixir might be lost to the world. The impulse to believe or to suspend disbelief is that strong below the border. Perhaps it's the Lourdes, the pilgrimage effect. You've come all the way to a strange place and you're more likely to experience a miracle here than in Elm City General Hospital back home.

Well, at least I wouldn't die without a taste of the real thing, because at that point Mildred was called away to another room, the Captain and Renee disappeared, and Marilyn emerged from another part of the clinic brandishing a big bottle of brown liquid.

"Want to taste?" she asked, removing the cap and giving me a sniff.

It smelled like cough medicine, the awful elixir terpenhydrate my parents had to force down my throat.

At last, a taste. Marilyn took my palm and turned the lip of the bottle over onto it. I hesitated, looking at the ring of sticky residue she'd left. I took a lick.

It was bitter like elixir terpenhydrate, strong like cough medicine. Not *too* bitter, on the other hand. I was finishing up the last sticky bit when the Captain and Renee emerged from a back room, their faces red, their hands clutching brown paper bags. Mildred wasn't anywhere to be seen.

Marilyn told us all it was time to move on to the next clinic if we wanted to finish by midnight. It wasn't until we were back in her car bumping down the hill that she told me what happened in the back room.

"Mildred is terrific, isn't she?" said Marilyn. "Did you see what she did for those two people?"

"What?" I asked.

"She gave them the medication. It was amazing. She took them into the back room and asked them what they'd been through, and they just burst into tears. They were sobbing and showing her their scars.

Then she gave them each a supply of the standard medication and told them to call her and come back free of charge.

A LOYAL DAUGHTER AND
HER COFFEE ENEMA CRUSADE

Before we'd left the Hoxsey clinic Nurse Mildred had given us directions to our next destination. We were bound for La Gloria. That's the name of the onetime resort hotel that has been converted to the Gerson coffee enema cancer therapy clinic.

To get to La Gloria we had to make our way through the maze of streets that surround the Hoxsey hilltop. Our directions called for us to look for a dead end and turn right before we hit it, but every street looked like a dead end, then turned out to be something else. Finally Marilyn asked a passerby for La Gloria, and we were on our way. "Everybody knows La Gloria," said Marilyn as we emerged at last on the Old Ensenada Road, which took us there.

One glance at La Gloria and you feel as if you're in a tropic deeper than Tijuana. Set back from the road, the well-trimmed lawns and the wide verandas reminded me more of a colonial planter's outpost—a German plantation in Southwest Africa, perhaps.

Charlotte Gerson Straus is the youngest daughter of the late Dr. Max Gerson. A tall, blue-eyed Rhine maiden, she could well have played the part of the wealthy planter's wife as she formally welcomed us into the clinic's spacious dining room for a late lunch. In the cool, tasteful interior with its polished wood floors servants brought us soup, salad and a carrot-liver juice concoction, part of the clinic's therapeutic diet. It sounds terrible, but it didn't taste as bad as the Hoxsey tonic.

Dr. Max Gerson was a German Jewish physician who originally specialized in detoxifying dietary cures for tuberculosis. One of those he cured of TB was Albert Schweitzer's wife. The saintly doctor became Gerson's advocate ever after, calling him "one of the most eminent geniuses in the history of medicine."

Gerson fled Europe in 1936 with his three daughters and soon after set up practice on Park Avenue in New York City and began applying his theories to a cure for cancer. In 1958 he published *A Cancer Therapy:*

Results of Fifty Cases and then made what turned out to be a fatal mistake. He accepted an invitation to discuss his therapy on *The Long John Nebel Show*, the pioneer midnight-to-dawn radio talk show that specialized in UFO contactees and bee venom arthritis cures, among other arcane phenomena. Immediately following that appearance, the AMA accused him of "advertising" and expelled him from its ranks. He died little more than a year later of chronic pneumonia.

What was Gerson's cancer cure secret? In the chapter of his book entitled *The "Secret" of My Treatment*, he says, "Of course, there is none!" But, of course, there is. Not a secret physical formula or elixir but a secret metaphysic that fairly sings out the influence of German romanticism.

The opening chapters of his book are a hymn to "the harmony in the metabolism . . . which reflects the eternal mystery of life," to "the Eternal Life" force, to "the concept of totality," to "the whole in its infinitely fine order." Cancer, he tells us, is not a disease of the particular organ or whatever part it first appears in, but of the whole individual; it merely shows up first as a localized tumor. Gerson believed, along with Einstein, that other romantic German Jewish scientist, in a "unified field theory"—his of health and disease. One can treat the tumor mass only by restoring the total metabolism, the wave of being that washes through the whole body.

But why coffee enemas? According to Gerson the caffeine absorbed by the hemorrhoidal vein travels directly to the liver, where, he said, it stimulates bile secretions to detoxify first the liver and then the rest of the body. The restored metabolism, boosted by massive infusions of raw vegetable and liver juices, then gets rid of the tumor without the aid of drugs.

It's all there in Gerson's book, but I was still a little shaken, as Charlotte Gerson led us on a tour of the clinic's rooms to come face to face with an item of furniture she calls "the enema bench."

Somehow the wooden severity of the enema bench reminded me of public stocks, the punitive confinement inflicted on those who fell from grace in early Puritan settlements. The secret of the continuing popularity of the Gerson therapy in the unorthodox world, despite competition from easy-to-take potions and pills, may be precisely due to the arduous, humiliating discipline it subjects the patients to—a testament to the ingrained assumption we inherited from Puritan forefathers and

Jewish grandmothers that no redemption, whether from sin or sickness, can be achieved without suffering.

In Max Gerson's case the healer, too, had to suffer for his cure. But his daughter Charlotte has made the redemption from that suffering, the vindication of her father's visionary legacy, a lifetime crusade. In fact, the only time I heard Charlotte abandon her demeanor of icy certitude, the only time she seemed to show any emotional excitement, was when she was describing a moment of symbolic vindication.

It was a particularly significant moment because it had taken place on a radio talk show, a West Coast version of the show that had doomed her father to persecution and fatal suffering. On this show, though, Charlotte said the climate had changed and she was on the offensive. She took the opportunity of the air time to deliver devastating attacks on the orthodox establishment that had expelled her father. "I really let loose at them," Charlotte said, a triumphantly Gersonian way of putting it.

Somewhat fearful of her severe Germanic demeanor and her icy blue eyes, I decided to test her goodwill by asking her about one old and one new controversy the Gerson method had aroused. First there was the *Death Be Not Proud* loss of John Gunther's 16-year-old son after a seeming remission under Gerson's care back in the forties. And then there were the news stories about deaths caused by coffee enema ODs just last year.

●   ■   ●

The John Gunther Jr. story is one she's particularly passionate about because, she claimed, her father went to his grave wrongly blaming himself for the boy's death. As you may have read in Gunther Sr.'s *Death Be Not Proud*, Gunther Jr. was brought to Dr. Gerson after he'd been given up for dead by orthodox doctors who had failed to stop the growth of a massive brain tumor. According to Gunther Sr., Gerson's treatment stopped the tumor from growing and enabled the boy to get off his deathbed and go back to school. Everything was going well until, Gerson said in his book, he made one fatal mistake: Against his better judgment he allowed another doctor to treat young John with pituitary hormones for a case of eczema he'd developed. "Six weeks later the tumor regrew. [After he died] the disaster threw me into a deep depression," Gerson wrote. "I almost lost the strength to continue this cancer work."

Poor Papa. Only after Gerson's death did the true story come out, daughter Charlotte claimed. "He took the blame—wrongly. The thing that had destroyed Johnny's body was the experimental nitrogen-mustard chemotherapy" the conventional doctors had failed with before they gave him up to Gerson.

"Johnny was the first person my father had treated after chemotherapy, and he wasn't aware that after chemotherapy the body is so destroyed it cannot heal. It took me more than 22 cases of healing after chemotherapy—with the same results—to find out that it's too late then."

And the two coffee enema deaths reported on television news?

"The news reports were very much distorted," she declared. "It was the case of a lady who had had some chemotherapy. We didn't want to accept her in the first place, but she begged us. The doctors had given up. She came to the clinic, and we put her on a very mild therapy so as not to reactivate the chemotherapy—we'd had bad experiences with that. She did fairly well and went home. About six weeks later she said she wasn't doing well, her glands were growing again. We said that we would need to put her back on a very strict therapy for at least a few weeks if we could, without reactivating the chemotherapy. She thought she could do it at home, and just as we've discovered, the healing reactions after chemo can be very violent, very toxic. She went into a coma. Patients often get low in chlorides, their potassium and sodium levels are okay, but down in Mexico we give them an I.V. with potassium chloride to build the chlorides right up. At home there's no doctor who knows to do this. Finally, she found a doctor, but she died in the waiting room.

"The health inspector went to her house and found she had been using coffee enemas and put that on her death certificate—'Death by coffee enemas.' The autopsy doctor indicated in his findings that she had widely disseminated cancer with liver metastasis, of which she died. Her husband wanted them to change the death certificate to 'Cancer.' But by the evening news it went out that not one patient but two or three had died of coffee enemas.

"Nothing but lies," she said. "Half-truths and lies. Anybody is welcome to come to the clinic and see that we have a 24-hour professional staff of doctors who know how to react. They should come, talk to the doctors, talk to the patients. My father always said . . ."

As we left La Gloria, neither the Captain nor any of the other cancer patient pilgrims looked excited about returning. They were respectful. Impressed. But none seemed eager to return for prolonged stretches on the enema bench.

A TALE OF TWO FAMILIES

We are in another part of Tijuana now, far from the jumble of streets, the tumbledown re-upholstery shops and the skeletal shells of the cars that are stripped and serviced there. We are close to the ocean, and across the broad plaza of Ernesto Contreras's Centro Medico Del Mar we could see the sunset-singed whitecaps. Here, in what one pro-laetrile magazine calls "balmy playas del Tijuana," we are also close to the most expensive residential district in Tijuana, immense, tastefully landscaped haciendas, the homes of many of the prosperous doctors on the Contreras clinic's large professional staff.

The clinic is a multilevel, luxury, mall-like affair with a facade dominated by a huge tile mosaic of a heroic nude in mortal combat with a zodiaclike crab. It looks like a close contest.

Dr. Contreras has come a long way since the mid-sixties, when he moved into a small furnished apartment so he could turn his own home into a tiny hospital to treat cancer patients with laetrile. The early missionary struggles are far behind him now, but the size of an enterprise like this full-scale ultramodern hospital, clinic, pharmacy, motel complex by the sea entails other problems—problems of empire and succession, and among them, it seems, is another one of those perplexing father-son struggles that plague the prophets of cancer cures.

Jerry and Diane Green weren't aware of any of this when they arrived in Tijuana with their leukemic child in January 1979. For the fugitive family who'd fled in disguise from court orders that their child be force-fed state-sanctioned medicine, for an earnest but innocent couple in their mid-twenties whose convictions had led them to risk their child's future on an underground railroad ride into the unknown, the first sight of Contreras's deluxe clinic complex, this Sloan-Kettering of the laetrile world, must have been reassuring.

And so, it seemed, was Dr. Contreras. He appeared to believe in all the holistic therapies they did, and he had the facilities to put them into practice. There were even soundproof, plush carpet, "white-noise" rooms where oceanic waves of hypnotically soothing static wash over the consciousness of tranced out cancer patients in visualization therapy as they imagine the white knights of their immune systems slaying cancer cell dragons in dream dramas.

Shelter at last from the storm, thought the Greens, a place for their child to heal. But there was something else available in this holistic heaven—the poison fruit that caused the postmortem trauma. Chemotherapy.

The basic situation was this: When three-year-old Chad arrived at Contreras's clinic in January, his leukemia was in a state of remission. He had been taking both chemotherapy (a court-ordered treatment) and laetrile obtained from underground sources.

No one could say for sure which one had induced the blessed remission, but the Greens were eager to get Chad off chemotherapy: They saw it as only a source of suffering, not as a cure. According to them Contreras agreed to "taper off" the chemotherapy for a few months and, if Chad's blood count and bone marrow levels remained stable, to cut it off altogether.

"He even encouraged us in our desire to take Chad off it," Jerry Green told me when I finally reached him in his sad Nebraska exile. "He told us the story of a young girl, a similar case, he had treated eleven years ago who was still alive."

And then, according to the Greens, there came a crucial consultation in July in which Contreras told them that their son was stable and agreed to cut off chemotherapy completely.

Then when Chad died in October, his parents, still stunned by the sudden death of their child, were further shocked to find that Contreras had held a postmortem press conference denouncing what he called *their* decision to cut off the chemotherapy.

In effect, Contreras was saying: Don't blame laetrile, don't blame me or my clinic, I warned those wayward parents against the choice they made. The resultant publicity did go beyond blaming laetrile—the Greens were singled out in their grief for going against the advice of their own doctor. One Boston newspaper referred to the parents as "this wicked couple."

Jerry Green is still trying to figure out Contreras's behavior. He hinted at "vested interests," fear of the power of orthodox medical wrath, even certain "villainous influences" on Contreras, certain powers behind the family throne the doctor couldn't control.

As our contingent of pilgrims filed in and seated itself facing Contreras across his desk we were all struck not by the sad-eyed drooping figure who feebly gestured us welcome but rather by the dramatic life-size portrait of a young, stunningly beautiful Mexican girl arrayed in a vibrantly colored off-the-shoulder Second Empire gown.

"My wife," Contreras said modestly, "when she was on the stage. As you can see," he added proudly, "she has Napoleonic and Indian blood."

Flanking this commanding vision were smaller snapshots of Contreras's children, a daughter and two proud-looking sons. According to what I've been able to piece together it's the two sons and their concern with the survival of the healing empire they stand to inherit that lie beneath Contreras's contradictory behavior toward Chad's family. The way I heard it Contreras sent his two sons off to the finest medical schools in Mexico City, hoping not only that they would return to stand by his side but that their obvious intelligence and sincerity would make them apostles of his cause even in the temples of the nonbelievers.

"Ernesto Jr. has been trained as an internal medical oncologist," Contreras said proudly. "He went into the lion's den and is winning over orthodoxy." Others told me that the son went into the lion's den and came out a lion, that he and the other son returned to Tijuana as converts to the temple of orthodoxy, that his allegiance was not to their father's amygdalin therapy but to the chemotherapy and radiation the holistic movement dreaded.

What was a father to do? He'd built his empire on the faith of thousands fleeing orthodoxy in search of "a place where holistic therapy is a reality." Yet the father's empire is fragile if founded only on amygdalin, if subject to sudden shifts in official favor, if a case like Chad's is allowed to "raise a stink." What interest should the father have put first when the spotlight was focused on him by such a case—the legacy he would leave to his sons or the sensibility of Chad's father?

Things seemed, well, melancholy in Contreras's office late that afternoon. The doctor displayed a disarming eagerness to please, but his eyes were mournful and his drooping jowls seemed to register tremors of sadness as he spoke. I had the feeling that he was suffering from a sense that his time of glory had passed and that he envied the rise of ambitious rivals on the metabolic cancer cure scene. He spent considerable time sniping at their methods, disparaging their lack of orthodox credentials.

"They are not trained oncologists. One is an allergist. Cancer is cancer. It should be treated by people who know it, by an oncologist, like my son Ernesto who is trained in this, at a place where they know how to handle all eventualities, not at one of those little clinics."

Contreras claimed that only at a comprehensive center like his could a patient get "the best of both worlds"—both chemotherapy and metabolic treatment, that they are not contradictory, that, in fact, he was getting exciting results combining laetrile with low-dose chemotherapy.

It was in the midst of Contreras's unexpected hymn to low-dose chemotherapy that I decided to ask him the big question about the disputed consultation and the death of Chad. Without the slightest hesitation he repeated the account the Greens had called "bold-faced lies." He insisted he had never agreed with their desire to stop Chad's chemotherapy. "I told them, 'Why don't we keep him as it is?' After all, there's nothing that beats chemotherapy in childhood leukemias. Children, for some reason, tolerate it, and I won't risk the life of a child to prove a point."

That last little barb—the implication that the parents were out to "prove a point" about holistic therapy rather than to save their child's life—is particularly galling to the Greens. They claimed Contreras stretched the bounds of accuracy in his autopsy of Chad to prove his own point. Contreras claimed his postmortem examination found Chad had died of "a massive involvement of leukemia." But an autopsy by the parents' American pathologist, Dr. Frank Raasch, found no conclusive signs the death had been caused by cancer, no conclusive cause of death at all.

The Greens, with the backing of Frank Sullivan, the former chief psychologist on Contreras's staff, claimed that Chad died because of the trauma of his state-enforced exile, that he longed so badly to return to his Massachusetts home that he just lost the will to live any longer in Tijuana, that the subtle sickness that killed him was homesickness. Sullivan even claimed that in the absence of other causes Chad's must be called "a psychologic death."

The Greens put it more simply. His father said, "Chad died of a broken heart."

He and his wife are left to live with theirs. For parents in their position, fleeing orthodox medicine, faced with life or death choices for their son as soon as they cross the border, the unorthodox world, like the streets of Tijuana, offers few reliable signposts. Some are crooked, some lead to dead ends, only a few insiders know the intrigues behind the treatments, who to trust for what.

When at last we emerged into the sunset-lit plaza of the Contreras complex, gloom seemed to shadow the faces of the pilgrims in our caravan. Dr. Contreras graciously offered to show us the psychotherapy wing in the basement of the clinic—the one with the white-noise rooms. But we all declined, too depressed, too hungry. For the cancer patients it was not so much what Contreras had said in his office, it was the long walk to and from that office—the corridors lined with gleaming hospital machinery.

The Captain explained his feelings: "He seems like a fine fellow, this Contreras, but to me this was too much like a hospital. Nobody who's been in a cancer ward likes going back, even for a visit. It was different at that woman Mildred's establishment." He was still clutching the brown-bagged bottle of Hoxsey tonic Mildred had slipped him two clinics ago. "She had a humanistic touch," the Captain said.

STONE DRAGONS AND METABOLIC TECHNICIANS

We were late. It was past sunset and our last destination was a good 40 miles down the coast just north of Ensenada. That last destination would turn out to be, by far, the strangest and, for me, the most bewildering.

The new Ensenada road is an unlit, two-lane blacktop. Our caravan seemed to be the only travelers on the road after sunset. We could hear the ocean off to our right, but we couldn't see it. In the darkness Marilyn unfolded the weird history of the place we were heading for.

She said the clinic there now—a luxurious, state-of-the-art establish-ment—is not the first to occupy Plaza Santa Maria, the breathtaking cliff overlooking the Pacific. Several strange and questionable health practitioners had come and gone before the present people took over.

In fact, said Marilyn, the legend goes that the site originally served as sacrificial killing grounds for the Aztecs. "Supposedly," she said, "it's meant to be a healing place so it can overcome the karma of its past."

Unfortunately, this karmic realignment did not have an auspicious beginning. The first place built there was "a fabulous health resort," Marilyn told me. But it failed. "Part of the legend," said Marilyn, "is that the spirits that guard the place will make sure that anyone who tries to pull a shtick will fail."

And, in fact, said Marilyn, Plaza Santa Maria has seen a succession of failed healers and clinic promoters who went a little weird. One disappeared completely. Then there was another one who arrived with a reputation for medical brilliance and took over the clinic for his version of cancer therapy.

"He'd dazzle you with this aura he had and brilliant medical talk, and then he'd whisper to some people he was a reincarnation of God or Christ and tell others that he was sent here from another galaxy."

Marilyn thought there was merit to his therapy. "But I began hearing from people that he'd examine them and tell them that for, say, $7,000 he'd make them completely well; for $4,000 he'd get you better but not all the way, that sort of thing."

"What happened to him?" I asked Marilyn.

"Well, he disappeared. I think he may be practicing in Ohio now."

And the people there now?

"Kelley's people are down there now," Marilyn told me. Kelley's people are the newest mass movement in the cancer cure world, perhaps the wave of the future. Kelley's people claim they've treated no less than 15,000 people (although they say a fire in 1975 burned most of their records before that year).

Kelley's system—with its ultrasonic spectograph blood analysis, its computerized diagnostic gimmicks, its metabolic subgroup typing—is the most sophisticated new synthesis of unorthodox techniques around. Some say Kelley lifted a lot from Gerson and others. But Kelley's got his own "original shtick," as Marilyn described it.

It's a clever one. He believes all people can be classified as one of ten metabolic subtypes, which are sort of the astrological signs of personal biochemistry. Of course, you have to fill out Kelley's 3,000-question questionnaire and submit it to him or one of his franchise operators to feed into his computers before you can know your sign. Along with your sign, Kelley's computer analysis will tell you where you have undetected malignancies or are in a premalignant state and what vitamins and raw gland extracts a person of your sign need take to prevent or cure it.

"Halting malignant growth is relatively simple," Kelley declares. All you have to do is take the approximately $400-a-month worth of supplements the Kelley computer prescribes for you—and which Kelley's people will be happy to sell you.

Still, for all the coziness of this computer cancer cure-cum-vitamin franchise operation, Kelley's people have had some trouble finding a safe haven for their central headquarters. Dr. Kelley started out as an orthodontist first in Fort Worth and then in Grapevine, Texas, with a theory he claims cured his own cancer and which he synthesized into "an ecological approach to the successful treatment of malignancy." After he came up with his theory of metabolic subtypes and the computer capacity to market it, mounting controversy over his methods drove him to move his operation to Winthrop, Washington. He also tried to create a Nutritional Academy in Illinois (basically the Hamburger University for the counselor franchisees of the Kelley therapy) and still maintains an International Health Institute in Dallas.

But there were limits to what Kelley's people could do in the United States. An invitation from the proprietor of the Plaza Santa Maria General Hospital to set up a treatment center offered Kelley's people the chance to work with exotic substances, esoteric procedures not permitted above the border, gave them a chance to get out from behind the computer terminals and really get their hands on cancer patients. We were unaware at the time of our visit that Steve McQueen, on his own unorthodox pilgrimage, would become that very month one of those patients, that McQueen would become, for better or worse, once it became public, Kelley's Chad.

● ■ ●

By the time we pulled up to the high iron gates guarding the Plaza Santa Maria clinic it was nearly 10 P.M. and the sentry had to be stirred from a nap.

"Dr. Kelley here?" Marilyn called out.

"He leave today," the sentry said.

"What about Dr. McKee," Marilyn asked. "We called ahead; he's expecting us."

The sleepy sentry mumbled something that sounded like "2001."

"Cottage 2001," Marilyn said.

We started winding around a smooth graveled drive, and even in the darkness I could tell the place was huge. We passed what looked like a small stadium sunk in cliff rock and surmounted by some spooky stone statues. "That's supposedly the site of the Aztec rituals," Marilyn told me. Past their stony scrutiny we wound around through several beautifully landscaped and terraced levels of cottages. The lights were off inside them. From the sound of distant breakers below it seemed we passed near a cliff-side ocean overlook, then curved around and up to a cluster of cottages and parked by the only one with a light on inside.

We climbed out of the car, and I could make out the sound of voices and laughter inside. I could make out the number "2001" on the doorpost, and I could see shapes passing behind the curtains. A woman's face parted the curtains, peered out and withdrew. Marilyn mounted the porch and rapped on the door.

From behind the window a man's voice said, "We're all off duty for the night."

Marilyn was not one to be denied so easily.

"Is Dr. McKee in there? We spoke before. These people have come all the way from L.A."

There was a long pause. Finally a sleepy-eyed, slightly built figure emerged.

"I'm Dr. McKee. Please lower your voices. The patients . . . they're all asleep . . . it's too late. We all have to be up early for rounds."

"We came all the way," Marilyn repeated. "These people have been looking forward to seeing the Plaza. They've been to all the other clinics."

Dr. McKee—a licensed M.D. who would later be identified as the "metabolic technician" supervising Steve McQueen's treatment and who is referred to by Kelley's own people as "a genius" surpassing even the founder in his mastery of metabolic wizardry—gazed down at our motley crew with a certain amount of wariness. We'd clearly intruded on something. He was not pleased.

Marilyn started toward the door.

"Out there," he hissed angrily. "We'll do it out there. In the amphitheater. Wait outside."

He disappeared. Several other figures appeared, stalked angrily out the door, stamped down the porch steps and into the night.

At last the good Dr. McKee emerged again and led us off on a trek to the stone amphitheater. There was a chill in the air, and not all of it was coming from the Pacific breezes.

We seated ourselves on the stone steps beneath the stars and the fierce stares of the stone statues. Dr. McKee rubbed his eyes and then— as if he'd switched on some Kelley program computer terminal that works in his sleep—he began to rattle off what kinds of things they do to patients. It was the most astonishing agglomeration of unorthodox cancer cure techniques I'd ever heard. This place was the Alice's Restaurant of cancer clinics. You can get anything you want.

What a rap. McKee started off with some Kelley terminology about individuation of metabolic subtypes and temporal mandibular adjustments. Then he got down to the menu. In addition to the massive doses of raw gland supplements, "we're still in the process of gathering our immunostimulants, but we can offer three different kinds of laetrile, using applied kinesiology to decide which is best for the individual patient. Then we have DMSO, GH3 from Rumania, superoxide dismutase. We have three different strengths of mistletoe extract, we've got the Muriana vaccine from Japan, which is a variation of BCG immunotherapy. Then, of course, we've got a full program of EDTA chelation, if vascular treatment is indicated. Let's see, oh, yes, the oxidated catalysts of the Koch remedy. We have quite a bit of those.

"We also offer the virostats for viral-related diseases, lymphomas, some melanomas, also plasmaphoresis, electrophoresis. We use applied kinesiology to discover reactions, then back in the metabolic area we also have live cell therapy, which is guided by Dietmar Schildwaechter, who has experience applying live cell techniques to degenerative diseases and cancer as opposed to mere rejuvenation. We give all the cancer patients here an injection of live thymus cells and an injection of a mixture of reticuloendothelial cells. These are live fetal cells, deep-frozen

and shipped under the same conditions as sperm for artificial insemi-
nation. The reticuloendothelial mixture has thymus, Kupffer cells from
the liver, spleen, bone marrow, placenta and umbilical cord. . . ."

Dr. McKee paused to yawn, rub his eyes and shake himself awake.
"Then, of course, for crisis situations we have allopathic treatments
together with supportive biological treatments. For instance, if I'm giving penicillin, I'm also giving propolis and extra thymus, extra vitamin
C and replacing intestinal flora. After I finish, I give an appropriate
dose of homeopathic penicillin to clear the disturbance. . . . We use
castor oil packs to open up lymphatic drainage over, say, the axilla in
breast cancer or over the liver. We have acquired a magnatherm unit,
which is a radio frequency diathermy machine that functions as a form
of localized hyperthermia, can heat tissue to a depth of four inches front
and rear. Heating makes the tumor more sensitive to other modalities."

Pause. Yawn.

"Pain is a situation I'm interested in dealing with more holistically
down line"—Kelley people tend to use computer management jargon
like "down line." "I'd like Norm Shealy to come in and teach us all
the ins and outs of his dolorology program. At present we're using
some acupuncture techniques, some neurotherapy techniques, which
involve subjecting local anesthetics to dermal acupuncture, injecting
procaine in trigger areas. We also have a full program of massage
therapy, psychotherapeutic emotional release, and we do use surgery in
some situations."

"Is that all there is?" I was tempted to ask. Dr. McKee's presentation
is impressively slick and encyclopedic even in his sleep. And yet there
was something slightly horrifying about that rapid-fire roll call of unorthodox remedies. Was there anything they wouldn't try here?

I remember what one of the Life-Force leaders had said about "the
cosmic kick" for cancer patients: "When you have cancer you can do
anything." Could it be that there's an equivalent cosmic kick for the
unorthodox doctors at a place like this—when a patient has cancer you
can do anything to them. It's a notion that might also explain some of
the horrible and unsuccessful chemotherapy and radiation experiments
orthodox oncologists are doing to patients north of the border.

I asked Dr. McKee how much the clinic charged. "Eight thousand
dollars a month," he said. "The live cell treatment is an optional extra—

a full set of fresh live cells runs about $4,000 complete," although you can apparently order certain organ cells a la carte.

Finally, someone asked Dr. McKee what the daily schedule for the cancer patient is at this clinic. I listened in disbelief: "They get up at seven in the morning for a coffee enema, followed by a rectal enzyme implant, followed by breakfast, followed by their intravenous. While they're on I.V.s, I have group rounds with them, which are finished by eleven, when there's a patient education class. "Then at one they have lunch. In the afternoon there's chiropractic and splint-balancing classes, massage therapy, psychotherapy sessions, work with the metabolic technician on whatever's going on. At four o'clock most of them take another coffee enema followed by another rectal enzyme implant, dinner at six, after which we have two of the metabolic technicians play music three nights a week, plus a video thing we're developing. At 3:30 in the morning they get up and take another rectal enzyme implant, and they take oral enzymes at the same time.

"Then they're up at seven for a coffee enema. Cancer patients stay on this schedule for an average of a month. Of course, we handle all the other degenerative diseases, arthritis, arteriosclerosis, multiple sclerosis. . . ."

MIDNIGHT AT THE BORDER: MARILYN'S DREAM

It was close to midnight when we left the stone dragons and the metabolic technicians in peace and started north for the border. I decided to leave it up to the Aztec gods to decide what the Kelley people were doing for the karma of the place, whether they were "pulling a shtick" as Marilyn had put it. My brain felt like it had had an enzyme implant from all the cancer cure theories it had been stuffed with in the past four days. There was one more clinic we'd been scheduled to see, a newly established rival laetrile/metabolic clinic in Tijuana. When we passed through the sleepy town at 1 A.M. the indefatigable Marilyn offered to get out and wake up everyone at that clinic and take us around, but we declined in favor of a fast border crossing.

It was a tense one, too. Not for me. I was at the wheel and merely sleepy. But for the two cancer patients in the backseat it was a matter of life and death. There had been another complicated seat switch in the caravan. Marilyn's food chests had been transferred to her trunk for the ride back so the Captain and Renee could sit in the back. As we approached the customs booth they tried to stash their brown paper sacks containing the Hoxsey elixir bottles in some inconspicuous place amidst the empty fruit and sandwich bags.

Marilyn cautioned us that it would be a mistake to volunteer to the customs inspector that we'd been to the cancer clinics. Every time she'd done that they'd taken her out of her car, given her and the vehicle a long and thorough search.

This kind of harassment arouses Marilyn's outrage—and her organizing instinct. She has an "I have a dream" vision of an all-out cancer patient revolt against the medical orthodoxy that drives them below the border in search of the hope it cannot offer. Marilyn thinks that cancer patients are restive, ready to coalesce into a civil rights—or terminal rights—movement, ripe for open revolt.

"My dream is," she told me, "if each cancer patient in the world would go down to Mexico to get the medicine of his choice, then come to the border and hold up for them to see whatever it was he thought was curing him of his cancer, whether it was Hoxsey or laetrile or whatever. Held it up in full view of everyone and said, 'You may shoot me if you like, but you're not going to take this away from me.' What does any one of them have to lose? If they'd only wake up to the knowledge that they are invulnerable."

"Invulnerable?" I asked.

"Yes!" she said. "Of course. They have nothing to lose. They'll come to the border and say, 'If you want to take this medicine from me, you're going to have to shoot me first. Your doctors say I'm going to die anyway, so go ahead and try to stop me.' "

Marilyn's extraordinary vision reminded me of a conversation I had once with a radical lawyer who was close to the Weather Underground. He recalled that back in the days before they went under, one particularly fanatic Weatherperson was constantly urging his collective to start recruiting terminal cancer patients to the fight against the beast. "They'd make the perfect guerrilla warriors," he'd argue. "They'll do anything, take any risk; they have nothing to lose."

"They're waking up now," Marilyn said. "Once they do, once they make that basic commitment to fight for their lives, once they realize that if they gave the disease to themselves they can take it away from themselves—it matters not what kind of therapy they try, they've got a chance to make it."

Our border crossing turned out to be anticlimactic and uneventful. The customs man waved us through. However alien I felt by that time, we didn't look like illegal aliens. The Captain and Renee sighed and reached down below their seats to reclaim the precious tonic bottles they'd stuffed down there. On the long drive back up to Laguna Hills, Marilyn fell asleep in the front seat, I struggled to stay awake behind the wheel, while in the back the Captain and Renee were pumped up by their successful Mexican mission. Clutching their tonics, they chattered away comparing notes on possible next moves.

●   ■   ●

I have set this particular down so fully, because I know not but it may be of moment to those who come after me, if they come to be brought to the same distress, and to the same manner of making their choice . . .

—DEFOE

If, as Marilyn says, it's the decision to fight one's cancer, not the theory one fights it with, that is decisive, one still has to choose some theory; one can't be what Marilyn calls a "shopper" forever. And so, after my marathon immersion in the cancer cure subculture, what's this shopper's favorite theory?

The theory that intrigues me most is less a cancer cure theory than a theory about the theories themselves, a megatheory about the phenomenon of unorthodox cancer cures. Something has to explain the anecdotal evidence, the dozens of people at the convention who told me face-to-face the stories of their cures—often by therapies with completely contradictory explanations of the disease. Something has to explain the stories told by the people on the Cancer Control Society's *White Sheet*, a list of scores of people who had all different kinds of cancer and who claim to have been treated with all different kinds of unorthodox therapies. Get the *White Sheet* yourself and call these people up (they've given the CCS permission to publish their phone numbers and invite people to call). You figure it out.

The only way I can figure the phenomenon out, my megatheory, might be called the Modified False Hope Cure Theory. I picked it up from the American Cancer Society while reading their *Unproven Methods of Cancer Management* pamphlet. I couldn't get over their outright concession that some quacks get "what seem to be good results." Sure, the American Cancer Society goes on to say these good results "are often based entirely on the subjective response of the patient, which may result from the false hope instilled in him" by self-deluded cancer cure prophets.

Well, so what? Does it matter how you're cured if you do get better? I'm willing to be gulled out of a malignancy by unorthodox healers if that's what it takes to get rid of it when orthodox medicine gives up hope. Problem is, we run into a Catch-22 situation here. False hope cures only work if you believe they're true cures. You can't say to yourself, "I'm going to set out to fool myself into being cured." You have to *be* fooled. But now that I know that, and now that I've told you, have I ruined it for us all? Can we ever again hope to be innocent beneficiaries of a false hope cure?

Fortunately, from the evidence of the cancer cure subculture, from the evidence of my journey into the Tijuana clinic scene, it seems clear that false hope springs eternal.

As long as orthodox medicine continues to fail with its fearsome and destructive therapies, there's a role for the deluded dreamers, the biomystic visionaries, the masked microbe detectors, apricot pit alchemists, mind cure mesmerists—all who keep supplying us with theory after elaborate theory about the elusive malignant plague. Somehow the periodic transfusions of false hope the cancer cure cults supply us with serve a purpose. Some of us may need a Tijuana of the mind, a place we can retreat to, to smuggle back some illicit hope when our own world doesn't offer much, a fertile poetics of faith and fraud to fool ourselves into fighting for our lives.

—*NEW WEST*
November 1980

THE LAST SECRETS OF SKULL AND BONES

Take a look at that hulking sepulcher over there. Small wonder they call it a tomb. It's the citadel of Skull and Bones, the most powerful of all secret societies in the strange Yale secret-society system. For nearly a century and a half, Skull and Bones has been the most influential secret society in the nation, and now it is one of the last.

In an age in which it seems that all that could possibly be concealed about anything and anybody has been revealed, those blank tombstone walls could be holding the last secrets left in America.

You could ask Averell Harriman whether there's really a sarcophagus in the basement and whether he and young Henry Stimson and young Henry Luce lay down naked in that coffin and spilled the secrets of their adolescent sex life to fourteen fellow Bonesmen. You could ask Supreme Court Justice Potter Stewart if there came a time in the year 1937 when he dressed up in a skeleton suit and howled wildly at an initiate in a red-velvet room inside the tomb. You could ask McGeorge Bundy if he wrestled naked in a mud pile as part of his initiation and how it compared with a later quagmire into which he so eagerly plunged.

You could ask Bill Bundy or Bill Buckley, both of whom went into the C.I.A. after leaving Bones—or George Bush, who *ran* the C.I.A.— whether their Skull and Bones experience was useful training for the clandestine trade. ("Spook," the Yale slang word for secret-society member, is, of course, Agency slang for spy.) You could ask J. Richardson Dilworth, the Bonesman who now manages the Rockefeller fortune, just how wealthy the Bones society is and whether it's true that each new initiate gets a no-strings gift of fifteen thousand dollars cash and guaranteed financial security for life.

You could ask . . . but I think you get the idea. The leading lights of the Eastern establishment—in old-line investment banks (Brown Brothers Harriman pays Bones's tax bill), in blue-blood law firms (Simpson, Thacher & Bartlett, for one), and particularly in the highest councils of the foreign-policy establishment—the people who have shaped America's national character since it ceased being an undergraduate power, had *their* undergraduate character shaped in that crypt over there. Bonesman Henry Stimson, Secretary of War under F.D.R., a man at the heart of the heart of the American ruling class, called his experience in the tomb the most profound one in his entire education.

But none of them will tell you a thing about it. They've sworn an oath never to reveal what goes on inside and they're legendary for the lengths to which they'll go to avoid prying interrogation. The mere mention of the words "skull and bones" in the presence of a true-blue Bonesman, such as Blackford Oakes, the fictional hero of Bill Buckley's spy thriller, *Saving the Queen*, will cause him to "dutifully leave the room, as tradition prescribed."

I can trace my personal fascination with the mysterious goings-on in the sepulcher across the street to a spooky scene I witnessed on its shadowy steps late one April night eleven years ago. I was then a sophomore at Yale, living in Jonathan Edwards, the residential college (anglophile Yale name for dorm) built next to the Bones tomb. It was part of Jonathan Edwards' folklore that on the April evening following "tap night" at Bones, if one could climb to the tower of Weir Hall, the odd castle that overlooks the Bones courtyard, one could hear strange cries and moans coming from the bowels of the tomb as the fifteen newly "tapped" members were put through what sounded like a harrowing ordeal. Returning alone to my room late at night, I would always cross the street rather than walk the sidewalk that passed right in front of Bones. Even at that safe distance, something about it made my skin crawl.

But that night in April I wasn't alone; a classmate and I were coming back from an all-night diner at about two in the morning. At the time, I knew little about the mysteries of Bones or any of the other huge windowless secret-society tombs that dominated with dark authority certain key corners of the campus. They were nothing like conventional fraternities. No one lived in the tombs. Instead, every Thursday and Sunday night, the best and the brightest on campus, the fifteen seniors in Skull and Bones and in Scroll and Key, Book and Snake, Wolf's Head, Berzelius, in all the seven secret societies, disappeared into their respective tombs and spent hours doing *something*—something they were sworn to secrecy about. And Bones, it was said, was the most ritualistic and secretive of all. Even the very door to the Bones tomb, that huge triple-padlocked iron door, was never permitted to open in the presence of an outsider.

All this was floating through my impressionable sophomore mind that night as my friend Mike and I approached the stone pylons guarding the entrance to Bones. Suddenly we froze at the sight of a strange thing lying on the steps. There in the gloom of the doorway on the top step was a long white object that looked like the thighbone of a large mammal. I remained frozen. Mike was more venturesome: he walked right up the steps and picked up the bone. I wanted to get out of there fast; I was certain we were being spied upon from a concealed window. Mike couldn't decide what to do with the bone. He went up to the door and began examining the array of padlocks. Suddenly a bolt shot. The massive door began to swing open and something reached out at him from within. He gasped, terrified, and jumped back, but not before something clutched the bone, yanked it out of his hand and back into the darkness within. The door slammed shut with a clang that rang in our ears as we ran away.

Recollected in tranquillity, that dreamlike gothic moment seems to me an emblem of the strangeness I felt at being at Yale, at being given a brief glimpse of the mysterious workings of the inner temples of privilege but feeling emphatically shut out of the secret ceremonies within. I always felt irrelevant to the real purpose of the institution, which was from its missionary beginnings devoted to converting the idle progeny of the ruling class into morally serious leaders of the establishment. It is frequently in the tombs that the conversions take place.

NOVEMBER, 1976: SECURITY MEASURES

It's night and we're back in front of the tomb, Mike and I, reinforced by nine years in the outside world, two skeptical women friends and a big dinner at Mory's. And yet once again there is an odd, chilling encounter. We're re-creating that first spooky moment. I'm standing in front of the stone pylons and Mike has walked up to stand against the door so we can estimate its height by his. Then we notice we're being watched. A small red foreign car has pulled up on the sidewalk a few yards away from us. The driver has been sitting with the engine running and has been watching us for some time. Then he gets out. He's a tall, athletic-looking guy, fairly young. He shuts the car door behind him and stands leaning against it, continuing to observe us. We try to act oblivious, continuing to sketch and measure.

The guy finally walks over to us. "You seen Miles?" he asks.

We look at each other. Could he think we're actually Bones alumni, or is he testing us? Could "You seen Miles?" be some sort of password?

"No," we reply. "Haven't seen Miles."

He nods and remains there. We decide we've done enough sketching and measuring and stroll off.

"Look!" one of the women says as she turns and points back. "He just ran down the side steps to check the basement-door locks. He probably thought he caught us planning a break-in."

I found the episode intriguing. What it said to me was that Bones still cared about the security of its secrets. Trying to find out what goes on inside could be a challenge.

And so it was that I set out this April to see just how secure those last secrets are. It was a task I took on not out of malice or sour grapes. I was not tapped for a secret society so I'm open to the latter charge, but I plead guilty only to the voyeurism of a mystery lover. I'd been working on a novel, a psychological thriller of sorts that involved the rites of Bones, and I thought it wouldn't hurt to spend some time in New Haven during the week of tap night and initiation night, poking around and asking questions.

You could call it espionage if you were so inclined, but I tried to play the game in a gentlemanly fashion: I would not directly ask a Bonesman to violate his sacred oath of secrecy. If, however, one of them happened to have fudged on the oath to some other party and that other party were to convey the gist of the information to me, I would rule it fair game. And if any Bonesman wants to step forward and add something, I'll be happy to listen.

What follows is an account of my search for the meaning behind the mysterious Bones rituals. Only information that might be too easily traced to its source has been left out, because certain sources expressed fear of reprisals against themselves. Yes, reprisals. One of them even insisted, with what seemed like deadly seriousness, that reprisals would be taken against me.

"What bank do you have your checking account at?" this party asked me in the middle of a discussion of the Mithraic aspects of the Bones ritual.

I named the bank.

"Aha," said the party. "There are three Bonesmen on the board. You'll never have a line of credit again. They'll tap your phone. They'll . . ."

Before I could say, "A line of *what?*" the source continued: "The alumni still care. Don't laugh. They don't like people tampering and prying. The power of Bones is incredible. They've got their hands on every lever of power in the country. You'll see—it's like trying to look into the Mafia. Remember, they're a secret society, too."

WEDNESDAY NIGHT, APRIL 14: THE DOSSIER

Already I have in my possession a set of annotated floor plans of the interior of the tomb, giving the location of the sanctum sanctorum, the room called 322. And tonight I received a dossier on Bones ritual secrets that was compiled from the archives of another secret society. (It seems that one abiding preoccupation of many Yale secret societies is keeping files on the secrets of other secret societies, particularly Bones.)

This dossier on Bones is a particularly sophisticated one, featuring "reliability ratings" in percentiles for each chunk of information. It was obtained for me by an enterprising researcher on the condition that I keep secret the name of the secret society that supplied it. Okay. I will say, though, that it's not the secret society that is rumored to have Hitler's silverware in its archives. That's Scroll and Key, chief rival of Bones for the elite of Yale—Dean Acheson and Cy Vance's society—and the source of most of the rest of the American foreign-policy establishment.

But to return to the dossier. Let me tell you what it says about the initiation, the center of some of the most lurid apocryphal rumors about Bones. According to the dossier, the Bones initiation ritual of 1940 went like this: "New man placed in coffin—carried into central part of building. New man chanted over and 'reborn' into society. Removed from coffin and given robes with symbols on it [sic]. A bone with his name on it is tossed into bone heap at start of every meeting. Initiates plunged naked into mud pile."

THURSDAY EVENING: THE FILE AND CLAW SOLUTION TO THE MYSTERY OF 322

I'm standing in the shadows across the street from the tomb, ready to tail the first person to come out. Tonight is tap night, the night fifteen juniors will be chosen to receive the one-hundred-forty-five-year-old secrets of Bones. Tonight the fifteen seniors in Bones and the fifteen in each of the other societies will arrive outside the rooms of the prospective tappees. They'll pound loudly on the doors. When the chosen junior opens up, a Bonesman will slam him on the shoulder and thunder: "Skull and Bones: Do you accept?"

At that point, according to my dossier, if the candidate accepts, he will be handed a message wrapped with a black ribbon sealed in black wax with the skull-and-crossbones emblem and the mystic Bones number, 322. The message appoints a time and a place for the candidate to appear on initiation night—next Tuesday—the first time the newly tapped candidate will be permitted inside the tomb. Candidates are "instructed to wear no metal" to the initiation, the dossier notes ominously. (Reliability rating for this stated to be one hundred percent.)

Not long before eight tonight, the door to Bones swings open. Two dark-suited young men emerge. One of them carries a slim black attaché case. Obviously they're on their way to tap someone. I decide to follow them. I want to check out a story I heard that Bones initiates are taken to a ceremony somewhere near the campus before the big initiation inside the tomb. The Bonesmen head up High Street and pass the library, then make a right.

Passing the library, I can't help but recoil when I think of the embarrassing discovery I made in the manuscript room this afternoon. The last thing I wanted to do was reduce the subtleties of the social function of Bones to some simpleminded conspiracy theory. And yet I do seem to have come across definite, if skeletal, links between the origins of Bones rituals and those of the notorious Bavarian Illuminists. For me, an interested but skeptical student of the conspiracy world, the introduction of the Illuminists, or Illuminati, into certain discussions (say, for instance, of events in Dallas in 1963) has become the same thing that the mention of Bones is to a Bonesman—a signal to leave the room. Because although the Bavarian Illuminists did have a real historical existence (from 1776 to 1785 they were an esoteric secret society within the more mystical freethinking lodges of German Freemasonry), they have also had a paranoid fantasy existence throughout two centuries of conspiracy literature. They are *the* imagined megacabal that manipulated such alleged plots as the French and Russian revolutions, the elders of Zion, the rise of Hitler and the house of Morgan. Yes, the Bilderbergers and George De Mohrenschildt, too. Silly as it may sound, there are suggestive links between the historical, if not mytho-conspiratorial, Illuminists and Bones.

First consider the account of the origins of Bones to be found in a century-old pamphlet published by an anonymous group that called itself File and Claw after the tools they used to pry their way inside Bones late one night. I came upon the File and Claw break-in pamphlet in a box of disintegrating documents filed in the library's manuscript room under Skull and Bones's corporate name, Russell Trust Association. The foundation was named for William H. (later General) Russell, the man who founded Bones in 1832. I was trying to figure out what mission Russell had for the secret order he founded and why he had chosen that particular death's-head brand of mumbo jumbo to embody his vision. Well, according to the File and Claw break-in crew, "Bones is a chapter of a corps of a German university. It should properly be called the Skull and Bones chapter. General Russell, its founder, was in Germany before his senior year and formed a warm friendship with a leading member of a German society. The meaning of the permanent number '322' in all Bones literature is that it was founded in '32 as the second chapter of the German society. But the Bonesman has a pleasing fiction that his fraternity is a descendant of an old Greek patriot society founded by Demosthenes, who died in 322 B.C."

They go on to describe a German slogan painted "on the arched walls above the vault" of the sacred room, 322. The slogan appears above a painting of skulls surrounded by Masonic symbols, a picture said to be "a gift of the German chapter." "*Wer war der Thor, wer Weiser, Bettler oder Kaiser? Ob Arm, ob Reich, im Tode gleich*," the slogan reads, or, "Who was the fool, who the wise man, beggar or king? Whether poor or rich, all's the same in death."

Imagine my surprise when I ran into that very slogan in a 1798 Scottish anti-Illuminist tract reprinted in 1967 by the John Birch Society. The tract (*Proofs of a Conspiracy* by John Robison) prints alleged excerpts from Illuminist ritual manuals supposedly confiscated by the Bavarian police when the secret order was banned in 1785. Toward the end of the ceremony of initiation into the "Regent degree" of Illuminism, according to the tract, "a skeleton is pointed out to him [the initiate], at the feet of which are laid a crown and a sword. He is asked *whether that is the skeleton of a king, nobleman or a beggar*. As he cannot decide, the president of the meeting says to him, 'The character of being a man is the only one that is of importance' " (my italics).

Doesn't that sound similar to the German slogan the File and Claw team claims to have found inside Bones? Now consider a haunting photograph of the altar room of one of the Masonic lodges at Nuremberg that is closely associated with Illuminism. Haunting because at the altar room's center, approached through an aisle of hanging human skeletons, is a coffin surmounted by—you guessed it—a skull and crossed bones that look exactly like the particular arrangement of jawbones and thigh-bones in the official Bones emblem. The skull and crossbones was the official crest of another key Illuminist lodge, one right-wing Illuminist theoretician told me.

Now you can look at this three ways. One possibility is that the Bircher right—and the conspiracy-minded left—are correct: the Eastern establishment is the demonic creation of a clandestine elite manipulating history, and Skull and Bones is one of its recruiting centers. A more plausible explanation is that the death's-head symbolism was so prevalent in Germany when the impressionable young Russell visited that he just stumbled on the same mother lode of pseudo-Masonic mummery as the Illuminists. The third possibility is that the break-in pamphlets are an elaborate fraud designed by the File and Claw crew to pin the taint of Illuminism on Bones and that the rituals of Bones have innocent Athenian themes, 322 being *only* the date of the death of Demosthenes. (In fact, some Bones literature I've seen in the archives does express the year as if 322 B.C. were the year one, making 1977 anno Demostheni 2299.)

●   ■   ●

I am still following the dark-suited Bonesmen at a discreet distance as they make their way along Prospect Street and into a narrow alley, which, to my dismay, turns into a parking lot. They get into a car and drive off, obviously to tap an off-campus prospect. So much for tonight's clandestine work. I'd never get to my car in time to follow them. My heart isn't in it, anyway. I am due to head off to the graveyard to watch the initiation ceremony of Book and Snake, the secret society of Deep Throat's friend Bob Woodward (several Deep Throat theories have postulated Yale secret-society ties as the origin of Woodward's underground-garage connection, and two Bonesmen, Ray Price and Richard Moore, who were high Nixon aides, have been mentioned as suspects—perhaps because of their experience at clandestine underground truth telling). And later tonight I hope to make the first of my contacts with persons who have been inside—not just inside the tomb, but inside the skulls of some of the Bonesmen.

LATER THURSDAY NIGHT: TURNING THE TABLES ON THE SEXUAL AUTOBIOGRAPHIES

In his senior year, each member of Bones goes through an intense two-part confessional experience in the Bones crypt. One Thursday night, he tells his life story, giving what is meant to be a painfully forthright autobiography that exposes his traumas, shames and dreams. (Tom Wolfe calls this Bones practice a forerunner of The Me Decade's fascination with self.) The following Sunday-night session is devoted exclusively to sexual histories. They don't leave out anything these days. I don't know what it was like in General Russell's day, maybe there was less to talk about, but these days the sexual stuff is totally explicit and there's less need for fabricating exploits to fill up the allotted time. Most Sunday-night sessions start with talk of prep-school masturbation and don't stop until the intimate details of Saturday night's delights have come to light early Monday morning.

This has begun to cause some disruptions in relationships. The women the Bonesmen talk about in the crypt are often Yale co-eds and frequently feminists. None of these women is too pleased at having the most intimate secrets of her relationship made the subject of an all-night symposium consecrating her lover's brotherhood with fourteen males she hardly knows. As one woman put it, "I objected to fourteen guys knowing whether I was a good lay. . . . It was like after that each of them thought I was his woman in some way."

Some women have discovered that their lovers take their vows to Bones more solemnly than their commitments to women. There is the case of the woman who revealed something very personal—not embarrassing, just private—to her lover and made him swear never to repeat it to another human. When he came back from the Bones crypt after his Sunday-night sex session, he couldn't meet her eyes. He'd told his brothers in Bones.

It seems that the whole secret-society system at Yale is in the terminal stages of a sexual crisis. By the time I arrived this April, all but three of the formerly all-male societies had gone co-ed, and two of the remaining holdouts—Scroll and Key and Wolf's Head—were embroiled in bitter battles over certain members' attempts to have them follow the trend. The popular quarterback of the football team had resigned from Scroll and Key because its alumni would not even let him make a pro-coeducation plea to their convocation. When one prominent alumnus of Wolf's Head was told the current members had plans to tap women, he threatened to "raze the building" before permitting it. Nevertheless, it seemed as though it wouldn't be long before those two holdouts went co-ed. But not Bones. Both alumni and outsiders see the essence of the Bones experience as some kind of male bonding, a Victorian, muscular, Christian-missionary view of manliness and public service.

While changing the least of all the societies over its one hundred forty-five years, Bones did begin admitting Jews in the early Fifties and tapping blacks in 1949. It offered membership to some of the most outspoken rebels of the late Sixties and, more recently, added gay and bisexual members, including the president of the militant Gay Activist Alliance, a man by the name of Miles.

But women, the Bones alumni have strenuously insisted, are different. When a rambunctious Seventies class of Bones proposed tapping the best and brightest of the new Yale women, the officers of the Russell Trust Association threatened to bar that class from the tomb and change the locks if they dared. They didn't.

That sort of thing is what persuaded the person I am meeting with late tonight—and a number of other persons—to talk about what goes on inside: after all, isn't the core of the Bones group experience the betrayal of their loved ones' secrets? Measure for measure.

TUESDAY, APRIL 20: INITIATION NIGHT— TALES OF THE TOMB AND DEER ISLAND

When I return to New Haven on initiation night to stand again in the shadows across the street from Bones in the hope of glimpsing an initiate enter, it is, thanks to my sources (who insist on anonymity), with a greater sense of just what it means for the initiate to be swallowed up by the tomb for the first time.

The first initiate arrives shortly before eight p.m., proceeds up the steps and halts at attention in front of the great door. I don't see him ring a bell; I don't think he has to. They are expecting him. The doors open. I can't make out who or what is inside, but the initiate's reaction is unmistakable: he puts his hands up as if a gun has been pointed at him. He walks into the gloom and the door closes behind him.

Earlier, according to my source, before the initiate was allowed to approach that door, he was led blindfolded to a Bones house somewhere on Orange Street and conducted to the basement. There two older Bonesmen dressed in skeleton suits had him swear solemn oaths to keep secret whatever he was to experience in the tomb during the initiation rite and forever after.

Now I am trying to piece together what I know about what is happening to that initiate tonight and, more generally, how his life will change now that he has been admitted inside. Tonight he will die to the world and be born again into the Order, as he will thenceforth refer to it. The Order is a world unto itself in which he will have a new name and fourteen new blood brothers, also with new names.

The "death" of the initiate will be as frightful as the liberal use of human skeletons and ritual psychology can make it. Whether it's accompanied by physical beatings or wrestling or a plunge into a mud or dung pile I have not been able to verify, but I'd give a marginally higher reliability rating to the mud-pile plunge. Then it's into the coffin and off on a symbolic journey through the underworld to rebirth, which takes place in room number 322. There the Order clothes the newborn knight in its own special garments, implying that henceforth he will tailor himself to the Order's mission.

Which is—if you take it at face value—to produce an alliance of good men. The Latin for "good men" is "*boni*," of course, and each piece of Bones literature sports a Latin maxim making use of "*boni*." "Good men are rare," is the way one maxim translates. "Of all societies none is more glorious nor of greater strength than when good men of similar morals are joined in intimacy," proclaims another.

The intimacy doesn't really begin to get going until the autobiographical sessions start in September. But first there are some tangible rewards. In the months that follow tonight's initiation, the born-again Bonesmen will begin to experience the wonderful felicity of the Protestant ethic: secular rewards just happen to accrue to the elect as external tokens of their inner blessedness.

Fifteen thousand dollars, for instance. According to one source, each initiate gets a no-strings, tax-free gift of fifteen thousand dollars from the Russell Trust Association just for having been selected by Bones. I'd heard rumors that Bonesmen were guaranteed a secure income for life in some way—if only to prevent a downtrodden alcoholic brother from selling the secrets for a few bucks. When I put this question to my source, the reply was that of course the society would always help a downtrodden member with interest-free loans, if necessary, but, he added, the only outright contribution was a flat fifteen-thousand-dollar payment.

When I mentioned the fifteen-thousand-dollar figure to writer Tom Powers, a member of a secret society called Elihu, he, like members of

other secret societies, professed incredulity. But the day after I spoke
to him I received this interesting communication from Powers:

"I have checked with a Bones penetration and am now inclined to
think you have got the goods where the fifteen thousand dollars is
concerned. A sort of passive or negative confirmation. I put the question
to him and he declined to comment in a tone of voice that might have
been, but was not, derisory. Given an ideal opportunity to say, 'That's
bullshit!' he did not.

"The interesting question now is what effect the fifteen-thousand-
dollar report is going to have on next tap day. The whole Bones mystique
will take on a mercenary air, sort of like a television game show. If
there is no fifteen thousand, the next lineup of tappees will be plenty
pissed. I can hear the conversations now: outgoing Bones members
telling prospects there is one thing they've got to understand, really and
truly—*there is no fifteen thousand!!!* While the prospects will be winking
and nudging and saying, 'I understand. Ha-ha! You've got to say that,
but just between us. . . .'

"If Bones has got a cell in C.I.A.," Powers concluded his letter, "you
could be in big trouble."

Ah, yes. The Bones cell in the Central Intelligence Agency. Powers
had called my attention to a passage in Aaron Latham's new novel,
Orchids for Mother, in which the thinly veiled version of C.I.A. master
spy James Angleton recalls that the Agency is "Langley's New Haven
all over again. . . . Secret society'd be closer, like Skull and Bones."

"There are a lot of Bonesmen around, aren't there?" asks a young
C.I.A. recruit.

Indeed, says the master spy, with all the Bones spooks it's "a regular
haunted house."

If you were a supersecret spy agency seeking to recruit the most
trustworthy and able men for dangerous missionary work against the
barbarian threat wouldn't you want someone whose life story, character
and secrets were already known to you? You'd certainly want to know
if there were any sexual proclivities that might make the future spy
open to temptation or blackmail.

Now, I'm not saying the C.I.A. has bugged the Bones crypt (although
who could rule it out with certainty?). But couldn't the Agency use old
Bonesmen to recruit new ones, or might they not have a trusted de-

scendant of a Bonesman—just one in each fifteen would be enough—
advise them on the suitability of the other fourteen for initiation into
postgraduate secrets?

Consider the case of once gung-ho-C.I.A. Bonesman William Sloane
Coffin, who later became a leader of the antiwar movement. A descendant of an aptly named family with three generations of Bonesmen,
Coffin headed for the C.I.A. not long after graduation from Bones. And
the man Coffin tapped for Bones, William F. Buckley Jr., was himself
tapped by the C.I.A. the following year.

When I tried to reach Coffin to ask him about C.I.A. recruiting in
Bones, I was told that he was "in seclusion," writing his memoirs.
(Okay, Chaplain, but I want to let you know that I'll be looking in
your memoirs to see just how much you tell about the secrets of Bones
and the C.I.A., how loyal you still are to their secrets. Which side are
you on?)

●   ■   ●

In the late summer following his initiation, right before he begins
his senior year, the initiate is given a gift of greater value than any
putative fifteen-thousand-dollar recruitment fee: his first visit to the
private resort island owned and maintained by the Russell Trust Association in the St. Lawrence River. There, hidden among the Thousand
Islands, the reborn initiate truly finds himself on an isle of the blessed.
For there, on this place called Deer Island, are assembled the active
Bones alumni and their families, and there he gets a sense of how many
powerful establishment institutions are run by wonderful, civilized,
silver-haired Bonesmen eager to help the initiate's establishment dreams
come true. He can also meet the wives of Bonesmen of all ages and get
a sense of what kind of woman is most acceptable and appropriate in
Bones society and perhaps even meet that most acceptable of all types
of women—the daughter of a Bonesman.

A reading of the lists of Bonesmen selected over the past one hundred
forty-five years suggests that like the secret society of another ethnic
group, certain powerful families dominate: the Tafts, the Whitneys, the
Thachers, the Lords, for instance. You also get the feeling there's a lot
of intermarriage among these Bones families. Year after year there will
be a Whitney Townsend Phelps in the same Bones class as a Phelps

Townsend Whitney. It's only natural, considering the way they grow up together with Bones picnics, Bones outings and a whole quiet panoply of Bones social events outside the campus and the tomb. Particularly on the island.

Of course, if the initiate has grown up in a Bones family and gone to picnics on the island all his life, the vision—the introduction to powerful people, the fine manners, the strong bonds—is less awesome. But to the nonhereditary slots in a Bones class of fifteen, the outsiders—frequently the football captain, the editor of the *Yale Daily News*, a brilliant scholar, a charismatic student politician—the island experience comes as a seductive revelation: these powerful people want me, want my talents, my services; perhaps they even want my genes. Play along with their rules and I can become one of them. They *want* me to become one of them.

In fact, one could make a half-serious case that functionally Bones serves as a kind of ongoing informal establishment eugenics project bringing vigorous new genes into the bloodlines of the Stimsonian elite. Perhaps that explains the origin of the sexual autobiography. It may have served some eugenic purpose in General Russell's vision: a sharing of birth-control and self-control methods to minimize the chance of a good man and future steward of the ruling class being trapped into marriage by a fortune hunter or a working-class girl—the way the grand tour for an upper-class American youth always included an initiation into the secrets of Parisian courtesans so that once back home the young man wouldn't elope with the first girl who let him get past second base.

However, certain of the more provincial Bones families do not welcome *all* genes into the pool. There is a story about two very well-known members of a Bones class who haven't spoken to each other for more than two decades. One of them was an early Jewish token member of Bones who began to date the sister of a fellow Bonesman. Apparently the Christian family made its frosty reaction to this development very plain. The Christian Bonesman did not convince his Jewish blood brother he was entirely on his side in the matter. The dating stopped and so did the speaking. It's an isolated incident, and I wouldn't have brought it up had I not been told of the "Jew-canoe" incident, which happened relatively recently.

There's a big book located just inside the main entrance to Bones.

In it are some of the real secrets. Not the initiation rites or the grip, but reactions to, comments on and mementos of certain things that went on in the tomb, personal revelations, interpersonal encounters. The good stuff. I don't know if the tale of the brokenhearted token gay and the rotting-paella story are in there, but they should be. I'm almost sure the mysterious "Phil" incident *isn't* there. (According to one source, the very mention of the name "Phil" is enough to drive certain Bonesmen up the wall.) But the unfortunate "Jew-canoe" incident *is* in that book.

It seems that not too long ago the boys in a recent Bones class were sitting around the tomb making some wisecracks that involved Jewish stereotypes. "He drives a Cadillac—you know, the Jew canoe." Things like that. Well, one Jewish token member that year happened to be present, but his blood brothers apparently didn't think he'd mind—it being only in fun and all that. Then it got more intense, as it can in groups when a wound is suddenly opened in one of their number. The Jewish member stalked out of the tomb, tears in his eyes, feeling betrayed by his brothers and thinking of resigning forthwith. But he didn't. He went back and inscribed a protest in the big book, at which time his brothers, suitably repentant, persuaded him not to abandon the tomb.

Outsiders often do have trouble with the Bones style of intimacy. There was, for instance, the story of one of the several token bisexuals and gays that Bones has tapped in recent years. He has the misfortune to develop, during the long Thursday and Sunday nights of shared intimacy, a deep affection for a member of his fifteen-man coven who declared himself irrevocably heterosexual. The intimacy of the tomb experience became heartbreaking and frustrating for the gay member. When the year came to a close and it came time to pick the next group of fifteen from among the junior class, he announced that he was not going to tap another token gay and recommended against gay membership because he felt the experience was too intense to keep from becoming sexual.

There's a kind of backhanded tribute to something genuine there. The Bones experience can be intense enough to work real transformations. Idle, preppie Prince Hals suddenly become serious students of society and themselves, as if acceptance into the tomb were a signal to leave the tavern and prepare to rule the land. Those embarrassed at introspection and afraid of trusting other men are given the mandate and the confidence to do so.

"Why," said one source, "do old men—seventy and over—travel thousands of miles for Bones reunions? Why do they sing the songs with such gusto? Where else can you hear Archibald MacLeish take on Henry Luce in a soul-versus-capital debate with no holds barred? Bones survives because the old men who are successful need to convince themselves that not luck or wealth put them where they are, but raw talent, and a talent that was recognized in their youth. Bones, because of its elitism, connects their past to their present. It is more sustaining, for some, than marriage."

Certainly the leaders that Bones has turned out are among the more humane and civilized of the old Yankee establishment. In addition to cold warriors, Viet warriors and spies, there are as many or more missionaries, surgeons, writers (John Hersey, Archibald MacLeish) and great teachers (William Graham Sumner, F.O. Matthiessen) as there are investment bankers. There is, in the past of Bones, at least, a genuine missionary zeal for moral, and not merely surplus, value.

●   ■   ●

It's now a century since the break-in pamphlet of the File and Claw crew announced "the decline and fall of Skull and Bones," so it would be premature for me to announce the imminence of such an event, but almost everyone I spoke to at Yale thought that Bones was in headlong decline. There have been unprecedented resignations. There have been an increasing number of rejections—people Bones wants who don't want Bones. Or who don't care enough to give up two nights a week for the kind of marathon encounter any Esalen graduate can put on in the Bougainvillea Room of the local Holiday Inn. Intimacy is cheap and zeal is rare these days. The word is out that Bones no longer gets the leaders of the class but lately has taken on a more lackadaisical, hedonist, comfortable—even, said some, decadent—group. (I was fascinated to learn from my source that some Bones members still partake in certain sacraments of the Sixties. Could it be that the old black magic of Bones ritual has kind of lost its spell and needs a psychedelic dramatizing these days?)

And the reasons people give now for joining Bones are often more foreboding than the rejections. They talk about the security of a guaranteed job with one of the Bones-dominated investment banks or law firms. They talk about the contacts and the connections and maybe in private they talk about the fifteen thousand dollars (regardless of whether Bones actually delivers the money, it may deliberately plant the story to lure apathetic but mercenary recruits). Bones still has the power to corrupt, but does it have the power to inspire? The recent classes of Bones just do not, it seems, take themselves as seriously as General Russell or Henry Stimson or Blackford Oakes might want them to.

The rotting-paella story seems a perfect emblem of the decay. The story goes that a recent class of Bones decided they would try to cook a meal in the basement kitchen of the tomb. It was vacation time and the servants were not on call to do it for them. They produced a passable paella, but left the remains of the meal there in the basement kitchen, presuming that someone would be in to clean up after them. Nobody came in for two weeks. When they returned, they found the interior of the tomb smelling worse than if there actually *had* been dead bodies there. The servants refused to cook the meal for the next autobiographical session unless the Bonesmen cleaned up the putrefying paella themselves. The Bonesmen went without food. I don't know who finally cleaned up, but there's a sense that like the paella, the original mission of Bones has suffered from neglect and apathy and that the gene pool, like the stew, is becoming stagnant.

I began to feel sorry for the old Bonesmen: after a few days of asking around, I found the going too easy; almost too many people were willing to spill their secrets. I had to call a halt. In the spirit of Bonesman Gifford Pinchot, godfather of the conservation movement, I'm protecting some of the last secrets—they're an endangered species. I have to save some for my novel. And besides, I like mumbo jumbo.

It's strange: I didn't exactly set out to write an exposé of Skull and Bones, but neither did I think I'd end up with an elegy.

—*ESQUIRE*
September 1977

POSTSCRIPT TO "THE LAST SECRETS OF SKULL AND BONES"

A personal postscript. In October 1986 aboard Air Force Two, 35,000 feet over the Carolinas, I asked George Bush about Skull and Bones. It was probably a bit unfair to choose that particular situation. We were strapped into seats in the forward cabin; if, as legend had it, Skull and Bones members were required to exit a room when anyone pronounced the secret society's name in their presence, here the nearest exit was a seven-mile drop.

I had Bush trapped. (I was covering Bush on assignment for *The New Republic*, to write about his pre-presidential midterm election campaign swing.)

There were a couple of factors complicating the situation, though. One was named Barbara Bush. She had the window seat next to me in the cabin during the interview, and I couldn't help but notice her expression of disapproval—the knitted brow, the compressed lips—of the kinds of "character" questions I'd been asking her husband even before I got to Skull and Bones.

It wasn't so much her knit brow but her knitting needles I found most disconcerting. I could sense her disapproval with my questions in the stepped-up tempo and, well, pointedness with which she stabbed the needles through the fabric. At this point I can't recall whether it was crochet needles, knitting, or needlepoint; all I remember are the glint of those needles flashing like stillettos as I asked George Bush my Skull and Bones question.

But I had my own reasons for being uneasy about the Skull and Bones question. In a certain sense I felt Bush had suffered a bit unfairly from my story. I had written what I thought of as a story about the *decline* of one of the great mythic emblems of the Yankee Eastern establishment. Indeed, the subtitle of the story when it first appeared was "An Elegy for Mumbo Jumbo."

But, perhaps inevitably, conspiracy-minded right-wing groups had ignored the subtleties in the story and used Bush's Bones connection to *reify* the myth of Bones' occult power. During the crucial 1980 New Hampshire primary, when Bush's first run for the presidency had run aground, the right-wing Manchester *Union-Leader* had aired the Skull and Bones connection, quoting my story; other looney-right Trilateralist-conspiracy theory tracts had cited my story as proof that

Bush was a minion of what was portrayed as a conspiratorial secret society of diabolical internationalist bankers that ruled the world from behind the scenes, Protocols of the Elders of Connecticut-style.

And so it was with a bit of guilt that I asked the vice-president about the influence of his secret society on his life. Did Bones inculcate an ethos of leadership?

"Well, it wasn't about leadership per se," he said, "so much as about friendship." He recited a number of similar platitudes, then he cut it short, nodding to his furiously knitting wife and saying, "We're just not the type who likes to get into all this self-analysis stuff." Barbara Bush nodded vigorously back and returned to her needles.

The most shocking recent development to Bones-watchers—the one that, as far as I'm concerned, really rent the fabric of the Bones mystique more than anything I'd done—came during Bush's 1988 presidential campaign. In September 1988, *The Washington Post* published the first installment of a five-part Bob Woodward review of Bush's life and career. The shock in that first installment was that Woodward had interviewed many of Bush's class in Bones. And that they'd talked. Not merely talked, gabbed. Blabbed. About Bones, about the sexual confessional (they confirmed it), about Bush's experience in Bones, about the midlife crisis Bush was suffering during his vice-presidency when he summoned his Bones class to a kind of confessional session and confided in them that he was worried he'd sold his principles in an effort to conform to Ronald Reagan's. I was astonished by the way that— overawed, perhaps, by Woodward or by their sudden closeness to the next president (or both)—Bush's Bones brothers babbled about the very character analysis issues the Bushes seemed to deplore.

This, more than anything, was a true measure of the decline of Skull and Bones—when the glamour of the White House overshadowed the mystique of the Tomb.

And speaking of the sexual confessional, I must admit I think I was misled on one point in this story by one of my sources, an angry ex-girlfriend of a Bones man who was particularly irritated about having her private life bruited about in the sexual confessional. It was she who told me about the $15,000 postgraduate stipend for Bones initiates— which I now believe is an inaccurate generalization from one initiate she knew getting a $15,000 loan for a postgraduate grand tour.

The sexual confessional nonetheless continues to be a potent irritant to Bones girlfriends. In the years since my story was published, I've received two sets of photographs of the secret interior of Bones from two separate women-led break-in groups. I also learned the truth about the mysterious "Phil" incident referred to in the story. But on that embarrassing affair, I'm still sworn to silence.

DREAM DANCING

RICHARD ROFFMAN
AND HIS UNKNOWN FAMOUS PEOPLE

The first time I met Richard H. Roffman he was still representing Big Ed Carmel. You might remember Big Ed, the nine-foot-tall "gentle Jewish giant from the Bronx," from the celebrated Diane Arbus photograph of the big guy with his pint-size parents in their living room up on the Grand Concourse.

Back then, P.R. man Roffman was trying to promote interest in a film career for Big Ed, an effort that never got very far, no doubt due to the shortage of really good parts for nine-foot-tall men.

But it was not long before I discovered that Richard H. Roffman is a giant in his own right—a towering figure in a strange subculture of show-biz dreamers, would-be celebrities, and stand-ins for stars that Roffman runs out of his living room on West End Avenue.

Roffman is more than a P.R. man—he's the ringmaster of a self-contained, self-fulfilling world that offers the complete "celebrity treatment" to a client: gala openings at restaurants represented by Roffman's P.R. business, radio and cable-TV talent showcases on Roffman-purchased air time, guest shots on Roffman-hosted talk shows, conspicuous mention in "Roffman News Service" releases and appearance in celebrity-type "overheard while dining at . . ." anecdotes sent out by Roffman to show-business and gossip columnists (who cares if the items never run?—the fact that you have a press agent sending items about you to real columnists is halfway to real celebrity-hood right there). All of this is accompanied by accolades from a cult composed of fellow Roffman-client "celebrities" who treat one another as if they were all "real" celebrities and nourish one another's cherished mutual illusions.

The success of the Roffman apparatus is all the more extraordinary when you consider that the clients involved do not exactly have the stellar magnitude of the celebs who employ John Springer, Bobby Zarem, and other established P.R. hotshots.

There is Monde, "Genie of the Accordian" and inventor of "the celebrity handshake glove." There is Yoga-donis, "the singing psychic." There's Tino Valenti, invariably identified as "the society troubadour"; someone known as "Count Gregory"; Dr. Joseph Yellis, "podiatrist-humorist." Several other clients of hyphenated accomplishments include a "songwriter-furrier," a "singer-artist-civic leader from Guyana," and Dr. Murray C. Kaye, described as "civic leader and retail beauty-world industrialist-owner of Murray Kaye Way beauty salon and frequently a guest on radio and TV shows . . . to discuss current problems."

The most recent Roffman client roster includes these other current favorites, along with the inimitable Roffmanesque descriptions of their talents:

- —"Ugly George Urban, video cameraman heavy on adult material—wears silver suit."
- —"Jos Gabriele, equinologist expert on horse racing, former wrestler investment counsellor."
- —"Nat Lehrfeld, furrier who does sculpture out of seashells."
- —"Princess Audrey Kargere, colorologist."
- —"Harold Blum, cookie wholesaler."
- —"Gregg Peters, an Elvis Presley soundalike lookalike."
- —"Andrew Clay, young singer, a comedian, a John Travolta lookalike, soundalike, actalike."

In Roffman News Service press releases, the chance remarks of Roffman luminaries are accorded all the attention and awe given an Andy
or Liza by Suzy and Liz. Consider some of the following items culled
from Roffman releases over the years:

> Six vegetarian dachshunds are available for placement by
> noted singing psychic Adonaiasis. At a press conference held
> at the Lotos Eaters Chinese Restaurant, Adonaiasis, a tall,
> handsome, blond young man of muscular physique said:
> "I sadly must give up these wonderful dogs, for I am
> getting so very busy with my consultation and personal
> advisory services and can only find time to give personal
> attention to a very few loved ones of the canine world. . . ."
> The Whirling Dervish Society presented an award to
> Tino Valenti, the Society Troubadour, Raconteur, Character
> actor, Artist, Fashion Designer, Singer, Guitarist, Bicyclist,
> Lecturer, producer, director for being the Busiest Man of
> Quality Around.
> Vance Packard, the songwriter of many hit tunes (not
> the author of best selling books, yes there are two gentlemen
> with that same name) disclosed while dining at the Adam's
> Rib restaurant that he is planning to open a unique beauty
> salon in the early part of the year.
> Mikulas Grosz, a sightless violinist with a "genius" mind
> for discussions of all the problems of the day, even though
> they do not relate to music or the questions of the blind,
> will become a regular panelist on the Richard H. Roffman
> and His Friends Show which is taped at the 86th Street
> Hofbrau House restaurant. This is one of the first times a
> sightless personality has been a regular participant in a talk
> show according to informal research.
> Richard H. Roffman well known newspaper man, pub-
> licist attorney and theatrical producer has been on the air
> continuously since 1935 and is celebrating his 35th contin-
> uous year of radio broadcasting in this city. At a reception
> held at the 86th Street Hofbrau house he was honored by
> the Greater New York Citizens Society for distinguished
> service in the communications world. Presented with a ci-

tation by Dr. Murray C. Kaye, civic leader and retail beauty
world industrialist Roffman declared . . .

After reading these curious releases for a year or so, I began asking
reporters around town whether they'd heard of this Roffman guy. A
mystified look would cloud their expressions. What *is* the story on that
guy, they'd ask. Is he for real, or is it some kind of concept art? Have
you *seen* those releases?

I decided to get a glimpse of Roffman's world firsthand. And so, one
warm spring evening some time ago, I attended one of the many award
ceremonies that crowd the Roffman social calendar. This particular one
took place in a big banquet room in the back of a now defunct place
called Phil Gluckstern's Fancy Kosher Dairy Restaurant in the theater
district.

As I walked in, the first of many "entertainers"—I can't recall if it
was the songwriter-furrier or the podiatrist-humorist—was giving the
first of many tributes to "the wonderful Mr. Dick Roffman," following
which the entertainer would sing a song or tell some jokes, the audience
would applaud or laugh vociferously, and Mr. Dick Roffman would
then introduce the next "award-winning" performer with effusive
praise. Mr. Dick Roffman is a big, jolly giant of a fellow with a gleaming
bald dome and an unflagging geniality that gave an air of dignity to
the relentlessly amateurish proceedings.

The "celebrities" all seemed deadly serious about themselves. Roffman's attitude was harder to figure out. Was he deluding these people
or was he fulfilling their fantasies in a harmless, satisfying way? Was
Roffman a benign Walter Mitty or a conniving charmer cynically toying
with the dreams his clients entrusted to him?

I needed a closer look at the Roffman operation. I spent hours during
the day watching him weave his web of contacts and connections; I
followed him on his nightly rounds along the freebie, due-bill, and
press-review-party circuit; and, finally, I spent a strange night at a
Roffman-inspired "Tribute to Richard H. Roffman," where I learned
the secret of "Dream Dancing."

Dick Roffman begins his day by turning on his TV set and watching
with almost religious veneration *The Joe Franklin Show*. Joe is an idol
to Roffman, who often boasts of the time he was actually asked to fill
in for Joe at some promotional dinner at Luchow's. Besides, the show

is a good source of potential clients and may be a big-break guest shot for a current client.

With Joe's show over, Roffman turns on his two phone lines, and the calls start pouring in. Roffman spends the next six hours taking calls, making connections, setting up deals. It goes something like this.

Ring. "Yes, this is Richard H. Roffman. Yes, I *had* called earlier. To say I was representing a gentleman named George Friedensohn, an international monetary expert who is desirous of talking about the impending collapse of the Western world. He is available for a limited number of talk shows—what station is this again?"

Ring. "Hold one moment, please, that's my other phone. Hello, who is this? Mrs. Marvell? You're looking for a man who owns a stone quarry. Hold on, please. Hello again. Yes, Mr. Friedensohn is available for a limited number of talk shows. There's a real catastrophe approaching. Please get back to me. Hello again, Mrs. Marvell. Now, what's the point you're making about a stone quarry? There's a natural stone with a pink-and-white stripe? Yes, what is it you want me—for a lighthouse? Oh, for ranch houses? Okay. A man named Sam Shapiro at 60 East 42nd is in the mortgage-finance business and works with a lot of builders; he might be a good contact for that."

Ring. "Hello, dear. Hold on, Mrs. Marvell. You have a portrait of Shakespeare done by who? . . . I see, I see. So what is it you need? You need an art dealer, a fine-art dealer. Well, let me think about it—call me tomorrow morning. Hello again, Mrs. Marvell. Yes, *Sam Shapiro*. What's that? You need a lawyer to handle your extra money? I could handle your extra money. Oh, I see. You *owe* somebody money. Try a very fine lawyer named Milton Notarius—he's also in 60 East 42nd. N-O-T-A-R-I-U-S. Easy to remember. He happens to be a good friend of mine, and I'm sure he can guide you properly."

Roffman puts the phone down. "I get all kinds of calls after being in show business 40 years. Now this Mrs. Marvell, somehow she's come into some pink marble, or maybe it is somebody's given her the right to sell this pink marble for them if she can find a buyer. She's an older woman who never gives up, despite the fact that she's half-blind—she has an indomitable spirit. She's always working on deals. She's always trying to make money and bring people together. She loves to be the catalyst."

A description that fits Roffman himself, and so, since the phone is temporarily silent, I ask him how he actually makes a living.

"Well, I don't have any fixed fees. I always say to people if anything happens, remember me if you can, because I feel that if you tie people up to things you get to a point where they may rely on you and maybe you can't help them solve their problems. Then you're *misleading* them. I try to avoid that."

Ring. "Hello. Yes. Yeah. Oh yes. You talked to me about something at a yeshiva at Brooklyn Saturday night. Wait, I want to get all the information because one of my chief associates is going to cover it personally."

Ring. "Hold on, Bernice. Great. I've got on the phone the chief representative of an Israeli magician. [Picks up other phone.] What do you call it again? He's a what? Ah hah. [Back to second phone.] He's known as 'The Wizard of Ouz.' [Back to first phone.] Do you spell Ouz O-U-Z? Yes? And is it like Hebrew humor? I see a general English magic show for Jewish audiences. Just one second. I'll take all the information because my associate is on the other phone. [Back to other phone.] Bernice, this guy might be great on your cable-TV show. 'The Wizard of Ouz.'"

He seems ready to put the two phones together to make the connection. Decides against it, gives the Wizard's number to Bernice, and returns to the Wizard's manager.

When the phone is silent again, Roffman begins filling me in on his 40 years of wheeling and dealing and how he got to be the "Best Kept Secret in New York," as he likes to call himself, this hub, catalyst, social director for such a strange assortment of people.

His father, "the distinguished orchestra leader and composer" (as Roffman releases invariably describe the late Maurice Roffman), raised young Richard in the theatrical society of the early-twentieth-century Upper West Side. (Roffman doesn't look it, but he's in his sixties already.) Although the distinguished leader and composer never achieved stellar renown ("His most well-known composition was something you may never have heard of called 'Hula Formal' that he was personally commissioned to do by Arthur Murray to promote his hula lessons, I think"), nonetheless the late distinguished etc. was someone who was invariably *recognized* as something of a celebrity in the neighborhood.

"As a child the greatest thrill of my life was to walk with my father on Broadway and have people recognize him," Roffman recalls.

In fact, Roffman reveals he was something of a celebrity himself back then: "I was an actor as a child in a number of early Vitagraph movies and one or two *Our Gang* comedies."

Now he has his own gang of sorts and . . . *ring* . . . one of them is on the phone now.

It's Tino Valenti, invariably described by Roffman as a "society troubadour" although he is vague as to what that means.

"Yes, Tino. Are you feeling better? A package? Sure I'll bring it over. It's not a large package. Good, I'll bring it over. No, not much going on tonight. There's that restaurant opening and then the party at the Yugoslav mission, but that's about it. Fine, Tino, see you later."

Tino, Roffman tells me, is a show-business friend of long standing. "He was Rudolph Valentino's stand-in back in the thirties."

"His stand-in?" I ask. "You mean his understudy or stunt man?"

"Not exactly," says Roffman. "Tino didn't really *look* like Valentino, but he didn't have to. They just needed someone to stand in his place so they could set up the scene while Rudy was getting ready to come out of his dressing room."

"Did Tino give himself that name because of Valentino?"

"Well, it was a very important influence on his career, which needless to say was not as fabulous as Rudy's, but Tino has many friends and admirers, and he's truly what we like to call a multi-talent, singer-guitarist-entertainer-raconteur-all-around troubadour, as I like to say."

Roffman returns to the Richard Roffman saga.

There were sensational celebrity-chasing exploits as a young reporter for Hearst's *Journal American* in the early thirties, and finally his first venture into what was to be 45 consecutive years of broadcasting.

His first radio show had the hauntingly evocative title *Real Stories From Real Life*.

"It was a big show; there were many, many famous people who were on it. Many well-known actors and actresses got their start with me on that show."

Who, for example? I asked.

"Well, I'd have to search my files to find a name, but it's true that *at least* six men and six women whose names became well known in film and theater, although not so much in television, started out in radio and were busy from this show."

Famous as *Real Stories From Real Life* may have made some of its actors, it wasn't exactly a gold mine for Roffman himself, and he pursued, in the meantime, some enterprising ventures with some very curious gadgets, inventions, and sales promotions.

His biggest success, he says, was promotion for an invention he describes as "a pressure cooker that was unexplodable." Unfortunately, the next venture was either way ahead, or way behind, the times.

"We called it 'Re Nu Cell.' It was a plastic machine with gadgets such that you attach a glass cup to the skin and there's alternate suction and pressure that's supposed to be beneficial. It was based on ancient truths or something like that."

Roffman concedes, "This thing was never as successful as the Diner's Club or apple pie," but he does note proudly that "we never had trouble with the medical authorities."

There was a brief stint as P.R. man for the Stork Club in the midforties after he left the *Journal American*. There was a job as promotion editor of *Modern Knitting* ("We got Klavan and Finch to knit on the air—it was a radio first"). His radio interviews provided him with clients and a way of giving clients their first big-time exposure on the air, even if most of Roffman's show had to be bought with his own money. Many of them, realistically, couldn't hope for much more. He began to develop a whole social life centered on his clients.

I asked Roffman how he managed to attract such a curious range of people.

"Well, for one thing, I'm listed in the Yellow Pages as a publicist. I'm listed in two different ways, actually. I'm listed under "Public Relations" and also under "Publicity," and I also list in one of the ads the kinds of accounts in which I specialize."

Another secret of his success, Roffman confides, is that he makes sure he gets himself listed with every U.S. consulate around the world as a New York City P.R. man specializing in show business and inventions, so that foreigners seeking to come to the land of opportunity to market themselves or their products will be more likely to call him up. This explains the number of exotically based people Roffman represents. A Sephardic Jew from Bombay, a Finnish woodworker, a Yugoslav baker, etc., etc. Why does Roffman content himself with this sort of clientele? "I could have gone in for the big celebrities," he says. "I could have gone for the big clients. But I'm content to be the Woolworth of the publicity business rather than the Tiffany."

By four in the afternoon, after nearly a hundred calls, Roffman declares he will take no more. It is time to make his rounds. His rounds, from the sampling I did following him, seem to consist of generous helpings from the freebie-due bill circuit, created by other P.R. enterprises. He's on the press lists for every promotion party, art opening, and P.R. event imaginable, in addition to representing a seemingly endless array of uptown Chinese restaurants and other eating places that issue "due bills," or meals in exchange for service or promotional work. That afternoon we attended a promotional cocktail party at Adam's Apple, a frequent beneficiary of "heard at" items in the Roffman News Service releases, then an opening party at an East Side Jamaican restaurant with a hearty dinner, gratis.

Capping off this particular evening was a reception party at the Yugoslav mission on upper Fifth Avenue. I never found out for whom or what the reception was, nor why Roffman was invited, although he does seem to have a number of Yugoslav clients, including a guy who wants to market a line of Balkan frozen foods.

The reception is quite elaborate and formal. Not much English is spoken, but there is definitely much strong slivovitz making itself felt as formally dressed waiters press glass after glass into visitors' hands. I meet a man named Wambly Bald, who says he's known Roffman since their tabloid-reporter days. I express my continued mystification as to the nature, extent, and reality of the Roffman world.

"You have to understand his secret," Wambly Bald tells me.

"His secret?"

"Don't listen to anything he tells you," says Roffman, looming up out of the reception throng and then passing on to greet a Balkan buddy.

"You have to understand his secret," Wambly Bald repeats. "He's the Pied Piper."

"The Pied Piper?"

"The Pied Piper of New York. That explains why they all follow him and live their lives around him. He's the Pied Piper."

Not entirely satisfied with that explanation, I looked forward to the upcoming Roffman Birthday Tribute for a chance to meet with these allegedly spellbound grown-up children who make up the Roffman world. The Birthday Tribute was being thrown by the Friends of Richard H. Roffman in association with several civic groups that were headed by Murray C. Kaye and other Roffman associates. It's not clear whether Roffman throws these tributes for himself or they're thrown for him, but in typical Roffman fashion both tributee and tributors benefit, since the Friends of Richard Roffman get to perform their songs, dances, and comedy acts before an appreciative audience they might not command at some more neutral booking.

In any case, this tribute was to be held in the basement banquet room of the Factoria, a short-lived pasta palace on East 58th Street.

The party was going strong when I arrived that night. Before I could make my way through the crowd, a small, determined-looking man with iron-gray hair approached me, handed me a mimeographed leaflet, and warned me about "the Atlanteans" at the party.

"They look like ordinary people but they're spies from Atlantis. They have ways of recognizing each other and communicating that we don't know."

"How do you know I'm not one?" I asked.

"You might be. I might be. You can't tell. Read this."

He pointed to his leaflet. An open letter to the U.N. General Assembly. He demanded the right to present evidence that the original astronauts who had landed on the moon had been kidnapped and replaced by look-alike aliens who were actually Atlantean spies.

And, indeed, Roffman's world of make-believe and look-alike celebrity was not unlike a secret Atlantean subculture beneath the surface of New York life. The Roffmanites all had their common signs and mutual recognitions. A submerged kingdom of their own.

The very next person I came across at the tribute enforced this sense of an invisible realm.

It was a Cowboy Jack Willis, the ex-prizefighter-poet and lecturer on health and nutrition. I had run into Cowboy Jack once before—at a "Gala Bon Voyage Party for Joe Franklin's Cruise Down Memory Lane" on a Greek liner about to depart down said lane via Joe's clips of Silent Era Stars. Cowboy Jack wasn't going on the cruise. He and some other Roffmanites were circulating like Atlanteans among the revelers. I asked Jack what he was doing at the Birthday Tribute, and discovered he was a longtime Roffmanite and a true fan of the gentle giant of West End Avenue. In fact, Jack had come to the Birthday Tribute with a freshly minted poem, an ode to Richard Roffman he planned to read to climax the night's festivities.

Cowboy Jack began to give me a full-voiced preview of the ode. " 'Hail to thee, Sir Richard Roffman,' it begins," he confided. "I compare him to King Arthur and his Knights of the Round Table. I see him as a reincarnation of one of King Arthur's Knights." The poem ended with the imagery intact: "Happy Birthday, Sir Richard the Roffman/ May your heart never shed any tears."

One after another, the Roffmanites I met at this tribute expressed their gratitude to their cult leader for helping them "make it." They'd always dreamed of being in show business, they'd say, and "Dick Roffman made my dreams come true."

Some Roffmanites I met at the tribute:

There was George Friedensohn, "the international monetary expert prepared to predict the impending collapse of the Western world on talk shows." Friedensohn, appropriately, turned out to be an intense, brooding fellow much given to scowling when his prophecies were not taken seriously enough. He flew into a raging tirade about my insensitivity to impending monetary doom when I ventured to ask him how much he charged for his "private consultations" on pre-apocalyptic investment strategies. When he calmed down, he did tell me he was pleased with Roffman's P.R. work for him. "His was by far the lowest bid," the canny monetary expert confided, "and he has succeeded in getting me on some real talk shows."

Then there was Eddie Rane, tirelessly promoted in Roffman releases as "the new Russ Columbo voice." I confessed to Eddie I wasn't familiar with the original Mr. Columbo. "He was said to have the most perfect voice of all back in the thirties," Eddie told me. "If he had stayed around, Crosby wouldn't have been Crosby; *he* would have been Crosby. But he died at age 24. People say I look and sound just like him." Eddie looks like he's safely past the fateful age at which the original expired. But he carries on and pronounces himself pleased at the "bookings" he gets at Roffman-related activities.

There was a woman who, with surprising reticence, would describe herself only as "someone who's been in show business a long time and who has known Roffman 'from the beginning.'

"What do I think of him? I think he's a jerk, that's what," she said.

A jerk?

"For being too nice to people. He's too good to too many people. They take advantage of him. He doesn't know how to take care of himself. He could have had the biggest clients if he wanted. From when he started out. But he likes these people even if he never makes a dime off them."

There was a final conversation I had that night, after the tributes to Roffman were read, sung, declaimed, and the performers performed to one another's applause. As I was leaving, I ran into a Roffman connection who described himself as a "big booker of 'socials'" for specialized singles groups (100 doctor and dentist widowers to meet 100 widows who have money to invest in plays, etc.). Roffman, it seems, has an extensive matchmaking practice of this sort, with all his contacts, plus restaurants willing to host socials and clients to entertain. The "socials" organizer was telling me about the "musico-chemico-emotional" science of making these socials genuinely sociable. "Background music is the key," he declared. "You've got to have the right ground fertilized for romance." He'd been experimenting for years with types of various background music for the get-acquainted stage of the socials, and he was convinced that there was one tape more than any other which made magic between people.

"What was it?" I asked.

" 'Dream Dancing,' " he said.

" 'Dream Dancing'?"

"Yes. By Ray Anthony and his orchestra. Don't ask me why, but with 'Dream Dancing,' if you've got a decent list-maker to start out with, you can't miss."

Dream Dancing. Roffman's clients are, most of them, Dream Dancers of one sort or another, Roffman himself the composer and choreographer of the background music, the Ray Anthony of their celebrity waltz.

—*NEW YORK MAGAZINE*
December 1979

POSTSCRIPT TO "DREAM DANCING"

Recently one Saturday afternoon I came across, on Manhattan's Paid Access Channel J, the "21st anniversary celebration" of the "Richard H. Roffman and His Friends Cable Talent Show." I was pleased to see this unique Dickensian (in the best sense) institution still going strong and bizarre as ever. The highlight of the new talent that the ever-youthful septuagenarian Roffman introduced was a young man who had perfected the ability to whistle Sinatra songs through his nose.

It's perhaps worth noting that at last, at least one former Roffman client has achieved real fame, or at least notoriety—the man described as the "John Travolta lookalike, soundalike, actalike," Andrew Clay, is now "The Diceman," Andrew Dice Clay.

Secrets of the
Little Blue Box

The Blue Box Is Introduced:
Its Qualities Are Remarked

I am in the expensively furnished living room of Al Gilbertson,* the creator of the "blue box." Gilbertson is holding one of his shiny black-and-silver "blue boxes" comfortably in the palm of his hand, pointing out the thirteen little red push buttons sticking up from the console. He is dancing his fingers over the buttons, tapping out discordant beeping electronic jingles. He is trying to explain to me how his little blue box does nothing less than place the entire telephone system of the world, satellites, cables, and all, at the service of the blue-box operator, free of charge.

"That's what it does. Essentially it gives you the power of a super operator. You seize a tandem with this top button," he presses the top button with his index finger and the blue box emits a high-pitched cheep, "and like that"—cheep goes the blue box again—"you control the phone company's long-distance switching systems from your cute

---

* His real name has been changed.

little Princess phone or any old pay phone. And you've got anonymity. An operator has to operate from a definite location: the phone company knows where she is and what she's doing. But with your beeper box, once you hop onto a trunk, say from a Holiday Inn 800 [toll-free] number, they don't know where you are, or where you're coming from, they don't know how you slipped into their lines and popped up in that 800 number. They don't even know anything illegal is going on. And you can obscure your origins through as many levels as you like. You can call next door by way of White Plains, then over to Liverpool by cable, and then back here by satellite. You can call yourself from one pay phone all the way around the world to a pay phone next to you. And you get your dime back too."

"And they can't trace the calls? They can't charge you?"

"Not if you do it the right way. But you'll find that the free-call thing isn't really as exciting at first as the feeling of power you get from having one of these babies in your hand. I've watched people when they first get hold of one of these things and start using it, and discover they can make connections, set up crisscross and zig-zag switching patterns back and forth across the world. They hardly talk to the people they finally reach. They say hello and start thinking of what kind of call to make next. They go a little crazy." He looks down at the neat little package in his palm. His fingers are still dancing, tapping out beeper patterns.

"I think it's something to do with how small my models are. There are lots of blue boxes around, but mine are the smallest and most sophisticated electronically. I wish I could show you the prototype we made for our big syndicate order."

He sighs. "We had this order for a thousand beeper boxes from a syndicate front man in Las Vegas. They use them to place bets coast to coast, keep lines open for hours, all of which can get expensive if you have to pay. The deal was a thousand blue boxes for $300 apiece. Before then we retailed them for $1,500 apiece, but $300,000 in one lump was hard to turn down. We had a manufacturing deal worked out in the Philippines. Everything ready to go. Anyway, the model I had ready for limited mass production was small enough to fit inside a flip-top Marlboro box. It had flush touch panels for a keyboard, rather than these unsightly buttons sticking out. Looked just like a tiny portable radio. In fact, I had designed it with a tiny transistor receiver to get one AM channel so in case the law became suspicious the owner could switch on the radio part, start snapping his fingers, and no one could tell anything illegal was going on. I thought of everything for this model—I had it lined with a band of thermite which could be ignited by radio signal from a tiny button transmitter on your belt, so it could be burned to ashes instantly in case of a bust. It was beautiful. A beautiful little machine. You should have seen the faces on these syndicate guys when they came back after trying it out. They'd hold it in their palm like they never wanted to let it go, and they'd say, 'I can't believe it. I can't believe it.' *You* probably won't believe it until you try it."

You Can Call Long Distance For Less than You Think

"You see, a few years ago the phone company made one big mistake," Gilbertson explains two days later in his apartment. "They were careless enough to let some technical journal publish the actual frequencies used to create all their multi-frequency tones. Just a theoretical article some Bell Telephone Laboratories engineer was doing about switching theory, and he listed the tones in passing. At - - - - - [a well-known technical school] I had been fooling around with phones for several years before I came across a copy of the journal in the engineering library. I ran back to the lab and it took maybe twelve hours from the time I saw that article to put together the first working blue box. It was bigger and clumsier than this little baby, but it worked."

It's all there on public record in that technical journal written mainly by Bell Lab people for other telephone engineers. Or at least it was public. "Just try and get a copy of that issue at some engineering-school library now. Bell has had them all red-tagged and withdrawn from circulation," Gilbertson tells me.

"But it's too late. It's all public now. And once they became public the technology needed to create your own beeper device is within the range of any twelve-year-old kid, any twelve-year-old *blind* kid as a matter of fact. And he can do it in *less* than the twelve hours it took us. Blind kids do it all the time. They can't build anything as precise and compact as my beeper box, but theirs can do anything mine can do."

"How?"

"Okay. About twenty years ago A.T.&T. made a multi-billion-dollar decision to operate its entire long-distance switching system on twelve electronically generated combinations of six master tones. Those are the tones you sometimes hear in the background after you've dialed a long-distance number. They decided to use some very simple tones—the tone for each number is just two fixed single-frequency tones played simultaneously to create a certain beat frequency. Like 1,300 cycles per second and 900 cycles per second played together give you the tone for digit 5. Now, what some of these phone phreaks have done is get themselves access to an electric organ. Any cheap family home-entertainment organ. Since the frequencies are public knowledge now—one blind phone phreak has even had them recorded in one of those talking books for the blind—they just have to find the musical notes on the organ which correspond to the phone tones. Then they tape them. For instance, to get Ma Bell's tone for the number 1, you press down organ keys F^5 and A^5 [900 and 700 cycles per second] at the same time. To produce the tone for 2 it's F^5 and C^6 [1100 and 700 c.p.s.]. The phone phreaks circulate the whole list of notes so there's no trial and error anymore."

He shows me a list of the rest of the phone numbers and the two electric organ keys that produce them.

"Actually, you have to record these notes at 3¾ inches-per-second tape speed and double it to 7½ inches-per-second when you play them back, to get the proper tones," he adds.

"So once you have all the tones recorded, how do you plug them into the phone system?"

"Well, they take their organ and their cassette recorder, and start banging out entire phone numbers in tones on the organ, including country codes, routing instructions, 'KP' and 'Start' tones. Or, if they don't have an organ, someone in the phone-phreak network sends them a cassette with all the tones recorded, with a voice saying 'Number one,' then you have the tone, 'Number two,' then the tone and so on. So with two cassette recorders they can put together a series of phone numbers by switching back and forth from number to number. Any idiot in the country with a cheap cassette recorder can make all the free calls he wants."

"You mean you just hold the cassette recorder up to the mouthpiece and switch in a series of beeps you've recorded? The phone thinks that anything that makes these tones must be its own equipment?"

"Right. As long as you get the frequency within thirty cycles per second of the phone company's tones, the phone equipment thinks it hears its own voice talking to it. The original granddaddy phone phreak was this blind kid with perfect pitch, Joe Engressia, who used to whistle into the phone. An operator could tell the difference between his whistle and the phone company's electronic tone generator, but the phone company's switching circuit can't tell them apart. The bigger the phone company gets and the further away from human operators it gets, the more vulnerable it becomes to all *sorts* of phone phreaking."

A GUIDE FOR THE PERPLEXED

"But wait a minute," I stop Gilbertson. "If everything you do sounds like phone-company equipment, why doesn't the phone company charge you for the call the way it charges its own equipment?"

"Okay. That's where the 2,600-cycle tone comes in. I better start from the beginning."

The beginning he describes for me is a vision of the phone system of the continent as thousands of webs, of long-line trunks radiating from each of the hundreds of toll switching offices to the other toll switching offices. Each toll switching office is a hive compacted of thousands of long-distance tandems constantly whistling and beeping to tandems in far-off toll switching offices.

The tandem is the key to the whole system. Each tandem is a line with some relays with the capability of signaling any other tandem in any other toll switching office on the continent, either directly one-to-one or by programming a roundabout route through several other tandems if all the direct routes are busy. For instance, if you want to call from New York to Los Angeles and traffic is heavy on all direct trunks between the two cities, your tandem in New York is programmed to try the next best route, which may send you down to a tandem in New Orleans, then up to San Francisco, or down to a New Orleans tandem, back to an Atlanta tandem, over to an Albuquerque tandem, and finally up to Los Angeles.

When a tandem is not being used, when it's sitting there waiting for someone to make a long-distance call, it whistles. One side of the tandem, the side "facing" your home phone, whistles at 2,600 per second toward all the home phones serviced by the exchange, telling them it is at their service, should they be interested in making a long-distance call. The other side of the tandem is whistling 2,600 c.p.s. into one or more long-distance trunk lines, telling the rest of the phone system that it is neither sending nor receiving a call through that trunk at the moment, that it has no use for that trunk at the moment.

When you dial a long-distance number the first thing that happens is that you are hooked into a tandem. A register comes up to the side of the tandem facing away from you and presents that side with the number you dialed. This sending side of the tandem stops whistling 2,600 into its trunk line. When a tandem stops the 2,600 tone it has been sending through a trunk, the trunk is said to be "seized," and is now ready to carry the number you have dialed—converted into multi-frequency beep tones—to a tandem in the area code and central office you want.

Now when a blue-box operator wants to make a call from New Orleans to New York he starts by dialing the 800 number of a company which might happen to have its headquarters in Los Angeles. The sending side of the New Orleans tandem stops sending beep tones to a tandem it has discovered idly whistling 2,600 cycles in Los Angeles. The receiving end of that L.A. tandem is seized, stops whistling 2,600, listens to the beep tones which tell it which L.A. phone to ring, and starts ringing the 800 number. Meanwhile a mark made on the New Orleans office accounting tape notes that a call from your New Orleans phone to the 800 number in L.A. has been initiated and gives the call a code number. Everything is routine so far.

But then the phone phreak presses his blue box to the mouthpiece and pushes the 2,600-cycle button, sending 2,600 out from New Orleans tandem to the L.A. tandem. The L.A. tandem notices 2,600 cycles are coming over the line again and assumes that New Orleans has hung up because the trunk is whistling as if idle. The L.A. tandem immediately ceases ringing the L.A. 800 number. But as soon as the phreak takes his finger off the 2,600 button, the L.A. tandem assumes the trunk is once again being used because the 2,600 is gone, so it listens for a new series of digit tones—to find out where it must send the call.

Thus the blue-box operator in New Orleans now is in touch with a tandem in L.A. which is waiting like an obedient genie to be told what to do next. The blue-box owner then beeps out the ten digits of the New York number which tell the L.A. tandem to relay a call to New York City. Which it promptly does. As soon as your party picks up the phone in New York, the side of the New Orleans tandem facing you stops sending 2,600 cycles to you and starts carrying his voice to you by way of the L.A. tandem. A notation is made on the accounting tape that the connection has been made on the 800 call which had been initiated and noted earlier. When you stop talking to New York a notation is made that the 800 call has ended.

At three the next morning, when the phone company's accounting computer starts reading back over the master accounting tape for the past day, it records that a call of a certain length of time was made from your New Orleans home to an L.A. 800 number and, of course, the accounting computer has been trained to ignore these toll-free 800 calls when compiling your monthly bill.

"All they can prove is that you made an 800 toll-free call," Gilbertson the inventor concludes. "Of course, if you're foolish enough to talk for two hours on an 800 call, and they've installed one of their special antifraud computer programs to watch out for such things, they may spot you and ask you why you took two hours talking to Army Recruiting's 800 number when you're 4-F. But if you do it from a pay phone, they *may* discover something peculiar the next day—if they've got a blue-box hunting program in their computer—but you'll be a long time gone from the pay phone by then. Using a pay phone is almost guaranteed safe."

"What about the recent series of blue-box arrests all across the country—New York, Cleveland, and so on?" I asked. "How were they caught so easily?"

"From what I can tell, they made one big mistake: they were seizing trunks using an area code plus 555-1212 instead of an 800 number. Using 555 is easy to detect because when you send multi-frequency beep tones off 555 you get a charge for it on your tape and the accounting computer knows there's something wrong when it tries to bill you for a two-hour call to Akron, Ohio, information, and it drops a trouble card which goes right into the hands of the security agent if they're looking for blue-box users.

"Whoever sold those guys their blue boxes didn't tell them how to use them properly, which is fairly irresponsible. And they were fairly stupid to use them at home all the time.

"But what those arrests really mean is that an awful lot of blue boxes are flooding into the country and that people are finding them so easy to make that they know how to make them before they know how to use them. Ma Bell is in trouble."

And if a blue-box operator or a cassette-recorder phone phreak sticks to pay phones and 800 numbers, the phone company can't stop them?

"Not unless they change their entire nationwide long-lines technology, which will take them a few billion dollars and twenty years. Right now they can't do a thing. They're screwed."

CAPTAIN CRUNCH DEMONSTRATES
HIS FAMOUS UNIT

There is an underground telephone network in this country. Gilbertson discovered it the very day news of his own arrest hit the papers. That evening his phone began ringing. Phone phreaks from Seattle, from Florida, from New York, from San Jose, and from Los Angeles began calling him and telling him about the phone-phreak network. He'd get a call from a phone phreak who'd say nothing but, "Hang up and call this number."

When he dialed the number he'd find himself tied into a conference of a dozen phone phreaks arranged through a quirky switching station in British Columbia. They identified themselves as phone phreaks, they demonstrated their homemade blue boxes which they called "M-F-ers" (for "multi-frequency," among other things) for him, they talked shop about phone-phreak devices. They let him in on their secrets on the theory that if the phone company was after him he must be trustworthy. And, Gilbertson recalls, they stunned him with their technical sophistication.

I ask him how to get in touch with the phone-phreak network. He digs around through a file of old schematics and comes up with about a dozen numbers in three widely separated area codes.

"Those are the centers," he tells me. Alongside some of the numbers he writes in first names or nicknames: names like Captain Crunch, Dr. No, Frank Carson (also a code word for free call), Marty Freeman (code word for M-F device), Peter Perpendicular Pimple, Alefnull, and The Cheshire Cat. He makes checks alongside the names of those among these top twelve who are blind. There are five checks.

I ask him who this Captain Crunch person is.

"Oh. The Captain. He's probably the most legendary phone phreak. He calls himself Captain Crunch after the notorious Cap'n Crunch 2,600 whistle." (Several years ago, Gilbertson explains, the makers of Cap'n Crunch breakfast cereal offered a toy-whistle prize in every box as a treat for the Cap'n Crunch set. Somehow a phone phreak discovered that the toy whistle just happened to produce a perfect 2,600-cycle tone. When the man who calls himself Captain Crunch was transferred overseas to England with his Air Force unit, he would receive scores of calls from his friends and "mute" them—make them free of charge to them—by blowing his Cap'n Crunch whistle into his end.)

"Captain Crunch is one of the older phone phreaks," Gilbertson tells me. "He's an engineer who once got in a little trouble for fooling around with the phone, but he can't stop. Well, this guy drives across country in a Volkswagen van with an entire switchboard and a computerized super-sophisticated M-F-er in the back. He'll pull up to a phone booth on a lonely highway somewhere, snake a cable out of his bus, hook it onto the phone and sit for hours, days sometimes, sending calls zipping back and forth across the country, all over the world. . . ."

Back at my motel, I dialed the number he gave me for "Captain Crunch" and asked for G- - - - - T- - - - -, the name he uses when he's not dashing into a phone booth beeping out M-F tones faster than a speeding bullet, and zipping phantomlike through the phone company's long-distance lines.

When G- - - - - T- - - - - answered the phone and I told him I was preparing a story for *Esquire* about phone phreaks, he became very indignant.

"I don't do that. I don't do that anymore at all. And if I do it, I do it for one reason and one reason only. I'm learning about a system. The phone company is a System. A computer is a System. Do you understand? If I do what I do, it is only to explore a System. Computers. Systems. That's my bag. The phone company is nothing but a computer."

A tone of tightly restrained excitement enters the Captain's voice when he starts talking about Systems. He begins to pronounce each syllable with the hushed deliberation of an obscene caller.

"Ma Bell is a system I want to explore. It's a beautiful system, you know, but Ma Bell screwed up. It's terrible because Ma Bell is such a beautiful system, but she screwed up. I learned how she screwed up from a couple of blind kids who wanted me to build a device. A certain device. They said it could make free calls. I wasn't interested in free calls. But when these blind kids told me I could make calls into a computer, my eyes lit up. I wanted to learn about computers. I wanted to learn about Ma Bell's computers. So I built the little device. Only I built it wrong and Ma Bell found out. Ma Bell can detect things like that. Ma Bell knows. So I'm strictly out of it now. I didn't do it. Except for learning purposes." He pauses. "So you want to write an article. Are you paying for this call? Hang up and call this number."

He gives me a number in an area code a thousand miles north of his own. I dial the number.

"Hello again. This is Captain Crunch. You are speaking to me on a toll-free loop-around in Portland, Oregon. Do you know what a toll-free loop-around is? I'll tell you."

He explains to me that almost every exchange in the country has open test numbers which allow other exchanges to test their connections with it. Most of these numbers occur in consecutive pairs, such as 302 956-0041 and 956-0042. Well, certain phone phreaks discovered that if two people from anywhere in the country dial those two consecutive numbers they can talk together just as if one had called the other's number, with no charge to either of them, of course.

"Your voice is looping around in a 4A switching machine up there in Canada, zipping back down to me," the Captain tells me. "My voice is looping around up there and back down to you. And it can't ever cost anyone money. The phone phreaks and I have compiled a list of many many of these numbers. You would be surprised if you saw the list. I could show it to you. But I won't. I'm out of that now. I'm not out to screw Ma Bell. I know better. If I do anything it's for the pure knowledge of the System. You can learn to do fantastic things. Have you ever heard eight tandems stacked up? Do you know the sound of tandems stacking and unstacking? Give me your phone number. Okay. Hang up now and wait a minute."

Slightly less than a minute later the phone rang and the Captain was on the line, his voice sounding far more excited, almost aroused.

"I wanted to show you what it's like to stack up tandems. To stack up tandems." (Whenever the Captain says "stack up" it sounds as if he is licking his lips.)

"How do you like the connection you're on now?" the Captain asks me. "It's a *raw* tandem. A *raw* tandem. Ain't nothin' up to it but a tandem. Now I'm going to show you what it's like to stack up. Blow off. Land in a faraway place. To stack *that* tandem up, whip back and forth across the country a few times, then shoot on up to Moscow.

"Listen," Captain Crunch continues. "Listen. I've got a line tie on my switchboard here, and I'm gonna let you hear me stack and unstack tandems. Listen to this. I'm gonna blow your mind."

First I hear a super rapid-fire pulsing of the flutelike phone tones, then a pause, then another popping burst of tones, then another, then another. Each burst is followed by a beep-kachink sound.

"We have now stacked up four tandems," said Captain Crunch, sounding somewhat remote. "That's four tandems stacked up. Do you know what that means? That means I'm whipping back and forth, back and forth twice, across the country, before coming to you. I've been known to stack up twenty tandems at a time. Now, just like I said, I'm going to shoot up to Moscow."

There is a new, longer series of beeper pulses over the line, a brief silence, then a ring.

"Hello," answers a far-off voice.

"Hello. Is this the American Embassy Moscow?"

"Yes, sir. Who is this calling?" says the voice.

"Yes. This is test board here in New York. We're calling to check out the circuits, see what kind of lines you've got. Everything okay there in Moscow?"

"Okay?"

"Well, yes, how are things there?"

"Oh. Well, everything okay, I guess."

"Okay. Thank you." They hang up, leaving a confused series of beep-kachink sounds hanging in mid-ether in the wake of the call before dissolving away.

The Captain is pleased. "You believe me now, don't you? Do you know what I'd like to do? I'd like to call up your editor at *Esquire* and show him *just* what it sounds like to stack and unstack tandems. I'll give him a show that will *blow his mind*. What's his number?"

I ask the Captain what kind of device he was using to accomplish all his feats. The Captain is pleased at the question.

"You could tell it was special, couldn't you? Ten pulses per second. That's faster than the phone company's equipment. Believe me, this unit is *the* most famous unit in the country. There is no other unit like it. Believe me."

"Yes, I've heard about it. Some other phone phreaks have told me about it."

"They have been referring to my, ahem, unit? What is it they said? Just out of curiosity, did they tell you it was a highly sophisticated computer-operated unit, with acoustical coupling for receiving outputs and a switchboard with multiple-line capability? Did they tell you that the frequency tolerance is guaranteed to be not more than .05 percent? The amplitude tolerance less than .01 decibel? Those pulses you heard were perfect. They just come faster than the phone company. Those were high-precision op-amps. Op-amps are instrumentation amplifiers designed for ultrastable amplification, super-low distortion and accurate frequency response. Did they tell you it can operate in temperatures from $-55°C$ to $+125°C$?"

I admit that they did not tell me all that.

"I built it myself," the Captain goes on. "If you were to go out and *buy* the components from an industrial wholesaler it would cost you at least $1,500. I once worked for a semiconductor company and all this didn't cost me a cent. Do you know what I mean? Did they tell you about how I put a call completely around the world? I'll tell you how I did it. I M-F-ed Tokyo inward, who connected me to India, India connected me to Greece, Greece connected me to Pretoria, South Africa, South Africa connected me to South America, I went from South America to London, I had a London operator connect me to a New York operator, I had New York connect me to a California operator who rang the phone next to me. Needless to say I had to shout to hear myself. But the echo was far out. Fantastic. Delayed. It was delayed twenty seconds, but I could hear myself talk to myself."

"You mean you were speaking into the mouthpiece of one phone sending your voice around the world into your ear through a phone on the other side of your head?" I asked the Captain. I had a vision of something vaguely autoerotic going on, in a complex electronic way.

"That's right," said the Captain. "I've also sent my voice around the world one way, going east on one phone, and going west on the other, going through cable one way, satellite the other, coming back together at the same time, ringing the two phones simultaneously and picking them up and whipping my voice both ways around the world and back to me. Wow. That was a mind blower."

"You mean you sit there with both phones on your ear and talk to yourself around the world," I said incredulously.

"Yeah. Um hum. That's what I do. I connect the phones together and sit there and talk."

"What do you say? What do you say to yourself when you're connected?"

"Oh, you know. Hello test one two three," he says in a low-pitched voice.

"Hello test one two three," he replies to himself in a high-pitched voice.

"Hello test one two three," he repeats again, low-pitched.

"Hello test one two three," he replies, high-pitched.

"I sometimes do this: *Hello* hello *hello* hello, *hello*, hello," he trails off and breaks into laughter.

WHY CAPTAIN CRUNCH HARDLY EVER TAPS PHONES ANYMORE

Using internal phone-company codes, phone phreaks have learned a simple method for tapping phones. Phone-company operators have in front of them a board that holds verification jacks. It allows them to plug into conversations in case of emergency, to listen in to a line to determine if the line is busy or the circuits are busy. Phone phreaks have learned to beep out the codes which lead them to a verification operator, tell the verification operator they are switchmen from some other area code testing out verification trunks. Once the operator hooks them into the verification trunk, they disappear into the board for all practical purposes, slip unnoticed into any one of the 10,000 to 100,000 numbers in that central office without the verification operator knowing what they're doing, and of course without the two parties to the connection knowing there is a phantom listener present on their line.

Toward the end of my hour-long first conversation with him, I asked the Captain if he ever tapped phones.

"Oh no. I don't do that. I don't think it's right," he told me firmly. "I have the power to do it but I don't. . . . Well one time, just one time, I have to admit that I did. There was this girl Linda, and I wanted to find out . . . you know. I tried to call her up for a date. I had a date with her the last weekend and I thought she liked me. I called her up, man, and her line was busy, and I kept calling and it was still busy. Well, I had just learned about this system of jumping into lines and I said to myself, 'Hmmm. Why not just see if it works. It'll surprise her if all of a sudden I should pop up on her line. It'll impress her, if anything.' So I went ahead and did it. I M-F-ed into the line. My M-F-er is powerful enough when patched directly into the mouthpiece to trigger a verification trunk without using an operator the way the other phone phreaks have to.

"I slipped into the line and there she was talking to another boyfriend. Making sweet talk to him. I didn't make a sound because I was so disgusted. So I waited there for her to hang up, listening to her making sweet talk to another guy. You know. So as soon as she hung up I instantly M-F-ed her up and all I said was, 'Linda, we're through.' And I hung up. And it blew her head off. She couldn't figure out what the hell had happened.

"But that was the only time. I did it thinking I would surprise her, impress her. Those were all my intentions were, and well, it really kind of hurt me pretty badly, and . . . and ever since then I don't go into verification trunks."

Moments later my first conversation with the Captain comes to a close.

"Listen," he says, his spirits somewhat cheered, "listen. What you are going to hear when I hang up is the sound of tandems unstacking. Layer after layer of tandems unstacking until there's nothing left of the stack, until it melts away into nothing. Cheep, cheep, cheep, cheep," he concludes, his voice descending to a whisper with each cheep.

He hangs up. The phone suddenly goes into four spasms: kachink cheep. Kachink cheep kachink cheep kachink cheep, and the complex connection has wiped itself out like the Cheshire cat's smile.

THE MF BOOGIE BLUES

The next number I choose from the select list of phone-phreak illuminati prepared for me by the blue-box inventor is a Memphis number. It is the number of Joe Engressia, the first and still perhaps the most accomplished blind phone phreak.

Three years ago Engressia was a nine-day wonder in newspapers and magazines all over America because he had been discovered whistling free long-distance connections for fellow students at the University of South Florida. Engressia was born with perfect pitch; he could whistle phone tones better than the phone-company equipment.

Engressia might have gone on whistling in the dark for a few friends for the rest of his life if the phone company hadn't decided to expose him. He was warned, disciplined by the college, and the whole case became public. In the months following media reports of his talent, Engressia began receiving strange calls. There were calls from a group of kids in Los Angeles who could do some very strange things with the quirky General Telephone and Electronics circuitry in L.A. suburbs. There were calls from a group of mostly blind kids in - - - -, California, who had been doing some interesting experiments with Cap'n Crunch whistles and test loops. There was a group in Seattle, a group in Cambridge, Massachusetts, a few from New York, a few scattered across the country. Some of them had already equipped themselves with cassette and electronic M-F devices. For some of these groups, it was the first time they knew of the others.

The exposure of Engressia was the catalyst that linked the separate phone-phreak centers together. They all called Engressia. They talked to him about what he was doing and what they were doing. And then he told them—the scattered regional centers and lonely independent phone phreakers—about each other, gave them each other's numbers to call, and within a year the scattered phone-phreak centers had grown into a nationwide underground.

Joe Engressia is only twenty-two years old now, but along the phone-phreak network he is "the old man," accorded by phone phreaks something of the reverence the phone company bestows on Alexander Graham Bell. He seldom needs to make calls anymore. The phone phreaks all call him and let him know what new tricks, new codes, new techniques they have learned. Every night he sits like a sightless spider in his little apartment receiving messages from every tendril of his web. It is almost a point of pride with Joe that *they* call *him*.

But when I reached him in his Memphis apartment that night, Joe Engressia was lonely, jumpy, and upset.

"God, I'm glad somebody called. I don't know why tonight of all nights I don't get any calls. This guy around here got drunk again tonight and propositioned me again. I keep telling him we'll never see eye to eye on this subject, if you know what I mean. I try to make light of it, you know, but he doesn't get it. I can hear him out there getting drunker and I don't know what he'll do next. It's just that I'm really all alone here. I just moved to Memphis, it's the first time I'm living out on my own, and I'd hate for it to all collapse now. But I won't go to bed with him. I'm just not very interested in sex and even if I can't see him I *know* he's ugly.

"Did you hear that? That's him banging a bottle against the wall outside. He's nice. Well forget about it. You're doing a story on phone phreaks? Listen to this. It's the *MF Boogie* blues."

Sure enough, a jumpy version of *Muskrat Ramble* boogies its way over the line, each note one of those long-distance phone tones. The music stops. A huge roaring voice blasts the phone off my ear: "AND THE QUESTION IS . . ." roars the voice, "CAN A BLIND PERSON HOOK UP AN AMPLIFIER ON HIS OWN?"

The roar ceases. A high-pitched operator-type voice replaces it. "This is Southern Braille Tel. & Tel. Have tone, will phone."

This is succeeded by a quick series of M-F tones, a swift "kachink" and a deep reassuring voice: "If *you* need home care, call the visiting-nurses association. First National time in Honolulu is four thirty-two P.M."

Joe back in his Joe voice again: "Are we seeing eye to eye? 'Si, si,' said the blind Mexican. Ahem. Yes. Would you like to know the weather in Tokyo?"

This swift manic sequence of phone-phreak vaudeville stunts and blind-boy jokes manages to keep Joe's mind off his tormentor only as long as it lasts.

"The reason I'm in Memphis, the reason I have to depend on that homosexual guy, is that this is the first time I've been able to live on my own and make phone trips on my own. I've been banned from all central offices around home in Florida, they knew me too well, and at the University some of my fellow scholars were always harassing me because I was on the dorm pay phone all the time and making fun of me because of my fat ass, which of course I do have, it's my physical fatness program, but I don't like to hear it every day, and if I can't phone trip and I can't phone phreak, I can't imagine what I'd do, I've been devoting three quarters of my life to it.

"I moved to Memphis because I wanted to be on my own as well as because it has a Number 5 crossbar switching system and some interesting little independent phone-company districts nearby and so far they don't seem to know who I am so I can go on phone tripping, and for me phone tripping is just as important as phone phreaking."

Phone tripping, Joe explains, begins with calling up a central-office switch room. He tells the switchman in a polite earnest voice that he's a blind college student interested in telephones, and could he perhaps have a guided tour of the switching station? Each step of the tour Joe likes to touch and feel relays, caress switching circuits, switchboards, crossbar arrangements.

So when Joe Engressia phone phreaks he *feels* his way through the circuitry of the country. In this electronic garden of forking paths, he feels switches shift, relays shunt, crossbars swivel, tandems engage and disengage even as he hears—with perfect pitch—his M-F pulses make the entire Bell system dance to his tune.

Just one month ago Joe took all his savings out of his bank and left home, over the emotional protests of his mother. "I ran away from home almost," he likes to say. Joe found a small apartment house on Union Avenue and began making phone trips. He'd take a bus a hundred miles south into Mississippi to see some old-fashioned Bell equipment still in use in several states, which had been puzzling him. He'd take a bus three hundred miles to Charlotte, North Carolina, to look at some brand-new experimental equipment. He hired a taxi to drive him twelve miles to a suburb to tour the office of a small phone company with some interesting idiosyncrasies in its routing system. He was having the time of his life, he said, the most freedom and pleasure he had known.

In that month he had done very little long-distance phone phreaking from his own phone. He had begun to apply for a job with the phone company, he told me, and he wanted to stay away from anything illegal.

"Any kind of job will do, anything as menial as the most lowly operator. That's probably all they'd give me because I'm blind. Even though I probably knew more than most switchmen. But that's okay. I *want* to work for Ma Bell. I don't hate Ma Bell the way Gilbertson and some phone phreaks do. I don't want to screw Ma Bell. With me it's the pleasure of pure knowledge. There's something beautiful about the system when you know it intimately the way I do. But I don't know how much they know about me here. I have a very intuitive feel for the condition of the line I'm on, and I think they're monitoring me off and on lately, but I haven't been doing much illegal. I *have* to make a few calls to switchmen once in a while which aren't strictly legal, and once I took an acid trip and was having these auditory hallucinations as if I were trapped and these planes were dive-bombing me, and all of a sudden I *had* to phone phreak out of there. For some reason I had to call Kansas City, but that's all."

A Warning Is Delivered

At this point—one o'clock in my time zone—a loud knock on my motel-room door interrupts our conversation. Outside the door I find a uniformed security guard who informs me that there has been an "emergency phone call" for me while I have been on the line and that the front desk has sent him up to let me know.

Two seconds after I say good-bye to Joe and hang up, the phone rings.

"Who were you talking to?" the agitated voice demands. The voice belongs to Captain Crunch. "I called because I decided to warn you of something. I decided to warn you to be careful. I don't want this information you get to get to the radical underground. I don't want it to get into the wrong hands. What would you say if I told you it's possible for three phone phreaks to saturate the phone system of the nation. Saturate it. Busy it out. All of it. I know how to do this. I'm not gonna tell. A friend of mine has already saturated the trunks between Seattle and New York. He did it with a computerized M-F-er hitched into a special Manitoba exchange. But there are other, easier ways to do it."

Just three people? I ask. How is that possible?

"Have you ever heard of the long-lines guard frequency? Do you know about stacking tandems with 17 and 2,600? Well, I'd advise you to find out about it. I'm not gonna tell you. But whatever you do, don't let this get into the hands of the radical underground."

(Later Gilbertson the inventor confessed that while he had always been skeptical about the Captain's claim of the sabotage potential of trunk-tying phone phreaks, he had recently heard certain demonstrations which convinced him the Captain was not speaking idly. "I think it might take more than three people, depending on how many machines like Captain Crunch's were available. But even though the Captain *sounds* a little weird, he generally turns out to know what he's talking about.")

"You know," Captain Crunch continues in his admonitory tone, "you know the younger phone phreaks call Moscow all the time. Suppose everybody were to call Moscow. I'm no right-winger. But I value my life. I don't want the Commies coming over and dropping a bomb on my head. That's why I say you've got to be careful about who gets this information."

The Captain suddenly shifts into a diatribe against those phone phreaks who don't like the phone company.

"They don't understand, but Ma Bell knows everything they do. Ma Bell knows. Listen, is this line hot? I just heard someone tap in. I'm not paranoid, but I can detect things like that. Well, even if it is, they know that I know that they know that I have a bulk eraser. I'm very clean." The Captain pauses, evidently torn between wanting to prove to the phone-company monitors that he does nothing illegal, and the desire to impress Ma Bell with his prowess. "Ma Bell knows the things I can do," he continues. "Ma Bell knows how good I am. And I am *quite* good. I can detect reversals, tandem switching, everything that goes on on a line. I have relative pitch now. Do you know what that *means*? My ears are a $20,000 piece of equipment. With my ears I can detect things they can't hear with their equipment. I've had employment problems. I've lost jobs. But I want to show Ma Bell how good I am. I don't want to screw her, I want to work for her. I want to do good for her. I want to help her get rid of her flaws and become perfect. That's my number-one goal in life now." The Captain concludes his warnings and tells me he has to be going. "I've got a little action lined up for tonight," he explains and hangs up.

Before I hang up for the night, I call Joe Engressia back. He reports that his tormentor has finally gone to sleep—"He's not *blind* drunk, that's the way I get, ahem, yes; but you might say he's in a drunken stupor." I make a date to visit Joe in Memphis in two days.

A PHONE PHREAK CELL TAKES
CARE OF BUSINESS

The next morning I attend a gathering of four phone phreaks in - - - - - (a California suburb). The gathering takes place in a comfortable split-level home in an upper-middle-class subdivision. Heaped on the kitchen table are the portable cassette recorders, M-F cassettes, phone patches, and line ties of the four phone phreaks present. On the kitchen counter next to the telephone is a shoe-box-size blue box with thirteen large toggle switches for the tones. The parents of the host phone phreak, Ralph, who is blind, stay in the living room with their sighted children. They are not sure exactly what Ralph and his friends do with the phone or if it's strictly legal, but he is blind and they are pleased he has a hobby which keeps him busy.

The group has been working at reestablishing the historic "2111" conference, reopening some toll-free loops, and trying to discover the dimensions of what seem to be new initiatives against phone phreaks by phone-company security agents.

It is not long before I get a chance to see, to hear, Randy at work. Randy is known among the phone phreaks as perhaps the finest con man in the game. Randy is blind. He is pale, soft, and pear-shaped, he wears baggy pants and a wrinkly nylon white sport shirt, pushes his head forward from hunched shoulders somewhat like a turtle inching out of its shell. His eyes wander, crossing and recrossing, and his forehead is somewhat pimply. He is only sixteen years old.

But when Randy starts speaking into a telephone mouthpiece his voice becomes so stunningly authoritative it is necessary to look again to convince yourself it comes from chubby adolescent Randy. Imagine the voice of a crack oil-rig foreman, a tough, sharp, weatherbeaten Marlboro man of forty. Imagine the voice of a brilliant performance-fund gunslinger explaining how he beats the Dow Jones by thirty percent. Then imagine a voice that could make those two sound like Stepin Fetchit. That is sixteen-year-old Randy's voice.

He is speaking to a switchman in Detroit. The phone company in Detroit had closed up two toll-free loop pairs for no apparent reason, although heavy use by phone phreaks all over the country may have been detected. Randy is telling the switchman how to open up the loop and make it free again:

"How are you, buddy. Yeah, I'm on the board out here in Tulsa, Oklahoma, and we've been trying to run some tests on your loop-arounds, and we find 'em busied out on both sides. . . . Yeah, we've been getting a 'BY' on them, what d'ya say, can you drop cards on 'em? Do you have 08 on your number group? Oh that's okay, we've had this trouble before, we may have to go after the circuit. Here, lemme give 'em to you: your frame is 05, vertical group 03, horizontal 5, vertical file 3. Yeah, we'll hang on here. . . . Okay, found it? Good. Right, yeah, we'd like to clear that busy out. Right. Now pull your key from NOR over to LCT. Yeah. I don't know why that happened, but we've been having trouble with that one. Okay. Thanks a lot, fella. Be seein' ya."

Randy hangs up, reports that the switchman was a little inexperienced with the loop-around circuits on the miscellaneous trunk frame, but that the loop has been returned to its free-call status.

Delighted, phone phreak Ed returns the pair of numbers to the active-status column in his directory. Ed is a superb and painstaking researcher. With almost Talmudic thoroughness he will trace tendrils of hints through soft-wired mazes of intervening phone-company circuitry back through complex linkages of switching relays to find the location and identity of just one toll-free loop. He spends hours and hours, every day, doing this sort of thing. He has compiled a directory of eight hundred "Band-six in-WATS numbers" located in over forty states. Band-six in-WATS numbers are the big 800 numbers—the ones that can be dialed into free from anywhere in the country.

Ed the researcher, a nineteen-year-old engineering student, is also a superb technician. He put together his own working blue box from scratch at age seventeen. (He is sighted.) This evening after distributing the latest issue of his in-WATS directory (which has been typed into Braille for the blind phone phreaks), he announces he has made a major new breakthrough:

"I finally tested it and it works, perfectly. I've got this switching matrix which converts any touch-tone phone into an M-F-er."

The tones you hear in touch-tone phones are *not* the M-F tones that operate the long-distance switching system. Phone phreaks believe A.T.&T. had deliberately equipped touch tones with a different set of frequencies to avoid putting the six master M-F tones in the hands of every touch-tone owner. Ed's complex switching matrix puts the six master tones, in effect puts a blue box, in the hands of every touch-tone owner.

Ed shows me pages of schematics, specifications, and parts lists. "It's not easy to build, but everything here is in the Heathkit catalog."

Ed asks Ralph what progress he has made in his attempts to reestablish a long-term open conference line for phone phreaks. The last big conference—the historic "2111" conference—had been arranged through an unused Telex test-board trunk somewhere in the innards of a 4A switching machine in Vancouver, Canada. For months phone phreaks could M-F their way into Vancouver, beep out 604 (the Vancouver code) and then beep out 2111 (the internal phone-company code for Telex testing), and find themselves at any time, day or night, on an open wire talking with an array of phone phreaks from coast to coast, operators from Bermuda, Tokyo, and London who are phone-phreak sympathizers, and miscellaneous guests and technical experts. The conference was a massive exchange of information. Phone phreaks picked each other's brains clean, then developed new ways to pick the phone company's brains clean. Ralph gave *MF Boogie* concerts with his home-entertainment-type electric organ, Captain Crunch demonstrated his round-the-world prowess with his notorious computerized unit and dropped leering hints of the "action" he was getting with his girl friends. (The Captain lives out or pretends to live out several kinds of fantasies to the gossipy delight of the blind phone phreaks who urge him on to further triumphs on behalf of all of them.) The somewhat rowdy Northwest phone-phreak crowd let their bitter internal feud spill over into the peaceable conference line, escalating shortly into guerrilla warfare; Carl the East Coast international phone relations expert demonstrated newly opened direct M-F routes to central offices on the island of Bahrain in the Persian Gulf, introduced a new phone-phreak friend of his in Pretoria, and explained the technical operation of the new Oakland-to-Vietnam linkages. (Many phone phreaks pick up spending money by M-F-ing calls from relatives to Vietnam G.I.'s, charging $5 for a whole hour of trans-Pacific conversation.)

Day and night the conference line was never dead. Blind phone phreaks all over the country, lonely and isolated in homes filled with active sighted brothers and sisters, or trapped with slow and unimaginative blind kids in straightjacket schools for the blind, knew that no matter how late it got they could dial up the conference and find instant electronic communion with two or three other blind kids awake over on the other side of America. Talking together on a phone hookup, the blind phone phreaks say, is not much different from being there together. Physically, *there* was nothing more than a two-inch-square wafer of titanium inside a vast machine on Vancouver Island. For the blind kids *there* meant an exhilarating feeling of being *in touch*, through a kind of skill and magic which was peculiarly their own.

Last April 1, however, the long Vancouver Conference was shut off. The phone phreaks knew it was coming. Vancouver was in the process of converting from a step-by-step system to a 4A machine and the 2111 Telex circuit was to be wiped out in the process. The phone phreaks learned the actual day on which the conference would be erased about a week ahead of time over the phone company's internal-news-and-shop-talk recording.

For the next frantic seven days every phone phreak in America was on and off the 2111 conference twenty-four hours a day. Phone phreaks who were just learning the game or didn't have M-F capability were boosted up to the conference by more experienced phreaks so they could get a glimpse of what it was like before it disappeared. Top phone phreaks searched distant area codes for new conference possibilities without success. Finally in the early morning of April 1, the end came.

"I could feel it coming a couple hours before midnight," Ralph remembers. "You could feel something going on in the lines. Some static began showing up, then some whistling wheezing sound. Then there were breaks. Some people got cut off and called right back in, but after a while some people were finding they were cut off and couldn't get back in at all. It was terrible. I lost it about one A.M., but managed to slip in again and stay on until the thing died . . . I think it was about four in the morning. There were four of us still hanging on when the conference disappeared into nowhere for good. We all tried to M-F up to it again of course, but we got silent termination. There was nothing there."

THE LEGENDARY MARK BERNAY
TURNS OUT TO BE "THE MIDNIGHT SKULKER"

Mark Bernay. I had come across that name before. It was on Gilbertson's select list of phone phreaks. The California phone phreaks had spoken of a mysterious Mark Bernay as perhaps the first and oldest phone phreak on the West Coast. And in fact almost every phone phreak in the West can trace his origins either directly to Mark Bernay or to a disciple of Mark Bernay.

It seems that five years ago this Mark Bernay (a pseudonym he chose for himself) began traveling up and down the West Coast pasting tiny stickers in phone books all along his way. The stickers read something like "Want to hear an interesting tape recording? Call these numbers." The numbers that followed were toll-free loop-around pairs. When one of the curious called one of the numbers he would hear a tape recording pre-hooked into the loop by Bernay which explained the use of loop-around pairs, gave the numbers of several more, and ended by telling the caller, "At six o'clock tonight this recording will stop and you and your friends can try it out. Have fun."

"I was disappointed by the response at first," Bernay told me, when I finally reached him at one of his many numbers and he had dispensed with the usual "I never do anything illegal" formalities with which experienced phone phreaks open most conversations. "I went all over the coast with these stickers not only on pay phones, but I'd throw them in front of high schools in the middle of the night, I'd leave them unobtrusively in candy stores, scatter them on main streets of small towns. At first hardly anyone bothered to try it out. I would listen in for hours and hours after six o'clock and no one came on. I couldn't figure out why people wouldn't be interested. Finally these two girls in Oregon tried it out and told all their friends and suddenly it began to spread."

Before his Johnny Appleseed trip Bernay had already gathered a sizable group of early pre-blue-box phone phreaks together on loop-arounds in Los Angeles. Bernay does not claim credit for the original discovery of the loop-around numbers. He attributes the discovery to an eighteen-year-old reform-school kid in Long Beach whose name he forgets and who, he says, "just disappeared one day." When Bernay himself discovered loop-arounds independently, from clues in his readings in old issues of the *Automatic Electric Technical Journal*, he found dozens of the reform-school kid's friends already using them. However, it was one of Bernay's disciples in Seattle who introduced phone phreaking to blind kids. The Seattle kid who learned about loops through Bernay's recording told a blind friend, the blind kid taught the secret to his friends at a winter camp for blind kids in Los Angeles. When the camp session was over these kids took the secret back to towns all over the West. This is how the original blind kids became phone phreaks. For them, for most phone phreaks in general, it was the discovery of the possibilities of loop-arounds which led them on to far more serious and sophisticated phone-phreak methods, and which gave them a medium for sharing their discoveries.

A year later a blind kid who moved back east brought the technique to a blind kids' summer camp in Vermont, which spread it along the East Coast. All from a Mark Bernay sticker.

Bernay, who is nearly thirty years old now, got his start when he was fifteen and his family moved into an L.A. suburb serviced by General Telephone and Electronics equipment. He became fascinated with the differences between Bell and G.T.&E. equipment. He learned he could make interesting things happen by carefully timed clicks with the disengage button. He learned to interpret subtle differences in the array of clicks, whirrs, and kachinks he could hear on his lines. He learned he could shift himself around the switching relays of the L.A. area code in a not-too-predictable fashion by interspersing his own hook-switch clicks with the clicks within the line. Independent phone companies—there are nineteen hundred of them still left, most of them tiny island principalities in Ma Bell's vast empire—have always been favorites with phone phreaks, first as learning tools, then as Archimedes platforms from which to manipulate the huge Bell system. A phone phreak in Bell territory will often M-F himself into an independent's switching system, with switching idiosyncrasies which can give him marvelous leverage over the Bell System.

"I have a real affection for Automatic Electric equipment," Bernay told me. "There are a lot of things you can play with. Things break down in interesting ways."

Shortly after Bernay graduated from college (with a double major in chemistry and philosophy), he graduated from phreaking around with G.T.&E. to the Bell System itself, and made his legendary sticker-pasting journey north along the coast, settling finally in Northwest Pacific Bell territory. He discovered that if Bell does not break down as interestingly as G.T.&E., it nevertheless offers a lot of "things to play with."

Bernay learned to play with blue boxes. He established his own personal switchboard and phone-phreak research laboratory complex. He continued his phone-phreak evangelism with ongoing sticker campaigns. He set up two recording numbers, one with instructions for beginning phone phreaks, the other with latest news and technical developments (along with some advanced instruction) gathered from sources all over the country.

These days, Bernay told me, he has gone beyond phone-phreaking itself. "Lately I've been enjoying playing with computers more than playing with phones. My personal thing in computers is just like with phones, I guess—the kick is in finding out how to beat the system, how to get *at* things I'm not supposed to know about, how to *do* things with the system that I'm not supposed to be able to do."

As a matter of fact, Bernay told me, he had just been fired from his computer-programming job for doing things he was not supposed to be able to do. He had been working with a huge time-sharing computer owned by a large corporation but shared by many others. Access to the computer was limited to those programmers and corporations that had been assigned certain passwords. And each password restricted its user to access to only the one section of the computer cordoned off from its own information storager. The password system prevented companies and individuals from stealing each other's information.

"I figured out how to write a program that would let me read everyone else's password," Bernay reports. "I began playing around with passwords. I began letting the people who used the computer know, in subtle ways, that I knew their passwords. I began dropping notes to the computer supervisors with hints that I knew what I know. I signed them 'The Midnight Skulker.' I kept getting cleverer and cleverer with my messages and devising ways of showing them what I could do. I'm sure they couldn't imagine I could do the things I was showing them. But they never responded to me. Every once in a while they'd change the passwords, but I found out how to discover what the new ones were, and let them know. But they never responded directly to The Midnight Skulker. I even finally designed a program which they could use to prevent my program from finding out what it did. In effect I told them how to wipe me out, The Midnight Skulker. It was a very clever program. I started leaving clues about myself. I wanted them to try and use it, and then try to come up with something to get around that and reappear again. But they wouldn't play. I wanted to get caught. I mean I didn't want to get caught personally, but I wanted them to notice me and admit that they noticed me. I wanted them to attempt to respond, maybe in some interesting way."

Finally the computer managers became concerned enough about the threat of information-stealing to respond. However, instead of using The Midnight Skulker's own elegant self-destruct program, they called in their security personnel, interrogated everyone, found an informer to identify Bernay as The Midnight Skulker, and fired him.

"At first the security people advised the company to hire me full-time to search out other flaws and discover other computer freaks. I might have liked that. But I probably would have turned into a double double agent rather than the double agent they wanted. I might have resurrected The Midnight Skulker and tried to catch myself. Who knows? Anyway, the higher-ups turned the whole idea down."

You Can Tap the F.B.I.'s Crime Control Computer in the Comfort of Your Own Home, Perhaps

Computer freaking may be the wave of the future. It suits the phone-phreak sensibility perfectly. Gilbertson, the blue-box inventor and a life-long phone phreak, has also gone on from phone-phreaking to computer-freaking. Before he got into the blue-box business Gilbertson, who is a highly skilled programmer, devised programs for international currency arbitrage.

But he began playing with computers in earnest when he learned he could use his blue box in tandem with the computer terminal installed in his apartment by the instrumentation firm he worked for. The print-out terminal and keyboard was equipped with acoustical coupling, so that by coupling his little ivory Princess phone to the terminal and then coupling his blue box on that, he could M-F his way into other computers with complete anonymity, and without charge; program and reprogram them at will; feed them false or misleading information; tap and steal from them. He explained to me that he taps computers by busying out all the lines, then going into a verification trunk, listening into the passwords and instructions one of the time sharers uses, and then M-F-ing in and imitating them. He believes it would not be impossible to creep into the F.B.I.'s crime-control computer through a local police computer terminal and phreak around with the F.B.I.'s memory banks. He claims he has succeeded in reprogramming a certain huge institutional computer in such a way that it has cordoned off an entire section of its circuitry for his personal use, and at the same time conceals the arrangement from anyone else's notice. I have been unable to verify this claim.

Like Captain Crunch, like Alexander Graham Bell (pseudonym of a disgruntled-looking East Coast engineer who claims to have invented the black box and now sells black and blue boxes to gamblers and radical heavies), like most phone phreaks, Gilbertson began his career trying to rip off pay phones as a teen-ager. Figure them out, then rip them off. Getting his dime back from the pay phone is the phone phreak's first thrilling rite of passage. After learning the usual eighteen different ways of getting his dime back, Gilbertson learned how to make master keys to coin-phone cash boxes, and get everyone else's dimes back. He stole some phone-company equipment and put together his own home switchboard with it. He learned to make a simple "bread-box" device, of the kind used by bookies in the thirties (bookie gives a number to his betting clients; the phone with that number is installed in some widow lady's apartment, but is rigged to ring in the bookie's shop across town; cops trace big betting number and find nothing but the widow).

Not long after that afternoon in 1968 when, deep in the stacks of an engineering library, he came across a technical journal with the phone tone frequencies and rushed off to make his first blue box, not long after that Gilbertson abandoned a very promising career in physical chemistry and began selling blue boxes for $1,500 apiece.

"I had to leave physical chemistry. I just ran out of interesting things to learn," he told me one evening. We had been talking in the apartment of the man who served as the link between Gilbertson and the syndicate in arranging the big $300,000 blue-box deal which fell through because of legal trouble. There has been some smoking.

"No more interesting things to learn," he continues. "Physical chemistry turns out to be a sick subject when you take it to its highest level. I don't know. I don't think I could explain to you how it's sick. You have to be there. But you get, I don't know, a false feeling of omnipotence. I suppose it's like phone-phreaking that way. This huge thing is there. This whole system. And there are holes in it and you slip into them like Alice and you're pretending you're doing something you're actually not, or at least it's no longer *you* that's doing what you were doing. It's all Lewis Carroll. Physical chemistry and phone-phreaking. That's why you have these phone-phreak pseudonyms like The Cheshire Cat, The Red King, and The Snark. But there's something about phone-phreaking that you don't find in physical chemistry." He looks up at me:

"Did you ever steal anything?"

Well yes, I—

"Then you know! You know the rush you get. It's not just knowledge, like physical chemistry. It's forbidden knowledge. You know. You can learn about anything under the sun and be bored to death with it. But the idea that it's illegal. Look, you can be small and mobile and smart and you're ripping off somebody large and powerful and very dangerous."

People like Gilbertson and Alexander Graham Bell are always talking about ripping off the phone company and screwing Ma Bell. But if they were shown a single button and told that by pushing it they could turn the entire circuitry of A.T.&T. into molten puddles, they probably wouldn't push it. The disgruntled-inventor phone phreak needs the phone system the way the lapsed Catholic needs the Church, the way Satan needs a God, the way The Midnight Skulker needed, more than anything else, response.

Later that evening Gilbertson finished telling me how delighted he was at the flood of blue boxes spreading throughout the country, how delighted he was to know that "this time they're really screwed." He suddenly shifted gears.

"Of course, I do have this love/hate thing about Ma Bell. In a way I almost *like* the phone company. I guess I'd be very sad if they were to go away or if their services were to disintegrate. In a way it's just that after having been so good they turn out to have these things wrong with them. It's those flaws that allow me to get in and mess with them, but I don't know. There's something about it that gets to you and makes you want to *get to it*, you know."

I ask him what happens when he runs out of interesting, forbidden things to learn about the phone system.

"I don't know, maybe I'd go to work for them for a while."

"In security even?"

"I'd do it, sure. I'd just as soon play—I'd just as soon work on either side."

Even figuring out how to trap phone phreaks? I said, recalling Mark Bernay's game.

"Yes, that might be interesting. Yes, I could figure out how to outwit the phone phreaks. Of course if I got too good at it, it might become boring again. Then I'd have to hope the phone phreaks got much better and outsmarted me for a while. That would move the quality of the game up one level. I might even have to help them out, you know, 'Well kids, I wouldn't want this to get around but did you ever think of—?' I could keep it going at higher and higher levels forever."

The dealer speaks up for the first time. He has been staring at the soft blinking patterns of lights and colors on the translucent tiled wall facing him. Actually there are no patterns: the color and illumination of every tile is determined by a computerized random-number generator designed by Gilbertson which ensures that there can be no meaning to any sequence of events in the tiles.

"Those are nice games you're talking about," says the dealer to his friend. "But I wouldn't mind seeing them screwed. A telephone isn't private anymore. You can't say anything you really want to say on a telephone or you have to go through that paranoid bulls–. 'Is it cool to talk on the phone?' I mean, even if it is cool, if you have to ask 'Is it cool?' then it isn't cool. You know. Like those blind kids, people are going to start putting together their own private telephone companies if they want to really talk. And you know what else. You don't hear silences on the phone anymore. They've got this time-sharing thing on long-distance lines where you make a pause and they snip out that piece of time and use it to carry part of somebody else's conversation. Instead of a pause, where somebody's maybe breathing or sighing, you get this blank hole and you only start hearing again when someone says a word and even the beginning of the word is clipped off. Silences don't count—you're paying for them, but they take them away from you. It's not cool to talk and you can't hear someone when they don't talk. What the hell good is the phone? I wouldn't mind seeing them totally screwed."

THE BIG MEMPHIS BUST

Joe Engressia never wanted to screw Ma Bell. His dream had always been to work for her.

The day I visited Joe in his small apartment on Union Avenue in Memphis, he was upset about another setback in his application for a telephone job.

"They're stalling on it. I got a letter today telling me they'd have to postpone the interview I requested again. My landlord read it for me. They gave me some runaround about wanting papers on my rehabilitation status but I think there's something else going on."

When I switched on the forty-watt bulb in Joe's room—he sometimes forgets when he has guests—it looked as if there was enough telephone hardware to start a small phone company of his own.

There is one phone on top of his desk, one phone sitting in an open drawer beneath the desk top. Next to the desk-top phone is a cigar-box-size M-F device with big toggle switches, and next to that is some kind of switching and coupling device with jacks and alligator plugs hanging loose. Next to that is a Braille typewriter. On the floor next to the desk, lying upside down like a dead tortoise, is the half-gutted body of an old black standard phone. Across the room on a torn and dusty couch are two more phones, one of them a touch-tone model; two tape recorders; a heap of phone patches and cassettes; and a life-size toy telephone.

Our conversation is interrupted every ten minutes by phone phreaks from all over the country ringing Joe on just about every piece of equipment but the toy phone and the Braille typewriter. One fourteen-year-old blind kid from Connecticut calls up and tells Joe he's got a girl friend. He wants to talk to Joe about girl friends. Joe says they'll talk later in the evening when they can be alone on the line. Joe draws a deep breath, whistles him off the air with an earsplitting 2,600-cycle whistle. Joe is pleased to get the calls but he looked worried and preoccupied that evening, his brow constantly furrowed over his dark wandering eyes. In addition to the phone-company stall, he has just learned that his apartment house is due to be demolished in sixty days for urban renewal. For all its shabbiness, the Union Avenue apartment has been Joe's first home-of-his-own, and he's worried that he may not find another before this one is demolished.

But what really bothers Joe is that switchmen haven't been listening to him. "I've been doing some checking on 800 numbers lately, and I've discovered that certain 800 numbers in New Hampshire couldn't be reached from Missouri and Kansas. Now it may sound like a small thing, but I don't like to see sloppy work; it makes me feel bad about the lines. So I've been calling up switching offices and reporting it, but they haven't corrected it. I called them up for the third time today and instead of checking they just got mad. Well, that gets me mad. I mean, I do try to help them. There's something about them I can't understand—you want to help them and they just try to say you're defrauding them."

It is Sunday evening and Joe invites me to join him for dinner at a Holiday Inn. Frequently on Sunday evening Joe takes some of his welfare money, calls a cab, and treats himself to a steak dinner at one of Memphis's thirteen Holiday Inns. Memphis is the headquarters of Holiday Inn. Holiday Inns have been a favorite for Joe ever since he made his first solo phone trip to a Bell switching office in Jacksonville, Florida, and stayed in the Holiday Inn there. He likes to stay at Holiday Inns, he explains, because they represent freedom to him and because the rooms are arranged the same all over the country so he knows that any Holiday Inn room is familiar territory to him. Just like any telephone.

Over steaks in the Pinnacle Restaurant of the Holiday Inn Medical Center on Madison Avenue in Memphis, Joe tells me the highlights of his life as a phone phreak.

At age seven, Joe learned his first phone trick. A mean babysitter, tired of listening to little Joe play with the phone as he always did, constantly, put a lock on the phone dial. "I got so mad. When there's a phone sitting there and I can't use it . . . so I started getting mad and banging the receiver up and down. I noticed I banged it once and it dialed one. Well, then I tried banging it twice . . ." In a few minutes Joe learned how to dial by pressing the hook switch at the right time. "I was so excited I remember going 'whoo whoo' and beat a box down on the floor."

At age eight Joe learned about whistling. "I was listening to some intercept nonworking-number recording in L.A.—I was calling L.A. as far back as that, but I'd mainly dial nonworking numbers because there was no charge, and I'd listen to these recordings all day. Well, I was whistling 'cause listening to these recordings can be boring after a while even if they are from L.A., and all of a sudden, in the middle of whistling, the recording clicked off. I fiddled around whistling some more, and the same thing happened. So I called up the switch room and said, 'I'm Joe. I'm eight years old and I want to know why when I whistle this tune the line clicks off.' He tried to explain it to me, but it was a little too technical at the time. I went on learning. That was a thing nobody was going to stop me from doing. The phones were my life, and I was going to pay any price to keep on learning. I knew I could go to jail. But I had to do what I had to do to keep on learning."

The phone is ringing when we walk back into Joe's apartment on Union Avenue. It is Captain Crunch. The Captain has been following me around by phone, calling up everywhere I go with additional bits of advice and explanation for me and whatever phone phreak I happened to be visiting. This time the Captain reports he is calling from what he describes as "my hideaway high up in the Sierra Nevada." He pulses out lusty salvos of M-F tones and tells Joe he is about to "go out and get a little action tonight. Do some phreaking of another kind, if you know what I mean." Joe chuckles.

The Captain then tells me to make sure I understand that what he told me about tying up the nation's phone lines was true, but that he and the phone phreaks *he* knew never used the technique for sabotage. They only learned the technique to help the phone company.

"We do a lot of troubleshooting for them. Like this New

Hampshire/Missouri WATS-line flaw I've been screaming about. We help them more than they know."

After we say good-bye to the Captain and Joe whistles him off the line, Joe tells me about a disturbing dream he had the night before: "I had been caught and they were taking me to a prison. It was a long trip. They were taking me to a prison a long long way away. And we stopped at a Holiday Inn and it was my last night ever at a Holiday Inn, and it was my last night ever using the phone and I was crying and crying, and the lady at the Holiday Inn said, 'Gosh, honey, you should never be sad at a Holiday Inn. You should always be happy here. Especially since it's your last night.' And that just made it worse and I was sobbing so much I couldn't stand it."

Two weeks after I left Joe Engressia's apartment, phone-company security agents and Memphis police broke into it. Armed with a warrant, which they left pinned to a wall, they confiscated every piece of equipment in the room, including his toy telephone. Joe was placed under arrest and taken to the city jail where he was forced to spend the night since he had no money and knew no one in Memphis to call.

It is not clear who told Joe what that night, but someone told him that the phone company had an open-and-shut case against him because of revelations of illegal activity he had made to a phone-company undercover agent.

By morning Joe had become convinced that the reporter from *Esquire*, with whom he had spoken two weeks ago, was the undercover agent. He probably had ugly thoughts about someone he couldn't see gaining his confidence, listening to him talk about his personal obsessions and dreams, while planning all the while to lock him up.

"I really thought he was a reporter," Engressia told the Memphis *Press-Scimitar*. "I told him everything. . . ." Feeling betrayed, Joe proceeded to confess everything to the press and police.

As it turns out, the phone company *did* use an undercover agent to trap Joe, although it was not the *Esquire* reporter.

Ironically, security agents were alerted and began to compile a case against Joe because of one of his acts of love for the system: Joe had called an internal service department to report that he had located a group of defective long-distance trunks, and to complain again about the New Hampshire/Missouri WATS problem. Joe always liked Ma Bell's lines to be clean and responsive. A suspicious switchman reported

Joe to the security agents who discovered that Joe had never had a long-distance call charged to his name.

Then the security agents learned that Joe was planning one of his phone trips to a local switching office. The security people planted one of their agents in the switching office. He posed as a student switchman and followed Joe around on a tour. He was extremely friendly and helpful to Joe, leading him around the office by the arm. When the tour was over he offered Joe a ride back to his apartment house. On the way he asked Joe—one tech man to another—about "those blue boxes" he'd heard about. Joe talked about them freely, talked about his blue box freely, and about all the other things he could do with the phones.

The next day the phone-company security agents slapped a monitoring tape on Joe's line, which eventually picked up an illegal call. Then they applied for the search warrant and broke in.

In court Joe pleaded not guilty to possession of a blue box and theft of service. A sympathetic judge reduced the charges to malicious mischief and found him guilty on that count, sentenced him to two thirty-day sentences to be served concurrently, and then suspended the sentence on condition that Joe promise never to play with phones again. Joe promised, but the phone company refused to restore his service. For two weeks after the trial Joe could not be reached except through the pay phone at his apartment house, and the landlord screened all calls for him.

Phone phreak Carl managed to get through to Joe after the trial, and reported that Joe sounded crushed by the whole affair.

"What I'm worried about," Carl told me, "is that Joe means it this time. The promise. That he'll never phone-phreak again. That's what he told me, that he's given up phone-phreaking for good. I mean his entire life. He says he knows they're going to be watching so closely for the rest of his life he'll never be able to make a move without going straight to jail. He sounded very broken up by the whole experience of being in jail. It was awful to hear him talk that way. I don't know. I hope maybe he had to sound that way. Over the phone, you know."

He reports that the entire phone-phreak underground is up in arms over the phone company's treatment of Joe. "All the while Joe had his hopes pinned on his application for a phone-company job, they were stringing him along, getting ready to bust him. That gets me mad. Joe spent most of his time helping them out. The bastards. They think they can use him as an example. All of a sudden they're harassing us on the coast. Agents are jumping up on our lines. They just busted - - - -'s mute yesterday and ripped out his lines. But no matter what Joe does, I don't think we're going to take this lying down."

Two weeks later my phone rings and about eight phone phreaks in succession say hello from about eight different places in the country, among them Carl, Ed, and Captain Crunch. A nationwide phone-phreak conference line has been reestablished through a switching machine in - - - -, with the cooperation of a disgruntled switchman.

"We have a special guest with us today," Carl tells me.

The next voice I hear is Joe's. He reports happily that he has just moved to a place called Millington, Tennessee, fifteen miles outside of Memphis, where he has been hired as a telephone-set repairman by a small independent phone company. Someday he hopes to be an equipment troubleshooter.

"It's the kind of job I dreamed about. They found out about me from the publicity surrounding the trial. Maybe Ma Bell did me a favor busting me. I'll have telephones in my hands all day long."

—*ESQUIRE*
October 1971

POSTSCRIPT TO "SECRETS OF THE LITTLE BLUE BOX"

This story has had the most curious sort of ongoing repercussions. A recent biography of Steve Jobs, cofounder of Apple Computer with Steve Wozniak, describes how the Jobs-Wozniak partnership was first forged when, as California teenagers, they read "Secrets of the Little Blue Box" in *Esquire*, sought out the missing tone codes (which I'd deliberately left out of my story) in technical journals, and began manufacturing little blue boxes in Jobs's garage. (Jobs later confirmed this to me in person.)

Then there's "Captain Crunch," already a living legend when I first wrote about him, now a kind of mythic founder figure of computer hacker culture, which grew out of the outlaw-technology mystique of phone phreaks. Crunch's trajectory is emblematic of the divided nature of hacker consciousness. This one-time subversive techno-outlaw went legit—indeed, became establishment; he's still spoken of with awe, but these days it's as one of the patriarchs of the personal computer software revolution, having put his genius to work in programming the breakthroughs that made the p.c. user-friendly to the masses.

The other side of hacker-phreak consciousness—the outlaw, rebel romantic, sometimes Dark Side of the Force—can be found embodied in the visionary sensibility of cyber punk fiction (like William Gibson's *Neuromancer*) and the more diabolical of the computer virus creators (like the nihilist hackers who designed the AIDS-data-destroying computer virus of late 1989).

But to me the real heroes of the story are still the blind phone phreaks like Joe Engressia who created their etheric outlaw network not for dazzle or for fraud, but for the kind of extrasensory communion they achieved up on a tandem. Their like has been lovingly immortalized in a novel by Thomas McMahon called *Loving Little Egypt* (Viking), which, the author says, was inspired by reading "Secrets of the Little Blue Box."

HISTORICAL
LABYRINTH

● ■ ●

WHO WAS MARIA'S LOVER? THE CONTROVERSY OVER HITLER'S ANCESTRY

In April 1985, Harper and Row published a trade paperback reprint of *The Mind of Adolf Hitler*, a secret OSS-sponsored psychological study compiled by Dr. Walter C. Langer in 1943 and declassified in 1972.

The publisher's back-cover copy claims "this unique document sheds fascinating light on such facets of Hitler's strange psyche as . . . his hatred of Jews." The promo copy then proceeds to quote, without qualification, this sentence from the OSS report as evidence of the "fascinating light" it sheds:

"If it is true that one of the Rothschilds is the real father of Alois Hitler (Adolf Hitler's father) this would make Adolf a quarter-Jew."

Just a few months earlier, halfway around the world in Saudi Arabia, another variation of this rumor about Hitler's ancestry surfaced in the Saudi *Gazette*, an English-language daily published in Jeddah. In this case the allegation appeared in a letter printed under the half-inch high headline:

WAS HITLER A JEW?

The letter-writer, a self-described West German citizen who signed himself "A. Dusseldorf, Riyadh," informs us that he has been apprised of "evidence to prove that Hitler himself was a Jew. . . . Hitler's mother was a poor Austrian woman, a Christian employed as a maidservant in a wealthy Jewish household. . . . The actual father . . . was one of the Jewish sons of the old man. . . ."

The apparently unrelated appearance of these two items in such disparate quarters is testimony to the survival power of a disturbing subcurrent of Hitler aprocrypha: the "Jewish ancestry" myth.

Indeed, as recently as 1989 a purportedly scholarly book published by Cambridge University Press (*The Roots of Evil*) cites as fact "Hitler's illegitimate birth [and] . . . his belief (probably false) that his paternal grandmother was Jewish." (In fact, it was not Hitler but his father who was born illegitimately; and it is the identity of his paternal grandfather, not grandmother, that is at issue.)

Suspicion about his origins haunted Hitler throughout his public life and has plagued historians and biographers long after his death. As early as 1921, factional opponents of Hitler within the embryonic Nazi party raised the specter that he was in fact "a real Jew"—an accusation that was given public circulation by the opposition socialist newspaper.

In fact, questions about Hitler's "racial purity" troubled him—and those close to him—until at least as late as 1943, when the Gestapo undertook, with the knowledge of Himmler and Borman, the last of its seven separate investigations into the unresolved question of Hitler's genealogy. None of these was able to discover or produce for Hitler the "Aryan documentation"—documentary proof of racial purity dating back three generations—of the sort required of the lowliest of SS recruits.

Hitler's inability to produce positive proof of his racial purity and the continuing doubts raised about his official genealogy—in particular the question of the identity of his paternal grandfather—made him vulnerable to periodic episodes of public embarrassment and private blackmail threats. Hostile newspapers (particularly the London press), hostile intelligence organizations, disaffected members of Hitler's own family, as well as intraparty enemies had, at one time or another, attempted to make use of the potentially embarrassing "Jewish blood" accusation against Hitler during his lifetime.

And eight years after Hitler's death, the publication in West Germany of the memoirs of his personal attorney Hans Frank—with its extraordinary account of Frank's own investigation into the Hitler family genealogy, an investigation that, Frank said, seemed to substantiate the rumor of a Jewish ancestor—touched off a controversy among historians and scholars that has yet to be resolved conclusively, although I believe I can offer here a more persuasive explanation of the evidence than I have seen in the literature to date.

Needless to say, the real significance of the questions about Hitler's origins is not in the actual identity of the name on the family tree but in the effect doubt about his origins had on Hitler's psyche: the extent to which doubt about his own "racial purity" might have contributed to the genesis and obsessiveness of Hitler's anti-semitism.

What made Hitler's anti-semitism so uniquely murderous? How and when did Hitler become an anti-semite? How central to his policy was the desire to eradicate the Jews of Europe? These basic questions are still the subject of continuing debate among historians, biographers, and Holocaust scholars. I tend to agree with the proposition "No Hitler, no Holocaust." And I roughly concur with the "intentionalist" school of historians who argue that Hitler's personal drive to accomplish the eradication of the Jews of Europe was central and instrumental to the killing process (as opposed to the "functionalists," who see the Holocaust as a kind of byproduct of wartime circumstances and autonomous local and bureaucratic imperatives). But one doesn't have to be an intentionalist to believe that the origin and dynamic of Hitler's anti-semitism is an important question.

But it is one to which there are not agreed-upon answers, little certainty. How much of it was the product of anti-semitism in the culture that surrounded him, how much of it was generated by pathology within him? How did the two interact?

"The meaning of Hitler's anti-semitism to his psyche has been sought by many commentators," a 1983 survey of the literature reported. "Some have soon admitted defeat. Others have offered complicated speculations to fit their preconceptions."

I think I can fairly say I found myself approaching the question without any preconceptions, because in a way it snuck up on me in the course of my research into the more mundane question of who was Hitler's grandfather.

It began when I came upon the Hans Frank story in the course of researching a novel set in the first year and a half of the Hitler regime. It was a period in which anti-Hitler intrigues still abounded, and rumors of Hitler's "family secret" figured in some of them. When I began looking into the Hans Frank story, I was surprised to find such deep division over basic facts of Hitler's biography. William Shirer, for instance, never mentions the Hans Frank story in *The Rise and Fall of the Third Reich*, although he garbles even the official version of family history he tries to present. John Toland and Robert Waite both put a great deal of credence in the Hans Frank story, while Lucy Dawidowicz tends to dismiss it. On the continent, Austria's Franz Jetzinger believes Hans Frank's truthfulness; Germany's Werner Maser believes he's disproved it.

Then I began to notice garbled versions of the "Jewish ancestry" story showing up in such diverse places as a Harper and Row reprint and a Saudi newspaper. I began to see the way elements of this apocryphal theme had been perverted to fit anti-semitic formulations. The German-born Saudi *Gazette* letter writer, for instance, makes the contemptible suggestion that since Hitler had "Jewish blood," the Jews, not the Nazis, were responsible for the Holocaust.

The fact that the ancestry question has been abused in this fashion is cause for alarm as well as disgust. But on the other hand, to shrink from investigating the truth about Hitler's origins because the question has been perverted by bigots is almost to accept the sick premise of Nazi racial theory: that if Hitler had a Jewish grandfather, Jewish "blood" *can* somehow be held accountable for Hitler's crimes. In fact, from my examination of the literature in English and German, I think it can be shown that it's impossible to prove who Hitler's grandfather was—and that the *uncertainty*, not putative Jewishness, was what exacerbated his murderous pathology. But in any case it seems to me Jews shouldn't be inhibited from investigating the origins of the crime against them, and the facts, as far as they can be determined, should not be left to be a kind of playing field for the neo-Nazi imagination.

Nonetheless, since discussion of the question is potentially controversial, I showed an early draft of this essay to some fellow Jews to ask them for their reaction. None of them regarded investigation of these questions as offensive, but one of my readers said something to me about *my* motives for pursuing the question that was probably true, although I hadn't articulated it to myself.

This was a woman whose parents were refugees from Hitler's Germany; she'd been brought up with first-hand stories of Nazi terror. She said that the attempt to explore, if not explain, the origin of Hitler's anti-semitism helped demystify something she had experienced as an inexplicable, murderous hatred unaccountably directed at her, at her family, and her people. Dissecting the pathology of his hatred, she said, was somehow helpful in dealing with the legacy of that hate. Upon reflection, I think it was that same need for an explanation that was impelling me into the labyrinth unlocked by the question: who was Maria's lover?

●　　　■　　　●

Certain facts in the matter are no longer in dispute. On June 7, 1837, an unmarried Austrian peasant woman named Maria Anna Schicklgruber gave birth to an illegitimate child in her native village of Strones, twenty-five miles south of the German border. She did not identify the child's father on the baptismal register inscribed that day in the parish church in nearby Dollarsheim. The line for "Father" was left blank. Instead, she gave her newborn son, Alois, her own surname, Schicklgruber, as was the local custom when the mother could not or would not identify the father of her bastard child.

Nor, five years later, did the paternity question become clearer when Maria Anna married a local peasant laborer named Johann Georg Hiedler. The newlywed couple did not change the name of Maria's son from Schicklgruber to Hiedler, as might have been expected if Hiedler had fathered the child in a premarital relationship with Maria. Hiedler showed no interest in adopting or legitimizing Maria's child during his lifetime. In fact, after Maria died, he sent the boy off to live with his brother, Johann Nepomuk Hiedler.

Then forty years later, the brother-in-law did something that added a new layer of mystery to the question of the conception of Maria's child: he tampered with the original birth entry for Alois in the parish registry. One day in 1876, Johan Nepomuk Hiedler entered the Dollarsheim parish registry, accompanied by several illiterate witnesses. He persuaded the priest in charge to cross out the word "illegitimate" on the entry for Alois and to write a special note to the effect that before he died Georg Hiedler, long dead in 1876, had acknowledged fathering Maria's child, thus making Alois legitimate *"per matrimonium sequens,"* as the official Nazi party version of the family tree puts it—i.e., legitimate because of the subsequent marriage of the biological father to his mother. Maria's son emerged from this rewriting of the birth registration with a new, if problematical, legitimacy and a new name: Alois Hitler (apparently the priest's misspelling of Hiedler, which Alois then adopted).

While the fact of the name change itself may well have been innocuous, the reason for it has never been satisfactorily explained. One early Hitler biographer, Rudolph Olden, spoke of local talk that a legacy of some sort had been involved, but no such legacy or any other explanation for the change has yet been adduced.

Why the mystery and intrigue surrounding the parentage of Adolf Hitler's father? Who *was* Maria Schicklgruber's lover?

"Various candidates have been suggested," notes West German historian Werner Maser in his controversial review of the question. "Among them a 'Graz Jew' by the name of Frankenberger; a scion of the seigneurial house of Ottenstein; and even a Baron Rothschild of Vienna. But if there is one fact on which at least some biographers are agreed: it is that Adolf's paternal grandfather was not the man officially regarded as such, namely the journeyman miller Johann Georg Hiedler."

Although Maser's solution to this mystery—he believes Johann Nepomuk (the brother-in-law of Maria) was the biological father—is open to question, his phrase "one fact on which at least some biographers are agreed" sums up, in its imprecision, the state of the scholarship on the mystery of Maria's lover and the genealogy of Adolf Hitler.

But the more important issue is the state of Hitler's *own* knowledge of his complicated family history. The literature—memoirs, biographies, intelligence archives—is remarkably silent on this question. It is not even clear how early Hitler knew of his father's illegitimacy and the name change from Schicklgruber to Hitler that took place thirteen years before his birth—although, as we shall see, we do have testimony to his rage when these facts became public.

Still a name change, while unusual, doesn't necessarily imply the existence or consciousness of a "Jewish problem" in his ancestry. The only direct testimony in the literature to suggest Hitler had an *early* awareness of that sort of skeleton in the family closet appears in John Toland's 1976 biography of Hitler. Toland, who managed to unearth a number of previously overlooked sources on the Hitler genealogy question, quotes a certain Dr. Schuh to the effect that Hitler "suffered all his life from painful doubts, did he or did he not have Jewish blood."

Aside from this, the only other account we have that suggests an early awareness of a Jewish identity problem can be found in the memoir of a small-time Viennese hustler named Hanisch, who knew the teen-aged Hitler as a fellow denizen of Viennese flophouses and cafes.

In a three-part series published in 1939 issues of the *New Republic* titled "I Was Hitler's Buddy," Hanisch, who sold Hitler's drawings and paintings in the streets of Vienna, remarks that Hitler wore a full beard back then and a black caftan-like coat. "Hitler at that time looked very Jewish," Hanisch tells us. More than once, he says, Hitler was mistaken for a Jew: "I often joked with him that he must be of Jewish blood since such a large beard rarely grows on a Christian chin."

Hanisch's observation, as well as others by his Viennese vagabond companions—including one who suggested that the distinctive Hitlerian mustache was designed to "minimize" what Hitler considered "Jewish looking" nostrils—are particularly significant because in *Mein Kampf* Hitler pinpoints this period in Vienna as the moment of his awakening anti-semitic consciousness. Before Vienna, he says, growing up in provincial Linz, he rarely encountered or thought of Jews. In Vienna for the first time, he encountered "real" Jews and real anti-semitism. In fact, he traces the origin of his Jew hatred to a single illuminating vision on the streets of Vienna:

> Once as I was strolling through the inner city, I suddenly
> encountered an apparition in a black caftan and black ear-
> locks. "Is this a Jew?" was my first thought . . . but the
> longer I looked at this foreign face, scrutinizing feature for
> feature, the more my first question assumed a new form:
> "Is this a German?"

Suddenly—for the first time, Hitler claims—he began to see Jews as something alien, foreign, menacing.

Hitler's account of the origin of his anti-semitism in the vision of this "apparition" gains additional resonance if we bear in mind Hanisch's report that it was Hitler himself, wearing a black caftan-like cloak, whose ambiguous figure on the Vienna streets raised exactly that question—Is this a Jew?/Is this a German?—in the minds of others. That black-caftaned specter that, Hitler reports, triggered his hatred of Jews might well have been his nightmare vision of himself *as* a Jew.

Whatever the place it occupied in the privacy of his psyche, doubt about Hitler's racial identity began to become a factor in his public career almost from its inception.

The year 1921 marked a decisive shift in Hitler's political fortunes. In the two years since he'd joined the small racist fringe group calling itself the German Workers' Party in 1919, Hitler had attracted a growing notoriety as a rabble-rousing orator specializing in vitriolic attacks on the Jews. By 1921, he had become the most visible, but not yet the most powerful, leader of what was still a small-time hate group, now called the National Socialist German Workers' Party.

But in the summer of 1921 he made his move: he demanded the party acknowledge his primacy, make him its "*Fuehrer*." There was opposition from among the old-guard leadership of the party. One of the factions opposed to Hitler's power play produced a street leaflet titled "Adolf Hitler—Varrater [Traitor]?"

Hitler, the leaflet claimed, "promotes the interests of Jewry and its henchmen. . . . And how is he conducting this struggle? Like a real Jew."

The text of this leaflet and an account of the anti-Hitler factional fight inside the NSDAP appeared in a July issue of the socialist Munich *Post*. "Shortly before he took over the party in late July 1921," according to Werner Maser, "a number of the NSDAP chiefs put it about that he had Jewish antecedents. . . . Between July and December 1921 there were frequent rumors in Munich about Hitler's Jewish descent."

Although these rumors didn't succeed in derailing Hitler's bid for one-man rule of the NSDAP, once the doubt about his origins had become a part of public and private discourse about him, he was never able to eradicate it.

In part, this difficulty grew out of the fact of his foreignness: he was a fanatic proponent of German nationalism and Aryan supremacy who was neither German by birth nor typically Aryan in appearance. These paradoxes might not have presented the problem they did had they not been compounded by Hitler's own vagueness about his family history and his failure ever to produce positive proof of his Aryan genealogy.

In *Mein Kampf*, for instance, he fails even to name his grandparents, referring to his father's father only once as "a poor cottager" (when, in fact, the evidence suggests that Johann Hiedler never owned a cottage of his own, as the term "cottager" suggests, but is more accurately described as an itinerant peasant laborer).

Hitler's reticence about his family background in *Mein Kampf* caused some skeptical journalists to investigate the Hitler family history. It wasn't long before it became known that his father's name was originally Schicklgruber.

According to early Hitler biographer Rudolf Olden, "an ingenious journalist published the fact in a liberal newspaper in Vienna. It was not correct to say 'Heil Hitler,' he wrote, but 'Heil Schicklgruber.' "

This mocking exploitation of the ambiguity surrounding his father's parentage seemed to touch a nerve in "The Brown House," Hitler's Munich headquarters. According to Olden, "two young members of the party attacked the editor [who printed the Schicklgruber story] with truncheons in the cafe in which he used to sit after dinner. The incident had no further consequence except that the change of name was now reported in all the newspapers."

While there was no explicit mention of Jewishness in the "Heil Schicklgruber" stories, they helped create a climate of mystery and uncertainty over Hitler's origins and thus removed even rumors of Jewishness from the realm of utter implausibility, creating a sense that Hitler had something to hide.

That what was hidden might have been "Jewish blood" was, needless to say, particularly tormenting to Hitler, who was even more obsessive in his hatred of *Rassenschande*, "the racial shame" of mixed blood, than he was in his hatred of Jews themselves.

"*Blood-sin and desecration of the race are the original sin in this World*," he proclaimed in shrill italics in *Mein Kampf*.

Repeatedly in that screed he denounces the products of intercourse between Jews and Aryans. Nature, he says,

> . . . has little love for [such] bastards. Especially the first
> products of such cross breeding, say in the third, fourth and
> fifth generation, suffer bitterly. . . . With their lack of blood
> unity they lack also unity of will power. . . . In all critical
> moments in which the racially unified being makes correct,
> that is, unified decisions, the racially divided one will become
> uncertain, that is, he will arrive at half measures. *In innu-
> merable cases where race holds up, the bastard breaks down*
> [italics in original].

It is in this context of several years of hostile curiosity on the part
of the press and the exacerbated sensitivity on Hitler's part over the
issue of his origins that the curious Hans Frank episode began to unfold
in 1930. It was in that year that Hitler won his first major electoral
victory, one that suddenly brought him and his party close to the brink
of power in the depression-stricken Weimar Republic. It was a victory
that focused world attention for the first time on the question of who
he was and where he came from.

The London press was particularly avid on the subject of the shadowy
origins of this obscure Austrian with the comic mustache and the father
named Schicklgruber who was suddenly within striking distance of
power in Germany, clearly eager to refight the Great War. (One London
paper, the *Evening Mail*, went so far as to print a photograph of a
headstone from a Jewish cemetery in Rumania that had the name "Adolf
Hitler" carved upon it, followed by an inscription in Hebrew. The
accompanying caption asked, "Is this the grave of Hitler's Jewish grandfather?" and gleefully played upon the irony of the rabid anti-semite
being descended from a Jew; it seems that Hitler was not an utterly
uncommon surname among Eastern European Jews.)

All the publicity about Hitler prompted two distant relatives living
in England to come forward and attempt to profit from the family
connection.

Brigid Hitler was the Irish-born ex-wife of Adolf Hitler's half-
brother, Alois Jr., the son of Alois Schicklgruber by a marriage before
the one that produced Adolf. (Brigid would later author a largely spu-
rious postwar memoir of her adventures with Adolf, none of which is
relied upon here.)

Alois Jr. fathered a son, William Patrick Hitler. This mother-son team of Brigid and William had already caused trouble for their German relations. In 1924, the year after the Beerhall Putsch had given the Hitler name international notoriety, their attempt to resume contact with Alois Jr. resulted in a bigamy accusation against him in Germany, where he was then living with a German wife, with resultant publicity embarrassing to Adolf. And then in 1930, in the midst of the crucial German election campaign, the English relatives surfaced again. They began talking to the London press about "their family," about "uncle Adolf." Word reached Hitler headquarters in Munich from Hearst representatives that the London mother-son team was going to be writing about the "family history"—always a worrisome topic since the Schicklgruber episode.

And then worry turned to alarm. A letter arrived for Hitler from the half-nephew, William Patrick Hitler. According to several accounts, Hitler regarded the letter as a threat, blackmail. He summoned his lawyer.

"One day, it must have been towards the end of 1930," Hitler's one-time personal attorney Hans Frank has written, "I was called to the residence of Hitler at Princeregenten Theatre. He told me, with a letter lying before him, [of] a 'disgusting blackmail plot' in connection with one of his most loathsome relatives, with respect to his own ancestry."

Hans Frank tells us the source of this blackmail was "a son of Hitler's half-brother Alois who was gently hinting that in view of certain allegations in the press it might be better if certain family matters weren't shouted from the roof tops. The press reports in question suggested that Hitler had Jewish blood in his veins and hence was hardly qualified to be an anti-semite. But they were phrased in such general terms that nothing could be done about it. In the heat of the political struggle the whole thing died down. All the same, this threat of blackmail by a relative was a somewhat tricky business. At Hitler's request I made some confidential inquiries."

Before we get into the results of these "confidential inquiries" as reported by Hans Frank, it might be worthwhile to look at the circumstances in which Hans Frank made these disclosures, since his bizarre, still-controversial, account of his solution to the mystery of Maria's lover is the most explicit version of the "Jewish ancestry" myth extant.

Appointed chief Nazi party attorney in 1928, Hans Frank parlayed his position as legal confidant to Adolf Hitler into appointments as Bavarian minister of the Interior, then as Reichsminister for the Administration of Justice. Later, as governor-general of conquered Poland, he presided over the slaughter of millions of Poles and Jews.

Convicted and scheduled to hang on the gallows at Nuremberg for these crimes, Hans Frank entered into conversations with G. M. Gilbert, an American psychologist assigned to the Nuremberg prisoners by the tribunal, and an American Franciscan army chaplain, Father Sixtus O'Connor, about his role in the rise of Adolf Hitler and the horrors of his regime. At the encouragement of the priest and the psychologist, he produced a thousand-page pencil-written manuscript filled with memories, reflections, and soul searching, a memoir torn between professed abhorrence of what Hitler had wrought and yet continued admiration for his "greatness," however twisted. It was not designed for, nor even offered as, a plea for clemency. In fact, it never saw the light of day until 1953, seven years after Frank went to his death. While the original pencil-written manuscript remained in possession of Gilbert until he donated it to the Yad Vashem Holocaust memorial in Israel in 1961 (when he went there to testify at the Eichmann trial), a copy was smuggled out to Hans Frank's own family by Father O'Connor and was published in West Germany in 1953 under the title *In Sight of the Gallows*.

Frank's manuscript contains accounts of a number of instances in which he was entrusted with covering up potentially scandalous aspects of leading Nazis' personal lives. There were nasty rumors and innuendos in the Munich papers following the mysterious gunshot death of Geli Raubal, Hitler's young niece—and some said mistress—in her bedroom in Hitler's apartment residence. Threats from Hans Frank silenced those who were skeptical of the official verdict of "suicide."

But this new "loathsome blackmail threat" about Hitler's genealogy was to prove a more difficult assignment. Because the "confidential inquiries" he undertook at Hitler's request led him to investigate the whole mystery of Maria's lover, and to conclude on the basis of what he said was documentary evidence that there was a substantive foundation for the threat to expose Hitler as a *Mischling*—mixed breed or "mongrel," with Jewish blood.

"Intensive investigation elicited the following information," Hans Frank wrote at Nuremberg:

Hitler's father was the illegitimate son of a woman by the name of Schicklgruber from Leonding near Linz who worked as a cook in a Graz household. . . . But the most extraordinary part of the story is this: when the cook Schicklgruber (Adolf Hitler's grandmother) gave birth to her child, she was in service with a Jewish family called Frankenberger. And on behalf of his son, then about nineteen years old, Frankenberger paid a maintenance allowance to Schicklgruber from the time of the child's birth until his fourteenth year. For a number of years, too, the Frankenbergers and Hitler's grandmother wrote to each other, the general tenor of the correspondence betraying on both sides the tacit acknowledgment that Schicklgruber's illegitimate child had been engendered under circumstances which made the Frankenbergers responsible for its maintenance. For years this correspondence remained in the possession of a woman living in Wetzelsdorf near Graz who was related to Hitler through the Raubals. . . . Hence the possibility cannot be dismissed that Hitler's father was half Jewish as a result of the extramarital relationship between the Schicklgruber woman and the Jew from Graz. This would mean that Hitler was one-quarter Jewish.

It is hard to imagine an attorney-client conference more fraught with tension than the one in which Hans Frank says he presented Hitler with a report that he, the world's leading Jew-hater, was himself part Jewish. And that there were documents that seemed to prove it.

How did Hitler respond to this unwelcome news? This is the most fascinating, most overlooked aspect of Frank's controversial account.

Astonishingly, according to Frank, Hitler did not deny it. He did not claim that the paternity correspondence upon which Frank based his report that Maria had a Jewish lover was a forgery. He did not dispute Frank's report that a Jew had made payments to his grandmother Maria to support her child, his father. In fact, according to Frank, Hitler *confirmed* that such payments were made.

But, Hitler told Frank, there *was* an explanation—not a simple explanation, but one that could account for the existence of the potentially damaging child-support correspondence and yet exempt Hitler from the apparent implication of that correspondence: that he had "Jewish blood."

According to Frank, Hitler's explanation was that he "knew from conversations with his father and grandmother that his father had not been born as a result of sexual intercourse between the Schicklgruber woman and the Jew from Graz." The conception was actually the result of "a premarital relation" between Maria and the man she would later marry, Johann Georg Hiedler, the peasant laborer who was indisputably non-Jewish.

As for those child-support payments Maria got from the Jewish family, Hitler explained he had been told that they were actually extracted from the Jews under false pretenses. Maria Schicklgruber falsely accused the nineteen-year-old son of her Jewish employer of impregnating her in order to extract money from the evidently wealthy Jewish family. And, according to Hitler's explanation, "the Jew paid without going to court probably because he could not face the publicity that a legal settlement might have entailed."

While this explanation might have provided a technical basis for denying he had "Jewish blood," it was not exactly the kind of airtight distinction that would leave the mind of the world's leading anti-semite untroubled by doubt. Conceding, as it seems to, the likelihood that Maria Schicklgruber had two lovers at the time of conception, one Jewish, one Aryan—it would be difficult to extort child support if there had been no intercourse—it consigns the issue of paternity to unresolvable doubt: the only one who might have known for sure who fathered the child was Maria Schicklgruber, and the implication of Hitler's explanation is that even she might not have known.

Hans Frank himself seems uncertain what to think of Hitler's explanation of the paternity correspondence with the "Graz Jew." At one point he tells us he believes Hitler's explanation: "That Adolf Hitler certainly had no Jewish blood in his veins seems to be so strikingly evident that it needs no further explanation." But then he concludes his account of the whole episode by telling us, "I must say that it is not absolutely impossible that Hitler's father was in fact half Jewish. Then his hatred of Jews would have arisen from outraged blood-relative hate psychosis. Who could interpret all this?"

Before we attempt to meet that challenge—Who could interpret all this?—let's look at a strangely similar "Jewish blood" blackmail plot against Hitler that, according to the OSS report *The Mind of Adolph Hitler*, was developing about this time, a plot that, if one believes the OSS source materials, would subsequently play a role in the struggle over the fate of Central Europe in the midthirties.

According to the 1943 OSS report on Hitler, the pre-*Anschluss* Austrian government had initiated an investigation of the Austrian-born *Fuehrer*'s family background, and—with access to sources in his birthplace beyond Hitler's control—had come up with a startling conclusion about the identity of Maria's lover.

The OSS file on the matter was compiled before Hans Frank's 1946 confession and was based on at least two sources: one-time pro-Hitler industrialist Fritz Thyssen and one-time Heydrich aide Hans Jurgen Koehler. According to them, the OSS report states:

> Chancellor Dollfuss had ordered the Austrian police to conduct a thorough investigation into the Hitler family. As a result of this investigation, a secret document was prepared that proved that Maria Anna Schicklgruber was living in Vienna at the time she conceived. At that time she was employed as a servant in the home of Baron [Salomon] Rothschild. As soon as the family discovered her pregnancy she was sent to her home in Spital where Alois was born. If it is true that one of the Rothschilds is the real father of Alois Hitler it would make Adolf a quarter Jew. According to these sources Adolf Hitler knew of the existence of this document and incriminating evidence it contained. In order to obtain it he precipitated events in Austria and initiated the assassination of Dollfuss. According to this story he failed to obtain the documents at that time since Dollfuss had secreted it and had told [his successor, Chancellor] Schuschnigg of its whereabouts so that in the event of his death the independence of Austria would remain assured.

But according to several sources the matter didn't end there. One British biographer of Heydrich—Charles Wighton, who claims an "SD officer" as his source—tells us:

By the second half of 1937 the Austrian government [of Schuschnigg] was aware that Hitler planned a major move against his native country—and the highly incriminating dossier on Hitler was brought into play. A copy of the document was made and sent to Mussolini. . . . As the Austrians were certain would happen, the Duce sent the file to Hitler. By way of Rome it was made clear that in certain eventualities the dossier would be made public to the whole world.

This threat was serious enough, according to Fritz Thyssen, to cause Hitler to take extraordinary measures to end it before he engineered the *Anschluss* of Austria:

When he [Hitler] asked the Austrian chancellor to come to Berchtesgaden in February 1938 he intended to get possession of the document. In order to get hold of it, he began by ordering the arrest of Countess Fugger, Chancellor Schuschnigg's friend who later, after he was taken prisoner by the Gestapo, became his wife. The compromising document was then given to Baron von Ketteler, the secretary of the *Fuehrer*'s Ambassador to Vienna, Herr von Papen. It is quite possible that Papen took care to have the incriminating papers photographed before having them carried to Berlin to Ketteler. It is clear that the unfortunate Schuschnigg, faced by his terrible adversary at Berchtesgaden, was deprived of his one weapon against him—the threat to publish the Dollfuss document which would have revealed Hitler's true origin to the world.

Charles Wighton claims to have debriefed one of Heydrich's men who saw this fateful dossier. He tells us that:

According to the SD man who saw the dossier, the document suggesting that Hitler's unknown grandfather probably stemmed from at least the palace—if not the House—of Rothschild, had a marginal note written in pencil. It was in the unmistakable writing of Chancellor Dollfuss. "This

material [the margin note went] ought to cheer the writers
of history who sometime in the future want to publish the
true life story of Hitler. Here is the psychological explanation of Hitler's fanatical hatred of the Jews. Hitler, born
in peaceful Upper Austria, was filled even in his childhood
with a burning hatred of the Jews. Why? This may be the
answer. . . ."

Whether we believe Wighton's account or not, might this in fact be
"the answer"? Is it "the psychological explanation for Hitler's fanatical
hatred of the Jews"? Again there are really two questions here: Are
the stories of a Jewish grandfather—whether he was a Rothschild or a
Frankenberger—true? And did Hitler fear they might be true?

Many aspects of the Rothschild story arouse immediate skepticism.
The source is a hostile intelligence agency. It seems unlikely that the
Rothschild and the Frankenberger stories could both be true, unless
one wished to argue that the Frankenberger of Graz in the Hans Frank
story might have been related by birth or business connection to the
Rothschild palace in nearby Vienna. Or that the Rothschild story was
a garbled version of the Frankenberger story, fabricated by the Austrian
secret police from a fragmentary second-hand account of what Hans
Frank heard.

Whatever the case, the most significant elements of the Rothschild
dossier story in the OSS study are the accounts of Hitler's reaction to
the rumors of its existence.

The OSS sourcebook includes, for instance, this account by French
journalist Andre Simone from his book *Men of Europe*:

It seems by the way that the Austrian Chancellor Dollfuss
guarded Hitler's police record like a treasure. It is quite
possible that this cost him his life. For in May 1934 I saw
a report of the French Minister to Vienna on a conversation
with Dollfuss. The Chancellor complained bitterly that Hitler's henchmen were after him because he refused to hand
Hitler's police record to them. A few weeks after I was
shown this report by a high official of the Quai d'Orsay,
Dollfuss was murdered by Viennese S.S. men on the express
order of Hitler's deputy leader Rudolph Hess.

A further indication of the fairly widespread currency of this rumor can be found in the diaries of Bella Fromm, diplomatic correspondent for the Ullstein newspapers in Berlin. In her entry for August 15, 1934, she writes:

> Richard came to see me, all hot and flustered. "Bellachen, Hitler has Jewish blood in his veins. Paul Wiegler our fiction editor has found out through Viennese friends!
>
> "Hitler had a very beautiful grandmother. She was vain, ambitious, and money greedy. She had a job as a lady's maid in Vienna at a wealthy, non-Aryan banker's house. It is known that she brought an illegitimate child into her marriage with Schicklgruber. Well, that offspring of her romance with the Jewish banker was Adolf Hitler's father."

While this version sounds indeed as if it were transmitted, melodramatized by a "fiction editor," the skeletal outline—the poor serving girl, the rich Jew, the illegitimate mixed-breed offspring—is the same as that in the Hans Frank story and the Rothschild version.

It is almost as if there were some common precursor, some Ur-version of this story, which was the source for the Frankenberger, the Rothschild, and the "non-Aryan banker" variants.

Even more curious, as Professor Robert Waite has pointed out (in *Hitler: The Psychopathic God*), is how closely the Jewish ancestor stories follow the script of the pornographic fantasies Hitler loved to read in Julius Streicher's *Der Sturmer*. Week after week Streicher would print lasciviously illustrated "true stories" of innocent Aryan maidens finding themselves first in the employ of a wealthy Jew and then in his enforced embrace. It's a fantasy that occupies a prominent place, Waite points out, in *Mein Kampf*, where Hitler writes of the "black-haired Jewish youth lurking in wait for the Aryan maiden, his eyes alight with satanic joy." (Note that in Hitler's own version of the fantasy it is a black-haired *youth* who seeks to defile the Aryan maiden, as opposed to the standard *Sturmer* version, which usually featured rich old men. According to Hans Frank it was "the nineteen-year-old son" of Frankenberger who was responsible for Maria's pregnancy.)

While Hitler's preoccupation with this particular fantasy doesn't necessarily bespeak consciousness of a Jewish seducer in his own family tree, Waite adduces a couple of other extremely curious manifestations of Hitler's obsession with the Aryan serving girl-Jewish employer seducer theme.

Consider Hitler's verbal assault on Mathias Erzberger, the man who led the delegation that signed the November 1918 armistice, the so-called "stab in the back":

"Fate," said Hitler, "has chosen a man for that treachery, Mathias Erzberger . . . the illegitimate son of a servant girl and a Jewish employer."

Waite also notes a 1935 codicil to the Nuremberg Racial Laws, added at Hitler's insistence, that specifically forbids unmarried Aryan females under forty-five from being employed as servants in the household of Jewish employers. Maria Schicklgruber was forty-two when she gave birth to Hitler's father.

In word and deed, Hitler acted as if the sexual coupling of an Aryan serving girl and a Jewish employer was not merely a crime, not merely *Rassenschande*, "racial shame," but more like original sin. How much of this fantasy that preoccupied Hitler can be traced to uneasiness about his own family history? How much historical truth is there in the Jewish ancestry story?

The Austrian "Rothschild dossier" may be dismissed as disinformation disseminated by a hostile intelligence agency; the Hans Frank story is more difficult to disqualify on that basis. It comes from a confidant and ally of Hitler who went to the gallows still believing in his "greatness."

Can we believe the Hans Frank story? German- and English-speaking scholars and historians have been arguing over this question ever since his memoir was published in 1953. Among the most skeptical has been the West German biographer of Hitler Werner Maser, who believes Hans Frank made the whole story up. He supplies a peculiarly twisted motive for the purported fabrication:

> While in Nuremberg under the tutelage of Father O'Connor, Frank was patently remorseful and devout. Hence he may conceivably have been seeking, not only to disembarrass his fellow Catholics for all times of Adolf Hitler, the Catholic mass-murderer, but also to foment unrest, anxiety, and a lasting sense of guilt among the Jews.

Setting aside for a moment the outrageous and perverse implication that an imputation of Jewishness to Hitler's paternal grandfather should somehow cause "a lasting sense of guilt among the Jews" for their own murder (a belief shared by the Saudi *Gazette* letter-writer), could there be some basis for Maser's attack on Frank's motivation?

The most comprehensive and convincing testimony on this point comes from Frank's secular confessor, the American-born, German-speaking psychologist G. M. Gilbert, who attended Frank during his trial and incarceration at Nuremberg, during the time he wrote his memoir.

The Nuremberg authorities had assigned Gilbert to counsel the accused war prisoner. Having won Hans Frank's confidence, the psychologist encouraged the condemned prisoner to write down his memories and reflections on the rise of Hitler, particularly those events he witnessed and participated in.

Gilbert was interviewed by Toland on the subject of Hans Frank's account of his "confidential inquiries" into Hitler's ancestry.

"You believe this investigation *did* take place?" Toland asked Hans Frank's psychologist. "You're the only one in the world who can tell us that."

Yes, he believes it, Gilbert responds: "While he was prone to exaggerate many things," the psychologist recalled of Frank, "and of course to glamorize his own role, this is something he thought of no great consequence and he said, 'Well, I guess stranger things have happened than hatred of one's own race.' He [Frank] was inclined to believe the results of his investigation. He [Hitler] wouldn't acknowledge having Jewish blood but the mere fact that she [Maria] was in a position to blackmail a Jew, evidently having had relations with him, is enough to stir up this violent anti-Jewish sexual hatred in Hitler."

What about Hans Frank's motives in telling the whole story? Toland asked Frank's psychologist.

> "It was a way of expiating his guilt," Gilbert said. "He had to explain to the world, to help people understand how this man [Hitler] was able to influence so many."

Gilbert found Frank's explanation of the source of Hitler's anti-semitic obsession convincing. "Especially when he [Hitler] was already committed to being a violent anti-semite with his whole ego structure depending upon this, the idea that it [the Jewish grandfather story] could have been true could have been resolved in his sick mind only by showing, as Frank said, that he was the worst anti-semite in the world, so how could he possibly be a Jew."

Of course Maser's conjecture that Hans Frank invented the story of the "confidential investigation" can't be ruled out entirely. Nonetheless, there exists some significant external corroboration of the events Hans Frank relates.

There is, for instance, the OSS interview with the "loathsome relative" who, according to Frank, had written the "blackmail" letter, precipitating his confidential investigation. The never-published OSS debriefing took place on September 10, 1943, in New York City, several years after the nephew William Patrick Hitler had fled Germany, shortly before he enlisted in the American army to fight his uncle. A summary of the debriefing can be found in the "OSS Sourcebook," the collection of raw intelligence materials, interviews, and archival material about Hitler from which Dr. Langer compiled his analysis, *The Mind of Adolf Hitler*, and which was made available to me by Professor Waite, who succeeded in getting it declassified.

In the debriefing, William Patrick Hitler tells the story of how, in 1930, he and his mother suddenly found themselves drawn into a tense encounter with their German relative Adolf.

According to the OSS summary of the debriefing:

> In the late 1920s when Adolf began to rise in popularity sufficiently to get into the English newspapers, they wrote to Adolf. . . . In 1930 when Hitler suddenly became famous with over 100 seats in the Reichstag they thought it was an opportunity of making some money by giving an interview to the Hearst press. Negotiations were underway but they felt the need of additional information and wrote to Alois asking for further details about Adolf's youth. The reply came in the form of a demand from Adolf to come to Munich immediately for a conference. . . . Upon their arrival in Munich they found Adolf in a perfect rage.
>
> The gist of what Adolf said was now that he was gaining some importance the family need not think that they could

climb on his back and get a free ride to fame. He claimed that any release to the Hearst newspapers involving his family would destroy his chances for success in view of Alois's [bigamous] record, and that negotiations with the Hearst syndicate had to be stopped immediately, and the great problem was how this could be done without arousing suspicions. It was finally suggested that William Patrick and his mother return to London and tell the Hearst people that it was a question of mistaken identity and that they had discovered that the Adolf Hitler who was the leader of the Nazi party was not the uncle they had supposed but an Adolf Hitler who was no kin of theirs whatever. Hitler was pleased with this solution and . . . handed Alois 2,000 pounds to cover their expenses . . . [and] instructions to give Mrs. [Brigid] Hitler what was left over when their expenses had been paid. . . .

It is interesting in this regard that in the November 30, 1930, edition of Hearst's *New York American*, there appears an article titled "Adolf Hitler" by Alois Hitler, apparently a sanitized substitute for the one proposed by the English relatives.

In any case, although William Patrick Hitler does not characterize the 1930 encounter as blackmail, he does describe a 1930 transaction, in which he accepted money for silence and denial.

But the episode did not end there. Two and a half years later, there was a renewal of the peculiar relationship between Adolf Hitler and his English relatives, and this time it looked even more explicitly like blackmail.

Two developments in the interim had exacerbated Hitler's sensitivity over the family history issue. First was the publication in 1932 of a major biography (*Der Fuehrer*) by an unsympathetic journalist, Konrad Heiden, who made a point of raising—and not explicitly dispelling—the question of a Jewish ancestor. Heiden's biography was widely read and translated abroad (Heiden made the additional assertion, later proved to be unfounded, that Hitler had a Jewish godfather living in Vienna). The second factor that made Hitler even more vulnerable to the renewed threat from the English relatives was his sudden ascension to the Reichschancellorship and to the glare of publicity that came with it. That first year Hitler's grip on his office was by no means secure, his power not yet consolidated; he still served under Hindenburg's nominal authority. A family scandal, particularly one that could turn him into a figure of ridicule, would be especially threatening.

The English relatives seemed to sense this, because it was shortly after Hitler moved into the Reichschancellory on January 30, 1933, that they made another approach. According to the OSS summary of the interview with William Patrick Hitler:

> Mrs. [Brigid] Hitler chafed more and more under her poverty . . . and thought Adolf might be willing to pay something to keep her quiet. . . . Hitler replied and invited William Patrick to Berchtesgaden for a summer vacation. . . . Hitler . . . told William Patrick that . . . since he insisted on making demands on Hitler that he could see no way out of it except to tell him the truth . . . that his father Alois Jr. was not really the son of Hitler's father but a boy who had been orphaned as an infant and whom Alois Sr. had taken into his home. . . . He only wanted to make it clear to William Patrick that he had absolutely no claim on him as an uncle and that they were in fact not related at all.

This rather strained attempt by the newly elected Reichschancellor to rid himself of a loose-cannon relative by denying his blood relationship seems to have backfired.

> After his return to London [the OSS summary tells us], William Patrick and his mother checked on this report through the British Consul General in Vienna who, after some time, said the story was impossible, because no adoption papers were on record and the baptismal certificates were clear [that he was a blood relative]. . . .
>
> William Patrick has also a photostatic copy of Adolf's baptismal certificate. . . . It also shows that Hitler's godfather and godmother are probably not Jewish, as Heiden and many others have claimed, but a family named Prinz who lived on Lowengasse 28 Vienna III.

Apparently William Patrick used these documents on Hitler family history to good advantage with his uncle: "Hitler arranged a job for him at the Opel Auto Company," the OSS interview reports.

And William Patrick's knowledge of Hitler family history does seem to have served as some kind of extortion lever for him:

> Over and over again Hitler warned him about trying to cash in on their relationship. . . . He said he then acquainted Hitler with the fact that he had documents from the British Consul to the effect that his story about his father [being no blood relation to Adolf] was not true and that copies of these documents were deposited with the English government as well as with his mother in London. From that time on, Hitler became more tolerant of him and whenever he began to rage about William Patrick's activities, he had only to mention the documents in order to get Hitler to calm down.

The OSS interview concludes by saying that William Patrick "was under the impression that it was this knowledge [of family history] that made Hitler fear both of them [William and his mother] because he is absolutely intent on keeping both his present family and his background a deep, dark secret."

Melodramatic and self-serving as it is, William Patrick Hitler's statements to the OSS do tend to corroborate Hans Frank's story in two important respects. First, whether it's characterized as "blackmail" (Hans Frank) or "negotiations" (William Patrick Hitler), there does seem to have been a tense contest of wills going on between Adolf Hitler and his London relatives over the question of family history. And, second, Hitler acted as if he had something to fear from them, treating the otherwise powerless mother-son team as if they had the power to cause him great harm.

In light of this, Hans Frank's assertion that he undertook a "confidential investigation" of the Hitler family history in response to the alarm the London relatives caused Hitler rings true. But what about the more controversial aspect of his story: How much credence can we place in Hans Frank's claim that "intensive investigation" turned up proof in the form of paternity payment correspondence that Hitler had a Jewish grandfather?

Needless to say, Hans Frank did not have the correspondence in his possession in his death-row cell in Nuremberg when he was writing his memoir. Did he in fact ever have it in his possession? Did he show it to Hitler?

Franz Jetzinger, the Austrian archivist and historian (author of *Hitler's Youth*), is convinced that Frank must have had the letters and showed them to Hitler:

> It should be noted that Hitler made no attempt to deny that his grandmother had some kind of relationship with "the Graz Jew" or that the Jew had given her money at regular intervals over a considerable period. . . . The conclusion is inescapable that the evidence which Frank produced must have been solid beyond all possibility of denial. Then what evidence? The letters perhaps. . . .

Whether or not Frank showed them to Hitler, the letters have never turned up, and no one else but Hans Frank has emerged to say he saw them. What about the Jewish family Hans Frank claims assumed financial responsibility for Hitler's father—can their existence be established independent of Hans Frank's account?

Those like Lucy Dawidowicz, who reject the Hans Frank story, have tended to rely on the research of one Nikolaus Pedarovic to support their dismissal. Pedarovic, a historian at the University of Graz, studied the records of the Jewish community for the Graz district and found no Frankenberger family in residence as far back as they go—1856. Although Maria Schicklgruber's child was conceived twenty years earlier, in 1836, Pedarovic contends that centuries-old anti-Jewish decrees prohibited Jewish residence in the entire province of Styria (which encompassed Graz) before 1856.

But Austrian archivist Jetzinger responds to Pedarovic's objection by asking, "first of all, how many Jews resided there illegally, and secondly, whether the family of Adolf Hitler's grandfather [the Frankenbergers] were not converted Jews professing Christianity?"

Even Maser, who disputes the whole Jewish grandfather hypothesis, concedes that Jews were allowed to re-enter [the province] for a few weeks at a time, at mid-Lent and the feast of St. Giles when they were admitted to the annual fairs at Graz. . . . There is, of course, no reason why a Frankenberger should not have attended the 1836 September Fair in Graz and there met Maria Anna Schicklgruber. Alois Schicklgruber (later Hitler) was born on 7 June 1837. Hence, there might conceivably have been an encounter in September of the previous year.

If the absence of a Frankenberger family from Jewish archives (Simon Wiesenthal made a similar search in 1967 and found no trace of a family of that name) is not necessarily a fatal objection to Hans Frank's account of the paternity correspondence, it might still be objected that the documents themselves may have been forgeries. Hans Frank may be telling the truth about what he read in them, but the correspondence might have been manufactured by Hitler's enemies or by confederates of "the loathsome half-nephew" to substantiate the threat his blackmail letter represented.

There is some fragmentary evidence to support such a hypothesis. In particular, there is Hans Frank's remark that the paternity correspondence was "for years in the hands of a member of the Raubal family." The Raubal family consisted of Hitler's half-sister Angela (daughter of Adolf's father, Alois Sr., by a previous marriage), Angela's husband, and their two children, Leo and Geli. After his release from prison in 1925, Hitler lived with this family in an apartment building in Munich for almost seven years. In 1931, his niece and ward Geli Raubal was found shot to death in her bedroom, a suicide according to the local authorities. But stories appeared in the opposition press that linked Hitler to the teenaged Geli romantically and implicated him in her death. According to William Patrick Hitler's interview with the OSS, he came to know the Raubal family and he mentions one startling fact about them: young Leo Raubal blamed Hitler for his sister Geli's death.

Hans Frank tells us the source of the incriminating paternity correspondence was someone "in the Raubal family." We know that William Patrick Hitler wrote letters threatening to reveal deep, dark family secrets and that William Patrick Hitler was acquainted with a member of the Raubal family who harbored a grudge against Hitler because he believed him guilty of perpetrating a dark deed upon a family member. And so it's not inconceivable to speculate that these connections were the matrix that resulted in Hans Frank's acquisition of the "paternity correspondence," whether real or forged.

Nonetheless, even if we take the skeptical position that the paternity correspondence Hans Frank describes was not authentic, that he was taken in by some sort of forgery, we still must contend with Hans Frank's report of Hitler's *reaction* when confronted with the existence of this "evidence" for a Jewish grandfather. Hitler did not deny it, didn't insist the correspondence must be a forgery. In fact, according to Frank, he confirmed the essence of it: a Jewish family did make child-support payments to Maria Schicklgruber because they were led to believe their young son had impregnated her. Hitler's only objection to the story the correspondence seemed to tell was that the actual conception of his father "was not a result of sexual intercourse between [his grandmother] and the Jew from Graz"; that the Frankenberger family had only been tricked or browbeaten into accepting responsibility for the pregnancy.

Can we believe Hans Frank's account of Hitler's astonishing admission? Werner Maser seizes on one element of Hans Frank's account to attempt to discredit it. According to Frank, Hitler said he learned the facts of the pregnancy-extortion scheme "from his conversations with his father and grandmother."

"The suggestion that Adolf Hitler ever conversed with his grandmother," Maser wrote, "is utterly absurd since she had already been dead for 42 years by the time he was born."

In other words, says Maser, because Frank's version of Hitler's explanation contains a historical impossibility, Hans Frank's whole story must be fabricated.

Jetzinger, however, takes the same "utterly absurd" report that Hitler heard this explanation from Maria and puts a different interpretation on it: it was not Hans Frank who was fabricating but Hans Frank accurately reporting *Hitler's* fabrication:

> Hitler [Jetzinger tells us] was lying when he claimed that he had it on the word of his father and grandmother, the latter having died over forty years before he was born, and his father when he was not yet fourteen, and it is incon-

ceivable that any father, let alone a man of Alois Hitler's reserved and rigid character, would have remarked to his young son, "Whatever you hear to the contrary, your grandfather was not a Jew."

Since Hitler's explanation had to be a lie, Jetzinger tells us, he must have had guilty knowledge that his grandfather was in fact a Jew:

Hitler's unsavory explanation to Frank must then have been concocted on the spur of the moment with the intention of firstly giving Hans Frank to believe that Hitler already knew the story of the Jew, and secondly of discrediting it.

Maser believes Hans Frank fabricated his account of Hitler's explanation; Jetzinger believes Hans Frank was telling the truth, but Hitler's explanation was a lie.

But there's a third possibility, one that in all the literature I've read on the controversy I've never seen proposed—and yet one that I've come to believe makes more sense as a way of accounting for the pathology of Hitler's anti-semitism.

What if Hans Frank were telling the truth, as he recalled it, and what if Hitler's explanation were the truth as *he* knew it?

The possibility that Hitler believed the extortion explanation for the paternity correspondence is open to two principal objections, neither necessarily conclusive.

Jetzinger's objection that the story had to be a hasty lie (because Hitler was, of necessity, lying when he said he heard it from a grandmother who died before he was born) does not take into account the possibility that Hitler heard the story from his father or another family member with its origin *ascribed* to his grandmother. Hans Frank's locution—"an account from the grandmother"—does not necessarily imply a first-hand telling.

Another principal objection to accepting the possibility that Hitler may have believed his "explanation" for the paternity correspondence is the implausibility of Hitler's admitting such a sordid version of his family history, even to his confidential attorney. Why did he not just denounce the "correspondence" as a forgery rather than admit his grandparents were petty extortionists who exploited his grandmother's sexual contact with a Jew for profit?

Hitler's decision to deploy this unseemly defense instead of crying forgery *does* make sense, however, if he believed the extortion story was true. Were that the case, not only would he tend to believe the paternity correspondence was not forged, he would have reason to fear that even if he convinced Hans Frank it *was* a forgery there would probably be someone somewhere—family members in Austria or England, for instance—who would be able to corroborate the fact of the financial transaction.

Better, from Hitler's point of view, to acknowledge the veracity of the correspondence but give it an explanatory twist that would refute the most obvious and damning implication of the correspondence: that the Jewish family was making child-support payments because one of them was *actually* the father of Hitler's father. The ingenuity of Hitler's explanation is that, however much a discredit it is to the moral purity of his grandmother, it preserves the possibility that the *racial* purity of his father was not compromised by the affair—by maintaining that even though his grandmother might have had a sexual relationship with a Jew, her *pregnancy* was, in fact, the result of a concurrent sexual relationship with an Aryan.

There are, in addition, several other reasons for believing that Hitler believed the extortion scenario behind the paternity payments.

First, there is his treatment of the loose-cannon English relatives, particularly the nephew, William Patrick Hitler. According to the latter's account to the OSS, his communications to Hitler made no explicit references to Jewish ancestors; Hitler, nonetheless, reacted to these communications as if they were "disgusting pieces of blackmail." The implication is that Hitler knew there was an embarrassing secret and that he assumed the nephew's vague references to "family background" must have been knowing allusions to it. Hitler's subsequent rather solicitous treatment of the nephew—seeing to it that the youth (who could not land a job in England) was employed first by a bank, then by an Opel dealership in Berlin under Hitler's watchful eye—indicates that he had cause to be concerned about what damage the nephew might do if not taken care of.

(There is some evidence that William Patrick is still alive and living in the United States under another name. John Toland hinted to me that as part of his effort to investigate the Hans Frank story he'd located and been in contact with William Patrick Hitler, but Toland declined to assist me in my as-yet-unsuccessful efforts to contact him.)

Another reason for thinking Hitler believed the story he told Hans Frank is his reported reaction to the rumor that the Austrian secret police had a dossier that proved his paternal grandfather was a Rothschild. While it is extremely unlikely that any such "evidence" was anything more than disinformation fabricated by a hostile intelligence agency, reports from several sources suggest Hitler took it seriously as a threat. The only explanation for his fearfulness about it would be an awareness on Hitler's part that there may well have been a relationship between his grandmother Maria and a wealthy Jew, and the possibility that someone somewhere—and most probably in Austria—could document such a relationship. How could he know the "Rothschild" supposedly identified in Dollfuss's dossier was not related at least by association of some sort to the wealthy Jewish family his grandmother extorted child-support payments from?

Finally, there is the evidence of Hitler's behavior in relation to the Jewish question, the peculiarly psychotic nature of his anti-semitism. Not that any anti-semitism can be said to be rational, but there is something about the obsessiveness of Hitler's that suggests that it is founded upon obsessive doubt of his own racial purity.

Consider Hitler's state of mind if, in fact, he believed the extortion "explanation" he gave Hans Frank. While Hitler might insist to Frank that his explanation obviated any concern that he had "Jewish blood," in fact, it could not have completely quelled his doubts. He would of necessity have to believe that his grandmother had a sexual relationship with a Jew *and* with the Aryan man she married. As Gilbert points out, extorting money because of a pregnancy would have been less likely if there had been no sexual contact. And so Hitler would have to take on faith the claim passed down to him that his grandmother was able to know with certainty that her pregnancy was caused by the Aryan and not the Jew. It would be in her interest to claim confidence in making such a distinction, but such confidence, particularly in an age of relative ignorance in reproductive timing, is open to question.

If Hitler devoted any thought to the matter he would recognize that, while his explanation did offer an escape from the *prima facie* implication of the paternity correspondence—that his grandfather was a Jew—the explanation could not offer absolute certainty that his grandfather was an Aryan. In fact, the "explanation" consigned the matter to a state of unresolvable doubt.

That Hitler did devote some thought to this question, that he sought to find some means of resolving that doubt, is strongly suggested by several disquisitions in *Mein Kampf* on the characteristics and behavior of "half-breeds."

It is in the midst of one such rambling denunciation of the consequences of *Rassenschande*, "racial shame"—sexual intercourse between Aryans and Jews—that Hitler discloses what he calls the "infallible signal" by which the debilitated character of their offspring makes itself manifest:

> The first such products of such cross breeding, say in the third, fourth and fifth generation [interesting he begins with the third generation—which would be *his* generation in relation to his grandmother Maria], invariably reveal their mixed breeding by one infallible signal. In all critical moments in which the racially unified being makes correct, that is, unified decisions, the racially divided one will become uncertain, that is, he will arrive at half measures."

Mein Kampf is filled with Hitler's obsessively repeated denunciations of half-breeds and the "halfheartedness" and "half measures" he believes their mongrelized blood produces. If we accept the possibility that Hitler himself could never be certain—in a historically or biologically conclusive sense—whether he himself was or was not a third-generation product of an act of "racial shame," there would be only one way for him to resolve his doubts about his own identity: the search for *characterological* evidence, for the "infallible signal" in his own behavior of the presence of Jewish blood.

Would his own actions in moments of crisis reflect any hint of "halfheartedness"? Could his own decisions, particularly in relation to "the Jewish question," ever be characterized as "half measures?"

Looked at in this light, Hitler's unrelenting search for "total" and "final" solutions to the Jewish question can be seen as a reflection of his obsessive need to find a solution to his *own* Jewish question—his never-ending need to prove by his behavior the racial purity he could never establish with historical certainty.

Such a state of mind helps explain such otherwise inexplicable decisions as his order at the height of the crisis on the Eastern Front in late 1944 to divert desperately needed railway cars from his hard-pressed troops holding off the Russians to the transport of Jews to the gas chamber.

An even more telling instance has been noted by historian J. P. Stern. In December 1944, "all half-Jewish serving officers and men were ordered to be dismissed from active service, while boys of fourteen and old men in their sixties were pressed into the *Volksturm* (homeguard)."

Given the choice between total commitment to the defense of the Reich and total commitment to the destruction of Jews, Hitler, in essence, chose self-destruction over behavior that might be interpreted as halfhearted commitment to the Final Solution. He chose to go to his death believing in the wholeheartedness of his Aryan nature rather than seek to survive, suspecting himself of the halfheartedness of the half-breed.

There exists some testimony to suggest that others in the Nazi leadership shared this pathological thought process. Consider the troublesome allegations about S.S. Chief Heydrich's alleged "Jewish blood."

On June 6, 1932, according to historian of the S.S. Heinz Hohne, Rudolf Jordan, *Gauleiter* of Halle-Mersberg, wrote to Gregor Strasser, chief of the party organization: "It has come to my ears that in the Reich leadership there is a member named Heydrich whose father reputedly . . . is a Jew. It would perhaps be wise for the personnel department to check this matter."

While Reinhard Heydrich, head of the Gestapo and chief architect of the Final Solution, was officially cleared of this allegation by party genealogist Achim Gercke, rumors of Heydrich's Jewishness persisted throughout his career.

It is known that Heydrich's father became a rabid anti-semite to compensate for all the talk about his supposed Jewishness; and it seems that his son's anti-semitism grew out of a similar process (as a naval cadet young Heydrich was given the derisive anti-semitic nickname "Izzy Suss"). In fact, it seems that the suspicion of Heydrich's father's side of the family may have been unfounded, but there *is* some reason to believe his maternal grandmother, Sarah, may have been of Jewish descent.

According to a number of reports, Heydrich, the "young blond god of death" of the Third Reich, the most cold and ruthless hater of Jews in the Nazi hierarchy, was tormented by the possibility that there might in fact lurk a Jew within him. There is a story recounted by Hohne to this effect, a story said to illustrate the almost schizophrenic madness to which Heydrich's self-doubt and self-hatred led him:

> One day when under the influence of drink, Heydrich stag-
> gered into his brilliantly lit bathroom and came up against
> his reflection in the great wall mirror. He snatched his
> revolver from the holster, and fired twice at the mirror.

The speculation was that somehow Heydrich had finally seen the spectral Jew he had become convinced he harbored within.

Nor were Hitler and Heydrich the only members of the party leadership who suffered from suspicions of Jewish blood. There was Hermann Goering, for instance. In Leonard Mosley's recent biography, *The Reichsmarshall*, there is a fascinating account of how Goering, as a secondary-school student, was traumatized by public exposure of the fact that his godfather was a Jew—and by subsequent private whispers that his Jewish godfather was actually also his biological father. Rumors about Jewish ancestors dogged Goebbels because of his more-semitic-than-Aryan appearance; there were also suspicions about Himmler, Hess, and Ley. Hitler's one-time bodyguard and confidant Emil Maurice was said to have a Moroccan Jewish mother, and even Hans Frank's ancestry had come into question (which might raise the question of whether his "Frankenberger" story about Hitler was perhaps somehow generated from a projective identification: "Frankenberger" a Judaized version of "Frank"). An anti-semitism fueled by doubts about their own "Jewishness" seems to have been a pathology that infected almost the entire leadership of the Nazi party.

But Hitler and Heydrich's cases are the ones with the most terrible significance. It seems no accident that the two co-architects of the Final Solution, the two most fanatic and relentless Jew haters, both suffered from acute and maddening doubts about the putative presence of "Jewish blood" in their veins. In fact, the two of them, Hitler and Heydrich, seem to be bound together by their own doubts, and their knowledge of the other's doubts about them, into a kind of mutually reinforcing *folie a deux*: each knew the other was under suspicion, each suspected himself, each was feverishly alert for any sign of "halfheartedness" in his or the other's behavior. In order to exterminate the doubt about the "Jew within" themselves, they proceeded to exterminate the Jews of Europe.